The Strange Woman

Ben Ames Williams

Houghton Mifflin Company

Books by Ben Ames Williams

SPLENDOR

THE STRUMPET SEA

THREAD OF SCARLET

COME SPRING

THE STRANGE WOMAN

TIME OF PEACE

AMATEURS AT WAR (*Edited*)

LEAVE HER TO HEAVEN

PRINTED IN THE U.S.A.

By Way of Acknowledgment

THE STRANGE WOMAN was originally projected as an attempt to present a picture of life in Bangor and the Penobscot Valley through the years immediately preceding and during the Civil War, just as *Come Spring* had done for the town of Union during the Revolution, and *Thread of Scarlet* for Nantucket during the War of 1812.

But before the actual writing began, the central character assumed command of the book. Instead of the period 1855-1865, it was found necessary to cover fifty years of time; and the whole work became much more a study of character than a historical novel.

Bangor and some of the people who lived there are in these pages; but Jenny, John Evered, their sons, Isaiah and Ephraim Poster, Judge Saladine and Meg and Beth, Jenny's father and mother, Lieutenant Carruthers, and most of the minor characters in this book are completely fictitious, and are not in the slightest degree drawn from any actual individuals, whether of those days or of these.

There seems no point in making even a partial bibliography of books, manuscripts, and newspapers which were consulted in working up the background of this novel; but grateful acknowledgments are due to Mrs. Fannie Hardy Eckstorm for many suggestions as to source material and for contributions from her own wide knowledge of the life of Bangor and of lumbering upon the river; to Olive M. Smythe of the Bangor Public Library for her generous assistance in locating material in the library; to Mrs. Marion Cobb Fuller of the Maine State Library at Augusta for her ready answers to many inquiries on points that arose while the novel was being written; to Miss Elizabeth Ring of the Maine Historical Society for helpful suggestions; to Miss Maude Goggins of Ellsworth for answering a number of questions about the family of Colonel John Black; to Harry M. Smith of Bangor for an explanation of the mechanics of the speculative boom in Bangor in the Thirties and for other useful information; and to Louis Felix Ranlett, Librarian of the Bangor Public Library, and L. T. Ibbotson, Librarian of the University of Maine, for their readiness and courtesy at all times.

BEN AMES WILLIAMS

CHESTNUT HILL
MASSACHUSETTS

Contents

I

Lieutenant Carruthers

'For the lips of a strange woman drop honey,

And her mouth is smoother than oil:

But her latter end is bitter as wormwood,

Sharp as a two-edged sword.'

— PROVERBS

I

DURING her lifetime only seven men — and no women — really knew Jenny Hager for what she was; and Lieutenant Vincent Carruthers of His Majesty's frigate Endymion was the first of the seven. No man of lesser qualifications could have been so quick to recognize Jenny's essential attributes. The Lieutenant was a handsome young man of twenty-three, tall and a little lank, with a hawk nose and pink cheeks. His chin, seldom demanding the attention of a razor, was smooth; but there was a suggestion of downy beard just in front of each ear. His hawk nose was useful to him as an officer, enabling him to assume a severe and commanding demeanor simply by composing his countenance to match its bold and ruthless proportions; but in those lighter moments — which occurred as frequently as he could contrive — when he was more anxious to persuade than to command, he looked more like a shy and decidedly attractive boy than like a Lieutenant in the Royal Navy. This disarming aspect, lulling all suspicions, had conquered as many feminine hearts as his more martial bearing had his country's foes.

He had entered the navy as a volunteer, first class, in 1804, at the age of thirteen. He did this with the blessing of his father — his mother having died of lung fever — because the elder Carruthers thought his son was sickly and that a navy life would either kill him or make a man of him. He served as midshipman and master's mate on a succession of His Majesty's ships, achieved his seniority as a Lieutenant while cruising in the Baltic in 1810, and was entered on the Endymion early in 1813 for service on the American station.

After his first stay in Halifax, his feminine acquaintance there was as wide and as generous as that of any officer in the fleet, regardless of rank; but this surprised no one. The Lieutenant's success in such matters had long been the envy of his fellow officers, and he had been a marked man since the day — or the night — when Captain Hunter of the Implacable found the sixteen-year-old midshipman making himself at home in a bed-chamber to which the Captain had thought he himself had the only entry. The resulting unpleasantness might have been worse but for Mr. Carruthers' pretty and precocious discretion. He tactfully pointed out to his infuriated superior that any public discussion of the matter would — since the Captain's attachment to the lady in question was of long standing and was well known — subject the Captain himself to as many amused chuckles as though he had been presented with a pair of horns; and it was not till after Mr. Carruthers had been assigned to another ship that the tale leaked out.

Since then the young man had been rated among the foremost swordsmen in His Majesty's Navy; but the British occupation of Bangor on the third and fourth of September, 1814, afforded him his first opportunity for a foray into American territory. He was to die rather unpleasantly from a bullet in the abdomen in the bloody fight between the Endymion's boats and the Prince of Neufchatel, off Nantucket, five or six weeks later; but no premonition marred his enjoyment of the brief Bangor stay during which he met Jenny.

He was quick to mark in her an unusual quality. His immediate impression was that she reminded him of someone, and during their first hour together he tried to clarify that memory. That Russian woman in whose bed he had supplanted the Captain of the Implacable had dark hair with hidden, warmer lights in it, as Jenny had; but also Jenny's hair prisoned a faint delicious perfume which made him remember a young English woman, the wife of an Admiral of the Blue, with whom he had spent more than one long blissful evening in an old garden at Malta. There was a Contessa in Naples whose cheek had an ivory warmth like Jenny's; and a lass fresh from the farm had kissed him once at Portsmouth, and the corners of her mouth were moist as Jenny's were. When he held Jenny in his arms so many memories came trooping back to him. In one way or another she reminded him of each of the charming women he had known. She was a distillation, concentrating in her person all that had been most enticing and delicious in them. She was the essence of scores of pretty wantons, each one of whom for a moment he had loved, with all their outward beauty, with their seductive inner flame.

And also he thought he discovered in her that thin wire of heartless cruelty which each of them had possessed. He had found that a woman was sometimes kind to a man, not because she wished to please him, but because she wished to wound and to betray some other man. In her lover's arms, outwardly enraptured and abandoned, she was as apt as not to be thinking in the innermost chambers of her malicious soul of that other who would suffer if he could see her thus. The caresses she gave the one were whiplashes for the other. He thought there was this mocking cruelty in Jenny, too.

The profound impression which Jenny made on the Lieutenant was the more remarkable because of the fact that she was at the time only four years old.

II

The Endymion, to which the Lieutenant was attached, was one of the British fleet consisting of three seventy-fours, two or three frigates, three or four smaller fighting ships and ten transports, which made into Castine Harbor at sunrise on the morning of September 1 and demanded a surrender. The American fort there was held by Lieutenant Lewis with twenty-eight regulars, while ninety-two militiamen from Bucksport, commanded by Lieutenant Little, were quartered in the Court House. The militiamen, at the first sight of the British fleet, started eagerly home to Bucksport; but Lieutenant Lewis and his regulars waited till the enemy began to land troops before blowing up the magazine and taking the same road.

The British after this quick success pushed their advantage. The United States corvette Adams was just then laid up at Hampden for repairs. General Gosselin went to occupy Belfast and prevent any possible interference by militia from Lincolnville or other towns to the westward, while a flotilla of shallow-draft vessels, barges and guard boats, presided over by the Dragon, 74, started up the Penobscot with a force of five hundred soldiers and a lesser number of sailors and marines to seize or destroy the Adams and to sweep the river clean of American craft.

Lieutenant Carruthers, commanding on this expedition a division of boats from the Endymion, watched with a lively pleasure the unfolding beauty of the upper Bay. The boats entered the wide river and the shores came near, the forests of spruce and pine often descending unbroken to the water's edge. An occasional tract of land had been cleared and put under cultivation, and now and then at lonely farms men and women and children were visible, watching from a distance as the flotilla passed. Twice or thrice the Lieutenant saw a mounted man galloping in haste up the river road, presumably to give warning of their progress.

The flotilla anchored that first night in Marsh Bay, and in the late afternoon of September 2, the British made their landing at Bald Hill Cove. They spent a rainy and uncomfortable night, and next morning, soon after dawn, in a thin river fog, the land forces advanced to attack with a punctilious formality the American militiamen and the sailors off the Adams who were waiting to receive them.

Lieutenant Carruthers and his division of boats with the rest of the British flotilla kept pace with the soldiers on shore till they drew the fire of the great guns off the Adams, some of which had been mounted on the wharf at Hampden. At the first fire, the flotilla halted and lay on their oars just out of range until the American militia, after a few harmless shots had been fired, flatly turned tail and ran. Captain Morris of the Adams, his flank thus exposed, spiked his guns, set the Adams on fire, and led his men across Sowadabscook Stream and away toward Bangor.

The flotilla then came on and the men landed below the village almost as soon as the soldiers marched into it. Having had little opportunity to discharge their weapons at an enemy, since the militiamen fled before the range was closed, the soldiers let off their pieces without discrimination at the houses of the village and at the swine of all ages and degrees which ran at large in the streets. Some bullets found their mark, and it was not long before bayonets had done a rough dissection on the tenderest pigs, and gobbets of meat spitted on ramrods were cooking over many little fires. For fuel the soldiers — scorning the firewood convenient in every shed — dragged out of the houses highboys and lowboys, chairs and tables, and knocked them to pieces. The morning air was soon laden with an appetizing odor of roast pork. The easy victory had left the men rather hilarious than bloodthirsty, and after hunger and thirst had been satisfied, they looked for sport. A dozen of them took possession of Crosby's mill and fed feather beds into the first run of stones to see whether it was possible to make flour out of feathers; and the air around the mill was so full of white down that the Lieutenant as he passed was reminded of a light fall of snow. He paused to watch half a dozen men tearing up books and stuffing the torn paper into a martin house atop its pole. They set it on fire as a small but lofty beacon to celebrate their recent victory.

But Lieutenant Carruthers, with that fine fragrance of roast pork in his nostrils, was hungry; so he called two of his men, directed them to cut a few chops off a convenient carcass and follow him, and turned into Marm Grant's house where he found the good dame cooking breakfast for some of the regimental officers. A pretty girl, badly frightened and with tear-stained cheeks, was serving them. When Lieutenant Carruthers entered, Captain Ward of the rifle company of the Sixtieth was saying:

'. . . so we caught a farmer named Oakman, or Oakes, or some such name, to guide us to the bridge — with a bayonet nudging him between the shoulder blades; but when we met their skirmishers he tried to run, and we shot him.' He laughed. 'He rolled over and over down the hill, like a rabbit caught in mid-leap!'

The girl who was serving them at that began to cry again, with cascading sobs, and Lieutenant Carruthers put his arm around her shaking shoulders. 'There, my dear, you've nought to fear now,' he said. 'Be sure we'll treat a girl as pretty as you with the nicest tenderness. Dry your tears.'

She clung to him as to a rescuer, and the other officers protested in shouting laughter at the Lieutenant's quick success, but Marm Grant said harshly:

'Stop that cackling, the lot of you, or I'll douse this hot grease in your faces! She has a right to cry. She's Beth Oakman and that was her pa you killed that you think's so funny!'

The officers stopped laughing, and the Lieutenant patted the girl's bowed head. 'There, my dear!' he said. 'They did not know who he was. Come sit with me till you're yourself again.' He led her to the high-backed settle, and Captain Ward rose, objecting:

'What's the justice in that? We kill the old bull and you get the heifer! Share and share, I say!'

But Marm Grant turned on him with a spider full of frying chops and glared at him so ominously that he sat down again. So Lieutenant Carruthers, with pretty Beth Oakman weeping on his shoulder, thought his stay in Hampden promised well; but he had scarce begun to endear himself to her when he received orders to move on to Bangor, and reluctantly the Lieutenant took himself away.

III

When Lieutenant Carruthers and his forces proceeded up the river, the fog had blown off. A little before noon, his boats rounded High Head and he had his first sight of Bangor town. The village of seven or eight hundred people sprawled pleasantly across low hills on either side of Kenduskeag Stream, with scattering farms, bordered by the black masses of the forest, strung along the roads to Hampden and to Old Town, and to Levant and Six-Mile Falls. Some of the houses in town were no more than cabins, but most of them were more substantial, and there were a few larger buildings — stores, the Court House and Jacob Chick's Hotel. A number of vessels — sloops, and a brig, and a ship recently launched

and not yet rigged — were at anchor in the river; and others were
tied up at wharves, or in various stages of construction in the shipyards on the stream which flowed through the town. Piles of fresh-
sawed lumber, gleaming yellow, suggested the principal industry of
the place.

The Lieutenant proposed to land where a tall pine marked the
ferry; but as he veered in toward the shore there he saw a white
flag flying from the window of John Barker's store on the Point
opposite, so he turned that way. Himself the first ashore, he surveyed his surroundings with a curious eye. From the landing a
muddy road led up to the store. The river was behind him, the
tributary stream on his left. Across the stream he could look up
Water Street and see the British soldiers just arriving, men and
women moving sullenly to stand and watch them pass.

Then John Barker himself and Captain Greene Sanborn and
Robert Lapish came down to the landing to assure the Lieutenant
of the complete submission of the town, and to invite him to enter
Mr. Barker's store and refresh himself. The young man looked
down his hawk nose at them as sternly as possible, warned them
that the least hint of opposition would let loose the severest retri-
bution, and then left his subordinates to form the men and bring
them after him while he picked his way fastidiously through the
mud up to the store. There he shared a glass or two of grog with
the three Bangor men while his sailors were paraded outside to
wait his pleasure there.

IV

The first house beyond John Barker's store was Timothy Hager's,
and the head of the column, when the men marched up from the
landing and halted, almost reached it. Moll Hager, Jenny's mother,
stood in her open door to look at them. The sailors were a nondescript lot, most of them in round blue jackets, white trousers and
tarpaulin hats; but there was variety in their bright waistcoats,
checked shirts and neckerchiefs. A fair half of them were barefooted. Moll, still a young woman, in a snug tow dress buttoned
down the front over many petticoats, with her hair disordered and
her cheeks flushed from the fire where she had just put kettle
bread to bake, inspected them with a grim detachment, ignoring
the fact that they were as interested in her as she was in them.

Then Jenny wriggled past her mother and ran toward the head
of the column in laughing excitement and with outstretched arms.
The little girl had a strange and haunting beauty, with dark hair
and blue eyes and a skin like ivory, at once pale and warm; and on

each cheekbone there was a delicate line like an elongated and extremely faint dimple, which appeared when she smiled and made her seem about to burst into tears. She was delighted now at having escaped from her mother, and when Moll darted after her in dismayed pursuit, she threw herself for sanctuary into the arms of the tall sailor at the head of the line. He laughed and swung her high, her petticoats flying; and she clasped her arms around his neck and buried her face against his ear and cried in a wriggling triumph:

'Jenny run'd away from mommy!'

Moll tried to recover her baby, tugging at the sailor's arms. 'Give her to me!' she pleaded breathlessly. 'Jenny, you little wretch, come here to mommy!'

But Jenny clung fast to her sailor, and he laughed and passed her to the man behind him, good-humoredly blocking Moll, pushing her away.

'Sure, ma'am, she's the friendly one!' he said amiably. 'Let the men be having a look at her. It's long since they've handled a baby — and some of them might have left one or two of their own at home, and that might be many a year ago.'

He was a handsome youngster, and his smile was friendly enough, and Moll Hager was no older than he, and smiled as readily. So Jenny was passed down the line from man to man, and she had a kiss for those who pleased her and a frown for the others; while Moll moved watchfully beside her.

v

When Lieutenant Carruthers came out of John Barker's store it was to see his force already thus disorganized by feminine friendliness. He inspected the woman with an expert eye. She seemed to him not particularly attractive, and he judged she was older than he. The Lieutenant had found that in itself no demerit, if there were compensations; but she was flushed and flustered and rather untidy, and he might have waited to look farther but for the striking beauty of that baby the men were dandling. The woman was obviously the baby's mother, so he stepped forward and rescued Jenny from the men; and she came to his arms as readily as to any other, patting his cheek approvingly, fingering his single epaulette, looking to see whether he had a pigtail like the sailors. She was a bewitching youngster, and more for her sake than for the woman's he doffed his cocked hat with a sweeping gesture.

'Madame, I trust you have been put to no alarm,' he protested in a grave solicitude.

'No,' she said. 'The men wanted to see the baby, and she likes men. But she'd best be indoors.'

'Pray accept my escort,' he said with elaborate courtesy, and he delivered Jenny to her and walked with her to her threshold. She would have dismissed him then, but he asked:

'Is your husband home?'

The woman shook her head. 'No. He's gone . . .' She hesitated, said only: 'He's not here now.'

'I need to find quarters for myself and for my men,' Lieutenant Carruthers explained. 'May I come in and discuss the point with you?'

She hesitated, then nodded her consent; and the Lieutenant followed her across the threshold into a compact warm room with a wide fireplace where a bake-kettle was buried in the ashes and a steaming pot hung on the crane. A teakettle was set on the hob, and a spider and a warming pan leaned at one side.

Moll, once they were indoors, set Jenny down. 'There, you little imp!' she said harshly. 'Now mind you stay where you belong!' She gave the baby a cuff in the petticoats, and Jenny cried delightedly.

'Mommy spank Jenny?'

'I will if you go out again,' Moll declared, and Jenny gleefully bolted for the door, as eager to earn that punishment as though it were a reward. Moll darted after her and caught her. 'She's a limb!' she told the Lieutenant. 'She'll bedevil me all day long to get a spanking! It's the game she likes best.' She swept Jenny up again, turned her over her arm and paddled her affectionately, while Jenny squalled in pretended pain. 'There, Miss!' she exclaimed in mock ferocity. 'That'll teach you!' And to the Lieutenant: 'Will Your Honor sit down?'

The Lieutenant laid his hat aside. 'I'm wet from this morning's rain,' he confessed. 'May I dry myself while we discuss my business?' He unbuttoned his long cloth coat, edged with white; and she took it to hang near the fire. He pulled off his boots and set them on the hearth and drew a chair near, and Jenny went to pluck at the crown-and-anchor buttons on his coat admiringly. Moll irritably slapped her small hand.

'There now, leave be!' she said sharply; and Jenny ran to the Lieutenant and climbed on his lap, and he laughed and kissed her. She accepted the kiss so greedily that the Lieutenant was conscious of a surprising pleasure. There was in this child in his arms a sort of flame, and her lips were firm as a woman's, with none of the softness like rose petals and the lavish moistness of a baby's kiss.

He looked at her in a wondering interest while the woman cleared the kettle top of ashes to see how her bread did. It was finely browned and she lifted it out and carried it to the table, passing it from hand to hand when it became too hot to hold. Jenny sat erect on the Lieutenant's lap, facing him, her small hands touching his cheeks and nose and eyelids teasingly, laughing when he shut his eyes tight; and he forgot the woman in his pleasuring with the child till Moll, returning to sweep clean the hearth again, asked sullenly:

'Was the fighting bad at Hampden?'

He chuckled. 'Fighting? That rabble militia ran so fast our soldiers never saw them!'

'They came galloping into town like sheep with a dog after them,' she agreed in a dry scorn. 'Stripping off their uniforms and throwing away their muskets — them that had held on to them till then!' She laughed without mirth. 'A fine sight to see! Did they stand up to you at all?'

'They made some pactice at us with the great guns, but did no harm. I heard we lost one rank and file, and Captain Gell of the Twenty-Ninth Grenadiers was wounded.'

'Was there many killed?'

He shook his head, dandling Jenny amiably. 'I told you, they outran us!' Then he remembered the girl at Marm Grant's. 'Only there was one of your farmers down-river, a man named Oakman. They made him guide our troops and he tried to get away and they shot him.'

'Fighting's an old story, like as not, to you?'

'Aye, I've seen my share of it, these ten years.'

She looked at him incredulously. 'Ten years? You're no more than a boy now!'

'I'm twenty-three,' he assured her. 'We're blooded young, so we grow up with a stomach for it.' She was busy, moving to and fro about the neat small room, and his eyes returned to Jenny, curled in his arms. When thus he looked down at her now she was lying quietly, watching the way his lips moved, searching all his countenance. She met his glance and smiled and her smile was as composed and serene as a woman's, with mystery in her eyes. Then in a quick movement she buried her face against his shirt, and he laughed and hugged her close. 'This little one has no misliking for an enemy,' he said, amused and pleased. 'How old is she?'

'Just gone four.'

'Our English children are still babies at her age.'

'She's baby enough,' the woman agreed. 'But she'll go to any

man, any time, and always would from the time she could squeal.'
She eyed him narrowly. 'After you had the Adams, what did you
come on to Bangor for?'

'Why, your damned privateers have made us trouble, and half
the rivers and bays along this coast are nests for them. We came
to root them out.'

'Joe Leavitt fitted out a privateer last year,' she told him, 'and
my Tim has a piece of a sloop building in Joe's yard that he says
he'll take privateering.'

'That sloop will be burnt on the ways when I report her purpose.'
Her back was turned to him. 'Burn it, then!' she said shortly.

He smiled quizzically. 'You've no great love for your neighbors
— or your husband?'

'I hate the lot of them!' she said, and with a slow violence she
added: 'I hate the place and the people in it and all about them,
and everything they think and do and say. I wouldn't care if you
burned the town and all in it.'

Jenny, on his knee, snug in the curl of his arm, watched her
mother and she watched the Lieutenant, puzzled by their tones.
'Mommy mad?' she asked uneasily.

He held her closer, reassuringly. 'Your mother's much too pretty
to be mad at anyone,' he assured her.

The woman tossed her head. 'That's as may be. My prettiness
never got me anything.'

They heard shouting in the street and loud voices raised and
some drunken singing, and Lieutenant Carruthers remembered
that he should report his men to Captain Barrie; but he was comfortable here and Jenny pleased him and he was reluctant to leave.
Also, with Jenny in his arms, he thought her mother had a sullen
beauty, with her heavy hair and her angry eyes; and there was a
way she had of moving, and her tow gown fitted snugly about her
pleasant bosom.

'It might buy you many pretty things to match it, if you put it
up in the right market!' he said.

'I'm not likely to have a chance. Another year or two here, and
another brat or two, and I'll be as wore out as the rest of them.'

'You're lonesome and lorn,' he said, and his tone was full of understanding. 'I know well the feeling. My mother died when I
was not much older than this baby, and a boy needs a mother —
just as a man needs a woman. But a sailor's never long enough in
one place to find one to love him.'

She laughed shortly. 'You'd not be long in finding one, if you
had a mind, wherever you might be, with that boy's face of yours.'

Her eyes were angry; but when he smiled she softened, and he said gently:

'Is that why you've treated me thus kindly?'

'It might be,' she confessed, smiling invitingly; but an unaccustomed reluctance kept him from pushing his advantage.

'You've a fine town here,' he suggested, 'to be so far in the wilderness. How many people?'

'Too many!' she said shortly. 'They're an idle, lying, rum-drinking, thieving lot! The distillery across the way just up the street is kept busy making rum as fast as they can drink it.'

'I didn't see any church steeple, from the river?'

'There's no church,' she assured him. 'And if there was, the ministers are as bad as any. Elder Noble, him that named the town after a hymn tune he liked, used to buy four and five gallons of rum a month at Treat's. My Tim says he's seen the charges on the books against him. He used to claim he gave it to sick folks when he visited them, but if he did, the sick folks drank a-plenty! And Elder Boyd was worse than him, making a hussy out of every woman in the town till the council put him out. That was before my time, but they say he was so bad Amos Patten wouldn't even write down the things he did, in the book!'

Lieutenant Carruthers chuckled. 'Perhaps he believed in the laying on of hands — in the wrong places.'

'He believed in bedding wherever he could,' the woman assured him, and added grudgingly: 'But Mr. Loomis that's just lately come to preach here is a good enough man.'

'It's clear you don't like the town?'

'They're a lazy, drunken, worthless lot, every man of them. They farm and fish and cut a few trees and saw them into boards, and the rest of the time they drink rum and brag. There's not twenty decent, hard-working men in the place.'

'What kind of fish?' he asked. There was a trout stream in England where he had spent fine days.

'Salmon and shad and alewives, mostly. They spear salmon up at Treat's Falls. You can fill a boat with them any time; and they'll kill maybe five hundred in a day. Then my Tim drifts a net sometimes. That's quickest, unless a sturgeon gets into it. They're all full of fish, the river and the Stream.'

'What's the name of the river that runs through the town?'

'Kenduskeag Stream. The plantation used to be called after it till Elder Noble named the town Bangor.' Jenny squirmed on his lap, and she said sharply: 'Jenny, don't plague the Lieutenant! Get you down!'

Lieutenant Carruthers protested: 'Leave her as she is. It's a long time since as pretty a girl has perched on my knee!' And he asked: 'Was your husband one of that rag-tailed lot that ran so fast this morning?'

She shook her head. 'He's not a running man. If he'd been there, you might have had a warmer time.'

'A pity he wasn't. We hadn't enough to do to work up an appetite! Is he from home?'

'He's gone off to Boston.' She sighed, a little too loudly. 'So I'm left lone in a town full of murdering soldiers and none to protect me.'

The invitation was clear enough, too clear. The Lieutenant preferred more difficult game. A sportsman does not shoot a sitting bird. He might have taken a polite departure but for Jenny. The child on his lap was warm and vibrant and lavish, pressing close to him, magnetic and possessive, drawing him to her, holding him fast. Perhaps there was in the woman, waiting to be aroused, some of Jenny's quality. He said strongly:

'No protection? Why, damme, you have my protection, ma'am! My word on't, none shall touch you — except in kindness.' And he asked: 'That good man of yours, d'ye think he will be back this day — or may I quarter here?'

'If I said you could not, you'd still have your way,' she reminded him. 'There's none here to stand against you.'

'I'd take nothing by violence from a lady, ma'am.'

'Well, there's no knowing when he'll be back, to be sure,' she confessed. 'But we've poor quarters here, a small house as you see, and just the one bedroom and a trundle bed for Jenny. Yet I suppose I must give up my bed to you, if you want it so.'

'We can speak of beds when it is time for them,' he said reassuringly.

Moll smiled, and Jenny, looking intently at her mother, suddenly pulled herself up to kiss him, pressed her cheek to his. 'Jenny likes you, and mommy likes you,' she announced.

The Lieutenant chuckled. 'Gad, I'm glad to hear that!' he declared. 'For I like the two of you. I'm not sure which I like the better!' He remembered again that he must report for orders, and he put Jenny from his lap. 'But now, Miss, I've my duties to do.' He knocked the dried mud off his boots and pulled them on and rose, and Moll Hager brought his coat for him. 'My compliments, ma'am,' he said, 'and my gratitude for your hospitality. D'ye know that gratitude is said to be a lively anticipation of future favors?'

'I'm sure you'll be welcome when you come back, if that's what you mean.'

'That will be soon,' he promised her. 'But — duty first, devotion afterward.' He swung his hat to his head, bent to kiss Jenny goodbye, and turned away.

VI

When Lieutenant Carruthers left the Hager door, he saw that his sailors had crowded into John Barker's store; and they were helping themselves to the stock of boots and shoes there when the Lieutenant entered to bid them fall in. John Barker met him in a trembling good nature. The Lieutenant said, with an amused eye on these proceedings:

'I trust my men have made no trouble, sir?'

'Oh no, no, to be sure!' Barker protested. 'Very good customers! I've done a month's business in an hour.' His voice became confidential. 'They've no money, they say; but I'm keeping a careful memorandum of all their purchases, to charge them to the King.'

The Lieutenant said gravely: 'Excellent! It's a pleasure to deal with a man of business.' He spoke to a master's mate at the door. 'Fall in the men,' he said. 'Leave a guard on the boats, and a man in front of the house yonder to see it's not disturbed. I'll make my quarters there.'

Mr. Barker touched the Lieutenant's elbow. 'Colonel John and Captain Barrie are quartered at my home,' he explained. 'The Court House and the school buildings have been put at the disposal of the men.'

'Nevertheless I'll quarter here,' the Lieutenant assured him. 'But I must report to my superior — if you'll be so kind as to guide me to your residence.'

Mr. Barker eagerly agreed; and he and Mr. Carruthers started up Poplar Street, splashing through the mud, the column of sailors following. Mr. Barker was voluble at the Lieutenant's side, pointing out Trafton's store, and the distillery below the road beside the Stream where a pack of soldiers were trooping in and out, as exuberant as schoolboys in an unguarded orchard. After they crossed the toll bridge, Main Street ahead of them, well lined with stores and with a tavern or two, was filled with men.

John Barker said with a placating tolerance: 'The men are goodnatured, Lieutenant; no harm in them, full of fun. They sampled Mr. Trafton's goods, but said his prices were too high and left him!' He laughed in a hollow fashion at this jest. 'You understand, Lieutenant, we're good Federalists here, most of us, with no love for the war, and no hatred for the British.'

But the Lieutenant only nodded in an abstracted way.

They found Captain Barrie on the steps of Mr. Barker's house, at the corner of Main and Water Streets; and before the Lieutenant could speak, Mr. Barker told Captain Barrie, in an anxious desire to please:

'Captain, there's some sauce in my garden below the house here. You're welcome to it!'

Captain Barrie eyed him mockingly. 'I want none of your sass!' he roared. He was a blustering, loud man, forever breathing out threatenings and slaughter, earning by his demeanor a reputation among his country's enemies for bold and ruthless brutality; but like a barking dog he seemed more dangerous than he was, and his worst threats were seldom followed by performance.

Mr. Barker, however, did not know this. 'I mean to say, the vegetables!' he humbly explained. 'You can take what you want.'

'To be sure I can. They're mine already! Be off with you!' Mr. Barker moved a little aside and lingered uncertainly, and Captain Barrie turned to the Lieutenant. 'Mr. Carruthers, had you any trouble at your landing or since?'

'Not at all, sir. In fact, I was treated most hospitably. A lady whose husband is absent offered me comfortable quarters — though I fear my night's sleep may be interrupted!'

'Ho!' the Captain chuckled. 'You've a gift that way, Mr. Carruthers!' Mr. Barker still stood by and for his benefit Captain Barrie shouted: 'But if you're molested, say the word, Lieutenant, and I'll act. If a dog on the streets so much as wets a British soldier's shins, we'll burn the town over their heads.'

Mr. Barker at this dreadful threat scuttled away, and the Captain asked Lieutenant Carruthers in a lower tone: 'Would your prospective hostess by any chance be young and pretty? Or even young? I've seen nothing but whiskered beldames in the town!'

'Why, pretty enough,' the Lieutenant assured him, 'and young enough.' He added, as one reports a curious natural phenomenon to an expert: 'And she has a daughter, a baby that's forever wanting to be kissed and dandled. There's something about her that rouses a man more than you'd think possible.'

'Eh? The woman or the baby?'

'Oh, the woman's well enough, but I meant to say the baby. She's four years old.'

Captain Barrie chuckled. 'Precocious lot, these wilderness wenches; but that would never do for an Englishman! She'll have to wait till we come again to give her what she wants.' He became serious again. 'Now, Mr. Carruthers, between dame and babe, I doubt you've had any time for our business here?'

'I await your orders, sir.'

'The town's submitted,' the other told him. 'They've surrendered all arms, muskets, guns. A bold tanner by the name of Zadock Davis hid some four-pounders under a bridge down the road, but we soon persuaded him to show us where they were. Every able-bodied man in town's entered himself as a prisoner of war and given parole. We'll take what shipping we want, burn the rest where it lies. There's a schoolhouse somewhere to shelter your men. Make someone guide you to it. I've given orders that no liquor is to be served to the men.'

Mr. Carruthers smiled to himself. Between where they stood and the Stream, along Main Street, there were shouting, drunken groups of soldiers everywhere; and quite obviously Captain Barrie himself had violated the prohibition he now imposed. 'I'm sure no liquor will be drunk by anyone,' the Lieutenant said gravely.

Captain Barrie laughed. 'Let's have a look in the tavern yonder and make sure,' he suggested, and Lieutenant Carruthers followed him across the way. When they came in, Tom Hatch was presiding at the bar and the room was packed with Hessian soldiers who gave way as the officers entered. Tom had just pulled a cork. Captain Barrie took the open bottle from his hand.

'What's this?' he demanded, and drained half the bottle at a gulp. 'Why, by Gad, it's rum!' he cried, in a sudden passion. 'I said no liquor for the men, and I'll have my orders obeyed!' He wrenched out his sword and strode behind the bar and with smashing blows cut off the faucets of the rum barrels there resting on their sides. 'Orders!' he repeated thickly. 'Obedience! See to it!'

With the bottle in one hand, his sword in the other, he turned to the door. Before Lieutenant Carruthers followed him out, Tom Hatch was already putting buckets under the spouting faucets, while the soldiers mopped up the flood on the floor and squeezed the last drop down thirsty throats. Outside, Captain Barrie finished the bottle and tossed it away.

'I want every drop of liquor in town destroyed, Mr. Carruthers,' he said. 'See to it. I've shown you what measures to take.'

'Very well, sir. Any other orders?'

'Quarter your men and leave with me someone who will know where to find you. We'll move out of here tomorrow.' He hiccoughed loudly. 'And pleasant dreams, Mr. Carruthers!'

'Thank you, sir, but I'm afraid there'll be little sleep for me tonight. I'm not one to neglect my duty!'

'A soldier's first duty in an enemy town is to compel submission. See to it, Lieutenant!' The Captain winked, and hiccoughed again and turned away.

VII

Lieutenant Carruthers, when he left Captain Barrie, swung back toward the toll bridge, stopping at half a dozen stores to carry out the orders to destroy whatever liquor he found, bidding his men pour it into the street. The sailors in his command took the opportunity to help themselves to odds and ends which in each establishment attracted their attention; but after he had stopped at half a dozen stores, he met Lieutenant Symms of the Bulwark in the act of opening a pipe of brandy for his men. When the other heard Captain Barrie's order, he said cheerfully:

'To destroy all liquor? Well, what else are we doing? There's only one proper way to destroy good liquor. Just give us a little time and it will all be gone!'

Mr. Carruthers was ready enough to agree. Lieutenant Symms' procedure in fact accorded well enough with Captain Barrie's example. He instructed the other to see the men quartered for the night, and crossed the toll bridge and turned down Poplar Street toward Moll Hager's home, his duty done.

They were burning the vessels lying at anchor in the river, and the Lieutenant saw rising columns of smoke ahead of him, shot through with the red anger of the flames. On the Point, and across the Stream by the ferry landing, scores of townsfolk were gathered to watch that destruction, the men with shamed and haggard faces, the women with tears of helpless rage, the children with wide enchanted eyes. A brig was a fountain of fire, and the hull of a ship recently launched was burning fiercely, and half a dozen smaller craft were all blazing from stem to stern. The crackling roar of the flames was a ravening and dreadful sound; and the silent folk along the shore, helplessly watching the burning ships, heard behind them in the town the loud tumult of the drunken, looting soldiers.

VIII

The Lieutenant dismissed his man on guard at the Hager house, and at his knock the woman opened the door, and Jenny ran to meet him and he swept her up and tossed her high and caught her coming down and kissed her. The woman was near and Jenny cried:

'Kiss mommy too!'

Lieutenant Carruthers laughed, and dropped his arm around the woman's waist and obeyed that command.

'That little wretch!' Moll protested, bridling. 'She's at some devilment the day long. She's too much for me to handle!' She freed herself from the circle of his arm. 'Shame on you, Jenny, to say such a thing! You ought to be smacked. What will poppy say?'

'Poppy's gone to Boston,' Jenny retorted. Lieutenant Carruthers removed his coat and hat and pulled off his boots and sat comfortably down before the wide hearth, and Jenny climbed on his lap, lying back across his arm, her chin uptilted, smiling at him. He laughed and kissed her under the chin, and she wriggled and squealed in ecstatic protest, and the woman said:

'I thought you'd maybe be hungry when you came.'

'I'm a starving man!' he agreed.

'Then hold her, while I put a bite on the table,' she directed, and presently she bade him sit down to beef roasted on a spit above the coals, and garden sauce and cornbread and sweet butter, and there was a flake of wild honeycomb from a tree Tim Hager had found a month ago, and steaming tea. Jenny stood across the table, on tiptoe to bring her chin above the level of the board, watching his every mouthful; and the woman served him. When she came beside him he circled her waist with his arm, but she pushed his hand almost absently away. Dusk fell, and the glare from the burning vessels was in the windows. The woman lighted a candle on the table, and when he had eaten she cleared away. From across the stream and up in town they heard remotely the tumult of hoarse voices as full dark came down. She poured hot water in the big wooden bowl to wash the dishes he had used, and she said:

'This will be a bad night for Bangor town, with drunken sailors and soldiers in the streets and everywhere and no one to say nay to them.'

'The men will soon be asleep,' he predicted. 'They're full of rum, and that will quiet them. They stood to in the rain half the night, and fought a skirmish this morning, so they're ready now to rest a while.'

She said scornfully: 'It was nought to tire them out to send that lot of ours scrabbling! They're puling fools, with their musters and their marching and their bragging what they'll do!' She looked at him sidewise. 'Will you be staying here for long?'

'No. We'll leave tomorrow.'

'You'll be going back to Castine.'

'We'll be there a while,' he agreed. Jenny was warm in his arms, half asleep, now and then wriggling a little to settle herself more comfortably into the hollows of his body. He looked down at her, touched her dark hair, and still watching Jenny, he said indolently: 'This is a sweet armful. Tell me about that husband of yours, off in Boston town. Is she like him more than you?'

The woman for a moment did not speak, and when she did there was no expression in her tones. 'Tim's a big man with a roaring voice,' she said. 'The backs of his hands, even his fingers, are covered with stiff black hair like pig bristles, thick as reeds in a swamp, stiff enough to scratch me when he touches me.' She had turned away, did not look toward the Lieutenant. 'He's a hasty man,' she said, in that flat voice so curiously free from bitterness to match her words. 'A hasty, hard, violent man with no gentleness in him; and he'll laugh to split your ears.'

'How old?'

'Old enough so he was a man before I was Jenny's age.'

'Handsome?'

'I might have thought so, once; but mostly it was his talk that beat me down till I had no more strength to say no to him.' She repeated bitterly: 'He's a hairy man, with more whiskers in his nose and his ears than a boy like you will ever have on your chin, and all as stiff as bristles on a pig.'

The Lieutenant chuckled comfortably. 'A woman would as soon sleep with a hedgehog!'

She said, as though he had not spoken: 'He married me in Norridgewock and brought me here. That was my mother's doing, making him bring me away so Norridgewock would not know when Jenny was born.' She faced him slowly. 'I'd have left him before, if there was a place to go. I'm a woman now, not a girl that he can scare into a shivering jelly in his arms.'

'You have it in mind to leave him?'

She said grimly: 'Aye, if anyone asked me.' Her eyes were a challenge to him, straight and bold. He realized suddenly, his throat full, that she was by candlelight pretty enough. Put her in the right gown, with her hair more seemly dressed, and there would be some beauty in her. That damned husband of hers had given her a weary time. She was entitled to be gay and merry for a while; and if there was in her any of that quality he discovered in her daughter, in this baby in his arms, she would know how to please a man. He looked down at Jenny, wondering whether this was true, thinking that Jenny moved him more than her mother ever could. The baby's eyes were tight closed.

'She's asleep,' he said.

The woman nodded. 'Fetch her,' she directed. 'I'll pull out her bed and tuck her in.'

Jenny did not seem to wake while he carried her to the bedroom, nor when presently at Moll's bidding he laid her down on the low trundle bed. The woman stooped to arrange the coverlet, and he waited till she was done, standing so close to her that her skirts brushed his knee. She stood up at last, close to him, speaking in low tones.

'There, she'll sleep till day,' she said. 'There's nothing could wake her now.' And she added slowly: 'Try the bed, see if it suits Your Honor.'

'It will suit,' he said, waiting no longer. The room was dark except for the light that came through the doorway from the fire burning bright in the other room. In that darkness after a moment the woman whispered breathlessly:

'Your cheek's as — smooth as Jenny's!'

The Lieutenant chuckled, and Jenny, where she lay on the trundle bed beside them, murmured drowsily: 'Kiss Jenny too.'

II

Tim Hager

II

Tim Hager

I

BIG TIM HAGER, Jenny's father, was a giant of a man, nearer seven feet tall than six, with a massive frame, and tremendously strong. His size commanded respect; but like most very big men, Tim was more conscious of his bulk than of his strength, always uneasily suspecting that other men were secretly laughing at him, and desperately afraid their mockery would come out into the open where he must deal with it. As a defense against that contingency, he went shouting truculently through the world, trying — with a surprising secret humility of spirit — to measure up to the opinion of himself which he attributed to others. He might have been as easily daunted as an elephant in the presence of a mouse, but he was so big and so powerful that no one had ever ventured to stand up to him; and he had not since his boyhood struck a blow or given one. In any argument he beat his opponents down by voice alone, and though they might wish to resort to violence none did so.

In the presence of women, an overpowering shyness confused his movements and tangled his tongue; and he avoided them whenever it was possible. Until he met Moll Cornish — and he was by that time well into his thirties — he was as helplessly tongue-tied in the presence of a pretty little serving maid as of a deacon's wife, and except for some embarrassing adolescent experiments, he was when he met Moll still ignorant of the mysteries into which she initiated him.

He came to Norridgewock from a farm near Canaan where he had lived with his mother till she died, and his great size and strength immediately made him conspicuous, while his obvious terror of all womankind was like a challenge to every girl in town. Moll, playing a skilful game, broke down his defenses; but Tim thought himself the victor, and he was as gleefully greedy as a colt first loosed to pasture in the spring, till the day when Moll and her mother told him that he must marry her.

Tim submitted without protest. He was as much afraid of Moll as he was intoxicated by her kindnesses, and the thought of marriage terrified him; but it was also instinctive with him to try to do what he was expected to do, to try to measure up to his obligations. Not even after they were married and had removed to Bangor did Tim cease to be afraid of Moll, but he hid his fear as though it were a crime. Like most big men he was by instinct tender and gentle; but he stifled these instincts, thinking them weaknesses. Ribald masculine assurances that women liked to be mastered and that his size made him in such matters the envy of lesser men formed the pattern of his conduct toward his wife; and his habitual ardent violence broke down little by little any affection Moll may once have felt for him.

But he did not suspect this. He thought that he was the pattern of what a husband should be, and that Moll during his absences lived only for his return. The half-dozen men who, having flattered their vanity by taking the place which he occasionally left vacant, could have told him otherwise, took care not to do so; and Moll, though she sometimes dreamed of a moment when she would tell him to his face how she hated and betrayed him, had never found the courage to risk the destructive rage of which his size made him appear capable.

II

In the four years since he came from Norridgewock to Bangor, Tim had prospered. He had a gift for handling animals, and he could get more work out of a yoke of oxen than most men. He worked as a teamster, saved money, built himself a small house, accumulated four yokes of oxen and hired men to drive them, and when the war and the British blockade rendered sea transport dangerous and risky, he entered the business of freighting goods to Boston. All honest imports from England had ended when the war began; but there was a heavy demand for British goods, and birch canoes brought smuggled wares from Fredericton to be hauled on to Boston at seven dollars the hundredweight.

Tim was not satisfied with this fair profit, and in the summer just past he and half a dozen others whom he persuaded to the venture bought in Fredericton silks and laces, sewing silk, needles and other wares to the value of several thousand dollars, but of small and convenient bulk. Some careful carpentry contrived well-concealed hiding places on his ox carts; and on this trip to the westward Tim took along the whole consignment. He stood to net himself and his associates, after these goods were sold in Boston, a handsome sum.

Tim had no scruples against smuggling. He was by politics a Federalist, with the most profound contempt for the Democratic Party and all its works, and especially for customs officers who

might seek to interfere with his activities. Before his departure, after a cheerful evening at Tom Hatch's tavern, he boasted of his plans; and John Barker, one of his partners in the current venture, led him outside and chided him for talking too much.

'First thing you know,' he warned the big man, 'you'll have the customs men after you and lose our goods and our profit too!'

'Them?' Tim echoed, in his blaring voice. 'Why, if they open their mouths to me, I'll grab them by the ears and stick my heel down their throats and pull them on like an old boot! They're nought but a lot of lousy pimps and spies, looking for a chance to make a good grab for themselves, like hungry wolves looking for a lamb to eat up! That's what you get from the Democrats!' But then, since he liked to be thought a man of character as well as parts, he added vigorously: 'But I'll say this, John. I don't rightly favor smuggling! It's all politics with me.'

III

Tim was on his return from that trip to Boston when the British occupied Castine. He heard at Lincolnville the news that an enemy fleet was making up the eastern Bay; he was at Belfast next afternoon when the Burhante frigate with two transports full of soldiers came to occupy Belfast town; and he reached Hampden late the following day to find several hundred militiamen already there. Captain Charles Morris of the Adams corvette, and General Blake commanding the militia, had called together the leading citizens of Hampden to consider what should be done; and Tim invited himself to that meeting.

When he entered, Captain Morris was speaking. The Captain was a good commander and an able man. His ship, pierced for eighteen guns but actually carrying twenty-four, and with a crew of two hundred and fifty-eight men, had captured during her summer's cruise a ship, two brigs and a schooner before she grounded on Isle au Haut in stormy weather and forced him to work up the river to make repairs. The news that the British were at Castine reached him in good season, and he immediately called on General Blake to muster the militia for an attempt to save his ship. Her guns had already been removed in preparation for hauling her out, and before Tim arrived in Hampden some of them had been dragged up to the hilltop by the meeting house whence they could deliver a raking fire at any force seeking to ascend the river, while the rest were mounted on the wharf.

Captain Morris was desperately anxious to save his ship and he

used his utmost eloquence to persuade the doubtful folk of Hampden to join him in resistance now.

'We're well placed to meet any force they bring against us,' he assured the gathering, as Tim elbowed his way through the crowd at the door. 'Our guns can smash them out of water if they try to come up the river, and General Blake's men can stand them off and protect my flank if they come by land.' Some heads wagged doubtfully, and he cried earnestly: 'Why, gentlemen, the position couldn't be better, if we're resolute and bold!'

Tim wagged his head in firm approval, anxious to play in this hour the part which he thought men would expect of him; but an old man with a half-circle of whiskers under his chin rose and said doubtfully: 'Trouble is, Cap'n, half the milishy haven't got guns — and wouldn't know what to do with them if they had.'

'I can supply muskets enough,' Captain Morris promised. 'My own men won't need them. They'll be busy serving the guns. And as for not knowing what to do with them —' His voice thickened in a sudden passion. 'Why, God Almighty, men, you're all Americans, used to hunting, used to range the forest! You mean to tell me there's an American anywhere who doesn't know how to aim a gun and fire it? What's happened to us since Bunker Hill?'

Tim Hager, standing head and shoulders above the group at the door, called in that rousing great voice of his: 'We'll handle 'em, Cap'n! We'll roll 'em down-river fast's they come up!'

But the old man came to his feet again. 'Well now, I'll tell you how it is, Cap'n Morris,' he confessed. ' 'Course, you're naturally anxious to save your ship, but dad burn it, we're worried about the town! If we fight 'em and get licked, what they'll do to us'll be a-plenty! And if we fight 'em and lick 'em, they'll just fetch some more men and ships up from Castine till they do us, and that'll be worse for us than getting licked the first time. Now, what I say —' His eyes swung around the crowded room. 'What I say is, we treat 'em right and they'll treat us right!'

There was a murmur of approval, but Tim Hager shouted in loud scorn: 'Don't let Old Whiskers down you, Cap'n! We'll back you. Give it to 'em!'

Captain Morris looked at him in a dry approval. 'You're big enough to whip them without our help, my friend,' he remarked. 'I wish we had more like you!' Then he gravely faced the others again. 'But, gentlemen, it's a mistake to trust to British courtesy — and we'll not! Our batteries will keep their ships from coming up to the town and the militia must drive back their soldiers.'

Tim, encouraged by the Captain's word, came crowding forward

and he clapped Captain Morris on the shoulder.

'We'll do it, Cap'n!' he cried again, and he faced the crowd. The sound of his own voice could always comfort him, and he was suddenly drunk with it now. A man like him, big enough to lick a bull moose in fair fight, had to set an example to lesser men.

'What did your fathers and grandfathers do to 'em at Concord?' he demanded, challenging the listeners. 'Eh? What did they? Why, they sent 'em tumbling back to Boston. Well, we'll do the same! We'll make 'em wish they'd never left Castine. We'll show 'em, by God, that one good free American can lick ten hired soldiers of any damned King! Bring 'em on!'

His bellow filled the room and rang through the village. 'Why, I was to Belfast when I see them heading up the river,' he declared. 'I didn't have to come on here and get into it, but I came a-running! Says I to myself, "There they go," I says. "Well, their mothers'd better kiss 'em good-bye, because there's half of them never will get home again. But I'll have to hurry," I says to myself, "or the folks up at Hampden will have kicked the dog water out of 'em before I get there!" So I came loping through the woods like a God damned moose, to have a piece of the fun!'

His voice was a booming roar. 'Come on!' he cried. 'Give me a musket, Cap'n. We'll show the lousy bastards, if I have to lick the lot of them alone!'

By sheer noise, he overpowered all objection. The townsfolk came to their feet in bloodthirsty zeal, and there was some shouting tumult for a while, till the crowd emptied into the street to look for rum which would fortify their sudden martial resolution.

IV

When the mob had gone, Captain Morris kept General Blake behind; and Tim, proud of having swayed the crowd by his eloquence, and full of a sense of leadership, stayed to hear what they would say.

'Do you think you can hold your militia?' Captain Morris asked the General. 'Will they stand?' He was a good commander, and he could trust his trained men, but he was too well seasoned as a fighter to expect soldierly virtues from the militia. General Blake was an older man. He had served in the Revolution, and was the hero of one legendary exploit on which his nickname hung. With a squad of men he had surrounded a farmhouse where four British officers were playing whist, and he crept up to an open window just as one of them asked what were trumps. The General, then a sergeant, shouted: 'Black Jack, by God!' and bounded through the window, making them all his prisoners. He was Black Jack to his men — and to his friends — from that day on.

But that was long ago, and the General was an old man at Hampden here today. He echoed Captain Morris' question in an indignant tone, shouting down his own misgivings.

'Can I hold them? Damme, man, they'll not need any holding! They'll stand their ground, yes and die in their tracks, like good Americans.'

Tim echoed this assurance. 'Leave it to me, Cap'n,' he said strongly. 'Any man that tries to crab it, I'll give him a boot in the backside. With me behind them, they'll eat the Britishers for breakfast. I'll make 'em more scared of me than they are of the King's men.'

Captain Morris smiled faintly. 'Well, those are fair words,' he admitted. 'But — have you ever heard bullets spatting all around you?'

Tim laughed. 'Why, I'll catch 'em in my teeth!' he cried. 'I can spit a lead ball farther and harder than most guns will shoot it.'

The Captain nodded. 'If you fight as well as you talk, we'll do fine,' he said crisply. He looked at General Blake, splendid in epaulettes and braid. 'A suggestion, General,' he remarked. 'Your uniform will attract the enemy fire. It might be wiser to remove your insignia before the fighting starts.'

The old man reared his head and snorted scornfully. 'Captain,' he retorted, 'I have never gone upon the field of battle in disguise!'

The Captain bowed. 'My apologies, sir,' he said, and Tim cried: 'Why, Godamighty, Captain, what'd the men think if they saw the General afraid of being shot at!'

'To be sure,' the Captain assented. He added in a slow amusement: 'You yourself will make a mark they'll find hard to miss, my friend.' He turned to the General again. 'Now, let us consider our dispositions. I'll put Lieutenant Lewis to command the guns on the hill by the meeting house, and Lieutenant Wadsworth on Crosby's Wharf.'

'Colonel Grant and Major Chamberlain command my militia companies,' the General assured him. 'Lieutenant Brown will direct the Bangor Light Artillery. You'll find we'll do all that men may.'

'I'm sure of it,' the Captain agreed, and he added: 'I don't think they'll come on tonight, but I'll send picket boats down the river, and your videttes will give us ample warning if they come by land.' He turned toward the door. 'Now I'll serve out muskets to those of your men who have no weapons, and we'll see what we will see.'

v

Tim Hager, flushed with his oratorical triumph and fortified with half a dozen noggins of rum, presently attached himself to Major Chamberlain. His secret doubts of his own courage were long ago forgotten, and he was loudly confident of the event, reassuring the Major.

'We'll stand like rocks, Major,' he promised. 'We'll lay them down as easy as laying popple shoots with a brush hook! But Major, there'll be lead and iron flying like ice in a sleet storm. We've got to put the womenfolks out of harm's way.'

'That's done, Hager,' Major Chamberlain assured him. 'They're all gone to Mr. Lane's house, back about a mile on Sowadabscook Stream. They're safe enough there.'

'You've done well,' Tim acknowledged. 'I've the prettiest wife in Bangor town waiting for me, and a baby besides. I'm a family man, Major; and I'll fight like a lion to protect my family; but if I knew they were in a bullet's way, I'd have no stomach for battle at all — and you'll find other men feel the same. Where did you say they are? At Josh Lane's?'

'Yes, about a mile up the Stream.'

'Good!' Tim repeated. A sailor from the Adams handed him a musket, a handful of balls, powder flask and spare flints. Tim laughed. 'I'll not need this if I can get my hands on them,' he boasted. Nevertheless he proceeded to charge the gun. 'You've done well, Major,' he said again. 'Now I'll just go talk to the boys, see to't their dander's up so they'll be ready for anything. If I can get these men mad, they'll fight like the devil himself!'

Through the early evening hours he busied himself in this fashion, going along the waiting lines and clapping men on the back so vociferously that they staggered and coughed for minutes afterward. 'Lias Browning from Brewer, handling his musket dubiously, confessed that he was not used to firearms. 'I don't even know how to load the danged thing!' he admitted.

Tim laughed at his ignorance. 'Watch me, man!' he commanded. 'Do what I do.' He loaded his piece as an example to 'Lias, and moved on. Rain had begun to fall, and he found a group of men huddling in the open door of Mr. Godfrey's barn and damned them for a pack of shivering cowards, afraid of a little water; but the rain was chill, and he stayed there with them. A nervous skirmisher down beyond Pitcher's Brook saw a cow moving through the night and let off his gun, and the report, muffled and remote, silenced the shivering men. The distant shot prompted Tim to load his

musket, and he rammed home the bullet with an excessive violence
to prove his courage to himself.

Then he realized that his mouth was dry as dust, so he slipped
away and went foraging. The jug he found in the cellar of a
deserted house in the village was no more than a quarter full when
it came into his hands, and a little dab of rum like that wouldn't
be any good at all for even two men. It wasn't really enough for
Tim. He finished it within the hour, staying in the cellar till the
jug was drained.

He was reluctant to leave his refuge even then. If there was
going to be any shooting, the cellar was a mighty safe, comfortable
place. But those trembling cowards out in the rain wouldn't be
worth a whistle in the morning unless someone kept their spirits
up, and Tim knew himself the man to do it. Before leaving the
cellar he poured a charge of powder into his musket and rammed
a ball well home and checked his flint and filled the pan, to be
ready for action when the time for action came.

He marched out in the rain and struck up a roaring song.

'I often have been told that the British seamen bold
    Could beat the tars of France so neat and handy, O;
But they never found their match till the Yankees did them catch
    For the Yankee tars for fighting are the dandy, O.'

He swaggered toward the meeting house, and his singing was a
brazen outrage in the night and rain.

'Oh, the Guerriere so bold on the foaming ocean rolled,
    Commanded by Dacres the grandee, O,
With as fine a British crew . . .'

Someone shouted from the lee of the meeting house: 'Hush up
that God damned noise! You'll have them turning loose on us!'
Tim was abashed, and he hoped no one knew it was he who had
been singing. He found the men of Major Chamberlain's company, and went from one group to the next, and discovered a
youngster of seventeen or eighteen, huddled against the foot of a
great oak and shaking with nervous tears. Tim pounced on him.

'Hey, what's this? What's this?' he demanded. 'Crying like a
woman! I'll give you something to cry about!' He hauled the boy
across his knee and paddled him roundly, the youngster struggling
to be free and swearing with a sobbing violence; and Major
Chamberlain came to investigate the disturbance, and Tim freed
his victim and the boy squalled through tears of rage:

'You big ox, you lay a hand on me again and I'll blow you in two!'
'That's more like it, sonny!' Tim told him in grave approval,

and he appealed to the officer: 'See what I mean, Major? I was just trying to get him mad. Get 'em mad and they'll fight like good ones.'

Major Chamberlain said quietly: 'You look out for yourself, Hager, and the men will do the same.' He moved away, and Tim, loading his musket against the time of need, spoke indignantly to the group of men who had gathered around him.

'That's the thanks a man gets, trying to help! The Major's had a drop too much, boys, if you ask me; but we can handle the God damned British without him!'

They answered only with mutters, and Tim moved on, a little unsteady on his feet, stumbling in the darkness. He climbed the hill, following the line marked by clustering huddles of men in every spot that offered shelter from the rain; and the ghostly murmur of voices as he passed made him shy like a nervous horse, and once he tripped over a boulder which projected through the sod and fell his length, heavily, his musket flying. He salvaged it and moved on at random till he came to the road and the meeting house and found a number of men and officers there with the guns, an eighteen-pounder off the Adams, and the four-pounders of the Bangor Artillery Company. He laid his hand on the great gun, and the cold wet iron was clammy and chilling so that he shivered. He wished someone would make a noise, and hoping other voices would join his, he sang in low tones:

'"Oh," cries Hall unto his crew, "we will try what we can do,
 If we beat these boasting Britons we're the dandy, O."
The first broadside ——'

But a voice with the accents of command called: 'Silence, you there by the gun!' So Tim stopped singing and drifted away down the hill again. His teeth were chattering together — perhaps with cold — and every shadow moving in the night made his heart pound. He descended toward the river with no purpose in his mind; and he came to a cart shed not far from the water and groped his way into it and found it half full of men. He stumbled in among them, and around him in the darkness low voices murmured, telling bloody tales heard from fathers and grandfathers of battles during the Revolution and in the older Indian days; and Tim listened and licked his dry lips and dreaded coming dawn. Then the rum in him and the snug warmth of the shed and the heat generated in his steaming clothing lulled him to snoring slumber.

VI

When he woke, Tim knew instantly and instinctively that he was alone; and to find himself thus deserted in the face of the enemy was frightening. It was still dark, yet there was a hint of brightness in the sky. The wind had come southerly, warm and bland. In his first alarm at finding himself abandoned, he hurriedly loaded his musket and then with an elaborate stealth crept out of the shed.

There was light enough so that he could see the shape of near-by things, black in the morning fog. He found with a vast relief that the men were still here, the line extending up the hill from the river to the meeting house. He located Major Chamberlain's company and took his stand with them. Dawn came gray through the fog, and a foggy dawn after a rainy night is a bad time to wait for soldiers to come and shoot at you. Tim's teeth began to chatter again, and he wondered what a man could do about breakfast, and then suddenly he was violently sick. As though he had given a signal, he heard another man retching, up the line; and a moment later another; and there were sneezings and coughings and the rattle of equipment from men invisible in the fog; and someone spat and elaborately cleared his throat and spat again. Major Chamberlain came along the line with two men carrying heaps of cornbread on a hand barrow, and everyone took a handful, but Tim's stomach turned over at sight of the bread soggy with rain and he did not touch it.

It was still dim and misty when a little after seven a spatter of shots sounded from beyond Pitcher's Brook. Tim in haste began to load his gun. He had some trouble with it. There seemed to be an obstruction in the barrel so that the ramrod would not go in as far as it should. While he was still bewildered by this, Major Chamberlain moved along the line of men to steady them, and Tim appealed to him.

'Look a-here, Major!' he said huskily. 'This God damned musket's no good! Give me a gun that will shoot. I want to get me a couple of Britishers for breakfast!'

The Major took the gun and tried it, twisting the screw end of the ramrod into the obstruction, tugging. He pulled out a lead ball and its patch, and turned the gun with its muzzle down and a little stream of powder ran out.

'Why, you drunken fool!' he said harshly. 'This gun's already loaded.' Then in sudden recollection: 'I've seen you load it twice, myself!' He measured the depth to which the ramrod would go. 'Man, there must be six or seven charges in it! How many English-

men did you expect to kill with one shot?' The men around were
grinning at Tim's discomfiture, and the Major passed the musket
back to him. 'Here, draw the charges and make your piece ready,'
he said, more gently. 'You'll have a chance to use it damned soon
now.'

He turned away. Down the hill beyond the brook, from men
hidden in the fog, more shots sounded. Tim, with a hooting and
derisive audience, began to try to clear the barrel of his musket,
but it was a tedious and trying business. An acorn, loosened by a
squirrel, dropped off the oak tree under which he stood and rapped
him sharply on the shoulder, and he barked in hoarse panic and
clapped his hand to the spot and looked for blood, and the men
around him laughed aloud, and Tim grinned sheepishly and then
mustered his courage again.

'By God, that's more like it!' he cried. 'I knew if I could get
you boys to laughing you'd forget to be scared. Let 'em come now!
We'll give it to 'em!'

He was still fumbling with the musket when the great guns down
on Crosby's Wharf began to thunder. The musket fire beyond
Pitcher's Brook had been disquieting, but at this loud clangor the
raw militiamen huddled in uneasy groups, showing the whites of
their eyes.

And then suddenly the fog thinned, and looking down toward
the brook they caught a glimpse of the British columns approaching
the bridge. Up to the right by the meeting house the eighteen-
pounder bellowed, and the lesser guns let go, jarring the ground
with their detonations. Major Chamberlain came smartly along
the line.

'Wait till they're handy, boys,' he said over and over. 'Don't
shoot till they're close. Wait till you can't miss, and pick your
man and drop him.'

The fog shut in again, and when it thinned once more, the
British were filing across the bridge, deploying into orderly ranks,
moving firmly forward. Guns were going, down there, too; and
the smoke from them, carried toward the militiamen by the light,
southerly breeze, became a curtain which hid the advancing enemy
completely. This curtain of fog and smoke rolled up the slope,
concealing everything behind it. It drew nearer. There was something dreadful in the advance of that cloud which hid no one knew
what terrors. Before it, the American line insensibly sagged backward. To face flesh and blood would have been easier than to face
that screening fog from which hideous death might at any moment
emerge.

When the men near him sagged back, Tim threw away his still useless weapon and sagged with them. To stand unarmed before so many enemies was too much to expect of any man! Major Chamberlain raced along the line, commanding, laughing, pleading; and he checked them for a moment, but Colonel Grant's company on their flank was sagging too. When the line bent back too far and stretched too thin, it tore apart and broke into huddling groups; but even these groups did not stand. Each one, finding itself for a moment left to face that creeping fog and smoke behind which the enemy was advancing, sought to overtake the others; and as though in a game of leap-frog, the groups left behind raced after those which were gone. The withdrawal gained speed, and suddenly, most of them without having fired a shot, four or five hundred American militiamen were trampling the officers who tried to stop them, bolting in headlong flight for the bridge across the Sowadabscook and the Bangor road.

Tim ran with them, but he was slow of foot and lesser men outstripped him. When he reached the first house of the village and saw an open cellar way, he plunged into it like a rabbit into its hole. The potato bin was full. Tim leaped in among the potatoes and began to burrow, seeking any hiding place. Outside the house, the rout swept on.

VII

The bridge was a bottleneck through which the fugitives must pass. When Major Chamberlain reached it, he hoped to make a stand there, and he tried to rally the bolder spirits. He had perhaps a dozen doubtful men in hand when he saw Tim Hager plunging toward him, tearing his way through the pack of those who were trying to cross the bridge all at once. Tim had lost faith in potatoes as a hiding place when he remembered that the British soldiers might prod among them with their bayonets. He had no wish to be spitted, with a potato on the same bayonet for garnishing, so he took to flight again; and the congestion at the bridge enabled him to overtake there the other fugitives.

When the Major saw him coming, he recognized in Tim a potentially valuable ally. 'You, Hager!' he cried. 'Help me hold these men!' Tim paid no heed, rushing across the bridge, and the Major shouted: 'Halt, Hager! Halt, I say!'

Tim, without checking his lumbering run, bawled at him: 'Halt be God damned! Why, Major, this is dangerous! You'll get us all killed!'

And when the Major would have stopped him by brute force, he brushed the smaller man aside and so was gone.

VIII

Behind him in the town, and from Crosby's Wharf, there was still some firing; and the Bangor road was choked with fugitives, looking fearfully over their shoulders as they ran. Tim decided that the road was no place for him. He was so big that he offered more than a fair target for British bullets. He turned blindly upstream and made for the nearest woods, seeking to conceal his mighty frame. Probably the soldiers would chase the militia clear to Bangor and hang the lot of them. Tim did not want to be hanged. He pushed on up the Sowadabscook, at first with no goal in mind; but then he remembered that the womenfolk and the children were at Josh Lane's house. If they were safe there, a man ought to be.

By the time he reached the house, Tim's wits were working again. If the British did happen to come here and found him, his mud-stained clothing would prove he had fought against them and they would hang him after all. When he came to the house, everyone was out in the yard, staring off toward the village, and questions poured on him.

'Why, we'd have whopped them easy,' he announced. 'But Colonel Grant's men took and run, and what was left of us couldn't handle them alone, so they're chasing everyone to Bangor, hanging every man they catch!' He pushed through the weeping, trembling women and took Josh Lane's arm and led him indoors. 'They'll hang me, too, Josh,' he cried, 'if they see the mud on my clothes! You've got to give me something to put on.'

'Why, I ain't got a thing,' Josh protested. 'Only my wedding suit, and no two of my suits would make a coat for you.'

'Where is it?' Tim insisted. 'I can wedge into it.'

'No, and you can't,' Josh insisted, but Tim gripped his arm with an overruling violence and Josh ruefully submitted.

When Tim began to fight his way into the suit, and Josh heard the first seam go, he groaned, but Tim said reproachfully:

'Godamighty, Josh, wouldn't you rather see a seam ripped than see me hung? Well, I would! Be sensible, man!' His great legs were compressed into skin-tight breeches, and the coat was so small that his arms were drawn backward by it, his wrists projecting halfway to the elbows. 'Now, where's a place to hide?'

IX

Tim was in the darkest corner of the cellar an hour or so later, when a British patrol came and dug him out and marched him back to Hampden with a bayonet pricking his hams. He and seventy-five or eighty other prisoners were crowded into the cabin of the Decatur, which had made port at Hampden weeks before with a cargo from Bordeaux, and which had been held there since then by the British blockade. The prisoners had scant room even to stand, and none to sit or to lie down; and they were kept with neither food nor water, and with very little air, all night.

But next day before the Decatur was burned they were ferried ashore to be paroled. Tim, a ludicrous figure in Josh Lane's best broadcloth suit, of which half the seams were irreparably ripped, was among a group still under guard on the wharf, when the flotilla of boats which Lieutenant Carruthers had taken up to Bangor came down-river.

Tim saw Moll and Jenny in the stern sheets of the Lieutenant's boat. His first reaction was a hopeless despair at discovering these two whom he loved thus prisoners of the invaders; but then he realized that Moll did not look like a wretched prisoner. She was glowing with some inner happiness, dressed in her best, close by the Lieutenant's side.

The boat touched just below where Tim stood, and the Lieutenant landed on the wharf to report to Captain Barrie for orders. Tim's size made him conspicuous, and Moll saw him and began to laugh at his ridiculous costume; but when Jenny recognized him she held out her arms and called delightedly:

'Mommy, there's poppy!'

So Tim could not escape attention. He asked hoarsely: 'Moll, what you a-doing in that boat?'

Moll did not answer. The Lieutenant and Captain Barrie were at one side with Colonel John, and the Lieutenant turned to see what was going on. Colonel John asked him crisply:

'What is this affair, Mr. Carruthers?'

'Why, the lady has asked our protection, sir,' the Lieutenant told him. 'She begged to be given transportation to Castine, where she has relations.'

'Relations?' Tim echoed, perplexed and yet indignant too. 'She ain't got any more relations in Castine than a sturgeon has wings! Moll, you get out of there and come along home with me.'

Colonel John smiled in amused understanding. He spoke to the woman. 'Is the Lieutenant correct?' he asked.

'Yes, he is,' she told him stoutly. 'I want to go to Castine, and to Halifax too! My uncle lives in Halifax!'

'Is this clown who has outgrown his garments your husband?'

'Yes, he is, but I want nothing to do with him.'

Jenny cried plaintively: 'I want my poppy!' She sought to escape from her mother's grasp, to climb up on the wharf; and Colonel John spoke to Captain Barrie.

'We're asked for a judgment of Solomon, Captain,' he remarked. 'If the woman wants sanctuary with us, I think we ought to grant it, don't you?'

'I'm sure Mr. Carruthers would say so,' Captain Barrie agreed with a chuckle. Tim tried to speak, and Captain Barrie said harshly: 'Silence, you, before we stretch that thick neck of yours!'

'But the baby seems to prefer the father,' Colonel John pointed out. 'Suppose we let her go to him for a minute?'

So Jenny was passed up to Tim, and she clung to him; and Moll called persuasively: 'There, Jenny, now you come back to mommy.'

Jenny cried: 'No! I hate you!' She buried her face in Tim's shoulder, wailing wretchedly: 'I want my poppy!'

Colonel John nodded. 'All right, we'll let him have the baby, since she decides it so. I suppose the woman must do as she likes.' He spoke to Moll. 'Madame, do you wish to stay behind with your baby?'

Moll Hager hesitated, looking at Tim and then at the Lieutenant; but her hesitation was not long. 'I wouldn't stay with that hairy bull for twenty babies,' she said lightly. 'But Jenny'd rather go with me, only she's a little scared of the boats. Jenny, you come here to mommy.'

But Jenny clung to Tim, her arms around his neck, her face buried under his ear, shaking her head. 'No! No!' she insisted. 'I hate you! I love my poppy!'

Moll flushed angrily. 'Let him keep the brat,' she said. 'She'll make him sorry he ever fathered her!'

The Colonel nodded. 'I wish you joy of your conquest, Lieutenant,' he said in a dry distaste. 'You're doing this giant a favor, ridding him of her.' He turned to Tim. 'Have you made your parole?' he asked shortly.

'Yes, Your Honor.'

'Then take the little girl and be off with you!'

Tim appealed hopelessly to his wife. 'Moll, you'd ought to come along home,' he urged.

But Moll only laughed, and Captain Barrie told Tim: 'Go while you can, man!'

So Tim turned away, Jenny close in his arms. He crossed the bridge and took the Bangor road and left the town behind. Jenny's sobs slowed and she hiccoughed in his ear and whispered softly:

'I love you, poppy.'

Tim strained her close in a wakened hunger and longing. His cheek was white and hard. Behind him smoke from burning ships rose in black billows to the sky. With Jenny in his arms, he trudged home to Bangor to face mirth and shame.

2

It was dusk when Tim came tramping into town with Jenny, now asleep, in his arms; and he was glad to avoid notice, wretchedly conscious of the sorry appearance he must make in Josh Lane's best broadcloth, so much too small for him, and sadly split and wrinkled now. He thought the town must know by this time the story of his cowardice, and of that musket which he had loaded so often but never fired; and he shivered with shame at the memory. He had tried so hard to stifle his fears, to play the leader and the strong man, till flat panic overcame him. When he passed Hatch's tavern, he heard loud drunken voices within as men boasted what they would do to the British if they came another time; and he listened and heard this one say that General Blake was to blame for the panic, and another damned Major Chamberlain, and a third said Colonel Grant had run faster than any of them.

Tim dreaded to hear his name mentioned, but in the days to come he would find that his own cowardice at Hampden was forgotten in the poltroonery of so many others. Those who like him had fled occupied themselves in seeking to make a scapegoat of their officers. Also, Moll's departure had won for Tim the sympathy of the town. Others had lost their goods and their ships, but he had lost his wife; and this gave him a certain distinction in the public mind. A dozen good women offered to undertake Jenny's care, to give her a home; but he refused, for already Jenny began in many ways to take Moll's place in his life, winning him to smiles, making him forget her mother.

He and Jenny stayed on in the little house, and Tim hired Mrs.

Hollis to keep house for him and Jenny. She was a widow woman with grown sons and daughters of her own, and she lived with one of her sons on Hancock Street not far from Tim's home. She came to cook his meals, to clean and tend for him; but Jenny from the first insisted that Tim should put her to bed at night and dress her in the morning. Mrs. Hollis was scandalized by this.

'It ain't fitten for you to see that young one naked!' she protested. 'It ain't right and proper, Tim, and I won't be under the same roof with such goings on.'

But Tim was unwilling to lose any part of this increasingly sweet communion, and Jenny, seeming not to miss her mother at all, was devoted to him. If she woke before he did, she was apt to leave her small bed and climb into his, pressing against him in his sleep, touching with one small finger the stiff hairs in his nostrils, drawing her finger along his lips till he began to stir uneasily and to puff and snort and lick his lips and brush at them with his hand, and so woke at last. When he found her thus happily tormenting him, and because it pleased her to the point of ecstasy, he might assume a ferocious anger, and spank her with awkward gentleness till she pretended to weep and he could comfort her.

He liked best of all the Saturday nights when he bathed her, in a great tub before a blazing fire; and when he was inadequate she instructed him to do thus and so, and Tim obeyed. When the bath was done he wrapped her in a rough towel and dried her small body, delicate and soft yet wiry strong; and when she was dry she might wriggle away from him and run to and fro about the firelit room, her white skin bright in the radiance of the flames, while he laughingly pursued her, afraid of hurting her if he caught her too abruptly, till he penned her at last in some corner, or under the great bed in the other room, or perhaps in the bed itself where she had dived for sanctuary.

Mrs. Hollis, witnessing these occasions while she washed the supper dishes, said they were two heathens. 'She's every bit as bad as you are, Tim Hager!' she declared. 'And it ain't decent! I'll stand about so much of such goings on, and then I'll walk out on you and there you'll be. Bringing up that child as if she didn't know the meaning of clothes! If I don't keep my eye on her every minute all day, as like as not she'll get away from me and wriggle out of every stitch and go running around as naked as the day she was born.'

But she never carried out her threat to leave them to their own devices. Tim's helplessness awoke her protective, maternal instinct; and Jenny won her completely.

II

Moll had never been a church-goer, but Tim, facing the task of bringing up Jenny in the way she should go, thought it his duty for her sake to become a member of Mr. Loomis' congregation. He took Jenny with him to the meetings in the Court House. Also, Martha Allen had commenced a few months before to conduct the first Sunday School in Bangor, and she welcomed Jenny into her class. It was through his church attendance that Tim first had news of Moll. One Sunday in mid-October, an early cold spell made it necessary to build fires in the portable stoves which heated the court-room where the meetings were held, and the hall outside. During meeting, Tim, in the rearmost seats, heard movements in the hall; and a few moments later his nostrils caught the unmistakable odor of sausages cooking.

To stimulate Tim's new interest in right and godly living, Elder Loomis had persuaded him to join the recently organized Bangor Moral Society and Tythingmen, whose responsibility it was to try to enforce a seemly observance of the Sabbath; and to cook sausages in the portals of the church was surely not a fit way to behave, so Tim slipped out into the hall to admonish the individual guilty of this profanation.

He found Haty Colson cooking his dinner on the small stove there. Hatevil Colson was one of those simple-minded, harmless folk so often to be found in small towns. Mrs. Hollis called him 'love-cracked.' He lived an itinerant life, wandering across the countryside, eager to tell anyone who would listen how a girl named Spinny Goldthread — of whom no one had ever heard except from him — had jilted him. He was a petty thief, but since he seldom stole anything but food — which would have been gladly given him — he was tolerated and treated always with a kindly sympathy.

So, although Tim might have hustled another man brusquely out of doors, he spoke to Haty mildly now, telling him he ought to go cook his sausages somewhere else. Haty looked at him with shrewd, rolling eyes, and without responding to this suggestion said in a sly tone:

'I see Moll Hager down't Castine. Know her, do ye? Like to have some news of her?'

The British, having destroyed all possibility of attack by sea, had garrisoned Castine with a force under General Gosselin and sent their fleet back to Halifax. This much Tim knew, and now at Haty's word a sudden hope stirred in his heart.

'See her, did ye?' he asked.

Haty laid his finger to his nose. 'I'm a-telling you, ain't I?' He turned his sausages and chuckled to himself. 'I went down there because I had something to say to that General,' he boasted. 'I made it up by myself, too, one day when I was to Belfast, and they told me what his name was. But I didn't tell anybody what I was going to say to him. I just put for Castine, laughing to myself fit to kill when I thought how he'd look when I said it to him.'

Tim asked urgently: 'What about Moll?'

'I didn't see her till after I'd seen the General,' Haty assured him, and then with sudden, shrill impatience: 'Drat it, man, I didn't go there to see her! I went to see this General. Well and I got there and I made them take me right to him. They didn't want to, but I made 'em, so they did.' He began to laugh in anticipation. 'So they did,' he repeated. 'He, he, he! So they did, and I says to him, "Be ye General Gosselin?" I says, and he says — he, he, he! — he says: "Yes, I be," he says. "What can I do for you?" So I says — he, he, he! — I says: "Well, if you're the goslin', then damn the goose that hatched ye!"'

He shook with laughter, and picked up a hot sausage in his fingers and tossed it from hand to hand for a moment, then nibbled at it gingerly. Tim laughed politely and he asked again:

'Did ye see Moll?'

'Yup!'

Tim brushed his mouth with his hand. 'How'd she look?' he asked huskily.

'Why, good!' Haty assured him. 'She looked good!' Then he chortled again. 'Not what Elder Loomis would call "good"!' he admitted. 'But purtier'n I ever see her.'

'What was she doing?'

'Just getting into a boat,' said Haty calmly. 'Just getting into a boat and rowing out to a great ship and sailing off to Halifax! And that's the last I see of her.' He finished his sausages and rubbed his hands on his coat. 'There, I've et,' he said. 'Much obliged for the use of the stove. Now I've got some business. I'll have to go.'

III

Tim was not surprised by Haty's news. Moll had said that day at Hampden wharf that she would go to Halifax. Nevertheless he did not even now give up all hope of her return; and when late that month Amos Patten, as the town's emissary, departed for Halifax to seek from Sir John Sherbrooke some amelioration of the conditions of the bond Bangor had given to guarantee delivery of vessels that were building in the town when the British came to Bangor, Tim sought him out and asked him to try to find some news of Moll. Amos promised sympathetically to do so.

He returned in December — his mission had slight success — and told Tim what he had learned. News had come to Halifax while Amos was there of the death of young Lieutenant Carruthers when the Endymion's boats attempted to capture the privateer Prince of Neufchatel off Nantucket early in October. But as for Moll, Amos said Tim would be wise to forget her as quickly as possible.

'She's forgot you long ago,' he said. 'I saw her, Tim. She's a bad one. She's forgot you, and she'd already forgotten the Lieutenant before the news came he was dead. There's a master's mate she's took up with now.'

Tim asked no more questions; but sometimes in the years that followed he wondered whether Moll were still alive, wondered to what wretched depths she had descended. He never heard of her in any way again.

3

THROUGH the ten years after Moll left him, Jenny came to mean more than life to Tim. Not even the period when she was losing baby teeth and getting new ones — which seemed at first so much too large for her — made her less beautiful in his eyes. Till Moll went away, Tim had thought little of his daughter; but now they were thrown into an increasingly close communion, and from the first she lavished on him a generous affection which made Tim her slave. There was for him an indescribable delight in her caressing tendernesses. She had an amusing trick of climbing on his knee, circling his neck with her small arms, hugging him tight and kissing him and then sitting back to look at him, her head on one side, as though trying to read his mind; and at what she saw she might laugh and hug him again. There were times when she did not wish him to touch her at all; but there were other times when she lay in his arms and went to sleep, warm and soft and small, and the big man might sit for an hour holding her so before he carried her to her bed.

During her childhood they drew closer all the time; but at first Tim was sometimes away from home. Leaving Mrs. Hollis to care for Jenny during his absence, he and his ox teams hauled from Augusta, by rude wilderness roads, the printing press and types with which Peter Edes presently began to publish the Bangor *Weekly Register*, the first newspaper in town. With the end of the war, water freight to Boston took the place of the land journey; so Tim turned to business nearer home. Bangor's best export crop was lumber. Farming promised so poorly that after the nearer forests were cleared there had been many migrants to Ohio; but those who stayed at home began to extend their lumbering up the river, and Tim's ox teams were in demand. New mills were being built, and vessels came to carry loads of sawed lumber to the westward. The navigation of the river below Bangor was doubtful and uncertain, and Tim had a hand in making the first survey, checking depths of water and marking dangerous ledges. He owned shares in several vessels, and he prospered modestly.

But the heart of his life was always Jenny, and as she grew older he began to refuse to accept work that would take him long away from her. He ran a net in the mouth of the Stream to catch salmon for the market, and Jenny liked to go out with him to bring in his take. Once when a great sturgeon became entangled in the net he noosed a rope around its tail, and the sluggish fish towed the boat up and down the river for an hour, to Jenny's shrill delight. After that — although sturgeon were a nuisance and were apt to tear the net — Tim was always glad to catch one. If Jenny were not with him, his shout would bring her running down to the bank for another ride. It was a game of which she was slow to tire, and Tim never wearied of watching her pleasure in it.

She had, even as she grew older, few playmates. Mrs. Hollis and Tim kept her at first close at home. Doctor Rich, who had tended most of the militiamen wounded at Hampden, later moved to Bangor and lived near them, and when Jenny was seven Isaiah Poster built a house and store just beyond Doctor Rich's home; but there were not many residences in the immediate neighborhood. Mr. Poster had a son named Ephraim, a year or so younger than Jenny, and there were children in the Rich household; but with these exceptions Jenny had no friends her own age.

But older people knew her and liked her. She was regular in attendance at Miss Allen's Sunday School, regularly in her place by Tim at church; and she had ingratiating ways. If she had faults too, the womenfolks agreed that this was because of her upbringing. Mrs. Hollis' stories of Tim's tender and scrupulous care of the little girl amused and touched them. They liked Jenny, and Tim too.

II

Tim had, though he never realized this, one enemy. When Jenny was ten years old, Maine achieved statehood; and at the same time, with a developing self-consciousness, men began to predict the heights to which the new state might aspire. Isaiah Poster was one of these. He was New Hampshire born, and he had come to Bangor in 1804, foreseeing even then that the great pine forests of the province of Maine would make rich men out of those who knew how to exploit them.

But he was before his time. He found a wilderness village of three or four hundred people, scratching at rocky farms; and the glowing reports from the new state of Ohio lured him west. From there he wrote jocosely to Amos Patten: 'The corn grows so tall out here it needs a ladder to pick it. Down near Chillicothe a farmer dug a big beet — he had to quarry it out in chunks — and his boy fell into the hole and the farmer had to let down a bed cord to pull him out. I never saw it myself, but they say that up Sandusky way the pigs are so big you can roast the outsides of 'em and the pigs never know it, so they run around with knives and forks stuck into 'em, and when a man wants a snack he just slices off a piece.'

He stayed ten years in Ohio, but in 1817 he returned to Bangor and built a house and a store on Poplar Street opposite the distillery. Bangor men had begun to be farm-conscious, and Jacob Chick and Will Thompson vied with each other to see which would be the first to serve green peas to patrons of their taverns; but at the same time, men dreamed of fortunes in pine; and one group — Judge Kinsley; former Congressman Francis Carr, who despite his record as a supporter of the war had signed the submission when the British were in Bangor; Amos and Moses Patten who had been ruined by the depredations of the British in 1814 but who were now on the way to recoup their losses; Isaiah Poster, John Barker, and Mr. Williamson, who would be in turn Postmaster, Senator from Penobscot County, the second Governor of the new state, and finally a Congressman, and who was then already engaged on his monumental history of Maine — bought jointly twenty thousand acres of wild lands as a speculation against the future.

But Isaiah also made scattering purchases on his own account.

He preferred to buy selected tracts rather than to acquire land at random; and the year Jenny was eleven, he persuaded Tim Hager to go up-river and look out good pieces of pine for him. Tim did not want to go, preferring to stay at home with Jenny; but Isaiah persisted till Tim's resistance was at last worn down. He was six weeks gone, and he missed Jenny, missed her prettily affectionate ways, and her trick of sitting on his lap for a while after supper, and of coming into his bed in the morning. He was as lonely for her as an uxorious husband for his wife, and he thought more of her than of what he had come to do.

On his return Mrs. Hollis gave a good account of her. 'She's better off with you away than with you here,' she told Tim, mocking his solicitude.

Tim held Jenny on his knee. 'Did you get lonesome for me?' he asked her, and she hugged him and said she had been awful lonesome.

'But I played with Eph lots,' she said. 'And Uncle Isaiah let me eat gingersnaps at the store.'

He felt a momentary jealous resentment. 'Call Isaiah "Uncle," do you?'

Jenny nodded. 'He wants me to,' she said. 'And he's nice.'

Mrs. Hollis explained that Isaiah — since it was he who had sent Tim away — had felt responsible for Jenny's well-being during her father's absence; and that reminded Tim to go and report to his employer. But he had little of value to tell Isaiah. The vastness of the untouched forests up-river had confused him. 'There's big pine everywhere,' he told Isaiah. 'Millions of trees. I dunno as I saw any one place that was better than another.'

Isaiah felt himself cheated by this vague report and said so; and he berated Tim with a violence which increased when the big man sat passive under his reproaches.

'Well,' Tim said at last, 'I c'n see how you might feel that way, but I dunno how I c'n help it. I done the best I could, but if you didn't get your money's worth, I'll make it up to you.'

'You've wasted my money and my time!' Isaiah told him stormily. 'I'd have been a year ahead of myself if you'd done what I told you to do. Why, damn it, Hager, you've cost me a lot of money!'

There was, his tone implied, no higher crime than this; and Tim felt guilty about it. He considered himself bound to repay Isaiah; and the result was that he became in small ways Isaiah's man, fetching and carrying as Isaiah required — and without pay.

But Tim, happy to be at home with Jenny again, did not greatly mind this. She seemed to understand, with the uncanny intuition

which children so often possess, that she had taken her mother's
place in his life; and sometimes, as though she saw how it moved
him, she pretended to be Moll. Coming into his bed in the morning, waking him with the caressing touch of her small hands, she
might say: 'Now you hold me and hug me like you did mommy.'
Or, thrusting her small arm under his neck: 'Now I'll be mommy
and hold your head on my shoulder!' She began to rule him abso-
lutely; and when she scolded him, Tim stood abashed before her,
and Mrs. Hollis shook with amusement at them both and told her
friends it was a sight to see that young one make her father stand
around. In spite of her sharp tongue, she was as proud of Jenny
as Tim was, devoted to the child.

III

Jenny began her formal education in Aunt Betty Minot's school,
and when she was twelve Mr. Baldwin opened his Young Ladies'
Academy — for boys as well as girls — and she became a regular
attendant. The classes met in a room on the third floor of the
brick store building Joe Leavitt had built on Washington Street,
near the river; but later the Academy moved into the one-story, hip-
roofed building where Aunt Betty Minot had formerly presided.
Jenny was at first almost the youngest of the children there. She
had a quick, acquisitive mind and she easily achieved equality with
her immediate elders. The tuition was twenty cents a week, but
Jenny, since she lived at home, had not to pay the nine shillings a
week board which was the standard figure charged by Judge
Kinsley and others who provided lodging for students from the
towns down the river.

Through her new contact with older girls, Jenny acquired a
sudden interest in clothes, and Tim realized that as she grew older
her demands would increase. Once he had been an enterprising
man, full of plans and projects; but Moll's going left him for a
while with no real ambition. Now, in the perception of Jenny's
increasing needs, he wanted to make money.

It was natural that he should turn to the lumber business, for
talk of pine was in the air. The fact that he himself owned no
timber land was not an obstacle. Benjamin Bussey of Roxbury
and such outsiders had bought lands north of Bangor, but a man
who wanted a few trees cut them where he would. None thought
the theft of standing timber a crime. Pine on the stump was so
nearly valueless that to steal it was like taking a breath of air,
and could hurt no one. Maine, on achieving statehood two or

three years before, had refused to pay Massachusetts four cents an acre for eight million acres of wild lands within her borders, because the price was held to be too high; so when Tim that winter hired a crew of men to lumber off a vein of big pines west of the horseback a few miles above Old Town, and set his oxen to haul them to the river so that they could be floated down to the mills in the spring, it did not occur to him to seek out the owner of the land, whoever he might be, and offer to buy it.

He put all the financial resources he could muster into this project, borrowing heavily; and he arranged by correspondence to sell his lumber, when it should be cut and sawed, in Boston. The bargain was concluded before he set axe to the first tree. When in the early summer he saw the lumber loaded on the Little Cherub schooner, which Joseph Leavitt had built three years before, he went with his cargo to Boston to consummate his bargain. His cut had been a big one, and he was jubilantly sure of a handsome profit.

The market, since he made his dicker, had advanced; but Tim — having already agreed with the purchaser upon a price for "merchantable lumber" — did not expect to be able to take advantage of this fact. Sharp dealing by his Boston correspondent gave him the opportunity. Bangor lumber merchants had suffered for years from unfair classification of their cargoes after they were delivered in Boston; and the surveyor there, after inspecting Tim's cargo, set aside a full half of it as 'refuse.' The purchaser paid for the 'merchantable lumber' and then proposed to take the refuse at a lower price; but Tim laughed at him.

'I'll be damned if you will!' he retorted, his voice booming in its old way. 'I didn't contract to sell you refuse. If this is refuse, I'll just keep it myself and see if I can't get a price for it.'

He readily found a purchaser at a figure higher than that which had been paid for the rest of his shipment, and he was exultant, but not for long. He took payment, in both cases, in bills of the Bangor Bank; but when he went to the New England Bank to redeem the bills at the current discount, he found that redemption had been stopped — and there was a report that the bank had failed.

'Why, there can't be a thing wrong with the Bangor Bank!' Tim protested. 'Not with the men that's back of it! Sam Dutton's a good man, and so's John Barker, and Joe Leavitt's got money enough to buy the whole bank if he was a mind to, and Deacon Adams never done a crooked piece of business in his life!' He pounded his big fist on the counter in a sort of desperation, and his brow was dripping.

The cashier smiled drily. 'They're too big for their britches,' he said. 'Why, man, the bills they've got in circulation you'd think they had all the specie in the United States in their vaults! Now some of their debtors have failed, and if you ask me, their bills aren't worth what it cost to print them.'

Tim wiped his mouth with his hand. 'Then what am I going to do to get my money?' he protested.

'Well, I understand there's going to be a meeting at the Marlboro Hotel of the others like you who hold the bills. But they can't do anything but talk. My advice to you is to forget it, cross it out, go home.'

Tim nodded dumbly and went out into the street again, crushed and hopeless. He sought the purchasers of his lumber and humbly asked for payment in specie, but they hooted him down. He stayed in Boston long enough to attend that meeting in the Marlboro Hotel, but its proceedings only confused him; and at last, in a stupor of despair, his dreams shattered, he took passage for home to lick his wounds.

The schooner made up the river as far as Hampden on the evening tide, and anchored there to wait for morning; but Tim landed and walked the rest of the way, remembering as he trudged through the gathering dusk another night, now eight years gone, when he had walked this road with Jenny in his arms. Then as now his head had been bowed and the world had seemed a dark and hopeless place.

It was night before he came to Bangor, but he did not go directly home. He had to talk to someone. Isaiah Poster's business ability had impressed Tim, and the big man stopped to see him and to ask his advice.

He told Isaiah his story, but he got small comfort. Isaiah said scornfully: 'Why, you were a damned fool to let them do you, Tim. Nobody'd take the bank's bills as a gift!' His shrill, rasping tones were like a file. 'Your money's gone, Tim. Tear up the damned bills and burn them. That's all they're good for.' And he added: 'Here, have a drink, man. You're shaking like you had the fever!'

Tim filled a cup and drained it. Since that shameful night at Hampden he had avoided rum, drinking sparingly or not at all; and the strong liquor burned his throat now and set him coughing and strangling.

'Take another,' Isaiah advised, his old eyes masked. 'To kill the taste of that one. Help yourself.'

Tim obeyed him gratefully, and this drink went more easily. In the old days, hard liquor had made Tim feel good, warm and comfortable and sleepy; but this produced in him a submissive despair. Struggle and effort became futility. He asked other questions, but Isaiah assured him his case was a hopeless one, and when he was well fuddled, the older man said:

'All the same, Tim, you're a friend of mine. I hate to see things go hard for you. Maybe, give 'em time, the bank will redeem some of their bills — if you can wait long enough.'

'Can't do nothing but wait,' Tim grunted, and poured himself another drink.

'Well, I'll tell you,' Isaiah said largely, 'I'll take a gamble on it, Tim. If you say so, I'll take the bills off your hands — at a discount.' And he added hastily: 'If it was anybody but you, I'd not touch 'em; but I'll take 'em at ninety per cent off — give you ten cents on the dollar — if you want me to.'

A crumb was better than no bread; and the rum had fuddled Tim. In the end he agreed.

IV

When Tim came out of doors to walk the short distance down Poplar Street to his own house, it was late. His head felt swollen and tremendous, and the sky was a confusion of whirling stars, and Doctor Rich's house swayed back and forth like a ponderous inverted pendulum against the sky. Mrs. Hollis, during his absence, had used his bed, lodging with Jenny — who now had a larger version of the trundle bed which had served her as a baby — in the single bedroom the small house contained.

They were both asleep when Tim came home, but he rattled the door and Mrs. Hollis hurried to lift the bar and let him in. She was scandalized at his condition; but Tim, ignoring her and her protests, pushed past her into the bedroom and kicked off his boots and lay down and almost instantly was snoring. When Mrs. Hollis realized that she could not even wake him, so that she was left without a bed, she dressed in a fuming indignation and went home through the dark streets of the sleeping town alone.

Tim slept soddenly till morning, and he might have slept all day, but in his dreams he thought that he was smothering. He struggled against this, gasping for breath, and as his senses, bemused as much by sleep and by exhaustion after despairing days as by the liquor he had drunk, cleared a little, he realized that it was Jenny who was pressing her hands on his mouth and nose. He twisted his head away and growled:

'Don't do that, Jenny. What's the matter?'

She laughed and lay down beside him. 'Wake up, poppy!' she insisted. 'It's daylight, and you've still got your clothes on, and you were making awful noises! What did you bring me from Boston?'

He was suddenly at that question completely sober. What had he brought her from Boston? Why, failure, ruin, poverty! In a terrible and tormenting loneliness he drew her close in his arms. She wore a single garment, and the night had been warm, and since there were no open windows in the room, her nightgown was faintly moist with perspiration. She was small, so small that his arms wrapped completely around her, encircling her, and his hand touched her breast.

He had not noticed any change in the lines of her figure of a girl child; but under his hand there was a faintly swelling softness. He knew with the blinding force of an overwhelming enlightenment that Jenny was no longer a child, that soon she would be a woman now.

4

ONE result of Tim's drunken homecoming that night was the expulsion of Mrs. Hollis from his household. He and Jenny were still abed when — fuming at the indignity to which she had been subjected the night before — she appeared at the bedroom door. She saw them together and proceeded to give Tim a piece of her mind. Tim, still stupid from the dregs of rum, took this supinely; and he did not defend himself at all. But Jenny, seeing her father passive under Mrs. Hollis' scolding, suddenly sprang out of bed and faced Mrs. Hollis, crying:

'You stop that! You stop scolding my poppy!'

Mrs. Hollis scarcely heard her. 'You hulking ox!' she said to Tim. 'You guzzling, drunken clown! For sixpence I'd walk out of this house and never put foot inside it again, and then where'd you be?'

Jenny, furious at being ignored, thrust at her, beating at her with small fists. 'Go on, get out!' she retorted. 'Get out! We don't want you here!' She tried to push Mrs. Hollis toward the door. 'Get out!' she insisted, almost screaming. 'Go away! I hate you!'

Mrs. Hollis doubtfully — because she loved Jenny well — appealed to Tim. 'Tim Hager, are you going to let that young one talk to me like that?'

But before Tim could answer, Jenny ran to the hearth. She snatched up the warming pan, brandished it with both hands, charged at Mrs. Hollis. Her eyes were blazing and she was white with rage; and in the face of that charge, Mrs. Hollis picked up her skirts and fled.

Jenny banged the door triumphantly behind her and went to comfort Tim, persuading him at last to lie down and sleep a longer while; and she kissed him and said in soft tenderness:

'There! We don't need any old Mrs. Hollis! I'm going to take care of you.'

When an hour later Mrs. Hollis came hopefully to the door again, thinking the storm might have passed, it was to find Jenny busy by the cooking stove, one of the first to come to Bangor, which Tim had bought a year before. Tim was still asleep, and Jenny would not let her into the house. Mrs. Hollis tried to appease the child.

'Why, Jenny, somebody's got to take care of you two, cook and mend and tend!'

'I'll do it,' Jenny told her. 'I'll do it myself.'

'Where's he gone now? Let me talk to him.'

'I won't either,' Jenny insisted. 'I put him back to sleep. He's awful tired.' Her face twisted and those faint lines on her cheekbones made her seem about to burst into tears. 'I'm going to take good care of him. I want to! Please go away!'

So Mrs. Hollis in the end reluctantly departed, and till Jenny left the small house on her wedding day, she and Tim lived there together and alone. He liked to watch her, busily absorbed in keeping house for him, and Jenny seemed to enjoy it. She made of it a game, pretending to be Moll, sometimes scolding him as Moll had scolded him, sometimes lavishing on him pretty and precocious caresses, coming into bed with him in the morning, demanding to be kissed; and sometimes she might complain: 'That's not the way you used to kiss mommy. Kiss me the way you did her!' Then he would kiss her hard, and they would laugh together at this make-believe.

II

Tim had gone into debt to finance his lumber enterprise, and the sum Isaiah paid him for the bank's bills was not sufficient to satisfy his creditors. Only by the sale of his oxen and of his shares in small vessels built or building could he meet all claims. He was left with no occupation, but Isaiah put him to work in the store at a small wage. When in November the bank resumed redemption of its bills, Tim went hopefully to Isaiah. 'I kind of thought you might want to do something about it,' he explained.

'Don't see how I can,' Isaiah demurred. They were in the corner of the store that served him as office; and he drew the jug from under the counter and poured Tim a drink and passed it to the big man. 'It wa'n't rightly a business deal. 'Course, if it had been, you wouldn't have any horse to shoe now at all; but as 'twas, I just the same as gave you the money, and it looks to me I'm entitled to keep what I got. Have another drink.'

Tim passed his cup, silenced once for all. He never found the courage to speak of the matter to Isaiah again.

III

In the months that followed, the big man almost visibly disintegrated. There was in Tim a humble yearning to play a fine part in the world, to do what he worthily should. His own cowardice at Hampden, although others as craven as he excused it and forgot it, remained in his memory to taunt him. He had tried there to be brave and strong, and to give strength and courage to other men; but he had failed, and he could not forget that failure. In the same way he had tried to be a good husband to Moll. The fact that his neighbors gave him after Moll's departure a full and kindly sympathy rather than the derision he expected softened the blow of her desertion, but it could not make Tim forget that he had failed as a husband as completely as he had failed to play a brave man's part.

And now as a man of business he was a failure too. Others might excuse him, and blame Isaiah — who boasted of his bargain — but Tim did not excuse himself, even to himself.

And there was worse. More than his sense of past failures, it was his shamed recognition of the nature of his feeling for Jenny which as she grew older speeded the swift process of decay in him. He fought against it, but Jenny by her every action made his fight the harder. She delighted in provoking him to gusty caresses, laughing gleefully when he caught her close in a rib-cracking embrace. She bemused him with pretty tricks of coquetry; and she had always that trick of watching him, her head on one side in a speculative way, as though she were appraising the storms she could arouse in him.

Thus, once when she had come to wake him in the morning, sitting on the side of his bed, leaning down to kiss him, she said with warm eyes:

'I love you, poppy. Do you love me?'

'Yes, certain.'

'A lot?'

He put a strong check upon himself, and this effort at restraint made his voice sullen. 'Certain I do!'

Her head cocked and she smiled mischievously. 'As much as I love you?' she challenged; and then: 'As much as you loved mommy?'

Till suddenly he could not meet her eyes, and he sat up, pushing her angrily away. 'Be off with you!' he shouted. 'Let a man be!'

She laughed, and pulled his hair and kissed his cheek, and then fled into the other room. He dressed in a morose and grumbling humor, and when he emerged from the bedroom he was still scowling. Jenny came to him, looking at him curiously.

'Poppy,' she asked, 'why do you get mad when I'm sort of love-making with you?' There was no reproach in her tones, but an intent inquiry. 'Don't you like me to?'

He stared at her, baffled and helpless, and then with no word at all bolted out of the house. Behind him he heard her laugh a little as he fled.

He came as time passed to be more often thus defensively angry. Sometimes his rages faintly frightened Jenny; but as though trying to understand them, she provoked them again and again. Tim found no way to ease the thirst in him except with rum, till he became a scandal to the town, and people spoke of how much Jenny endured, and how loyally she served her father. It was at once a wonder and a pity to everyone that a thirteen-year-old girl should have to spend her days taking care of a drunken no-good like Tim, and Jenny had many offers of help and counsel; but she declined them all, and as her devotion persisted, so did her stature grow in the public mind.

That winter, the Selectmen included Tim's name in the list of those intemperate drinkers to whom storekeepers were warned not to sell rum; but Tim had no need to buy liquor. There was always a convenient supply in Isaiah's store.

IV

The day came when Tim's last vestiges of self-respect suffered a final blow. The market for good sawed lumber — despite the larcenous Boston surveyors who by their classifications frequently reduced the value of a shipment by a third or a half — was showing a steady improvement. Isaiah owned an increasing acreage of timber lands, but his holdings were far up-river. There was, however, an ample supply of good pine within easy distance of Bangor, and though the owners began to engage caretakers to guard their property, stealing lumber was still a common and a profitable pursuit.

Isaiah, hiring men to do his thieving, dabbled in this petty larceny; and in the early spring of 1824 he set Tim and Ned Lawrence to fell a number of trees on a fine tract above Old Town. Tim objected. He said he couldn't go off into the woods and leave Jenny alone; but Isaiah said Jenny could sleep at his house while Tim was gone, and Jenny agreed to this. So Tim and Ned spent a fortnight in the forest, working along the banks of a brook large enough to float the logs down to the river. They were far enough from the river itself to escape easy discovery; but they would need oxen to move the logs to the brook, and when they had felled as many trees as they could hope to handle, they came back to Bangor to get a team.

Sam Stetson was guardian of the tract upon which they had trespassed; and he had enlisted the services of two Indian boys to help him keep an eye on the holdings for which he was responsible. Before Tim and Ned came to Bangor, one of the Indians discovered them at work in the forest and subsequently trailed them to town, where he reported to Sam Stetson.

Tim by his great size was easily identified; and Sam went to Isaiah's store, knowing he would find Tim there. He did not flatly accuse the big man of the depredations; but in Tim's hearing he said cheerfully to Isaiah:

'Well, I been saved some work, up-river.'

'So?' Isaiah spoke warily. 'How's that?'

'Why, I figured to get out a few logs this month to pay me for watching the timber, the way I do every year, but somebody's saved me the trouble of falling the trees.' He laughed. 'I aim to keep an eye on them till they get the logs to the river, and then take over. Let them do the work and I'll take the logs.'

Isaiah cackled in due appreciation. 'Smart work, Sam,' he agreed, with a side glance at Tim. 'Be a joke on them, all right.'

Sam elaborated his story, sure that by so doing he would warn off the thieves and that the logs would be left where they were till he could handle them; but when he left the store, Isaiah turned on Tim in a storm of reproaches.

'A fine hand you turned out to be!' he cried. 'Cutting lumber for Sam Stetson on my time! You and Ned get along up there and get them logs to the mills, or you don't get a shilling pay out of me.'

Tim was doubtful. 'If Sam's watching for us, I dunno as I want to get into any trouble,' he confessed. 'Seems like Sam'll just grab the logs, even if we do get them to water. Looks to me we'd best leave them lay.'

'By Godfrey mighty, you'll not!' Isaiah raged. 'Them's my logs, cut on my time, by men I'd 'greed to pay. You turn 'em over to Sam Stetson and I'll charge the lot of them to your account, Tim! You can't do me! You try it and you'll find I'm a hard man!'

Tim grumbled: 'Dunno what we can do?'

'You going to let a little half-pint of a man tell you what to do? If you've got the backbone of a jellyfish you'll go get them logs. Yes, and if Sam bothers you, you'll learn him manners. If you don't, you ain't no use at all, and you can just keep out of my sight from now on!'

So Tim and Lawrence drove an ox team out of town along the Old Town road that night; but Sam Stetson was not asleep, and he saw them go and followed them. Isaiah had goaded Tim to a sullen truculence, and Ned Lawrence was by instinct a combative man. Also, Isaiah made sure before they started that they were well supplied with rum. In these months, as Tim drank more and more heavily, rum produced in him a dangerous and violent humor; and his own doubts of the wisdom of this current enterprise turned, after he had drunk enough, into a reckless and cruel rage against Sam.

He and Ned were in the act of hauling the logs to the brook, next afternoon, when they discovered that Sam was watching them. Tim was handling the ox team, Ned Lawrence barking the logs so that they would slide more easily. It was Ned who spied Stetson slipping through the thin-leaved underbrush; and he told Tim, in a whisper, his discovery.

'You go along t'the brook,' he said. 'If he trails after you, I'll sneak up on him and lay for him. We'll teach the lousy spy some manners, Tim!'

Tim, scowling sullenly, agreed; and Sam fell into the trap. He had no warning till, as he was watching Tim drag the great log down to the brookside, Ned fell on him from behind. Their scuffling cries brought Tim in haste, and he found them rolling on the ground, Sam for the moment uppermost.

Tim brought his ox goad, a well-seasoned staff six feet long and an inch thick, hissing down on Sam's shoulders; and Sam bawled with pain and released his hold on Lawrence, and Tim pinned him and held him while Ned took the goad and beat him to a sobbing helplessness. If Ned had been as much inflamed with drink as Tim, they might have killed the man; but Ned had wit enough to stop in time. They left Sam moaning on the ground, and proceeded calmly with their labors.

Sam crawled away and limped back to Bangor town; and when they presently returned, they were arrested and at the June term of court they were tried on charges of aggravated assault. Their guilt was plain enough, and Chief Justice Mellen, since stealing timber was an increasingly common offense, took the opportunity to make an example of them. Jenny was in court and heard his stern words.

'This practice of secretly depredating on lands to which you have no claim is in the eye of Heaven no less than stealing! How can you answer to your wives and children' — his eye turned from Tim to Jenny — 'who must be left without protection, and deprived of ordinary comforts, during that imprisonment which you must suffer for your misconduct? I sentence you to pay the costs of this proceeding and to serve twenty-five days in jail. Let this be a warning to you!'

The jail was not a strong place, and prisoners escaped from it almost at will; but Tim was crushed by the disgrace of his sentence. Sitting long days in silence, he served his time. Jenny stayed alone in the small house during his imprisonment, refusing Mrs. Hollis' offer to keep her company, declining Uncle Isaiah's sympathetic invitation to live with him. She won new respect in the town by coming every day to see Tim and to bring his meals, and to try in teasing, laughing ways to make him smile.

But after that term in jail, there was no longer any sound fibre in Tim at all.

v

Jenny had been for years now a regular church-goer. At first she went with her father, sitting demurely through the long services; but of late she usually went alone. Her regularity and her devotion were a part of the virtuous part which in the town's eyes she played, and they won for her the loyal approval of all the congregation.

After Tim's imprisonment she persuaded him to a more regular attendance than had been his recent habit. Tim yielded more to

please her than for any other reason; but Elder Loomis, the first
time Tim appeared in the congregation, preached directly at the
big man in burning and unmistakable terms, and Tim, with Jenny's hand pressing his arm and many eyes upon him, found a per-
verted pleasure in his own sudden eminence. That summer and
fall he came regularly to meetings; and the town became accustomed to see him and Jenny trudging through the streets side by
side.

Sunday, the second of January, a snowstorm swept the town;
and they ploughed through deep drifts on the way to church.
Through the same storm Elder Loomis walked up from his home
on Union Street, and they overtook him, and Tim broke a way for
him to the door. The older man was tired, panting heavily from
the hard climb. They took their seats, and a moment later the old
minister stepped into the pulpit and sat down.

But at once Tim saw his head droop and he sagged sidewise,
and Jenny at Tim's side cried:

'Oh, he's sick! Help him!'

Tim came uncertainly to his feet, following others who rushed
to the pulpit. He picked up the old man in his arms and carried
him into the entry; but the minister did not recover consciousness
and presently he died.

When Tim and Jenny turned homeward, she was convulsed
with grief, weeping, with streaming tears. It was her first experience of death, and the effect was overwhelming. Before they
reached the house she was near hysteria, wringing her hands, wailing helplessly; and once indoors she flung herself across the bed
in a rising paroxysm, writhing and twisting as though she were
herself in torment. Tim tried clumsily to comfort her. He himself
was shaken by what had happened, and he was bewildered and
helpless in the face of her tears; and when he could not quiet her,
his own helplessness made him angry, so that he passed from
soothing urgencies to harsh commands, bidding her be still and
cease her cries.

'Stop that caterwauling!' he commanded furiously. 'Or I'll give
you something to howl about!'

'Oh, he's dead, he's dead!' she wailed.

'Well, what of it? I guess other men have died before now, and
will from now on! You don't have to carry on like a spleeny cat
having kittens! Get some sense into you, Jenny!'

She flamed at him. 'You're a fine one to talk! He was a good
man, but you're just a great, drunken, stealing loafer! Oh, I wish
you were dead! I hate you!' She scrambled off the bed and ran

at him, pounding him with small fists. 'I've worked and slaved for you!' she screamed. 'I ought to have run away from you long ago. Uncle Isaiah says so, and everybody! You're a no-good, lying, thieving, useless man!'

He stood helpless before her storming rage, and she struck him hard in the face. Instinctively he cuffed her, slapping her cheek so that she was knocked sidewise and fell; and she lay on the floor, screaming monotonously, with long, hollow, rasping cries.

'Hush up!' he shouted hoarsely, maddened by her tears. 'Hush up before the whole town hears you! Folks'll think I'm killing you!'

She screamed monotonously, without words; and Tim jerked her to her feet. In a desperate rage, feeling himself stripped naked before the eyes of the town by those screams which everyone must hear, he carried her to the bed and threw her there face down, pressing her mouth into the pillow to silence her.

'Hush up!' he bawled, and when she twisted her head sidewise and screamed again, he cried: 'Oh, God damn you, stop that yelling!'

And he began to beat her with the flat of his hand, holding her head with one hand, slapping at her as she squirmed and twisted. Her struggles, the vibrations of her small body, the sight of her slim legs when by her own twistings and kickings her petticoats were thrown into disorder, woke in him something dark and hideous. He beat her till she lay bruised and exhausted, weeping with long, racking sobs.

5

THAT emotional convulsion into which Jenny had been thrust by the death of Elder Loomis marked a change in the relationship between her and her father. Tim himself was full of shame for his violence; but Jenny forgave him with a generous sweetness, and she seemed thereafter, instead of hating him, to seek out new and charming ways to please him and to make him love her more. She kept him much at home, rueful when he must go to his work at Isaiah's store, kissing him when he departed and when he returned; and for a time that dreadful moment was not mentioned between them.

It was Tim who spoke of it at last. Jenny had come one morning to sit on the side of his bed and to wake him, tickling his lips with a broom straw while he pretended to be asleep and tried not to grin; till at last she laughed and leaned down to kiss him.

'Wake up, sleepy bear!' she said.

He threw his arm around her neck and held her for a moment and kissed her again. 'You're mighty good to me, Jenny,' he told her.

'Of course I am. Why shouldn't I be?' Her voice was beginning to have a maturer quality, deeper than it had used to be. She spoke softly always, so softly that unless he were attentive he might not hear her; and yet there was warmth and beauty in her tones.

'After the way I mauled you that day, I didn't know as you'd have any more use for me.'

'I deserved it,' she said. 'I needed it.' She laughed. 'Besides, I never did mind being spanked! Remember? I guess it's good for me. You ought to do it oftener!'

He shook his head. 'I'll never lay a hand on you again.'

'Don't be too sure! I may do something terrible, any time! I'll bet I could make you spank me if I wanted to.'

'I never will,' he insisted.

She slid off the bed and stood up. 'Well, I won't try now!' she promised. 'You'd best get dressed. It's high time.'

He basked in her forgiveness, happier than he had ever been. Yet to be always near her, though it was bliss, was torment too. Sometimes after they were abed and she was asleep, Tim would lie long awake, conscious of her near, listening for her quiet breathing; and a turbulence was in him, strange and terrible.

II

Yet she was not always thus agreeable, and occasionally he was bewildered and confused by a determination in her which he could not resist. Early in February there was to be a hanging at Castine. A man named Seth Elliot, drunkenly chastising his child, had beaten it till it died; and for this he was to pay with his neck. From all the nearer towns, people proposed to gather for the spectacle. Tim would never have thought of going. He had no stomach for horrors. But Jenny heard of the hanging and she begged him to take her to Castine.

'It ain't a thing for a girl to see,' he protested. 'It'll be sickening and awful, Jenny.'

She laughed at him in a teasing gaiety. 'I want to go,' she urged. 'And you ought to see it, poppy, so you'll remember next time and not spank me too hard! Why, if I told folks the way you beat me that day, they'd all say you ought to be hung yourself.'

This was, Tim thought, true enough. It had seemed incredible to him that no one had heard her screams; and the thought that she might tell the town what he had done alarmed him now. There was no threat in her tone, nothing but laughter; but he saw a shrewd calculation in her eyes.

'I felt awful about that after, Jenny,' he told her. 'I was so mad I didn't rightly know what I was doing.'

'You weren't really mad,' she assured him, speaking half to herself as though thinking aloud. 'You were just sort of crazy, because I was yelling so; and you were hating me and kind of loving me at the same time.'

He stared at her in a stark realization that what she said was true. There had been as much desire as wrath in him that day, and that she should know this before he did was startling. Half-frightened, he made no new objection, and they went to Castine together, joining with others who drove down the road in sleighs till they came to the foot of the ice that clogged the river, crossing the head of the bay by boat. It was an unpleasant company of drunken men and noisy women, shrill and loud, and in Castine a full two thousand people gathered around the scaffold; but Tim's bulk and Jenny's zeal edged them through the crowd to the front ranks. Tim was made sick by what he saw, but Jenny watched with a pale intentness, wetting her lips with the tip of her tongue, her fingers like wires on his arm, shaking with some strange excitement and turning away at last with a sigh as though of appeasement and satiety; and on the weary trip back to Bangor she was relaxed and drowsy at his side.

After that day, for no reason he could put in words, Tim insisted that she should have the bedroom to herself. 'You're getting to be a big girl now,' he said awkwardly. 'It ain't fitten for you to go on sleeping in the same room with me.' She protested that they were more comfortable so, but for once he had his way. He gave over his big bed to her, took for himself the one she had been using and moved it out into the room where they lived and cooked and ate. But Jenny insisted that the door between the two rooms should stand open still.

III

By the time Jenny was sixteen, she was as tall as she would ever be, slenderly and beautifully formed, with warm cheeks and masses of dark hair and eyes of a clear and shaking purity. Her countenance, which was in repose like a still pool where a man could find reflected anything he chose, became when she smiled alive and entrancing. Those delicate lines like dimples, just below the cheekbone, visible only when she smiled, gave her expression a peculiar poignancy, suggesting always the imminence of tears.

And there was always in her that thin, vibrating wire whose keen note Lieutenant Carruthers had been the first to hear. The Lieutenant had tried in his thoughts to define it; but Tim, as now when she approached womanhood he heard it more and more plainly, could not begin to put it in words. Yet he heard it as clearly as the Lieutenant, and he was even more strongly moved. There are certain musical resonances, single notes or chords, which will provoke a dog to utter lugubrious howls of grief or pain. Tim with Jenny was like a dog hearing these notes played upon an instrument. He did not tip back his head and howl as a dog does; but his nerves were thrummed so that their vibration shook him and he was possessed by a hunger and longing that was almost insupportable.

He tried to fight it down, tried to drown it; but the rum he drank gave him no ease. The harsh liquor was like a thin stream of water poured on a raging fire, dissipating itself in steam at the instant it meets the flames. Yet there was seldom a day that he was not befuddled and he came to be of little use around the store. When the great forest fire which burned over the whole wilderness from Passadumkeag to Lincoln consumed the standing timber on some wild lands to which Isaiah had acquired a title, Isaiah felt himself robbed and ruined; and in a fit of economy, he discharged Tim. The big man, driven to earn a living as he could, turned back to his old love for netting in the river. He and Jenny made a net together. Tim whittled out the shuttles, and taught Jenny the simple knot that must be tied, and they worked long hours, sitting facing each other, the finished net rising in a soft pile between them. Jenny was able, after she learned the trick, to accomplish half again as much as he. Too often he forgot his work in watching her hands, in watching the way her arms and wrists moved, and the shadows in her hair; and she caught him at this, and laughed and told him he must work harder, and came to kiss him and to tug at his hair teasingly, and Tim trembled at her touch as a nervous colt trembles under the trainer's hands.

When the net was finished, she often went with him to drift for salmon or for shad. One night in October he and she were astonished to take almost two hundred shad. Some people claimed these were run-down fish, outward bound after spawning; but the fish were in fine condition and brought a good price in the markets of the town.

One result of their success was that Isaiah Poster hired Tim back again and set the big man to fish for him; and in the following summer Tim and others who followed his example made tremendous catches. Some of them began using seines, and in May one record haul took seven thousand shad and a hundred barrels of alewives. But the effect was to break the price. Shad were worth no better than fifty cents a hundred, and alewives were more often used for fertilizer than for food.

Isaiah, since fish were no longer worth the catching, took Tim back into the store; but at night Tim and Jenny might still go drifting, and for Tim these nights when they were together on the river were one long intoxication. Whenever he was with his daughter there was a beating in his veins like the drumming of a cock partridge on a hollow log, dimly heard in the still forest in the spring. He thought Jenny guessed this, for she took an impish delight in plaguing him, practicing upon him a thousand coquetries, leaving him at last dazed and helpless, just as a bull in the arena is dazed by the passes of the matador and made ready for the death stroke at the end.

IV

That summer the circus came to Bangor; a Grand Caravan of Living Animals that included an elephant, an assortment of monkeys and baboons, lions, tigers and an ichneumon, a display of wax statues and a troupe of tumblers.

Tim took Jenny to see the sights. The elephant was the particular attraction, and when they reached the ground, a crowd had gathered around him at his picket and were feeding him indiscriminate tidbits, gleefully watching the gravity with which he received each offering, reaching out his wrinkled trunk with the appendix so like a human fingertip at the end. Jenny and Tim came near, and a sailor from one of the vessels which were anchored in the river, and who was already unsteady on his feet from too frequent potations, saw Jenny and with the instinct of all young males to do something conspicuous under feminine eyes, drew from his pocket a twist of Black Jack and offered it to the great beast.

The elephant reached for it, and the sailor snatched it away, holding it just out of reach, tantalizing the huge creature till it shuffled and blew an angry blast. The sailor protracted the game, spurred by the cheers and laughter of the crowd, and one of the circus men came to find out what was irritating the elephant and without seeing what the sailor offered said harshly:

'Hey, rube! Give it to him if you're going to!'

So the sailor allowed the elephant to take the tobacco. 'Now let's see if he can spit!' he said, and everyone watched with a lively interest.

The elephant, having tucked the Black Jack into its triangular mouth, for a moment gave no sign. Then, without warning, it lunged forward against the chain which held its hind leg to a picket stake, and at full reach whipped its trunk around the sailor's arm. The man, dragged off his feet, bawled with pain and fright; and the elephant swung him high and brought him crashing down. The man's legs struck the great beast's tusks, and the bones snapped like matches, before the sailor's body slapped the ground. He lay senseless, and the elephant lurched forward to kneel on him; but by that time the attendant was there to beat the animal back and drag the man away.

The crowd had scattered in every direction, and Tim had turned to run, tugging at Jenny; but her arm slipped from his grasp, and when he swung back he saw her watching, and shivering in a sort of ecstasy, staring at the broken man upon the ground. She was pale and still and yet somehow transfigured too, her swimming eyes half-closed.

By that time the sailor had been lifted to safety, and men were tending him; but Jenny did not move, and at what he saw in her inflamed eyes Tim was more afraid of her than he had been of the elephant a moment before.

Then the crowd returned, to praise Jenny because she had stood her ground, to laugh at their own fright and say how brave she was. But Tim knew better. She had not been brave. She had watched the breaking of that sailor man with a dreadful delight; and next morning she came to wake Tim, sitting on the edge of his bed in her thin shift, appearing to be serenely unconscious of the scant garb of which his every sense took notice, and made him tell her over again all that had happened, as though she had not seen it for herself.

'Did it break his legs?' she asked. 'Both of them?'

'Yes,' Tim said uneasily. 'One of them, the bone stuck out through.'

'Did it break his arm too?'

'Just pulled it out of the socket, they said.'

'Was it going to kneel on him?'

'Why, it tried to,' Tim admitted. 'But the man driv it back. Gosh, Jenny, what do you want to talk about it for?'

'What if it had?' she insisted, in a dreaming tone, her hand absently stroking his cheek.

'Why, if it had, I guess it'd have killed him.'

'Mashed him?'

'Yes.' Tim began to shiver at her tone.

'Mashed his insides out?'

'Guess so, if they hadn't got him away.'

She lay down beside him, her head on his shoulder, her finger tracing the outlines of his jaw. 'Did you ever see a man mashed that way?'

Tim was trembling at her touch, yet he was sick too with a sort of terror as he answered her. 'Saw a tree fall on a man once, a man named Frohock, over't Norridgewock. He tried to jump out of the way, and tripped up and fell and it caught him.' He coughed. 'Caught him across the shoulders,' he said. 'Time we got to him he was dead. You could pretty near have picked him up in two pieces.'

'What did he look like?' she insisted.

'His eyes popped out. I got sick. I couldn't look at him after I saw that.' He added unwillingly: 'There was a piece of his shoulder blade stuck into the tree when we came to bark it. We had to dig it out.' He sat up suddenly, brushing her away. 'God damn it, Jenny, what do you want to hear about things like that for? Makes me sick, just remembering!' He stepped out of bed on the farther side, staring down at her.

She lay still, her arm across her forehead shadowing her eyes, smiling up at him with that smile which suggested tears. 'I like to hear about things like that,' she said in her still, slow tones.

Tim made an explosive sound. 'Go get some clothes on you!' he told her. And when she did not move: 'Get up. Go on!'

She obeyed him. But after that day Tim was always afraid of her, half-dreading to come home. He drank more and more. For a time, the rum had seemed not greatly to affect him, but now when he rose in the morning his hands were apt to shake so violently that he could not button his clothes, could not hold a cup without spilling the contents. Also he lost his appetite, eating less

and less, and the flesh melted off his bones, and his skin sagged
emptily. So day by day his destruction sped.

v

There was the yeast of growth in Bangor in these years of Jenny's
girlhood, and many changes. The growing lumber business meant
that every spring troops of lusty woodsmen came down-river, and
that for the whole summer the harbor was crowded with ships,
and sailors filled the town. For the entertainment of these men,
an increasing number of establishments began to arise along the
waterfront; and since Tim Hager's house was on Poplar Street near
the river and the Stream, Jenny sometimes saw sights which
puzzled her. She and Tim might be wakened by shouting laughter
in the dark hours of the night, and sometimes sailors came pounding on the door, though Tim's giant figure appearing in the
doorway was enough to scatter them.

On the night after one of the annual musters of the militia there
was something like a riot that centred around a house which had
been built on the Point beyond John Barker's store, and Jenny
heard the shouts of brawling men, and the crash of a breaking
door, and the screams of women; and she came from her room
to the front window to see what was happening. The street outside the house was full of people, shadows in the darkness, running to and fro. She stayed there till Tim too awoke, and called
to her to go back to bed.

'But I want to watch,' she urged. 'What are they doing? What
are they fighting about? What are the women screeching for?'

'It's nought for you — or for any decent folk,' he assured her.
'Go on back to bed.'

She yielded for the moment; but her curiosity drove her next
morning before Tim was awake to walk down past the store to the
house which had been the focus of the disturbance. The house
was closed and shuttered, and except that she saw a man with a
bruised and battered countenance asleep or dead in a clump of
alders below the road, she found no answer to the riddle of the
night.

Then one day Doctor Rich, next door, sold his house and moved
to Main Street, and she asked Tim why the doctor had moved
away. Tim said evasively:

'Why, I sh'd judge he didn't like the neighborhood.'

'Why not?'

'It's getting to be mostly stores and wharves and shipyards down
here.'

She pressed him, but he would tell her no more than this till a month later, when the empty house found occupants and she questioned him again.

'Some women have moved in,' she said. 'Four anyway, because I've seen them. And they had a party there last night. I'm going over and borrow some tea, sometime, and get acquainted.'

Tim said harshly: 'No and you're not! You stay away from them.'

After a moment she asked: 'Why do you act so secret about it?' Then she said, laughing a little: 'I know it must all be wickedness, or you'd tell me! You might as well tell me. I'll find out for myself, somehow!'

Her word provoked him to a blind and choking rage. 'It's nothing to you!' he said fiercely. 'Leave them be.'

'I'll find someone to tell me,' she warned him.

'Any man that does, I'll break his neck for him,' he declared. 'And yours too! Now shut up your mouth or I'll handle you.'

She said, laughing again: 'You haven't beat me since the night Elder Loomis died. You can't scare me. I'm not afraid of you.'

Tim, remembering that night, remembering her slim body writhing under his blows, could not speak, and she said no more.

VI

Jenny had that liking for a uniform which is common to most women; but Tim, remembering her mother and Lieutenant Carruthers, saw this trait in her with a sullen misgiving. Uniforms appeared in Bangor at the annual muster of the militia, or at the drills three times a year. Since militiamen had broken in disgraceful flight at Hampden, the service was unpopular with everyone except those who nursed political ambitions and took this easy road to public notice. Yet some military duty was required from every man, and the volunteer companies offered an attractive and fashionable substitute. Captain Zebediah Rogers organized the Independent Volunteers, and Jenny made Tim take her to see the presentation of their standard. The company marched through the streets to Judge Dutton's house where Miss Julia Dutton, representing the young ladies who had devised the standard and arranged to have it painted by the artist, Mr. Hardy of Hampden, made what seemed to Jenny an elegant address. 'The young ladies of Bangor,' she said, 'yet retaining a fresh recollection of the horrors excited by an invading enemy in war ...' Tim moved uneasily at that reference, and Jenny's hand tightened on his arm and she smiled up at him reassuringly, while Miss Dutton went on to speak of 'That sex upon whom we must at all times depend for protection,' and summoned the members of the company, not to careers of war and destruction, but to 'practise the principles and enjoy the pleasures of virtuous peace.' Ensign David Nye, accepting the standard, gallantly vowed that 'the enemy shall find that we strike our colors only to those by whom they were presented!' Everyone cheered, and Jenny, clinging to Tim's arm, jumped up and down and cried that the Ensign was wonderful. Tim was glad when the occasion was over and glad to point out to her a day or two later the young Ensign, no longer in uniform, driving one of his father's teams and completely stripped of martial glamour.

But Jenny's delight in uniforms persisted, and when she was eighteen, she had a chance to fill her eyes with them. The northeastern boundary disputes, provoking talk of a new war with England, revived a martial spirit in Bangor town. When Mr. Baker of Madawaska was carried off to Fredericton and charged with stirring up sedition and insurrection, there were shouts for vengeance; and when the Provincial authorities seized for debt a cow owned by a man named Arnold, who lived on the Aroostook River forty miles within the claimed American line, the loud patriotic fervor waxed. Fourteen militia regiments in the eastern counties were mustered and reviewed as proof that Maine was prepared to fight for what she deemed her rights; and the Government at Washington ordered four companies of infantry of the regular army to move to Houlton.

Early in May the first of these companies reached Bangor by schooner. They stayed only overnight before starting the long march north, and Jenny had the scantiest glimpse of them; but when late in July three more companies arrived, their officers were persuaded to spend some days in Bangor. The soldiers pitched their camp in the open land between Penobscot and Somerset Streets, out Broadway; and Captain Staniford good-humoredly put them through a series of drills and parades, while the band played for an hour or two every evening to entertain all comers.

Jenny insisted on going every day to watch the drills, and in the evening to hear the band; and Tim jealously went with her. He was uneasy with so many uniforms about, and he shook with rage because she attracted every masculine eye. When during the band concert Thursday evening Lieutenant Bloodgood, commanding one of the companies, ventured to pay his compliments to her and invited her to promenade, Tim harshly bade him take himself away. The Lieutenant looked at this unkempt giant of a man with a beautiful girl upon his arm. 'Sir,' he protested, 'may I not offer so lovely a lady this small courtesy?'

'No, you mayn't,' Tim told him flatly. 'Be off with you! She'll have no truck with Lieutenants.'

He led Jenny away, bidding her come home; and she looked up at him, smiling teasingly. 'You want me all to yourself, don't you, poppy?' she said in her warm, low tones.

'I'll have no Lieutenant dandling you!'

'Mommy went away with a Lieutenant, didn't she?'

He was often startled to see how she read his thoughts, and he flinched at her word now, and said sullenly: 'She was never better than a hedge sparrow, ready for the first man that'd have her!'

'Was she like the women in Doctor Rich's house?' Her tone was grave, inquiring.

'Full as bad, or worse,' he agreed; but then in sudden anger, realizing what knowledge her word implied: 'What do you know about such? I told you to keep away from them!'

'But when mommy went away,' she reminded him, not answering his question, 'you felt sad! So I guess you loved her, anyway.' She laughed softly. 'Even if she was a sparrow!' She linked her arm in his, pressing his arm against her side affectionately. 'But I've made it up to you, haven't I? Do you love me as much as you loved mommy?'

He said hoarsely: 'I've forgot her long ago, Jen.'

She nodded with pleasure. 'I liked it when you were so mad at the Lieutenant tonight. I knew it was because you love me so much yourself that you were sort of jealous of him.' They were at home, turned indoors; and she lighted the candle and told him smilingly: 'I know the way you feel about me.'

She kissed him, on the mouth. Her mouth was always faintly moist at the corners; and when she had gone into her room, Tim brushed his lips with his hand, trembling where he stood. That kiss had roused him beyond endurance; and he knew he could not go to bed, could not stay in the same house with her so near. He turned hurriedly out of doors. The night was still and humid, with scarce any breeze; and he went up to Isaiah's store. The store was dark, but Tim made into the cellar and tapped a rum barrel there to still the tumult in him. Later, his pulse shaking him, he went down to the river and took his boat. Tide and river were running out, but it was cooler on the water, and Tim let his oars trail and finally lifted them inboard and drifted with the current; and he sprawled in the bottom of the boat and presently fell asleep.

He woke at dawn far down-river, and cursed his own folly and set out to row back upstream; but the way was long. When he came up to Hampden he put ashore for meat and drink there; and he saw the wharf where Moll had flouted him, fourteen years ago, and bitter old memories made him drink more than he ate.

It was past sunset when he came laggard home. Jenny was not there, but in the fuddled confusion of his senses he ignored this, seeking water to quench his raging thirst. When he found it, his hand shook so that he spilled half the cup, and held it at last with both hands to bring it to his lips. The draft cooled his raw throat, but it was sour and nauseous in his poisoned stomach and the taste in his mouth offended him. Nevertheless, the water a little cleared his head, and he remembered the night before, and the dapper young Lieutenant; and his blood thickened with a murderous and choking passion. It was as though the expanding jaws of a vise were tearing his breast apart, and he caught at his throat like a man strangling.

Then he heard far away the sound of the band, and knew Jenny must have gone to listen again; and he came out into the dusk and stumbled blindly up Poplar Street to hunt for her; but the thirst which tormented him, and the terrible need of more and more alcohol to steady his quivering nerves and his spasmodically shaking hands, made him forget her again. There was rum in Isaiah's store. He turned that way.

The door was barred, but Tim, as though it were the young Lieutenant who denied him admittance, smashed at the panels with his fist. Although he broke the skin across his knuckles, he felt no pain, and the door yielded and he went in.

He drew a noggin of rum and spilled half of it, slopping it on the floor. He gulped what was left and repeated the dram, waiting for his hands to stop shaking; but they did not, and he sat down on the floor beside the barrel and drank deep. He forgot time, and when Isaiah came home and discovered the broken door and fetched a candle to see what had happened, Tim was still sitting on the floor, his head lolling stupidly.

Tim stared at the candle flame with wide owl's eyes, the whites darkly congested; and Isaiah snorted with disgust.

'You, is it?' he cried. And then, as though at a sharp memory, and in a shrill rage: 'Well, it's a fine time for you to sit there stiff with drink, and Jenny carrying on the way she is!'

Tim's eyes fixed on him unwinkingly; and Isaiah's voice like a file rasped through the silence. 'Slipping off into the trees with one of the officers!' he said. 'Oh, I had my eye on her. I saw him kissing her, back where they thought they were out of sight, and her laughing and pushing him away.'

Then he fell back in a sudden alarm, for Tim's face was terrible. The big man climbed to his feet with a careful precision, stiff as rods. He walked toward Isaiah, as deliberately as though each step were a conscious and planned action, calling for all his powers. Isaiah moved hurriedly to one side; but Tim passed him as though he did not exist. He reached the door and went out. He walked off the top step like a somnambulist, and Isaiah heard him fall to the ground with a clattering thump; and then Tim laboriously pulled himself to his feet and stalked away.

His mind, he would have said, was clear enough. Jenny had been needing a lesson for a long time. Well, she should have it! She was his, not for any other man at all. He forgot the Lieutenant's part in Jenny's offense. The officer was nothing, an impersonal figure, vague and unimportant. It was Jenny with whom Tim meant to deal.

His mind controlled his body. He stayed erect by a profound effort of will. He moved up Exchange Street, and along Main to Stetson Square and out Broadway to the encampment. The band was still playing, and there were torches and bonfires for illumination; and though the crowd had thinned and the more conservative townsfolk were long since gone to their homes, the throng had at the same time become noisier, decorum long since forgotten. Tim pushed through the laughing groups, disregarding whoever stood in his path.

He looked everywhere for Jenny without finding her; and he arrived at last at the dull conclusion that she had gone home, so he turned down Broadway again, implacable and deadly. When he came to his own door and entered, a candle was burning on the mantel, so he knew she was here and had left it to light him in. He took it and moved slowly to the bedroom door.

Jenny was in her bed, asleep, curled in a ball, her dark hair loose upon the pillow. The night was warm and she slept without covering, one leg drawn under her, the other extended. Her thin shift, open at the throat, fell away from one white shoulder.

Tim stared at her for a long moment; and then the light waked her, and she looked up and saw him. She turned on her back and stretched like a cat, yawning sleepily, smiling at him.

'Hello,' she said, in her low, half-whispering tones.

The word and her husky voice acted on Tim like sparks on powder. In an abrupt, explosive violence, he flung the candle blindly across the room. The flame was blown out before it struck the wall, leaving all in darkness. He lunged toward where she lay and caught Jenny's arm, dragging her off the bed; and he cried in a hoarse and blasting madness:

'God damn you, letting them soldiers tumble you!'

She was on her knees, trying to rise; but he held her arm with a hard grip, shaking her to and fro so that she could get no footing. He jerked her clear of the floor and twitched her to him, gripping both her arms, shaking her so that her head was flung back and forth as though her neck were broken.

'You're no better than your ma!' he said through grating teeth. 'You God damned doxy, I'll show you!'

He set her on her feet, shifting his grip on her arms; and she found her voice in a fury to match his own. 'I'll kill you, saying so! Let go of me!'

'Men after you like dogs — and you kissing them behind every tree!'

'You're after me yourself!' she cried in a strident bitterness. Her word paralyzed him for a moment, and she laughed in his face. 'Oh, I've seen you, always watching me, peeking to see what you could see, licking your lips at the sight of me! You're worse than any of them!'

What she said was true, and he knew it, and the knowledge drove him mad with hunger and with shame. His teeth grated. He slapped her, hard, yet still holding her with one hand.

'I'll learn you!' he cried. She wrenched free and he plunged after her and struck at her blindly in the darknes, his hand smashing into her face. 'I'll flog the skin off your back!' he said thickly. 'You God damned whoring bitch!' He caught her arm and leg and lifted her, carrying her through the kitchen door. She tried to cling to the jamb and he jerked her away, and holding her arm, dragging her along the floor behind him, he sprang across the room. There was an ox goad in the corner, and he found it and lashed at her with it. She scrambled to her feet, still in his grasp. The night was dark, and no light shone in the room. In that blackness she twisted to evade him, fighting in a sobbing silence, tirelessly; and under each blow her body arched as tensely as a bow, rigid with pain. He held her arm with his left hand, turning as she circled around him; and she pressed close to him to get inside the arc of his blows, and so at last she set her teeth in his hand.

At that sharp pain his hold slackened and she tore free from him and darted toward the door. He tried to catch her, lumbering across the room; but a keener agony struck him, so that his chest and side and arm were a blaze of pain. As she fled she heard him fall. Then she caught the handle of the door and whipped it wide, and jerked it to behind her; and barefooted, in her torn shift, her nose streaming blood from his blow that had caught her in the face, the taste of blood from her cut lips in her mouth, her legs welted by the goad, she ran blindly through the night, not knowing where.

III

Isaiah Poster

I

Isaiah Poster, when he came back to Bangor from Ohio in 1817, found it a scattering village of perhaps a thousand people; but he foresaw the future of Maine pine and — since most of that pine would have to come down-river to be milled and shipped — of Bangor too. The town was sure to grow, so he began at once to buy pasture and farm land which would one day be salable as building lots, and to buy wild lands up the river, financing his purchases with the profits from his store and from his systematic thefts — through such agents as Tim and Ned Lawrence — of pine off public and private lands.

The habit of secrecy which he acquired in those early years grew upon him, and long after there was any need to do so he hid as many as possible of his operations behind a modest anonymity. He bought stumpage through straw men, and only the woods boss who cut his pine knew that Isaiah owned the stumpage and financed the winter's cut and the spring drive. He owned — by private arrangement with the nominal owners — three mills at Old Town. Through Budd Parsons, and without letting his name appear, he participated in the organization of the Penobscot Boom Corporation, planned by a group of a dozen small operators to whom the Legislature was quick to grant a charter; but immediately afterward, as a silent partner of Rufus Dwinel, Isaiah bought the valuable charter from the original incorporators and thereafter, until he sold out to Mr. Dwinel, he shared in the profits it returned.

As his capital increased, so did his interests expand. One day in June, 1827, he counted sixty-four vessels anchored in the river to receive their cargoes of lumber, and he perceived a neglected opportunity and began to buy into the shipping industry, taking a share in bottoms built and building, scattering his risks with a shrewd discretion.

Thus like an octopus he extended his tenacles in every direction, taking his profit out of pine all the way from the stump to the Boston market, till he must have been rated, by anyone who knew all his resources, as one of the dozen richest men of the town.

II

Isaiah was when he returned from Ohio a small man with a tight, narrow mouth and a rocky chin under which a half-moon of sandy whisker extended from ear to ear. In the intervening years the whiskers had turned gray, and now in his early sixties he was except for a fringe of thin white hair completely bald, and he wore a black skull cap to protect his pate from drafts. As his teeth one by one disappeared, his jaws had clamped more tightly shut so that he gave the impression of putting a lock upon his tongue. This appearance did him no injustice. He was in fact as secret and furtive as he was greedy and shrewd.

He put up a store on Poplar Street and built a house beside it, his household consisting of his son Ephraim and a woman named Mrs. Wetzel. She was twelve years younger than Isaiah, with the buxom cheeks and full figure which bespoke a tremendous vitality. She had become Isaiah's housekeeper soon after his wife died in Ohio, and her enemies there were quick to put the worst construction on the relationship between them. It was rather to defy their slanderous tongues than from any fondness for him that she presently invited him to her bed. 'I might as well have the game as the name,' she said sharply. When in her later forties she became more querulous than generous, he welcomed the curtailment of their relationship, yet habit still led him sometimes to her arms until she died.

One Friday morning a few years after they came to Bangor she complained of a cold, and it was worse next day. Isaiah suggested calling in Doctor Rich, but Mrs. Wetzel insisted on sending instead for a man named Nathaniel Oak, who had recently come to town and set himself up as a steam doctor, attracting an astonishing number of feminine patients. When Doctor Oak had examined Mrs. Wetzel he wagged his head in a doleful way and administered an emetic. He stayed with her all Saturday night, repeating the emetic at intervals of an hour, and by daylight Sunday morning Mrs. Wetzel was in a state of physical collapse.

Isaiah protested with some violence: 'You keep on, and you'll kill her! She can't stand it, Doctor. She'll vomit up her insides!'

But the quack told him wisely: 'It's necessary, Mr. Poster. At some time in her life Mrs. Wetzel has taken opium, and it's still in her system, and the medicine I've given her has to fight to get rid of that poison. Once we get it out of her, she'll be all right.'

Isaiah, as helpless as most men where feminine ailments are concerned, was silenced; and Doctor Oak gave Mrs. Wetzel another emetic. Then he subjected her to his steam treatment. He and Isaiah swathed her in blankets, upon which, a little at a time, the Doctor poured scalding water until the blankets were saturated, careful to do this so slowly that she was not actually blistered. He continued this until Mrs. Wetzel's face and head, which protruded from the cocoon of blankets in which he had wrapped her, were streaming perspiration; and her breathing had become so labored and painful that it seemed ready to stop altogether. Then he whipped the blankets away and dashed cold water over her.

Immediately afterward, he poured capsicum down her throat. 'We have to do this,' he told Isaiah, 'in order to keep up the internal heat while we cool her off outside; but we can't leave the capsicum in her too long or it'll burn her up.'

So he gave the moribund woman another emetic, and then repeated the steam treatment. He labored with her along these vigorous lines until Monday night, when she died. Isaiah was dazed, not so much by his loss as by the emotional experience of witnessing, and even participating in, this ghastly procedure; and it was weeks before he was able completely to forget it.

III

When Isaiah came to Bangor, Jenny was seven years old; and since his store was so near her home, she and Isaiah's son Ephraim — a few months younger than herself — soon became acquainted. The store fascinated her, and Isaiah first became conscious of her as a young one who was almost as much of a nuisance as Eph, forever underfoot there. He might drive them both out of the store with angry hoots; but Mrs. Wetzel liked Jenny, as did most women, so when they were banished from the store the little girl and Ephraim fled to Mrs. Wetzel, and Jenny came to think of the Poster house as almost a second home.

Isaiah's impatience with her, however, did not long persist. The old man, even then well into his fifties, began to find that Jenny held his eye. Since he was small, standing no more than two inches over five feet, while Tim Hager was big and physically powerful, he would have disliked Tim in any case; but his early interest in Jenny, who so patently adored her father, perversely accentuated this feeling. He hired Tim to work for him, largely because to be able to give Tim orders and see them obeyed and to be able to scold Tim as a shrewish wife scolds her hulking husband, without fear of physical reprisals, gave him a profound and almost sensuous satisfaction. When the chance came to strip Tim penniless, he seized it with a relish; and thereafter, to furnish Tim with rum and watch the big man degenerate into a shaking, maudlin hulk gave Isaiah a pleasing sense of virtuous power.

Even before Mrs. Wetzel died, Isaiah began to make friends with Jenny, welcoming her at the store, giving her sweetmeats, taking her on his knee, teaching her to call him 'Uncle Isaiah.' When he proposed to Tim to go up-river on that lumber-stealing expedition, and the big man objected to leaving Jenny alone, Isaiah suggested that she stay at his house; and she did so, taking Mrs. Wetzel's old room, eating her meals with him and Ephraim — Isaiah had engaged Mrs. Hollis to come in by the day after Mrs. Wetzel died — while Tim was gone; and to have the child under his roof gave the old man an astonishing pleasure. Through Tim's progressive degeneration afterward, on occasions when the big man had drunk himself into a stupor and Jenny came to the store to take him home, Isaiah might walk down Poplar Street with her, propping Tim on one side while she supported him on the other, and help her put her father to bed. He derived a curiously exciting pleasure from these intimate moments when they worked together, pulling off Tim's boots and removing his clothing while he lay helpless.

As Jenny ripened into young maturity, she was in Isaiah's thoughts more and more, and he watched her with a jealous eye. When he saw that his son Ephraim had likewise become conscious of her increasing beauty, he decided that it was high time the boy saw something of the world; and he sent Eph away to Harvard College in Cambridge.

Afterward — since Mrs. Hollis slept at home — Isaiah was at night alone in the house; and he sometimes thought, as one dreams of the impossible, that it would be fine to have Jenny under his roof again.

IV

On that Friday night which marked the last day of the stay of the three companies of soldiers in Bangor before they proceeded to Houlton, Isaiah walked up to their encampment to listen to the band concert. He saw Jenny in the crowd, and spoke to her and she to him; but because he was afraid that to do so would provoke smiles from those who saw them together, he made no effort to keep her by his side. Yet when she moved away he followed her, since it was happiness to him to watch her, to see the way she moved and the turn of her head and the rich shadows of her hair; and when Lieutenant Bloodgood spoke to her, an astonishing

storm of jealous anger shook the old man. His reaction was completely instinctive. There was a bitter taste in his mouth and a
dryness in his nostrils and a nervous twitching of his hands. He
watched them, hating the Lieutenant — and Jenny, too — with
a curdling violence. Jenny seemed to him, suddenly and with the
force of revelation, to be somehow sacred; and for any man to
touch her was like a profanation of which she, since she permitted
it, was as guilty as the officer who now held her hand in the crook
of his arm. Isaiah blamed her even more violently than he blamed
the Lieutenant.

He saw them draw apart into the cover of a clump of trees near
the encampment ground. In that retreat the Lieutenant tried to
kiss her. Jenny, though she laughed, fought free and darted away;
but Isaiah moved angrily forward and intercepted the young officer
with a scolding violence of shrill rage which startled the Lieutenant
and held him in his tracks long enough so that Jenny escaped.
Isaiah himself, still angry, tried then to find her, searching once
more through the crowd, but without success.

When he went back to the store, he was torn by the jealous
passion which shook him. He blamed Jenny for her dallying and
told himself she should be punished for it; and when he found Tim
sunk in a drunken stupor in the store, he seized on opportunity,
telling Tim what he had seen, leaving Jenny's chastisement in her
father's hands.

v

After Tim was gone, Isaiah was for a while so weakened by his
own emotions that he could not stand; and he sat down limply in
the chair which Tim had left and stayed there, imagining Tim
finding Jenny, imagining the big man's rage at his daughter,
mumbling in an avid relish of his own thoughts. When he left the
store and went to his house and to bed, he did not sleep; and he
was still wide awake when he heard running steps outside the
house and then the thud of bare heels on his stoop, and hands
beating at the door, and Jenny crying his name:

'Uncle Isaiah! Uncle Isaiah!'

He lighted a candle and without waiting to dress went to the
door, a grotesque figure in his nightcap, his shirt flapping around
his shins. He lifted the latch and Jenny came stumbling in. Blood
had stained her cheeks and throat and had dripped down on the
shift which was her only garment. One of her sleeves was torn half
away where Tim's great hand had gripped her, and her shift was

ripped down the side so that Isaiah saw angry weals across her bare white legs, and long scratches where Tim had dragged her across the floor. He stared at her for an instant in an almost triumphant satisfaction, relishing these evidences of what she had suffered. Then she flung herself into his arms, sobbing without tears, the sobs shaking and convulsing her whole body, clinging to him, hiding her face against his breast, crying:

'Don't let him in! Don't let him in, Uncle Isaiah! He'll kill me! Don't let him in!'

Isaiah, one arm around her, closed the door and barred it. That Jenny should have come to him in her distress filled him with a greedy excitement and with satisfaction too; but also he was embarrassed, thinking what the town would say if anyone saw Jenny here half-naked in his arms. When she would not let him go, holding him fast as though in him her only safety lay, and crying out in an hysterical terror which he could not soothe, he began to be frightened. He wished Mrs. Hollis were here, to help him take care of the hurt girl and to wrap the mantle of her respectability about them both. That good woman's home on Hancock Street was not far away. She was accustomed to come to Isaiah's house by a path which cut directly from her door to his; and Isaiah thought if he could leave Jenny for a moment he might fetch her. But when he spoke of this, Jenny would not let him go.

'No, no!' she cried. 'Don't leave me alone! Please, Uncle Isaiah! He'll come after me!'

So, as the next best thing, he led Jenny into what had been Mrs. Wetzel's room. She was so wretched that a gentle tenderness began to supplant in him every other feeling, and he persuaded her to lie down on the bed there, and as she grew quieter, he went to put water to heat. When it was warm he bathed her bloody face, and while she lay with closed eyes, still shuddering with sobs and seeming to be unconscious of his attentions, he washed her feet and wiped the scratches and weals on her legs, tending her as gently and as impersonally as a woman.

When she was clean and her hurts were soothed, he covered her over; and without speaking again of Mrs. Hollis, for fear to do so might wake Jenny's fears again, he sat with her until at last, clinging to his hand, she fell asleep. Dawn by that time was near. The night had been long, but now there was light in the eastern skies, and the windows were pale rectangles, even though here in the room the candle still burned. As day brightened she seemed to sleep more heavily; and at last he went to dress, and looked in at her again, and then hurried to summon Mrs. Hollis.

VI

Jenny slept for hours. Isaiah was uneasy at this, and thought perhaps she had been hurt in some way not apparent and should have a doctor's attention, but Mrs. Hollis would not let him rouse her, refusing even to open Jenny's door.

'The poor lamb needs all the rest she can get,' she said. 'We'll let her sleep as long as she can.' They heard distinctly the strains of the military band as the three companies of regulars took the Old Town road on their march to Houlton. 'Did she tell you what happened?' she asked.

Isaiah shook his head. 'No, she didn't tell me anything; just came crying at the door for me to let her in, and saying he'd kill her.'

'Did he come after her?'

'No.' Isaiah's jaw set. 'If he had, I'd have put a slug through him! The town's stood too much from Tim Hager already.' He forgot that it was he who had set Tim on her, swelled now with a virtuous indignation at the big man.

'No one ever will know what that poor baby had to stand from him.'

'He'll never touch her again!' Isaiah swore. The sight of Jenny's hurts and the fact that she had turned to him in her extremity had aroused in him a passionate and possessive tenderness, and he wished now to cherish her and to protect her in every possible way. 'If the town can't deal with him, I can. I'm not going to have such goings on, right next door as you might say.'

Mrs. Hollis nodded with an almost unctuous satisfaction. 'He's been a hard man to her, ever since Moll Hager left him. There was some that thought Moll was wrong to go, but they didn't know him as well as I do. Oh, I've seen what this poor darling went through! She was as scared of him as a mouse is of a cat, and always trying to make him like her; making up to him till your heart would turn over to watch them together, and him so sour and grumbling, yelling at her all the time.' She wagged her head. 'What's to be done about her I don't know. After all, he's her father. You can't just take her away from him.'

'There'll be a way found,' Isaiah said strongly.

'There has to be,' she agreed. 'What she needs is someone to love her and take care of her right. It's a sin and a shame, her living down there anyway, with the women in the houses by the river, and sailors, and men as drunk as Tim Hager up and down the street all night. It's no fit place for her, growing up with that going on right under her eyes!'

Isaiah nodded soberly. Jenny's distress and the way she clung
to him last night had awakened in him emotions he had thought
dead forever. 'Aye,' he agreed. 'Something must be done, but
what's to do?' And he said cautiously, wondering what Mrs. Hollis'
reaction would be: 'It's a pity some good man wouldn't come along
and marry her.'

Mrs. Hollis looked at him with quick, shrewd eyes. For a moment she did not speak, but then she said: 'If it comes to that,
there's no man or boy in town she likes as well as you. Whenever
I see her it's Uncle Isaiah this and Uncle Isaiah that.'

Isaiah shook his head. 'I'm an old man,' he reminded her, but
his fingers twisted together.

'Old or young, she could go farther and fare worse,' Mrs. Hollis
declared; and she added hearteningly: 'But it'd be a burden on
you, to be sure.'

He cleared his throat, but he said no more. She kept her eye
upon him watchfully till he rose at last and took his hat. 'You
stay here, be here when she wakes,' he said. 'She'll want someone.
I'll be back.'

'Are you going down to tell Tim Hager what you think of him?'

'No. I'm done with him! And so is she! No, I'm going to talk
to Deacon Adams and maybe Amos Patten.' Amos that year was
First Selectman, and he and Isaiah were old friends. 'I'll see if
there isn't something we can do to take care of her. It's sure she
can't be let go back to live with him!'

VII

Isaiah, as he walked through the town, kept a sedate and sober
countenance, but there was in him a pounding turbulence. Not
till today had he thought of marrying Jenny — or of marrying
anyone; yet he was an old, lonely man, and if he might borrow
some of her youth for a while, he could repay her in worldly goods
beyond the most avaricious dreams. But he was not lost in folly.
For him simply and plainly to marry a girl forty-five years younger
than himself would be to make himself ridiculous in the town —
unless to do so could be made to appear a virtuous and altruistic
action. But if Mrs. Hollis approved, as obviously she did, so would
other women; and if now Deacon Adams, standing for the church,
and Amos Patten, representing the town government, gave his plan
their countenance, then he could risk the smiles of lesser men.

He went first to Deacon Adams. The Deacon had visited Bangor in 1803, walking up from his then home in Bucksport to inspect the place with a view to settling; but he reported to his wife on his return: 'The town's no better than Sodom, with Lot living there in the person of Deacon Boyd.' So he decided against a removal to Bangor at that time; but ten years later, when Mr. Loomis had been called to head the church, Mr. Adams came to town and became presently a Deacon. After the death of Elder Loomis he had assumed the leadership of the congregation; so it was natural for Isaiah to turn to the Deacon for advice today.

He told Deacon Adams what had happened, and he said at last: 'I'll take the child into my own home, if that's the only thing to do. She's like my own daughter to me, calls me Uncle Isaiah any time she comes into the store.'

The Deacon nodded soberly. 'Someone must take her in, to be sure; but it wouldn't be suitable, Isaiah, for her to be alone in the house with you.' He added: 'And I can't take her. I would if I could, but my home is not a happy place. You and all my good friends know how it has been with Mrs. Adams since we first came to Bangor. It's as if there were a cloud over her mind. She was unwilling to come to live here, saying it was a judgment on her for her sins; and since the day we came I have never been able to comfort her. Night after night I hear her beside me weeping, and whispering: "Would God it were morning!" And all day she whispers: "Would God it were evening!" She's had no peace nor comfort these fifteen years, and I would not bring any young woman to look for happiness in such a home as mine.'

Isaiah nodded in a sympathetic agreement. 'But we must find some way,' he said. 'I thought you'd go along with me to talk to Amos Patten, see what he can say.'

The good Deacon agreed. Amos heard Isaiah's story with clucking, sympathetic sounds and a wagging head. 'To be sure, she could come on the town,' he said, when Isaiah was done. 'But that would be a pity, too.' As a town officer it was a part of his responsibility to keep expenses down. 'Isaiah, it was to you the poor girl turned in her hour of need. Perhaps that's like a sign that you are meant to take the responsibility.'

'Deacon Adams thinks it would not be suitable for me to take her into my home, a young girl alone there with me.' Isaiah hesitated, choosing his words, watching them both. 'But I'd not shirk my duty,' he said, 'if you think it is my duty. I'm an old man, and it's likely I won't be here long; but as long as I live, I could see to it that she had a proper home. If having her in my house would scandalize the town, I'd even be willing to marry her — unless there's some young man she prefers. To have a good home and an honorable name might mean much to her.' He added: 'And she'd be well fixed, too, when I died, and no need ever to turn to Tim Hager again.'

When he had spoken, he waited apprehensively to hear what they would say. Amos rubbed his chin doubtfully. 'Have you said anything of marriage to the girl?' he asked.

Isaiah shook his head. 'I've said nought to her. Why, Amos, she came to me in the small hours of the night, beaten and bruised and bloody, holding on to me as if I was her father; and she's no more to me than my own daughter might have been. I'm too old for the desires of the flesh. It's just that marrying her might be the wisest way to give her the home she ought to have.'

Deacon Adams nodded, as though assenting to his own thoughts. 'And since she turned first of all to you, it must be that she has some liking for you, Isaiah,' he commented. 'Maybe this marriage is the Lord's own will.' His head moved soberly up and down. 'It must always be the part of the elders to bear the burden of guidance of the young. I have guided the lives of my own children since I became a father, praying and laboring for their conversion and repentance and faith in Christ, training them for usefulness here, and for Heaven hereafter. This child has been diligent in attendance at meeting, but there may well be waywardness in her. Her mother was a wanton, and her father is a drunkard. Perhaps this sacrifice may be required of you, Isaiah; that you undertake not only her protection but even her chastening. If you were her husband, your authority would outweigh her father's. As our Lord battled with Satan, so you can battle with her drunken father for her soul!'

Isaiah hesitated, as though in doubt, and Amos urged: 'Yes, Isaiah. Jenny needs the firm hand of such a man as you.'

'I don't know as she'll have me,' Isaiah humbly confessed. 'But when I saw the state she was in, her legs all cut and bruised from Tim Hager's beating, I couldn't turn her from my door. I bathed her hurts and put her to bed like a baby.'

Deacon Adams rose. 'You did well,' he said strongly. 'We will go home with you, to see if she is healed. It may be necessary to labor with her, to add our words to yours, till she sees the wisdom of our plan.'

VIII

When the three old men came to Isaiah's house, they found that Jenny had not yet waked; but Mrs. Hollis was there on vigilant guard, and they talked to her in low tones for a while. Mrs. Hollis openly approved their project. 'It's the best way,' she said, and added frankly: 'I dunno as you're the husband a girl like her would pick, Isaiah; but you'd be good to her, long as you lived, and she'd heir your prop'ty when you die.'

'All the same,' Isaiah confessed, 'you can't expect her to relish marrying an old curmudgeon like me.'

Mrs. Hollis tossed her head. 'She will if she has the sense to skin a cat,' she declared. 'And I think she will. Outside of standing all she did from Tim Hager, Jenny's got a head on her shoulders.'

Amos Patten cleared his throat. 'Suppose we talk to the girl herself,' he said. 'See what she has to say.'

Mrs. Hollis agreed to that. 'It's high time she was waking, anyway,' she said. She turned to the closed door of the room where Jenny lay. 'You wait till I see how she is,' she told them. 'I haven't been in to her yet.'

She went into the other room, but almost at once they heard her cry of dismay at what she saw, and they followed her. Jenny was awake, lying quietly and very small in Mrs. Wetzel's great bed, looking up at them. Her face was a mask of hurts. Her nose and her lips were swollen from Tim's blows, and her lips were marked with red wounds where her teeth had cut them, and there was a bruise across her cheek that darkened one eye. When the old men came in, Mrs. Hollis was sitting on the bed with Jenny in her arms, crooning over her tenderly; and she bade Isaiah bring a lump of butter.

'So I can rub this black and blue mark,' she said, 'and keep it from getting any worse.'

He obeyed her, the Deacon and Amos staying by the bed; and when Isaiah returned, while Mrs. Hollis applied the unguent, she poured out upon Jenny a flood of comforting solicitudes. Yet her curiosity, even in this moment, was alive, and she had questions, too. What had happened? Why had Tim done this dreadful thing?

Jenny said warily, watching them all: 'I don't know. He just came home and I was asleep, and he was drunk.' Her eyes shifted from one face to the other. 'He tried to hold me down on the bed, and I fought and got away from him, but he caught me and he took a stick and beat me till I bit his hand and he let go and I got away.' Then when they shook their heads in grave sympathy, as innocently as a child she pushed down the bedclothes and extended one bare leg for them to see the angry marks upon it. 'He beat me awful,' she said, in low, still tones. 'I guess he'd have killed me if I hadn't got away.'

Amos Patten, staring at the marks on her tender flesh, asked hoarsely: 'Did he chase you?'

'I don't know. I ran out of doors, and it was dark and I just kept running, and the only place I could think to come to was you, Uncle Isaiah.'

'He ought to be birched,' Mrs. Hollis declared. 'It'd take six men to do it, him as big as he is, but I'd like to see it done!'

Deacon Adams cleared his throat. 'Did he ever beat you before, child?'

Jenny looked at him. 'Yes. Lots of times. He beat me the day Elder Loomis died, because I cried.'

'You mean he whipped you because you grieved for that good man?'

'Yes.'

The Deacon shook his head as though unable to credit such depravity. 'Was that the only other time?'

'Oh, no!' Jenny assured them. 'Whenever he came home drunk, if I didn't suit him he'd take a stick to me. The time he wanted to take me to Castine to see the man hung, I didn't want to go and he beat me then till I had to. He beat me lots of times.' She twisted as though in a spasm of terror and cried: 'Don't let him get me again! He'll kill me, next time!'

Isaiah touched her hand. 'I'll take care of you, Jenny. We've decided you're to stay here and live with me.' He smiled. 'Would you like that?'

She looked at him for a long moment. 'He won't let me,' she said. 'Once I told him if he hit me I'd come to live with you, and he said he'd kill me if I did. He said he's my father and I have to live with him.'

Deacon Adams stepped nearer. 'When a woman marries, my child,' he said, 'she leaves all others and cleaves to her husband and he to her. Isaiah says that if you are willing, he will marry you. If you marry Isaiah, your father can never touch you again.'

Jenny's eyes held his, and seconds ran to minutes before she stirred or seemed to breathe. Then she turned her head slowly, as though dreadfully weary, to look at Isaiah; and he said huskily: 'I don't know as you'd want to, Jenny, but I'd be good to you.'

She looked at Mrs. Hollis, appealing for an understanding word; and Mrs. Hollis suddenly gathered the girl in her arms. 'You men go in the other room,' she said. 'The poor lamb doesn't know what to make of it, and her so hurt and all. You just let me talk to her, till she knows what she wants to do.'

IX

Jenny and Isaiah were married late that afternoon. She was still too weak and shaken, aching with the stale pain of the hurts which at first had left her numb, to rise from bed; and she lay very small and still, more like a child than a woman, while Isaiah stood by the bedside and the words were spoken.

Afterward he and Deacon Adams and Amos Patten and John Barker walked down to Tim Hager's house to deal sternly with that man, to tell Tim that Jenny would not come home to him again. They found the door a little ajar, and since no one answered their knock, Deacon Adams pushed it open and went in.

Tim lay with his great shoulders and arms and head across the bed, his legs along the floor, as though he might have crawled this far after he fell. They needed not to touch him to know the truth. The big man was dead.

2

JENNY had come to Isaiah's house almost naked, and she never sought to bring any of her own belongings from her former home. Mrs. Hollis assembled a wardrobe for her in time for Tim's funeral, which Jenny insisted on attending, rising from bed to do so; and she bore herself there with a grave, sweet composure which made Isaiah tenderly proud, and won the sympathetic approval of everyone who saw her. Tim's death was so flagrant an example of the evils of intemperance that it had shocked the town, and even at his funeral this was pointed out and a moral lesson drawn. Jenny, her head bowed, heard herself held up as an example of the suffering and of the fortitude demanded of a drunkard's family.

For a few days afterward she stayed abed, seeming dazed and half-stupefied by her experience and by her father's death; but then her strength began to return, and Isaiah looked forward to her recovery with an eagerness which he had not thought himself capable. If when she was well again she accepted his laborious ardors with no more than a kindly tolerance, he did not complain. Certainly she seemed to like him, she was dutiful, and she was pleasingly grateful for his steady thoughtfulness and solicitude.

He was delighted with her, and the possession of what he had so long almost unwittingly desired changed his outlook on the world. He found in himself a new expansiveness; and forgetting for her sake his thrifty ways, he began a few weeks after their marriage to build a new house, a fine brick house with a chimney on each end, on Main Street near the home of Deacon Adams. Increasing business congestion in the Poplar Street neighborhood, and the nightly disorders there, made the house by the store no longer a desirable location; but also that house was small, and Isaiah wanted a home more in keeping with his place in the community and better worthy of his bride. John Hamm was the builder. Isaiah spared no expense, and the house was among the handsomest in town. It was shaped like a T, the top facing the street, with the storerooms, the woodshed and the stables in the wing behind; and Isaiah in the exuberance of his new happiness ordered furnishings sent from Boston, so that some of the things he acquired became the envy and the wonder of his friends.

His possession of Jenny brought him a sense of permanence and peace. His temper as the weeks passed assumed an equable balance that was rarely shaken, and he found a warming happiness in all she did and in all she was. Their life together, as well privately as publicly, was decorous and seemly. He had always been a regular church-goer and Jenny now sat beside him in his pew. Deacon Adams one day spoke approvingly to Isaiah of the mysterious providence of God, which had arranged matters so well.

II

Jenny, as Mrs. Isaiah Poster, had a position in the community which she filled admirably. The dramatic circumstances of her marriage, and her sudden elevation from the daughter of the town drunkard to be the wife of Isaiah Poster, made her a notable figure. Those who already knew her liked her, and those who now came to know her soon shared that liking.

Isaiah was proud to see that she rose to her responsibilities. It pleased him that when, after Tim's death had served as a horrible example of the evils of drink, the project of forming a county temperance society began to gather strength, she had a part in it; and he was quick to yield when she worked upon him to discontinue the sale of liquor in his store. When Bert Chick, under his patronage, opened a new establishment, she made Isaiah insist that Bert advertise for sale 'refreshments of every kind with the exception of spirituous liquors, which by the way are no refreshment and will not be kept either on the counter or under the counter.'

He took her proudly with him to the meeting in the Court House where a committee was appointed to draft a plan for the organization of the county temperance society, and to the subsequent meeting when the society was organized. He spoke at the meeting, unctuously referring to Jenny's life and to her sufferings as an example of the evils the society was formed to remedy; and Jenny beside him sat with her head demurely bowed while many eyes turned her way.

When it was possible, he took her with him everywhere. Once he had business in Old Town; and he showed Jenny the Indian village on an island in the river, and enjoyed her fastidious distaste for the squalor and dirt she saw everywhere, smiled at her surprise at the fact that the Indians lived not in huts of bark and boughs but in actual small houses set with the gable ends toward the street that crossed the island, and chuckled at her doubtful approval of the Catholic chapel and of the image of the Virgin set in the wood of the cross planted in the cemetery. When he and she returned from the Indian village to Old Town, three itinerant musicians were giving an entertainment there. Jenny suggested that she and Isaiah hear the singers, and they did so. The most popular performer was a man named Cruta, with a repertoire of popular if faintly ribald songs: 'The King and Countrymen,' 'Down in Fly Market,' 'Sitting on a Rail' and a dozen others. Isaiah cackled at them, but afterward — to his secret delight — Jenny chided him for this; and when the performers a few days later moved on to Bangor and set up a theatre of rough boards on the corner of Main Street and Union, she made him report to the congregation that the performance was not one which self-respecting folk should attend.

When Miss Clarke gave a course of ten historical lectures in the schoolhouse on State Street, though there were some who thought it deplorable that a woman should put herself forward as Miss Clarke did, Jenny persuaded Isaiah to subscribe for the course and they attended the lectures. They likewise joined the Lyceum, and the Literary Club.

But in addition to her constant appearances, silent but devoted, at Isaiah's side, Jenny had activities of her own. In the second year after they were married, a niece of Mrs. Amos Patten died of consumption which was attributed to the fact that she had laced herself too tightly; and an attempt was made to organize a society for the reform of female dress, to crusade against the wearing of busks, boards and stays, and equally against the custom of supplementing the deficiencies of the female figure with cushions, pillows, bolsters and other padding.

Jenny was the moving spirit in this enterprise, and she counted on Mrs. Patten's support. Mrs. Patten was an older woman, in her early forties. She was a daughter of Captain Isaac Hatch and her brother Tom and her mother still kept that tavern on Main Street where Captain Barrie had cut the spigots off the rum barrels with his sword; so she was not a whole-hearted convert to the temperance cause of which Jenny was already a leading advocate. Nor was she enthusiastic about Jenny's proposal to reform female dress, and though Jenny had some youthful converts, Mrs. Patten remained skeptical.

'It's all very well for you, child,' she warned Jenny. 'And for young scrippets like you! You've a waist like an hourglass, and a nice high front, and you're not flat behind like most women; but wait till you've had a few babies and begin to get a middle-aged spread. You'll be driven to stays and ruffles and bustles like the rest of us!'

Nevertheless the society was duly organized, and there were enthusiastic meetings for a while; but the young wives who were the most ardent supporters of the new doctrine presently found that physical facts overruled their zeal, and one by one, as the members themselves waxed, the membership waned.

III

In April of the second year after Jenny and Isaiah were married, the First Parish Meeting House burned. The fire was blamed on an incendiary. Five years before, a half-witted boy named Friend Watson had set fire to Mr. Chick's stable, and that fire spread and burned over all the territory between Main, Fish and Water Streets. The boy was locked up at the poorhouse as of unsound mind; but he had had imitators since. They were prompted perhaps by a desire to witness the pleasant hullabaloo which attended a conflagration; but whatever the motives, arson was the most common major crime in Bangor, and the fire which destroyed the church had certainly been set. The Selectmen offered a five hundred dollar reward for the discovery of the criminal, but he was never found.

The church burned to the ground, destroying the organ and partially fusing the bell which Mr. Bussey had given the congregation, but plans for a new church were at once put under way, and within a few months it was completed. It stood on the old location, a square building with a white steeple at each of the four corners. Isaiah told Jenny: 'It looks to me like a table turned upside down, with the legs sticking up in the air.' But no public dissatisfaction with the architecture was voiced. Calvin Edwards made the new organ, and Mr. Bussey's bell was recast, though the splendor of its original tone could never be recaptured.

The new structure was paid for by the sale of pews; and Isaiah was proud of the fact that Jenny took the lead in selling them, working through the wives of the members upon their husbands, organizing a pew committee which was so successful that after the hundred and thirty-four pews had been sold, not only was the church paid for but some two thousand dollars additional was turned over to the church treasury. By her activity in this work, the position which Jenny all her life would hold as a leader among the women of the congregation was established beyond disputing.

IV

Jenny, born in Bangor, had never been farther away than Castine in one direction, Old Town in the other, till three years after her marriage Isaiah took her with him on a business trip to Houlton. He had not planned to do so, but she proposed it. 'There's been so much talk about Houlton and the boundary disputes and all that I'd like to go,' she said; and when Isaiah hesitated, she protested teasingly: 'You're afraid I'll see some of those handsome soldiers there, the ones that were here three years ago.'

This had not occurred to him, and the possibility disturbed him now; but to prove to himself that he did not fear the competition of uniforms, he agreed that she should go along. They were three days on the way, travelling by stage over the military road which had been cut by the troops since their coming and which except for an occasional stretch that was still unfinished and miry was good enough, lodging at night in crowded small taverns where Jenny was sometimes the only woman in the place.

Houlton was a town of about fifty houses, with a fort and a custom-house, and Mars Hill, bold on the horizon to the northward, lifted its crown above the forested lands between. Isaiah's business there was to meet a Scot named Gillies whom he had dispatched some weeks before to make an exploratory trip through the northern wilderness in search of pine lands worth the purchasing. They were beforehand, and they put up at the tavern to wait his arrival. At the common table the first evening they were joined by a man with his wife and two sons, and the man immediately fixed his attention so sharply on Jenny that Isaiah stiffened in resentment. The man seemed to be in his middle forties, astonishingly untidy in his dress, yet with a certain grace and zest in all his movements. His nose was his dominant feature, beneath a broad, square brow and above a narrow, mobile mouth embraced in deep lines that ran down from his nostrils.

He continued to stare at Jenny so intently that Isaiah, sitting beside her, pulled his brown wig — which Jenny had soon after they were married persuaded him to substitute for his familiar skull cap — tighter on his head with an angry gesture; and the movement attracted the other man's attention. He spoke to Isaiah, smiling in a sudden fashion full of charm.

'Sir,' he said, 'I should like to make a drawing of your daughter. My name is Audubon, and drawing is my profession. It is true that I prefer to draw the likenesses of birds and of animals, but I draw people too, supporting myself in this way on the travels necessary to find the subjects I seek. Yet your daughter is of such a beauty —— '

Isaiah interrupted him with a harsh violence. 'This is my wife, man, not my daughter!'

The other looked at him and then at Jenny, and there was a twinkle in his eye; but his tone was grave and full of respect. 'My apologies, sir, and my compliments too. You are a brave man! Yet I would still beg your permission to make a likeness of Madame.'

Isaiah was confused, beyond his depth. 'I don't know about that,' he admitted; but Jenny said smilingly:

'Let him try it, Isaiah. I've never seen myself through anyone else's eyes.'

Audubon added his urgencies to hers, and as a warrant of his capacities, he showed Isaiah the portfolio of drawings which he had just completed in his travels through the Provinces. He made a sketch of Jenny next day, Isaiah sitting jealously near; and even before it was done, Isaiah, watching it approach completion, proposed to buy it. Mr. Audubon of course assented, but when he suggested a price of twenty-five dollars, Isaiah objected with such violence that Audubon bowed and said in an edged tone:

'Then take it, my friend, with my compliments! I give it to you as a tribute to a very beautiful young woman.'

'Don't want it as a gift!' Isaiah protested. 'I'm willing to pay a fair price!'

Audubon shrugged. 'Who is to say what is a fair price?' he countered. 'Perhaps it is worthless, perhaps priceless. You and I are too near the subject to judge.' He turned to Jenny. 'Let

Madame decide,' he proposed, and put the sheet of drawing paper in her hands.

Jenny when she took it was smiling; but after she had looked at it her smile faded. She studied her image for a long moment, and then, still staring at it, she said in her quiet tones: 'Buy it, Isaiah.'

Isaiah hesitated. 'Fifteen dollars?' he suggested, turning to the painter.

But before Audubon could reply, Jenny repeated, no more loudly but with a cold violence in her very quietness: 'I said, buy it, Isaiah!'

She watched them with level eyes while the money was paid over, the full price. Then she asked: 'Now is it mine?'

Audubon, a little puzzled, said: 'But certainly, Madame.'

Jenny nodded, and then, very carefully, she tore the drawing from top to bottom, and across again and again in an increasing violence till the whole was reduced to scraps. She threw them on the floor. She rose from her chair and took one step toward Audubon. Her cheeks were blazing.

'If my husband were a younger man he would kill you,' she said in controlled tones. 'If I were a man I'd kill you myself!'

Isaiah stared at her, dumb with astonishment; but Audubon after a moment laughed, and he bowed. 'Thank you, Madame!' he exclaimed. 'I perceive that my portrait was a good one!'

Isaiah, completely bewildered, looked from one to the other, protesting querulously: 'What's that for, Jenny? What did you go and do that for?' But for a moment Jenny did not speak. She stared at the scattered fragments on the floor; and then suddenly her anger passed and she smiled and touched the artist's arm.

'You and I have eyes,' she said quietly, and turned and left the room.

Isaiah delayed a moment to say something apologetic about feminine vapors; but Audubon, careful not to smile, bowed again and said politely:

'Sir, I think Madame — unwittingly and certainly unwillingly — paid me a very high compliment.'

Isaiah blinked, more perplexed than ever; but before he could pry further into this mystery, a boy brought word that the man he expected had arrived. Audubon went with him to meet the woodsman.

v

Donald Gillies was a small, lean, tireless Scot, at this time in his later thirties; and he had long since demonstrated to Isaiah his reliability. He had a dry humor, and such a keen appreciation of his own jests that others less perceptive sometimes thought he laughed not at anything that had been said but at his listeners. With a party of sixteen men, carrying as provisions two hundred and fifty pounds of bread and a hundred and fifty pounds of pork, he had started up-river from Old Town in canoes, weeks before. They ascended the Penobscot almost due north to the Seboois Lake region, threaded the lakes northwesterly, carried across to Allegash waters, and came down that stream and the St. John's, with occasional portages, to Woodstock, whence they crossed to Houlton.

Audubon and Isaiah listened to Mr. Gillies with an equal interest now. 'About twelve hundred miles I make it, for the whole trip,' the little Scot told them. 'And I'll draw you up a map, Mr. Poster, that will tell the tale better than words.' Of much of the territory they had visited there were as yet no surveys. 'I'll lay it out by days' journeys,' Gillies explained. 'I kept compass courses and bearings all the way, and tallied all the pine in sight.'

Audubon asked eagerly how this was done; and Gillies explained: 'Why, we'd climb tall trees and take a look around; or hills or mountains. The pines stand up fifty-sixty feet, sometimes more, over everything else.' He told Isaiah: 'I took a look at some of it that was handy; all good clean stuff. Didn't see a concussy tree the whole time.'

The artist had many questions about the wild life of the region visited, both birds and beasts; and Gillies was amused at his interest in such unimportant matters. 'I'd not know one bird from another,' he declared. 'I might have heard a pigeon-woodpecker rattle and never notice it, and like as not there were eagles and fishhawks along the way, and I mind seeing a few broods of scurry ducks on the river.'

Audubon demanded to know what scurry ducks were; but Gillies shook his head. 'All I know, they're hard eating,' he declared. 'We did shoot a few, tried 'em every way. The first, we skinned 'em and put 'em in the stew-pot with a flat rock on top and boiled 'em till we could stick a knife through the rock.' He slapped his knee and laughed, but Audubon looked at him in such a puzzled way that he sobered again and added: 'After that we'd skin 'em out and tie a string to 'em and let 'em hang in rips of the quickest water we could find all night, and then go out in the morning and cut the string!' He chuckled once and added: 'We found some trout that had worked theirselves to death chawing at those ducks all night, but even the trout were too pore to eat after that.'

He laughed again, till he saw that Audubon was not amused.

'But animals, then?' the artist insisted. 'Surely you saw many wild creatures?'

Gillies shook his head. 'I did not,' he said. 'I was looking for pine, mind you.' Then his eyes twinkled and he made one last attempt at humor. 'The only animal I had an eye for at all was a porcupine, but then that's one kind of pine.'

VI

Jenny's experience with Mr. Audubon had a sequel. Isaiah reproached her for destroying the drawing just after he had paid a round price for it; and he insisted that he had liked it well.

'Of course, Jenny, it wasn't so beautiful as you are, but all the same, it pleased me,' he said.

Jenny was apparently contrite enough. 'Something about it made me hate it,' she said. 'I didn't know myself in it. I didn't like myself. But next time, I won't lose my temper, Isaiah.'

Isaiah was not sure there would be a next time, since though Audubon had travelled with them as far as Bangor he was now gone on his way. When Isaiah spoke of the incident to Amos Patten, however, Amos offered a substitute. 'If it's a likeness of Mrs. Poster you're wanting, take her to Mr. Hardy,' he suggested. 'He's a good hand at it, and he could do fine for you, to be sure.'

So that summer Jenny sat for her portrait a second time. Jeremiah Hardy, although he lived in Hampden, had opened a studio on York Street, walking the seven miles to and from his home each day. He was at that time in his early thirties, and fairly launched on his career. As a youngster of fourteen in Hampden, he had seen the British overrun the town, and had watched from a safe distance the casual skirmish which led to the flight of the American militia. He had even then begun to show an aptitude for draughtsmanship, and also for engraving; and his first plates were graved on sheet copper which he salvaged from the wreck of the Adams, diving at low tide to strip off the sheathing on her bottom. At sixteen he painted a portrait of his sister, Mary Ann, which pleased his father so much that he was sent to Boston to study at Mr. Brown's Academy; and he opened a studio for a while in Boston, till he came home to marry Catherine Wheeler in Hampden and settle there.

He was a man with a wide, flexible mouth and a long upper lip under his hawk's nose. His eyes, a little inclined to frown with the intensity of the gaze which he turned upon his sitter, were widely spaced and keen; and Isaiah, when he went with Jenny while she sat for him, saw with some misgivings that she watched the artist with a grave absorption, occasionally cocking her head a little on one side in that way which was always natural to her. Half-fearing she would treat the canvas as violently as she had Mr. Audubon's drawing, Isaiah made it a point to be present at every sitting. When Mr. Hardy, so that he could watch the play of her features and her changing expressions, led Jenny to talk, and Isaiah saw in her an animation he himself had never evoked, he stirred uneasily. He was relieved when the portrait was done, and he paid Mr. Hardy's fee, thirty dollars for the portrait and sixteen dollars for the frame, with never a word of argument, and took the portrait home with a sense of escape.

Jenny had chosen to be painted in a black dress of heavy silk, with puffed sleeves and a tight-fitting bodice buttoned down the front, topped with a lace yoke and collar. For her sittings she put her hair in prim order, parted demurely in the middle and drawn back so that her ears showed. Her hair was naturally almost straight, but she arranged for these sittings soft curls above each ear and in front of the heavy knot at the back of her neck. The portrait emphasized her broad brow and strong mouth and chin; and the strange purity of her countenance, which would always persist, was perfectly caught by the painter's brush. Only in the faintly lifting brows, which, rising from the bridge of her nose toward her temples, curved scarcely at all, and in the eyes, which, while they were wide and frank, yet had on closer scrutiny no expression whatever, was there a suggestion that Mr. Hardy had sensed and perhaps had caught and laid on canvas something in Jenny that was calm, remote, potentially cruel and unshakably strong.

If she saw this in the finished likeness, she did not protest, and to Isaiah the portrait seemed perfection. It was admired by everyone who saw it, and he hung it over the mantel in the big dining room, directly above Jenny's usual seat at table; and when he sat facing her, looking from her to the painting above her head, he saw her in duplicate and did not know which was the more beautiful, the reality or its counterfeit.

But at the same time he was made uneasy by the fact that Jenny spoke often of Mr. Hardy, and that sometimes she insisted on Isaiah's taking her to the studio to see any new work upon which the artist might be engaged. Isaiah was so delighted with the portrait of Jenny that he felt he had driven a sharp bargain with the painter, and he had a certain sense of guilt whenever he met

Mr. Hardy; but also Jenny's persistent interest in the man himself was faintly disturbing.

He had a like alarm when some time after the portrait was finished Ephraim came home for a few days' stay. Since Ephraim first went to Boston, Isaiah had encouraged him to stay there and to use his free time in travel. He told Ephraim this was a part of a young man's education, refusing to admit even to himself that he remembered the boy's awakening interest in Jenny, which had been interrupted when he sent Ephraim away.

Ephraim came home on this occasion without advance notice; and when he saw the painting he studied it, looking from it to Jenny as though perplexed by what he saw. Jenny watched him, and Isaiah watched them both, and he said at last sharply:

'Well, what's the matter, Eph? What are you staring at?'

'I can't decide whether it's like her or not,' the boy told him. He laughed. 'I don't think it is,' he said to Jenny. 'If you were like that, I'd be afraid of you.'

Jenny smiled and said in those quiet tones which were always pitched so low that her listeners had need to be attentive in order to hear: 'Why, Eph, you don't ever have to be afraid of me.'

Isaiah, suddenly alert, looked from one of these young people to the other with narrowing eyes. When Jenny was with Mr. Hardy, and when she talked with Ephraim now, he heard in her voice something which alarmed him. While they discussed the portrait together, he reflected with relief that Ephraim would be going back to Cambridge soon.

VII

Isaiah had had since they were married no cause to complain of Jenny. She was always serene and composed, thoughtful of him in little ways, grateful for everything he did; and she was as she passed from girlhood into womanhood so completely beautiful that he swelled with pride like a turkey cock when he appeared in public with her by his side. Marriage had in some ways rejuvenated him. He felt younger, was full of a restless energy, tireless in all business affairs; and he thanked her for this, told her more than once:

'Why, Jenny, you make me feel like a colt again!'

She had never denied him anything. They slept together in the high canopy bed in the big upstairs room; and Jenny in her sleep never moved, nor did she wake if he was sometimes uneasy beside her. There was a smaller room opening off theirs, where he kept his possessions and where he prepared for the night. Usually she came upstairs before him, while he extinguished the candles or the whale-oil lamps and bolted the doors; but he was apt to hurry after her, and when he was undressed he went in and climbed into bed to lie watching her leisurely preparations for the night. He used to laugh to see how long it took her to be ready to come to bed, and she might smile with him, but she never hurried. He particularly liked to watch the curve of her arms and the turn of her head as she brushed her hair and separated it and braided it in two heavy braids. Then she would snuff the last candle and in the darkness he heard her — or if a moon were shining saw her — take off the figured silk wrapper she had put on over her nightgown when she undressed, and so come to bed beside him; and on chilly nights he would press near her, warming himself against her young body.

He was apt to be cold at night, and in winter he wore a nightcap and heavy underwear under his nightshirt and used the warming pan to prepare the bed before he got into it. Even in summer he kept the windows closed, resenting and fearing any breath of outside air. Jenny had always accepted his wishes in this respect, and their nights together rested and restored him; but after Mr. Hardy had made her likeness and after Ephraim's few days at home there began to be a change. She who had always slept so quietly now no longer did so. She stirred and twisted in her sleep, assuming strange positions, her knees in the small of Isaiah's back crowding and fretting him. If he moved away from her she followed him, so that sometimes he got up and went to the other side of the bed and lay down there; but when he did so, even in her sleep — she was so persistent that he sometimes thought she was awake and plaguing him — she would move toward him again, her knees nudging him till he had no peace at all.

When he was driven at last to protests, she said contritely: 'Oh, I'm sorry, Isaiah! I think it must be because there's no air in the room. Sometimes I dream I'm smothering.'

He protested that no people of sense had air in their bedrooms, and she agreed that this was true; but her restless movements continued night after night until he was driven to opening a window a crack, and then wider and wider. She began after that to sleep as she had used to, without movement; but he was cold, and if he drew near her to warm himself, her elbows and knees jabbed him in the ribs or in the back. His nights were spoiled; and at last in self-defense he proposed to set up a smaller bed in his dressing room and sleep there.

'Why, we might try it,' she agreed. 'I do want you to be comfortable, Isaiah!'

Isaiah had forgotten how pleasant it could be to sleep alone. In the smaller room, with doors and windows closed and sometimes — even in summer — with a fire in the little stove, he could have the stifling heat his cooling blood desired.

So the arrangement, begun as an experiment, persisted. Isaiah might still go in to watch her do her hair, but when she was ready for bed he retreated to his sanctuary where he could have things as he chose.

VIII

After her father's death, the small house in which they had lived became Jenny's property. Isaiah had long since made Tim give him a mortgage deed to it, but because he saw how it pleased her to think of the house as her own, he never told her so, left its disposition completely in her hands. She herself never returned to it at all, but she sent Mrs. Hollis to put it in order, and at regular intervals to keep it so; and Isaiah saw to it that necessary repairs were made from time to time.

The house had no occupant until the third year after Tim died. Then Jenny found a tenant for it, a woman named Lena Tempest. Isaiah, from the first, had fondly insisted that Jenny do nothing more laborious than polite needlework. Her hands, at once soft and strong, were his delight, and he would not have them marred; so Mrs. Hollis when they moved into the new house came to live with them and took complete charge of the establishment. At first she cooked and cleaned and did everything herself; but the work was more than she could handle alone, and eventually she engaged Lena Tempest to come in by the day and do the washing.

Lena Tempest was a newcomer to Bangor. She was a woman in her late thirties, who, when she found herself mysteriously denied maternity by nature, embraced all mankind in a general affection in which there was much more of the mother than the wanton. She was Scandinavian, tall and fair, with fine blue eyes. Her mother had after her father's death run a boarding house in Springfield, patronized by Connecticut River lumbermen, where Lena at eighteen took the part of a little man named Connell against Dan McIsaac who was twice his size. Connell came out of that encounter with a broken arm and two cracked ribs; but he might as easily have been killed if Lena had not smashed McIsaac's head with a chair so hard that she cracked his skull. Connell gratefully insisted that she marry him, and she did; but he was drowned on the drive the following spring, and Lena — who had been disturbed since her marriage by the fact that McIsaac never recovered his wits after that buffet she had given him — took her victim in hand and they lived together and continued the management of the boarding house which by her mother's death had come under Lena's direction. For eight years she was the loyal slave of Dan McIsaac's moods, whether tyrannical or amorous; and only after his death did she accept the devotion which Jeff Tempest had offered long before. Jeff was a lovable big man, but he quickly drank up or gambled away all Lena's savings. After the boarding house had followed the rest, Jeff, hearing of the rising lumber trade on the Penobscot, decided to remove to Bangor, and she came with him. He was killed when a log rolled on him in one of General Veazie's mills at Old Town; and since then Lena had earned her living by doing odd jobs of household work around the town.

When she came to labor in the Poster home, a curious intimacy sprang up between her and Jenny, and they spent many hours in talk together. Isaiah at last discovered this and expressed a surprised disapproval.

'What do you want to set and talk to her for?' he protested.

'Why, I like her,' Jenny told him. She added — and he had a faint suspicion that she was teasing him: 'Of course she's not what we call a good woman. She says she was never married to Jeff Tempest, and she's had a strange, hard life, with rough men.'

'Why, that's scandalous, Jenny!' he protested. 'You ought to get her out of the house!'

'Oh, no,' she insisted. 'You see, she looks at such things in a different way. She's not the sort that just go with men for money, Isaiah. She says it's the same as marrying a man, if you like him and want to make him happy.'

Isaiah was shocked at such words from Jenny, whom he had thought completely innocent, and he felt it his duty as a leading citizen and a good churchman to insist that Lena be banished; but Jenny would not consent to this.

'It's not her fault,' she insisted, and she said: 'Why, she talks about her men just the way I talk about you, and when she's living with one of them she never looks at any other man.' And when he tried to muster some violence of condemnation, she said, with her head on one side, looking at him wisely: 'But Isaiah, she's with her men the same way Mrs. Wetzel was with you.'

He had not guessed that she knew or even suspected the truth

about Mrs. Wetzel, and Jenny was still so like a child, with that
purity of countenance which always distinguished her, that he
found it hard to speak of these matters under her calm and steady
eyes. She suggested that he talk with Lena himself, and he agreed
to do so.

Lena easily won him. There was in her a long understanding of
mankind, so that she knew how to make Isaiah laugh and like her
as Jenny did. He might sit for an hour watching her as she labored
at her tubs, her strong white arms soap-flecked; and he chuckled at
the tales she told of her life in Springfield, and of the rough and
lusty rivermen, and of the women whose profession it was to please
them.

But she had, she assured him, put all that behind her. It was
now her ambition to save enough money out of her small earnings
to be able to set up for herself in the laundry business. Jenny and
Isaiah in the end made this possible. Lena lodged in the basement
of a rooming house that was at best semi-respectable, on Broad
Street on the west side of the Stream and near the river. Toward
the end of March a heavy fall of warm rain precipitated a sudden
rise of water in the river, and on the first of April the jam of ice
above town gave way and in a groaning, grumbling mass came
trundling downstream. But below town the ice jammed again; and
behind it the water rose with an astonishing rapidity. It overflowed
the wharves, sweeping away lumber and shingles piled there during
the winter for shipment as soon as the river should open for navigation, and toppling one sloop that was on the stocks over on its side.
So rapidly that there was no time to move anything to higher
ground, the water flooded the cellars and the lower floors of houses
near the shore; and Lena was among the sufferers.

When Isaiah came home that night, Jenny told him what had
happened to Lena. 'The flood washed her out,' she said. 'Everything she owns is not only wet but caked with mud, and she can't
live in that room any more. So, Isaiah, I've an idea. I like Lena,
and she's always been wanting to set up a laundry business. I'm
going to let her rent my house. It's high enough so it never gets
flooded out, and it ought to be lived in, anyway. She'd take good
care of it, and it would make her happy too.'

Isaiah, who never long opposed Jenny in anything, agreed; and
the result was that Lena was presently established in Tim Hager's
small house on Poplar Street, taking in washing from the young
bachelors of the town. In the years that followed, as Bangor
grew, so did her business; and she hired first one and then another
young woman to help her. When the house became too small for

her, Isaiah gave Jenny the money to enlarge it, and he went one day to inspect the alterations.

He found that Lena had four girls working under her direction, and there was a youthfulness and a friendliness about them which seemed to him suspicious. 'I sh'd think you'd want women that looked more like they could do enough to earn their keep,' he urged.

But Lena said good-naturedly: 'They earn their keep, Mr. Poster. Don't you worry about that. And Lord love you, my customers are all single gentlemen. You know yourself that a young man would rather talk to a pretty young woman than a hard-working old one, any time!'

'All the same, I want no scandalous goings on in this house,' he said severely; and she laughed and assured him that any girl in her house would behave, and that none but gentlemen should call upon them, or she would know the reason why.

Isaiah told himself that to push the matter further, to attempt to evict Lena, would involve making explanations to Jenny which his wife was still too young and innocent to hear; so he decided to shut his eyes and let the new arrangement stand.

IX

Bangor in these years was growing at an accelerating pace, and it was becoming increasingly conscious of this fact. Isaiah one evening proudly read aloud to Jenny from the columns of the Penobscot *Journal*, which had just begun publication, a leading article which said:

> The activity of trade in Bangor at the present time is cheering to its citizens, and excites the admiration of strangers. A large share of our merchants are in the very comfortable condition of having as much as they can do. Our streets exhibit the bustle of a city, and a fleet of shipping is constantly in the harbor. Boats and rafts are passing on the river at all times, in all directions. A large number of buildings are in progress, including several blocks of stores. Six or seven brickyards within this village are in constant operation. A spacious hotel, we believe the largest in the State, is well filled. Laboring men are in great demand, and at the highest wages.

'Now that Barnes is a smart man!' said Isaiah, as he slapped the paper approvingly. The *Journal's* editor was Phineas Barnes, a graduate of Waterville, recently come to town. 'A paper like that is what this town needs. Bangor's going to be the biggest city in

Maine, and maybe in New England. The best pine in the world is in Maine, and folks have got to have good punkin pine if they're going to get along at all; and we're the ones will cut it and make it into lumber and sell it to 'em.'

Jenny, sitting across from him, busy with a bit of needlepoint, nodded her smooth head. 'Yes, Isaiah,' she said, 'and it's men like you who have done it, too; seeing what was going to happen, helping it along.'

Isaiah, as always, beamed under her praise. 'We've just begun,' he declared. 'I was talking with General Veazie today about the Brewer Bridge and the business it's brought to town. I thought that bridge was a big idea, but now he's figuring on a railroad to Old Town, and maybe to Houlton, and there'll be railroads coming through from Augusta by and by. The only thing holds us back now is the river's froze up all winter so's we can't ship lumber out. Fix it so we can load it right on the steam trains, and there'll be no stopping us at all.' He sat dreaming, and he looked again at the paper in his hand. 'I won't live to see the whole of it,' he admitted. 'But the way things are going, there'll be ten thousand people here in Bangor, even in my time. I was counting up with Amos Patten, day before yesterday. There are right on to seventy stores and shops in town now, and fifty-one houses and stores building, one place and another. We can saw forty million feet of boards, up at the mills in Stillwater and Orono, not counting all the other mills on the main river and on the Kenduskeag. This coming winter there'll be four hundred yokes of oxen working in the woods, hauling logs against the drive next spring.' He chuckled gleefully. 'That means business, and profits, and I'll get my share of them.' He looked at her fondly. 'You're going to be a rich woman when I die, Jenny.'

'Don't talk so, Isaiah! I want you to live a long time.'

He cackled happily. 'I aim to. Since I married you, I feel like a colt sometimes.'

She smiled. 'You're always saying that!'

'Well, I do!' he insisted. 'I've got more ideas than I could work out if I lived to be a thousand.' He added, more soberly: 'But I don't want to die and leave you with a lot of prop'ty to take care of. You wouldn't know how to do.'

'I'll have Ephraim to help me,' she reminded him.

He stared at her, suddenly angry, not at her but at the thought of her and Ephraim together after he was gone. 'Him!' he said explosively. 'I wouldn't give shucks for him! Since he went off to Harvard College he's too high and mighty for Bangor. Chance is he'll want to go and live in Europe or somewhere, and think himself too good for this town! No, you can't count on Eph, Jenny. But don't you worry!' He rose, his anger gone, and came and patted her shoulder affectionately. 'I'm going to fix it so you'll be all right. I'm going to sell off the most of my house lots here in town. The lots Mr. Bulfinch surveyed brought good prices, and I've got better land than any of that. And I'll sell off the heft of my timber lands. There's no sense in holding on too long. We might get another fire like that one a few years back that burned over a couple of my townships. Pine on the stump is worth something, but a fire can burn it up awful quick. I'd rather have boards stacked at the mills, or else the money in hand.'

'Don't you think Ephraim will come home when he's through college?' she asked, not lifting her eyes from her work.

He resented her speaking of his son again, and he looked down at her bowed head for a moment with angry eyes before answering. 'I don't know's he will, and I don't know's he won't,' he said then shortly. He turned away, crossing to his own chair, picking up the paper he had dropped. 'I don't know as I want him to,' he said, almost sullenly. 'You and me are well enough as we are!'

She glanced toward him, her head on one side, studying him as though trying to read his thoughts till his eyes turned uneasily away. He wished fretfully that she would not keep talking about Ephraim all the time.

IV

Ephraim Poster

I

EPHRAIM POSTER was born in the summer of 1811, on a farm in Cuyahoga County in the new state of Ohio. He was the only child of Isaiah's second wife, who died when he was born. Isaiah's children by his first wife, resenting his early remarriage, had disliked their mother's successor, and they disapproved even more violently of Mrs. Wetzel, whom Isaiah brought into his home as soon as Ephraim's mother died. The result was an estrangement between them and Isaiah which — coupled with the fact that Isaiah presently sold his farm and went back to Bangor, so that they never saw him again — made Ephraim in effect an only child.

Mrs. Wetzel, who hid behind a pretended scorn of her neighbors and the barbed-wire fence of a sarcastic tongue a keen loneliness, took charge of Ephraim while he was still a baby; and since in her eyes he could do no wrong, he never underwent any stiffening discipline. If Isaiah barked at him, Mrs. Wetzel was quick with comforting; and if Isaiah threatened punishments, Mrs. Wetzel's arms were always a sanctuary. To Isaiah himself the woman was no more than a habit; but to Ephraim she was the fountain of all good, and his love for her, selfish though it may have been, was the dominant fact of his boyhood.

He was when Isaiah came back to Bangor just six years old, and Jenny was his first playmate. She ruled him completely, largely because she always knew exactly what she wished to do; and as long as he was too young to range far from home, he had few acquaintances among boys his own age. Those who knew him jeered because he preferred a girl's companionship to theirs; and when he grew a little older and began to go abroad, Mrs. Wetzel's solicitude in such respects as comforters around his neck, mittens, felts and rubbers and the like, marked him as a fair target for derision. He had no defense against the bullying to which as a result he was subjected. To fight back was beyond his wildest dreams. He was not even articulate. When he was accused of anything, whether seriously or in jest, Ephraim could only grin in a watery way and exclaim: 'Who, me? Gee!' This habit became so firmly fixed that he acquired a nickname: 'Me Gee!' This, still further contracted, became at last simply 'Gee!', and he was till he went away to college Gee Poster to every boy on the east side of the Stream.

His childhood was beset by fears, usually imaginary. For instance, water always had terrors for him, and though he might be shamed into wading knee or waist deep, he never learned to swim. When in summer other youngsters took slabs cast aside by the sawmills and using them as floats paddled out into the Stream to ride the current down to the Point, Ephraim might run along the bank in a breathless excitement to see their adventures on the way; but he never attempted to imitate them.

In the same way the forests near town seemed to him dark and fearful places; and when others went exploring there, he never joined them. Inevitably his fellows discovered his fears and played upon them. Once, in a curious desire to see what he would do, some of them dragged him — at first in silence — as far as the border of the wood. There, when he began to cry, they smothered his screams and carried him into the thicket and tied him to a birch; but his struggles to escape were so violent that they were alarmed and released him, imposing silence on him by threats to repeat the outrage if he ever told anyone what had happened.

There was one occasion when the bullying which his youthful cowardice evoked almost led to his death. Three older boys — Nat Barker, young Joe Leavitt and Eddie Patten — were swimming off the Leavitt shipyard. A small raft of logs loosely floored with boards was moored along the wharf; and they persuaded the trembling Ephraim to climb down the ladder nailed to the piling and join them on the raft. He did so, and then because he was so obviously afraid, they began to pretend to push him off the raft. His pleas for mercy excited them to such an extent that they carried the game too far. Ephraim went overboard, and he came up under the raft.

The logs were sufficiently wide apart so that, while he could not squeeze up through the space between them, his head did appear there. Eddie Patten caught him by the hair and supported him, warning him to keep his mouth shut so that he would swallow no more water; and the three boys, keeping tight hold on his hair, having sometimes to push him under and past an obstacle before pulling him to the surface again, worked him to the end of the raft and hauled him aboard.

Ephraim was by that time too scared to cry; and all four of them, stark naked, completely forgetting their clothes in the excitement of this rescue, raced up to the Poster home to tell Mrs. Wetzel their great adventure. That good woman had been cleaning house. They found her in the kitchen and, while Ephraim clung to her and sobbed, the other three, all talking at once, told the story. Ephraim's danger — even though it was past — made her for a moment insane with relief that he was still alive. In a dreadfully calm deliberation she locked the kitchen door, took a birch switch with which she had been beating rugs, and lashed the three rescuers till the birch was frayed and broken and their white bodies were crisscrossed with red streaks, while Ephraim, safe in a corner, looked on in a horrid fascination.

This did not endear either Mrs. Wetzel to the mothers of the boys, nor Ephraim to them; and from that day, though he was never seriously molested, he was an outcast in the town.

II

It was not until Ephraim came into his teens and Jenny was more and more often at the store with her father that the boy began to feel an adolescent interest in her. This manifested itself either in attempts — whenever she was near — to do something remarkable in order to attract her attention, or in a shy and grinning silence. His interest in Jenny was intensified when Mrs. Wetzel died. The woman had always given him a tenderness she never showed to anyone else, not even to Isaiah. When he suffered from the indispositions of youth she took care of him; and long after he emerged from babyhood he still liked to curl in her lap, feeling the warmth of her body, cushioned against the mysterious softness of her bosom. Within himself at such times there were stirrings which he found deeply pleasurable; and to be near her, in physical contact with her, provoked an instinctive reaction in his boy's body to her lavish womanliness.

So he missed her when she was gone, missed these puzzling pleasures; but it was not long before he discovered that to touch Jenny's hand, to come near her, to tussle with her in amiable play gave him that same sense of warm, assuaging comfort. His preoccupation progressed until the simple sight of her was enough to produce in him a glassy-eyed state almost somnambulistic. Isaiah's announcement — after he became conscious of Ephraim's infatuation — that the boy must go away to Cambridge, to Harvard College, provoked in Ephraim a dismal grief; but it was a grief for which he found no utterance. He left Bangor on the Boston packet Madawaska in June, to be tutored in Boston in preparation for his admission to Harvard's classic halls.

When his father wrote that Tim Hager was dead and that he had married Jenny, Ephraim hated Isaiah for days; and for a longer while his passion for Jenny devoured him like a flame.

III

Ephraim by the time he entered Harvard was as big as he would ever be; a slender young man not much taller than his father. Mrs. Wetzel had often told him that he had been a sickly young one, and a trouble to raise. His mother, she said, was puny; and the same adjective might have been applied to him. His color was never good. He was subject to heavy colds, which were slow to cure themselves. His cheeks were pale, although even in winter he had a mask of freckles laid like a veil across his nose; and his eyes were a watery blue, his hair a lifeless, stringy brown.

If he had stayed in Bangor, the cheerful contempt of his fellows must eventually have crushed out of him any trace of self-confidence; but at college among strangers he could begin afresh. When he realized this, he gained courage and began to seek ways in which he might distinguish himself. He presently discovered — and demonstrated — that he could drink incredible quantities of liquor without apparent effects. This gave him standing in some undergraduate circles. Also, as is so often the case with men who are otherwise physically insignificant, he displayed, after his new-found friends had introduced him to Boston brothels, a precocious prowess which added to his fame; and his exploits were the boast and the envy of his intimates.

Thus, in one way and another, he achieved an unpleasant distinction among his college mates; and he enjoyed it. He forgot Jenny, or if he thought of her at all, it was fleetingly, while he lay in the embrace of other arms; and when Isaiah suggested that he might better use his vacation periods for travel than in coming back to Bangor, Ephraim offered no objection. Except for that one brief occasion when he saw Mr. Hardy's portrait of his father's wife, he did not go home at all.

IV

Ephraim was saved from complete ruin in these years by the influence of John Evered. With three of his fellows he went into Boston one evening, and they dined at the Bell in Hand. Afterward, they all went out into the street to seek new diversions. Within three blocks, two of the group had accepted feminine companionship. Bill Pease and Ephraim proceeded arm in arm till a girl spoke to them, and Ephraim produced a coin and spun it.

Bill won, so Ephraim was alone when John Evered touched his arm. Ephraim looked up at the other man in surprise. 'Hullo,' he said. 'Who are you?'

'My name's Evered,' the stranger explained. 'John Evered. I've seen you at college, and I was in the Bell in Hand just now. I want to talk to you.'

'Who, me?' Ephraim protested. His youthful habit of reacting to anything like an accusation with this ejaculation had persisted; but now he remembered to be sophisticated. 'Good evening, Mr. Evered,' he said with punctilious dignity. 'What can I do for you?'

Evered hesitated. He was a head taller than Ephraim, with broad shoulders and strong hands. 'Come back to Cambridge with me,' he said, and he added: 'You're making a damned fool of yourself, Poster. I've seen you in classes. You haven't noticed me, but I've seen you. You've got brains, if you want to use them. This sort of thing is foolishness.'

Ephraim laughed. 'You talk like a parson,' he said loftily. 'Perhaps you are. Now suppose you take the next turning, and I'll go my own way. I've business with a friend.'

Evered shook his head. 'No, I'm taking you back to Cambridge,' he said.

'Who, me?'

'I'm taking you,' Evered told him calmly, 'if I have to knock you down and haul you home in a cart.'

Ephraim, to his own surprise, was pleased by this threat. 'Why?' he demanded. 'What do you want?'

'I want to talk some sense into you.'

The smaller man shook his head. 'Really, I'm much too drunk to talk sense.'

'You'll be sober by the time we get to Cambridge,' Evered promised him. 'We'll walk.'

'Who, me? Walk?' Ephraim laughed again. 'Not me, my friend!'

But Evered insisted, and he laid a great hand on Ephraim's arm. 'You'll come if I have to carry you,' he said.

Ephraim had never any stomach for physical violence, so they walked to Cambridge; and when they came to Ephraim's room, Evered stayed with him, talking insistently about the folly of dissipation. Evered managed to be wise without being righteous. He said nothing at all about morality, but he said a great deal about health, not only physical but mental; and he spoke of capacities and their use and abuse, and of the responsibilities they entailed. Something about Ephraim had attracted him, months before, when in the course of their college work their paths crossed; but had not found any way to make Ephraim's acquaintance till tonight his own distaste for what he saw gave him courage. There was strength in him which somehow imposed itself upon the other, arousing in Ephraim dreams and ideals long forgotten. They talked till dawn.

After that first encounter they were friends, and they presently arranged to room together for the rest of Evered's college career. When on his visit to Bangor, Ephraim saw the portrait of Jenny which Mr. Hardy had painted, he came back and told John Evered about her.

'I've known her ever since I was six years old,' he said. 'Her father was a drunken giant who worked for my father in the store. Her mother was no good, ran away with one of the British officers who came to Bangor in 1814. She and I used to play together. When we grew up, I realized of course that she was pretty; but my God, John, she's lovely now!'

'How old is your father?'

'Sixty-five or so. She's about my age, a little older.' Ephraim added: 'She's had her likeness painted, by a man named Hardy. The picture's beautiful, but it scared me. It's no more beautiful than she is, but there's something about it — I don't know what it is, maybe the eyes - that makes her look like . . .' He hesitated. 'I started to say like a damned whore, but it's worse than that. She looks like one of the women that run houses.'

Evered smiled. 'I shouldn't think your father would like such a picture.'

'Oh, I guess he doesn't see what I see in it. He thinks the picture's wonderful — and so does everyone else.' He added seriously: 'I went to see Mr. Hardy. He's quite a man. I wanted to find out whether he knew what he'd done. I told him the picture seemed to me to be like her, but I said there was something about it I couldn't quite understand. Know what he said?' John shook his head and Ephraim went on: 'He told me that a painter tries to put on canvas what he sees, but that each person who looks at the picture afterward may see in it something different. He said: "The painter and his subject make the picture together. I sometimes think there's a mystical communion between them, with all barriers removed. In the same way the spectator and the painting collaborate, the spectator putting some of himself into what he sees."'

John laughed. 'That was rough on you, if you had seen in it what you say!'

Ephraim nodded thoughtfully. 'Maybe that's true. I'm apt to see a wanton in every woman I meet.' He laughed grimly. 'If I try, I usually find one, too!'

'You have dangerous capacities, Eph,' John Evered told him soberly. 'You can drink a lot without showing it. Unless you watch yourself, that will betray you in the end. And you can seduce almost any woman who seems to you worth the trouble. That's even more dangerous.'

'By God, I think you're right!' the other agreed; and he said, almost wistfully: 'I wish one drink made me drunk, and I wish there was only one woman in the world whom I could win — providing I could find her. I need women, John. I always have.'

v

When Ephraim was ready to leave Cambridge, Isaiah wrote suggesting that he travel and see something of the world; but Ephraim, remembering Jenny, decided to go home. He had no chance to discuss this with Evered, who had left college a few weeks before. The other might have advised Eph to adopt his father's suggestion, might have made the young man realize the danger in a return to Bangor. But Ephraim persuaded himself that he went home to take his place by Isaiah's side, to begin to learn the management of his father's large affairs. Without answering Isaiah's letter, he boarded the Albion, Bangor packet. In spite of his fearful anticipations of the journey — terror of the water still obsessed him — the prospect of seeing Jenny awoke a strong excitement like hunger in his veins.

2

THE Albion packet with Ephraim aboard caught a fair southeaster to help her up the Bay; but at dusk the breeze failed and at full dark the packet anchored in Fort Point Cove. A dozen brigs and schooners were waiting there to make up to Bangor to load lumber, or already loaded they were praying for a good slant to beat down the Bay; and Ephraim was astonished at their number. On his single visit home he had seen that Bangor had grown, but now to find so many craft waiting to move up the river was visual evidence that the lumber trade had tremendously increased.

He stayed late on deck that night, hearing an occasional shout of laughter from the near-by vessels, or the creak of oars as some visiting captain returned to his own craft; and he was early awake and on deck. The southerly came to life again with the dawn, and they filled away with the flood tide just beginning to run.

The breeze, except for the eccentricities caused by high lands on either side, helped them all the way. On this tide and wind they met no vessels outward bound; but they saw craft at anchor in every sheltered cove, loaded deep with sawed lumber and shingles, waiting to go out with the tide if the wind would let them. Off Bucksport a dozen vessels, large and small, were sheering to their cables in the currents that eddied across the anchorage ground abreast of the turn; and a few miles above, the Albion's master took his speaking trumpet and let loose a cascade of profanity fit to blister the paint on the sides of a ship anchored fair in the narrow channel, while they crept closely by.

The Albion's master knew every quirk of the tides and every foot of the channel; and Ephraim, standing in the bow, watched with a fearful interest his bold manoeuvring, shivering with apprehension every time they passed near exposed ledges. The river was well sprinkled with slabs and bark and edgings, refuse from the mills above; and once or twice they broke through solid rafts of this drift, floating in a loose assembly acres in extent. Sawdust filled the water everywhere, changing its color. Some of it was on the surface, while the rest, saturated and waterlogged, was carried in solution as it slowly settled toward the bottom. In the narrow shoal channel above Hampden the water was full of it, constantly churned up by passing bottoms and by the racing tides. The master, alert to his marks, brought them past the Three Fingers; and a tide-walker thumped the packet's bottom so that Ephraim's heart pounded in his throat, and then they began to see the vessels massed in the river off Bangor town.

Ephraim stared ahead with a quickening astonishment. There seemed to be hundreds of craft of every description, from stately ships to simple sloops, at anchor or tied up side by side along the wharves. Everywhere along the shores he saw the bright lumber of new buildings under construction. A group of other passengers had joined him in the packet's bow; and he saw something feverish in every countenance, as though they looked upon the promised land. He had heard enthusiastic reports, even in Cambridge, removed as collegiate circles are apt to be from contact with the world, of the coming boom in Bangor and in timber lands; but now his eyes — and the greedy countenances of the men about him — for the first time made those rumors real.

II

When the packet docked, runners from the Exchange Coffee House and from the other hotels fought over the baggage of every passenger. Ephraim left his gear aboard, to be sent for presently, and walked up Poplar Street on his way home. On Tim Hager's house, enlarged now by the addition of a two-story wing behind, he saw Lena Tempest's sign, 'Laundering for Young Gentlemen,' and a pretty girl with fair hair waved to him in a friendly fashion from the doorway. The street was dry and dusty, and it was thronged with people, while through the crowds moved vehicles of a dozen kinds. Carts loaded with shingles or sawed lumber or with produce of the near-by farms picked their laborious way; and when he reached Main Street coaches, barouches, curricles and carriages of every description passed to and fro.

When he came to his father's house on Main Street, Isaiah and Jenny were at dinner; and Isaiah in his skull cap — he wore the brown wig only when he went abroad, still clung to the skull cap at home — rose in surprise from his chair.

'Came home, did ye?' His tone was not cordial. 'I thought you'd be on your way to Europe or somewhere by now.'

'Who, me?' Ephraim laughingly protested. 'No, I decided to come home and go to work.' He shook his father's hand and went to greet Jenny, sitting at the other end of the table under Mr. Hardy's portrait. When he took her hand, she drew him gently toward her, and with a quick pleasure he leaned down to kiss her cheek; but it was her lips, a little moist, which were lifted to meet his.

Isaiah grunted at the other end of the table, and Jenny said: 'I was sure you'd come home, Ephraim. Isaiah told me you meant to travel for a while, but I didn't think you would.'

'He wanted me to travel,' Ephraim agreed. 'He wrote and told me to.' Jenny looked at Isaiah with expressionless eyes, then smiled a little. 'But I decided to come home without any arguing.'

'Didn't you want him here, Isaiah?' she asked curiously. Isaiah grunted again, and she rang a little glass hand bell with a tinkling note, and a girl with black hair and a tipped nose came in. Jenny said: 'Put a place for young Mr. Poster, Ruth. Here, by me. Ephraim, sit down. I think you've grown heavier since you were last home.'

Isaiah said morosely from the end of the table: 'You'll find little to keep you in Bangor, Eph.' Isaiah was nearing seventy, a spry little old man with a crackle in his voice. 'After your fine ways in Cambridge, you'll be hard to please in this town.'

'Bangor's grown, even this year,' Ephraim commented. 'The packet was crowded with men coming to buy timber lands. The talk aboard was of nothing else.'

'Aye,' Isaiah agreed, pride for the moment overcoming his jealous ill temper at his son's return. 'Five or six thousand people here already and more coming. The hotels are full, and houses going up everywhere. I'm about ready to start selling off my building lots.'

Jenny watched them while they talked, and Ephraim commented: 'The talk was more of trading in timber lands than in building lots.'

Isaiah snorted. 'Land, my foot! It's bonds they mean. They're not caring about the land. It's the price, whether it goes up or down, that they're interested in. Price is all they know! The Coffee House is packed all day with them, dickering for bonds.'

'What's a bond?' Ephraim asked curiously.

Isaiah cackled: 'You'd best go back to Cambridge and learn something. Say a man owns a township. He makes a bond to give a deed for it at a certain price a year from now, or five years, or ten. He sells that bond and pockets the money, and the man that bought the bond sells it to someone else, and that keeps on till there's no sense to it.'

'Who gets the land in the end?'

'Whoever has the bond when the time comes to make a deed — if he wants a deed and can pay for it. But half the time a man will make a bond for a deed without owning the land at all, and maybe sell the bond and skip with the money.' Isaiah added hotly: 'They're crazy, the lot of them, and getting crazier every day!'

Jenny said in her low tones: 'I'll take you with me this afternoon, Ephraim, to show you what a town we have.' She explained to Isaiah: 'Mrs. Ingraham looked for a shipment of millinery and fancy goods on the packet. I want to see them as soon as they're unpacked.'

Isaiah protested crabbedly: 'Eph has something better to do than help a woman buy a bonnet!'

But Jenny insisted: 'I shall need his advice. He can tell me what Boston ladies prefer to wear.' She added, smiling at Eph: 'He's young enough to pay attention to such things, I know.'

III

They drove into town that afternoon in the curricle, with the calash bonnet raised to keep off the sun, and Pat Tierney on the box. As the demand for labor in the growing town increased, Bangor was receiving an increasing number of Irish immigrants. They were, despite a certain garrulous pugnacity, a cheerful and a hard-working lot; and men who wanted a job of work done were glad to have these new citizens. But there were others in the town who worked as little as possible, yet who now protested that the newcomers were taking jobs away from honest folk; and along the waterfront and wherever work was in progress daily brawls occurred.

Pat Tierney was somewhere in his later forties, and he had come from Ireland two years before. An old injury to his foot gave him a severe limp and incapacitated him for manual labor; but he was a master hand with horses, and he kept Isaiah's stable, his animals and his carriages in the best of order. He was not married, living in a boarding house on the east side of the Stream; and he was devoted to Isaiah — and to Jenny too.

She thought today that Ephraim might wish to make some purchase for himself. 'And I want you to see that Bangor is not too far behind Boston,' she explained. So at the Phoenix Block she sent him to inspect Mr. Sargent's broadcloths and cassimeres, and his assortment of fashionable vestings and stocks, while she herself was busy at Mrs. Ingraham's. There presently he had to approve the bonnet she had chosen. Then they went together to Nourse and Smith's bookstore, where she bought the latest reviews and magazines; and she stopped to consult John Stevens about a broken silver spoon which he was to repair. She bought ten pounds of sea-fowl feathers at Aaron Lowell's establishment on Main Street; and at Jesse Wentworth's Ephraim persuaded her to purchase a French print. After they had stopped at Wright's to order some West India goods, she said softly:

'And now I must show you something of the town.'

So she told Pat Tierney which way to turn, and they drove out Broadway to see the fine new houses built or building there; General Veazie's towering mansion, and Mr. Sylvester's, and next door to it the house he had built for his sister, Mrs. Guild. They passed one house, of brick with two chimneys, and Ephraim said:

'That's like ours.'

'Mr. Hamm built them both,' she assented, and she directed Pat to drive down Essex Street past other houses Mr. Hamm had put up. Then they crossed the Stream and went out Hammond Street past the Seminary and drove a little way into the country beyond, before turning back into the town.

She told him many things about the houses which they passed and about the people who lived in them; and he listened as he could. Sitting close beside her under the bonnet of the curricle, with the broad back of Pat Tierney and his square shoulders obscuring everything ahead, they were in a sort of solitude which Ephraim relished. She wore, he thought, some delicate scent; yet he could not be sure of this. It might be merely the distilled essence of her beauty; that beauty which was compounded of the dark masses of her hair, and the curve of her lips always a little moist at the corners like the lips of a greedy child, and the way when she smiled those faint indentations on her cheekbones made her seem on the point of tears till Ephraim wished to take her in his arms and comfort her. They were so near one another that her shoulder touched his, and when the carriage swayed around a corner, she leaned toward him and the pressure was increased. He thought of that moment when on his arrival he had seen that she expected him to kiss her, and how when he bent to do so her lips rather than her cheek met his; and he wished he were still on the packet, still to come to her and receive that warming welcome.

It was not until they neared home that he remembered with a faint sense of foreboding that she was his father's wife.

IV

During the weeks that followed, Ephraim tried to fit himself into the pattern of his father's business. Isaiah had since his marriage put the management of his store into other hands, devoting all his energies to the ramifying details of his larger affairs. He had a sort of office in his home, at one side of the front door, with an iron vault built into the wall where his books and ledgers and his letter books were kept; and he spent there most of his waking hours, writing many letters in his precise hand that began to be a little tremulous, meticulously copying each one into a letter book afterward. Ephraim, the morning after his homecoming, went to him there to propose that the older man begin his training in business affairs.

Isaiah did not welcome the suggestion. 'There's nought for you to do,' he said harshly. 'I've managed by myself this long. I don't need any young fool to help me now!'

Ephraim grinned appealingly. 'I'm not such a damned fool, sir,' he said. 'You can teach me things.'

'Nobody taught me anything,' Isaiah assured him. 'I taught myself, and you can do the same.'

'Who, me?' Ephraim echoed. 'Well, I'll try. I may have to ask you to tell me about some of the books and what they mean; but I'll study them all, learn all I can.'

'You'll do no such of a thing!' Isaiah told him flatly. 'I don't aim to have any young jackanapes sticking his nose into my business.'

Ephraim said reasonably: 'But after all, sir, you're getting old. I'll have to learn about your affairs if I'm to handle them properly when you die.'

'Who said you were a-going to handle them, when I die or ever?'

Ephraim grinned appeasingly. 'Why, I took that for granted. If I'm not, then certainly I don't want to bother you — or waste my time.'

'Waste your time? What's your time worth to anybody? What did you ever do but waste it?'

Ephraim hesitated. 'Possibly you're right.' He thought suddenly of John Evered, and said honestly: 'It's true I did waste a lot of time, my first two years at college. But I did some good work these last two years. And it was your doing that I went to college, sir. I'd have come home more often, too, if you had wanted me. I don't think you wanted me to come even now. Why not? What is it I've done that has offended you?'

'You think yourself too good for this town!'

Ephraim protested: 'I don't think I'm good enough.'

Isaiah burst out in a sudden storm of anger. 'I know your kind, nothing in your heads but dandling and kissing! I tell you right now, young fellow me lad, I'll have none of that in my house. You try it and I'll bring you up with your toes a-digging! You hear me?'

He paused, as though expecting a reply; but before Ephraim could speak, someone knocked on the closed door. Isaiah barked a summons and Jenny came in, came to his side.

'There, Isaiah,' she said in her low tones. 'It's bad for you to get all excited! Shame on you, Ephraim, to torment him!' Isaiah fumed, and she laid her hand upon his shoulder, standing at his side and a little behind him, looking at Ephraim. 'Your father's a fine man,' she said. 'And he has much business on his mind. You must never disturb him so.'

Her tones were calm and grave, yet she was smiling faintly,

some message in her eyes; and Ephraim thought he understood. She meant that Isaiah was old and crotchety and must be humored. 'Who, me?' Ephraim protested. 'I didn't go to bother him.'

Isaiah grunted and mumbled, yet under her hand he was calmer too. 'I'll give you a chance,' he said. 'Can you copy a letter and make no mistakes?'

'I think so.'

'I'll put you at it. We'll soon see! But mind you, boy!' Isaiah's voice rose in new wrath. 'One mistake's the last. Mind what I say!'

v

Thereafter, Ephraim assumed the task of copying Isaiah's correspondence. Since there was not space in the office for them both, he worked in his own room, painstakingly comparing each copy with the original after his task was done. This was laborious, and Jenny came to him there, on the fourth day, to offer her help.

'I don't want you to make any mistakes,' she explained, 'because it would upset Isaiah so. He talks angrily, but really he loves you, Ephraim.' When she spoke his name, he thought it had a beauty he had never heard in it before. 'So I'll help you. I can read the letters to you while you watch the copy. Between us we can make sure there are no mistakes in any one.'

He welcomed her help, and her company; and thereafter they were thus together and alone for at least some time every day. Isaiah, busy in his office downstairs, never knew this. As he grew older, his world was constricting, his horizons narrowing. He regularly complained, for instance, that his spectacles were always so dirty that nobody could see through them; and although he heard Jenny well enough, as though there were a vibration in her tones to which his ears were attuned, he was apt to insist that everyone else talked so low that a man couldn't hear what they said.

So he was unconscious of any sounds in the big house, of anything that went on outside the office where he sat all day behind a closed door.

Also, another result of Isaiah's increasing deafness was that he slept easily and long. In the short evenings he was apt to drop off in his chair, till Jenny roused him to say that it was time he went to bed. He always grumbled at doing so, maintaining the fiction that he went upstairs only to please her; but he never delayed long. Once abed, he seldom waked till Jenny roused him in the morning; so sometimes after he was asleep she would come down-

stairs again, and she and Ephraim might read over the letters he
had copied that day; or they might talk awhile, Jenny asking many
questions about the young man's travels, or about his life in Cambridge and his friends there.

Once he told her about John Evered. 'I'd have gone to the Devil
properly, if it hadn't been for him,' he said. 'I was chasing after
women, and drinking a lot, and on the downhill road.'

She asked about John, and he answered her; and she asked too
about those sins of his. He took a certain pride in confessing his
iniquities, as men will always boast — under a mask of penitence
— of their ill deeds, even while they conceal their good ones.

'I'm glad you don't drink now,' she said. 'We're trying to drive
rum out of Bangor. There's a county temperance society; but I
want them to change the name. Temperance is just the first step
toward excess. It's only in abstinence that men can find any safety,
Ephraim.' Her tone was one of friendly counsel and warning.
'Men who boast that they take only one glass may believe they tell
the truth, but they are deceived. John Evered did well to draw
you back in time. Moderate drinking is the seed of drunkenness.'

He grinned in that attractive way which always marked him.
'I never was a moderate drinker,' he said. 'I could drink twice as
much as would make most men drunk, and never know it.'

She asked curiously: 'Did you really like that kind of woman,
Ephraim? I know some base men do, but — did you?'

'Who, me?' He hesitated, coloring a little; then he said auda-
ciously: 'Why, Jenny, all women are like that, only some of them
never find it out. I liked them, yes, till John Evered talked some
sense into me.'

She said slowly: 'I used to see such women with men near our
house when I was little; but the men were always drunk, and
usually the women too.' She relaxed in her chair, her head far
back, her eyes upturned. 'I used to watch them and wonder
about them,' she said in low tones, and suddenly, without moving
her head, her eyes looked down over her cheekbones and met his.
He was jarred as though by a physical blow, and for a long moment their eyes held.

Then quietly she rose. 'Good night, Ephraim,' she said, and
went from the room.

VI

One evening when he had been a month or so at home, Jenny
and Ephraim were reading together the letters he had copied, and

Isaiah was asleep upstairs when they became conscious of a distant sound, hoarse and turbulent and curiously frightening. Jenny heard it first, looking up from the letter she was reading aloud while he followed his copy; and then he too heard that sound. It seemed to be compounded of many voices, swelling at times into a single roar. Ephraim after a moment rose and went to the door and stepped outside; and she followed him, standing on the stoop, and then, as he moved across to the corner of the house to hear the better, coming by his side.

The uproar came from the direction of the Point, half a mile away. The night was dark, the general blackness broken only by a lighted window here and there; but over the intervening roofs and trees they could see a faint glare as though from some illumination in that direction; and they heard an occasional far shout, or a splintering crash, and now and then a woman's distant scream; and they were conscious of nearer sounds, the sounds of voices and of running feet as others drawn by this disturbance hastened toward the scene.

Jenny touched Ephraim's arm. 'Come,' she said. 'We'll go down there.'

'What is it?' he asked uneasily.

'I don't know,' she said. 'But once when I was a girl there was a fight down there in the night, a crowd of men fighting; and next morning I saw a man all beaten and bloody, still lying in the alders. Come.'

He brought a shawl which she drew about her head and they set out, Jenny with her hand on his arm hurrying him along Main Street to the head of Poplar. By that time they were particles in a stream of people rushing to see what was going on. At first the stream moved freely, but when beyond the Coffee House the crowd grew more and more dense, their advance was retarded. By the time they came to Barker's store the street was packed; but once they had passed the corner by the store, they moved more easily through the milling tumult all around them.

The focus of the disturbance was on Carr's Wharf. Torches gave some flickering light, and nearer, at the landward end of the wharf, a bonfire illuminated faces all around them in the crowd. Ephraim said in Jenny's ear: 'Hold your shawl close so no one will know you.' She did so. As other newcomers joined the spectators, earlier arrivals were explaining what was going on; so they had only to listen, had no need to ask questions. A young man near them shouted cheerfully to some inquirer:

'Why, one of Ma Hogan's girls stole his money off a sailor off the Merry Andrew brig, and they're taking the house to pieces looking for it! They've got crows and axes and sledges and whatever! There won't be much left of that house if they keep on.'

Jenny, pressing Ephraim's arm, urged him nearer; and they made their way to the front ranks of the watching crowd. While others went on down to the wharf to take a hand in the work of destruction there, they stopped, half-concealed by people still in front of them, yet able to see what went on.

The woman called Ma Hogan had come to Bangor the year before and put up this house of rough sawed lumber which the mob now sought to demolish. It was a two-story structure, but the roof pitched only one way so that it was more like a shed than a house. On the wharf level the ground floor was divided into two rooms. One was a kitchen and the other combined the functions of bar, dining room and dance floor. A fiddle could usually be heard squeaking there till the small hours, and the hoarse laughter of men and the shrill emptiness of feminine mirth came all night long through the rough walls. At the farther end, outside the house, a steep stair led to the second floor which was cut up into small bedrooms under the low, slanting roof.

Ma Hogan ruled her customers — sailors from the vessels at anchor here or lumbermen just in from the river or the woods — with a fist as heavy as a man's; and for allies she had two husky individuals who did not scruple to use clubs when clubs were needed. Unruly men were apt to find themselves quickly and decisively spilled out of a door on the water side of the wharf and they usually emerged from the river with their belligerent ideas effectually cooled. If now and then it proved that one of those subjected to this treatment could not swim, no one was likely to discover the fact; and unless he could save himself, the river might carry him quietly to sea. 'Them as can't stand a ducking,' Ma Hogan used to say, with a fine philosophy, 'had best behave theirselves the way a gentleman should.' Her establishment had prospered, and so had she, and not a few of her sayings were already a part of the folklore of the town. She tolerated no complaints. 'Them as orders my vittles eats them,' she frequently declared, 'and them as drinks my rum likes it, and them as takes a fancy to one of my girls treats her like a lady or I'll know the reason why.' She coupled with arrogance a sublime generosity and was as ready to give as to sell the wares her establishment provided. Her business creed was simple. 'I'll give any man anything he wants, or I'll lend any man money — once!' She allowed no fighting in her place, nor any offensive language. 'Not counting swearing and such,' she always explained, 'because a man can call a girl a God damned little bitch and mean nothing but that she's the sweetheart he's always been looking for. But bad language I won't stand, and I hate nast'ness.' It was her boast that a man could spend a winter's pay in her place in twenty-four hours — and get his money's worth — if he were man enough.

But Ma Hogan and her establishment faced ruin and destruction now. Men with axes and crowbars swarmed upon the roof, while others smashed the windows and doors. Whenever a window was ripped out, or a door torn away, or shingles came showering from the roof, the crowd on the wharf dragged the débris to the bonfire to feed the flames there; and over the whole scene hung the continuous and appalling sound of the voice of the mob, compounded of many voices, some laughing, some drunken, some murderous with anger that grew by what it fed on.

A man near Ephraim and Jenny, just arrived, demanded to know where Ma Hogan's girls were; and someone answered him:

'They dragged 'em out and swung 'em over the side of the wharf with ropes, gave 'em a good ducking and turned 'em loose. Ma Hogan's still in there, though. You can hear her yell.'

The inquirer, a little ratlike man, screamed excitedly: 'God damn the Irish, anyway!' He darted forward to lose himself in the mob upon the wharf. Someone freed a rafter of the doomed house and pried it up and over, and it carried a section of the roof itself, which fell into the crowd, exposing in the upper room which it had covered the posts of a bed. Men dragged the mass of boards and shingles to the fire, and someone threw the bed down to the crowd on the wharf and it too went to feed the flames. In that sudden glare Ma Hogan herself appeared in the roofless upper room, belaboring the men who were there trying to pry loose another rafter; and one of them turned and struck her in the face so that she fell. She rose unsteadily and came to stand facing the crowd, and in the light of the flames Ephraim saw her face a mass of blood, her dress torn, her hair disordered and hanging in straggling strands about her shoulders. She stood embattled there above the mob, and at sight of her a cry rose, like the cry of maddened animals.

The woman shook her fists in the air and screamed inarticulately. Her scream brought a sudden shuddering hush, and everyone heard her word.

'You God damned rats and cowards! You going to stand there and see them tear my house down? Ain't there a God damned one of you with guts and blood in him enough to help me?'

Someone laughed, and she whirled toward the sound. 'Laugh, you stinking bastard! Come up here where I can see you and I'll give you something to laugh at!' And then in a fierce appeal: 'Ain't there one single solitary Irishman in the lot of you? No, by God, or he wouldn't stand there and let men treat women so, that never did them any harm!'

There was a shamed stirring in the crowd, but at first no one moved. Behind the woman, the wreckers wrenched loose another great segment of the roof and slid it over the plate, and it dropped to the wharf and was caught by many hands and carried toward the fire; and Ma Hogan turned to attack again, and single-handed, the men at their work of destruction. She picked up a broken rafter and swung it over her head, but a sailor grappled her, and a man shouted:

'Heave the old bag overside! That'll cool her off!'

Four of them caught her up by arms and legs, and they swung her, one, two, three. They threw her off the roof and she fell fifteen or twenty feet with a rousing splash into the waters of the river. Her screams were choked as she struck the water, and a great shout of laughter rose. Jenny's fingers tightened hard on Ephraim's arm, and someone threw a rope to the woman in the water and dragged her to the wharfside at its landward end, and she climbed up on the wharf again and stood, the centre of a hooting ring of men; and a man near Jenny and Ephraim in the crowd growled:

'Faith, I'll stand no more of that! A hundred men against one woman! Who's for it?'

A dozen others started forward with him, not together, but singly here and there; and Ephraim thought all of them were Irishmen. They plunged past the fire toward Ma Hogan's side, and instantly the tumult on the wharf, which though destructive had before been good-natured enough, became a battle, where fists and then clubs flew with a fine impartiality.

Ephraim felt Jenny beside him stir as though with a half-caught breath; and he looked down at her and saw her standing in a sort of ecstasy, her eyes shining. He tried to drag her away but she whispered passionately: 'No, no, no!' not looking at him, watching the conflict. The mob consisted mostly of sailors from the vessels here to load with lumber; but when now half their number of Irish laborers charged forward to take Ma Hogan's part, from the crowd of spectators raftsmen and woodsmen and rivermen surged forward on their heels. The smaller group of rescuers, thus attacked from behind and facing a superior enemy in front, were overwhelmed in a moiling confusion of blows given and taken.

Men began to go over the edge of the wharf, sometimes knocked backward by a blow, sometimes driven by the impetus of a kick, sometimes heaved bodily by three or four men at once.

One man broke through and tried to escape, running toward where Jenny and Ephraim stood, and another threw a club and it caught the fugitive in the shoulder with a crack of breaking bones, and he went down and tried to rise. He was on his hands and knees when the foremost of his pursuers jumped on him, feet first, knocking him flat. Then two or three men jumped up and down on him and kicked at him till he ceased to struggle and lay supine and senseless on the ground, not twenty feet from where Jenny and Ephraim stood.

The crowd swirled between, shutting off their view, and some-one shouted: 'God damn the Irish! Let's kill every one in town!' The crowd of spectators began to stir and mill like angry bees, and Ephraim gripped Jenny's arm.

'Come away!' he urged in a sudden alarm. 'This is getting worse all the time. Come home!'

She brushed him aside with a sort of violence — she was as tall as he and quite as strong — gliding forward to where the senseless man lay on the ground. Ephraim followed her, and as the crowd surged around them, he saw that she was on her knees, peering at the unconscious Irishman in a dark absorption. The man was breathing hardly at all. He lay limp and helpless as a rag, and his face was a mask of blood, his lips cut and torn, his eyes swollen, his nose crushed. The fire gave light enough to see, and Ephraim was sick at the sight. He caught Jenny's arm again, drew her to her feet, swung her roughly toward him.

'Come home!' he cried.

For answer, she flung her arm around his neck, dragged his head down, pressed burning, breathless lips to his, holding him for a moment helpless in that searing embrace. Then before he could move she turned and ran. He stood a moment paralyzed, till she was lost in the crowd.

He searched for her awhile in vain, at last turned homeward. There was in him amazement and yet terror too. Ephraim knew enough of light and laughing passion; but Jenny, in that moment when she held him fast, had been like a devouring flame. He half-dreaded seeing her again.

On Main Street, near their own door, he overtook her. She was walking unsteadily, her feet dragging as though from some great weariness. He caught her arm to support her.

'Are you hurt?' he asked.

She shook her head. 'No, I'm all right.'

They came into the silent house. She started at once up the stairs, holding to the rail, pulling herself upward step by step. In spite of himself, he spoke her name in a husky whisper:

'Jenny!'

But she did not turn. In the hall above he heard a moment later the quiet closing of her door.

3

EPHRAIM was not a complex young man, and after his brief experience of outright dissipation he had acquired from John Evered some firmness and strength. In that moment when Jenny kissed him, he forgot everything but her; but lying long awake that night, he remembered that she was his father's wife; and before he slept he decided that life here in the same house with her and his father must become intolerable. If he stayed, there could be but one end; and the thought, even while it inflamed him, filled him with shamed horror too. He made up his mind to go away.

He came down in the morning determined upon this; but when Isaiah and Jenny appeared together at the breakfast table, she was as she had always been, serene and beautiful, wearing a purity of countenance which made him doubt his own memory of what had happened the night before. She bade him good morning as she always did, and Isaiah barked at him, and they sat down. It seemed to Ephraim incredible that she should be this morning so composed. He did not in the least understand what had happened the night before; assumed — as wiser men might have assumed — that Jenny had for a moment yielded to an overwhelming passion for him which she could not control. If she had now said openly to her husband: 'Isaiah, Ephraim and I love each other. You must let us be happy together,' it would not have surprised him so much as the fact that last night had left upon her no mark at all.

The meal began. Ruth came in to serve them, and Ephraim, his eyes on his plate, heard Jenny ask her quietly:

'What is it, Ruth? You've been crying.'

'It's Pat Tierney, ma'am,' Ruth unsteadily explained. 'There was trouble in town last night, and crowds of no-goods hunting down all the Irish, and they caught poor Pat and broke his leg for him.'

Isaiah cried sharply: 'Eh? What's that? Speak up, girl! What are you talking about?'

Ruth began to cry openly, dabbing at her eyes. She told the story, and Jenny, pretending ignorance of the events of the night before, asked as many questions as Isaiah did. Ruth said that after the destruction of Ma Hogan's house was completed, the mob's lust for violence remained unsatisfied; and men had run to and fro through the town, searching out the boarding houses where most of the Irish lodged. Pat had been decently at home and in bed when they routed him out and threw him — as those four men had thrown Ma Hogan off the wharf — out of his own window.

'So he sent word, Mis' Poster,' she explained, 'that his leg's broke and he can't come if you was to want him today.' She added fearfully: 'And there's some hurt worse than him, they say, and crowds chasing the Irish on the streets everywhere, and fighting and all.'

Isaiah's wrath rose with her every word, till Jenny dismissed her at last. 'Poor Pat!' she said, when the girl was gone. 'I must go see him, see that he's well taken care of.' She said chidingly to Isaiah: 'That's what can happen in a town full of grogshops; drunkenness and fighting, and men hurt and killed. You have to expect it.'

Isaiah told her in shrill scorn: 'Don't talk like a fool! With the town full of sailors and lumbermen all summer long, you've got to have places like that. If you didn't, they'd go somewhere else to spend their money. It's good for business.' He admitted that every lazy idler in town hated the Irish. 'But they're good workers, and we need 'em.' He arrived at last at a conclusion which satisfied him. As a town, Bangor had nothing like a police force. 'But we've got to have one,' he declared. 'That means a city gov'ment. It's high time, too. Town meeting's so big now, with every man jack wanting to talk, that you can't get any business done. A city gov'ment's what we need, and I aim to see we get one.'

II

Ephraim took no part in this discussion, watching Jenny, wondering at her ability to dissemble so that no one could have suspected her of any first-hand knowledge of the events the night before. But when breakfast was done and before they left the table, he spoke of his decision to leave home, coming to the point abruptly and without preamble.

'There's a matter I want to talk to you about, sir,' he told his father in grim resolution. 'I've been thinking I might go back to Boston and find work there.'

Isaiah stared at him. 'Want to leave, do you?' he echoed scornfully; and then in a sharp ire: 'Might have known you would, soon's you got so you was some use to me! What do you want to leave for?'

Ephraim had not expected to be asked for reasons. His father had resented his homecoming; he supposed the older man would welcome his departure now. 'Why, I've been thinking it over,' he said lamely.

Isaiah grunted. 'Go if you're a mind to,' he said gruffly; but there was something almost like pain in his tones, and Jenny spoke quietly.

'I think your father needs you here, Ephraim,' she said.

Her voice, the way she spoke his name, was enough to weaken Ephraim's resolve. 'Who, me?' he protested. Then to Isaiah: 'I didn't know I was any use to you, sir.'

'Well, you might be some day,' Isaiah told him grudgingly, 'if you keep on. I'll say this for you, you don't make mistakes. But if you don't like, here, why, then go to Boston and be damned to you! I won't stay you.' His voice rose in shrill exasperation. 'Only, if you go, don't look to come meeching back again. If you go this time, I'm through with you.'

Ephraim repeated: 'Why, I didn't know you wanted me. I won't go right away, anyway. If I'm any help to you, of course I'll stay.'

Isaiah said harshly: 'Suit yourself. I got along without you once, and if I have to, I can again.'

He stumped away to his office. Ephraim would have followed him, but Jenny spoke his name and he hesitated. She looked at him with frank candor.

'I think,' she told him honestly, 'that it's because of me you want to go away.' He did not speak and she said: 'I was — excited last night, Ephraim. I ask you to forget it — for your father's sake. He needs you. He has done so much for me, I wouldn't want to send you away from him.' She smiled appealingly. 'He leans on you more and more, Ephraim,' she said. 'On you and me. We must help him, keep him happy, every way we can.'

So Ephraim stayed on.

III

The disorders in the town continued for a day or two, till the group of sober and resolute men whom Captain Bryant organized to patrol the streets restored peace again. Isaiah did not forget his belief that Bangor needed a city government; but in the profitable business season, as is the way of democracies, leading men of the town were too occupied with their own affairs to give much time to a discussion of the public good, so for the moment nothing was done.

When Isaiah saw that Ephraim had abandoned his plan to go away, he began to entrust his son with more and more of his affairs. Also, there was another change in his attitude toward the younger man. At first after Ephraim's homecoming Isaiah had watched him and Jenny with a jealous suspicion; but now, as though regretting his former distrust and wishing to make up for it, if Jenny proposed to go somewhere and asked for his company, he was apt to send Ephraim as his substitute.

'Your mother wants to see Mr. Moulthrop's paintings and waxworks,' he might say. 'I'm too busy for such nonsense. What anyone wants to see wax dummies of a lot of pirates and murderers for, I don't know, but she read a piece in the *Journal* about them and she's bound to go, so you keep her company.'

Ephraim was glad to do so, glad to be with Jenny. She studied the figures of the two pirates, Gibbs and Mourley, complete to the red streak left by the ropes around their necks, with a strange, still interest; and a scene representing the Salem murder held her for long moments intent. They went together to other entertainments of a lighter character. They heard James Kendall of the Boston Band play the bugle in the First Baptist Meeting House, heard Monsieur Canderbeck perform on harp and violin. Jenny professed to enjoy these performances, and discussed them in appreciative terms with her friends among the audience afterward. Ephraim alone would have found them wearisome; but with Jenny at his side they seemed to him delightful.

He and she were constantly together. Isaiah, perhaps because he was secretly sensitive about his increasing deafness, stayed more and more at home. Pat Tierney's broken leg robbed them for a while of the use of the carriages; and Isaiah used this as an excuse to give up going to church, declaring that it was too far to walk. Except for an occasional visit to the Coffee House or to the bank, he seldom ventured out. Jenny on the other hand, since Mrs. Hollis relieved her of all household cares, often went abroad. If it was for a round of calls upon the wives of the leading citizens of the town, she went alone; but for the Lyceum lectures, for the meetings of the temperance society in which she was intensely interested, and even sometimes for her shopping expeditions, she asked Ephraim's company.

He went with her, too, on more personal errands. Ephraim found that there were a surprising number of families to whom she played good angel, and who — whether she came laden with bounty or not — welcomed her affectionately. She commanded not only the gratitude and affection of these needy folk whom she befriended, but the friendship and respect of everyone they met. Jenny had earned as a child a reputation for devotion to her father; she was known now as a fine and loyal wife to Isaiah. There were enough Bangor folk who remembered Isaiah's sharp dealings in the past and who knew his greedy penuriousness to feel that a young woman as beautiful as Jenny deserved credit and honor for being so good a wife to a disagreeable old man.

They went together several times to see Pat Tierney, propped in a chair with his broken leg in a heavy splint; and the Irishman was apt to say: 'Sure, ma'am, and it's worth breaking a leg to see your face here! Like as not when this one is well I'll break the other so you'll come again.'

Jenny laughed and told him he had a charming tongue. 'Are all Irishmen so polite?' she protested.

'There's no politeness in it, ma'am,' he assured her. 'But as for politeness, if it's politeness to know a pretty face when you see one, there never was an Irishman who wouldn't do that, ma'am!'

They found him one day in a high humor, and he told them the reason. 'Sure and I'm on my way to make my fortune,' he declared, 'and me flat on my back too!' And he explained: 'Them that came to see me talked so much about land and bonds and all that I had to buy a small bond of my own with my savings, so now I can talk business as big and bold and free as any of them.'

Jenny's point of view on the increasing speculative fever was borrowed from Isaiah, who was torn between his certainty that the speculators were fools and the cupidity which was aroused in him by the tales of enormous profits being made on every hand. So she chided Pat now for risking what he had worked so hard to earn and save; but Pat said with a cheerful impudence:

'Risk, is it? Why, if I lose the whole, there's always yourself to put me back to work and maybe pay me a dollar more, so in no time I can save as much again!'

She laughed and warned him not to be too sure; and on the way home she told Ephraim that speculation was no better than gambling, and that it would be the ruin of them all.

Ephraim disagreed. Since the gamblers dealt in bonds rather than in the land itself, even the poorest man in town could have a hand in the speculation, and he pointed this out to her. 'That means there are a hundred buyers for every seller,' he argued. 'If I were Isaiah, I'd be buying and selling all the time.'

She warned him never to tell his father that. 'He's just beginning to have some confidence in you,' she reminded him. 'I don't want him to doubt you again.'

Her advice was sound. The old man came home that same day, after one of his increasingly rare trips down town, in a sputtering anger.

'The whole world's crazy!' he declared at the supper table. 'That black man that cleans out spittoons down at the Coffee House quit his job today. He'd heard so much talk about bonds that he was bound to have one, and Bert Chick wrote one out and gave it to him free and clear. It don't even pretend to be a bond for a conveyance. Bert just wrote on it: "I do solemnly swear, promise, obligate, testify, certify and with due mendacity assert that this paper is a good and valid bond, and know all men by these presents that I avow this to be my sworn bond and utterance for three years after date with interest at cent per cent so help me Hannah!" So the negro thinks he's too rich to clean out spittoons any more, and he quit his job.'

'I declare,' Jenny protested, 'it's a shame to abuse the poor colored men!' She was beginning even then to take her stand in the occasional discussions of slavery. When at the time of Maine's elevation to statehood the Southern Congressmen had insisted that Missouri also come in as a state to maintain the balance between the friends of slavery and its enemies, the question had become a live issue in Bangor. Of the few colored men in town, Abraham Hanson was the best known. He had come to Bangor seven or eight years before and opened a barber shop near the Court House, where his good humor and his infectious chuckle won him as many patrons as did his skill with razor and scissors. Someone had written for him a rhyming advertisement which, under the heading, 'To be shaved or not to be shaved,' appeared in the *Journal*. He was so conspicuous a figure in the life of the town that Mr. Hardy painted his portrait, splendid in a high white stock. When sympathy for the Greeks was at its height, he announced that he would put in one day's work for their benefit; and on the day set he refused all pay, insisting that he was working that day for the Greeks. This was so manifestly absurd that men began to say, in good-humored contempt, that a man was 'as simple as Abe Hanson.' Jenny referred to him now. 'They're so easy to fool! Even barber Hanson is a simpleton! I should think Mr. Chick would be ashamed to make sport of the poor man.'

But Isaiah snorted scornfully. 'Serves him right for a dunce!' he exclaimed; and he added: 'Not but what that bond's worth as much as most of them. Man came in from Boston on the packet today, and Jim Frye made him a bond on fourteen acres, more or less, of land out at the end of Washington Street, that piece that Walter McGaw owns, at three hundred dollars an acre, and sold the bond to him for two hundred and fifty dollars. Jim took him out and showed him the land, too. But he don't own it any more than I do.'

Jenny asked: 'Won't he have to make the bond good?'

'With what?' Isaiah chuckled. 'Jim never saw two hundred and fifty dollars in his life before. He's gone off to Boston to blow in the money!' His voice was shrill in a sudden rage. 'Why, ten per cent of the bonds they're buying and selling ain't worth the paper they're written on.'

Ephraim listened to these and other tales without comment, but when he could, he went to the Exchange, standing like a swimmer by the margin of a cold pool who tests the water with his foot, trying to muster courage to dive in.

IV

There was another fever in his blood. As the days and weeks passed and they were more and more together, thoughts of Jenny entered into every part of him. Isaiah's deafness this year grew rapidly worse, so that he heard less and less of what was said around him; and his eyes were dimming too. He bought new spectacles and discarded them and bought others and discarded them in turn, insisting that no one knew how to make a proper pair of specs nowadays. He refused to admit that his own faculties were failing, and insisted that he could hear as well as ever and see as well, and that the trouble was people mumbled their words, and kept the shades down so that rooms were dark. He thought modern candles were of inferior quality, no longer giving as much light as they had used to; and on sunny summer days he might insist that there was a great forest fire somewhere up in the woods, that smoke dimmed the sun. Ephraim discovered one day that at a little distance his father did not recognize him; and he found that if they were all together, he and Isaiah and Jenny, at table or in the sitting room, he and Jenny could talk in low tones without being overheard at all.

The effect was to lend a certain clandestine note to the simplest passage between him and Jenny. If in Isaiah's presence, but in such tones that he could not hear, she and Ephraim discussed her intention to go to Wright's store that afternoon to inspect a new consignment of West India goods, or the fact that Ephraim had heard at John Bright's news room reports that the Selectmen would prohibit driving carriages faster than a walk within half a mile of Kenduskeag Bridge, their harmless conversation became a secret and a furtive thing. Sometimes Isaiah caught the murmur of their voices without hearing their words, and demanded to know what they were saying; but this only lent zest to the game. It was always Jenny who answered him; but she might tell him the truth or not, and if she invented a conversation for his benefit, the effect was to intensify in Ephraim his feeling that there lay between them a secret understanding.

Either with Isaiah or without him they were much together. They checked Ephraim's work for mistakes, and as Isaiah entrusted more and more of his affairs to his son they studied ledgers and documents of all kinds, and gravely discussed questions of business policy and the ramifications of Isaiah's many interests. At such times they might sit side by side, books or papers spread before them; and Ephraim felt the faint tingling warmth of her nearness, and his nostrils caught that delicate fragrance which, artificial or not, always hung around her. He might find himself staring at her hands as they unfolded some document and opened it, watching the exquisite articulation of the bones in wrist and fingers, the perfection of her every movement. When the sun struck across her cheek, he could see the faint down there, so delicate that except by reflected light it was invisible. Except on occasions when she took particular pains with her toilet, she did not curl her hair, but drew it back smoothly to the rich knot on the back of her head. The lobes of her ears below the heavy strands were as softly tinted as the petal of a rose, and the curving lines of her ear delighted him when while she was intent on the papers spread before them he turned to look at her. They were at such moments so near together that he could sometimes see the pulse beat in her throat, below the slant of her jawbone, or in the nook where her collar bones met. He was intensely conscious of the perfection of the bony structure of her body; the roundness of her skull, the swelling of her forehead above the outer corners of her eyes, the bones in her forearm turning over one another when she turned her hand, her rib case elastic and flexible accommodating itself to her quiet inhalations. There was no part of her of which, even without thought, he was not aware; and every part of her seemed to him to combine to produce a celestial harmony, at once so entrancing that its very sweetness was cloying, and at the same time so faint that only by an aching tension could it be heard at all. When he was apart from her, it was almost a relief to escape for a while from her spell. With her, he was like a man in a dark room, whose eyes and ears and all his senses strain to discover the presence near him of some other occupant. He was by her still, magnetic presence maddened as one is maddened by half-heard sounds, by the murmur of voices when the words spoken cannot be understood, by objects in such shadow that their outlines cannot be clearly seen, by fragrances which have a haunting familiarity yet which cannot be identified. His was no possessive passion, no longing to seize and command her. It was rather that all of him wished to surrender to her. He was like a man in a river in spate, holding fast for safety to some great rock while with all his heart and soul he wishes to let go his hold, to be swept away, to drown.

The rock to which helplessly he clung was the fact that she was his father's wife! Again and again, alone in his room through white nights, he vowed to himself that he would go away, quickly, before harm came; but he never again proposed to his father that he go, nor to Jenny herself. His resolutions, made while he lay sleepless and tormented, vanished and were forgotten when he saw her at the breakfast table, her cheek fresh and her eye clear so that he thought of a freshly opened flower on which the dew still lay. When he was with her, to think of leaving her was intolerable. It was only when he was alone that he weakly swore to himself that he wished never to see her more.

v

In the early fall, almost casually, Ephraim found in another direction some surcease from the storms Jenny provoked in him. There were on the second floor of the big house several bedrooms. Isaiah and Jenny occupied those at the west end of the house, where the stair came up from the lower hall. Another, next to Jenny's, was immediately above the front door; and this, reserved for guests who never came, was seldom used. Ephraim's room was at the east end of the house and in the corner overlooking the street. Beside it there was another which was the particular domain of Mrs. Hollis, and where she kept her household accounts, stored the linen and bedding, and did her daily stint of mending. There or in the kitchen she was during the day usually to be found, although at night she went to her own home.

But there was a third floor in which two smaller bedrooms had been finished off. The cook, a certain Mrs. McGaw whom Mrs. Hollis had engaged, lived at home, coming early every morning, staying till her kitchen was all in order in the evening; but a month before Ephraim's homecoming, Ruth Green had been installed in one of those upper rooms.

This was at Jenny's suggestion. Ruth was Mrs. Hollis' granddaughter. Her father was dead, and her mother and two or three younger children lived with Mrs. Hollis. Mrs. Hollis first brought Ruth to the house when an attack of rheumatism crippled her.

'I can't hardly hobble,' she told Jenny. 'So I can't wait on table, but I'll show Ruth how to do.'

Jenny from the first liked the girl, and when she found that Ruth was clever with a needle, and could run a hot iron over the most delicate fabrics without scorching them, she entrusted the care of her garments entirely to the girl. Eventually she suggested that Ruth come to live in the house. 'Mr. Poster's getting old,' she told Mrs. Hollis. 'And he might be taken bad sometime in the night, and me alone with him. I'd like to have Ruth here, in case I need her to go fetch the doctor. Knowing there's someone else in the house will make me feel easier.' So it was settled.

Mrs. Hollis had been glad to see Ephraim again. She had sometimes when he was a youngster taken his part against boys who bullied him — as most boys did. She thought when he returned that he was a mite peaked-looking, and her maternal heart went out to him. When one day he showed signs of a slight cold, she kept him abed and fussed over him and poured into him some nauseous draught which she was sure would cure him, and rubbed his hollow chest with a mixture of tallow, camphor and turpentine in which she had the greatest faith.

Ruth liked Ephraim too. She was a pretty girl, with a quietly appealing beauty. He came to think that she was in many ways like Jenny. They were about the same size, the same coloring, with the same slenderness. Ruth had never seen any town but Bangor, and Ephraim with his background of Cambridge and Harvard College was in her eyes an impressive figure. He had even visited New York, not once but three times; and once he had gone as far as Philadelphia and Washington. The fact that he worked at his copying in his room meant that when she came to make his bed and put the room in order he was often there; and when he began to notice her and talk to her, she found courage to ask him questions.

He was pleased and a little flattered by her interest, and she made her tasks in his room last as long as possible while she listened to the tales he told. The day he first kissed her, she turned pale and trembled in his arms, and said he mustn't and pushed him away; and he laughed at her and told her she was the sweetest thing he had seen between Bangor and Washington and that she deserved to be kissed, and she told him he was terrible. Thereafter when on other occasions he repeated the offense, she was at first frightened and uneasy; but the day came when she clung to him in a soft happiness, her lips tremulous under his.

That sudden half-surrender startled him, and he warily decided to let the girl alone. This was as much a fear of consequences as any scruple; but he told himself she was just a friendly child, still in her teens, and that he liked her — and liked Mrs. Hollis — too well to make them both unhappy. He took care thereafter not to be in his room when she came to do her morning tasks, giving her no chance to be alone with him; and her eyes when she served him at table or when they met and passed elsewhere in the house were faintly bewildered and reproachful at this change in him. Yet Ephraim clung to his resolutions, trying to put her out of his mind.

VI

It was, indirectly, Jenny who broke down his vows at last. He had gone with her to a meeting of the temperance society at the Hammond Street church, where Judge Appleton talked on the dangers of moderate drinking, and the Reverend Mr. Pomroy discussed conditions in Bangor, declaring that forty-odd stores sold liquor openly, and that at night, especially along the waterfront, there were so many drunken men that no woman alone could walk safely there. Afterward Jenny and Ephraim strolled slowly home together, and with her hand lightly on his arm she spoke of what Mr. Pomroy had said, and of her childhood in the house down toward the Point, and how as the town grew roisterers had more and more often been about.

'And my father drank too much, for many years,' she said, 'till when he got up in the morning his hand shook terribly; and although I know he loved me, sometimes he would beat me awfully.' Ephraim felt a stormy rage at Tim Hager, and she explained: 'He beat me the night he died. I got away from him and he was chasing me and just dropped down dead. I didn't know it. I was running away from him, running to your father. I'd always called your father Uncle Isaiah. He married me so he could take care of me, you know. He married me before he knew — before anyone knew — that my father was dead.' She added simply: 'So I know what rum can do, even to a good man. Some day we'll stop men selling it here in Bangor, if I have anything to do with it.'

'I used to drink a lot in college,' he reminded her; and — finding an almost sensuous satisfaction in the confession — he added: 'And run after women. If John Evered hadn't straightened me out, I'd have gone straight to the Devil.'

She nodded. 'I know. You told me before.' Then she said in her low tones, her hand pressing his arm: 'It's hard to think of you as — doing these things. You're such a fine young man.'

'Who, me?'

She smiled at this familiar ejaculation. 'Yes, you.' She added after a moment: 'You know, Ephraim, I'm very fond of you. I think taking care of Isaiah together has brought us close. I think we will always be fond of each other.'

His throat was full, and he coughed to clear it. 'You're mighty good to him.'

'He seems so much older, these last few months.'

He tried to laugh. 'Don't worry. He's tough as a tamarack root! He'll live another twenty years.'

She did not speak for a moment. Then she asked intently: 'Do you think so, Ephraim?'

Her tone startled him. He said hurriedly: 'Why — yes, I do. There's nothing wrong with him.'

They walked on in silence for a while through the dark streets, the thought that Isaiah might die in both their minds; and her hand rested on his arm. When they approached the house, its windows were dark.

'Isaiah has gone to bed,' she said quietly.

The night was warm, with a blustery wind, the elms above them tossing; and she was so near him that her skirts brushed his legs as they walked along. He opened the door and they went in and she laid aside her hat of chip straw with a broad soft brim and a bright flower fastened to the side of the round, flat crown. She turned to him smilingly, and he caught that faint, exciting fragrance which she always seemed to wear.

'I've often thought, Ephraim, since you came home,' she said, looking up at him, 'that if you hadn't been away at Harvard College that night my father beat me I might have married you instead of Isaiah!'

'Who, me?' he gasped, staring at her, feeling his cheeks burning, trembling like a tree under the first stroke of the axe.

She waited for a moment, but when he said nothing more, and did nothing, still smiling, she spoke softly. 'Good night.' She turned and lifted her skirts and went away from him up the stairs.

VII

Ephraim stayed where he was for a long time before he lighted his night candle and snuffed the others and followed her. When he passed her door, his eyes turned toward its blank, white surface and it was as though he looked through its panels and saw her, slim and white and beautiful as she stepped out of the circle of her skirts and petticoats on the floor about her feet. In his own room he closed the door and set the candle down, watching its flame in a sort of fascination while he took off his coat and waistcoat and hung them on a chair.

He stood for a while in the middle of the room, carefully, like one who keeps precarious balance on a narrow foothold and as though with any movement he might fall. Jenny's words had let loose a storm in him, a storm almost too violent to endure. There are some women whose eyes are, when they wish, nakedly eloquent, carrying a message of surrender. Ephraim had once said to John Evered: 'I see a wanton in every pretty woman I meet, and usually I find it, too.' There could be no doubt what he had seen in Jenny's eyes tonight. He knew with an intoxicating certainty that if at the stair foot just now he had taken her in his arms, she would have been all surrender. If he had kissed her then, her door would not have been closed when he came up the stairs.

Yet — she was his father's wife. That too he knew; and one certainly battled with the other in him, rendingly. His brow was wet. He licked his lips, grinned weakly.

'You damned fool!' he muttered, in hoarse tones.

He looked toward the bed, moving that way, intending to finish undressing and try to sleep. He always slept with two pillows under his head, and Ruth when she came to put his room in order in the morning always found them one atop the other. Thinking to please him, when at night she removed the spread and turned back the covers she now usually put his pillows as he liked them; but tonight they lay end to end, and he lifted the nearest to rearrange them.

When he did so, he saw a slip of paper that had been hidden under the pillow. He lifted it and carried it across to the candle on the dresser to read it. It was unsigned, but he knew Ruth must have written it. Six words:

'What makes you mad at me?'

He stared at the paper, slowly understanding. Since that day when for the first time she responded to his kiss, he had avoided being alone with her, and he had seen the hurt bewilderment in her eyes. He crumpled the bit of paper, held it in the candle flame, dropped it, watched it burn black and die. The big house was silent, but outside, branches thrashed in the wind.

Ruth's room was just above his own. The stairs to that third floor were opposite his door. He thought suddenly, and the thought was like a flame running through his veins, how much Ruth was like Jenny. Jenny! He heard her intoxicating words again: 'If you hadn't been away at Harvard College, I might have married you.' For a moment his suffused eyes were almost blind. The candle seemed to burn red. He sat down, and his throat was so congested that when he leaned over to remove his shoes, his breath stopped stranglingly.

After his shoes were off, he sat a moment longer. When he acted, it was not by decision but as though compelled against his will. He blew out his candle, crossed and softly raised the latch and opened the door. In the dark hall he paused a moment, closing the door behind him without a sound, then went silent-footed up the attic stair to Ruth's small room.

4

THERE was in Isaiah a strong frugality which revolted at such ostentatious display as formal entertaining. To Jenny herself he denied nothing, meeting her every wish, lavishing upon her all and more than she desired; but when she now and then proposed a dinner to which they might invite their friends, he shouted at such foolery.

'Why, that means a lot of cackling womenfolks, jabber, jabber, jabbering like so many hens!' he said. 'No, ma'am, not in my house!'

Jenny asked mildly: 'Do I jabber, jabber, jabber, Isaiah?'

' 'Course you don't. But there ain't many women as sensible as you, Jenny. I won't have it, I say.'

So for the most part Isaiah and Ephraim and Jenny were alone in the big house; but in the fall of this year, as with the approach of cold weather the season of active business neared its close, Isaiah spoke to Jenny one day, bidding her arrange a dinner to which he proposed to invite a group of his friends.

'I'll ask 'em myself,' he said. 'Don't know yet who all there'll be; but maybe ten or a dozen.'

'Their wives too?'

'No, no women. Only you, Jenny. I wouldn't feel right sitting at my own table unless you was at the other end of it with your picture over your head.' He added: 'Have some good candles in the stands on the mantel, Jenny, so your picture'll be lighted up. I want 'em to see what a handsome woman my wife is.'

Jenny smiled. 'I seem so to you, Isaiah; but others may not think so.'

'Then they'd be a pack of fools,' he told her stoutly. 'But there won't be any fools here that evening. Amos Patten will be here, for one.' Amos was by this time a leading citizen of the town, President of the newly organized Savings Bank, merchant, and a leader in town government. 'And Ben Wingate,' Isaiah added, 'and Captain Bryant, and General Veazie if he'll come, and Judge Williamson and some more of them. Sensible men, Jenny. It's time sensible men got together and made something of this town.'

'I'll feel strange and queer, the only lady at table.'

'I'd feel a sight stranger if you weren't there. No, Jenny, you do as I say.'

II

Jenny obediently made her plans; and she and Mrs. Hollis discussed for days the food that should be served, while Jenny consulted with Ephraim as to wines. There were when the company sat down sixteen guests at the extended table with Isaiah at one end and Jenny at the other. Mr. Hardy the painter sat beside her, and Captain Bryant who had organized the force which put down the riots was on her other hand, while General Veazie and Judge Williamson, whose history of Maine had been published the year before, flanked Isaiah. Ephraim was halfway down one side between Amos Patten and William Abbott. Mr. Abbott was now the First Selectman; and George Brown and Royal Clark, the other Selectmen, were side by side across from Ephraim; and there were others. Jenny and Mrs. Hollis had planned a surfeit of good victuals, with two saddles of venison and a tremendous partridge pie as the backbone of the meal. To help Ruth serve, Mrs. Hollis had enlisted three other girls as pretty as she.

When the glasses were filled, General Veazie rose in his place, harumphing for attention, his glass in his hand. He was a newcomer to Bangor from Old Town, but he was already a figure of importance in the local world of business. He had begun life as a sailor in the West India trade, with certain stowage rights so that he was able to make small private ventures. With the proceeds he set himself up as a manufacturer of cigars, opened a store in Topsham, and used his profits to buy shares in trading vessels. During the War of 1812 he achieved the rank of General in the militia. In 1826, attracted by the growing lumber business, he moved to Old Town and bought the Jackson Davis mills and privileges. Mills would always be his passion, and whenever he heard of one for sale he bought it, so that he would come at last to be by all odds the largest mill-owner in Maine. After six years in Old Town, as his interests widened, he had moved to Bangor, bought a house on Harlow Street, presently built a bigger house at the corner of York Street and Stetson Square, and as of right took a place among the leading citizens.

He was at this time in his middle forties. He had a huge, blocky head, and his jutting, clean-shaven jaw and his clamped lips testified to the driving force in him, while his eyes, the right narrowed and piercing, the left wide open and with a questioning and half-quizzical lift to the lid, showed the shrewd ability which marked his career. When he had the attention of them all now, he lifted his glass to Jenny. 'Gentlemen,' he said, 'I beg you to rise and toast with me our hostess, the loveliest flower in Maine!'

They were on their feet with a shout, their glasses high; and Jenny smiled and color flooded her cheeks. Ephraim caught her eyes, and hers for a moment held his before passing to one man and another till every man thought she had smiled for him alone. Mr. Hardy beside her watched her thoughtfully; and once he looked up at the portrait above her head and back at her again. He had seen her glance meet Ephraim's, and thereafter he studied the young man for a while, looking from him to Jenny.

General Veazie at Isaiah's right began to talk on his favorite subject. 'Land's all right, and pine's all right,' he said loudly. 'But the mills will make the money. Since I bought out Jack Davis I've built two or three mills, and I'm putting up a couple more next year.'

Isaiah suggested: 'You and Wadleigh?'

General Veazie made a careless gesture. 'Why, we've pulled together some; but Wadleigh's got a bee in his bonnet. He figures to branch out for himself any time, I judge. I'll get along with him as long as I can, but we'll come to a bust-up soon. Trouble with Wadleigh, he's always wanting to go to court!'

Everyone laughed, for the General's own reputation as a hard fighter and a confirmed litigant was already established, and young Rufus Dwinel said in a dry tone: 'You're as hungry for a lawsuit as a bear for honey, yourself, General. The lawyers will take your hide, some day.'

The General's great laugh boomed again. 'You're a fine one to talk, my gentle sucking dove!' Dwinel, not yet thirty years old and already a successful man of business, had a reputation for a temper as violent as his business judgment was shrewd. He, with Isaiah as a silent partner, had bought the franchise of the Penobscot Boom Corporation soon after it was granted, and they secured a new charter for a boom at Pea Cove, but Dwinel presently bought Isaiah's interest and soon after sold out at a substantial profit to General Veazie. His irascible disposition was well known; so at the General's word now there were smiles but no open mirth; and Jenny, quick to prevent the threatened explosion, spoke the length of the table to Judge Williamson, referring to his history.

'I have read it every word,' she said. 'Certainly every Maine man must do so, too.'

The Judge smiled with pleasure. 'I'd be well pleased to think even every man in Bangor would read it — if each one of them would buy the copy he read!' he declared.

George Thatcher said he had bought not one copy but two. 'I presented one to my relative, Mr. Thoreau of Concord,' he explained, and he added smilingly: 'I doubt Mr. Thoreau has read it, but his son Henry — he's no more than a boy, studying in the Academy there — wrote to thank me for sending it to them.'

Nat Harlow told Judge Williamson amiably: 'You'd have more subscribers if you had written only the second volume. No one in Bangor today has time to read about anything that happened before the price of timber land began to climb!'

That turned the talk to speculation, and Jenny said in an undertone to Mr. Hardy at her side: 'I declare, I hope Mr. Dwinel and General Veazie won't come to blows!' Then, to hold the artist in conversation, she asked: 'Did I ever tell you, or did Mr. Poster, that your likeness of me was not the first that was made? Mr. Audubon made one of me in Houlton.' She added: 'But I was angry when I saw it. I tore it into bits.'

'Why?' Mr. Hardy inquired.

'I did not like the person he drew.'

'Mr. Audubon is a great artist,' he commented. 'I saw his port-folio, his drawings of birds and animals, when he passed through here. He had the gift of putting down exactly and faithfully whatever he saw.'

She smiled. 'Perhaps. But I did not like what he saw in me. I forgave him — after I had destroyed his likeness — but if there is in me what he drew, then I want no one to know it.'

He bowed faintly. 'I am sure no one could see in you anything but beauty and virtue,' he assured her; but then, as though in dismissal, he turned and spoke to George Thatcher on his other side.

She watched him for a moment with still eyes, and then Captain Bryant spoke to her. He was a young man more bold than discreet, with something in him of the demagogue. It was only because of his energy in handling the mob after the riots around Ma Hogan's establishment that Isaiah had invited him here tonight. He would not stay long in Bangor. A few years later he organized a movement to demand that surplus public revenues be turned back to the people, and earned from his followers the sobriquet, 'Grand Eagle,' but when the project collapsed he went West where some marauding Comanches took his scalp.

Tonight he was a little intoxicated — by the wine he had drunk, by Jenny's beauty, and by that feeling of importance which his inclusion in this company gave him. He asked her now in a low tone: 'Has your husband told you why he brought us together?'

She countered, without directly replying: 'Has he told anyone?'

'It is, I think, an open secret,' he assured her. 'Since the riot at Carr's Wharf, and the violence which followed it, many of us think we must make a city here. It's to discuss that that we are met tonight.'

'Would a city be so different?'

He explained: 'To be sure. If we were a city, we could elect delegates who could work more readily than our crowded town meetings. Then we need to take measures for the public safety; a police force, and an organized fire brigade; and we need a body of ordinances, and someone to see that they are obeyed.' Isaiah had suggested that Captain Bryant himself would make a first-rate Chief of Police, and the idea pleased the young man.

She smiled. 'We need so many things,' she agreed. 'Sidewalks, and lamps to light the streets, and paved streets, too, to be rid of the mud in spring and after every rain, and the dust all summer. Do you know that I must keep my door and my windows closed even on the hottest days, to shut out the dust that every passing carriage raises?'

He nodded. Mr. Hardy saw the hot admiration for her in his eyes. 'And we need a market house,' he said, 'and public squares, and a proper cemetery. But most of all we need to lay down rules of conduct and to enforce them.'

'To shut up the rum shops!' she suggested.

'That may come in time,' he agreed, as judicially as possible, sipping his Madeira. 'But not at once. We must make a start with little laws, till good people have the habit of obeying them. To be law-abiding is a habit, you know; yet it is a habit that must be taught.' And he said: 'We will begin with laws easy to obey, laws to provide for weighing hay brought in to be sold, and for measuring cart loads of wood so that the buyer knows what he gets, and to punish those who mix wood and bark with their hay to make the load seem bigger.'

'The farmers won't like that.'

He chuckled, made a defiant gesture. 'Then let them keep their wood and hay at home!' And he added: 'Another thing, we must stop the ringing of bells for sport, let them be rung only to summon folk to church, or to give an alarm of fire.'

She said eagerly: 'I know a law you ought to have; to stop men from riding horses at a gallop through the streets, or from driving full tilt, scattering people everywhere. A sleigh last winter drove directly in front of Mrs. Wingate as she crossed Main Street on the way to church, and so close to her that it tore her broadcloth cape to tatters and her cloak and her silk under-cape, and then raced away without ever stopping at all.'

'Certainly,' he assented, 'we must put an end to that.' He laughed, said in an amusing imitation of Ben Wingate himself: 'We can't have ruffians tearing Mrs. Wingate's capes!'

She smiled with him. 'There were no bells on the sleigh,' she explained, 'so she had no warning.'

'Come!' he said, his voice rising. 'Soon you and I will have planned the whole body of our laws! We must have bells on sleighs, to be sure!'

'And we mustn't let men stop their teams and carts on walks and crossings to unload, so that ladies have to walk around them.'

'Certainly not!' They were both laughing together now. 'And we won't let small boys coast down hills and knock their elders off their feet.'

'I'm not so sure of that,' she protested. 'I used to like to go sliding when I was a child.'

'There!' he exclaimed. 'I will see to it, this winter, that you try it again. Suppose — now that we have organized our future city, we organize a sledding party for the first snow!'

They began at once to do so, deciding where to go, and who should be of the party. They were so animated and so merry together that they drew the attention at first of those nearest them and then of others; and one by one conversation ceased, everyone looking toward these two, until like a rising tide silence crept up the table to where Isaiah sat and he became conscious of it and without being able to hear what these two said, watched them with peering, angry eyes.

Captain Bryant, turned toward Jenny, seeing only her, was unconscious of this hush along the table; but Ephraim saw Jenny suddenly realize that only they two were talking. She ceased to smile and her countenance became composed, and Captain Bryant looked around in surprise and then in confusion and was silent too.

Ruth and the others were clearing the dessert dishes away. Isaiah spoke to Jenny.

'Now, Mrs. Poster, our dinner's done and we must get to business. Thank you for your company, my dear.'

His dry tone was so manifestly a rebuke that Jenny caught her lower lip between her teeth, and Ephraim saw her color change to red and then to white. She rose at once, spoke evenly.

'Then it appears that I must bid you good evening, gentlemen.'

They stood as she moved toward the door; but after she was gone Jeremiah Hardy watched for a while the door where she had disappeared, with grave, dispassionate eyes.

III

The matter which the men discussed that evening came to fruition presently. The Selectmen had been among the company at Isaiah's table, and in November they called a special town meeting to see if the town would apply to the next Legislature for a charter. The vote was carried. The only other business was to change the name of Poplar Street. It became Exchange Street, in recognition of the fact that the Exchange Coffee House was the centre of that lively speculation which had already so powerfully stimulated the growth of the town.

In mid-December the form of the proposed act of incorporation was settled at another meeting of the town; and in February the Legislature prepared to consider the measure which would make Bangor a city. Isaiah had from the first taken an active part in these procedures; and he and Jenny went to Augusta to watch the Legislature pass the act. The trip was a hard one for the old man, since the stage left Bangor at seven o'clock in the morning and was all day upon the road, arriving in Augusta long after the early winter dusk. Ephraim did not go with them on this trip, and while they were gone he was alone in the house, Mrs. Hollis pointing out that for Ruth to stay there while Isaiah and Jenny were away was bound to start talk.

'Not but what Ruth's a good girl,' she assured him, 'and I don't mean to say I wouldn't trust you, Ephraim. But you know the way people are.'

Her word left Ephraim with a sorry taste in his mouth. There had been more than one occasion when after an evening with Jenny he crept secretly up the attic stair. At first, once his ardor had overcome her doubts and fears, Ruth's rapturous and trusting happiness had made her seem to glow, so that he thought Jenny or Mrs. Hollis must notice the change in her; and he cautioned Ruth not to look at him at all when others could see her. It seemed to him everyone must mark the glad surrender in her eyes.

He never went to her without hating himself for doing so; and it was never Ruth he sought, but those things in her which were like Jenny. Coming to her in the darkness it was often true that he did not speak at all, since her voice might have shattered the illusion he cherished. Usually he slipped presently downstairs to his own room again; but if, as sometimes happened, he slept, she was careful to rouse him at first dawn so that he could leave her before anyone in the big house was astir.

He would not let himself think of what the outcome might be. Ruth herself asked of him nothing except present happiness; but he never completely overbore her rueful certainty that they did wrong. She had the stern conscience bred and disciplined by generations of God-fearing folk; and though she yielded to him because she loved him too much to deny him anything, yet sometimes she wept with shame and sorrow even in his arms. He had taught her to accept him silently — he said this was so none could hear their whispering voices in the silences of night — so she stifled her sobs, but her eyes filled and overflowed.

She was glad that while Isaiah and Jenny were away she would not be alone in the big house with him. 'It would be fun,' she told him, 'pretending we were already married and that this was our house and that we were living here. But I'm always afraid, Ephraim. I'm afraid all the time.' She and Mrs. Hollis had come to get his breakfast — Mrs. McGaw, the cook, was taking these

days of Isaiah's absence as vacation — and Ephraim was at the desk
in Isaiah's office where she had come with her dustcloth and mop.
'I hate having to be ashamed and afraid.'

'It won't always be so,' he told her. 'Father likes me better all
the time. Some day soon I can tell him. And Ruth, we needn't be
ashamed, loving each other.'

'Will we have a house of our own when we're married, Ephraim?'

'You'll have everything you want,' he assured her. He drew her
near and kissed her lips, as cool as a child's; and after she was gone
he thought he might be wise to marry her. Perhaps to do so would
ease and end the anguish which every moment with Jenny evoked
in him. If he married Ruth he could at least recapture the self-
respect of which his desperate hunger for his father's wife began to
rob him.

He arrived at a fixed decision that this thing should be done.
Isaiah would not object. Ephraim was sure that his father would
be glad to see him married and settled down. He decided to discuss
it with Isaiah as soon as the older man returned.

IV

The day Isaiah and Jenny were expected, the stage was late. It
was due at six o'clock in the evening; but deep snow delayed it,
and that afternoon and early evening a cold northeaster drifted
the roads, and locked an icy grip upon the land. The passengers
were all shivering when they belatedly arrived, and Isaiah was fairly
paralyzed with cold, his old blood, already chilled by encroaching
age, failing in the fight to keep him warm. He was so nearly
helpless that he could not stand, and Ephraim persuaded the stage
driver to go on to the house. There Ephraim brought out a chair
and they put Isaiah into it, and he and the stage driver carried the
old man indoors and up the stairs.

Mrs. Hollis had a great fire going in Jenny's bedroom there, and
they laid Isaiah on her bed, and Jenny and Mrs. Hollis undressed
him and wrapped him in blankets warmed before the fire. Mrs.
Hollis, saying there was a time for everything, brought a great
pitcher of hot lemonade well shot with rum; but even after drinking a glass of it he was still cold, and he petulantly insisted that
Jenny must sleep with him to keep him warm. In the end she did
so.

Ephraim, after he helped carry his father upstairs, had gone
down again, leaving to the womenfolks the task of tending the old
man. Alone there, he tried in some astonishment to measure the

effect upon himself of seeing Jenny now after her absence. A hot
wind blew through him, tearing every thought except of her away.
He waited, pacing up and down, unable to keep still, for her to
come downstairs again; but she did not, and Mrs. Hollis appeared
at last to say:

'Well, there, we've got the poor man warm at last; but I'm
afraid to think what will come of it. Cold as ice he was, all over.
You put your hand on him anywhere and it was like sticking it
into snow. I don't know how he'll be tomorrow.'

'Is — she with him?' Ephraim asked.

'Abed with him, to be sure, holding him like a baby in her arms,
keeping him warm. Eh, but it's a good thing for an old man to
have a fine young wife to warm him when he's cold.'

At her words, a sort of madness seized Ephraim. That Isaiah,
an emaciated, bald, toothless, half-deaf, half-blind old man should
lie in the circle of Jenny's young arms, his lips mumbling against
hers or mouthing her smooth shoulder, seemed to Ephraim a
hideous profanation. He forgot that Isaiah was his father, forgot
everything except a pounding hatred of the old man. Mrs. Hollis
babbled on, but he answered with muttered, meaningless words, till
she thought his confusion was concern for Isaiah, and comforted
him.

'There, don't you worry! She'll take care of him. You'll see,
he'll be all right again in the morning.'

She said she would stay the night in the spare bedroom, in case
Jenny needed her. It was long before he followed her upstairs.
When he passed Jenny's door, he heard Isaiah cough a little, heard
Jenny's murmuring voice as she comforted him.

v

Despite Mrs. Hollis' prophecy, Isaiah was not all right in the
morning. Nevertheless he insisted on getting up and dressing; and
Ephraim met them at the breakfast table. Jenny seemed tired,
and her eyes showed traces of a weary night. Ephraim suggested
that Isaiah should summon a doctor, but the old man snarled
scornfully at such nonsense; and after breakfast he took Ephraim
into the office to give an account of what had happened during his
absence. They were closeted there all morning, and Isaiah's temper
was at its worst. He found every possible fault with his son, shouting
at him again and again in a shrill and querulous fury. Yet there
was more petulance than strength now in the irascible old man;
and at intervals he was interrupted by uncontrollable fits of cough.

ing which left him gasping and breathless, pressing his hands to his chest as though to crush the deep pain there.

That afternoon he was flushed, and Mrs. Hollis decided he was feverish and told him so; but not till dusk did he surrender and, with Jenny and Mrs. Hollis helping him on either side, crawl feebly upstairs to bed.

Even then he would not have a doctor, but next morning he accepted the inevitable and told them to call Doctor Mason. John Mason was both doctor and apothecary, living with his father, the Reverend William Mason, on High Street. During the cholera scare a year or two before, when the disease appeared in Lower Canada, he had been sent to New York by the town to get all possible information as to how cholera could be prevented and treated. He came now and examined the old man and looked grave, and prescribed repeated doses of New England Pectoral Syrup and Cough Pills to relieve Isaiah's cough, and Hall and Holdens' Improved Compound Syrup of Sarsaparilla as a tonic to build up his strength. When Isaiah objected to the taste of that, the doctor shifted to Swaim's Panacea. He was regular in attendance, coming twice and thrice a day to dose the old man, keeping him swathed in heavy masses of blankets and quilts, with mustard plasters on his chest, and warming his bed at intervals all day.

But despite all his attention, Isaiah's fever raged. Even in delirium he would not let Jenny from his side; and Mrs. Hollis was by day as constant in attendance as Jenny herself. When solicitous inquirers came to the door, Mrs. Hollis or Ephraim met them, Jenny staying always, night and day, with the sick man; and Mrs. Hollis told these callers proudly how devoted Jenny was.

'I'm scared she'll get sick too,' she declared. 'She's with him all the time, and not getting enough sleep to amount to anything, nor eating enough to keep a bird alive.'

It was true that Jenny suffered under this ordeal — which she nevertheless insisted upon enduring. She grew thin, so that her cheekbones and the firm lines of her jaw became prominent; and there were dark shadows under her sunken eyes. Ephraim, watching her day by day, was devoured at once by his anxieties for her and by his angry resentment because Isaiah, even though unknowingly, subjected her to such torments.

Rarely he went into the room — Jenny's room, with her intimate possessions all about — where the sick man lay. Isaiah after the first days did not know him, knew no one at all. Yet his hand clung tight to Jenny's, and if she had to leave him for a moment he fretted restlessly, his old fingers, all bone and gray dry skin, clutch-

ing feverishly at nothing till she returned to put her hand in his
again. No one shaved him; and a thin, gray beard sprouted on his
cheeks and chin above the semicircle of chin whisker extending
from ear to ear which he always wore. His bald poll was covered
by a wool nightcap which Mrs. Hollis had knitted for him. His
eyes seldom opened, but his mouth worked constantly, the dry lips
opening and shutting, revealing the toothless gums. His nostrils,
as the flesh on his face shrank away, seemed to dilate and become
unnaturally large, with long white hairs in them. His head on the
pillow was hideous, a mask like the skull of a body already partially
decomposed, so that Ephraim was sick to look at it. This was no
longer his father. This was a corpse which refused to die, and he
hated it and wished to put it away underground where its corruption would be hidden, would no longer offend the eye of living
man. Standing beside the bed, looking down at the dreadful thing
which lay there, he whispered in his thoughts like a soundless
prayer:

'God damn your soul, why don't you die!'

Yet that thin frame still prisoned the life which had animated it
so long, refusing to let it go; while these others in the house, and
Jenny most of all, lost strength and vigor day by day, as though
Isaiah were replenishing the vital essences which ebbed out of him
by sucking, like a hideous vampire, the life out of them all.

VI

On the twenty-fifth of February, the day after the town voted
to accept the act which would make Bangor a city, Doctor Mason
came in the late afternoon. Ephraim took him upstairs and left
him with Jenny and the sick man. Mrs. Hollis was in her own
room, catching a scrap of sleep. When Doctor Mason came down
again, dusk had fallen. Ephraim met him in the hall and asked:

'Well, can you tell how he is?'

The other said soberly: 'I've tried all I know. There seems to be
no good in anything. Your father's a sick man, Mr. Poster. I
doubt he'll last the night.'

Ephraim felt a leaping surge of relief at the prospect that this
long ordeal might be nearly ended; but he shook his head in a suitable despair.

'Is there no more to be done?'

'Deacon Adams told me today the whole town's praying for him
night and morning. There will be gatherings in many homes
tonight for prayer. Man can do no more for him, but God can.'

When the Doctor was gone, Ephraim went slowly up the stairs. The door of Jenny's room, where the old man lay, was closed; but he opened it quietly. He stood there in the doorway and in the candlelight met Jenny's eyes. Isaiah mumbled meaningless words, and Ephraim said in a low tone:

'The Doctor thinks he'll die tonight.'

Jenny looked at the sick man; and then, still watching him, she rose, freeing her hand from his. His fingers clutched at nothing, and she rubbed the hand he had held with the other, as though it were unclean. She stared down at Isaiah, and Ephraim came nearer, watching her, seeing her sway weakly.

'He's — he looks awful!' she said huskily. She turned toward Ephraim, reaching out to him as though for help; but then before he could catch her she bent like a reed and bowed and fell forward on the floor at his feet.

He uttered a low cry, kneeling by her, picking her up in his arms. He stood up, lifting her easily, as strong as four men in this hour. The door into Isaiah's small room, adjoining, was open. During the old man's illness she had slept there, on Isaiah's bed, when she slept at all. Ephraim carried her through the door and laid her down along the bed.

But as he did so, and before he could release her and withdraw his arms which had supported her, her arms came around his neck and held him; and her eyes opened, looking up into his. She did not at once draw him to her, but she held him so that he could not escape. There was no candle burning in this room, but enough light came through the door so that he could see her eyes, dark shadows in her white face.

She held him near, in the circle of her arms. One of his arms was under her shoulders, one still under her knees as he bent over her. He did not try to free himself. He saw her lips move, and then she whispered tensely:

'I hate him, Ephraim. I hate the sight of him and the touch of him. He's so ugly and old!'

He could not speak, leaning above her awkwardly, his weight precariously balanced. He felt her body lift a little toward him, yearningly; and suddenly her arms around his neck tugged his head down. She pulled him off balance so that it was as though he fell, his legs no longer supporting his weight, his lips crushing hers like a blow. Her lips were dry and cracked and a little parted, and her teeth bruised his lips in that long kiss, and her arms were steel bands around his neck, half-strangling him. He got his feet under him again, pressed down with his hands on the bed in a smothered panic, unable to breathe, trying to escape her. Then her lips moved under his, and she whispered softly:

'If he dies, Ephraim, I can marry you.'

'Who, me?' he muttered, paralyzed and trembling.

She almost laughed. 'You always say that, you scared boy!'

He caught her fiercely close, all bonds for a moment loosed, straining her in his arms in a long embrace; and she held him as though she would never let him go. But then suddenly she pushed him away, murmuring: 'Quick! I hear Mrs. Hollis.'

Mrs. Hollis, in fact, was coming along the hall. Ephraim darted toward the door into Isaiah's room, was in time to meet her as she entered.

'Mrs. Poster fainted,' he said carefully. 'I carried her in, put her to bed.' And he added, looking toward the bed where his father lay: 'Doctor Mason thinks he'll die before morning.'

He was astonished at his own tones, cold and steady and calm. It seemed impossible that in this moment, when every nerve in his body was jangling like snapped wires, he could speak so quietly.

5

ISAIAH did not die that night. Ephraim and Mrs. Hollis stayed with him, Jenny for once surrendering to sleep; and in the small hours, Mrs. Hollis discovered that Isaiah was perspiring. The fever had broken.

She cried exultantly: 'So he'll get well, if he's careful, Ephraim. That shows you how much a doctor knows!' She went into the small adjoining room to wake Jenny and tell her the glad news; and Ephraim heard her say: 'Wake up, child. Listen! He's broke out in a sweat. I've seen enough old men sick the same way to know the signs. He's going to get better!'

Jenny, drugged with sleep, echoed stupidly: 'Get better? Isn't he going to die?'

'That he is not!' Mrs. Hollis assured her. 'He'll be as well as ever, and better, maybe, and he has you to thank for it, taking care of him every minute.'

Ephraim heard Jenny wail wretchedly: 'Oh, I wanted him to die! Why doesn't he die?'

Mrs. Hollis cried tenderly: 'Hush now, darling! You're so wore out you don't know what you're saying. You go back to sleep again. You've done your job, taking care of him. Now I'm going to take care of you.'

So Jenny was silenced, and Mrs. Hollis came back into the sick-room. She was right in her prognosis. Isaiah when he woke knew them. He was still helplessly weak; but during the days that followed he mended fast, and Mrs. Hollis plied him with rich broths, and strength flowed back into him. He was not yet able to go abroad at the first balloting for city officers on the tenth of March, but in the next election he cast his vote for Allen Gilman, who was elected Mayor. By the time the ice went out of the river on the eighth of April, he was — or seemed to be — as well as he had been for years.

II

But Jenny did not recover so rapidly as he. She lay for days listless and dull, having no interest in food nor even in life itself; and Mrs. Hollis cared for her, letting no one see her.

'The poor baby's just wore down to nothing,' she told Ephraim. 'She's nought but skin and bones, and she won't more than pick at her vittles. I did think maybe seeing him would help her, but she's that sick in her mind that she said she never wants to see him again! She'll get over that when she's herself again. She mostly sleeps, or lets on that she's asleep, the whole day long; and the dear lamb needs every minute of it. She'll be better by and by.'

Ephraim wondered whether Mrs. Hollis was right in thinking that Jenny's unwillingness to see Isaiah was only a symptom of her great weariness. Remembering that moment when he had carried her to her bed, that moment when her thin and nervous arms drew him down and her parched lips bruised his, he thought Jenny had come to hate Isaiah, as youth may hate age and its wasted, desiccated ugliness.

The story of Jenny's devoted attention during Isaiah's illness was well circulated; and when as her energy began to return she could see her friends again, even though for a further while she did not come downstairs, the good women of Bangor called to praise her for her courage and to commiserate with her weakness now.

Ephraim had not seen her during these weeks; but as Mrs. Hollis and presently Isaiah began to report that she was better all the time, he at once longed for and feared the moment when they would meet again. The memory of how she tugged him down and kissed him was like a great bell clanging in his ears. He thought again, as he had thought before, of going away, never to return; yet to do so was something of which he knew in his heart he would never be capable. There was no moment when he was not conscious of his danger. He was like a swimmer in the outer fringes of a whirlpool who might still if he were resolute and strong escape, yet who allows himself to drift in wide circles which — imperceptibly narrowing — bring him always nearer the vortex, till he is caught beyond salvation.

During this period when he saw her not at all, half hoping to involve himself in a trap which would at the same time offer him security from the thing he at once dreaded and desired, he went more and more often to Ruth at night. Mrs. Hollis was living in the spare room, and she was up at all hours and might have discovered him; and he told himself he wished she would, so that he would have to marry the girl. Also, if Ruth became pregnant, marriage would be demanded of him, and he thought of marriage to Ruth as a safe harbor to which he might flee. Yet he would not seek this refuge without compulsion.

His hours with Ruth brought him no satiety. It was easy in the darkness to pretend that she was Jenny; but the pretense inflamed him without bringing him content. During this interval when he did not see Jenny at all, she possessed him more completely than ever before.

III

Yet when Jenny at last began to come downstairs for a while in the afternoon, Ephraim avoided being alone with her. He attached himself to Isaiah, staying close by his father's side; and Isaiah came to rely upon him more and more. They drew together, and a bond began to form between them, as though Isaiah in his old age clung hard to that part of himself which after he was dead would still survive in the person of his son.

If Isaiah did not need him, and if he knew Jenny was to come downstairs, Ephraim left the house and went into the town that was a city now. With the opening of navigation, new floods of men were arriving, attracted by the tales that had gone abroad of fortunes to be made here; and the fever of gambling, which during the winter had somewhat abated, revived. At the same time, the city came to life in other ways. When the drives came down-river, the driving crews swarmed into the grogshops and gambling houses and brothels on Exchange and Washington and Hancock Streets to spend the money earned by their winter in the woods; and the nights were full of noisy turbulence. At the same time many of the newcomers from Boston drove up to Argyle or to Pea Cove to see the logs penned in the booms there, and to visit the mills and watch the saws rip the great logs into boards. When sawed lumber was to be brought down-river, it was rafted till it made a solid platform pegged and roped together; and sometimes the progress of these huge rafts from the mills to Bangor where vessels lay waiting to be loaded was made a picnic, with two or three dozen guests invited to ride down the river, and bountiful refreshments, solid and liquid too.

Isaiah, at General Veazie's urgency and on Ephraim's advice, sold his mill interests in April to the General, keeping the cash in hand against its reinvestment. The General invited them all to one of these rafting parties, and Jenny wished to go, saying that a day on the water might help restore her strength again. Isaiah refused to be bothered with such foolishness. He said Ephraim might take her; but Ephraim, who was always uneasy when he was on the water, and who still avoided her, declined.

Jenny, watching him quietly, repeated that she would like to make the trip. 'I know it would be good for me,' she said. 'But I can't very well go alone.'

'It's a waste of time,' Ephraim protested, almost harshly, and Isaiah nodded in vigorous approval.

'That's the way to talk!' he declared. 'Let a young man learn to use his time and he'll go far. If you waste a dollar, you can always get it back again if you're smart; but you waste a minute and it's gone.'

Jenny said no more, but she looked at Ephraim in a way that disturbed him, with a level and half-scornful appraisal in her eyes. He thought she guessed his fear of her, and blamed him for it too.

IV

In a desperate desire to break the spell which bound him, Ephraim sought new ways to please his father; and he succeeded, and in so doing, as we do love best those we serve well, began to love the old man. Isaiah's obvious affection for him made the more bitter that hunger for Jenny which he could not long forget. To escape from her, and from his thoughts of her, he spent more and more time at the Coffee House, and wherever traders gathered in the town.

The speculative fever this year was rising, carrying steadily upward on its flooding tide the prices of timber lands. Sam Smith's counting room at the corner of Harlow and Prospect Streets was one of the trading centres. Sam and his brother Ed were of a boldly speculative turn of mind, ready at any time for large risks in a promising venture. They had recently built at their own expense the Central Bridge across the Kenduskeag, to make a more convenient route from the west side of the stream, where most of the hotels were located, to their place of business; and they thought it a good investment. Sam Smith and Amos Davis of W. P. Lawson & Co. had planted the seeds of this speculative mushroom, when they discovered a way to make it possible for persons with even a little money to buy wild lands. They took options on several tracts in the forested regions to the north, paying one-fourth down and giving mortgages for the balance, and proceeded to sell these lands in odd lots to small buyers. Colonel John Black, whose big house in Ellsworth was famous all over eastern Maine and who was the agent for the Bingham heirs, had originated this policy of selling off land in small lots; but Smith and Amos Davis were the first to buy on a large scale simply for the purpose of selling. Their lands cost them as little as twelve cents an acre, seldom more than twenty-five; yet in this summer of 1833 the same lands were being bought and sold at prices as high as a dollar an acre, and in lots as small as fifty or a hundred acres and as large as whole townships.

One day in May, Ephraim met in the counting room a man named Holbrook. Sam Smith introduced them. Sam just then was intoxicated by his easy success, confident of the future.

'Here's a man Isaiah ought to talk to, Ephraim,' he said. 'Mr. Holbrook spent most of the winter up-river on a survey, travelled on snowshoes, went everywhere. I know Isaiah thinks land prices are too high a'ready, but I take notice he's not anxious to sell. I tell him he's right not to sell. This is the time to buy. Some of this land that's going begging at ninety cents and a dollar now will be worth ten dollars in ten years.'

Ephraim agreed. 'And father's as sure of the future of pine as any man, Sam,' he said. 'He's been buying Maine lands for a good many years — and selling damned little.'

'Take Mr. Holbrook out to see him,' Sam urged. 'He'll tell you some stories that will astonish you.'

He left Ephraim and Holbrook together. Holbrook was a big man, broad-shouldered and powerful, yet with a surprisingly soft face, and too much flesh upon his bones. Ephraim thought it surprising that the man should carry any excess weight after his winter in the woods; but the hour's talk they had together made him forget everything except the tales he heard. Holbrook had explored a region which the lumbermen had not yet reached, far up the West Branch of the Penobscot; and on good tributary streams capable of carrying the logs to the main river, he had located pine forests which he described in such terms that Ephraim's eyes shone. He spoke of townships with a stand of a hundred million feet of pine, some with more, some with a little less. He himself had bought one township for a group of Boston men, and he estimated it would cut eighty million feet.

'And it was about as poor a piece as I saw, at that,' he declared. 'But at fifty cents an acre it took all the money my backers had put up.'

Ephraim made a mental calculation. A township ran to about twenty-two thousand acres. Holbrook must have paid eleven thousand dollars. 'Is it bought and paid for?' he asked with a new respect.

Holbrook admitted that he had acquired only a bond for a deed, paying three thousand dollars cash; but the bond ran for a year and the price was agreed.

'Will your backers lumber it?' Ephraim asked.

Holbrook shook his head. 'They've just about got my report by now; but I'm looking for them to tell me to sell it — if I can get a fair price — and buy a better lot. No one knows the pine up there but me, so if I can sell this bond at a couple of thousand profit, I can buy another township I located, where the pine will run a hundred and twenty million easy.'

v

When he and Holbrook parted, Ephraim's imagination was on fire. He had watched the prices of timber land pyramid until prices began to seem more real than the land itself. The land in which they dealt was a hundred miles away. The money was here. He went home planning how he might interest Isaiah in this transaction; and he opened the subject cautiously, reporting some of the tales he had heard. Without naming Holbrook, he repeated some of the man's reports, hoping to arouse his father's interest; but Isaiah laughed in dry scorn.

'I've made a study of timber lands for twenty years,' he declared 'And of surveys too. It takes a good man to size up the pine on a township, to see if it's concussy or not, and whether it's worth buying. Mr. Gillies could do it. I'd take his word any time. But the lot that spends their days drinking rum down at the Coffee House and bragging about the pine they've seen, half of them don't know a cat spruce from a hackmatack. Any time a man tries to sell me land, he's got to show me the land, or else let a man I know look at it for me.'

Ephraim pushed the point as far as he dared, till his father's rising petulance warned him to silence; but it seemed to him a shame that with the money from the recent sale of Isaiah's mill privileges lying idle, no advantage should be taken of the opportunities that here went begging every day. Isaiah had always held him on a tight financial rein, paying only after endless questioning the bills he incurred, grudging even a small sum for money in pocket. So he had no money of his own, could not act for himself; yet the itch for action was on him.

He had opened the matter at the dinner table, and he sat silent through the rest of the meal, so absorbed that he did not notice that Jenny was watching him. They rose at last, and Isaiah turned toward his office. He had fallen into the habit of sleeping for an hour every afternoon on the couch there, while Ephraim worked at a small desk which had been installed for his use. They went into the office together, and Jenny came to spread over Isaiah a heavy, knitted shawl as large as a blanket, and she tucked in his feet and adjusted his skull cap.

Jenny stayed till Isaiah fell into the quick, light sleep of age, and then she came to Ephraim's side — he had turned to the papers on his desk — and touched his arm. He looked up at her in surprise. She beckoned him toward the door, and when he hesitated, she nodded insistently and almost threateningly.

He rose and followed her. She closed the door behind them and they were alone. It was the first time they had been alone since Isaiah's illness weeks before.

VI

Isaiah's office opened off the front hall, at one side of the front door. Next to it there was a big, high-ceiled room with tall windows and a huge fireplace of black marble. On the mantelpiece stood two whale-oil lamps with crystal prisms, ornamented with gold leaf. The room was lavishly furnished; a marble-topped table with a Phyfe base, half a dozen Chippendale chairs, a pier table under a tall glass that hung between two of the windows, a Queen Anne wing chair, a Heppelwhite wall cabinet in which some

fine china and glass was kept for rare occasions and with candela-
bras of Waterford glass on top, a lampstand beside the wing chair
where Isaiah usually sat through his short evenings, the bed-chair
which he had used during his convalescence, a Heppelwhite desk
against one wall. Wide doors opened into the dining room where
Mr. Hardy's portrait of Jenny hung.

When Jenny and Ephraim came into the big room now, Ruth
Green was still clearing the dining table. Jenny did not speak at
once. She crossed to stand before the tall glass, looking at her
own reflection there with an impersonal interest. She raised one
hand and touched her hair which never needed rearrangement.
Ephraim watched her uneasily, and once he caught Ruth's eye
as the girl moved about the dining room; and he wondered remotely why Ruth had not long before this become pregnant and
insisted on his marrying her. He told himself in a sullen desperation that he would have been glad to do so, would be glad to do so
now if he had her condition as a weapon with which to overrule
Isaiah's possible objection.

Till Ruth finished and departed, Jenny was silent. Ephraim
sat down in the wing chair, a few paces from where she stood before the glass. She turned at last, leaning back against the table,
her hands resting on its edge behind her, her head tilted a little
backward, so that she looked down at him over her cheekbones.
He was instantly conscious of every part of her, the facial bones
outlined by cheek and chin and brow, the round line of her
shoulders and the swelling of her breasts under the closely fitted
dress she wore, the bones in her arms and wrists, her fingers
curved over the table edge, her body bent backward by her posture. Her eyes were steady, and he thought suddenly that there
was scorn in them, and a soft stir of anger. Her voice when she
spoke was very low.

'You have tried not to be alone with me, Ephraim,' she said accusingly.

'Who, me?' he stammered, in an automatic reaction. Under the
shock of this direct attack, strength went out of him; and his eyes
fell, so that he stared at the pattern in the carpet on the floor. He
heard her come nearer till he saw the hem of her dress and her
full skirt near his feet.

'Yes, Ephraim, you,' she told him in a gentle amusement.

'I ought to go away,' he muttered.

'Why?' His face twisted miserably, and he made no reply. Her
voice was no more than a murmur. 'Because of what I said, when
we thought Isaiah would die?' she asked. He nodded, and she

whispered: 'He will die some day.' When still he did not speak, she said accusingly: 'You are afraid of me?'

'Yes,' he admitted hoarsely.

She laughed, yet so softly he scarce heard her. She extended her hand and let it rest upon his shoulder, and her finger touched the lobe of his ear, lightly tracing its outline, pressing it gently aside. Her fingertip was warm. She whispered: 'Why are you afraid?'

He said, tremblingly at first and then in sudden desperate relief that the words were out: 'I can't stand it much longer, being near you all the time.'

She spoke reassuringly, as though appeasing a hungry boy. 'Yet he is old, Ephraim. He will not live very long.'

He looked at her blankly. 'That's an awful thing to say, Jenny.'

A swift anger showed in her eyes. 'You poor little rabbit!' she whispered; and then in a cool, almost a mocking tone: 'When will you come to be a man, boy?' And more gently: 'Yet I do not want you frightened, Ephraim. I told you once — remember? — that you need never be afraid of me.'

He whispered: 'What do you want?'

She spoke in a quiet challenge. 'What do you want, Ephraim? Are you afraid to tell me?' The word was a whiplash laid across his cheek.

His eyes met hers at last, and he saw in hers a flickering fire like the play of heat lightning along a far horizon. He said in a breathless tone: 'You hate father, don't you?'

She nodded. 'He ought to have died,' she said, and then she added: 'But I could learn to hate you, too. Or any coward. Do you want me to?' Her tones were cold as ice.

He clenched his fists. 'I've loved you since that time I came home from college, Jenny.' The words, once loosed, poured out of him. 'I've loved you and been afraid of you too.' She smiled, and smoothed the shoulder of his coat with the palm of her hand as he went on: 'The times you've kissed me — even that day I came home to stay — when I think of them it's like a spark in powder. And I can't stop thinking of them!' He pounded his knees weakly with his fists. 'But God damn my soul to hell for saying so!'

She turned away with a quick, contented movement, turned to the nearest chair, seemed about to sit down. She stood there with her back to him, her head bent as though in thought; and his eye followed the lovely line of her side, from shoulder to waist. When she faced him, there was something new in her eyes and in her tone.

'You were trying to persuade Isaiah to do something,' she remembered. 'With all that talk at dinner.' Her manner said that they were allies now, that all was settled between them. 'What was it? What did you want him to do?'

The sudden change, the return to everyday affairs, was like a reprieve. He seized on it, spoke eagerly, telling her what Mr. Holbrook had said, insisting that Isaiah was missing an opportunity for a handsome profit. She listened, yet he thought she was thinking more of him than of what he said. He talked at length, clinging to matter-of-fact words so that other words need not be spoken, till at last there was no more to say.

She nodded then. 'I see. You think Isaiah should do this?'

'I'm sure there's a big profit in it.'

'Isaiah's getting so old,' she said. 'He needs you to make decisions for him, Ephraim. He would approve this, after it was done.' And she asked: 'Has he the money to do what you want?'

'Yes — lying idle in the bank.'

She smiled. 'He trusts you more and more. Do you know what I think? If you had the authority to draw on his account, you could buy this fine land for him without his knowing.'

'But I haven't the authority,' he reminded her.

She came nearer him again. 'I will persuade him to give it to you,' she promised. 'You and I between us must see to it that his affairs are rightly handled. He will give you the authority if I ask him. If you had it, would you do this?'

He hesitated. 'I don't know.'

She said chidingly: 'Still so full of doubts? So easily afraid? A man must sometimes be bold, Ephraim!'

He nodded hurriedly. 'All right; yes, I guess I would.'

'Then I will persuade him,' she promised; and she said in a teasing tone: 'You know, Ephraim, three times — the day you came home, and the night at Carr's Wharf, and the night we thought Isaiah would die — three times I have kissed you. I wish some day you would kiss me.'

He came storming to his feet, all a leaping flame; but she eluded him, stepping quietly backward, saying in matter-of-fact tones: 'Not now. Now it is time to wake Isaiah.'

6

IN THIS matter of giving Ephraim authority to draw upon his funds, Isaiah was stubborn for a while; but Jenny pressed him tirelessly. To do what she proposed, she pointed out, was no more than sensible and wise. 'Suppose you got sick again, Isaiah?' she urged. 'Something might happen while you were out of your head that needed tending to, but Ephraim couldn't do anything.' She persisted day by day, and in the end, by argument and by cajolery, she won her point.

Yet Isaiah's surrender was conditional. 'Mind you,' he told Ephraim, 'you're not to use this power only when I tell you to — or if I'm sick and can't decide.'

After that warning, Ephraim would have retracted his promise to buy Mr. Holbrook's bond; but Jenny laughed at his fears, mocking him in smiling ways, her tone faintly derisive, yet light and tender too. He found in her in these days an extraordinary secret gaiety, and a provocative beauty and warmth which clouded all his senses. Invitation dwelt always in her eyes, and he had opportunity enough to do what half of him wished to do; yet there was still in him a tenacious loyalty to his father which held him in restraint. When now she urged him to go to Mr. Holbrook, he referred to Isaiah's word.

'He told me not to use the money unless on his order,' he protested, 'or if he were sick again.'

A sort of passion darkened her cheek. 'Must you always keep telling me what he said!'

He muttered in a puzzled tone: 'Something's different in you, Jenny, since he was sick. Before, you always seemed to like him, really; but now, when you talk about him you almost — grit your teeth!'

She nodded, speaking softly and absently as though in self appraisal. 'I used to like him when I was a child, because if I let him kiss me, he'd give me goodies at the store; and when he married me, I knew he'd be good to me if I let him do what he wanted. But after I knew you, Ephraim, I hated sleeping in the same bed with him, so I used to kick and toss to keep him awake; and because he hated fresh air I kept our windows open, till finally he went into the other room, slept there. After that he didn't come to me often. It was bad when he did, but it was funny too.' Her tone suddenly hardened. 'But then the night we came home from Augusta — when I had to sleep with him, hold him all night in my arms — I wished him dead.' She shuddered, and Ephraim remembered his own repulsion at the sight of the wasted old man, and she finished strongly, her eyes as cold as ice: 'And now when he comes to me it's as if a dead man touched me. There's never a minute of the day that I don't wish he were dead, that there was just you and me.' A blazing passion rang in her whispered cry: 'I wish he were dead, Ephraim!'

Sometimes when he was with her his blood pounded through his body, shaking him, and his vision was obscured as by a red veil; and it was so now. He wiped his eyes with both hands, as though to see the better; and he pleaded:

'But Jenny, he's my father!'

'Yes,' she assented. 'As long as he's alive.' Her tone was pitiless. She murmured in a keen longing: 'But how long must he live, Ephraim? That little spark of stale life in him, a child could pinch it out!'

His eyes met hers in a horrible silence. They were in the big room, standing together by the table; and he felt a chill wind blow upon the back of his neck. She came a little toward him, her voice no more than a whisper, half smiling so that those small indentations showed in her cheeks as though she were about to cry; and she repeated very softly:

'How long must the old man live — live between us, Ephraim?'

He dared not let her touch him. He moved a step backward to escape, said desperately: 'I'll go see Mr. Holbrook today.'

She looked at him with a bleak scorn naked in her eyes, then turned quietly away.

II

June came booming up the river, and life in Bangor was on the flood. Every packet brought a new flood of speculators and potential citizens; and the town that three years before had numbered no more than as many thousand people was approaching the eight thousand mark. Hundreds of houses and store buildings and new wharves were everywhere under way. The streets had been churned to a quagmire as the frost went out of the ground, and there had been no time nor inclination to scrape and level them. Pot-holes were filled with branches cut off and thrown loosely in; cedar poles formed a corduroy foundation in the wetter spots where springs or surface drainage sent trickles across the road. The mud turned to dust and back to mud again with every rain, and the heavy teams hauling lumber and rock and brick for construction work churned holes which there was never time to fill. Footpaths by the roadside were the only sidewalks, and in the busy streets these disappeared so that pedestrians picked their way along in front of the stores, forever dodging teams or carriages, crossing where they could.

And everywhere, at street corners, in the taverns, wherever two men met, the trading went on and paper passed from hand to hand. There was a current of excitement in the air so intense that most men were infected; and the fever in their blood burned so hot that they might stay all night at the Coffee House or at one of the other taverns or at John Bright's news room, in endless talk of what had been and what might be.

Pat Tierney, who after his leg healed had returned to work as Isaiah's stable man and coachman, quit his job to devote his time to speculation. His first venture had prospered, and so had others since. Pat himself became close-mouthed with success; but Sam Smith told Ephraim:

'He's made ten thousand already. Right now he owns bonds on half a township. Pat's a smart Irishman. He'll be one of the big men in Bangor in his day.'

Ephraim wetted his lips. He had made his deal with Holbrook, paying five thousand dollars for the Boston man's bond. Holbrook jibbed a little, when the dicker came to be concluded, protesting that Ephraim had waited so long that the bond was worth six thousand dollars now; but Ephraim had enough of his father in him to be a good trader, and in the end Holbrook was glad to take his profit and turn the money back into a new speculation.

Money as such began to have little value in the public mind, and those who were infected rushed to turn every dollar they could find into bonds; but Ephraim, after using a part of Isaiah's funds in hand, went no further. He was haunted by a sense of guilt for what he had done, and also by a zealous eagerness to turn over the transaction at a profit, and thus justify his venture; but while there were buyers enough for small parcels when the required investment ran into hundreds, not many were prepared to risk thousands; and also, there were more men with bonds to sell than with money to buy.

Isaiah remained awhile in ignorance of what Ephraim had done. In ordinary times the transaction could not have been long hidden from the old man; but circumstances combined to make possible concealment now. The money which Ephraim had used had been in the Commercial Bank. Isaiah had gone with Ephraim to give Ned Richardson, the cashier, a written authorization which permitted his son to draw out the funds; but since his sickness his hearing was almost completely gone, so he seldom ventured to town where he might be forced to talk to someone. To this extent, circumstances protected Ephraim; but also he had spoken to Mr. Richardson, warning him to silence.

'Father's failing fast,' he explained. 'So we don't bother him unless we have to. He can't discuss anything without getting excited, and that tires him out.'

The cashier said drily: 'If he knew his money was buying bonds for land he didn't know anything about, it'd kill him, like as not.' Mr. Richardson had the banker's mind, which distrusts easy profits and discounts hopeful dreams; and he had thus far been able to keep a level head through the rising hysteria. 'Isaiah never did hold with buying a pig in a poke!'

'We have reliable information about this tract,' Ephraim assured him, trying to sound like a sober business man. 'But don't speak of it to him — unless of course he asks you.'

The banker, though he might distrust the young man's judgment, had no reason to be suspicious of Ephraim himself. So though he saw Isaiah once or twice, Ephraim's warning and the fact that Isaiah, to cover his own deafness, was apt now to monopolize every conversation with a shrill monologue, kept him from speaking of the matter to the old man at all.

III

In July the new steamboat Bangor, Captain Barker, came up the river. Captain Barker claimed that she was the first iron steamboat built in the United States; and this fact led crowds to troop down to the wharf to see her. She was of about four hundred tons, with a tall black smokestack and two masts which were rigged with sails for emergency use; and to familiarize potential patrons with her comfort and speed, an excursion to Castine and Belfast was arranged.

Bangor folks were skeptical about steamboats. The packets Free Trade and Madawaska still plied regularly to Boston; and they were well patronized. With a sailing vessel a man at least knew that sooner or later he would catch a fair wind and reach his destination; but with steam, let the engine break down and there you were! But Captain Barker, proud of his command, laughed at these doubts; and when Jenny heard of the proposed excursion she suggested that she and Isaiah and Ephraim go. Isaiah refused; but he told Ephraim to take Jenny, since her heart was set upon it, and Ephraim, despite his fear of the water, doubtfully agreed.

The day proved to be fine. The Bangor cast off her lines at eight o'clock in the morning and turned down-river. There were about four hundred passengers aboard, as many ladies as gentlemen; and Ephraim and Jenny joined a group on the forward deck to escape the smoke and cinders and to watch each succeeding reach of the river unfold. For a while the conversation was exclamatory, centering upon the beauty of the day, discussing how much cooler it was on the water than on land and what a fine breeze the steamboat's speed produced, commenting on the beauty of the scene and on the farms and towns along the way.

Mrs. Nathaniel Harlow — whose husband, a Revolutionary soldier, had been granted the land east of the Stream and north of the bridge — with a warm merino shawl around her head and shoulders occupied a place of honor forward. Jenny had sent Ephraim to bring a chair for her from the cabin, and she sat there like a queen. She was an apple-cheeked old woman with a small, pursed mouth and a prim sense of her own importance as the widow of one of the first settlers in the town. Jenny and Ephraim stayed near her, and Jenny was solicitous to see that she was protected from the wind. George and Mrs. Thatcher joined them. Mrs. Thatcher, two or three years younger than Jenny, was a handsome woman with a rough, merry tongue. Mrs. Harlow's son Nat and his wife presently appeared to urge that the old woman find a more sheltered spot, but she refused.

'I want to see all there is to see,' she declared. 'And this child' — she touched Jenny's arm affectionately — 'is taking good care of me!'

So they all stayed with her; and Mr. and Mrs. Joe Littlefield, who conducted the Female High School, joined them. Mrs. Littlefield was excited over the fact that Mr. Caleb Cushing, recently returned from two years in Europe and a member of the Massachusetts House of Representatives, was coming to lecture before the Bangor Lyceum on his experiences abroad.

'I'm so pleased!' she said. 'I heard him lecture last summer when I went to Boston. He's a most remarkable man, and so interesting.' She smiled at Ephraim and said: 'I hope other young gentlemen like yourself will come to hear him. Usually there is no one to hear the really good things except ladies and workmen.'

'I shall bring Ephraim,' Jenny promised. 'If we can leave Mr. Poster. So often he needs me.'

Mrs. Harlow said approvingly: 'You've given years of your life to caring for people older than yourself, my dear. Some day you will be rewarded.'

Mrs. Thatcher laughed so merrily that her word gave no offense. 'When Mr. Poster dies, you mean, Mrs. Harlow? Everyone says only General Veazie and two or three others are better off than he!'

The old woman said reprovingly: 'That remark does not become you, 'Becca!' She patted Jenny's hand. 'Certainly this dear child expects no reward.' She looked up at Jenny in a frank affection. 'I think it is just your nature, my dear, to be thoughtful of older people — as you have been today of me.'

Jenny smiled and said: 'I like old people best. They're so frightened and lonely, really. It must be terrible to grow old till all the people your own age, whom you have known so long, are gone.'

Mrs. Harlow nodded. 'And till you're just a nuisance to your children,' she said, bridling.

Nat Harlow laughed, and dropped his hand on her shoulder. 'You're an old hypocrite,' he told her. 'Fishing for compliments! You know you're the best thing in our lives.'

Mrs. Littlefield had been silent too long. 'But I do think it's so awfully important to have good lectures and go to hear them,' she insisted. 'Literary topics, specially, just inspire me! I think we all need literature in our lives.'

Mrs. Thatcher said with her infectious chuckle: 'I'd like books better if the people in them were more like the people I know. I wish people in books had more stomach aches and fewer fine sentiments!'

Jenny suggested in her quiet tones that books were meant to make us forget the unpleasant daily things — like stomach aches. 'I agree with Mrs. Littlefield,' she said. 'If we can interest men in good books, they won't spend so much time in taverns. We'll never stop rum-selling by organizing temperance societies, or even by passing laws.'

Mrs. Harlow sniffed. 'I just refuse to patronize any merchant who sells liquor,' she said. 'If enough of us did that, it would soon bring them to time.'

Her son took mild issue with her. 'You'll never stop rum-selling as long as most men want a few drinks every day,' he argued.

Jenny commented: 'Mr. Harlow is right, just as Mrs. Littlefield is right. But literary pursuits, lectures, musical entertainments, if we have enough good ones, will little by little gently win the rum-drinkers away from the taverns. I'm sure of it.'

Mrs. Harlow said vigorously: 'Exactly! My dear, you've a head on your shoulders. No man ever preferred a tavern to an attractive home. When a married man takes to drink, look to his wife for the reason. If she's a good, fine woman, then maybe there's something wrong with his business.' She laughed with the chirping mirth of merry old women. 'Oh, I've seen my share of men that rum ruined!' she declared. 'There was Jim Budge — Captain Budge, he used to be — died the year before you married Mr. Poster, Jenny. He was a militia captain in the Revolution and a man of parts for ten years after, till his business went to pot and he took to drink and went crazy of it finally.' She added: 'He got so he'd steal anything he could lay hands on. Tom Bartlett gave him six salted fish one day if he'd promise not to steal anything out of the store for a week; but next day Jim brought 'em back, told Tom: "Here, take your fish. I can do better!"' They laughed with her at the familiar tale, and she concluded: 'Mighty few men take to rum if they can do better. Unless of course the Devil's in them in the first place!'

Mrs. Thatcher briskly exclaimed: 'The Devil's in the lot of them, if you want my opinion! Besides, I think it does a man good to get drunk once in a while.' She smiled mockingly at her husband. 'Not that Mr. Thatcher ever tries it. He knows what would happen to him if he did. But a man who was drunk the night before is always so full of good resolutions next day! In fact, I think men in a fit of remorse make mighty good company.'

The old woman chuckled, nodding. 'Mr. Harlow had a drop too much now and then,' she admitted. 'Everyone did, when I was a young woman; but the good men outgrew it.' She added thoughtfully: 'It's curious that we women don't outgrow our vices. A man can be a scapegrace boy and turn out all right in the end; but let a woman get her fingertip in the tar barrel, and soon she's black all over.'

Mrs. Thatcher laughed. 'Perhaps she liked the sample,' she suggested, 'and had the courage to want more! Men are always scared, after the fact. They're all a pack of cowards, if you ask me.'

IV

Jenny, when at last they were alone, reminded Ephraim of that remark. The steamboat had touched at Castine, had crossed the Bay to Belfast, now was homeward bound up the river; and the breeze had tossed up enough of a sea, even in these sheltered waters, so that the crowd on deck was thinned. When the Bangor passed Fort Point Cove, Ephraim and Jenny stood in the peak of the bow, elbows on the rail; and there was no one near them. Jenny looked at him sidewise, smiling a little, and said:

'I think Mrs. Thatcher was right, Ephraim. Men are all cowards.'

'Who is it does the fighting?' he argued. 'Who wins the battles?'

'Oh, fighting is just habit! Anybody can be brave with people watching.' Her eyes left his, turning to the river ahead, and she said wistfully: 'But you love me, and you know I love you; yet you're sorry you told me so.' She added in quiet accusation: 'For weeks after Isaiah was sick you wouldn't be alone with me at all. Even since we've both known how we feel, you leave the house early, come home late; or you stay all day with Isaiah, avoiding me. Today we've never been quite alone till now.'

'We're not alone now,' he warned her uneasily, turning to look back along the deck. 'There're at least fifty people watching us.'

'Yet not hearing us, Ephraim.'

He protested in a quiet desperation: 'We can't talk like this, Jenny! I've hated myself ever since that day I told you I loved you.'

'Was it a lie?'

'No, it was the truth. But I ought not to have said it.'

'What's the harm in words?' she urged. 'Isaiah has only a few days more to live — or a few weeks, or a few months — but you and I have years of life, Ephraim. Can't we dream of them, plan for them?'

'There's nothing to plan!'

She smiled scornfully. 'I think there've been men who loved a woman so much they wouldn't let anything stand in their way. Not even their father.'

He urged wretchedly: 'You're too fine to talk like that!'

'Isn't there something fine and sacred about — love like ours?'

'There's something sacred about being married to a man,' he countered, clinging hard to the things of which he was sure.

Her low tones hardened. 'There's nothing sacred about a marriage that brings a toothless, cold old man to mumble over me with dry lips and to scratch at me with his cold and creaky hands.' Her eyes met his hotly. 'If you weren't afraid of what Isaiah would do to you, you wouldn't wait for me to tell you this.'

'What can I do?'

'Take what is yours,' she whispered.

He said after a moment, almost pleadingly: 'Listen, Jenny! We're young. We can wait! Father won't live very long.'

'A minute is long. An hour is long. A day is long.' Her bleak voice was so low he scarce heard her words. 'Ephraim, Ephraim, there's so little life in him. A touch would end it. Why must he live longer?'

He shivered, suddenly cold; and when Mr. and Mrs. Thatcher came forward to join them he welcomed them as rescuers.

v

The Bangor tied up at her dock at six o'clock, and the passengers flocked to congratulate the Captain, to praise the new boat, to exclaim about the pleasures of the day. When they left the wharf, and for a part of the way home, Ephraim and Jenny had the company of other passengers going in their direction. Only for the last few rods did they walk alone, and then they did not speak. When Jenny said good-bye to Mrs. Harlow and the others her voice had been gentle and serene. It seemed to him impossible that she could have said to him what she had said, and still speak in such seemly fashion to these others now.

Yet she had said the same thing to him before. Lieutenant Carruthers twenty years ago had glimpsed in Jenny the woman she would come to be, at once wanton and cruel and yet calculating too. Tim Hager, less perceptive, had attributed to his own depravity the emotions she provoked in him; and shame, and terror of himself — and of her — had broken him and destroyed him. Isaiah had desired her, and had found peace in possessing her and in receiving the passive submission of this child who became his wife. But Ephraim was the first to whom she had revealed herself deliberately and completely, to whom she showed herself naked and shameless and more merciless than death itself.

Yet he could not believe his own senses now. He tried to tell himself that he must be mistaken, that his ears had heard amiss. Jenny was in the eyes of everyone except himself a considerate and wise and devoted young wife, a woman of whom people like old Mrs. Harlow approved. It was impossible that such a woman could invite him to foul his father's bed, to take his father's life.

He walked beside her haltingly, and they came to the door together and he lifted the latch and she went in. Isaiah's office opened into the hall. His door stood wide when they entered. Jenny turned at once that way, going in to lean down to the old man and speak into his ear.

'It's been a wonderful day, Isaiah!' she said happily.

Ephraim in the hall heard his father's rasping voice, shrill with rage. 'Where's Eph? Eph, come in here!' When Ephraim entered the study, he saw that Isaiah was in a towering fury. Then the old man cried in a harsh wrath: 'You damned thief! Come here to me!'

7

WHAT had happened was simple enough, but it was a long time before they had from Isaiah the whole story. He began by berating Ephraim for stealing his money, and by haranguing Jenny for persuading him to lay himself open to such a loss. Since he could hear nothing that Ephraim said, and since Jenny herself for a while said no word at all, they did not interrupt him; and the deaf old man, so full of fury that he looked like a malignant mummy in a skull cap, talked on and on.

Not till he had talked himself out did Jenny attempt to question him. He told them then what had happened. 'Man name of Eaton came to see me this morning,' he said. 'Wanted to dicker with me for a township of timber land he said I owned, way the hell and gone up the West Branch! I told him he was crazy, told him I didn't own any pine up there, and he said I did; said Eph here had bought it from a man named Holbrook, bought a bond for the deed for five thousand dollars!'

She nodded. 'Yes, Ephraim did,' she agreed. 'But he bought it for you, Isaiah.'

'Where'd he get the money?' the old man demanded. 'Eph ain't got a cent to his name.' And before she could reply, he shouted in his shrill, crackling tones: 'Don't lie to me! It won't do you a mite of good to lie to me, Eph! I knew damned well, minute I heard, what you'd done; so I went to see Ned Richardson. Sure enough, you took my money to do it with! That's plain thieving!'

Ephraim said defensively: 'You can make a profit on it, father. That deed calls for a price of fifty cents an acre; and worse land is selling for a dollar and better now.'

But Isaiah of course did not hear him, and shouted his son down. 'Don't lie to me,' he repeated. 'Thieving, I call it!' He turned on Jenny again. 'And you helped him!' he cried. 'Keeping at me till you talked me into letting him handle my money! Can't you wait till I'm dead and gone, before trying to get your hands on my prop'ty?' He looked from one to the other in a jealous suspicion. 'Conniving together to rob an old man! You'd ought to be ashamed of yourself, the both of you. I'd like to know what's been going on behind my back, anyway!' His wrath rose again, his old eyes flashing. 'I know you, Eph. You don't fool me a minute. Oh, I've seen you watching Jenny like a cat watches a mouse hole, as if you'd like to eat her alive!' His rage fed on itself and he banged his hand feebly on the table. 'I won't have it, you hear me! You can't pull the wool over my eyes.'

Jenny spoke in his ear. 'What did Mr. Eaton want, Isaiah?'

'Wanted to know would I sell,' he said sullenly.

'Did he make you an offer?'

A curious expression, at once shamefaced and sly, came across the old man's sunken countenance. 'What if he did?' he demanded. 'What's that got to do with it?'

'How much did he offer you?'

He tried to whip up his wrath again. 'What's that got to do with it?' he repeated. 'Eph as good as stole my money, and you helped him. Oh, I'm onto the both of you! But you can't fool me. You don't fool me a minute.'

She insisted, her lips close to his ear: 'What did he offer to pay?'

'Well, he said he'd give me a thousand-dollar profit,' Isaiah confessed. 'But that don't have a thing to do with it! It's thieving all the same!'

Jenny laughed quickly, her triumphant eyes flashing for a moment to Ephraim's. 'You gave Ephraim the money to use,' she told Isaiah, 'and he bought some property in your name, and it was a good buy, because you've already made a profit on it. Shame on you, calling names! I'd think you'd be proud of Ephraim for being clever, instead of carrying on like this, so crazy.'

He cackled harshly. 'Now I'm crazy! Is that it?' His eyes narrowed. He challenged Ephraim. 'Well, and I suppose you'd take his offer?' he exclaimed. 'You'd take it and think you were smart?' Eph nodded a strong assent, too relieved at this lucky outcome of his venture to think clearly; and Isaiah slapped his desk again. 'There!' he cried. He pointed his finger accusingly at Ephraim. 'There, Jenny! He's the crazy one! Not me! Just because he sees a profit, he's ready to sell and get out. Answer me one thing! Would this Eaton pay me six thousand if the bond wa'n't worth more? No sir! I'll take charge of this dicker from now on. I'll show you how business is done, young fellow my lad!'

Jenny asked curiously: 'What are you going to do, Isaiah?'

'Do? Why, what would any sensible man do? I don't aim to sell anything till I have some idea what it's worth. I'm going to find out what that land is worth. That's what I'm going to do!'

II

It was to investigate the value of this township of pine that Isaiah and Eph made the long trip up the West Branch in late July. Isaiah had proposed to send Mr. Gillies; but the Scot was already in the wilderness, cruising for Rufus Dwinel. The half dozen other men whom Isaiah might have been willing to trust were likewise engaged; for the speculation in timber lands had set on foot an intensive exploration of the north country, and every competent man had been sent up-river in June.

When he could find no trustworthy agent, Isaiah announced his intention of going himself, with woodsmen who knew a sound pine when they saw one, to make his own survey; and he said Ephraim should come along.

'It's time you learned what a pine on the stump looks like,' he told his son. 'Maybe you made a lucky buy this time, but you'll never get far in the lumber business without you know trees.'

Ephraim did not want to go. He had always been uneasy on the water. Even that trip on the Bangor to Castine and to Belfast had awakened fears alive in him ever since his boyhood; and he demurred as long as he dared, till Isaiah said in a sudden explosion of rage:

'No more talk out of you! I don't aim to leave you here with Jenny all the time I'm gone. Don't try to teach your grandmother to suck eggs! I don't allow to be made a fool of by the two of you. You'll come, and no more talk about it.'

Ephraim was as unwilling to stay behind with Jenny as to risk the perils of the river; but he still tried for a while to persuade Isaiah to give up the expedition, to send some trusted agent. His own fears translated themselves into concern for Isaiah; and he told Jenny she should persuade the old man not to go. 'We'll be sleeping in a tent,' he said, 'and the black flies and mosquitoes and things will eat him alive, and he'll get cold and wet. He'll get sick again, sure.'

'It's done him good, just thinking about it,' she insisted. They were all there at table, she and Ephraim talking together — as they often did — in tones so low that Isaiah's deaf ears caught not even the murmur of their voices. 'It will do him good to go.' And she added quietly: 'If he does get sick again, Ephraim, he'll not live through it. So — take good care of him.'

He did not answer her. The thought of Isaiah's death was always in his mind. She had put it there, and she kept it alive in a dozen ways. She was a madness in him now, a hot wind which blew through every part of him, giving him no peace nor respite. She watched the torment in his eyes with a faint, slow smile.

In the end it was settled that he and Isaiah would go together, travelling up-river by stages as far as possible, proceeding thereafter by canoe. The last Monday in July was set for their departure day.

III

During the interval of preparation, Ephraim spent as little time as possible at the house. There was in him a sense of impending crisis, and nameless fears plucked always at his sleeve. On the Saturday before they were to depart, he heard talk at the Coffee House of a man in Augusta who had killed his wife and who would be brought to trial presently. The man's name was Joe Hager, and it was remembered that Tim Hager, Jenny's father, had come from the Kennebec valley, from Norridgewock; and there was some speculation as to whether he and this Joe Hager were related. Ephraim listened to the talk, taking no part in it; but the brandy he had drunk began to burn in his veins and he called for another measure. Toward the end of his college years, after he came under the influence of John Evered, he had been sober enough; but during these months at home his passion for Jenny, just as it had driven him to Ruth's arms, led him to drink more and more.

Ordinarily he could drink intemperately without apparent effect; but tonight, for the first time in his life, he realized suddenly that his senses were becoming seriously confused. He welcomed this relief from his perplexities and courted it; and before he went home he had drunk more than he could carry, in a futile attempt to drown thoughts he could not endure.

The house was, save for a night light in the hall, dark when he reached it; and in the upper hall the doors into Jenny's room and into Isaiah's were closed. He wished to go in to see Isaiah, to make sure that he was all right. He blamed himself for leaving the old man alone in the house here, at the mercy of this woman in whose veins flowed the blood of murderers. But when he heard Isaiah's heavy snoring that was always so incredibly loud for such a small old man, it reassured him. He passed Jenny's door with sidelong glances, and in his own room his fear of her became a drunken fear for his own safety, so that he secured his door, pushing a table and two chairs against it to keep her from coming in.

Yet even after these precautions, and despite the liquor in him, he could not sleep. He lay at once shivering and perspiring, between an ague of terror and a fever for her which threatened to consume him altogether.

IV

They would start at early dawn on Monday morning; and after supper Sunday evening, Isaiah, stimulated by his coming adventure, sat long with them in the big room, full of gleeful anticipations. When at last he was weary, Jenny went with him upstairs. Ephraim, left alone below, turned into the office to put all in order there. He was some time at this. He might have finished more quickly, but without admitting it to himself he delayed. There had been many evenings when Jenny, having put Isaiah to bed, came down again to sit awhile with him; and secretly and despite his resolutions he hoped she would come tonight.

But for a while she did not, and at last he was ready to go upstairs. He snuffed the candle in the office, and went into the big room. The two whale-oil lamps, glittering with crystal prisms, were lighted on the black marble mantel there. He had extinguished one when he heard a sound in the hallway; the creak of a tread in the stairs.

He stood still, watching the door, knowing that Jenny was coming down; and his lips were parched and dry.

There was a small table in the hall on which rested a candle stand. This held seven candles; but Isaiah's frugality had long made it the rule that unless for special reasons only three of these should be burning at one time. On the table, night candles were placed every evening by Ruth as her last duty before she went to finish in the kitchen and then climbed to her attic room. Ephraim, standing by the mantel, could see through the open door the candles burning there; and then two of them were blotted out by Jenny's small figure as she appeared in the doorway.

When she saw him, she too stood still; but this was only for a moment. Then she came toward him. He was at the end of the hearth farthest from the door, his hand resting on the mantel shelf where he had just put out the lamp. She stopped by the lamp that was still burning, and raised her hand to it, and the flame died.

Except for the light of the candles in the hall, shining on them where they stood, this room was left in darkness. Beyond the candle beams, there were deep shadows. She turned that way, toward a curious article of furniture which was capable of being arranged as an armchair of spacious proportions, or as a couch with a sloping end to support the shoulders and head of the user. Until Isaiah's illness it had always been used as a chair, but when he began to come downstairs, Mrs. Hollis insisted that he have a place to lie down; and he had spent several days on this makeshift couch. It pleased him, and since then he sometimes used it to take a nap after meals.

Jenny now went to this couch and sat down upon it. She said quietly: 'Come near me, Ephraim.'

He followed her, trembling. He brought a chair to sit facing her. The night was cooler after a warm, humid day; but here in this closed room the cool of evening had not yet penetrated, and Ephraim's brow was wet. He mopped it uneasily. He was so close to her, his knee almost touching hers, that he caught the faint fragrance which whether natural or artificial she always wore, a heady and delicious perfume profoundly moving. She sat a little sidewise, supporting herself with one hand, the other in her lap. When his eyes became accustomed to the darkness, he could see her white hand moving a little as she thoughtfully smoothed the stuff of her dress along her knee.

He waited for her to speak. The candles threw some light into the end of the room where the fireplace was; and he could see the doorway and one of the candles reflected in the glass above the pier table that stood between the windows. She rose suddenly and went away from him, walking in a way that was like beautiful and sensuous music, walking in a way he had never seen before, nor imagined. Merely to watch her as she moved away from him filled him with a suffocating longing. She crossed to the pier glass and looked at herself for a moment in it, lifting her hands at last with a slow movement to press them on her breasts, pressing hard. She extended her arms slowly to full reach above her head, rising on tiptoes, stretching every muscle in her body; and he saw her waist draw slim, her shoulders narrow. Then her hands came down to her sides again and she returned toward him, still with that quality in her walk which he had never seen before. He thought of a cat. A cat might stretch itself so, might walk so.

She came to stand close to him, her back to the light as she looked down at him. He forced himself to speak, wetting his lips, shaping the words carefully.

'Is father asleep?' he asked. His voice croaked in his throat.

She nodded slowly. Her hand moved to rest on his shoulder, and her finger touched his throat under the jawbone at one side. He caught his breath, and she traced the line of his jawbone, touched his ear, pressed her hand against his cheek, cupped his chin in her palm. Her hand was cold.

'I'm glad of it,' he said hoarsely. 'He needs all the rest he can get. This is going to be a hard trip.'

She laughed without a sound. He could not have explained how he knew she was laughing. Her laughter was no more than a sort of easing of the tension in her. She sat down again upon the couch beside him, then leaned back, her body and shoulders and head supported by the inclined part of the couch. Every muscle in her body was relaxed. He thought that if he touched her, no matter where, she would be soft and warm. In that close and stifling room she gave off warmth as though she were a smouldering fire. Yet her hand had been cold as ice.

He mopped his brow again. She said: 'You're hot?'

'It's a hot night.'

'I think it must be growing cooler outside.'

He wished to escape into the dark, shaded streets; to walk quietly through their silences till the coolness of the night could enter into him and comfort him. Yet he did not move. She asked slowly:

'How long will you be gone, Ephraim?'

'I don't know. A month, father says; or a little less, or a little more.'

'Are you taking everything you will need?'

'The men will have everything, when we meet them.'

'When will that be?'

She knew as well as he every detail of their plans; but if they spoke of such harmless matters, they need not speak of other things. 'Tuesday night,' he said.

'Then you start up the river on Wednesday?'

'Yes.'

'In boats?'

He licked his lips, remembering how he dreaded the terrors of that long journey. 'In canoes,' he said. 'Indian canoes, made out of birch bark.' He had seen the frail things, so light that one man could swing them to his shoulders and carry them over a long portage without a pause for rest, so fragile that any wound would pierce their sides.

'How many men of you?'

'Eight. Four Indians to paddle, and father and me, and Mr. Duncan and Mr. Irish, the men father is taking along to cruise the land.'

'Will you go with them into the wilderness?' She lay completely without movement. In the half darkness he could see only the white blur of her face, her white hand. Her dark gown lost itself in the shadows.

'Wherever father can go. I'll stay with him.'

'Why will you be so long?'

'It may be less or more.'

She said without expression: 'Every hour you're away will seem to me too long to bear, Ephraim.'

His fist knotted on his knee, and her cold fingertip touched his wrist. Then her hand cupped his wrist and her fingertips pressed where his pulse beat. She spoke softly.

'Your heart is pounding, Ephraim. I think you too are sorry we must be apart awhile.'

'Father's dead set to go,' he said. He tried to speak in matter-of-fact tones. 'I think it's been good for him; the planning. I think the trip may do him good. He'll come home a new man.'

She withdrew her hand. 'I will tell you about your father, Ephraim,' she said in still, controlled tones. 'I will tell you about your father, and about my father too. I think you will understand my father. Twice he beat me. I think I knew even then why he beat me. I have always known things like that. I remember the English Lieutenant who took my mother away. I was only four years old then, but I remember him. It was twenty years ago, but I remember it. He stayed at our house that night with my mother, and we all slept in the same room, they in the big bed and I in my small one; and I remember her voice in the night, laughing.'

After a moment she went on: 'My father beat me because he wanted me, and because he hated himself for that. You are like him, Ephraim. He was ashamed of loving me, because I was his daughter, and you are ashamed of loving me because I am your father's wife. So you would like to beat me, too.' She laughed a little. 'I think sometimes you would like to kill me.'

He said hoarsely, in a shaking horror: 'What kind of woman are you?'

'You have always been afraid of me,' she told him. 'You were afraid when you saw Mr. Hardy's likeness of me. Some day, perhaps, you will kill me, Ephraim; but it will be because you are afraid.' She said dispassionately: 'You're afraid of so many things, aren't you?'

'I'm not afraid of you.'

'I was afraid, once,' she confessed, in a different tone. 'I was afraid the night my father died. I was afraid he would kill me. When Isaiah and Deacon Adams and Amos Patten came to talk to me, I was still afraid. I thought they might send me back to my father, so I told them lies about him; and I showed them the marks on my body where he had hit me. I knew that if they saw me covered with bruises, they would do anything for me.'

'How old were you?' He was fascinated as a bird is fascinated by a snake.

She said, laughter deep in her tones: 'Perhaps I did not know all these things then, but I do now. I have a friend named Lena Tempest. She is a very wise woman, and she knows the reasons men do things. Do you know her pretty little laundresses, Ephraim?'

'I know where she lives, in your father's old house.'

'Have you never been there?'

'No.'

'Yet you sometimes boast to me that you have known such women?' She went on easily: 'That is my house, since my father died. Lena used to work here for me; and sometimes when I am alone she comes here to see me now — and sometimes I go to see her.'

'You oughtn't to do that! Father would . . .'

'Oh, no one knows, except Lena, and now you. You see, I like to talk to her, to ask her questions. There are so many things I want to know, things she can tell me, about men.'

'You can't go to a place like that. What would folks say?'

She stirred as though in a deep amusement. 'No one would believe that I go there, not even if they saw me. I am a very respectable woman, Ephraim; the wife of Isaiah Poster, active in all good works, devout in church. Did you see on the steamboat how even old Mrs. Harlow thinks well of me? If you told them what I have told you, they would not believe it; and Lena and I would both say you were telling lies.' She added thoughtfully: 'Perhaps I am telling you a lie now. Perhaps there is more than one of me, Ephraim. Perhaps it is not I who likes to hear Lena Tempest talk about men. Or perhaps it is not I who goes sedately to church, and to the Lyceum, and to musical entertainments, and who is thought to be so respectable. Or perhaps it is not I who will be so wretched while you are away. Or perhaps it is not I who lies here now wishing you were not so much afraid of me.'

He repeated, defiantly: 'I'm not afraid of you.'

'There is nothing to be afraid of, Ephraim.'

He rose suddenly and turned away from her, his muscles twitching, walking with uncertain stumbling steps till behind him she spoke his name. He stopped, his back toward her, and she said softly:

'Come to me.'

He retraced his steps, slowly, as though under some unseen compulsion. She lay with her hand under her head, looking up at him. The light was behind him, but he could see her face, her eyes; and he saw that she was smiling. She lifted one hand to him.

Yet he knew suddenly that if he touched her hand it would be cold. He felt the cruel calculation in her; and hunger and terror fought in him and left him desolate as a corpse on a battlefield. He stammered hoarsely:

'What do you want?'

'I want your hand,' she whispered. 'I want to press it here against my heart, so you can feel how my heart pounds.'

He put his hands behind him, shaking his head in a stubborn desperation. 'No, I won't, Jenny! I won't touch you!' Then a sudden rage at her was in him. 'You persuaded me to steal father's money. It was just luck — just because everyone is land crazy — that you didn't make a plain thief out of me. But I won't do this! I've got to hold on to something. Let me go.' His voice was like a prayer. 'Jenny, let me go!'

The light behind him flickered. She said: 'The candles in the hall are burning down, burning out. It will be dark in a moment now.' He did not move and she sat up, extending her hand to seize his.

He backed away, two steps and then another. He turned then, surrendering to panic flight. Not stopping to find his hat, he bolted out of doors. The door behind him stood open. He strode away along the street, looking back at that open door as though afraid she would appear there to pursue him. The lighted rectangle of the doorway, seen at a narrowing angle, was visible for some distance. He was eight or ten rods away when the light disappeared, and he knew that she had closed the door.

v

Ephraim lurched through the dark streets like a man blind drunk. Until he came to Exchange Street he saw no lighted windows anywhere. There were lights in the Coffee House but he did not go in. Without purpose he walked down toward the river, past the store which still bore his father's name, till he came to the house where Tim Hager and Jenny had lived and where Lena

Tempest and her pretty laundresses now entertained the bachelors of the city.

He stopped there irresolute, half-minded to go in to quench the consuming fires Jenny had known how to light; but there was no ease for him in any woman but her. His muscles twitched and quivered, and his throat was swollen and congested, as though all the blood in his body stood still and multiplied itself, as though his flesh might be shattered by its bursting pressure. He stumbled on, shouldering through the loud and drunken sailors and rafts-men and woodsmen who with hoarse, hilarious voices made their way to this door and to that one, from behind which came the tinkle of music and loud cries and shrill feminine laughter, to end their night's carouse in casual arms; and he envied them the easy solace they knew how to find.

At Washington Street he turned, following the river; and the crowds thinned till at last he walked alone. When he came op-posite Boyd's Cove, the river came close to the street and the air was cooler. He stayed awhile there, staring at the dark and silent water, before moving on. He came by Newbury Street to Main a block or two beyond his father's house; but he could not yet bear to go home, so he swung away toward Old Town, heedless of time. Dust rose in puffs under his feet, and twice and thrice he met carriages, their lanterns visible a long way off, returning late toward Bangor. He walked on for a mile or two before at last his steps lagged and he moved slower and more slowly.

When he turned homeward again, he was drugged with weari-ness, and it was hours since he had left Jenny, and dawn was not far away; but the hot wind which she had roused in him still blew. He came back to his father's house and saw the windows of her room above him and stood a moment looking up at them. It was so dark that they were no more than shadowy rectangles; so dark that he could not see whether or not they were open to let in the cooler outer air. He knew she was long since abed, and Isaiah would be snoring in his little room next hers, huddled under blankets, his windows closed; and in her room in the attic Ruth would be. Perhaps, he thought, Ruth had stayed awake awhile, hoping he would come to her before his departure in the morning; but she too must be sleeping now.

He opened the door and stepped into the hall, black as the pit with no light anywhere. He closed the door behind him and moved softly toward the foot of the stair.

Then he stopped still, his heart suddenly leaping in affright, for there was someone near him. He had heard no sound in the silence, had seen nothing in the darkness; but he felt a presence here before him by the foot of the stair, and he caught the faint, intoxicating fragrance he could never mistake.

He waited for Jenny to speak, waited seconds that seemed eternities, till he heard a sound, heard the creaking of that tread halfway up the stair; so he knew she had retreated to her room, withdrawing before him as though in silent invitation.

After a moment, his breath pent, moving as silently as she, he followed her. Her door was open. When he came to it he could see the pale rectangles of the windows. There was no sound within, but he had not heard any straining of cords to suggest that she had climbed into the high canopy bed. She must be standing in the warm and fragrant darkness, waiting for him to come to her.

He took two steps into the room and saw her, a white figure dimly visible there by the bed; but then, despite the pounding in his ears, he heard Isaiah's snores from the other room. At that sound he turned instantly away, out into the hall again and — blindly groping — he made his way to his own door, feeling for it along the wall, finding it, going in.

He stood for a while in the darkness there, his back braced against the door panels, shaking and suffocated. Once his senses tightened when he thought he heard a sound in the hall outside the door, but the sound was not repeated. Still in darkness he removed his outer garments, and now he began to make haste. A grotesque terror possessed him. He could not endure the thought of lying here, feeling her nearness there at the outer end of the hall. She might come seeking him.

But there was a sanctuary to which he could escape. He thought of Ruth, in her room above, as a refuge and as assuagement too. In a breathless haste, he opened presently his door, and listened and heard no sound, and moved on tiptoe to the foot of the attic stair.

Ruth's door was open. On hot nights she often left it so, for her room was small and could be stifling. He came softly beside her bed, yearning toward her; but when he leaned over her where she lay she smelled like Jenny, and as though that familiar fragrance was a detonator, his cautious movements gave way in a sudden explosion of all the pent forces in him to an abrupt and unquestioning and unresisted violence.

VI

When an hour later Ephraim woke from the spent stupor of heavy sleep, there was gray dawn in the window. Ruth lay between him and the light, her dark hair loose upon the pillow under his cheek, her face turned away from him. He thought her still asleep; but since he and Isaiah were to make an early start, he rose on one elbow, ready to depart. At his movement she turned her head to look at him. He saw then, even in that faint light, that this was not Ruth but Jenny. A paralyzing astonishment for a moment held him motionless; but then he thrust away, sprang to his feet, recoiling as though from some dreadful vision, crying out the first question that came to his lips.

'Where's Ruth?'

Jenny said calmly: 'Her mother wasn't well yesterday. After you left me, I told her she could go home to spend the night.' She added: 'Then when you came home, I came to wait for you here. I was sure you would come.' She did not move, watching him quietly. He shook his head, groping, completely bewildered and helpless; and she explained in even tones: 'I have known for weeks that you were coming to Ruth's room, so I sent her home and took her place to wait for you.'

He knew he was forever lost, yet the question must be asked. 'Why?' he stammered pitifully. 'Oh, Jenny, why?'

She said, still unmoving: 'Because, Ephraim, I want you to do something for me, and you are afraid, so I wished to make you more afraid not to do it than to do it. Do you know what it is I want?'

He looked in terror toward the door, and she said evenly: 'You are thinking of Isaiah. He is still asleep. I must go wake him. You'll start soon.' Then she said: 'I will not tell him about what you've done to me before you go, Ephraim. Yet you know what he'll do when he knows.' Her low voice, as much as her words, chilled him through and through. 'When you come back, I'll tell him what you've done to me, Ephraim. You know what to expect. I'll tell him the day he returns. If he returns.'

His eyes dilated and he covered them with his hands to shut out the sight of her. He turned and fled headlong down the stairs to his own room.

8

EPHRAIM and Isaiah were a long ten days on the way up-river, and that was for the younger man a weary time. They rode in one canoe, while Alex Duncan and Tom Irish took the other. Two Indians paddled each craft. The passengers sat facing forward, and the rolled tent, the bedding, the bags of cooking dishes and the covered wooden pails full of supplies served as back-rests to support them. The canoes glided secretly up the long deadwaters, between blank forest walls, and sometimes a half-grown brood of scurry ducks scuttered for miles ahead of them in repeated alarms. They poled up the quicker reaches or landed at the foot of the worst falls and rapids to portage around, and the trip up-river was not alarming.

Nevertheless, Ephraim's old terror of the water returned tenfold, and he was wretchedly afraid. His days were one long torment, and for thinking of Jenny he could not sleep of nights. He lost weight and strength and his nerves were frayed and torn. Despair as much as terror harried him. He had dreamed for months that he would one day hold Jenny in his arms; but now that dream was bitter ashes in his mouth. Even in the half-mad violence of those moments when he still thought her Ruth, there had been something infuriating in her cold submission; and his subsequent awakening to the truth was a nightmare from which there was no escape.

But Isaiah was serenely unconscious of his son's despair. He gained strength on the trip, thriving on the long days out of doors, the tented nights, the hearty food; and also, the reports his men eventually brought put him in high spirits. The township which Ephraim had bought proved to be well stocked with pine of the first grade. The eighty million feet of which Mr. Holbrook had boasted might be an exaggeration, but not a serious one; and there was a tributary stream flowing into the Penobscot which would facilitate lumbering the tract. Isaiah greedily calculated that he might sell the stumpage for at least a dollar the thousand. If he could do that, his potential profit was enormous.

But to conclude such a transaction would take time. It might be years before lumbering operations reached so far into the wilderness. On the return trip down-river the old man thought aloud, calculating every possibility, weighing the advantages of the quick, sure profit to be derived from selling the bond Ephraim had bought against the long-term chances.

Ephraim, sitting behind his father, hardly listened. They were bound back to Bangor now, and when they came home, Jenny would tell his father what had happened; and that prospect was appalling. So the future daunted him; but also, he lived the immediate hour in constant terror of his life. When they breasted the current coming up-river, his fears had been bad enough; but now they glided with it, and this seemed to him to increase their danger. Once they struck boldly across an open lake, and a squall of wind caught them and slopped solid water into the canoe so that they were near swamping before they came to the shore and could empty the frail craft of water again. Isaiah took the adventure gleefully; but Ephraim in his imaginings died a dozen deaths. In mid-lake they passed the floating, partially decomposed body of a buck deer; and to Ephraim's fear-disordered mind that became his own body. He imagined the canoe overturning, felt the strangling water flood his laboring lungs, saw his body sinking with last spasmodic reflex jerkings of arms and legs to rest at last on the dark, slimed bottom of the lake till great sluggish fish with toothless mouths came to pluck and gulp at the soft, decaying flesh.

But if the moment on the lake was bad, every hour on the river was worse; for when they came to quick water they ran it, the Indians guiding the canoe with strong paddle strokes, missing huge boulders by so scant a margin that a dozen times a day Ephraim thought their destruction sure; and he imagined the canoe broken against these ledges and saw his own helpless body caught by the current and whirled downstream, to smash against the toothed rocks with sodden, bruising blows, and he imagined the egglike crunch of a cracked skull or the hideous grating grind of breaking bones in his arms and legs.

Sometimes the water was too heavy to be run, and then they portaged; and Ephraim thanked all the Gods there were for those reprieves. But the Indians who paddled them were in a hurry to be home, and Isaiah urged them on, promising a bonus for every day saved. A rivalry developed between the two canoes, each daring the other on, so that they risked running rapids around which they might better have carried, and again and again they escaped catastrophe by inches.

Ephraim usually sat behind his father, and since they both faced forward, Isaiah could not see his son's tortured countenance. But the Indian in the stern at their nightly camps told his fellows that the young white man was afraid, and during the day's run he was always alert to meet and counter any move Ephraim might make.

II

They were halfway home when disaster came. The pitch they were running was not particularly dangerous. There was a sharp drop at the top, but it was short, and then easier water ran for a dozen rods to descend through a strong sluice below. The first drop was sufficiently abrupt so that after the other canoe took it, Ephraim and Isaiah, a quarter-mile upstream, could no longer see even the heads of the paddlers.

As he watched that dreadful brink approach, Ephraim's hands tightened on the gunwale, and his lungs contracted and he could not breathe. The Indians chose their course to pass just to the left of a boulder that split the current at the head of the run. They came to it, and the bow of the canoe for a moment projected over nothingness before it dipped with a sickening sidewise lurch while the paddles swung it to take the angling current.

At that lurch, Ephraim's strained nerves snapped like tight wires. He screamed and tried to pull himself to his feet. The Indian in the stern shouted and struck him on the head with the paddle, thinking to stun him into passivity; but Ephraim saw the blow coming and tried to dodge, and lost his balance. Still holding to the gunwale, he fell overside, and the canoe turned over with him and swung sidewise and broke its back on a boulder in the way.

The four men and all the gear were thrown into the water together, and the strong current rolled them on, but Ephraim's desperate hold on the canoe was for a moment unbroken. When he too was torn away, his clutching hand caught the bail of one of the big wooden buckets still in the wrecked canoe, which had held flour and which was almost empty now.

He was still holding fast to this when the current brought him to the foot of the run, into somewhat easier water there; and the bucket's buoyancy fetched him to the surface. As soon as his mouth and nose were clear, he began to scream, and the naked, shameless fear-sound was terrible in the clean silence of the river and the forest. The current revolved him slowly. He tried to climb on the bucket, and forced it under, and came strangling to the surface a little farther downstream. Then someone clutched at the bucket with him, and under their combined weight it sank again, and again they drifted to the surface.

Ephraim saw a face near his, a blurred face seen only dimly through his terror-blinded eyes. He felt hands clutching at his, fighting to tear the bucket away, and he shouted hoarsely:

'Let go! God damn your soul, let go!'

He pounded at that blurred face with a clawing fist. He bent his head and bit at the clutching hands. Under his blows the face disappeared and the hand he bit let go, and the other man was gone. The bucket kept Ephraim near the surface. A swirling eddy swept him shoreward and his feet touched bottom, and then his knees scraped a boulder; and hugging the bucket like life itself he scrabbled up the shingle, out of the water. He bolted away from the river into the safe and secret shelter of the woods.

III

When Ephraim came back to Bangor, it was by stage, in the silent company of big Alex Duncan, who had gone with them up the river. Alex treated Ephraim throughout that homeward journey with the gravest courtesy, but the younger man was harried by his own thoughts, and by his certain knowledge of what must be in Alex's mind.

When the second canoe overturned, Duncan and Tom Irish and the two Indians in the other craft were already far down-river, below the second run of quick water; so Duncan saw nothing that happened. But he and the others heard Ephraim's screams and knew something was amiss; and they landed and ran back up the riverbank to the scene.

The two Indians had reached the shore near the foot of the relatively quiet water between the two rapids, letting themselves go with the current instead of fighting it while they angled toward the bank; but they had looked back and seen Ephraim batter at his father's head in that fight for possession of the wooden pail which would support one man but not two; so when Duncan and the others joined them they were able to describe what had happened.

Ephraim, plunging in blind panic into the forest, had disappeared, but there was still a chance Isaiah might be saved or his body found; so the men moved down-river, scanning the surface of the water for any sign of him. They put out in the other canoe to salvage some odd bits of gear which floated soddenly; but they saw no trace of Isaiah. His drowned body must have come down through the lower rips to settle to the bottom in the quieter water there. It would drag sluggishly along the bottom for days, till the processes of decomposition brought it to the surface, perhaps miles downstream.

When they were satisfied that Isaiah was gone, they turned back to find Ephraim. He had had time to recover from stark panic, and they met him, coming down-river along the bank. The Indians whose canoe he had wrecked were quietly angry because his frightened clumsiness had marred their reputation as good canoemen; but Alex Duncan had already silenced them before they came face to face with Ephraim.

They all met him gravely. He asked where his father was, and Duncan told him the truth. Ephraim sat down wretchedly on a boulder by the shore while the others decided what should now be done. They could not all continue their journey in one canoe; so it was decided that Duncan and Ephraim and two Indians should go on in the sound craft while Tom Irish and the other two canoemen followed more slowly on foot, watching for Isaiah's body along the way.

So Duncan and Ephraim pushed on. From Mattawamkeag to Bangor they travelled by stage, and it was a little past four in the afternoon when the stage set them down at the house on Main Street.

Duncan went directly to the door, Ephraim reluctant at his heels. Jenny had seen the stage stop and she opened the door to them. She said at once, speaking to Duncan:

'Where's Mr. Poster?'

The man tugged off his cap. 'Drowned, ma'am,' he told her ruefully.

Her cheeks suddenly flamed. 'What happened?' she whispered, not looking at Ephraim.

Duncan said in slow tones: 'Why, the canoe with them in it tipped over. I was downstream, didn't see it myself. Mr. Poster here was with his father. He can tell you.'

She looked at Ephraim, then back at Alex Duncan again. 'So he's dead,' she repeated.

'Yes, ma'am, he's dead,' he said. 'We didn't find him yet. I'm sorry. We hunted all we could.'

'I'm sure you did.'

Duncan pulled on his cap again. 'Well, ma'am, that's the whole of it. If they find him, they'll let you know.'

She nodded, and he turned to walk away; but he paused when

he heard her speak, paused and turned. Ephraim, as though to hide from the naked light of day, had tried to pass her, to creep indoors. She pushed him so strongly back that he staggered and almost fell.

'You can't come into this house,' she said in even tones. 'You wretched coward — you killed your father.'

She shut the blank door in his face. Ephraim stood helpless for a moment. Duncan spat and turned and walked away, and Ephraim was left on the doorsill there alone.

V

John Evered

I

JOHN EVERED was born in the winter of 1808, in a one-room log cabin with a lean-to shed, on the ridge west of the Whitcher Swamp in what was later to become the town of Fraternity, Maine. He was the third son in a family of nine children, and the first to be born after his father moved to Maine from New Hampshire. Almost at once after his birth his father removed again, this time to Freeport; and the Freeport house was the first home John remembered.

The heart of that house was the dining room, which was also the kitchen. The great fireplace at one end, with an oven built in at the side, was armed with cranes and with a clockwork jack actuated by weights to turn the spit, and it was equipped with pothooks and kettles for baking and for boiling, and with long-legged spiders and long-handled skillets and all necessary forks and spoons. The drop-leaf table, big enough to accommodate the growing family, was except at meal times pushed back out of the way. From hooks in the beams which supported the ceiling strings of apples cut to dry were hung in the fall, and sections of squash and pumpkin; and field corn and strings of onions were suspended around the walls.

This big room — the only room in the house where in winter there was any direct heat — was the focus of the family life; and John's mother might be busy at her cooking with two or three children from the cradle to the toddling age almost underfoot. The bedrooms were cold, so no one lingered long there on a winter morning, and the first move out of bed was to dash for the hearth. John's father before breakfast and again at night read a passage from the Bible, and made a short prayer; and John, kneeling during the prayer, used to feel shivers of warm happiness run up and down his spine as he listened to his father's sonorous and majestic tones.

These prayers were not necessarily solemn. John's father and mother believed — and taught their children — that religion, which to them meant kindliness and truth and courage and cheerfulness and simple decency, was not only a part of daily life, but a fine and heartening and merry part. John's father's cheerful prayers often made them all smile happily, or even chuckle; and John came to think of God as a friendly and an understanding older brother from whom in any emergency help could be expected for the asking — or even without it. He was a little puzzled by some of the things he heard at church, for the preacher spoke more of hellfire and eternal damnation than he did of friendliness and cheerfulness and tolerance; but John's father explained that that was just the minister's way of trying to scare cowards into behaving themselves.

'Some want their religion hot and smoking,' he told his sons. 'But I'll take mine just warm enough to taste good as it goes down. There'd be more folks go to church if the preachers didn't give them religion that was too hot to swallow. A man likes a steaming cup on a cold day; but he don't want to scald the rafters out of his mouth.'

John as a boy thought his father a fine man, and he never found reason to change that opinion.

Bedrooms opened off the big dining room where they spent most of their time indoors, and each was equipped with one and sometimes two huge beds; stout wooden frames through which cords were laced, with a tick of wheat or oat straw atop and then a feather bed filled with down from their own geese. When the frame worked loose, the screws which held it at the corners could be tightened with a bed key. John as a youngster never had a bed to himself, sharing his with one and sometimes with two of his brothers.

Cornbread and salt pork, with hasty pudding and milk — or, as he grew older, crust coffee — were winter staples, with potatoes as long as they lasted. Dried apples and jams and jellies and preserves supplemented this fare. Sometimes there was a crock or even a barrel of corned beef in the cellar beside the bins of roots — parsnips, turnips, beets and potatoes — that could be cooked with it. The cabbage seldom lasted beyond late fall; and fresh beef, even though frozen, had to be eaten promptly for fear of a thaw. Alewives salted down in the spring, and haddie and cod helped load the board.

John's clothes while he was a boy were made for him by his mother, and the big spinning wheel and the little one, as well as the loom on which she wove cloth or tow, had their place in the room that was the focus of their lives. She was a strong, clean, wise and frugal woman, deeply appreciative of the luxury which her husband provided — in such matters for instance as needles, of which she had seven, in different sizes. Her mother, John's grandmother, who lived with them, often said that times had changed since her day, when she used one needle for twenty-four years. John's mother taught him to knit before he was old enough to do any serious work around the farm; and although at first she turned the heels for him, he knitted his first complete pair of socks before he was eight years old.

II

John's father kept store in Freeport, but this was not his only interest. Freeport was a shipbuilding town, with yards forever active at Mast Landing and at Porter's. When John was nine, he began to show that he had a head for figures, and he often helped his father in the store. Most of the customers were on a barter basis, and this meant keeping for each one a running account of purchases, to be balanced when the customer brought in a load of hay, or some axe helves made in spare time on a rainy day, or a hay cart piled high with lime casks to be shipped to Thomaston. John learned to manage the entries in these accounts well enough. Also, his father taught him — and all the boys — the coopering trade. 'A man can make money and then lose it,' he used to say, 'or he can buy a farm and have it go back on him, or his store can burn down. But there'll always be a market for barrels, and a man that knows how to make 'em can always get along.'

John showed an aptitude for this work; as he grew older, he graduated from chores and from the bookkeeping in the store to work in the shipyards. He was at first no more than an errand boy there; but he began to round treenails in his idle time till he acquired a skilful axe hand. So he came by degrees to do a man's work in the yard.

Out of this experience there arose in him a passion for wood. He liked the smell of it and the feel of it, liked working it with his axe to a smooth and flawless surface, liked the scuff of chips under his feet, and the smell of sawdust and the pleasant crackle of shavings. He had begun to haunt the shipyards as soon as he was old enough to wander so far from his home; and in the pauses of the work there he listened — remembering, as young children do, so much more than their elders suspect — to the talk of the men. Much of that talk dealt with the exploits of the Dash privateer, which had been built at Porter's Landing; and he was old enough to remember the anxiety and then the grief when early in 1815 she disappeared in a gale and was never heard of again. He had known, as a boy of seven knows brave young men, John and Ebenezer Porter and John Bennett who were among the Freeport men aboard her when she sailed on that fatal voyage; and he felt at their deaths a personal loss mingled with an ennobling pride.

John left Freeport when he was seventeen years old to spend a winter lumbering in the forests far up the Connecticut. His older brothers had turned in that direction, and this influenced his decision. His mother worked for weeks to supply him with the clothes she foresaw he would need; and her parting present to him was a gold ring, a duplicate of rings which she had given to each of her older sons. She was a simple woman with a simple faith, the stronger for its simplicity.

'I give my boys rings,' she told John, 'because a ring is like a family. When it's broken, it has no more strength and goodness in it. A family is just a group of people all holding hands in a circle so that each helps the other. Dan and Walter are gone — and now you're going — but wherever you are you will always be part of our family, John; and even if we do not see you for many a year, we'll be helping you and strengthening you with our prayers, just as you will be helping us.' And she added: 'You'll marry, yourself, some day. Remember to choose a woman who'll always stand hand in hand with you; and remember that even when your children come and widen the circle of your family, one of your hands will always hold on to hers. So choose a wife carefully and wisely, John. The thing I'll pray for most will be for you to marry the right, good woman.'

III

John did not see his father and mother again for three years after his departure. That first winter he worked in the woods, beginning as a swamper; but before spring he was handling an ox team. He came down-river with the drive, and left it to work all summer in a shipyard at New London before returning to the north woods again.

He had decided by that time that he wished to go to college; and he saved money with this in mind. He had worked, even in the winter, since he was twelve, so he had little formal schooling; and it was necessary now for him to ground himself in certain fields before he could hope to get the full benefit from college work. He did this by diligence, alone.

Before going to Cambridge he came home for a fortnight's stay to find that his father had prospered and was now a leading merchant in Freeport and with widening interests.

'There's a big time coming for Maine, John,' the older man told his son. 'You go on with your college. You'll be through soon enough. Things are just starting now. But there's more pine up the Kennebec and the Penobscot than you ever saw in New Hampshire; and four or five years from now folks will begin to find it out. When you're ready, you take a look up our way. I'll know more about it by then. You've got a better head for figures than any of your brothers. You and me will make a good pulling team.'

They talked long that night. John's father had gone to Bangor during the summer, had pushed on up the river to see for himself the great pine forests to the northward; and already, quietly, he was buying state lands — not only from Maine but from Massachusetts — paying one-fourth down and pledging yearly payments on the remainder. 'Some are buying stumpage or taking permits,' he explained, 'but I'm buying the lands. Time enough to start cutting when the price gets up where it ought to be. The only risk now is fire and trespassing, but the land agents are after the trespassers. I went to see Colonel Black at Ellsworth. He's agent for the Bingham heirs. He's after the trespassers all the time, seizing outfits, or logs after they're cut, so his case will stand up in court. But I've been buying mostly so far up-river the trespassers haven't got that far yet.'

John went to Harvard with his head full of his father's plans; but during his second year in Cambridge the older man died, and when John came home to help check over his affairs, it became immediately manifest that the dream was ended. The annual payments could not now be met, and there was not yet a sufficient demand to allow a ready sale of land on which only instalments had been paid. John stayed out of college for most of a year, till the tangle had been straightened out. His brother Dan came home to assume the management of the store, and only then did John return to Cambridge.

IV

The attraction which Ephraim Poster from the first exercised on John Evered was not easy to explain. Evered was older than most of his college mates, and infinitely more mature; but he was a quiet, solid young man and he lacked the easy graces which would have won him many casual friends. He first saw Ephraim when the other spoke at a meeting of students gathered to protest at some detail of college management; and Ephraim's quick and lively tongue and his shy grin, coupled as it was with an impudent and effective effrontery, seemed to Evered, who was not articulate, astonishing and wonderful. For the months that followed, he never saw Ephraim without a stir of interest. He himself was usually alone, but the other was always one of a group of good companions, and John came to attribute to Ephraim virtues which the young man was far from possessing. But he was at the same time by no means blind to young Poster's patent vices. Without being a prig, Evered was nevertheless a decent man. In the lumber camps and on the river he had seen robust and flagrant vice with no particular reprobation, instinctively understanding that for the rough and half-savage men of the forest and the stream these occasional outbursts were to be expected, were even pardonable. A man who worked twelve or sixteen hours a day all winter long, toiling like an ox, seeing no one but other men like himself, could be forgiven for finding even in the stained and wretched women of the riverfront brothels something beautiful and worthy of desire; and John himself had known such women who were largely generous and loyal and, within their limits, fine, mothering the homeless and the lonely men who came hungrily to seek them out. There was one, named Lena Tempest, who kept a boarding house where he sometimes lodged, and whom he learned even to admire.

But he could not forgive in Ephraim what he was ready to forgive in rough woodsmen; and one night at the Bell in Hand, watching the other swill gross quantities of the heavy ale, Evered felt an almost personal pain which led him to follow Ephraim and his friends when they left the tavern, and finally to capture Ephraim as much by force as by persuasion, marching him home to Cambridge.

Their friendship in the months that followed came to mean much to both of them. Evered's character was built on a solid foundation broad enough and strong enough so that Ephraim acquired from him a new sense of responsibility and self-respect and personal pride. Evered on the other hand benefited too, becoming less the recluse, less the country boy, less silent and awkward — without in the process losing any of his strength. When it came time for him to leave Cambridge, these two parted with regrets, and planned to meet again.

v

John went home to Freeport, but not for long. Of all the land to which for a while his father had held title, little remained; but there was one tract of pine on the Kennebec which had been saved, and Dan and John agreed that John should take an outfit

into the woods and lumber it off. The enterprise had an indirect
result which determined the future course of Evered's life. When
he brought his drive down-river in the spring, he joined forces
with another drive of logs owned by the Bingham heirs; and at
the boom he met Colonel Black himself.

The Colonel recognized his name, said it was unusual. 'A man
named Evered came to see me in Ellsworth a few years ago,' he
said. 'He was buying state lands, wanted to talk to me about
handling trespassers.'

'He was my father,' Evered agreed. 'He died soon after.'

'So? Well, I'm sorry to hear it,' Colonel Black declared. He was
a conspicuous figure among those who interested themselves in
Maine pine. When on the heels of the Revolution Massachusetts
found herself heavily in debt, she organized a lottery for the sale
of fifty townships of Maine lands; but the lottery was a failure.
Less than five hundred tickets were purchased, out of some twenty-
seven hundred that were issued. Among those present at the drawing was William Bingham, a wealthy Philadelphian with an eye
to the future; and taking advantage of the disappointment at the
failure of the lottery, he bought at an average price of about twelve
and a half cents an acre those lands which were not drawn by
ticket-holders, as well as several of the best lots which had been
assigned to owners of lucky tickets. His purchases included over
two million acres, about equally divided between the watersheds
of the Kennebec and the Penobscot, and made him by all odds the
largest owner of wild lands in what was to become the State of
Maine.

Upon Mr. Bingham's death, Colonel Black became the agent
for the heirs. When John Evered met him for the first time, the
Colonel was just past fifty years old, a solid, thick-set, clean-shaven
man, bald on top of his head, but with tight curly hair above his
ears and at the back. The outer ends of his upper eyelids slanted
downward and the effect was to give his eyes a soft gentleness
which made John like him at once. His mouth was wide and
humorous, but his chin and jaw were framed in stern and heavy
lines. He was individually the biggest operator on the Union
River, which ran through Ellsworth, and in his capacity as agent
he was taking advantage of the rising appetite for Maine lands to
sell some of the colossal Bingham holdings — while at the same
time he was as ready to buy land that could be had at a fair price.
In 1828 he had sold some forty thousand acres, and his sales
would mount in the next two years to over seven hundred thousand acres. In one month during this period he sold almost one

hundred thousand acres, at an average price close to the two dollar mark.

John Evered was impressed when they met, not only by what he knew of the man, but by the other's pleasant kindliness. 'I'm sorry to hear it,' the Colonel repeated. 'Your father was a good man, a right-feeling man.' He looked at Evered thoughtfully. 'You're bigger than he,' he commented.

John nodded. He was in fact just over six feet, and now after months of hard daily toil he carried not an ounce of surplus flesh. 'Yes,' he assented.

The Colonel looked toward the river full of logs. 'Whose drive is this you've brought down with ours?' he asked.

John smiled. 'Well — as old Tom Hawkes in Freeport said about the horse — if you want to attach it, I don't know; but if you want to buy it, it's mine.'

The Colonel chuckled, and he asked a dozen questions. How many teams had John operated, how many men, how long a haul, how many feet would his drive scale? John answered him explicitly; and the Colonel looked at him with a new interest. 'You've a head for figures,' he commented. 'You seem to know exactly what you're doing.'

'I kept books in my father's store when I was ten,' John assented.

The Colonel pushed his questions till there were not many things about John which he did not know. In the end he said: 'Evered, come dine with me. You say you've no immediate, definite plans. I think I can use a man like you.'

The result of that interview and of the dinner that followed it was to determine — so far as his work was concerned — the course of John's future life. Colonel Black could not personally oversee the tremendous domain he administered.

'I need help, and I think you're the man for me,' he told John. 'For one thing, I've my own business — I manufacture some lumber at Ellsworth, have some mills there and plan more, and I take a turn at shipbuilding now and then — so I need someone to take detail off my hands. You'll have a salary — we'll discuss figures later — and a chance to buy stumpage at a low fee any time you want to. That will give you a foothold in the lumber business. I know your father had a bent that way. Now, what do you say?'

So John entered the service of the Bingham heirs, entered more immediately the service of Colonel Black; and before they parted he agreed that as soon as his immediate business was done he would come to the Colonel's home in Ellsworth to begin to familiarize himself with the estate's manifold affairs.

He went to Ellsworth in mid-July, travelling from Portland on the Bangor steamer; and he remembered that Ephraim's home had been in Bangor, and wondered whether his friend was there. But he had no time on his arrival to inquire, for when he stepped on the wharf a young man met him smilingly.

'By the look of you, you're John Evered,' he said.

'Why, I am, yes.'

'I'm George Black,' the other explained. 'Father sent me to meet you.' He clasped Evered's hand and led him to where a fine pair of trotters waited, harnessed to a light, well-sprung, two-wheeled curricle. The horses were eager, and a few minutes later they crossed the Brewer Bridge and sped away along the Ellsworth road.

VI

The weeks that followed were crowded with new experiences. Not only was John busy absorbing as much as possible from the ledgers in the Colonel's big iron safe, but also he was introduced to a way of life completely new to him. Colonel Black's house was a big square brick mansion, with a wide pillared veranda across the front and a one-story wing which was the Colonel's office. The house stood on a slope above Union River with a fine prospect toward Mount Desert, and trees had been cut away to give the eye free reach in that direction. Around the house were spacious grounds, where white pine was used effectively for hedges. There was a tremendous barn and carriage house behind. George, who had met John at Bangor, at twenty was already keenly interested in trotting horses, and he had a half-mile track laid out in the pine woods near the house where he and John sometimes went to exercise the horses in the early morning before breakfast time.

The household was a large one. George and Alex who were not yet married, and Charlie who never would be, lived at home; and the married sons and daughters lived near-by, so with children and grandchildren the big house was always well filled. But there were many guests too, coming for an evening, or for a day, or for days; and late in July Judge Saladine, who was Colonel Black's attorney, arrived from Bangor for a week's stay and his daughter Margaret came with him.

So all summer the big house sang with gaiety, and every evening there was likely to be music and some dancing. John was, without in the least suspecting it, a handsome young man, thoroughly likable; and there were some charming feminine attempts to break down his defensive reserve. Margaret Saladine was the most amusing and the most persistent of his tormentors. Her mother had died when she was a baby, and she was an only child. She was, John thought, limpidly beautiful, with the freshness of a fine, sunned morning after rain; and he was tongue-tied with delight in her presence.

She insisted one evening on trying to teach him to waltz, and he who with an axe in his hand or balanced upon a log as it floated down some strong river was as graceful as a reed, found himself in her nearness so clumsy that his ears burned.

'It's perfectly simple,' she assured him smilingly. 'If only you'll forget yourself — and not be so scared of me. I won't break if you touch me, you know!' She drew his arm around her, pressed his hand more firmly against her waist. 'Now it's just one-two-three, one-two-three,' she urged. 'Only don't count! I can see your lips moving. Just feel the music, without really paying any attention to it. Around and around, that's the way.'

When he stepped on her toes and stammered abject apologies, she assured him that he had not really hurt her at all. 'You just caught the edge of my slipper,' she declared. 'Now — one-two-three, one-two-three.'

He tried, perspiring with his own effort. They revolved in the same direction endlessly, till she protested: 'Now unwind us! Go the other way, please, quick. I'm dizzy!' But when he sought to do so, he stepped on his own feet and staggered and would have fallen but for her hand supporting him; and he was astonished to find how much strength there was in her slenderness.

She labored with him long and assured him that he did finely; but he was so palpably miserable that at last she relented, and made him find her a shawl and they went out on the veranda together, and she led him to talk about himself, to tell her about his father and his mother and about his boyhood. She seemed so interested in all he told her that he forgot to be afraid. Before his second dancing lesson was finished, he was more at ease with her. She had a merry tongue, and when he realized that no one else was doing so he could laugh at himself — and so made progress.

On another evening when there was a moon she said they must go for a drive, and Mrs. Black let them use her carriage, a high box-like buggy with three steps up which he helped Miss Saladine, and so narrow that they must sit close together. They drove down the river road, and when they were away from the house she made him let her take the reins, and she sent the good horse swiftly along the moonlit way, leaning a little forward, her eyes shining, her soft hair flying in the wind. John, watching her, thought he had never seen anyone so beautiful and so jolly and fine.

Afterward she gave up the reins to him and they came more slowly homeward, letting the horse cool down, talking quietly together; and they laughed together at John's massive gravity which she alone had been able to break through.

'I had to,' she confessed. 'You were so big and forbidding-looking that I was scared — as scared as you, really! I had to persuade you to smile a little, just so I wouldn't be scared. I declare, you frightened me so I'd wake up of nights just shaking, thinking of you!' And then she laughed gleefully and touched his arm. 'There! I didn't, really,' she confessed. 'I just said that to see if you'd blush to think you'd disturbed my maidenly dreams. Your ears are so pink, John! Even in the moonlight!'

He laughed with her. 'Why does a woman always want to make a man feel foolish?' he wondered.

'She only does it if she likes him very much,' she said, and he was warmly happy at her word. When she and her father went back to Bangor, he dreamed that after he was established there they would come to be good friends.

VII

John worked with Colonel Black day by day, till in mid-September the Colonel dispatched him to Boston on a business mission. George drove him up from Ellsworth and saw him aboard the steamboat, and John went to see his luggage safe bestowed. He came on deck again as the Bangor cast off her lines to depart.

When he did so, two men were helping a third up the gangplank, and John watched them. The man in the middle was clearly drunk. He was not only drunk, but he was soiled and dirty; and his legs would not support him, and he wept loudly as the two men half-carried him aboard. They dropped him on the deck and returned ashore again, and the drunk man rolled on his back and lay there, gurgling and choking with retching sobs.

Evered recognized him. The drunken man was Ephraim Poster.

2

WHEN Evered recognized in this shamelessly drunken man his friend of college days, he stepped forward where Ephraim lay. As he did so, two deck hands lifted the man to his feet.

'Where are you taking him?' Evered asked.

'Cap'n's orders, to put him in the hold.'

John did not attempt to interfere when Ephraim was dragged away; but he went to find the Captain. Captain Barker had just been succeeded by Captain Sam Howes — a change which provoked Captain Barker's friends to lively protests. They gave him credit for arranging to have the steamboat built and put upon this run, and a committee, self-appointed to investigate his removal, resolved that he had been discharged without good cause, and as a protest recommended patronizing the packets. But in spite of this feeling, the Bangor got an increasing share of the Boston business.

Evered waited till she was on her course down-river before speaking to Captain Howes; but when the other was no longer busy getting his ship under way, John approached him and introduced himself.

'I saw a friend of mine brought aboard,' he explained. 'Young Mr. Poster. Your men said he was to be put in the hold. Would it be possible for me to make some other arrangement for him?'

'Friend of yours, is he?' the Captain echoed. He made a snorting sound suggestive of laughter. 'Reminds me of the time old Joe Patten got drunk up't Old Town. Couple of his friends as bad off as him tried to take him home across the river and he fell out of the boat. One of them started to dive in after him — Joe had sunk out of sight — but the other says: "Hold on there, Bill. Wait till he stops bubbling!"' He laughed at his own tale. 'Maybe you'd better let your friend stop bubbling before you make any arrangements.' But then he realized that John was not amused; and as Colonel Black's representative the young man commanded a respectful deference, so he said: 'I'd be glad to oblige, but every bunk's taken. The hold's the place for him, the state he's in.' He added contemptuously: 'I'd not think you'd want to bother with him, after what he's done!'

'What has he done?'

'You've not heard?'

'No, nothing.'

The Captain's eyes were watchful on the channel. He said with a certain relish, glad of a new listener for this tale which he had thought everyone must know: 'Why, he's done a-plenty if you ask me — or anyone in Bangor will say the same.' And he explained: 'First off, he stole twenty thousand dollars off of his father, and lost it gambling on timber lands — and that's a trick that takes some doing, with land prices going up five-ten cents an acre between dark and dawn, one day after another. But then when the old man found it out — they'd gone off up-river to look at some pine — young Poster drowned him!'

Evered said in an expressionless tone: 'Drowned his father?'

'Yup,' the Captain assured him. 'Or just the same as, anyway.' He added confidentially: 'Mis' Poster claims it was an accident and that he's not to blame; but that's just because she's trying to stand up for him.' And he explained: 'What happened, they was coming down-river in a canoe with two Indians paddling, and they hit a little quick water, and young Poster let on to be scared. He give out a whoop and jumped up and oversot the canoe. Then, as if that wa'n't enough, when the old man come up, young Poster pounded him over the head till he went down again. He claims he was so scared he did it not knowing.' He touched Evered's arm in a strong affirmation. 'But there ain't anybody reely as scared of water as all that, if you ask me — and any man, woman or child in Bangor'll say the same.'

'Except Mrs. Poster,' Evered reminded him. 'It's her husband who was drowned — but you say she believes it was an accident.'

'That's just the goodness in her,' Captain Howes insisted. 'She's as fine a woman as you'll find in a month of Sundays, always going to see sick folks and doing good, one way and another.' He drew John aside so that the wheelman might not hear. 'It's her that talked me into taking him to Boston,' he explained. 'There ain't a man in Bangor has got a good word for him. First off, she blamed him too; but then when she saw how he took on — he's been as drunk as he is now ever sence it happened — she tried to get him home to sober him off. He wouldn't come, so she bought his ticket to Boston and gave me a thousand dollars in bills on Boston banks to give him when he gets there, and a letter to go with it. I say it's a good thing she got him out of Bangor. There was some talk of having him arrested for murdering the old man, first off; but they never did find Isaiah's body, not yet anyway; and you can't hang a man for murder without a corpus. So it's just as well to see the last of him, if you ask me — and anyone else will say the same.'

II

Despite the Captain's ill report, and despite the crowded condition of the boat, Evered was able to arrange for a proper bed for his friend; and he himself stripped off Ephraim's soiled clothes and sent them to be washed and cleaned and hung in the boiler room to dry. Ephraim slept till late the next day, and woke still unsteady from the stale fumes of brandy in him. They had run by that time into rough weather, a rising northeaster with rain and fog and driven, tumbling seas; and the tossing of the vessel and the clamor of the half-gale filled Ephraim with remembered terror and renewed the sickness in him. When he recognized Evered, he closed his eyes and refused to speak; so it was not till they reached Boston that these two had any talk together.

Evered had assumed responsibility for the younger man, and Captain Howes before he landed delivered to John the money and the letter which Jenny had put in his hands. When they docked in Boston, Evered took his friend in charge. He was shocked and pitiful to see how Ephraim had wasted since their last meeting. The other had always been small and frail, but now he was almost emaciated, with hollow cheeks and blackly shadowed eyes. John judged that Ephraim was at the end of a long debauch; and when — the other submitting in a stupid docility to his guidance — they were lodged in the hotel Evered chose, he saw that Ephraim's hands were shaking, his lips parched. He had till this moment offered neither sympathy nor chiding; but he said now, in a forced cheerfulness:

'What you need, Eph, is a good dinner under your ribs. You've eaten nothing that stayed with you since we left Bangor. We'll eat, and then we'll go out and get you some decent clothes.' He urged good-humoredly: 'Nothing like a new suit to cure a sick man.'

Ephraim was shivering with nausea. 'I don't want food,' he said. His voice was hoarse and broken. 'It's brandy I need, John.'

'A drink won't hurt us,' Evered agreed after a doubtful moment, watching the other's shaking hands. 'Stay here and I'll fetch a bottle.'

He went down the stairs, but when he came back to the room Ephraim was gone. Evered turned without hesitation and ran down the stairs again, sure that his friend had not had time to leave the hotel· and at hazard he entered the bar. He was in time to see Ephraim toss down a quick glass there. He came to the younger man's side and laid his hand on the other's arm.

'Couldn't you wait for me?' he protested cheerfully. 'Now I'll have to drink alone.'

Ephraim's face twisted. 'Damn it, John, let me go!' he pleaded. 'I don't want to stay with you.'

Evered laughed in strong reassurance. 'You're staying, all the same, Eph,' he said. 'It's a long time since we've seen each other, and I'm not going to let you get away so easily.' He added: 'Besides, I've a thousand dollars of your money the Captain gave me to hand you.'

'My money?'

'Yes. Mrs. Poster gave it to the Captain, and a letter for you. I have them in my pocket.' He said in a friendly tone: 'But I won't give them to you till we've had a visit together.'

'Money — and a letter,' Ephraim muttered. Then he laughed, and Evered saw in a sharp astonishment that Ephraim — whose capacity for liquor had been the wonder of his college mates — was already again a little drunk. 'From her, eh?'

'We'll have dinner,' John insisted. Food was Ephraim's need. 'We'll have a good dinner and you'll feel better.'

'Better?' Ephraim echoed, and he chuckled in ironic mirth. 'Better? Why, John, I feel fine! If I felt any better, I couldn't bear it.'

Nevertheless he submitted when Evered led him away; but when food was set before them — the chowder Evered suggested, as best for an empty and tormented stomach — Ephraim looked at it with loathing and barely tasted it. John, instead of pressing him to eat, began to talk, thinking to distract the other's mind. He talked not of Ephraim but of himself; of his winter up the Kennebec, his meeting with Colonel Black, his weeks at Ellsworth. 'You'd have had a time there,' he said. 'Lots of company, and more pretty girls than you could shake a stick at. I was a bull in a china shop, didn't know which hand was which; but you'd have had them around you like flies.' He had a cheerful ability to appreciate a humorous situation, even though the joke might be at his own expense; and he painted a ludicrous picture of himself, big and silent and ill at ease in a laughing company. 'I was like an ox with a bunch of spring lambs cutting didos all around him, not knowing which way to move for fear of stepping on one of them.' But Ephraim did not smile, so he went back to his days of logging on the Connecticut, describing the hilarious rioting when one of the driving crews hit a river town; and he spoke of their years together in Cambridge. He returned at last to Colonel Black again, talking enthusiastically and eagerly, trying to win the other to forgetfulness.

'It's like managing a kingdom,' he said. 'Colonel Black thinks of townships as other men think of acres. I've found the work I want to do in the world.' He added: 'You'd better eat something, Eph. You'll feel a lot better.'

Ephraim grinned. 'Why, I feel fine, John!' he repeated. Then he said, with a dry twist to the words: 'I've been in the land business myself. Made one deal that's worth a twenty-thousand-dollar profit any time.'

'Good man!' Evered exclaimed. 'You know, Eph, I always thought you had fine capacities.'

The other's lips writhed, and he wetted them. 'Capacities?' He laughed. 'Capacities for rum and women!' There was a sudden flame of anguish in his eyes. 'Why in hell do women fall in love with me, John? I'm just a rat; a slimy, stinking, useless little rat — but they do, God damn their souls to hell!'

Evered saw in the other now a need for speech that outweighed all other appetites. 'Had all you want to eat?' he asked.

'All I want?' Ephraim laughed, and then leaned forward tensely. 'I've had all I want of the whole damned world!' he said.

Evered nodded. 'We'll go upstairs,' he decided, and paid their charge and rose. Ephraim at his elbow said:

'Bring the brandy along.' He chuckled mirthlessly. 'Lend me your ears, John; and I will a tale unfold.'

III

The two young men talked together for long hours that night, or rather Ephraim talked and John listened; and though John drank little, the level in the brandy bottle steadily sank lower. At first Evered tried to check Ephraim's steady guzzling; but the other shook his head.

'It's no use, John,' he said. 'I'm finished. You can't help me now. If you try to stop me, sooner or later I'll get away from you. Be reasonable and I'll let you watch me go on over the edge.'

So Evered did not again interfere; and Ephraim told his friend the story of the year just gone, alternating between wretched bewailing of his own weakness and fierce accusations of Jenny.

'It was my own fault for going home at all,' he said. 'Father didn't want me to. He must have known all the time what she'd do to me.

You remember I told you, John, about that likeness Mr. Hardy made of her, and how it scared me? I was right to be scared, John; but I wasn't scared enough — or wise enough. And I remembered how beautiful she was, so I went home.'

He looked at John keenly. 'But you've probably heard the whole story?' he said suspiciously. 'How I killed my father? Have you?'

John gravely shook his head. This wreck of a man needed the ease of speech, the mercy of confession.

'God damn you, don't lie to me!' Ephraim cried. 'Somebody's sure to have told you.'

But John said steadily: 'Go on and tell me, Eph. If you want to.'

'Oh, I want to, all right,' Ephraim assured him. 'One reason, I just want to show you what a damned fool you are to think there's any good in me.' He began, absurdly, to cry, wringing his hands, tears streaming down his face, a small, emaciated, twisting wreck of a man like a worm on a hook.

'I'll always think there's good in you,' John insisted. 'Tell me, Eph.'

So Ephraim told him. He tried in floundering ways to describe how little by little Jenny had provoked in him a passion beyond controlling. 'And she did it on purpose!' he cried. 'God damn her whore's soul to hell — she meant to do it, whispering that if I hadn't gone away to college she would have married me, kissing me!' He leaned forward tautly, speaking in a low tone, and he told the tale of that night when the mob tore down Ma Hogan's house, and how Jenny kissed him at the end. 'Maybe that doesn't sound like much to you,' he confessed. 'Maybe you think I was crazy to think so much about it. I've had plenty of kisses — yes, and liked them too; but I didn't like that one! No sir!' He filled his glass again, swallowed a burning draft. 'It was awful, John. It was like drinking hellfire!'

And he said: 'After that I decided to go away, but she wouldn't let me go.' He hesitated, as though for the first time ashamed of his own words. 'There was a hired girl worked for us, slept in the attic. Her name was Ruth Green. I used to go up to her room at night when Jenny'd left me crazy. Ruth was a nice girl. I hoped I'd get her in a family way so I'd have to marry her; but I never did.' He said abjectly: 'Maybe I'm not man enough. I wasn't man enough to marry her without being made to, anyway.'

Evered offered no comment, wondering how he could help this lost man he loved.

'Then father got sick,' Ephraim explained. 'And I hoped he'd die — and so did she. She told me one night she'd marry me if he died.' He shuddered helplessly. 'She kissed me again and told me so, and when she kissed me I felt as if someone had hit me across the mouth with a red-hot poker. But father got well, and after that for a long time I kept away from her.' He said shrewdly: 'Up to then, John, she was in love with me. I know that. You can't fool me about that. But after that, I can see now, she hated me. She tried to get me to sleep with her, tried every way she knew; but she hated me all the same.

'And she fixed it so I had the handling of some of father's money, and she talked me into buying a bond with it, on a township way up in the woods. When father found that out, he called me a thief; but the way he found it out, someone wanted to buy it, offered him a profit on it. So he went up-river to look it over, and he took me along.'

He stared blankly at the big man, lost for a moment in his own thoughts. 'You might as well know the whole of it,' he said then. 'The night before we were due to start, she made love to me till I was crazy, trying to get me to take her. I didn't. I never did, John; not when I knew it. I'm no good. There's no backbone in me. But I wouldn't sleep with my father's wife! Not if I knew it!

'But that night I went up to Ruth's room, in the dark. She was Jenny's size, like her in a lot of ways. And we didn't talk at all. And when it came daylight, Jenny was there in bed with me. She'd sent Ruth home and taken her place, in the dark, before I went up there.'

Evered said no word, but he thought grimly that Ephraim must be lying; for the word he said was incredible — or seemed to be. Such a woman as this drunk man described was outside the range of Evered's experience. She had no relation to reality.

Ephraim saw the doubt in the other's eyes; for he said quickly: 'You think I'm drunk. Well, I'm drunk all right, and I'll drunker soon, and I hope I'll be drunk till I die and I hope that won't be long. But she was there, John. She was there when I woke up, there in bed with me.

'And she told me if I didn't kill my father while we were up in the woods, she'd tell him when he came home that I'd been with her.' He saw Evered's face stiffen in a sort of pain and he cried: 'You don't believe that, either; but it's God's truth! She'd hinted at it before, John, as good as asking me to kill him. Her name used to be Hager, and her father came from over Augusta way; and a man named Hager killed his wife over there this summer. Probably he was her father's brother or something. Murder runs in the family! It's God's truth, John. She tried to get me to kill my father!'

Evered met the other's inflamed and twitching eyes, fastened on him, begging to be believed; and he could not face them. He poured brandy in his empty glass, gulped a swallow.

'But I didn't kill him!' Ephraim cried, in a desperate appeal. 'Or at least I didn't mean to!' He said shamedly: 'I've always been scared of the water, John, even when I was a boy. I almost drowned once, and that made it worse. I was scared in the canoe on that trip — and I couldn't sleep anyway, or eat, for thinking of her. I was half crazy! Coming down-river, we tried to run a rapids and the canoe tipped over. They say I stood up in it. I don't remember. But I remembered being in the water, with a flour bucket holding me up, and father grabbed it, and I fought him for it, John. I didn't know who he was. I was crazy! But I beat him off till he let go and sank and drowned.' His eyes suddenly dilated. 'They've never even found his body!' he cried, like a scream, so loudly that Evered caught at him to silence him; and at that touch upon his arm Ephraim began to laugh through streaming tears, bowing forward till, his head buried in his arms and as though there were no strength left in him, he tipped forward out of the chair, his head thumping on the floor, and lay there shaking with terrible laughter and with helpless sobs.

IV

John did not sleep that night. He put Ephraim to bed, and the younger man, drugged as much by weariness as by drink, and purged and somehow eased by the flood of talk that had poured out of him, appeared at once to sleep. Evered sat by the table, thinking of what he had heard, trying to persuade himself that Ephraim spoke true. His mind did not altogether believe; but his heart did. In the wretched man's abject babbling there had been the ring of truth. He tried to imagine such a woman as Ephraim described, who could mask the blackest villainy behind a lovely countenance; but it was impossible for him to bring her to life in his thoughts. His mother, whom alone among womankind he had known well and long, was all goodness and serenity and strength; and not pain but peace dwelt in her. The girls he had known as a boy in Freeport were healthy, forthright country damsels whom he might kiss at a husking, blushing as hotly as they; but there were no dark depths in them. The woman to whom in river towns other men turned had never seemed to him so much vicious as unfortunate or easily affectionate or perhaps maternal. He had seen their gentleness in tending hurt men as well as their loud readiness for casual and mercenary embraces. Nothing in his experience prepared him to comprehend such a woman as this.

He thought Ephraim spoke what he meant for truth; but he knew well enough the depravity of which the other man was capable. A man saw in the world the things he looked for, and his every impression of life, of men or of women, was tainted and tinted by something within himself. To the pure all things were pure. Perhaps it was equally true that to the vile all things were vile. Ephraim had told him once, long ago, that he saw a wanton in every pretty woman he met. Was it not conceivable that Ephraim had seen in his father's wife what was not there at all?

Thinking of her, he remembered at last that he had her letter to Ephraim in his pocket, with the money Captain Howes had given him to deliver to the younger man. He drew the letter out and studied it. It was addressed to Ephraim in care of Captain Howes, in a neat, small hand, precisely legible, strong and controlled; and it was closed with a bit of crimson wax that bore the imprint of a seal in which the figure of a beaver gnawing at the slender trunk of a small tree had been deeply cut. But beyond these superficial indications it told John nothing. He wished to open it and read it, wished to scan the lines, to see what manner of words would be used and what message would be inscribed by such a woman as Ephraim had described.

He laid it on the table within reach of his hand, staring at it with unseeing eyes, looking from it to Ephraim snoring on the bed. It was hard for him to feel for the other now anything except a profound abhorrence; yet he mustered pity, too. Certainly life had bludgeoned that small, wasted man. A better than Ephraim might have been shattered by so many and such dreadful blows; but a friend if he were wise might help Ephraim back to strength and healthy sanity again, and Evered in his thoughts undertook the task, tried to plan what for the other's sake he might best do.

When the tall candle burned low, Evered snuffed it and sat in darkness for a while till day came in the windows. He did not stir until sunlight touched the room. Then he picked up the letter again. At the same time the sudden brightness roused Ephraim, and he grunted and opened his eyes. He blinked sleepily and tried to rise, and then lay back again and spoke steadily enough.

'Didn't you go to bed?'

'No. I sat here thinking.'

Ephraim saw the letter in John's hand. 'What's that?' he asked.

'The letter from Mrs. Poster, for you.' Evered rose to take it to the other man.

Ephraim did not move when John extended the letter. 'Read it,' he directed. 'Read it. See what she says.'

v

Dear Ephraim —

I have been sadly troubled with concern for you since you came home, and I have wanted to make my peace with you, without knowing how. The day you came to the door, my great grief for my husband made me unfair to you. I have regretted, every minute since, what I said to you — that you had killed your father — before I closed the door against you and went weeping to my room. Why did you not come in, Ephraim? Then, if ever, you needed understanding and charity and kindliness; and this is your home. Here above every place else in the world you could expect to find refuge.

Even before my tears had ceased to flow — for you know that though your father was an old man he had been always gentle and kind to me and I loved him well and grieved to know that he was gone — I sent Mrs. Hollis to call you to come to me; but you had gone. Since then I have asked Elder Pittridge to bring you to me; but he found you sodden with drink in the lowest taverns in the town, and when he wished to help you find yourself, you always rebuffed him.

I have not known what to do except to pray that when your grief passes you will come back to sanity again, and be once more the fine man of whom your father was so proud. You have had my prayers every day, Ephraim.

Elder Pittridge — I put much faith in his judgment — thinks you can never recapture your self-respect here in Bangor where every one blames you so unfairly for your father's death. I grieve sometimes to think that my hurt, angry word the day you came home has set the tune they sing. Elder Pittridge thinks you will be better if you go away for a while, and Deacon Adams, whom I have consulted, agrees with him.

So I have asked Elder Pittridge and Pat Tierney to see you aboard the Bangor when she sails today, and to put you in charge of Captain Howes, and to ask the Captain to give you when you land in Boston this my letter and also a little sum of money for your immediate expenses.

I must tell you, Ephraim, that your father treated you most unfairly in his testament. It was made while you were still in college, before you came home and won his love and trust by your industry and your devotion. He drew another will after his illness, and showed it to me. In that he provided well for you, arranging that you should manage his affairs and have a handsome income. I know he meant to go to Judge Saladine and execute it, but you know how sensitive he was about his deafness, so that he hesitated to talk business; and he must have put it off from day to day. I have not found it among his papers, so I can only think that he may have destroyed it in his anger at you, the day we took the trip to Castine and Belfast on the Bangor, when he learned that you had used his money to buy that bond.

So the old will, Judge Saladine says, must stand. In that he bequeathed to you and to each of his other sons the sum of one thousand dollars, saying that he started life with a thousandth part of that and that you should all be grateful and well pleased. But so far as you are concerned, Ephraim, I want you to know that I shall carry out the terms of the will he wrote and showed to me. If you will come home, in your own good time, the work he designed for you to do will be waiting for your hands. Until you do, your income — the income he planned for you to have — will be yours; and you can draw on Mr. Richardson's bank up to two thousand dollars a year.

Remember too that this is your home. You have a battle to fight, Ephraim; and I pray that God will give you strength to win it. Your victory can never be complete until you take and maintain your rightful place here in Bangor. Pray for strength and courage, Ephraim. You are young, with a long, fine life ahead of you, and by strength you can make the world forget all that is past.

You will have my prayers to help you. You were my husband's son, so I sign myself,

Your affectionate mother,
JENNY POSTER

VI

When John Evered began to read this letter aloud, standing near the window, Ephraim was still in bed; but almost at once he moved, rising first on one elbow, then sitting up on the edge of the bed, finally coming to his feet. Evered did not mark these movements. He continued to read, his eyes following the neatly written lines; and from the letter in his hands a sort of warmth seemed to emanate, not physical but of the spirit. Each word was so packed with gentleness and kindly strength and wise counsel and good comforting! This was, he thought, the sort of letter his own mother might under the same circumstances have written to him — except, knowing her inarticulate simplicity, he knew that such a letter would have been beyond her powers. Yet these were the things his mother would have wished to say to him if he — like Ephraim — had lost himself in cowardice and in folly.

So as he read he forgot Ephraim — and he forgot the things the other had told him — and he felt himself close to the writer of the letter in his hands, hearing her quiet words. But while he read, Ephraim crossed to the table. He stood there a moment listening, and his face twisted and became contorted with a sort of pain. The brandy bottle was under his hand, not quite empty. He lifted it to his mouth and let the scalding liquor run down his parched dry throat; and when the bottle was empty he looked at it stupidly, as though unwilling to believe the liquor in it was gone.

Then Evered finished the letter and turned to look at him; and Ephraim made a terrible sound like a gasping howl of inarticulate and insane rage. He threw the bottle with all his might blindly across the room. It struck the wall and did not break, dropped to the floor, rolled two or three feet till it collided with the leg of a chair and spun half around and rolled back an inch or two and oscillated slightly and lay still. Ephraim stared at it, and then he leaped toward it. He kicked it with his bare foot, heedless of pain, and the bottle went spinning under the bed to hit the baseboard on the other side. At the same time he burst into a flood of foul and sickening obscenity, sifting out of the dark recesses of his mind the most hideous words he could remember, pouring them out in a steaming, slimy stream till John, shocked at first into passivity, strode toward him and caught him and shook the frail little man into gasping silence; and Ephraim, his stomach revolting at the raw liquor he had poured into it, suddenly ejected it all, bending over John's arm, hanging there like a rag, vomiting upon the floor.

John held him tenderly. 'Steady, Eph,' he said. 'Easy. You'll feel better now.'

Ephraim coughed his throat clear. He spat stringily and spat again, and straightened weakly and faced Evered, his eyes blind with tears. 'Oh, she's such a whore, John!' he said hoarsely. 'I can't help it. She's such a whore! I told you what she did, wanting me to sleep with her, tricking me into it, trying to make me kill my father. And then she writes a letter like that. Probably she read it to Deacon Adams so he'd know how good she was! John, she's not human! She's not even a human being!' He took the letter, still in Evered's hand, and stared at it, turning it over and over. He dropped it, rubbing his hands together as though they had been scorched by contact with the paper on which it was written. He backed away from it warily.

John found himself full of a great compassion for Ephraim's

torment, so manifest in shaking hands and trembling limbs and writhing lips and staring eyes. He quieted the little man, led him to the bed, made him sit down and then lie down; and Ephraim turned on his face and began to cry like a small baby, to whom every woe is absolute and overwhelming. He wept aloud, with long, shuddering wails; he cried gaspingly:

'Oh, John, I tried so damned hard to behave right! I tried to come away. I tried so hard to be good!'

VII

For a long time Evered sat beside the bed till Ephraim from simple exhaustion slept again. John's hand was gentle on the other's small thin shoulder, feeling how the flesh was wasted away, the poor bones so near the skin; and while he sat there, his lips compressed in a firm line. There was no longer any incredulity in him. He might have doubted all the other said, but now he had seen the scars, the unhealed wounds which that woman had left on Ephraim's naked soul; and they were eloquent and could not be denied.

Ephraim slept, and that was mercy. John had, he remembered, business of his own to do; and he decided he might safely leave Ephraim here for an hour or two alone. But while he was preparing to depart, the other roused and lay watching him and said at last:

'Are you going, John?'

'Oh, awake are you?' Evered made his tone as matter-of-fact as possible. 'Yes, but I'll meet you here in a couple of hours.' He hesitated, said then: 'You'll want to get yourself some clothes. I've your money here.' He laid it on the table.

'Yes, that's right,' Ephraim agreed. 'I'll need some clothes.'

'We'll make plans later,' Evered said. 'I have some work in mind that you can do. I'll need your help. Go back to sleep if you can; but I'll be here in two hours at the longest.'

'I'll be here,' the other assented. He said, grinning that wry and curiously pleasing grin which Evered remembered: 'Don't worry about me, John.'

'Of course not. You'll be fine.' Evered came to touch the other's shoulder affectionately. 'Don't try to dodge me, Eph.'

'Who, me?' Ephraim protested, in the familiar, curiously boyish phrase. 'Gee, no! I'll be here when you come back.'

But when John returned, two hours later, Ephraim, and the money, and Jenny's letter, were gone.

3

John never saw Ephraim again. When he returned to the hotel
and found the other gone, his inquiries led nowhere. He spent a
week in Boston, then went to Freeport to see his mother, and afterward met Colonel Black in Augusta where the Colonel was pre-
senting applications for four townships of state lands which he
wished to buy. John had expected they would return from there
to Ellsworth; but Mrs. Black had decided on a Boston winter, and
they went back to find a suitable house and to see her and the
younger boys settled there. It was November before, bound for Ellsworth, they returned to Bangor again.

They arrived in early afternoon, and since the drive to Ellsworth was a long one, they stayed overnight, and Colonel Black
drove John here and there about the city. They saw a hectic
activity everywhere; knots of excited men on every street corner,
new buildings rising on every street. They stopped to inspect the
new Bangor House, now approaching completion. There were
drawing rooms and sitting rooms and special bathing rooms; and
the great kitchen, Manager Wood assured them, was as well
equipped as the kitchen in the White House. He said the hotel
would be opened on Christmas Day with a grand banquet for
every lady and gentleman in town, and urged them both to attend.

The Colonel could not. 'I'll be in Boston,' he said. 'But John
here will represent us.' John promised to do so.

The Colonel took John to call on business acquaintances, and he
left invitations for three who were not in their offices — General
Veazie and Rufus Dwinel and Amos Roberts — to sup with them.

'They're men you'll come to know, and you'll be doing business
with them,' he told John. 'General Veazie already owns most of
the saws at Old Town, and buys every mill that comes up for sale.
Rufe Dwinel's just finished building six double mills at West Great
Works. Matter of fact, I've got some money of my own in that
venture with him, but no one knows it except Rufe and me. Roberts only came to Bangor three years ago; but I'll pick him to be
one of the biggest operators on the river in ten years. He's a sound
man. He's a director of the Mercantile Bank, and I'm thinking

of backing him in starting a new bank. See what you think of them.'

John had hoped he and the Colonel might call on Judge Saladine, perhaps at his home, and thus see Margaret; and also as they drove here and there he scanned every woman they met, thinking always that they might encounter Mrs. Poster, who if Ephraim told the truth hid behind a lovely mask evil unspeakable. But they neither went to Judge Saladine's house nor met Jenny before they returned at last to the Exchange to await their guests.

The three gentlemen arrived together, and the Colonel told them heartily: 'John here is one of my young men. Just now I'm educating him, so he's on the move most of the time; but he'll be making Bangor his headquarters, beginning next year.' He warned John laughingly: 'Don't ever let the General find out we own any mill property, or he'll try to buy it — and steal it if he has to! Rufe Dwinel is honest enough, but he's as contentious as two cats in a bag. Amos Roberts here, he doesn't say much, but what he says most generally turns out to be true.'

Judge Saladine joined them for supper, and John hoped there might be a chance to ask for Miss Saladine; but at table where they sat long the talk was all man talk. John, watching these men whom he met that day for the first time, was particularly taken by Mr. Dwinel. Dwinel was not much older than John himself, and John thought him remarkably handsome, yet in a thoroughly masculine way. His eye was large and bright and keen, but hard and steady and with no mirth in it to match the quizzical line at the corner of his mouth. His hair was dark and naturally a little curly; and he wore a luxuriant side whisker in front of each ear which descended to cover the angle of his jawbone in a fashion which John thought admiringly he might some day imitate. Dwinel had a violent temper, but tonight nothing occurred to rouse it and he was genial and pleasant even to General Veazie whose loud voice and dogmatic pronouncements might sometimes strike sparks from the mildest man. Amos Roberts was the quietest of the three. He was taller even than John, with an impressive dignity.

General Veazie told them, with a booming chuckle in his voice, about his recent break with his former associate, Mr. Wadleigh. 'He and Purinton bought the Indian interest in Shad and Pine Islands last year,' he said. 'They've put in six saws — and they've grabbed three of my mills, claim they're on their land. But I'll lick 'em if I have to go to the Supreme Court to do it.'

Judge Saladine said in dry amusement: 'Colonel, I wish you liked a lawsuit as well as Sam does. He's a lawyer's idea of a perfect client.' And he told General Veazie: 'You'll have some hard doing in that suit, with Indians for witnesses. They won't stand without hitching.'

Rufe Dwinel suggested in a dry tone: 'Better get Bob Wyman on your side, Sam. He'd rather testify than eat; bragged after the last term of court that he'd been a witness in fourteen cases and only lost one of them!'

They laughed together, and Judge Saladine said: 'A good witness can win your case for you, Sam. I was charging a jury the other day and I said: "Now if the testimony of this witness was so and so, you will decide for the defendant," and the witness jumped up and yelled: "Why, Judge, that's just what I said, to a shaving!" After that, plaintiff didn't have a chance!'

General Veazie chuckled with the rest. 'But I never go to court unless I know I have the law on my side,' he said, and Judge Saladine smiled.

'That's all right if your opponent knew the law,' he suggested. 'Bert Jewett was prosecuting a fellow the other day for an outrage on a girl up in Orono. Moody was for the defense, and he argued that because the girl made no outcry, the jury must infer consent; produced an armful of law books to show that was the common-law rule. But when Bert came to that, he shouted at the jury: "I ask you, gentlemen, what did this girl know about the law? She never read these law books. She was just a poor, ignorant country girl. But, by God, gentlemen, if she had known what the law was she'd have yelled loud enough to be heard ten miles off!" And he got his conviction, too!'

The tales after that came thick and fast, and the good wine went around till John's eyes began to blur; but when Colonel Black called for a fourth bottle, Rufe Dwinel rose. 'Thank you, Colonel, no,' he said. 'I know my limitations.' The others came to their feet to say good night; and General Veazie said frankly:

'I sometimes have regrets in the morning myself, Rufe; but I'm never wise enough to foresee them the night before.'

John remembered a tale his father had used to tell. 'There was an old ship's carpenter in Freeport,' he said, 'used to take too much and feel bad afterward; but he couldn't leave it alone. One morning he was feeling particularly low in his mind, after a rough night, and he said to his wife: "By the Great Jehovah, Mary, I'm never going to touch another drop of rum as long as I live!" But then before she could say how glad she was, he realized that he'd taken in a good deal of territory, and he added one word: "Probably!"'

Everyone laughed, and John had a fine certainty that he had contributed something to the amusement of these men so much older in wisdom than himself. When the guests were gone, Colonel Black clapped him on the shoulder in full approval.

'Well, John, you're all right!' he said. 'You'll get along. Now we'll go to bed!'

II

They were up early for the long drive to Ellsworth. Colonel Black, as a matter of routine, went to Philadelphia on the first of January every year, to make a report to the Bingham heirs; and for that mission there was a mass of papers to be put in order, of summaries to be prepared. On John's earlier visit, the house in Ellsworth had been full of the family and of guests; but now November was bleak across the land, and John and the Colonel had the place to themselves. They worked together all day long, but toward the middle of the month Judge Saladine came down for a day or two of business talk; and at the first opportunity John ventured to ask for his daughter.

'Meg's in Washington,' the Judge told him. 'Visiting some friends. I'm meeting her in New York after I go to Philadelphia with the Colonel.' He added courteously: 'If you're in New York at that time, I'm sure she'd be pleased to have you call. She's spoken of you often since last summer.'

John, red with pleasure at this, promised to see them in New York, as the Judge suggested.

At dinner that day, Judge Saladine spoke of Isaiah Poster's death, said his body had never been found; and John saw that he and the Colonel had known Isaiah. 'I knew his son at Harvard,' he remarked. 'But I never met him — or Mrs. Poster.'

'She's a fine young woman,' Judge Saladine assured him. 'She made Isaiah a good wife.' He added gravely: 'Your friend, Isaiah's son, turned out rather badly, but she stands up for him. He was cut off, you know — I drew Isaiah's will — but she insists on providing for him.'

'I've heard Ephraim speak of her,' John assented, and said no more, trying to reconcile what Ephraim had told him with Judge Saladine's opinion.

He had another report of her — and he had news of Ephraim — a few weeks later. Early in December Colonel Black departed, with instructions to John to join him in New York as near the first of the year as possible. Left alone in the big house except for the servants, Evered was busy with his ledgers till a day or two before Christmas. The river closed on December 9, so he made arrangements to go to Thomaston overland and sail from there on the schooner Mary Ann, which would carry a load of lime to New York and which he was promised would wait for him.

He came to Bangor Christmas Day, stopping overnight for the formal opening banquet of the Bangor House. The banquet was an impressive affair, with Mr. Wood playing host to a brilliant company of ladies and gentlemen. John had thought it possible Mrs. Poster might be among them; and he had a lively curiosity to see her, but she was not at the banquet. He met, however, Mr. Richardson, cashier of the Commercial Bank; and he remembered that Ephraim was authorized to draw on that institution.

'By the way,' he said, 'I've lost contact with my old friend Ephraim Poster. I believe he banks with you. Can you tell me where he is?'

Mr. Richardson, he thought, hesitated for a moment; but he said then: 'In New York, I should say. He drew on us for funds a week ago.'

'I'd be obliged for his address,' John explained. 'I shall be in New York a week hence, and I can look him up.'

Mr. Richardson promised to send the address by messenger in the morning, and Evered asked one more question. 'Is Mrs. Poster among the ladies present this evening?'

The other shook his head. 'No, she goes nowhere — to no social gatherings — since her husband died.' He added, smiling slightly, for wines had flowed freely at the banquet: 'And her views on temperance are so strong she would hardly appear here in any case!'

'I haven't met her,' Evered explained. 'But of course I've heard much of her from Ephraim.'

'She's an admirable young lady,' the other told him with obvious sincerity. 'She's had more than her share of troubles and has borne them well.'

Evered hesitated, thinking of a hundred questions he wished to ask; but clearly Mr. Richardson had no slightest suspicion of that side of Jenny which Ephraim had described. So John said no more.

III

When Evered reached Thomaston, he went by prearrangement to the Georges Hotel. Captain Obed Manter of the Mary Ann had appointed to meet him there. Cap'n Manter was a little old man with a bald head which he kept covered with a tremendous coonskin hat, indoors and out; and when Evered first saw him he was in the midst of a violent argument with another man as old or older than he.

'Dad rot it, Willie!' he cried in a shrill rage. 'I told you to stay aboard her and get the hatches on! You know, well as I do, I plain had to come back here to pick up my passengers, and to see that man about going mate. Doggone George Hedge anyway, getting sick and us all ready to sail!'

'George ain't no sicker'n I be,' Willie retorted. They scolded each other in high, cracked voices. 'But he always did say he wouldn't ship on a hen frigate. Sence when did the Mary Ann turn into a passenger packet? A man's bad enough, but why in tarnation did you have to take a woman too?'

'That's my business,' Cap'n Obed told him, louder than ever. 'If I want to carry a woman, I guess't I can, and take no sarse from George Hedge, or any damned cook either!'

John Evered, smiling at their heat, approached them. 'You must be Cap'n Manter of the Mary Ann schooner,' he said. 'I'm Mr. Evered, your passenger.'

The two old men instantly were silenced. Cap'n Obed extended a limp, horny hand, and Evered grasped it, and the Captain said: 'Pleased to make your acquaintance. This is Willie Small, be'n going cook for me for thirty years.' Evered took Willie's gnarled, heavy hand, lifeless and unresponding, and Cap'n Manter explained: 'We worked the Mary Ann around to the shore village to load her, to keep clear of the ice that makes in the river here. We'll drive over first thing in the morning, before day.' He added: 'You make yourself t'home here. I'll see to't you're rousted out. I won't go off without you.'

Evered nodded and turned away. He saw Cap'n Obed dismiss old Willie Small with a restrained violence, and later, after he had gone up to his room and come down again, he saw the Captain in talk with another man, taller than Evered himself, big enough to make two of Cap'n Manter; and this man's voice was so loud that everyone in the common room heard what he said. He told Cap'n Manter his name was Brock. He was a New Londoner who had quit his berth on the Eliza schooner when she docked at Searsport, and now looked for a chance to work his passage home. Cap'n Obed asked him cautiously:

'What was the matter with the berth you had?'

'Couldn't hit it off with Cap'n Horne.' Brock told him in a cheerful tone. 'He was too careful to suit me.

'Well, I aim t'be keerful myself, as keerful as there's any need,' Cap'n Obed admitted. 'Know the courses around the Cape and Nantucket, do ye?'

'Like that!' Brock assured him, pointing to the palm of his hand.

'Well, I guess't you'll do, then,' Cap'n Obed decided. 'I ain't be'n beyond Boston in ten years, but I'm going to N'York this v'y'ge.'

His word made Evered remember with a quick pleasure that he too was going to New York, and that Margaret Saladine would be there. He had not forgotten her, nor any moment of their hours together; and he looked forward to seeing her again.

He found that he had an hour to spare before supper would be ready, and went out to stroll around the town. The state prison had been built ten years before, had been enlarged since then; and John looked curiously at its massive granite buildings. He saw a woman coming toward him in the dusk, and she stopped to stare at the prison. She wore over her small bonnet a heavy black veil, so nearly opaque that in the failing light he could see nothing of her countenance; but he was struck by the rigidity of her posture. She looked at the grim stone structure without a movement, as though her glance could pierce its walls. He was so impressed by this that after he had passed he looked back at her again, wondering why the prison should fascinate her so. Perhaps someone she knew was there immured.

When he returned to the tavern, Captain Copeland greeted him. John Copeland had built the Georges Hotel, on Prison Corner, at the time the prison was building, and of brick which he himself manufactured. He was a vigorous and enterprising man, combining a stage business and the responsibility of carrying the mail with his activities as tavern-keeper. To Evered as a representative of Colonel Black he was anxious to pay every courtesy and attention; and John had to assure him that his quarters were comfortable, his accommodations satisfactory.

'I walked past the prison,' he said. 'It's a gloomy-looking place.'

'And well it might be,' Cap'n Copeland agreed. 'And a miserable place for them in it. There's talk of making it over so it won't be so bitter hard on them. Now the prisoners every night have to be lowered down through a hole in the floor to cells no better than receiving tombs; no air, and damp, and cold. I don't hold with law-breaking myself, but a man had better be hung right off than treated so.'

John agreed that a more humane lodging for the guilty should be found. When he went in to supper, the veiled woman was seated near him. She raised her veil to eat and he saw a pale, still countenance of an extraordinary purity, like that of a girl in her teens, and of a beauty which—if it were more animated—would be striking. She did not raise her eyes during the meal, and when she was done she lowered her veil and left the room; but he found himself thinking about her after she was gone.

Cap'n Copeland knocked on his door at an unearthly hour to say it was time to be stirring; and the proprietor himself served the hot and hearty breakfast. Cap'n Manter and Mr. Brock appeared to join Evered at table; and later John and Mr. Brock were waiting by the capacious coach set on runners which the innkeeper had brought around from the stables, and which he himself would drive, when Cap'n Manter appeared. He was escorting a lady, the veiled lady whom Evered had seen by the prison the night before; and the old man said awkwardly:

'Mis' Poster, this is our passenger, Mr. Evered. And this is Mr. Brock, my mate.' He may have been conscious of the sudden alertness in Evered and in her at his word of introduction, for he looked from one to the other doubtfully. They bowed without speaking, and Mr. Brock said:

'Pleased, ma'am!'

Cap'n Obed said briskly: 'Well, we might as well get started.' He handed Jenny into the coach and the others followed. He and the mate faced backward. Evered and Jenny sat facing forward, side by side; and Evered's every muscle was tensely conscious that this woman whose sleeve touched his shoulder was the monster Ephraim had described.

4

It was already dark when they set out to drive to East Thomaston. For the first mile Cap'n Obed was talkative, and Mr. Brock now and then addressed a tentative remark to Jenny; but she answered him only by nods, spoke not at all. Evered, beside her, said nothing except when the Captain or Mr. Brock seemed to demand an answer; and presently they all became silent, the Captain and Mr. Brock surrendering to the oppressive silence of the others.

Evered during that drive was acutely aware of the woman by his side. He had thought her at supper last night comely enough, but he forgot that now, seeing her through Ephraim's eyes as of a deadly loveliness and wearing a beauty behind which lurked evil in its most treacherous and dreadful forms. Remembering Ephraim, he abhorred her, and his own present nearness to her, as a man abhors the snake which he sees writhing on the ground. He hated her with a sick loathing, so that it was hard for him to sit quietly.

In the seat facing them, Cap'n Obed and the mate huddled in a silent fortitude, enduring the bitter cold which stiffened their muscles and slowed the blood in their veins. Darkness bestowed upon each one of them a protecting solitude. To Evered's eyes his companions in the coach were indistinct and stiffly lurching shadows, while outside in the still starlight the snow-mottled spruce forests and the open farm lands glided slowly by.

When they arrived at the wharf, the Mary Ann was tied up to receive them, and once on her decks Cap'n Manter said briskly: 'Lively, now! Looks like snow to me. We'll get the hatch covers on and battened down.' Mr. Brock protested that daylight would be time enough for that, but Cap'n Obed said: 'No, I won't rest easy till she's snug. Carrying lime the way we are, you can't resk letting it get wet or it'll set us afire.'

Jenny had gone at once below, but Evered, to avoid her near proximity, stayed on deck awhile. The Mary Ann was a decrepit old craft, all cargo space amidships, with a narrow forecastle where two men slept, and a deck house aft from which a companion ladder descended into the cabin. This cabin was no more than a wide corridor running crosswise of the vessel, with a galley on the port side forward where Willie not only performed his functions as a cook but slept, and a small cabin beside it which Cap'n Obed and Mr. Brock would share. Aft were two other cabins; and the larger, to starboard, would be Mrs. Poster's while Evered took the other.

'We're kind of cramped,' Cap'n Obed confessed when Evered at last came below — relieved to find that Jenny was not visible. 'I don't most gen'ally figger to carry any passengers — nor to go all the way to N'York either — but Mis' Poster was dead set I sh'd carry her to N'York, and she's paying me so much I couldn't afford not to take it.'

Evered said quietly: 'I hope she doesn't object to my presence aboard.'

'No, she don't,' Cap'n Obed assured him. 'I ast her, writ her a letter when I got yours — she'd already made her dicker with me — and she said I could take you well as not, if there was room;

said she'd be glad to have any friend of Colonel Black's for a ship-mate.'

So she had known his name beforehand; but he reminded himself that Ephraim might never have mentioned him to her. He went on deck again as they got under way, dawn just breaking. The Mary Ann carried two stumpy masts, with no topmasts; so they had only to handle main and foresail and the jibs. Mr. Brock and Willie gave a hand when the work required it. The crew consisted of the three men aft, and a thin, gangling boy and a half-witted man who wore a meaningless yet curiously appealing smile and who slept in the forecastle. Evered never heard the boy called anything but Squid. The halfwit's name was Arthur.

A snow flurry chased them toward the open sea, and the spruce-clad shores on either hand disappeared behind its curtain. Cap'n Obed held the wheel, and after Willie gave them breakfast — Jenny had not yet appeared — Evered stayed with the Captain in the deck house which offered shelter from the storm. Snow cloaked them all that day, and not till mid-afternoon did Jenny emerge from her cabin.

Evered, on deck, had gone forward to stand awhile by the fore-mast. They were on the starboard tack, the wind southwesterly and not severe. When he turned aft at last, he saw Jenny leaning against the mainmast, holding to it with her hands behind her to steady herself, facing the wind; and she had laid aside her veil.

He hesitated, then went on to pass her. As he approached, she met his eyes. Snow crystals lay on her shoulders, and snowflakes had melted on her bright cheeks and hung there in drops like tears. She was rosy and glowing, and she was beautiful; but he was struck again by the extraordinary purity of her expression. Her eyes were wide and friendly and innocent as a child's; her mouth was like a child's mouth, delicate and soft and warm. She smiled when her glance met his; and when she smiled, small crescents like faint curved dimples indented her cheeks just below the cheekbones.

He had meant to pass her and go on, but without his own volition his feet lagged and he stopped in front of her; yet he did not speak, and after a moment she said:

'It's a fine wind.' Her voice was soft and low.

'Warmer, I think.'

Snow came for a moment more strongly into her face, and she wiped it away with her mittened hands, and then laughed gaily and took off one mitten and rubbed her nose hard with her hand. 'I always forget,' she said. 'The wool off my mittens sticks to my nose and itches so! I never remember till too late.'

She was so lovely and so friendly and charming that he had to force himself to remember Ephraim, and his face set in grim lines; but then Mr. Brock came and spoke to her.

'I'm taking the wheel now, Mis' Poster,' he said. 'Come aft and I'll give you that lesson in steering I promised you.'

She turned at once, looking up at Evered over her shoulder as though in smiling apology for deserting him. He changed his mind about going below, returned to his post by the foremast. The wind in his face was strong and scouring and he filled his lungs with it. There was an extravagant disturbance in him. He forced himself to think clearly, to remember all that Ephraim had said about her; yet he could not forget her eyes and her clean lips and that pure beauty which she wore. Ephraim must be mad! Of such a woman as this, the things he said could not be true.

Yet whether deliberately or not, he reminded himself, she had destroyed Ephraim. So — even though she might conceivably be as pure and innocent as she appeared — nevertheless corruption dwelt in her which could ruin a man. He put himself on guard.

II

Before he was again alone with her — they met at meals in the small cabin, or in the deck house or on deck, but there was always someone near — he had a chance to see how her presence aboard affected the other men. The boy and the halfwit forward watched her with goggling eyes, and he saw her in talk with one and then the other, smiling and nodding, winning them to eager speech. Mr. Brock, when he could persuade her to take the wheel, stood close beside her, sometimes reaching around her with both hands to steady the spokes; and he laughed more and more loudly all the time, like a man who is taking repeated drafts of some strong liquor. At the supper table he monopolized the conversation, telling her long tales in which he was always the hero, laughing at his own words while she listened with a half smile. Old Willie served her like a queen, and even Cap'n Obed fell under her spell, and she won from him a grudging chuckle now and then.

During the night they ran out of the snow into mild weather and light winds, and Mr. Brock next day was more concerned with Jenny than with his duties. He began to deride Cap'n Obed in open ways, winking at Jenny as he did so to make sure she appreciated and relished his words; and the old Captain scowled and muttered to Willie in the cabin. The next night the Mary Ann went creaking on her way, complaining in every seam; and Evered thought the weather had changed again, or was about to do so. They woke to fog and light winds and slatting sails, and after breakfast Evered returned to his cabin for a while, to spend some time on the papers he carried.

When he came out again an hour later, everyone had gone on deck except Jenny. She sat on the bench beside the table with a book in her hands, and she looked up and met his eyes and smiled; but he would have climbed the companion ladder to the deck if she had not spoken to him.

'Mr. Evered,' she said; and when he paused, she asked straight-forwardly: 'Were you not a friend of Ephraim's at Harvard College?'

He colored slightly. 'I am his friend, yes,' he said, emphasizing the second word, angry at her use of the past tense.

'He often spoke of a Mr. Evered,' she agreed. She said gravely: 'Will you sit down? I want to ask your help.' And she explained: 'You see, I am going to New York to find him now.'

So that was the explanation of her presence here aboard. She must have learned Ephraim's address from Mr. Richardson and was bound to find him and to finish the havoc she had begun. John asked sternly: 'Why don't you leave him alone?'

She looked at him with puzzled eyes. 'Alone? When he needs friendliness?' She said reproachfully: 'He told me that in college he was — behaving badly till you set him on the right path, so I know you are his friend. Now he has gone back to those old, ugly ways and needs help again. I want to help him, and I want you — for his sake — to help me help him.'

He stood above her, steadying himself against the lurching of the vessel, his feet apart, his legs braced; but for a moment he was uncertain what to say. She explained with a gentle gravity: 'I might not have the courage — or even the will — to try to save him for his own sake; but Mr. Evered, there's a girl, a nice girl named Ruth Green, who works in my house. I've learned since Ephraim went away that he betrayed her. There's still time for him to come home and marry her — if we can persuade him.' She added: 'She's a good girl. Her mistake was only that she loved and trusted him. Will you help me, Mr. Evered?'

He sat down then, facing her, his hands pressed hard upon the table, his lips dry. Because he felt himself weakly believing her, weakly finding her true and gentle and good, he fortified himself with anger. He wetted his lips and spoke, spoke in a rush of words.

'He's beyond help,' he said. 'You know that! It's your doing! You've — worse than killed him!'

For a moment she sat with no trace of expression in her eyes, as though her thoughts were far away. The Mary Ann tipped drunkenly in a long swell, and the yards — the sails empty of wind — came over with a creak and then with a shock as they brought up short. She said at last quietly:

'Go on, please, Mr. Evered. You — confuse me. What have I done to him? What is in your mind?'

'You made him love you!' he said, his voice thick, hating his own words, hating her.

Her eyes widened in perplexity. 'Love me? He was Isaiah's son, and I was fond of him on that account; but I think that is not what you mean?'

'It isn't!' His voice was blunt as a blow, but she did not wince.

'Then — what is it that you do mean, Mr. Evered?'

He chose his words to hurt her, to cut and bite like a lash, wishing to provoke her to tears, or to defensive protests, or to a passion of anger like his own. 'You made him want you!' he blurted. 'You drove him crazy with wanting you, fondling him, kissing him! But he tried to fight it. You were his father's wife, and he was decent enough to blame himself for the thing you woke in him. You stole his self-respect!' He waited for denials; but she did not speak and he went on: 'And you tricked him into stealing money from his father, and you tricked him into — worse than that. And finally you tried to drive him — with promises and then with threats — to kill his father. When he did it, it was an accident, but so many have blamed him that he is himself no longer sure it was an accident.' He finished in a sudden woeful grief: 'So he is lost! There is no hope for him at all.'

Her eyes were wide and steady, searching his countenance. She said at last in a gentle sympathy: 'You're devoted to him, aren't you?'

'I never liked a man so well.'

'What was this — this worse trick I played on him?'

His cheek flamed angrily. 'You know as well as I do!'

'Perhaps I do,' she assented. 'But — tell me what it was, this terrible thing I did.'

He hated her for driving him to put the thing in words. He hated her enough to do so. 'You took the girl's place,' he said harshly. 'You lay in her bed, let him find you there in the dark, not knowing — and then threatened to tell Isaiah what he had done to you unless he killed his father.'

She whispered in a sort of wonder: 'He told you all this?'

'Yes!' And when she did not speak, he challenged: 'Isn't it true?'

She made a curious gesture with both hands, a gesture that dismissed the question. 'It is what you believe,' she said. 'He has been your friend for a long time, and — you do not know me, so naturally you believe him.' She rose with a serene dignity. 'I will not ask your help again,' she said. 'I will just do what I can do alone.'

She picked up her book and went to her cabin. Evered was left staring at his own hands, clenched there on the table edge. If she had protested, had denied, had raged at Ephraim or at him, his conviction of her guilt would have been stiffened by her very denials. But she had denied nothing. She had said he must think what he chose; and by her refusal to defend herself he was left shamed, as though he had kicked an unresisting child.

III

A northeaster blew the fog into rain and the wind freshened. At dinner time — they were all at table, the boy called Squid at the wheel — Cap'n Obed told Mr. Brock to shape a new course, close-hauled as she would go, almost due easterly.

Brock laughed at him. 'Where you heading? Spain?' he demanded, and looked to Jenny for approval of his jest.

'I'll give the Cape plenty of room,' Cap'n Obed told him. He added: 'And you'd better have Squid and Arthur try the pumps.'

'We sucked her dry this morning,' Brock argued.

'We'll keep her dry,' Cap'n Obed warned him. 'If water gets to the lime, we'll have her decks hot in no time.'

Brock went grudgingly to see these orders obeyed; but when later Cap'n Obed decided to reef her, the mate again protested. 'You're too damned careful,' he declared. 'This won't hurt her!'

'Mebbe not,' Cap'n Obed told him. 'But I'd ruther be keerful than dead.'

So reefed she was; and their course was presently more southerly. In the relatively shallow waters under the Cape, great seas formed and broke in a piling roar; and the Mary Ann overtook them and climbed them and pitched into the trough beyond their peaks. Cap'n Obed at the wheel humored her, and Jenny in the deck house liked the drive of the wind and the climb — slow and slower —up each long swell, and the moment when they paused before tipping on and down. Evered, even from below, could hear her laughter, clear and happy and fine. She was untouched by that scene between them in the cabin, ignoring it as though it had never occurred; and he thought her laughter brave and valorous, and could not face her now.

In the late afternoon Brock took the wheel and Cap'n Obed came below; but Jenny stayed in the deck house. Brock did not humor the Mary Ann. Because Jenny liked those laborious ascents, those abrupt dives into the trough between the waves, he drove the schooner hard. Cap'n Obed went to his bunk to catch some sleep against the night that was coming; but Evered thought the schooner was taking a pounding. Then at last she fell off a great wave and came down with a smashing shock and a sound of splintering; and before Evered could move, Cap'n Obed had leaped to the companion ladder, John on his heels.

Evered was in time to hear the old man shout: 'Gol darn you, Brock, what you trying to do, break her back? Give me that wheel!' He pushed the other aside. 'Go hit the pumps, see if she's making any water.'

Brock was sobered by the heavy blow the old schooner had taken; and he put the men to the pumps, and himself spelled them. At the end of an hour, the mate came to the wheel house.

'She don't suck air yet,' he confessed.

Cap'n Obed spat. 'Pump till she does,' he said. 'I don't like the feel of her.' The wind had backed into the north and the rain began to turn to snow. He brought her to and took soundings. 'I'd haul off,' he told Evered, 'but she feels to me heavier all the time. We'll go ahead as we are. We'll be making into Nantucket Sound by morning, have a chance to head for somewheres if we have to.'

He said no further word of reproof to Brock; and Evered thought bitterly that the mate could not be blamed. It was Mrs. Poster, arousing in him a reckless madness, making him forget good seamanship, who had brought them to these straits. Evered had enough wit to appreciate their danger in a leaking old tub of a schooner and a rising gale.

The men were still pumping, Evered taking his turn with the others, when night came down. That night was a long one, and except for Jenny no one stayed below. The pumps spouted steadily, but even Evered thought the schooner was more sluggish all the time.

Just before daylight Jenny climbed the companion ladder to tell them that she could smell smoke in her cabin. Cap'n Obed went hastily below to investigate. She was right. The water had reached the lime. The cargo was afire.

IV

At daylight the wind was north by west, and it rose in force while they worked into Nantucket Sound. They kept the pumps going, and Willie during his respites from that toil went down into the galley and — choking in the smoke there — made coffee and heated beans. The deck forward was hot from the fire below, and all around the butt of the foremast the snow melted as fast as it fell. Their progress was slow and slower all the time. Evered, taking his turn at the pumps, did two men's work, glad of the hard labor and the deadly weariness which followed it. When the smoke below became so thick that no one could breathe in the cabin, Jenny stayed in the deck house where Cap'n Obed and Willie, too old and weary for the steady labor at the pumps, stood to the wheel. Brock thought they could point well enough to make Holmes' Hole. He said there was no harbor to leeward except Nantucket where the bar might trap them; and Cap'n Obed took his advice and kept her up to it as well as he could.

Evered was at the pumps when a little after noon the foremast suddenly tilted sidewise at a drunken angle, snapping stays like thread. The butt had burned through at the step; the mast leaned out over the rail. Brock leaped to fetch an axe and begin to cut the mast away, since if it went further overside, the leverage of the butt would rip open the decks and let air in to feed the fire; but he was clumsy at it, and Evered took the axe from him and with shrewd and violent strokes cut the butt through till the stick fell.

But it was still held alongside by the rigging, dragging there; and the Mary Ann lay helpless in the trough. One of the great seas that came solidly aboard her swept the halfwit away and they saw Arthur no more. Evered hacked at the tangle that still held the mast, and the wind thrust at him, and the seas battered him, and even through his soles he could feel the decks hot under his feet. They had been close-reefed, and when the wreck of the foremast was clear, the rag of mainsail took hold and began to drive her, but it seemed to Evered she went to leeward more than she went ahead. He turned into the deck house for a moment's respite.

'Can't you do better, Cap'n?' he shouted, over the roar of the gale. 'We're going down wind fast!'

'I don't dast sheet the mains'l home,' Cap'n Obed told him. Evered saw Jenny watching them both, and her eyes were serene and unafraid, meeting his steadily. 'I'd rip the mast out. If that happens, the old Mary Ann will look like a flower basket, fire pouring up out of her.' He added: 'She's deeper all the time, but if she'll float through the night, water in her might drown out the fire.'

Evered could not take his eyes away from Jenny. He knew well enough their danger, from the fire, from the gale, from the raging storm; and he was not afraid. But it was strangely frightening to think that she too might be lost, that that exquisite flesh might be scorched or battered or washed white and pulpy by the pitilessly pounding seas. He forgot her crimes, remembering only how she had faced his accusations, with an unpretending dignity, without protests or denials, without even anger, as though it were natural and to be expected that he should take his friend's word for her sins. She said to him in a low tone that nevertheless came clearly above the clamor of the storm:

'You've worked so hard! You're worth all the others together.'

He hesitated. 'I'm sorry you're in this,' he told her then, reluctantly. She nodded in calm understanding, taking his word at its surface meaning, seeming to see in it nothing more.

v

Dark came early, and soon afterward they saw a lighter line to leeward and knew it for the breakers and the snow-clad shore; but there was no way to claw off. The Mary Ann struck once, rose on a wave, came down a second time hard enough to bilge her, rose sluggishly once more and struck again and rolled wearily over on her side as though glad to rest awhile. Pounding seas drove her ever harder on the sand, coming sometimes in sheets of solid water pouring down her decks. The shock or the seas carried the boy named Squid overside as Arthur had gone; and he was lost in darkness on the instant, beyond any help at all.

They had one chance. A dory trailed astern, and Cap'n Obed and Brock worked it into their lee. The mate vaulted into it to bail out what water it had shipped; and into it they piled. Cap'n Obed was the last. He hated to leave the Mary Ann. She had brought him through some hard times, but now he was abandoning her helpless to her enemies, and tomorrow she would be no more than a litter of charred timbers scattered along the beach.

Yet even now, faithful to the last, she was a bulwark between them and the seas. Brock took the oars and headed for the beach; and the seas drove them headlong on. At the last the dory was lifted stern first and pitched over and over, throwing them all into the water. It came smashing down atop them as they floundered helpless there. Evered instinctively caught Jenny in his arms, swinging her aside, and they escaped that blow; but the gunwale of the heavy boat as it came down caught Brock in the back of the neck. When the others crawled and floundered to the shore, he did not follow. Evered saw his dark form in the breakers and dragged him out on hard clean sand; but the man's head hung limp. His neck was cracked, and it was clear that he was dead.

Just as they were sure of this, a glare suddenly broke through the decks of the Mary Ann; and they stood a moment watching her. The mainmast had gone at last; the decks were breached; and for a moment leaping flames played high. The next sea turned them to steam, but they flared up again, as though the sea and the fire like hyenas over a corpse fought for the carcass of the schooner. Those on the beach watched that unholy combat in a dreadful fascination for long moments, till the wind and their wet garments began to suck warmth and life out of them and warned them to be moving.

Without discussion they put the wind and the sea behind them, moving straight away from the water, not knowing where they were going, knowing only that this was land under their feet, that on this good land somewhere safety lay. They trudged through the wet packed snow, and the driven snow blinded them and the whiteness of the snow was the only light in the dark and storm-scourged world.

They came presently to water skimmed with ice, saw the black of open water beyond. Here was a barrier they could not pass. They stopped in a huddled group; and Evered felt Jenny shivering beside him. Cap'n Obed stood with bowed head, already crushed by the weight of the cold that tightened like a vise upon them all; but Evered looked right and left, and to the right, far away, dimly through the screen of the driving snow, he saw a radiance that was light.

An instant later that light was gone, snow once more shutting in between; but he shouted the word and turned them all that way. He supported Jenny, his arm around her. Cap'n Obed and Willie, with the dumb patience of old age, came on their heels, their heads down, pressing mutely on. The wind off the water was not so cold as it would have been off land; but it was laden with snow that plastered itself upon their garments, against their cheeks, in their eyes. Their outer garments stiffened with it and crackled as they walked. The footing was uncertain and the way was long and their feet were slow; but the light, visible more and more often through the blackness of the storm, was a promise of warmth and security waiting at journey's end.

There was water on their left, and the sand spit lay between them and the sea; but the low land gave them no shelter, and the wind was an enemy with which they locked in a steady grapple. Strength failed fast, but the light with its promises lured them on.

Then slowly the water on their left began to curve across their path. They followed the beach line till they encountered the first disturbed seas driving in from the Sound.

They had landed on Coetue; but here the sand spit ended. The warm security of Nantucket town was so near, scarce half a mile away beyond the light; but in the darkness and the storm they could see no sign of the town yonder, and the channel was a barrier they could not cross to come to safety there. Through the open water between them and that security great seas charged like massed cavalry with white manes flying. Beyond lay the town and safety, but there was no way to reach that haven. Behind them lay the weary miles they had come; and on either side they were penned in by the sea. They were like men at the bottom of a pit, with grinning death for company.

When John Evered turned from looking toward the light, he saw that they now were only three. Jenny was here, in the curve of his arm; and Cap'n Obed had sunk down on the beach and sat weakly at their feet. But Willie Small had fallen somewhere on the way, since they left the Mary Ann, quietly to die. Arthur, and then Squid, and then Brock, and now old Willie; these four were gone, and death rode the icy wind, hurrying hungrily to devour them all.

VI

Evered for hours now had found release from thought in action; in action that was largely instinctive, just as a man knocked senseless into the water may without ever recovering his wits struggle to the surface and, paddling weakly, there sustain himself till rescue comes. So long as he could labor at the pumps or to cut away the fallen mast and rigging or to lead them all along the beach toward the light which beyond the open water mocked them now, he needed not to think. He fought for his own life and for the lives of all of them: for Jenny at first no more than for Arthur, the smiling and good-humored halfwit; no more than for Squid, the gangling, dumb and speechless boy; no more than for Mr. Brock who because it was he who had let the Mary Ann break her back by falling off a wave was directly responsible for this disaster; no more than for valiant Willie Small, choking in the smoky galley to heat coffee and beans that they might eat; no more than for Cap'n Obed himself. Life was a quality which all men fought to protect. Life was a treasure beyond price, and when life and death were at issue, a man did not stop to count costs. A king might risk his life — yes, and lose it, too — to save a wretched foundling fallen into some hidden pit or pool. A sheriff might risk his life to save for a while the life of the felon in his charge and bring him safely to the gallows in the end. Deep-rooted in mankind there was this instinct, if life were endangered, to interfere and at any cost to save. Evered himself, once upon a time, had seen a strange tragedy. Among the crew in winter camp and on his first log drive down the Connecticut there was an individual named Thisbeus, a besotted and visibly diseased wreck of a man with only half a nose and no teeth, old in vice and lost to shame. He had been hired to help the cook, but the men and the cook revolted, refusing to let him handle any food that humans were to eat. Thereafter he cut and fitted firewood all day long, his shaking limbs barely equal to the task, so that he could hardly meet the demands of the voracious stoves. On the drive he helped handle the wangan, the long double-ended boat in which the cook brought his stores and gear down-river; and one day he had the bad luck to fall overboard. He could not swim, but he managed to clutch the end of a straggling log at the tail of the drive and cling to it as it drifted at slowly increasing speed toward a horseshoe of falls and tumbling rapids half a mile below. There was not a man of those who saw him drifting toward the falls who did not wish old Thisbeus dead. He had too long been an affront to the eyes of the living. Nevertheless, three of the best of them, racing down the riverbank, found a boat drawn up on shore and set out to try to intercept him just above the falls. They were too late for that, but the log to which he clung hung crosswise on a ledge at the head of the falls, and — although they knew there was slight hope the manoeuvre would succeed — they let the boat gently down to him, holding her against the current by rowing hard upstream. They reached him, too; and the wretched man caught the boat's stern and tried to climb in, while they redoubled their exertions to make way against the current. They gained two or three feet in an agonizing struggle that lasted almost a minute before an oar broke and they all went over the falls. Thisbeus alone drifted unhurt through the rapids and survived. The others died. Evered had been too late to take his place in that small boat, but he and twenty others, watching helplessly, saw the affair; and he remembered it now, thinking how blindly men fought to guard the flame of life and keep it burning.

Of those who had been on the Mary Ann, four men were dead,

and only he and Jenny and Cap'n Obed remained alive; but he would cling to life. He drew Jenny down on her knees beside Cap'n Obed; he sheltered her with his body against the wind and — shouting to be heard — he asked whether the Captain knew where they were.

'Nantucket's over there,' the old man said haltingly, through chattering teeth. 'You can't see it, but it's there. I was here once, twenty-two years ago. We're on the tip end of the sand spit opposite the town. They call it Coetue.'

'Can we go back, get to the other end?'

'It'd be too far for me — and nothing there but scrub and ma'sh meadows if we made it. We'd freeze as easy there as here.'

'How far?'

'Five-six miles, at a guess.'

Evered judged it was almost three miles to where they had left the Mary Ann, and the thought of returning that weary way was dreadful. In the darkness, unbroken except by the light's periodic flash, the town yonder might have been a thousand miles off. He stood up and shouted half a dozen times; but the wind caught the sound and shredded it, and Cap'n Obed said fretfully:

'Save your breath! Save your stren'th!'

Evered was too young to be passive. 'We've got to do something.'

'We'll set till we get cold,' the old man told him. 'Then we'll stomp around till we get warm again. We can last the night.'

Jenny made no sound, and Evered wrapped her in his arms, opening his coat to draw her against his body half within its folds.

'We'll freeze here,' he said.

The Captain cackled. 'Not me. I won't. You young ones might.' He seemed as his strength failed full of words. 'You're a fine pair of critters, young and full of sap; but where it's just a business of setting still and taking it, old men can stand more than young ones. An old man can go into his shell like a turtle, like a denned bear. He'll quit thinking and feeling, quit everything except just staying alive. Young ones think too much, and that scares 'em, wears 'em down.' He appeared to realize for the first time that they were but three, and he muttered: 'Where's Willie?' When Evered did not answer, he said wearily: 'We been shipmates long as I c'n remember, always stuck together.'

Jenny was shivering in Evered's arms, her body shaking in a long crescendo, still for a moment and then beginning again; and he thought how a dog shivers in its sleep. There was no surrender in him, yet for a while he remained passive, deliberately waiting to see whether in their wet garments the cold could be endured. He sat on the ground with Jenny between his legs, his feet crossed over hers, his arms around her, bowing forward over her so that she was bowed forward too. Cap'n Obed was lying down, curled in a ball, completely passive, no longer curious to know where Willie was.

They stayed thus for a long time, not speaking. Evered found that he grew colder till he was in torment. He spoke in Jenny's ear.

'Can you stand it?'

'I'm not — very cold,' she said as steadily as possible.

After a while he thought that he suffered less, and he realized suddenly that he was drowsy, ready to fall asleep. The realization brought him wide awake enough. He had heard all his life that before freezing to death a man went to sleep. He stirred, and the slightest movement was agony; so he knew that to stay here meant that before morning they would die.

When he spoke to Jenny, she was asleep. He climbed painfully to his feet, and lifted her by the shoulders and shook her and made her stand. He shouted at her and walked her up and down till she came back to life again, and she said — not complainingly:

'It hurts to move.'

'We're half-frozen,' he admitted. 'We've got to get to shelter somewhere.' Back up the long spit of Coetue — past the wreck of the Mary Ann, five miles or six or a dozen, it did not matter — they must go, must at least begin the journey. For to stay here was to die, and that must not happen. The life in them, a part of the great treasure shared by all the world, must be preserved. It was not themselves who must be saved, but the spark of life which was in their custody.

When Jenny could stand alone, Evered tried to rouse Cap'n Obed; but he could not. The old man's sleep — if it were sleep — was so profound that Evered could not break through its barrier. He turned to Jenny again, his arm around her waist, and led her along the beach, retracing the way they had come an hour or two before.

VII

That journey up the beach on the inner shore of Coetue was an ordeal without end. The snow began to ease, but the wind was bitter, bringing from the northwest a desperate cold which would be remembered for a hundred years, when Boston Harbor froze solidly over, and up in Bangor the thermometers registered forty-two below. It was already well below freezing, even here on

Coetue with open water on two sides, and it was colder all the time. Their wetted garments, stiff with ice, crackled when they moved.

As the snow thinned, they could distinguish the whiteness of the land and the shore ice from the darkness of the water. Evered, leading Jenny with his arm around her, found that the beach was not straight. It was a series of shallow crescents with projecting points between. He began to cut across these points as he came to them, saving every foot of the way.

Jenny for a while walked as well as he. They did not hurry, but they did keep moving; and the exercise stirred their circulation enough so that they were no longer cold, but the wind drained their strength and quickly wearied them.

Jenny faltered at last. 'My limbs are so heavy I can scarcely move them,' she confessed, and there was almost mirth in her tones. 'I have on so many petticoats! It's hard to walk.'

'Take them off,' he said.

She tried, but her fingers were clumsy with cold, and he sought to help her. Fumbling under her outer skirt in the darkness he could not find the buttons at her waist; and in the end he compromised by ripping her petticoats and her skirt short off just below the knee. Less encumbered, she was able for a while to proceed; and when she lagged again, he took her on his shoulders, her arms around his neck, his arms under her knees; and she rode thus pickaback awhile, till he was staggering with fatigue and had to put her down, and she walked with him.

He knew when they passed the broken wreck of the Mary Ann by the smell of smoke and of charred wet timbers on the wind; but they did not cross the spit to look at her. He remembered that they had seen no trace of Willie Small. Perhaps the snow had covered Willie, or perhaps they had missed him when they cut across the low points. They trudged slowly on, and it was as though theirs were the only two lives in the world, as though the night and the storm combined to crush the whole human race of which they were the last survivors.

When Jenny could go no farther, Evered took her on his back again; but she had not even strength to cling to him, and he knelt and lifted her laboriously in his arms and came painfully to his feet and stumbled on. He walked until his legs gave way and he fell; and he drew her close and lay still awhile, gasping for breath till his laboring lungs were at peace. When the bitter cold began to stiffen them again, he picked her up once more, once more went on.

He had no sense of distance nor of time, knew only that this life which was in their keeping must be preserved. It was not one life alone which he sought to save, nor two. In his disordered thoughts he and Jenny were the only survivors of an universal catastrophe. If they died, the world would be left tenantless; but if they lived, their two lives blending could populate the earth again. She ceased to be for him an individual, became to him the embodiment of woman, the mother of all life as man is its father. When his weariness betrayed him and he fell, sometimes atop her, he held her in a strong embrace, pressed between him and the earth; and there was in this close union of their half-frozen bodies a sort of sacrament that filled him with peace and with assuagement as though already their life fires had joined to give off other lives like sparks to light the world. When he picked her up and labored on, his arms supporting her embraced her too; and his heart yearned for her, and all the loves that man has known for women were alight in him for her.

He thought she felt this too. When they fell and rose, twice or thrice she walked awhile. 'You can't do it, John,' she said, clinging to him. 'You can't carry me always. You will wear yourself out. Let me do what I can.' So though the time came when she could not stand at all, it was still as partners that they went on. Together they kept the waning fires of life alive.

VIII

When Evered saw at last that the line of the beach swung to the right in an extended curve, he thought this was a deeper cove than any they had passed; and he left the water, holding a straight line, thinking to cross a projecting point of land as he had done before. But no water showed ahead, for they had come to the end of the upper harbor, where Coetue widens into Coskata; and when John was sure of this, strength for a while came into him.

He never knew how long he walked after he left the water before he came to the haystack. This was hummocky hay, marsh hay which some farmer had scythed the summer before and stacked here to be sent for during the winter and boated home. The stack stood up as a black shape against the snow-covered ground, and Evered veered toward it and came into its lee, and the blessed relief from the wind was so great that for a moment he was sick with gladness. He laid Jenny down, and he began to tear at the sheltered side of the haystack, dragging out great handfuls till he had a pile which would protect her from the snow on which she lay. He lifted her on it and piled more hay on top of her. He had by that time dug a shallow recess in the stack, and on a sudden thought he continued to dig deeper and deeper, throwing the hay on the ground beside him, tunnelling into the close-packed stuff, tearing and bloodying his hands, splintering his nails. When he remembered the stout knife in his pocket and began to use it he made more rapid progress, and his tunnel grew deeper. He burrowed like an animal. The dust of the hay filled his nostrils and made him sneeze, and as he dug deeper and deeper, he had to shove the loosened hay down past his body to the opening.

He dug until he could lie at length, his knees a little bent, and still be completely within the stack. Then he roused Jenny and set her on her feet and — since her dress was wet and stiff with ice — he stripped off her outer garments and her sodden shoes, and helped her slide feet-first into the den he had made. He pulled off his boots and coat and trousers and edged in beside her. He drew his coat in after them and turned it inside out to make a pillow that would protect them from the prickly stubble ends of the hay. Then he reached out again and gathered armfuls of the hay and — backing into the tunnel he had dug — wadded with it the opening, building the plug higher and higher, till at last the entrance to their refuge was sealed and the outer cold was completely shut away.

The tunnel he had dug was narrow. It was so snug that they lay pressed close together, and he drew her closer, seeking to wrap himself around her, to warm her with the warmth in him. She was cold in his arms awhile, shivering, with locked teeth; and he tore open the front of his shirt so that she lay against his breast. Her garments were wet and cold between them and he ripped them away till he and she were close as lovers, and he began to feel an answering warmth in her icy flesh. He drew her hands, as cold as some sluggish creature fresh lifted from the sea, between their bodies, and his arms circled her protectingly. She was woman, the mother, the giver of life; and he was man, the father. And they were alive. So long as they guarded and passed on the flame in them, man would not die.

From the deep springs of their two bodies life began to flow in a rising tide through their arteries. Life which forever renews itself thus renewed itself in them now. They were content to lie thus while life came back to them; but with life their strength a little returned, and he spoke at last.

'Warm?'

'Yes. But I thought I never would be warm again.'

'We're all right.'

'Where are we?'

'I don't know. This is a haystack. There must be a farm near. I'll find it in the morning.' He held her closer. Without knowing he spoke, compelled by that sense of an eternal unity between them which their shared ordeal had imposed, he said: 'I love you.'

In the darkness her lips, soft, warm, came to press his. 'I love you, John,' she answered, between kisses. 'I love you too.'

5

AFTER that night when her father died, and again after the long ordeal of Isaiah's illness, Jenny herself had been for weeks half-sick from nervous exhaustion. It was to be so with her now. Even when they were warm, she still shivered in those long crescendos, like a dog shivering in its sleep, till John thought the spasms of her small body in his arms would shatter it as a glass by vibration may be shattered.

'B-but I'm not c-cold,' she assured him. 'I'm all right, really I am. I'm just so dreadfully t-tired!'

Even when she slept at last, close against his breast, her soft breath warm on his throat where her face was buried, she continued to shake and shiver so that he was full of fear for her. Day came and he saw light through the interstices of the hay, but for a long time he did not stir, reluctant to wake her, dreading to leave her while he went to hunt shelter for them both.

So they were still there together when at last he heard voices near. The wreck of the Mary Ann had been sighted at full dawn, and though the wind was high, boats crossed the sheltered inner harbor to look for survivors along Coetue. They found Cap'n Obed and old Willie Small; and they found Brock's body where it lay on the beach near the wreck. The others, Arthur and Squid, they did not find; but they followed Evered's tracks and Jenny's and so came to the haystack in the marsh land at Coskata.

Before noon Jenny and Evered had been brought safely back to Nantucket town; but Jenny, weak and trembling, could not help herself at all, and when she was put to bed she clung to Evered's hand and wept that he should think of leaving her and whispered pitifully:

'I'll die, John, if you ever let me go!'

'I'll never let you go,' he promised. All the things Ephraim had told him were forgotten. The long ordeal of the night had fused them together; her very weakness bound him now. They were married late that afternoon, he standing by her bed as Isaiah had stood when she and the old man were married seven years before. They were married and then they were alone, and Evered held her in his arms, tenderly as a woman holds an ailing infant, all night long; and for days thereafter he never left her side.

II

They left Nantucket three weeks later. Jenny was still so frail that she must be carried aboard the New York packet. Evered had long since written Colonel Black, and he had an answer from the Colonel, congratulating him on his marriage.

'I know Mrs. Poster only by reputation,' he said, 'but she is one of the most respected ladies in Bangor. And incidentally one of the wealthiest. You may count yourself a fortunate young man. Judge Saladine and Miss Saladine join me in congratulations, at once on your escape from death and on your marriage.'

He added generously that John need be in no haste to report to him, promised to be in Boston in February and said he would hope to see the young man there.

So they need not have gone to New York, but Jenny insisted on doing so. 'We mustn't forget Ephraim,' she said. 'Nor Ruth Green. Her baby will come in March, but there is still time if we can find him.' And she added gravely: 'I remember, too, some of the things Ephraim told you about me, so I want us to see him together, John.'

'I was a fool to believe him,' he confessed. 'I don't think I ever really did believe him, not even at the first. He was half-mad with drink that night, not knowing what he said.'

'I hope we can find him — and help him find himsel.,' she murmured.

But they did not find Ephraim. In New York, Jenny was exhausted by the journey and unable to leave her bed; so John went alone to the address Mr. Richardson had given him. When he came to the place he was glad he had come alone. A negro woman admitted him with a bewildered giggle.

'I dunno as dey's any of de young ladies awake yit,' she confessed. 'We don' have many gemmen call dis time o' day.'

Evered asked for Mr. Poster. 'I'm a friend of his,' he explained. 'I understood he lived here.'

Her white teeth flashed in a cheerful mirth. 'Yas suh!' she said with emphasis. 'He sho did. He was de livingest man I ever did see — long as his money lasted. "Mistus Foah Poster," de young ladies called him! But he gone now.'

'Do you know where he went?'

'Tuh de bad place, I reck'n,' the negress assured him. 'He di'n't look like he'd live long when he lef' here. Tuk foah men to handle him, spite of his being so little and puny.' Ephraim, she explained, had gone stark crazy, and the Madame sent for the police and they overpowered him and carried him away.

He thanked her, gave her money, and went to the authorities. Ephraim, they told him, had died of the horrors ten days before.

John did not at once tell Jenny this, afraid of the effect upon her of the dark news. She was terribly thin and frail, so that it made him wince to see her arms like sticks, her collar bone like a slender bar under her skin. For a while in Nantucket she had declined all food; and when at his tender urgency she tried to eat, her stomach refused to receive any nourishment.

'I'm sorry, John,' she told him in wistful apology. 'I wish I could eat and get nice and plump for you. I'm not really a delicate woman, but it's always this way with me when something terrible happens. It was so the night my father died, and it was so after Mr. Poster was sick. I'm truly sorry, darling, but I can't help it.'

'Don't worry,' he urged. 'You're alive, and you're getting well, getting better every day. Soon you'll be fine.'

'I know how hard it is for you. I'm afraid I'm not a very satisfactory wife. But I will be, John, one day.'

'Don't worry about me,' he insisted. 'All I want is for you to get well.'

This was true enough. There was in him in these days of her weakness no ardent hunger, but only a clumsy tenderness and a yearning like prayer. Seeing her so weak frightened him, filled him with terrors he could not confess; and when he kissed her it was as gingerly as though she were a bubble which would vanish at the least touch. He never thought in these day of the things Ephraim had told him. They were forgotten, dismissed as the lunatic ravings of a madman. It was impossible that they could have been true of Jenny. Evered was no blind and fatuous lover; but in those hours of storm and wreck and death, Jenny had become a part of him and she was his wife. His wife — whatever she had done or should do — she would always be, to cherish and protect and to defend.

It was to protect her now that he concealed for a while the news that Ephraim was dead. Not till she was stronger, and not till her questions became insistent, did he at last admit the truth.

When she heard, she held fast to his hand, comforting him. 'There, John. Poor John! I'm so sorry. He meant so much to you!'

'I'm sorry for the poor girl.'

'We'll do everything we can for her,' she promised. 'Perhaps we can find some good man for her.' She said thoughtfully: 'We must go back to Bangor soon.' He spoke of Colonel Black and his business in Boston and she nodded. 'We'll go to Boston, then, when I am stronger,' she agreed, and smiled and said: 'Perhaps it is just as well not to go home to Bangor right away. Some of the good people there may be critical of me because I did not wait longer after Isaiah died. But if I had waited without you, John, I would have died myself.' And she asked: 'Where will we live, John? Where will our home be?'

'Where would you like to live?'

'In Bangor,' she admitted. 'I always have lived there. But I will live where my husband decides.'

He laughed in a quick, happy pride. 'I like the sound of that. You really are my wife, aren't you?'

'I'm going to be. Oh, John, I'm going to be the best wife ever was.'

'Colonel Black wants me to live in Bangor,' he told her. 'So you'll have your wish.'

Her eyes shone. 'But John,' she said, 'may we build our own home — please? I don't want to go on living always in the Poster house. I was never happy there — but I want to be happy all our lives, John, from now on.'

'I want you to be,' he said.

She was half-lying on the couch in their room. She lifted her arms, and he stooped to slip his arm around her and to kiss her lightly. She pressed her lips to his in a soft passion; but there was no strength in her, and she fell back and her eyes filled.

'Oh, John, I've so little to give you!' she whispered. 'Will I be better by and by?'

He held her gently, comforting her while she lay contented in his arms.

III

It seemed to him afterward that from the day when he told her Ephraim was dead, as though she had dreaded seeing that lost young man again, she began to mend. The change at first was more one of the spirit than of the flesh; but though she was still so terribly thin that to hold her in his arms the still nights through awoke in him only a great tenderness and compassion, yet he had no longer the frightening sense of weakness in her, of a flickering flame which might go out at any time. Within a few days she began to be interested in clothes. Her own things had been lost on the Mary Ann, the garments she had worn that night were ruined, and the substitutes he had bought for her in Nantucket were drab makeshifts.

'They're as sober as my weeds,' she told John gaily. 'I want to go home to Bangor decked in finery like a bride.' And she asked: 'Am I wrong, John, to have married you so soon after Isaiah died?'

'Never ask me if you're right or wrong, Jenny. For me, whatever you do will always be right.'

'I'm so glad we found each other. You know, John, I've always remembered the first time Ephraim spoke to me of you and told me how fine you were. I wanted to ask him so many questions about you, and I wanted him to invite you to Bangor, so that I could see you for myself. Was that wicked of me? I think I loved you already, John — even though I was really fond of Isaiah. The dear old man was always so good to me.'

She seemed to him like a child, depending on his opinions and advice as she depended upon his strength. He was required to consult with her about her purchases, and to approve everything she bought. She vowed that she would have nothing he did not like, but he found this was not strictly true. Once it was a bonnet upon which his opinion was demanded; and she donned it and faced him, radiant and smiling, and asked:

'There, do you like it, John?'

He answered honestly: 'Why — not very well. Not so well as the other.'

'Oh, don't you? Why not, darling?'

'Well, isn't it a little too —— ' He tried to put his feeling into words.

'Oh, do you really think so?'

'I'm sure it's not so becoming as it should be.'

She urged: 'But John, don't you like the color?'

'Why, the color's all right, but the shape . . .'

'But don't you see how prettily it is curved here, and the little ribbon bow there? Don't you think that's sweet?'

'I really don't like it, Jenny,' he insisted.

'But John, look! Look now and see it in daylight, here by the window. See how the shadow makes my face seem nice and round? See this, John. See that!' And she turned to and fro before him, insisting that he admire the many virtues of this charming bonnet, persuading him to abandon one objection after another till he had admitted liking so many things about the bonnet that he could no longer pretend he did not like the whole. Then she kissed him gratefully and happily and cried: 'There, I'm so glad you like it! Don't you just love it? I knew you would!'

He was amused by her, and delighted with her; and as with her quickening spirit her strength began to return, she put on day by day a vivid and compelling loveliness.

They came to Boston late in February, and though the journey fatigued her she was quick to recover. Colonel Black approved her highly, and Mrs. Black gave a splendid dinner in their honor. The gentlemen at table were all men of large interests, and the talk began with the French trouble. They conjectured whether France would grant the President's demands that American claims for vessels seized by Napoleon be settled, or risk an American war; and that led to a discussion of the potential effect of war on business, and then suddenly, since every man there was interested in Maine lands, the speculative prospects were the only topic and everyone listened while Colonel Black predicted the imminent collapse of the churning land market in Bangor.

'They're trying to charter new banks there now,' he said, 'to issue bills, to provide money for this crazy gambling. I went to Augusta to listen to the debates.' He chuckled. 'It was worth the trip to hear Representative Washburn. He made a blistering speech on the motion to postpone one of the incorporations. He said, by the way, that if all such measures now up for passage are passed, the banks in Penobscot County can issue up to a million, three hundred and fifty thousand in bills. That's absurd on its face. But then he went on to say that any man in Bangor thinks he ought to be permitted to start a bank if he can borrow fifty thousand in specie — the proposed laws require that sum to be paid in before discounts are permitted — and he said: "If we allow it, and there is fifty thousand hard money in Bangor, they will make the same fifty thousand do for each new bank, borrowing it from one another so that on Monday it will be the basis for incorporating the City Bank, and on Tuesday the Franklin, and Wednesday the Lafayette, and Thursday the People's, and Friday the Penobscot, and Saturday the Stillwater Canal. Then on Monday, if no more banks want to incorporate, they'll send the specie back to the actual proprietors." '

Even the ladies up and down the table laughed at this ironic exaggeration, and the Colonel went on; but John paid less and less attention to the talk. Watching Jenny in the candlelight, he felt his throat fill with delight in her. It seemed to him that these surroundings, the long table fine with linen and gracious with heavy silver and exquisite china, the hothouse flowers, the candles and the tinkling crystal prisms of the candelabra, the handsome gentlemen and the white shoulders of the ladies, combined to produce in his wife a bloom he had never seen before. Her eyes were glowing, her cheeks bright; and her low-cut gown revealed shoulders and bosom now well fleshed, where the bones no longer peaked the sunken skin. This transformation, it seemed to him, had come since they entered the Colonel's door. Till today she had been — or had seemed to him to be — still weak and small and delicate, so that he was afraid to touch her lest his awkward strength bruise her tender softness. He realized now for the first time that she was no longer thin, but she was naturally small of stature and delicate of mould. Certainly there was in her tonight no hint of the sighing invalid.

He watched her with a growing hunger, dreaming dreams the fulfilment of which till now, out of consideration for her weakness, he had deferred; he watched her till she met his eyes and met them fairly, and smiled at him with understanding and with promise too. So that night at last, when they were alone she came into his arms, holding him close, drawing down his head, kissing him in a new way, whispering breathless ardent words.

'John, I'm well again. John, darling patient John, you've waited so long. Oh, John, I love you now.'

IV

In March they went to Freeport to see his mother; and Mrs. Evered, at first faintly ill at ease with Jenny, was quickly won. These two spent long hours together while John went to and fro about the town renewing old acquaintances, or talked long talk with his brothers; or he might sit with his wife and his mother, watching smilingly their happy talk together, watching Jenny more radiant and blooming every day, her health and strength long since restored by her deep draughts at the healing spring of their love.

Mrs. Evered told Jenny all the tales of John's boyhood, those sometimes embarrassing reminiscences to which mothers cling so fondly and which they repeat over and over to the amused confusion of their sons; and Jenny told how she and John met on the Mary Ann. She brought alive for John things he had already forgotten.

'Poor Cap'n Obed was a little old man in a coonskin cap,' she said. 'Just old enough so that he knew he would soon be too old to go to sea, and in the back of his mind there was always that thought, so he tried to be very strong and commanding, as much to reassure himself as to impress us, I know. The mate was Mr. Brock, and he thought I was nice.' Her glance flashed teasingly at John. 'He insisted on teaching me to steer, and he made fun of old Cap'n Obed, showing off to me, just as little boys do when a new little girl is watching them.' John, remembering that it was Mr. Brock's recklessness which had brought the Mary Ann to disaster and five men to their ends, hoped Jenny would never guess this. 'And old Willie, the cook, was always grumbling, but he was so patient and he worked so hard. Then there was a boy, almost a grown man, with a big Adam's apple. They called him Squid. Cap'n Obed said that was because if he wasn't watched he did everything backward, in some wrong, thumb-handed way. He was always making mistakes, and they were always shouting at him.' Evered had not noticed this, and he thought how wonderful Jenny was to have seen in each of these men an individual. To him they had lumped themselves together; they were simply Captain, mate, cook and hands. 'And there was another man named Arthur; such a gentle, smiling man. He had a pet kitten in the forecastle. He showed it to me, the second day, before the storm. The poor man didn't even know what his last name was! People had always called him Arthur. But Cap'n Obed said he could do anything on the Mary Ann better than men with all their wits. The schooner was his home. He lived on her always, and Cap'n Obed took care of him and sent his pay to his mother. She was a widow woman in Cushing.'

She went on to tell of the disaster, describing its slow onset, and how John and the others strove to save the schooner, and how one man and then another came to death till only she and John were left alive, and how they fought to live, and did.

'John was like ten men,' she said. 'Like a giant, too great and strong for anything to beat and conquer. Do you blame me for loving him?' The older woman smiled fondly, and Jenny confessed: 'Perhaps we should have waited a longer while before being married. My husband died only last summer, you know. But I needed John too much to wait.' She looked at Evered, held his eyes with a long glance, smiling tenderly. 'I think I would still have died, afterward, if he had not been always by my side,' she said.

'John is a good man,' the little old woman agreed.

Jenny said soberly: 'When we were safe in the haystack that night, keeping each other warm, I remembered the men who had died, and it seemed somehow as though they died for us, as though John and I were meant to live.'

John's mother nodded. 'Aye, it seemed to be meant, certainly.'

Snow lay deep that winter all around, so they stayed much indoors. Men and beasts were all under the same roof, and through the shed they could come to the barn, where two horses stamped in their stalls, and six cows stood in the tie-up, and the oxen were housed in a lean-to, and the old sow had a pen of her own at the end of the barn floor, and the chickens and the geese here were sheltered too. The barn was warmed by the warmth from these creatures, and sun on fine days shone through the windows and through cracks in the walls, the sun rays alive with dancing dust motes. Once John and Jenny came there together and she wished to climb up into the mow. Above the tie-up, the hay had all been fed to the ruminant kine in their places below; but on the other side of the barn, the level of the hay was still high above the floor. John put up the long ladder made of tapering spruce poles with bits of board nailed across, leaning it against the beams of the barn frame and steadying it for Jenny to climb; and looking up at her as she ascended he whistled in teasing admiration and she cried laughingly:

'Shame, sir! Shut your eyes!' Then, when she was in the mow and he would have followed her, she protested: 'No, I don't want you up here! Don't come near me!' And she pushed the top of the ladder outward, delightedly defending the fortress of the mow against his assaults, thrusting the ladder beyond the balancing point so that it toppled and he had to drop to the floor. He set it in place again, his blood quickening in laughter, and tried once more to ascend; and she caught up the wooden-tined hay fork and thrust the head of the ladder out again so that when he came level with her they were six feet apart, the ladder precariously poised, held away from the beam against which it should have rested by the thrust of the fork; and he tried to treat with her, bargaining for permission to enter the stronghold she defended, and they parleyed laughingly till he treacherously caught the fork to twitch it out of her hands while she was off guard. But she thrust hard, thrust the ladder off balance; and though he held to the fork, the ladder tilted backward so that he had to slide hastily to the floor a dozen feet below while the ladder came down with a thump upon the beams across the way.

He shouted laughing threats, and she defied him. He set the ladder in a new place, at the end of the mow; and when she scrambled through the deep and yielding hay to meet him there, he suddenly snatched the ladder away and ran with it to the other end of the mow. Through the hay she could not move so swiftly, and before she reached the spot he had climbed high enough to catch hold on the barn post so that she could not push him away. She tried to tear his arm from the post it encircled, and bit at his hand; and he shouted in laughing pain and cuffed her, and she beat at his face with her small clenched fists, her eyes blazing, her teeth set, pounding at him hard. One fist struck him blindingly in the eye so that darkness was ablaze with flashing lights; and he fought his way around the ladder, straddling the beam, trying to catch her wrists, and she beat at him in a silent fury, no longer laughing now. He caught one hand and then the other, and she tugged to be free; and he launched himself at her, his weight carrying her backward upon the hay, and she writhed and twisted under him, fighting him still and with a silent, stubborn violence, till he pinned her at last, his legs pressing hers, his hands holding her crossed hands on her breast, and when she tried to bite his hands he thrust her own hands into her mouth and they lay a moment passive, their eyes meeting in the sunned darkness of the mow.

Then the red flames in her eyes died in laughter and she cried teasingly: 'Oh, John, you're going to have a black eye!'

'You little — wildcat!' he whispered. 'What a fighter you are!'

'Did I hit you some good ones, darling?'

'I saw stars!'

'Poor John! Here, I'll cure it!'

So she kissed his bruised eye, and it was healed, and she was forgiven, and they romped and burrowed in the hay, at first like children and then like secret lovers, and she reminded him of that night in the haystack when they were both congealed with cold.

'But I'm not cold now,' she said, and laughed huskily, and demanded: 'Are we pagans, John? Are we scandalous and terrible?'

'You're worse! You're a wildcat, scratching and biting and snarling!'

She laughed softly. 'I didn't mean really to hurt you!' She added, half to herself: 'Yet I think hurt goes with love. Don't you ever want to just pound and beat me, John? The way I did you? Wouldn't you love to?'

'No. Of course not.'

'Really? Well, I guess I'm different. I liked hitting you!' She laughed and kissed his eye again. 'I think I'd even like it if you hit me. But I didn't mean to hurt you! It's just because I love you so much I can't bear it!'

'I can stand it. I can stand anything except your not loving me.'

She said, after a moment: 'John — may I tell you something — strange and beautiful to me? I never knew what it was, before you.' He clipped her close in a quick delight, and she said: 'I know now I was never married to Isaiah at all.'

v

When they came in from the barn that day, Mrs. Evered looked up over her spectacles and saw John's eye and said in quick concern:

'Why, son, what happened to you?'

John laughed, his arm around Jenny's waist. 'I had a little trouble with this wife of mine,' he explained. 'But she's learned her lesson now!'

The older woman smiled, and her eyes returned to her knitting again. 'You children!' she protested. 'Playing like puppies in the hay! Bathe it in cold water, John, and rub it with butter. That will keep the swelling down.'

They were happy for four days in John's mother's house; and when they set out on the return journey to Boston, Jenny said: 'She's wonderful, John. No wonder you're such a fine man!'

'I think if I were ever hurt, I could always come back to mother and be healed.'

'I feel the same way about her,' she agreed. 'I hardly remember my own mother at all. John — when our babies come, help me to be like her, will you? Help me to be a fine mother to them.'

6

THE ice went out of the river that year on the seventeenth of April; but there were in Boston so many speculators eager to try their luck in the great gamble at Bangor that the first packets to sail were filled to overflowing, and not till early May were Jenny and John able to get accommodations. When they had their first sight of the city, Jenny exclaimed over the many new stores and houses and wharves which even from the water she could see under construction. 'If we'd stayed away much longer I wouldn't know the place,' she declared.

He said, echoing Colonel Black's opinion, that it was a mushroom growth based on speculation. 'And it can't last,' he assured her. 'Money's tighter all the time. That's partly because people are afraid of war over the French claims, but we're exporting gold besides.'

She smiled, holding fast to his arm with both hands as the packet worked toward the wharf. 'Women don't understand all those things, John. You'll have to manage my business for me.' She looked up at him in serene devotion. 'You'll have to manage all my life for me, John.' Then, discovering familiar faces on the nearing wharf, she began to point them out to him. She had left Mrs. Hollis in charge of the house, and had written to announce the day of their homecoming and to ask that the house be made ready for them; and she wondered who would be here to meet them now and suddenly discovered Pat Tierney himself, in his old livery as coachman and grinning broadly as he touched his hat to her. 'There's Pat!' she cried. 'See — just beside the gangway, John? Pat Tierney. He used to drive our carriages — till he got rich speculating in lands and quit the job — but I believe he's come to meet us now!' and when presently they stepped ashore and Pat met them, her first word was:

'Oh, Pat, I'm glad to see you!' And then: 'Pat, what's happened? Pat — don't tell me you've lost your money?'

He chuckled proudly. 'Lord love you, no, ma'am! I'm a rich man — richer than money could make me, to be sure. But — can't a rich man be proud to wear your livery, ma'am? And is there anything money can buy better than the chance to be your servant?'

She laughed delightedly and told John: 'He always says the nicest thing, the Irish tongue of him!'

Pat made his duties to John. 'Mr. Evered, sir to you!' He led them to where the horses waited, and they drove up the street, crowded with teams and carriages and men, and deep with muddy pot holes, with a few odd lengths of plank thrown down here and there to serve as sidewalks; and John thought there was an over-tone of hectic excitement in every voice they heard in the throngs through which the horses picked their way, men moving absently aside to let them pass. But when they turned out Main Street and began to escape from the revolving, aimless-moving crowds, Jenny asked:

'Honestly, Pat — why did you come to meet us today?'

'To please myself, to be sure. I've a cousin of mine from the old country to tend your horses now, and if he does not satisfy, you've only to speak to me. But it was in my mind to fetch you home today my own self.'

'Well, you were sweet!' she said, and she asked: 'How's Mrs. Hollis?'

'Why, poorly, ma'am,' Pat confessed. 'You'll see for yourself, so it's as well to know beforehand. She's cruel thin, and sickly to be sure.' He added in a low, sober tone: 'Eh, yes, she's not for long, I'm thinking. Mostly she keeps her bed, but nothing would do her but she'd make all ready at the house for you, and she'll be up and smiling to greet you at the door.'

'Oh!' Jenny's breath caught on the word, and her hand touched her throat in a sore distress. 'What's the matter with her, Pat?'

'I'd not know,' Pat admitted. He swung the horses into the drive. 'But you can soon see for yourself, for here we are, to be sure.'

The door swung wide to greet them, and Evered saw in the doorway a smiling, pretty girl curiously like Jenny in many out-ward ways; and behind her an older woman in garments too big for her, haggard and weary but with merry, brimming eyes. Jenny ran to greet them both, hugging Mrs. Hollis, making him known to them.

'This is Mrs. Hollis, and this is Ruth Green, John,' she said. 'I've told you how they always took care of me.'

Pat behind her spoke strongly: 'Begging your pardon, ma'am, not Ruth Green but Mrs. Tierney now.' She turned to see him chuckling with pride and delight, and cried out in surprise, and

Ruth blushed happily, and Jenny kissed her again and told them both:

'I'm so glad! You're a lucky man, Pat. Ruth was always dreaming about you. She cried for hours the time the men broke your leg.'

'Aye, she had her dreams and I had mine,' he agreed. 'But the money fever made me blind awhile, till I got well of it and could see the sweet one right under my nose all the time.'

Jenny took Ruth's arm. 'Come and tell me all about it,' she commanded, and she went off upstairs with Ruth and Mrs. Hollis, Pat summoning that cousin of his from the stables to help with their bags, and to go presently to fetch their trunks. John was left alone belowstairs, to inspect this house that would be at first their home. He stood for a long time before that likeness of Jenny which Mr. Hardy had painted, wondering at her perfectly recaptured beauty. The painter had even known how to fix in pigment the lucid purity of expression which was her outstanding attribute. John remembered fleetingly what Ephraim had said of this portrait, but it held for his eyes nothing sinister at all.

Jenny presently returned to him. 'Welcome home, John!' she said. She looked around the room with shadowed eyes. 'We'll live here till we can build for ourselves. I don't want to live here always.' She came to link her hand through his arm. 'I want to forget all of my life before I met you. I didn't really live till I met you, darling, after all.'

He said doubtfully that it would be a long time before he could afford to build a house; but she touched her finger to his lips to silence him. 'Please,' she protested, 'don't ever say "I" and "you" and "mine" and "yours"! I'm yours, John, all of me, and everything that's mine is yours too. I'll never be able to give you all I want to give you; but I'll give you myself and everything I have and only wish there were more to give.'

He kissed her, and in his arms she said: 'I'm so glad about Pat and Ruth, aren't you? He knows all about Ephraim, but before the baby came he asked her to marry him. The baby's a boy and they've named it Pat, and Pat's as proud of it as if it were his own — and proud of Ruth too.'

'He's a good man.'

She nodded. 'But John, I'm distressed about Mrs. Hollis. I put her to bed in the guest room next ours. She used to be so plump and cheerful. It's terrible to see her now. Ruth and I undressed her, and she's thin as a picked bird. She's cheerful enough; but poor thing, she says her feet keep going to sleep all the time.' She added ruefully: 'Ruth says the doctor can do nothing for her.'

But then she cried: 'There! I mustn't make sad our homecoming! Come see your office, John. It was Isaiah's but now it will be yours. You're going to be a busy man, taking care of all Colonel Black's affairs — and mine.'

II

John plunged in fact into an intense activity. Colonel Black, to keep in touch with the booming market for wild lands, spent several days every week at the Bangor House. The hotel was crowded, already succeeding the Exchange Coffee House as the centre of the speculative activities of the city; and the public rooms were full all day and most of the night of men who packed together in groups that forever formed and dissolved again; and the air was heavy with the steady talk of profits — always of profits — in the thousands of transactions that went on from day to day. Through May and into June — when the steamboat Bangor on her first trip brought three hundred more potential buyers — there were constant bidders for Bingham land. Colonel Black dealt with them, and John was always by his side.

The city itself was suffering from growing pains. Street lights had been put up at the busiest corners; there was talk of building sidewalks; and new construction — stores and business blocks and houses — was everywhere under way. Bangor was full of new enterprises. Freeman Duren came in one day to sell Colonel Black and John copies of the first city directory. He was a man of intelligence and cultivation, and with a bookish bent — though without any creative talent — which would lead him to produce such works as a Bibliography of Maine, and a brief History of Penobscot County, and to serve as secretary of the Bangor Historical Society when it was founded years later. He had come to Bangor in the August preceding, a young man of twenty; and he set himself up as a bookseller and with a boundless energy undertook at once to prepare this directory of the young city which was growing by the hundreds during each week of the summer months. When he came in today he proudly displayed the small volume.

'Everything you want to know about Bangor is right here,' he declared. 'A history of the town, the names of all city and county and state officers, a list of banks, advertisements from the principal merchants, stage routes and the hours at which the stages leave, city ordinances, and the name and business of every man in Bangor, fourteen hundred of them. Anything you want to know, gentlemen, is in this book!'

John and the Colonel each bought a copy, and the bookseller filled in their names in the labels pasted on the cover.

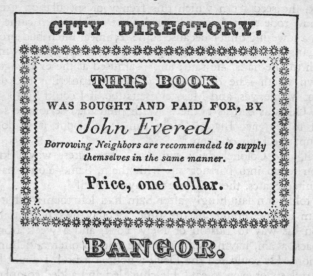

CITY DIRECTORY.

THIS BOOK

WAS BOUGHT AND PAID FOR, BY

John Evered

Borrowing Neighbors are recommended to supply themselves in the same manner.

Price, one dollar.

BANGOR.

'That's my own notion,' Duren explained, and he added frankly: 'It's as much a protection for me as for you, gentlemen. Where will the bookselling business ever get to, if people borrow books instead of buying them? Why, if you'd believe it, men will come into my store to look up a name in my directory and never offer to buy a copy. They'll spend hundreds — yes, and thousands too — to buy land they never saw; but they won't spend a dollar for a book like that, that they can hold in their hands.'

John, looking through the pages of his new purchase, commented: 'Must have been a job of work to get all this information together.'

'Why, it was and it wasn't,' Duren explained. 'Of course it meant knocking at just about every door in town; but that's not a bad idea for a young man who wants to get along. You get acquainted. I probably know more people to speak to than any man in Bangor — and I haven't been here a year yet.'

Colonel Black suggested that Bangor had already outgrown the directory; and Duren replied with a qualifying assent that John in later years came to recognize as habitual. 'Well, it has and it hasn't! You'll find just about everyone in my directory is still here; yes, and means to stay. But I didn't take any account of them that were just here to make their pile and go. We'll be rid of them some day, but most of the men in my book will still be here.'

John liked Freeman Duren, as he liked most of the men he met. He came to know well, and to be amused by, Sam Smith who had planted the seed from which this frenzy of speculation grew and who now rode the tide as a log rides the rapids. Sam came in one day in a towering anger because some technical hitch had prevented his buying a township offered for sale by the state. 'Makes me mad enough to bite nails,' he said; and — amused at the extravagance of his own wrath — he declared: 'I'd like to bankrupt the damned State of Maine, yes, and Massachusetts too, if I could find a way to do it! One's as bad as t'other.' With pretended seriousness he appealed to Colonel Black: 'How can I go about it, Colonel, to bankrupt the both of them?'

'Well,' the Colonel drily suggested, 'the surest way I know is for you to go into partnership with them, Sam. You'd bankrupt the United States, the way you're buying land!'

He told John laughingly after Sam had left them: 'That man's a steam engine, going all the time! Today he's here, tomorrow he's on his way to Boston or New York, and a week from now he's back again, having sold what he had to offer and hungry to buy more. He could sell the Devil a house on fire! I doubt he ever stops to sleep, or even to eat.' He chuckled and added complacently: 'Well, I'll sell him as much as he will buy and pay for.'

Sam came to them again and again. He was stocked with stories of successful speculation, which he spouted endlessly.

'You're touched in the head to sell an acre, Colonel!' he insisted. 'And it's worse to sell at the prices you're taking. Why, this thing has just begun! We've pine enough in Maine to build a house for every family in the country, and mills and water power to saw it into boards. I heard the other day about the winter's cut on one tract that was bought for two dollars an acre. They cut two hundred and twenty-seven thousand feet of pine off one acre; one acre, man; one little, miserable, two-dollar acre; and that pine, sawed into boards, is worth up to twenty dollars a thousand at the wharf! That's four or five thousand dollars' worth of lumber off a two-dollar acre. And yet you go on selling land!'

'Glad to sell you all you can pay for, Sam,' Colonel Black told him cheerfully. 'But, you know, you're talking the price up on yourself all the time.'

'I'll pay anything I can raise. Man, you're blind! D'ye know Mr. Chamberlain of Boston? He bought twenty-three thousand acres at forty-two cents in '32, then had to let it go. It brought eighty cents that winter, sold at one-fifty last summer, sold again at five dollars last week — and the buyer's asking eight today!'

He threw up his hands. 'And that's nothing, Colonel. Nothing!
I had one piece — I paid a dollar and a half, sold it at eight dollars
yesterday.'

'Did you get your money?' the Colonel asked drily.

'One-fourth down and three payments.'

'Bills?'

'Notes,' Sam confessed, and colored angrily at his own word.
'But damn it, the notes are good! I can discount them tomorrow!
Man, I've seen half a township fetch a hundred and eight thousand
dollars. I sold a full township to some New York men two weeks
ago at twelve dollars. That cost twelve cents, when Massachusetts
first sold the land. There's a two-hundred-thousand-dollar profit on
that one tract! Why, Colonel, I can name you five men in the
Bangor House right now who were bankrupts when they came
from Boston, and every one of them is worth a fortune today. Do
you know Brown of Vassalboro?' The Colonel shook his head.
'Well, he bought a township a few years ago for seven thousand
dollars. His father took it over and sold it a while back for ten
dollars per acre — thought he did well — but the buyer sold it again
for twelve dollars within the week.' He said impressively: 'Two
hundred and sixty-four thousand dollars! Why, Colonel, you
could have bought all the Massachusetts lands in Maine for a
hundred thousand less than that, fifteen years ago.' He laughed
like a drunken man, intoxicated with his own words. 'Did ye hear
about the two paupers? They got loose from the almshouse one
morning last week, and before they were caught that afternoon
they'd made eighteen hundred dollars!'

John heard these torrents of golden words day after day, but their
very violence was their own remedy; and Colonel Black laughed
at the tales and sold when he could — if the purchaser could pay.

III

Just as John plunged at once into a continual activity so did
Jenny, resuming her old contacts, renewing her old round of visits
to the many humble folk whom she befriended. She and John
went to church in diligent attendance. Even from the pulpit they
heard echoes of the speculative frenzy which filled the city. The
Reverend Pomroy devoted a sermon to the subject. He said — without naming names — that one of the deacons was setting an evil
example by trading in bonds.

'I thought it my duty to remonstrate with him,' he confessed.
'But he met me with an unseemly levity, distorting the words of

Saint Paul to say: "I would that thou wert almost and altogether such as I am, Reverend, except these bonds!" ' A smile appeared here and there in the congregation; and the minister saw this and was inspired to a blistering exhortation, denouncing not only the gambling but the fraud and chicanery which went with it, citing incidents. Sellers took prospective purchasers, strangers to the region, to inspect a fine tract — and then sold them, under pretense that it was the same, another piece of land altogether. Surveyors were bribed to make false reports. Men executed and sold bonds on land to which they held no title. One man sold house lots on the outskirts of the town without owning the land. The city, the Reverend Pomroy said, had become a second Sodom, with every other vice following the trail blazed by the vices of lying and cheating and gambling; and he predicted in a blazing prophecy the loss and ruin and destruction sure to ensue.

Jenny and John agreed profoundly with everything he said, John because he shared Colonel Black's views, Jenny because she shared the minister's reprobation of the increasing dissipation which followed in the train of this synthetic prosperity. They had returned to Bangor in time to see the lumbermen come out of the woods after their winter's work, and the district where Jenny had lived as a child, Exchange and Washington and Hancock Streets, was for days ablaze with drunken, fighting, gambling men. Sailors from the scores of vessels in the river joined the throng, and when the drives were down, the crowds of roisterers received new recruits. No unescorted woman was safe from annoyance on the streets, even by day; and Jenny, going to and fro among her friends, urged that it was time the ladies of Bangor took the temperance movement more strongly in hand. She prepared a petition which had seven hundred and fifty signers, all 'females of Bangor' and which was forwarded to Augusta, appealing to the Legislature to 'banish from our houses and our State the reproach and misery which the use of ardent spirits constantly imposes.'

Within a month after she and John came to Bangor she had resumed her place in the forefront of every movement for good in the city; but the temperance cause took most of her time. The State Temperance Society was gaining strength every year, and a score or so of Bangor's leading citizens had attended its meeting in Augusta in February. There were regular gatherings in the Hammond Street vestry where representatives from all the churches came together to advocate total abstinence even from cider and strong beer. Elder Lincoln Pittridge was the flaming leader of the cause; and it was his urgency which led to the inclusion of these mild potations in the pledge. He promoted the formation of the Youth's Temperance Society and the Young Men's Mutual Reform Society. He was a handsome man in his middle thirties, lighted by some inner fire; and Jenny — and John for her sake — came to know him well, and to respect his sincerity as much as his zeal.

IV

They had time, too, for their own affairs. Jenny was determined that they should build as soon as possible a house of their own, and they began to look for a site. Isaiah had owned several parcels of land around the outskirts of the city, and they inspected each of these possible locations. John's vote was for a certain piece of high land by the river; but Jenny pointed out, with a foresight which surprised him, that along the water wharves were sure to extend, and all that part of town would turn to business in the end.

'I used to live on Exchange Street when I was a girl,' she reminded him. 'And you know what it's like down there now, not fit for pigs!'

This was true. Even along Harlow Street, where it paralleled the Stream above Main, the dives which catered to sailors and lumbermen were extending. So their choice fell at last on a tract well beyond the then limits of the city, on the north side of the Old Town road.

The first time they drove out there, Jenny said: 'I made Isaiah buy this land we're going to see, John. It's all woods. Father used to bring me out here, when I was little, to explore; and we'd stop at the Howard farm on the way home and Mrs. Howard used to give us cookies and milk and tell us stories about Indians, and Mr. Howard would tell us about fighting with Wolfe at Quebec.' She laughed at a sudden memory and said: 'She told us about once an Indian came to the house and wanted breakfast, and just as he started to eat it another one came in and they began to fight over it, and while they were still fighting, another Indian came in and ate up all the breakfast! She was sweet. They came here to live before there was a town at all. Their daughter Mary — Mrs. Mayhew — was the first white baby born here. Mrs. Howard died when I was seventeen, and Mr. Howard only lived two or three months afterward.' Her hands were tight on his arm. 'Oh, John, I hope we'll live to be old, and die together! I know I wouldn't live a minute if you died.'

He smiled. 'I'm not thinking of dying soon, Jenny. And if I did — you're beautiful enough to bring a dead man back to life.' They were richly happy together in these long June days.

They explored the piece of land, some twenty or thirty acres, a dozen times, tramping through the thickets hand in hand. The pines which once had stood here were long since cut off, but they had been replaced by a fine stand of hardwood, beach and oak and maple. The spot which after many considerations they selected was on the crest of a low knoll, high enough and so placed that they would have a glimpse of the river when a few trees were cut away.

But the site had a defect. Exactly where the house would need to stand, one oak reared above its fellows. It was a majestic tree, its trunk straight as a pine and full forty feet to the first branches, clean and fine; and since the others near were lesser, they wished to save it.

'But it's in just the wrong place,' John pointed out. 'That's exactly where the house ought to be.' They had planned a frame house two stories high and shaped like an el, facing southeastward toward the river, the wing carrying back to shed and barn behind. 'It will come right where the el angles on,' he said. 'Unless we change our plan — or put the house somewhere else, lower down the knoll.'

There was in him a deep affection for fine trees, so that when he laid his axe to the base of a mighty pine it was regretfully; and he sometimes made in his thoughts a plea to the tree itself to be forgiven, just as savages about to kill an animal sacred to their eyes sometimes address to it an apology before they loose the deadly missile.

Jenny would have cut the great oak without a qualm, but John was so strong in his desire to escape from that necessity that she tried to discover some compromise. They came one late afternoon to the knoll, and brought a basket of supper and stayed till dusk to watch the moonrise, talking together in hushed voices in the silent wood. The evening was still and sultry, and he heard a far rumble and said a shower was coming, said they had best start homeward; but she would not.

'The tree will keep off the worst of it,' she urged. 'Let's stay, John. Let's pretend we're lost children, or secret lovers meeting here.'

So they sat on the warm ground at the foot of the tree while the moon through clouds pricked the forest with a pale, fairy light, and they were young together. He thought she was more beautiful than ever in these months when the secret they shared was still their own. She wanted him always with her, was jealous of their every moment apart and full of tender yearnings that could turn to a sort of fury when her knotted fists beat at him in passionate ecstasies, as though to inflict pain somehow contented and assuaged her.

When the thundershower came nearer, and the crashes followed more and more closely on the blazing lightning strokes, he was uneasy to be gone; but in a laughing madness, as though the tingling air charged her with electric fluid, she held him by her side; and when the first drops spattered on the leaves high above them she drew him close, whispering secretly:

'Cover me, John. Protect me from the rain.'

And for a while it was as though the thunder and the lightning were within them, reverberating through them as it reverberated among the wooded hills and passed at last across the river and so moved on and was gone; till with the passing of the storm sanity came back to them again.

The full beat of the shower had not touched them, and no more than a sprinkle of heavy drops penetrated the thick-leaved branches that were their shelter. 'You see!' she cried in happy triumph. 'We didn't get wet, hardly at all. The tree was like a roof over us.' And she exclaimed in a delighted inspiration: 'It was our rooftree, John! That's what it must always be — the rooftree over us. We'll build it into our house!'

He did not at once understand, and she urged, in a quick excitement at her own thought: 'We'll make a great timber out of it for a ridgepole, like the key of an arch. Our house will be like an arch, John, with the rooftree to hold it together.' She clung to him in a sweet ecstasy. 'You're my rooftree, John, holding our family together, standing against any storms.' She laughed in a soft tenderness. 'You've loved the big tree so! I think you're brothers, you and the oak! Will you always be strong for me?'

'It's too heavy for a ridgepole, Jenny,' he said doubtfully.

'You're so practical!' she protested. 'But so am I! We'll build our house strong enough to hold it up. I want our house strong to last forever, John. Please, let's do!'

There was a masculine slowness in him, and she had to persuade him long. He never quite understood this wish in her to erect the great oak's trunk as a symbol in the very structure of their home; but he could not in these months when she was doubly dear to him deny her anything.

So the tree was felled, and others conveniently near, and timbers were rough-hewed and left to season for a winter. She was impatient to see the work put under way; but John said they must give the wood months to dry out and toughen.

'It will be time enough next spring to frame the house,' he said;

and he laughed and told her: 'We'll have to use heavy stuff, Jenny.' He began to catch the infection of her eagerness. 'We'll need all oak, sills fourteen inches square, and posts a foot on a side, and a plate big enough for a ship's keel, to support that ridgepole you're bound to have.'

'It's the way I want it, John,' she insisted happily. 'I want the old oak for our rooftree, the keystone of our house, just as you will always be the strong, unshakable keystone of my life — and of our lives.'

7

MRS. HOLLIS died in August. She never left her bed in the guest room after their homecoming. Almost at once, mortification set in at her toes and she died horribly, and there was the smell of death in her room and in all the house as long as she lived.

Nevertheless she was happy during these last weeks of her life, hiding her suffering behind a mask of chuckling laughter, joking about her own agonies. 'I never looked to die a little at a time,' she declared. 'It's hard doing. Not everyone can manage it, I tell you!' And she said to Jenny: 'Not but I'd rather go the way Tim Hager did. Mind the night he just fell down and never got up again? That would be some easier for me — and for you, too, my dear.'

Jenny during the weary days stayed much with her, giving the dying woman what comfort she could, giving her own strength so unstintingly that John was concerned, and sought to persuade her for the sake of their baby to spare herself the ordeal. But Jenny laughed at his fears.

'I'll be fine, John, and so will our son,' she promised him. 'It makes me happy to comfort Mrs. Hollis all I can. I've known her since I was a little girl, you see.'

She seemed in fact to thrive on the devoted service she gave the dying woman; and sometimes John, coming home in the late afternoon, catching at once that faint smell of death which filled the house, would hear from the lower hall their laughing voices as in the room above they lived over again the days of Jenny's girlhood. That they should be thus gay together filled him with wonder. Jenny was ingenious in devising ways to amuse and divert the dying woman. Once Mrs. Hollis saw herself in a mirror and was distressed by her own shrunken, haggard countenance and her stringy white hair; and Jenny went to Mrs. Shaw on Main Street and bought a frizette and some French ringlets and fancy hair-work and pinned them on Mrs. Hollis' old head, and John came home and heard them laughing together almost in hysteria at the appearance she presented.

Mrs. Hollis liked to tell him about the years when Jenny was a child, and she told John how she rated Tim one night for his drunkenness till Jenny came to her father's defense. 'She fair drove me out of the house,' she confessed. 'She's a terror when she's roused, Mr. Evered. Afraid for my life I was!' She chuckled merrily. 'You'll best mind your manners or she'll handle you, big as you are.'

'She has me scared,' Evered admitted, smiling. 'If I don't do to suit her, she gives me a good pounding.'

Mrs. Hollis nodded. 'I never saw a man but was the better for a lick now and then!' she declared. 'I mind the time I broke a broomstick over Hollis — but he never came home with a drop in him too much from that day on.'

She had always in life borne herself decorously enough, but now, as though with the dissolution of the flesh so were the bonds long laid upon her loosed, her tongue ran freely. She spoke of the night when Tim died and Jenny came to Isaiah, and Isaiah fetched Deacon Adams and Amos Patten to consult with him about her fate. 'I have to laugh, thinking of the three of them standing staring at her like Susannah and the elders,' she said, mirthful at the memory. 'And this pretty innocent, not knowing what she did, putting out her sweet little leg all bruised and cut for them to see, and them weak as water at the sight of it! It was me told her to marry Isaiah. "You'll not have the fun out of it you would from a fine young man," I told her. "But he'll be good to you — if you can stand bedding with the old galoot now and then — and you'll still be young enough to find yourself a proper husband after he's gone."' She appealed to Jenny in a sudden anxiety: 'Was I wrong, my dear?'

Jenny touched her brow. 'You were never wrong. You always loved me, I know.' She looked toward John. 'You were right about my finding a proper husband, you see; and Isaiah was always good to me.'

'And you to him,' said the old woman stoutly; and she told John: 'You've a dear good wife in Jenny, Mr. Evered.'

'I know I have.'

'Many a poor woman in this town has reason to name her in her prayers, for she's always tending the sick and the old and weary — like me.' Despite her smiles, her eyes filled.

'I can never do enough for you,' Jenny told her warmly. 'I never can pay you for all you've done for me.'

John and Jenny summoned every doctor in town to see her, and she accepted their prescriptions cheerily enough. 'But there ain't a one of them knows what he's about,' she declared. 'They make wise faces and talk big, but I go on dying in my own way, just the same.' She chuckled in deep amusement. 'I've heard old Doc Perley up at Old Town say: "When disease in any form comes in contact with me it meets an all-powerful, all-conquering antagonist." You'd have thought that the folks he took care of would have turned out to be immortal, but they went on dying just the same.' And when the consulting doctors thought amputation might save her, or at least prolong her life, she said robustly: 'You'll leave me to die in one piece, thanks all the same!' And she laughed again and related how Doctor Bradford, during an operation, wished to lay aside his knife for a moment and absent-mindedly jabbed it into his patient's leg. 'And when the folks watching him said that was no way to do, he said: "Don't you give it a thought. That hole in him will get well before this one!"' When one day Doctor Mason told her frankly that there was not one chance in a hundred she would recover, she retorted briskly: 'Well, I'll take that chance!'

Her constant good humor made them forget her suffering. She was small and smaller day by day, but till delirium and at last coma heralded the imminent end she was always cheerful, had always an amusing word to say. John came to share Jenny's affection for her, and to respect the old woman's steady valor. When she died, he said to Jenny: 'She conquered death. I never knew it could be so ugly as hers was, but she made it seem beautiful.' He added: 'But I hope the long strain wasn't too hard for you.'

'It wasn't,' she assured him; yet he found that during the first days she told him over and over every detail of Mrs. Hollis' agony, dwelling on it again and again. He protested that she should at least try to forget the horrors she had witnessed; but she said:

'It does me good to talk about them, helps get them out of my mind.'

It was a relief to John when she began to forget, and when the

house was free at last from the smell of death which had haunted
it so long.

II

Despite her devotion to Mrs. Hollis, Jenny even during the old
woman's illness was alertly interested in all that went forward
in the city. She regretted that Mr. Manning of New York had
opened a school to instruct 'young ladies, misses and masters' in
the arts of dancing and waltzing. 'He says that he watches morals
and manners and deportment,' she told John. 'But his saying so
just shows the sort of thing dancing can lead to.'

John chuckled and told her how Margaret Saladine had under-
taken to teach him to waltz at Colonel Black's home in Ellsworth
the summer before; and she smiled, but she said: 'I'm glad you
didn't learn, John. Of course, dancing may be all very well for
ladies and gentlemen, but it sets a bad example to others.' She
added: 'I don't mean to criticize Miss Saladine. Do you think
I'm too much of a puritan, John?'

He told her she was neither too much nor too little of anything.
'You're exactly right,' he said; and he added: 'I saw Judge Saladine yesterday. You know they went to England last winter, and
she's staying in Paris till fall to cultivate her voice and to learn
French. He says she'll call on you when she comes home. You'll
like her, Jenny.'

'Oh, I do, already!' she agreed. 'Of course I only know her a
little. The ladies I saw most, as long as Isaiah lived, were his
friends' wives, older than I; but I always liked Miss Saladine so
much. I'll want to know her better.' She added smilingly: 'But I
shall see to it, John, that she doesn't put any more dancing in your
head, the little hussy!'

'She was mighty nice to me at Colonel Black's. I was just off
the farm, and I felt lost.'

She chided him gently. 'You don't ever need to be ashamed of
coming from a farm, John. Your mother's the finest woman I
know.'

'I wasn't ashamed,' he protested, reddening a little. 'You ought
to know that! I only meant that Miss Saladine was kind to me
when she might have been amused.'

She kissed him proudly. 'She'd better never let me see her laughing at my John or I'll scratch her eyes out!' And they laughed
together.

She and John went to the concert in the City Hall on the first of July, when a mixed quartette from Boston — Mr. and Mrs. Andrews, Miss Woodward and Mr. Comer — sang 'Hark, Apollo, Strike the Lyre!', 'On Fair Zurich's Waters,' 'Pretty Polly Hopkins,' and a dozen other selections. Jenny thought Mr. Comer's voice was no longer as good as it must once have been; but John laughed heartily at the comical aspects of the performance in which Mr. Comer led the clowning, and preferred the mirth to the music. He good-naturedly escorted her to the frequent sacred concerts, but they gave him no pleasure except through her. He was much more entertained by Mr. Nichols, the ventriloquist.

Twice during the early summer they went to Ellsworth, to stay a few days at Colonel Black's. John would have enjoyed these visits, proud of Jenny's beauty, proud of the admiration she aroused; but she confessed a firm disapproval of the Colonel's prodigal hospitality. 'People can have good times,' she insisted, 'without drinking all the time!' He was always a little surprised, and sometimes amused, at her severity, and once or twice he teasingly reminded her that she was not in all matters so austere; but she kissed him and said: 'It's different, darling, when it's you!'

III

Through that summer in Bangor the speculative tide ran high. To sell land — or to buy it — was the universal occupation, and prices continued to soar. Sam Smith bought from the Poster estate which John administered for Jenny eleven business lots at ten thousand dollars — Isaiah had originally paid four hundred and fifty dollars for the land — and came a week later to boast that he had sold them for thirteen thousand. Ransom Clark laid out Broadway Park, where lots were to be sold with a requirement that two-story brick houses should be erected on each one; but the lots went slowly. No one wanted to buy and build. Every buyer wanted to sell as quickly and as profitably as possible.

But the crowd in town was interested in other things besides business, and every form of entertainment was well patronized. During the summer several groups of young men went on excursions to Moosehead Lake. The steamer Moosehead had been put in service there; and a party might go and spend a week on her or a month, cruising around the lake, fishing, or drinking and carousing if they chose. The trip was not an easy one, involving a stage journey to Monson and a fifteen-mile walk to reach the lake. Tickets were on sale in the bay at the Bangor House and the accounts brought back by those who made the trip helped attract new customers. A dozen times John was urged to go, but he preferred to stay at home with Jenny; and when he told her in a chuckling amusement tales he had heard of what happened on these excursions, she was strong in disapproval. 'It's shameful to think of,' she said. 'Young men going up there to do nothing but drink for a week or two weeks on end!'

'Well, they fish too,' he reminded her.

'That's just an excuse,' she said.

John encountered one day at the Bangor House a man just returned from one of these trips, a young man with pretentious side whiskers whose name was David Crosby and whom he had known in Harvard. Crosby had been one of the wealthier students and his home was in Boston, and he and John had shared no common ground; but now John as Colonel Black's associate was a respected figure in the city, and Crosby sought him out with such a friendly greeting that John invited the young man to dinner. But he warned Crosby not to tell Jenny anything about this Moosehead excursion. 'She doesn't like that sort of thing,' he said.

'No more she should,' Crosby agreed. 'It was a rough time, Evered.'

He was delighted with Jenny, and she asked him at dinner whether he meant to settle in Bangor.

'No, I just came to see the excitement,' he said. 'We hear of nothing else in Boston! I came to be amused, but I'm catching the disease. You can't escape it, can't be twenty-four hours here without finding yourself — not knowing just how it happened — owning at least a quarter of a township; and about the time you realize it, someone grabs your elbow and wants to buy it from you at a profit.' He laughed and said: 'The queer thing is, no one seems to lose any money! Every seller makes a profit, or says he does.'

John laughed with him. 'But that's because they've stopped thinking of money as specie, or even as bills,' he said. 'Money now is all notes. You buy a deed and give your note for a thousand, and I buy it from you and give you my note for two thousand, and I sell it for three thousand and take a note in payment, and the man who bought from me does the same.' He said smilingly: 'Why, you and Mrs. Evered and I could be millionaires in an hour on that basis, just buying and selling to each other around and around in a circle, ignoring our debts and counting up our profits — if our hands didn't get tired of writing notes!'

'Then you expect the whole thing to blow up?'

'Money's tighter all the time,' John assured him. 'Sooner or later men will be called on to take up their obligations — and they won't be able to do it.'

He asked what the other had done since he left Cambridge, and Crosby said: 'I've travelled, mostly. I'm in cotton with my father, you know. I went to Mississippi last winter, on a buying trip.'

Jenny inquired in a quick interest: 'Did you see any slaves?'

'Thousands, everywhere.'

'Were they terribly abused and miserable?'

Crosby shook his head. 'No. They're a cheerful, happy lot, mostly.'

She asked in a voice so tense that John looked at her in surprise: 'Are they whipped all the time?'

'Sometimes, I suppose; but I never saw anything of the sort.' He added soberly: 'But I saw a white man whipped, in Natchez. That was pretty bad.' And while she listened with pent breath, he explained: 'He was a man named Foster. They said he had beaten his wife to death with a nigger whip. He was tried for murder, but he was acquitted, so a mob — they were all leading citizens, I was told — gave him a hundred and fifty lashes with cowhide whips, wore out two whips on him. Then they poured hot tar over him, and rolled him in feathers, and made him march through town, with a crowd trailing along and throwing rocks at him and yelling.'

Jenny asked in her low tones: 'Did you see him whipped?' John looked at her uneasily, thinking of their baby, thinking she should not hear such things, disturbed by the fascination which tales of violence always had for her; but Crosby said:

'Yes. The cotton broker I was dealing with took me to see it.'

She wetted her lips with her tongue. 'Did the whip cut his back? Did he bleed?'

John spoke quickly: 'Stop, Crosby! It's sickening to hear about. I suppose people who keep slaves don't mind such things, but I don't like the sound of them.'

'I don't like the thought of slavery myself,' Crosby agreed, 'but it's the only way to raise cotton. These damned abolitionists will ruin the country before they're through.'

Jenny took issue with him on that point. Her opposition to slavery and all its works was already definite and strong. John listened to their discussion, glad they no longer talked of whipping, wondering that she should become flushed and agitated over a question which seemed to him, absorbed as he was in business which engaged him every hour, so remote from their lives and far away.

IV

Despite her slenderness, the fact that Jenny was to have a baby would never be conspicuous; but John discovered that pregnancy affected her in other ways, making her at first intensely ardent and desirous, making her afterward easily irritable so that sometimes, quite without intention, he provoked her to angry outbursts which left him bewildered and unhappy. When one day in October he reported that a mob had attempted to tar and feather Garrison, the editor of the *Liberator,* for his abolition doctrines, she accused him of sympathizing with the mob and raged, with streaming tears. The pro-slavery and anti-abolition meeting at the City Hall a little later provoked her to fury, and she upbraided him because he continued to meet and to deal courteously with Mr. Jewett, Captain Louder, Samuel Upton and others who had spoken at that meeting.

She had, too, a morbid interest in ugly things. Early in November she insisted on attending the trial for murder of Isaac Spencer. The trial was held in the Baptist Meeting House, and the galleries were occupied by ladies; but John urged that for her to go to court was not only unseemly, but might have a bad effect on the baby. She silenced him angrily, demanding whether he expected her to sit all day at home and never go anywhere or do anything; and in the end inevitably she had her way. For the three days of the trial she was always in attendance, and when Spencer was sentenced to be hanged she came home in a strange excitement which John could not understand, and insisted on telling him how Spencer had looked when he heard his doom; and she described to him at length and in stark detail the hanging she had seen at Castine long ago. John's floundering attempts to lead the conversation to some other topic angered her, and he was helplessly silent at last under the storm he had provoked.

Her rages during these months were the more dreadful because, no matter how infuriated she became, she never raised her voice; and the impact of harsh words spoken gently was sinister and frightening. She was like a cruel and pitiless judge, impervious to the suffering and terror of those he sentences. John winced under the biting lash of her soft whispering wrath.

The most violent — and what to his relief proved to be the last of these outbursts — occurred in November. It was provoked in a circuitous way. Along with the price of wild lands, the price of pine was advancing; and this had put a premium on trespassing and the theft of timber. Colonel Black was active in prosecuting every such depredation on Bingham lands and it was a part of John's duties to attend court when an occasional marauder was brought to trial. The Colonel's policy was to seize the stolen property as evidence. He told John:

'You can't count on a jury anywhere in the lumbering counties, not even here in Bangor, unless your case is so strong they don't dare refuse a verdict. Juries are drawn from loafers and worthless men who hate the landowners. But if you secure the logs, even if the case goes against you, you've got your property back and they can't take it away from you.'

In accordance with this practice, when that summer the Colonel's agents located some logs which had been stolen off Bingham land and boomed in Sunkhaze Stream, he took possession, marked the logs with a B, and set a watch to protect them. The result, when the trespassers sought to recapture the fruits of their theft, was a bloody affray in which some bones were broken; and it led to court where John, at Judge Saladine's elbow, took a silent but effective part in securing the conviction of the men on trial.

One evening a few days later he went down to Carr's Wharf to give some instructions to a group of Colonel Black's men who were to start up-river in the morning; and a man whose conviction he had helped to secure recognized him as he passed under one of the new street lamps, and without warning kicked him from behind, violently.

John staggered forward, fell off the sidewalk of two-inch hemlock planks that had recently been built, bounded to his feet and turned toward his assailant. He was not by nature combative, but once roused there was a lively recklessness in him; and the fact that he now found himself facing not one man but three did not make him hesitate. He said evenly:

'Which one of you was it?'

The man, instinctively withdrawing at Evered's advance, cried hotly: 'Come on, boys, let's kill the bastard!'

Evered, as though this were enough identification, leaped forward and struck his assailant a crashing blow in the face. He felt a sharp pain as the bones in his hand let go, but he felt too the grate of bone in the man's shattered jaw. Then others joined the affray, and there was a strangling arm around his neck and he was down, and boots were thumping at his ribs. He pulled one enemy under him, kneeing the writhing body, smashing at the other's face while blows rained on his own head and shoulders; and the world was lost in a swimming mist and that man with the broken jaw was screaming somewhere, his screams a hollow, dreadful sound that gave John a hungry satisfaction.

He himself knew only by after report what in these brief moments he accomplished; but the tale of it would be told and retold, and would become such a legend in the town that not again in his lifetime would he have to meet any physical challenge. One man, as a result of his first blow, wore a twisted face and a wry neck as long as he lived. Another had a shattered arm, and a toothless gap in the front of his mouth where John's fist had landed; and the third, leaping on Evered from behind, was flung over his head and hurled headlong, smashing against the steps of Barker's store so that he did not walk for six weeks' time.

In that confusion in the dark, and before any rescue could come to him or any man could interfere, Evered himself — having beaten the man on the ground to insensibility — arose on wide-braced legs to look for a new antagonist. He himself had not gone scot free. His right ear was torn so that blood curtained his neck on that side; his hand was broken by the weight of the blows he himself had dealt; and there was a cut across his scalp just above the hair line with a skin flap hanging down, so that his face was a crimson mask and blood was in his eyes.

Yet he came to his feet, and braced his legs, and dared the world; and when helpful hands touched him, at first he fought them all away, till his senses cleared and he yielded to their ministrations.

They led him into a near-by house where Doctor Mason came to repair his hurts, and John found an old friend in a tall fair woman whom he had not seen for many years. She helped the doctor with bandages; and then Pat Tierney, who had heard of the affray, came to take John home. The night air brought John back to lucidity again, and he remembered that Jenny must not without warning see him in this state, so he waited outside the house while Pat went in to tell her that he was not as badly hurt as he seemed. At Pat's word she came swift to the door to meet her husband, and with a bandage on his brow and another on his hand, and limping from that kick which had taken him unawares, he faced her there. She caught him in her arms, crying out in tenderness, and she and Pat led him up the stairs; and when Pat was gone she helped John out of his torn and soiled and muddy clothes and so to bed.

Yet, though all she did was gentle and assuaging, after the first moment her words were not. She rated him for his folly in going down to the docks at such an hour, scolded him in a petulant indignation, said he should have remembered her and the dear burden she bore and protected her from such a shocking sight as he now presented. He guessed that it was her anxiety for him which prompted her to anger now and tried to reassure her, but she demanded, looking at him in a sudden sharp suspicion:

'Where did this happen, John? Who were the men? Why did they fight you?'

He could only guess, and he was too fair-minded to accuse any man without certainty, so he said he did not know who they were. She asked: 'Well, who tied up your hurts?'

He told her the fight had begun at the corner of Exchange and Washington Streets, by Barker's store. 'They took me into a house there,' he said, 'and sent for Doctor Mason.'

She looked at the bandage around his brow. 'Did Doctor Mason wear petticoats?' she insisted in sharp accusation. 'For this is a strip torn from one!'

So he explained: 'No, a woman in the house there bandaged me.' And he added: 'I knew her years ago, up on the Connecticut, when I was driving logs down that river. She used to run a boarding house for lumbermen.'

Jenny asked, suddenly intent, yet without raising her voice: 'What's her name?'

'Lena Tempest,' he said.

She spoke softly. 'Is she the one who pretends to do laundry work, to hide her real trade?'

'Why, I don't know.'

Her face was suddenly congested with rage. 'Well, I do! And I wonder you dare come from her bed to mine!'

'Jenny!' he cried. 'You know better than that!'

Her toneless voice made her fury the more dreadful. 'I know that since I, because I must bear your child, am now all misshapen and hideous so that I mean nothing to you, you go to this woman's house, and involve yourself there in some bestial brawl, probably fighting for her favors, and come home pretending to be hurt, seeking my sympathy!'

He saw the unreasoning passion of jealousy in her, urged wretchedly: 'Jenny, please!'

'Please! Please! Please!' she mocked. 'You can't lie to me! You're like all men, like the fool in his folly, forever seeking after the strange woman. Her lips drop honey, John, but her end is bitter as wormwood! Oh, men are all animals — and when one of us women, because she loved him, becomes ugly and swollen like a blister ready to burst — why, then you go looking for another!'

'You know that's nonsense, darling!' He sat up weakly in bed, trying to catch her hand; but she drew back, evading him. 'You never were so beautiful to me as now!' he told her warmly. She laughed in bitter scorn, and he said: 'Of course you can't understand a woman like her. No good woman can. But she's not so bad as most of them.'

'I understood her well enough, long ago! She did our washing here, till I sent her away because she tried to debauch Ephraim! I let her rent my house, not knowing what she was, till she gave it such a reputation that no decent person would buy it, and Isaiah made her a deed to it to be rid of its contaminations forever. And now my own husband comes to boast to me how fine she is!' Her voice was full of an acid scorn. She demanded in mock humility: 'Will you set her up as an example for me, John? Do you wish me to fill my house with wanton girls so that I can entertain a pack of brawling, whoring men? Is that what you want your wife to do?'

'Jenny please be reasonable!'

'Reasonable?' She laughed in a dry, chilling way. 'Am I to be as reasonable as your fine Lena? Is that what you mean?' The room moved dizzily around him, and he fell wearily back upon the pillow. 'Do you want me to invite every passer-by to my bed, as she does?' she insisted. 'Is that it? Have I not given you all the money a man could want? Are you so greedy that you wish me to earn more for you, even in that way, John?'

Lying with his eyes closed, unable to speak, he heard her come near him; and he opened his eyes and looked up at her and then drew his arm defensively across his eyes again, unable to face the haggard rage in hers. Till suddenly, all melting in a shamed contrition, she threw herself upon him, catching his head in her arms, close against her breast, sobbing piteously, small and helpless.

'Oh, John, John,' she sobbed, 'what makes me do it? Why am I so mean to you, my darling? John, John, John, I love you so! Please, darling, I didn't mean it! Please, I love you, I love you, I love you!'

In quick, grateful forgiveness his arms encircled her, soothing and assuring her; and the wounds her words had left were healed by their mutual tears.

v

There were no more of these storms. As though all the venom in her had by that explosion been released, Jenny was thereafter always gentle and serene, looking happily forward to their baby's coming; and as a man will, clinging to peace, John forgot that bitter hour, just as he had forgotten the dark things Ephraim told him about her long ago. They were happy together as autumn choked the last springs of life out of the world, and the river closed and Bangor entered its quiet winter months, and the days and nights were coldly still across the snow-muffled land where the horses' hooves made only a thumping rhythm, and sleighbells sang on every passing vehicle.

The baby was born in January, a boy, hearty and fine. For John's father and his older brother they named him Dan; and watching his wife as she gave the child her breast, Evered was filled with such pride and love as he had never known. Looking from the baby to him with smiling, eager eyes, she might demand: 'Isn't he sweet, John? Isn't he wonderful?' And when they stood by the small crib at night before turning to their own bed, she whispered: 'I want another, many others, John. Soon, darling. Soon!'

8

JENNY nursed her baby for only two months, weeping when her milk began to fail; but Ruth's older sister, though she had a baby of her own, was bountifully able to provide for Dan too, and she came to live awhile with them. Spring surged strongly up the river. The ice unlocked its barriers, the last drifts dwindled and were gone, the sun woke buds on every bough to greening life again.

As soon as the frost was well out of the ground, the new house was begun; the huge timbers were sized and fitted and the frame raised. John and Jenny savored every passing day, going often to watch the work or to admire what had been done. Sometimes they rode, Jenny in a fine new riding dress of ribbed gambroon, which he thought made her more beautiful than ever; and when they had inspected the new house they might go on along the farm roads, cantering side by side, a singing happiness in them. Sometimes they took the carriage, and then Dan went with them in

Jenny's arms. His cheerful company accented their happiness together, and John found Jenny more lovely day by day, ripely ardent as the tide of summer rose.

II

Jenny with a group of her friends, Mrs. Thatcher, old Mrs. Harlow and twenty others, had for years been accustomed to meet regularly as a sewing circle, gathering at the various homes in turn, sewing and talking for a while, with cakes and tea and even a glass of wine if they met at Mrs. Thatcher's or at some other house, where Jenny's own rigorous principles did not prevail, to end the afternoon. Jenny never served wine except to old Mrs. Harlow, who used to say that Doctor Rich told her a little was good for her.

'You may have it, of course,' Jenny told her. 'But I never trust a man who lets his doctor persuade him to drink. He's so anxious to find a reason why the same doctor should prescribe for him again.'

The old woman laughed with her familiar little mirthful chirp. 'Don't try to reform me, my dear,' she advised. 'I'm a lost woman, much too old to be saved.'

This conversation suggested to Jenny the idea which at a meeting at her home she eventually proposed. Before doing so she sought the advice of Elder Pittridge, who had already demonstrated his capacity for organization and leadership, and whose earnestness in the temperance cause had brought him and Jenny together.

'It just seems to me a pity,' she told him, 'that a group of women like us, intelligent and thoughtful and well intentioned, should waste our time and energy in many little ways when, if we were organized, there are so many things we could hope to accomplish.'

He agreed with her, and it was his suggestions which took concrete form when under Jenny's leadership the sewing circle adopted a formal name. They called themselves 'The Union Female Education Society' and adopted a statement of purposes, determining to concentrate upon 'the elevation and amelioration of the condition of destitute and degraded women in this city and vicinity.' They began at the same time to aspire to found some day an institution 'to educate the poor and ignorant and to reclaim fallen ones.' For this, funds would be necessary, and Jenny was active in arranging a concert at which Mrs. Lemon sang, a lecture by Mr. Asa Walker of California, and finally a fair at the Bangor House in March after Dan was born which raised twelve hundred dollars.

Their first successes encouraged them to organize the Bangor

Female Moral Society, for 'the prevention of licentiousness by showing in every proper way its fearfully universal and soul-destroying influence.' Margaret Saladine had returned to Bangor in May, and when she came to call on Jenny, she was easily persuaded to join this group.

'Of course, Paris has made me see that morals are largely a matter of geography,' she smilingly confessed. 'Certainly some of the things they do over there we would never do here; but all the same, it's worth while to have standards of some sort and to live by them. Any standard is better than none.'

There began this summer to be a real friendship between her and Jenny which John saw with pleasure. Margaret was a merry young woman, but she had too a steady strength. 'She sees the fun even in serious things,' Jenny told John one day. 'At first that startled me, but after you know her, she's fine.'

She liked to ask Margaret questions about Paris, and these two spent long hours together. John might come home and find them either upstairs admiring small Dan or waiting in the big living room for his own appearance.

'I should have gone long ago,' Meg sometimes said. 'But I wanted to see you, John!' She made no secret of her liking for him, said Jenny was lucky to have won him; but she was so open in this that Jenny was amused and pleased rather than in any least degree disturbed.

Meg described one day, to both of them, her efforts to teach John to dance at Ellsworth the summer before; and they laughed wholeheartedly at the picture she drew. 'It would have been quite as easy to train a bear!' she declared. 'He touched me as though he were handling live coals, and he seemed to have as many feet as a lobster — and no idea how to use them.' She tried to persuade John to help her show Jenny how that dancing lesson had proceeded; but he would not, so she played his part, holding an imaginary partner in her gingerly extended arms, stumbling around the room while they rocked with mirth.

After she had gone, Jenny said: 'She's so nice! I wonder why she hasn't married before now?'

'She will soon,' John predicted.

There were, in fact, young men enough in eager attendance on her, but none whom she preferred; and the friendship between these three continued and drew closer. The very differences between her and Jenny appeared to make them the more congenial. Jenny was much the smaller of the two, with dark hair and an ivory skin, quiet, speaking always softly. Meg was fair and tall and slender, and she laughed easily, and her voice had a warm, husky tone. John, proudly secure in his estate as husband and father, was no longer afraid of her; and he liked her well.

III

The winter Dan was born had been a quiet one, so far as business was concerned. John had only routine to attend. Colonel Black wrote from Boston that signs of a coming financial panic multiplied, and in Bangor men were uneasy, resenting the law which Congress had passed to prohibit the circulation of bills of a denomination less than five dollars. There was talk of defying that law, and risking the penalties attached. The secret anxiety which many began to feel provoked a restless eagerness to see active business once more resumed, and early in April some individuals, anxious to reopen water communication with the outside world, tried to shatter the ice in the river with gunpowder — and had trouble for their pains. When Congress voted to spend seventy-five thousand dollars a year for two years on the building of Fort Knox, opposite Bucksport, some thought the sums involved would give a fillip to business; but the temporary closing of the fine new Bangor House after a dispute between the proprietors and the landlord depressed the town. The river opened, and in June a hundred vessels were waiting at one time to load lumber, and the sailors combined with men just out of the woods or off the drive to make the lower part of town a roistering bedlam day by day; but the market for timber lands lagged, potential buyers and sellers no longer crowded the Coffee House, and there was little speculation done.

When the Stillwater Company advertised a 'great sale of permits, mill privileges, lands and lots,' at Lower Stillwater, seven miles above Bangor, the auction to be held late in June, Colonel Black and Judge Saladine and Mr. Richardson of the Commercial Bank and every sober citizen predicted that the sale would be a dismal failure. A careful map of the property to be sold, with every lot indicated and projected improvements drawn in, had been prepared, and the legend said largely:

> The advantages of this place for the location of Mills and Factories are not surpassed by those of any other place in New England. There is an abundant and never-failing supply of water. The advantages of the ground for factory sites are very superior, furnishing at a slight expense a solid stone foundation. Inexhaustible supplies of the finest pine timber are furnished by the Penobscot and its tributaries, the margins of

which and the country beyond are thickly covered for between two and three hundred miles with timber which must pass these mills to arrive at market.

The map was circulated weeks in advance, and the coming sale was discussed everywhere; but even Sam Smith, the boldest speculator of them all, said warily that the demand for land had lagged. He was sure it would revive again; but he counselled caution in the current lull. Such men as Ned Richardson, with his banker's point of view, were sure the sale would fall completely flat, and Colonel Black and John agreed.

So the event confounded pessimists and optimists alike. In advance of the day set, private sales proved so encouraging that the organizers of the company decided to back their hopes to the uttermost, and before the auction a banquet was spread for everyone who cared to attend. John and Colonel Black, with no intention to purchase, nevertheless joined the throng, and the banquet and its preliminaries were so prodigal — and so riotous — that the Colonel said cheerfully:

'My God, John, if they just sell enough lots to pay for the champagne they'll do well. Look yonder!' He pointed to where half a dozen waiters were hard at work opening bottles and emptying them into wide tubs out of which the encircling crowd — speculators, business men, brokers come from Boston for the occasion, sailors and seamen, lumbermen fresh from their winter in the woods or from the drive, and every rag-tag and bobtail in town — dipped the sparkling wine in mugs and drank it like water.

'There'll be men making bids today that won't even remember they were here, tomorrow,' John predicted; and the Colonel chuckled and said:

'Yes, and men with not a dollar to their names bidding thousands.'

General Veazie had come up behind them unseen, and he heard this and said: 'You're right, there, Colonel. Henry Head will tease the bids out of them.' And he chuckled and said: 'Hear about the time I had with Henry here awhile back? He auctioned the last four Williams privileges up at the Falls. Wadleigh and I both wanted them, and Wadleigh bid me up to twenty-seven thousand, and then Henry kept bidding till he ran me up to forty. Then I found out it was Henry bid me up, that Wadleigh stopped at twenty-six thousand; so I paid Williams twenty-seven thousand and told him that was as far as I'd go and he sued. We went to court over at Augusta, and the court ruled that Williams couldn't collect unless Henry had been bidding for him.

'Well, court let out and I knew Williams would head for Bangor to find Henry and tell him what to say. He'd hired an express team, so I did the same. Saw Williams three-four times on the road when he changed horses — or when I did. It was nip and tuck all the way, and neck and neck when we got here, but Williams had to go to John Bright's to find out where Henry lived, so I got to Henry's house before he did — and by the time Williams got there, I'd persuaded Henry to admit that he faked the bids and wasn't acting for Williams at all.'

The Colonel chuckled. 'That must have cost you something, Sam.'

General Veazie looked shocked and grieved. 'Why, it saved me thirteen thousand,' he assented. 'But Colonel!' His tone was full of pained reproach. 'Colonel, I hope you wouldn't go to say I'd bribe a man — or that Henry Head would take a bribe — now would you, Colonel?' They laughed together, and then the General exclaimed in a lower tone: 'Whoa! Here comes Rufe Dwinel, looking like an egg-stealing dog that's been fed an eggshell full of pepper! I'm getting out of his way. Look out for yourselves!'

He moved into the crowd and Dwinel joined them, his nostrils dilated with angry disgust. The Colonel asked: 'Well, Rufe, what do you think of this show?'

Dwinel looked at the half-drunken throng. 'They'll be no better than pigs in an hour,' he predicted. 'Ready for the sweat cure — and if it kills them, good riddance!'

'They'll be ready to buy — after Henry Head works on them awhile.'

'Henry on top of a bellyful of champagne is enough to make a fool of any man,' Dwinel assented.

John asked: 'Are you buying anything, Mr. Dwinel?'

'No. I never buy at auction. The bidding gets into your blood. You'll always go one step higher than you meant.'

Colonel Black nodded. 'Right!' he agreed. 'But Rufe — if we can catch some of the men who do buy today after they've sobered off, we might do ourselves some good. A lot of them will be glad to take a small loss and get out, to save a bigger one.'

'I doubt whether there'll be many sales,' Dwinel said, half to himself. 'Even a drunk man knows times are going to be bad.'

A big man in woods garb, with a mug of champagne in his hand and the contents of another splashed over his chin and his garments, lurched up to them and encircled Mr. Dwinel's neck with his arm. 'Rufe, you little old son of a bitch, have a drink with me!' he cried, and held the cup to Dwinel's mouth. Dwinel slapped it aside and it fell, spilling across the floor, and the man lugubriously protested: 'Now what did you want to do that for?'

Dwinel said precisely: 'Begone! Shrink back to your original nothingness, you bastard, and swear that you never were!'

The man, a head the taller, nevertheless mumbled apologies and backed away; and Colonel Black chuckled and said: 'You burned that gentleman to a crisp, Rufe. I thought he might jump you!' He added, surveying the eddying crowd: 'If a fight starts here it will be as bad as Old Town on a pay night.'

'I will be hell!' Dwinel agreed. He grinned faintly and added: 'They say hell is worse than Old Town and not as bad as Sunkhaze, but this may top all three before it's done!'

The preliminaries and the banquet passed, however, amicably enough. Cooks and caterers — and the viands they served — had all been imported from New York; and the press of men around the tables was awed into a respectful silence by the strange aspect of some of the confections; so when the actual auction began, they were orderly enough. Henry Head and Nehemiah Pillsbury — Head and Pillsbury, General Commission Merchants and Auctioneers, with an office in Market Square, opposite the Kenduskeag Bank — were in charge of the auction, and Mr. Head with a warming tongue whetted the appetite of the crowd.

'Well, gentlemen,' he said, when his hammering gavel brought silence, 'I don't need to tell you why we're here today, nor how fortunate you are to have this opportunity. You all know what Maine pine is worth. Every pine tree near a usable watercourse — providing it contains a thousand feet of sound lumber — is worth at least three dollars on the stump. I may say that private sales in advance of this auction have been at the average rate of four-fifty a thousand for stumpage; but call it three dollars. An acre of land with four three-dollar trees on it is worth twelve dollars; but many an acre has more than four. So timber land is the best possible buy. Even if you don't want to lumber off your tract, it's a good investment. Thrifty timber grows faster than the interest on your money.

'I want to say that I deplore as much as anyone the frauds that have in the past no doubt been committed; the swindles and deceptions as a result of which many reckless and improvident individuals have bought worthless land. But in many cases, rising values have rescued even such individuals from the consequences of their folly. Timber lands have not yet reached their fair and proper value. Although there is not this year that rage for speculation and for empty-headed gambling in lands which prevailed last year, yet our sound business men — like General Veazie yonder, and Mr. Dwinel — are still serenely confident of the future; and every day purchases are quietly being made by those who recognize an opportunity when they see it.

'We are selling off here today not only timber lands but mill and factory privileges. For the best of them, I warn you that you will be bidding against General Veazie. He won't make any bids himself — he's too smart for that — but his agents are among you, and if you hear some spirited bidding you may know the General wants that piece! I hope you won't let him have the choice lots too cheaply! Make the General pay through the nose. He can afford it!'

Laughter ran through the crowd, and John asked: 'Is he evening scores with the General?'

'No, just prodding these addled fools. I doubt if Sam wants anything that's up today.'

Mr. Head went on: 'Now, I want to give you just a few figures and then we'll begin. In case you don't know it — those of you who might hesitate to buy a mill privilege because it's outside your field — it costs about twelve to sixteen hundred dollars to put up a saw and lath mill — and a mill like that rents for a thousand to twelve hundred a year. That's — I'm no good at figures, but I know a bargain when I see one! — that's say eighty per cent on your money. The sixteen mills that are already working rent for over nineteen thousand dollars — and there'll be sixty-seven sawmills, lath and shingle mills in operation by the end of August.

'Now, gentlemen, my first offering — and if the first bidder is your next-door neighbor, who never bought a mill privilege in his life, and you wonder what he's doing here, he's probably bidding for General Veazie — will be . . . '

John stayed for an hour or two to watch what followed. He saw Pat Tierney in the crowd, and wondered whether Pat would make a bid. John liked the shrewd Irishman, and during the winter he had seen him many times and talked with him, advising him to realize on his speculations. Pat had taken his advice, vowing that he had all the money he and Ruth and their children would ever need. But watching Pat now, John saw a slow flush of excitement darken the other's countenance; and he was not surprised when Pat at last, after some lively bidding, bought in a factory site.

The enthusiasm grew, and before the auction had been long in progress Mr. Head was pulling bids from all around the room. When John and the Colonel at last departed together, the Colonel said, in a puzzled wonder, grinning at his own words:

'Well, by God, John, I think they're all crazy — but maybe I'm wrong!'

IV

It would be some weeks before the results of the sale were calculated; but a month after the auction the *Whig and Courier* printed complete figures. Before the public sale, permits had been sold to the amount of a hundred and forty thousand dollars, factory and mill sites to a total of sixty thousand dollars more. The auction doubled that figure, bringing total sales just over the four hundred thousand mark. This result, in the state of the money market, astonished everyone; and it gave a last spurt of new life to the speculative craze which had begun to die, persuading even the more conservative to enter at last the gambling field. Pat Tierney confessed to John one day that he was again extended the limit of his resources.

'When Ned Richardson starts buying, that's good enough for me,' he said. 'And they say he has.'

John found that men who had been most thoroughly persuaded that the land boom was a bubble apt to burst at any time were now the firmest converts. Speculation flared up in a new vigor — like the last flame of a dying fire. He had long since sold all Isaiah's holdings. That township on which Ephraim had bought the bond netted a paper profit of almost eighty thousand dollars, although two instalments of twenty-two thousand each were still to be paid. John was half-convinced by the new burst of enthusiasm after the Stillwater sale, but caution restrained him from making any purchases; and he watched as an outsider the last blossoming of the great boom.

V

Through the late summer of 1836 the weakness of some of the eight banks in Bangor, and the financial pressure which resulted when a million dollars of Government money was withdrawn from the state banks, gave warning enough of coming difficulties; but Jenny and John were happy in their own concerns. John sold the house Isaiah had built, for delivery January 1; and they went often to watch the new house, now almost ready, take shape and form. So long as the frame was still exposed, their friends had been apt to drive out to inspect it, and to laugh at the massive timbers; but Jenny told John:

'They don't bother me. It's the way I want it; strong and secure, to last forever, with our rooftree at the top — just as you're at the head of our family. Will you ever forget the afternoon the thundershower caught us here, John?'

'I'll never forget any minute I've spent with you,' he promised her.

They liked to take the baby everywhere they went pleasuring together, and as the new house took shape they explored it room by room, over and over, Dan in John's arms and crowing with delight, Jenny happy with them both.

The upper floors were finished first, and Jenny proposed that they move the furniture of their bedroom and Dan's small crib, and establish themselves there, returning to the Main Street house for the day and for their meals while the workmen finished the lower floor. John humored her — she was to have a second baby in February — in this as he did in all things; and on a fine sunny November day, with a great fire burning on the hearth of the big southwest corner room which would be theirs to welcome them, they made the move. The furniture was shifted during the day; and after supper, with Dan in Jenny's arms, they rode out of town. John drove himself, for young Tierney, Pat's cousin, had gone ahead to light the fire for them and to bring the carriage home. He would return for them in the morning, to fetch them back to Main Street for breakfast. 'Home for breakfast,' John said, giving instructions when the young man met them at the house, but Jenny as the carriage moved away corrected him.

'This is our home now, John,' she reminded him happily; and she said: 'I feel like a bride!' He opened the door for her to go in with Dan, but she said: 'No, you must carry me across the threshold, John. Carry both of us! All three of us!'

So he laughed and lifted her in his arms as Dan was in hers; and Dan crowed and gurgled delightedly, and John bore them in. Young Tierney had left candles burning in the lower hall, set on the floor — since the hall was still empty of furniture — and John carried his wife and his son up the wide stair to their room where the fine fire waited. He set Jenny on her feet there and stood watching while she began to take off Dan's wraps and prepare him for bed; and the flames danced a gleeful dance to welcome them. John went downstairs presently to snuff the candles in the hall; and from below he heard a sudden shrill cry of pain from Dan, and then his screams of anguish and Jenny's quick, excited comforting.

He raced up the stairs, his heart thrusting at his ribs in sharp terror. Jenny stood in front of the fire with Dan in her arms, soothing him while he wept and clung to her; and John caught them both and asked in a deep alarm:

'What happened, Jenny? What's the matter? What makes him cry so?'

'I don't know!' she declared. 'I haven't the faintest idea, John. A pin sticking into him, maybe. I took his little dress off and he just suddenly began to scream.' She tried to hush the baby. 'Danny, Danny, there, it's all right now!'

But as she spoke John saw in the firelight a mark on Dan's small, soft arm; and he leaned to look at it. Jenny in a guilty alarm tried to hide it from him, but he drew her hand away. Small spots of crimson showed on the baby's skin, and drops of red blood formed a circular pattern there. He cried incredulously:

'He's hurt, Jenny! He's bleeding.' And then in sudden, astonished understanding: 'Why, Jenny, you bit him!'

Danny still screamed and would not be consoled. John took him from her arms, and she clung to him and wept over her small son's grief and hurt and pain. 'I couldn't help it, John,' she sobbed. 'I was so happy, being here at last with you both, with both my menfolks, in our fine new home; and he was so sweet and soft and warm. I just couldn't help it!' And she wailed: 'Oh, Danny, Danny, darling, I didn't mean to hurt you so!'

Her tears drowned John's anger. He comforted her and Dan too, till they were both — through hiccoughing sobs — able to smile again. But a faint far terror was that night his bedfellow. He could dimly understand how in a sudden tender impulse Jenny might do to Dan what she had done. The impulses to love and to hurt, as he well knew, were in her strangely commingled.

But he could not forget, as in the past he had forgotten other things, that when he asked her what had happened, she had lied to him. It was the first time he had known her to lie.

9

When the panic of 1837 put an end to the dying boom in Maine lands, the heaviest losses in Bangor fell upon those conservative business men who had resisted the popular enthusiasm until the very end, only to yield at last to the intoxication that followed the Stillwater sale. But others whom the boom had earlier enriched were also ruined now, and Pat Tierney found himself a poor man again. He said cheerfully: 'Well, I was never meant to be a millionaire to be sure,' and went back to his old job as coachman for John and Jenny. Employment in town was slack, and public meetings were held to relieve the distress among the poorer folk. Specie payments were suspended by the Bangor banks and there was even a shortage of bills. Bankruptcies and assignments came thick and fast; and Bangor, which had ridden high during the early thirties — it was said that more men had made fortunes there in those years than in any other city in the country — now suffered the worst of the depression.

Between 1835 and 1840, the amount of pine that came downriver fell off fifty per cent, and pine was Bangor's life blood, so the city suffered; but then as though the abortive excitement which accompanied the bloodless Aroostook War stirred pulses and awoke latent energies, a new activity began. The lumber industry assumed an increasingly substantial character; and though the rapid growth of the early thirties did not continue, yet the town held now its gains.

II

For John and Jenny, the six or seven years during which their four sons were born were, except for an occasional stormy hour, serene and happy ones. There were fifteen months between Dan, the first baby, and Will. Tommy was born in April, 1839, and Mat two years and seven months later. They lived an intensive family life, Jenny absorbed in her children and yet finding time for her many outside interests, John as proud of the boys as he was intent upon his business affairs. Once, while Dan was still very young and Will was a baby, they went to spend a week with John's mother at Freeport; once or twice they left the children in good hands and took a trip to Boston and New York; and at first they paid regular visits to Colonel and Mrs. Black at Ellsworth.

But for the most part — though John had frequently to be away, over on the Kennebec Million, or up the Penobscot, or off to the eastward locating camps for the winter's lumbering — Jenny preferred to stay at home. They lived simply, taking little part in purely social affairs, and their most intimate friends were Meg Saladine and Elder Pittridge. These four, sometimes with the children and sometimes without, did many things together. The boys liked Elder Pittridge and it delighted him to plan for them small surprises. When he came to the house, his pockets were sure to hide small, delightful surprises for them. If John were to be away from home, he always told Elder Pittridge to look out for Jenny and the children. 'Keep an eye on them,' he might say. 'I'm a lot easier in my mind, when I'm away, Linc, knowing that you're going to drop in every few days.'

One summer afternoon when Mat was at the toddling age, John and Jenny were sitting on the lawn in front of the house, the boys playing together on the slope below them, when Elder Pittridge came up the driveway; and the children ran to meet him. He pretended to try to escape, loping away across the lawn at an awkward gait so that John laughed and said: 'Linc runs like a scared moose!' and Jenny smiled with him. Then Linc affected to stumble and fall, and the boys leaped on him, Dan first and then the others, Mat the last of all, digging into his pockets like dogs at so many rat holes, shrill with glee at what they found. They crawled and clambered over him while he sprawled on his back in pretended helplessness; and Jenny watched them happily; and John found himself looking from them to her with a proud affection. She was in her early thirties, but age had not yet touched her except that where a few years before she had been slender she now seemed thin, and where she had seemed soft and yielding she was now taut and firm. Her dark hair was as rich as ever, her eye as warm, and when she smiled, those faint inverted crescent dimples on her cheekbones still made her seem halfway to tears. Only her mouth had changed, losing its youthful fullness, drawing into a finer line.

She spoke at last to the children. 'That's enough now, boys. You'll wear Uncle Linc out.' There was a quiet compulsion in her tones to which all of them except Mat yielded without debate. The older youngsters drew off to savor the treasures he had brought, and he rose and brushed himself off and picked Mat up and, carrying the chubby baby, came toward where she and John sat. She told Dan to go bid Mrs. McGaw, who had succeeded Mrs. Hollis in charge of the household, bring out some birch beer and cookies. 'All of you go along,' she directed. 'Take Mat, too.' They trooped away without protest, and Elder Pittridge watched them go.

'They obey you like so many soldiers,' he said approvingly.

She nodded. 'They know they must,' she assured him. Her voice was even softer now than it had been, yet there was a calm and certain strength in her low-spoken words. 'I'm the disciplinarian,' she explained, smiling. 'John here spoils them terribly.' Her eyes met John's in tender amusement. 'But they know that if they don't do as I say, there's a little switch behind the woodshed door.' She added: 'They're devoted to you, Linc.'

He chuckled. 'And I to them,' he agreed. 'They're fine youngsters.'

'You like children, don't you?'

'Yes.'

John said: 'Jenny and I often think it's a pity you're not married, Linc, with children of your own.' And Jenny added:

'We've hoped that you and Meg might make a go of it. We're so fond of both of you.'

'Meg ought to be married,' Elder Pittridge agreed. 'She's a fine woman. I can't understand why she never has.'

'I can't understand why you never have,' Jenny gently amended. 'Why, Linc?'

He hesitated, said then reluctantly: 'Well, I was married, once. No one here knows it, but I married a girl in Albany. But — I was at odds with the world, in those days, drinking heavily. My wife left me, went back to her own people. She was quite right to do so.' He added: 'And when later I — came of age, mentally and spiritually — and returned to find her, she was dead.'

'I never knew that,' Jenny said in quiet sympathy. Mrs. McGaw brought the big tray, laden with ginger cookies and birch beer in a stone jug, and set it on the table Pat had built of birch poles and pine slabs to stand here on the lawn; and when the glasses were filled and Mrs. McGaw was gone, Jenny asked: 'But — do you never think of marrying again?'

'No,' Elder Pittridge said. 'No, I'll not marry again. Not even — if she would have me — Meg.' And he added: 'You see, my life has some dark spots in it. I've cleaned house as well as I can — but there are things that once done can't be undone. I know too well my own deficiencies to think myself worthy of any woman whom I would want to marry.'

John nodded understandingly, but Jenny protested: 'Yet, Linc, I think — next to John — you're the best man I know.'

III

John was tremendously proud of his sons. It was true, as Jenny told Elder Pittridge that day, that he seldom punished them. She often laughed at him for this, and once she said: 'When you say it hurts you worse than it does them, you really mean it, don't you, John?'

'I'm afraid I do,' he admitted. 'I never could understand how you can bear to whip them.'

'I don't enjoy it, of course,' she assured him. 'But I know it's for their own good, John. There are some things for which a switching is the only answer.' She added, smiling frankly: 'And it makes me feel better, too, when they've been particularly — devilish — to really let go. I work off a lot of bad temper on them, John. You ought to be glad, darling. If it weren't them it would be you.'

He smiled. 'I'd a sight rather it was me,' he said. 'But of course I suppose they do need it now and then.'

She came to touch his shoulder. 'There, darling, don't worry about it! One of us has to do it — and since I'm here alone with them so much when you're away, it's a good thing it's me.' She perched on his knee, said teasingly: 'Wouldn't you hate it if every time you came home I told you that Dan needed a whipping, and that maybe Will needed two, and Tommy three, and that you had to do it?'

He laughed. 'I'd never come home,' he confessed, 'if I knew that sort of job was waiting for me!'

She smiled and kissed his cheek, tumbling his hair. 'Never fear. I'll not put it off on you. I can handle them, John.'

Sometimes if he were at home when disturbances arose he wished to defend the boys against her stern justice; but she warned him not to interfere. Usually, though she was firm with him about this, she was full of understanding too; but their discussions on this and on other points were not always amicable. For the last few months of each of her pregnancies, Jenny was easily aroused to a blind, unreckoning anger when she might pour out a torrent of bitter, burning words. John learned at these times to walk softly and to avoid every possible offense. He recognized the fact that these rages were the result not of anything he had done but of the physical and nervous strain which child-bearing imposed on her; and he knew, too, that after the baby was born she would be again all tenderness and ardor. She was never able to nurse her babies long, and when she turned to his arms there could be a frightening hunger in her. Sometimes in their hours together she abandoned herself so recklessly that he was alarmed for her; or she might utter low, strangely feline sounds and beat at him with her fists till he pinioned her hands. He came to realize that she was in many ways two women, two distinct and separate individuals; and sometimes when they sat side by side in church together and he saw her so sedate and decorous, absorbed in the minister's every word, he remembered hours in which she had been otherwise, and had to hide a smile.

The occasional storms which swept through their lives, violent though they might be, seemed to him for a long time to leave no lasting trace. He knew — and came to be fondly amused by the knowledge — that sometimes she told him small lies; but that, he thought, was a part of the secret woman whom he alone would ever see. For the rest, for the woman the world knew, he held her dear and proudly as he held his sons.

IV

Until they had been eight years married, their differences were always quickly forgotten, as sunshine follows showers; but after Mat was born this was not so completely true. Scars, more and more frequently reopened, did not so quickly heal. They had still their rapturous, or their contentingly calm and peaceful hours; but there were long and longer intervals when Jenny might speak to John as she spoke to the boys, in calm and level tones which had the force of commands. She expected to be obeyed, and she was. John sometimes smiled at her tones, at her plain assumption of authority; but he did not contest it, content if she were content, happy only if she were happy too. He could be firm if the occasion seemed to demand it, and on these occasions his was apt to be the determining voice; but unless he must, he did not oppose her.

When at last circumstances produced a permanent rift between them, it was rather accident than any deliberate act on his part which made the trouble. In addition to his activities on Colonel Black's behalf, John managed the property which Jenny had inherited from Isaiah. Among Isaiah's assets had been shares in a score or so of vessels which were kept busy from the time the river opened till it closed, every year, in the lumber trade. The profits which they showed were so steady and so substantial that John, when he sold the Poster lands, extended Jenny's interest in this direction. Three or four vessels he bought outright; and in others he acquired for her a controlling share.

One of these vessels was the schooner Old Town, Captain Dan Philbrook. In June, 1844, she returned from a voyage to Savannah. She made up Bangor River in the late afternoon, and that evening Captain Philbrook came to the house to see John.

John and Jenny heard together his report — which was a confession too. 'You see, it's this way, Mr. Evered,' he said. 'After we got rid of our ice in Savannah there was some work needed to be done on the schooner. We'd had a rough time going down, got knocked around some. I hired a shipwright named Sagurs, James Sagurs. They told me he was a good man, Mr. Evered. Well, sir,

he had some colored men do the work for him, slaves he owned.'
John saw Jenny's lips tighten a little as she listened. 'There was
one of them named Atticus, a smart darky; and the men liked
him.' He rubbed his mouth in a deep embarrassment. 'I wouldn't
wonder if they filled him full of tall yarns, Mr. Evered, about
the way things are up here. Fact, I know they did. He told me so.

'But anyways, we got fixed up and sailed, and maybe some of
them helped him get aboard and kept him hid, because when we
were seven days on our way home, the mate found him, about half-
starved, down in the hold one day.'

Jenny made a low, compassionate sound, and John asked gravely:
'What did you do with him?'

'Why, we couldn't well put back,' Captain Philbrook pointed
out. 'So we fed him up and put him to work and brought him
along. He's a good worker, and the men like him. He's about the
cheerfullest man I ever saw, white or black.' He added appealingly:
'It'd make you choke, Mr. Evered, to see how glad he is to get
away.' He chuckled. 'Only, he's damned near froze,' he confessed.
'Wears all the clothes he can walk around in, even a day like this'
— the day was for the season warm and fine — 'and still shivers
all the time.'

'He's aboard now?' John asked.

'Yes, sir,' Captain Philbrook admitted. 'Matter of fact, I locked
him up. I 'lowed I'd better keep hold of him till I knew what you
wanted me to do.' He added: 'He begged me not to send him
back to Savannah. He says his master will cut him to ribbons for
running away.'

Jenny spoke quietly. 'We'll never send him back. He's here and
he shall stay.'

For a moment no one answered her, but then John said gravely:
'We can't steal another man's property, Jenny. The poor devil's a
fugitive. No doubt his master has guessed that he stowed away
aboard our schooner. Probably he'll come after him.'

'We'll hide him,' she declared. 'We'll not give him up, to be
whipped to death for the crime of wanting to be free.'

'He's not free aboard the schooner,' John reminded her.

'Then let him come ashore!' Jenny insisted, and she spoke to
Captain Philbrook. 'Bring him here, Captain. I'll put him to work
on my flower beds and lawn.' Her garden was her pride, and her
roses were famous. She had Bourbons and Bengals and Noisettes
as well as spreading beds of verbenas and petunias, and dahlias in
their season. John White, whose business was the laying out of
gardens and grounds, had bought a consignment of prize-winners

at the Grand Dahlia Show of the Massachusetts Horticultural Society, the year before; and Jenny had the pick of his purchases. Bangor folk out for a drive were apt to come this way simply in order to see the fine display. 'I need someone on the garden all the time,' she declared. 'Pat and I between us can't keep up with the weeds.'

John insisted: 'But it's our obligation as good citizens to hold him for his master, Jenny.'

Jenny's voice did not rise, but John heard the harder note in it. 'We have a duty to humanity, too,' she said in her low tones.

'It may mean trouble,' John warned her. 'Mr. Sagurs can probably attach the schooner for damages.'

'The schooner is mine, John,' she retorted, with no change of expression. 'I think sometimes you forget that. If I choose to risk its loss . . .'

Captain Philbrook watched them in disturbed astonishment. He had never seen Jenny thus aroused before, and he thought it was as though on a still, calm day at sea the surface suddenly were broken by many swirls as schooling fish are driven by some monster into panic flight. He rose uneasily, wishing to escape. 'Well, you can let me know,' he said, and took himself away.

v

When the Captain was gone, John still tried to convince Jenny; but he could not move her, and since she insisted, that night under cover of the dark he brought the negro ashore. Pat Tierney was waiting at an unused wharf above the town when a small boat from the schooner landed them; and he drove John and the negro out to the house. The slave was hushed and silent on the way, but at the house when Jenny met them he went on his knees to her in prayerful gratitude. Jenny protested and made him rise, and she led him to tell his story, questioning him with a gentle friendliness while John looked on

The slave spoke well enough so that he could easily be understood, and when Jenny commented on this, Atticus said readily: 'Yas'm, I uz a house boy, time I c'd walk, tekking keer of de chillun, and breshing flies and helping my mammy in de kitchen. I been wid de white folks mostly all my days.'

He walked with a shuffling limp and his cheek was scarred. Jenny asked him about these hurts. 'Did your master abuse you, beat you?'

Atticus said strongly: 'No, ma'am!' He put a rhetorical question. 'Whut he want tuh cripple me up for? He c'd sell me any time for fifteen hun'ed dollahs. I'm a good cahpentuh, ma'am. Mistuh Saguhs was too smaht tuh lay me up so's I couldn' wo'k.' He chuckled. 'No, ma'am, dis laig o' mine, mule kicked me in de knee when I uz a young one.'

'But that scar on your cheek?'

'I got dat from Big Pete, time he tried tuh git Nancy away f'om me.' He shook his head respectfully. 'Mistuh Saguhs tuk a black-snake whip an' licked de knife wo'k out o' Big Pete for dat. Pete was no use tuh hisself or anybody else only for a field hand!'

'Is Nancy your wife?'

'Yes, ma'am.'

'It must be terrible for you to leave her?'

The slave chuckled. 'No, ma'am. I got along fine wid Mistuh Saguhs, but Nance was in mah wool all de time. Da's why I stowed away on de schooner boat.'

John suggested: 'Then you wouldn't mind going back — if Mr. Sagurs would get rid of Nancy?'

But before the negro could speak, Jenny said in quiet indignation: 'Shame, John! The poor man is free. Do you suppose he wants to be a slave again? If he went back, he would be whipped to death.'

'Yas'm,' Atticus said hurriedly, 'I sholy would.' But then he asked in a doubtful tone: 'De only thing, is it dis cold heah all de time?'

'A lot colder,' John told him. 'Cold enough to freeze the river over three or four feet deep with ice!'

'M-m-m!' The negro made a rueful sound. 'Mighty cold for black folks. Y'all going tuh keep me heah?'

'Always,' Jenny told him. 'You'll never be a slave again.'

'Who my white folks gwine tuh be? Who gwine tek keer of me?'

'We are,' Jenny promised him. 'You'll live here and work for me.' And when John tried to speak, she said quickly: 'I'll have Pat show you. There's a nice room for you in the shed.'

When Atticus was gone, John said insistently: 'There'll be trouble about this, Jenny. I think you're making a mistake.' He urged with a smile: 'After all, he only came to get away from his wife. You heard him say so.'

'I heard, yes,' she said evenly. 'I think men often consider it amusing to speak so of their wives.' Then without a word, white with anger, she went quietly from the room and up the stairs.

VI

John felt sure that Mr. Sagurs would make the trip to Bangor to claim his property; but before this happened he himself had to go to Augusta on business. He told Jenny she must summon him home if Mr. Sagurs appeared, but he had had no word from her when he met Sam Smith in the State House corridors one day and heard from him that the Southerner was in Bangor.

'And he's bound to make trouble, John,' he said. 'He's a chubby little man; but that kind can be the meanest and the stubbornest when they want to.' He added: 'Every one in town knew the negro had been working for Mrs. Evered, taking care of her garden; but as soon as this Mr. Sagurs hit town, he disappeared. So Mr. Sagurs went to Judge Ware and swore out a warrant for the negro as a fugitive and gave it to Dave Piper to serve, but Piper couldn't find the negro, so he returned the warrant. Then Sagurs put a notice in the *Whig and Courier* that he'd pay a fifty-dollar reward for his slave; and he's staying at the Bangor House, waiting for news.'

John was concerned, afraid Jenny would commit some dangerous imprudence, and he decided to hurry home. Since there would not be a stage till tomorrow, he took an express team for the trip back to Bangor. It was well past midnight when he reached home; and he had to call under Jenny's window to wake her so that she would let him in. There was a wary reserve in her kiss, as though she had put herself on guard; and she asked quietly:

'What brought you home at such a time of night, John?'

'Why, I met Sam Smith,' he said frankly. 'He told me that Savannah man is here to get Atticus. Has he made you any trouble?'

'He sent Constable Piper with a warrant, but Linc had warned me that he was in town, so Pat hid Atticus in the woods. He's living in the haymow now.' She laughed a little. 'Mr. Sagurs is cooling his heels at the Bangor House, but he'll soon get tired of that and go home.' And she said, smiling, linking her arm in his, warm and sweet in her thin gown: 'Let's not talk any more about it tonight, John. Come to bed, darling. I've missed you. I'm ever so glad you're home.'

So they went up the wide stairs arm in arm. John thought he might in the morning persuade her to a sensible view; but in this he was wrong. She was inflexibly determined not to surrender the fugitive. Their discussion, begun when they woke, continued at the breakfast table where the boys listened in a trembling silence, frightened to see their mother and father thus at odds, till John saw this at last and for their sakes surrendered.

'Well, I'll see what I can do,' he said. 'I'll satisfy Mr. Sagurs somehow.' He smiled affectionately. 'Since you want Atticus, you shall have him. There'll be some way to content his master — and not turn law-breaker to do so.'

'I'd break every law there is to keep the poor man,' she retorted.

Pat drove John to town. During John's absences, Elder Pittridge usually attended to his office routine, and he was in the office this morning. John thought to get from him more information than Jenny had been able — or willing — to give; but almost at once Mr. Sagurs appeared. The round little man had a bulldog look about him, hanging stubbornly to his determination to recapture his property.

'I'm not a fool, Mr. Evered,' he said indignantly, when the preliminaries were over. 'I know there's a conspiracy against me here.'

John said uncomfortably: 'Your man worked around our garden and made no attempt to escape, so it seemed unnecessary to lock him up. Now I'm told that within the hour of your arrival he disappeared.'

'Some of your insane abolitionists have hidden him!' Mr. Sagurs said angrily. 'I tell you, Mr. Evered, this flouting of the sacred rights of the South must stop, and it will, even if the South has to withdraw from the Union to protect herself.'

'I'm not an abolitionist, Mr. Sagurs,' Evered assured him. 'I'm a business man. If slave labor is necessary to the successful conduct of business in the South, I would not disturb it; not as an institution. From our point of view up here, slavery is not necessary; but surely this is a difference of opinion which will settle itself.'

The Savannah man said stubbornly: 'There can be no honest difference of opinion in this case. I own a piece of property named Atticus. A thief — your Captain Philbrook — steals my property named Atticus, brings him to your town, and hides him away. If Captain Philbrook stole one of your horses and brought it to Savannah, I would be zealous to help you recover your property. I have a right to expect an equal zeal from you.'

John seized the point, and he suggested: 'Would you buy that horse from me, Mr. Sagurs; that horse of mine which someone might have stolen and taken to Savannah?'

'If I wanted it, and it was for sale.'

'Then I'll buy your slave from you. Make me a price. What is he worth?'

Mr. Sagurs hesitated, his small eyes suddenly shrewd. 'Suppose I said twenty-five hundred dollars?'

'I know little of slave values, but if that is a fair price, I will pay it.'

The chubby little man became purple with rage. 'Then, sir, if you are willing to pay so much, you know where my slave is! Atticus is not for sale at any price. I demand you deliver him to me!'

John said slowly: 'I would pay the price to satisfy you, Mr. Sagurs; not because I want the slave. If you accept the money, then Atticus will be free, you can go home content, and the affair is closed. I meant no more than that.'

Mr. Sagurs hesitated, but John thought uneasily that his eyes had calculation in them. After a moment he bowed. 'Your pardon, sir,' he said. 'Apparently I misunderstood you.' His color rose again. 'Nevertheless, Atticus is not for sale — and I bid you a very good day!'

VII

When the angry little man was gone, John looked at Elder Pittridge with a rueful smile. 'Jenny won't give him up,' he confessed.

'Was it her idea that you might buy the slave?'

'No. I was trying to find some way out.'

Elder Pittridge nodded. 'Sagurs is a sly, stubborn little man,' he said. 'I'd feel easier if Atticus were sent away up-river, out of his reach, where he couldn't be found.'

'I'll suggest that to Jenny when I go home at noon,' John agreed.

But before noon, Jenny came to town to find him. He had gone down to the Coffee House and Elder Pittridge sought him there, saying she was in the office and seemed much disturbed. At John's suggestion, they went back to her together. He had an unadmitted feeling that he might need the other man as an ally at his side.

Her word at first was quiet enough. 'John,' she asked, 'did you see Mr. Sagurs this morning?'

'Yes, he came here,' he assented.

Her lips suddenly were white. 'Then you told him where Atticus was!' she said accusingly.

He shook his head. 'Of course not. What happened, Jenny?'

'He came to the house — with Constable Piper. They went directly to the barn. I didn't see them till they came out, leading

Atticus away.' And she repeated in a stony accusation: 'You told Mr. Sagurs where he was.'

John said quietly: 'No, Jenny. You're mistaken. Linc was here when I talked with him.' He wondered why he thus called a witness to prove to her he told the truth. 'I tried to buy Atticus — offered twenty-five hundred for him — but I told Mr. Sagurs nothing.'

Her eyes narrowed. 'Twenty-five hundred dollars? John, you're a fool! When you offered him so much, Mr. Sagurs would know you could lay your hands on Atticus. Probably he led you on to tell him the truth.' John looked appealingly at Elder Pittridge; but before the other man could speak, she said in even, icy tones: 'You betrayed me, John; betrayed not this poor negro who trusted us, but me. I promised him he'd be safe. You've sent him back to be whipped to death. You betrayed my word — and me! And I can never forgive you, John. I never will.'

And while John stood silent in the face of her cold rage, she turned quietly toward the door, opened it and so was gone.

After a moment, Elder Pittridge touched John's arm reassuringly. 'It's all right,' he said. 'She'll feel differently in a little while, by the time she gets home.'

John nodded doubtfully. 'Yes, of course, I'm sure she will,' he agreed.

10

JOHN was frankly relieved that Atticus was gone; and he thought — or hoped — that Jenny's anger would be quick to pass, as her angers had passed before now. After all, his only crime had been that of being too transparent, of permitting Mr. Sagurs to guess the truth. He went home at noon prepared to make his peace with her. The boys met him at the door in a high excitement to tell him that Atticus was gone, and they all trooped in together to the big living room where Jenny was. John went to kiss her, and she gave him a cool cheek, and Dan — eight years old now and a tall, solid youngster — chattered by his father's side, telling him what had happened.

'And Mr. Sagurs just came into the stable — I was there with Pat — and shouted: "Atticus, you damn black rascal, come down out of there!"'

Jenny said calmly: 'Dan! I shall wash out your mouth with soap, to clean your lips of that word!'

But Dan hardly heard. His tongue raced on. 'And he did, father. He came running downstairs from the mow and yelling: "Bless Gawd! Bless Gawd! Ise gwine back tuh Savannah Gawguh! Too cold for old Atticus up heah!" And he went down on his knees and held on to Mr. Sagurs' hand, and Mr. Sagurs said: "I'll warm you, you lying, runaway niggah!" Only he didn't sound really mad, and Atticus kept laughing and saying: "Yas suh! Yas suh! You sholy will. Bless Gawd!"'

John chuckled and looked at Jenny. 'Well, I guess Atticus was really glad to go, then,' he said; but she looked at him with bleak eyes and did not smile. Instead she said simply:

'Come, Dan!'

Dan pleaded: 'But mother, I was just telling father what they said!'

She did not repeat her command, turned to the stairs; and Dan followed her, still protesting wretchedly. John and the others watched them go. When they came down a little later Dan was pale and nauseated by the evil taste of the suds, and his dinner had no appeal for him. He sat subdued and miserable through the meal; and Jenny's unforgiving silence put a repressive hand upon them all.

Nor did she relent thereafter. She made John remember, every hour of every day, his crime; and when he tried cajolery, tried tendernesses, tried to persuade her to smile again, she said evenly:

'I told you I'd never forgive you, John, and I never will.'

Yet outwardly, before the world, she was as she had always been. When the Governor of Georgia sent a demand that Captain Philbrook and John himself be surrendered for trial under the laws of that state, Jenny's loyal indignation was obviously sincere. The demand was of course refused, but it was not forgotten. Colonel Black had enemies, and they struck at him through John. Twice someone took advantage of the hours of darkness to paint the words 'Nigger lover' on John's office door; and for a while small boys jeered him in the streets. There were abolitionists in Bangor, increasingly vocal all the time — Jenny had always been among them — but there were others, leading citizens of the city, who either out of respect for the rights of the Southern States, or because as good business men they wished to keep things as they were, or because they perceived in the dispute an increasing possibility of bloody conflict, would have preferred to leave slavery untouched; and they blamed John for harboring the fugitive.

Jenny, as though to defy this adverse opinion, engaged a young negress to come to the house one day a week and do the washing. The girl's name was Mattie Hanson, and she was black as night, with an infectious chuckle and a plump comeliness. She had been born — of free parents — in Cambridge, and had worked in the family of a professor there who interested himself in teaching her to speak with some precision. She proved herself an excellent washerwoman, relieving Mrs. McGaw and Ruth Tierney of that part of the household tasks, and Jenny kept her on.

But though in these public ways she ranged herself on John's side, and although when the children were with them, after the first few days, she played a part for their benefit, when she and John were alone she was unrelenting. At night she lay frigidly beside him, and if he took her in his arms, hoping to win her to surrender both herself and her anger, though she submitted to his embrace it was with an aloof and maddening docility.

John began to be sure that her feeling had gone beyond mere wrath, that it was an obsession from which she would have been glad to escape if she could; and one morning at breakfast he tried clumsily to make her smile, teasing her affectionately about a single gray hair which he declared he could see above her brow, calling on the boys to corroborate him. They clustered laughingly around her; and Mat climbed on her knees, and John parted her hair with his fingers, bidding them look and see for themselves, till in a sudden angry violence, as though she had been tried beyond enduring, she struck him. She hit him in the body, so hard he gasped for breath, and she stood up, spilling Mat to the floor, facing them all.

'Don't touch me!' she said in low, clicking tones. 'Don't touch me at all, ever, any of you!'

And she fled up the stairs, leaving them abashed and unhappy together. Three-year-old Mat, still on the floor where he had fallen when she rose so abruptly, began to whimper in a tentative way, as though not sure whether he should cry or not. John — still looking at the door through which Jenny had disappeared — heard Dan comfort the youngster and assure him that he was all right; and John himself turned to say a smiling word to them before he drove unhappily away to town.

He was by Jenny's persisting anger more bewildered than anything else. It seemed to him incredible that she should — as she seemed bent on doing — wreck their life together because of Atticus. He went home to dinner that day, hoping to find her softened; but she sat stonily silent while he talked and laughed with the boys.

Normally, he would not have come home again that day till late afternoon; but Colonel Black summoned him to Ellsworth, and he returned early to get his bag. When he came up the drive, before he reached the door, he heard Mat screaming somewhere, heard Dan crying out in desperate pleading: 'Stop, mother! Please!' There was panic in Dan's voice, too; and John plunged into the house. He saw Will at the rear end of the hall, huddling fearfully in a corner there, and he himself ran swiftly up the stairs. He came to the open bedroom door.

An instant glance photographed that scene forever on his memory. Little Mat, naked, his small soft body crisscrossed with red welted lines, was writhing and twisting on the bed and screaming in a shrill, dry, terrible way. His cries had an inhuman quality. Beside the bed, her back toward him, Jenny was fighting to free herself from Dan's tight clutch on her arm. The boy held fast with both hands, gripping her arm just above the elbow. In that hand she held a birch switch with the leaves off but with all the little twigs left on, so that it was like a cat-o'-nine-tails, or some similar instrument of torture. She flung Dan to and fro, trying with her other hand to tear his fingers away; and he was sobbing and pleading with her. 'Please, mother! Please, mother, stop!'

Then Jenny saw John in the door and suddenly was completely passive, and Dan released her and ran to cling to his father, and Mat, his small body contorting in torment on the bed, emitted a succession of flat, toneless screams.

John, his arm around Dan, went to the bed and sat down beside Mat there, touching him quietly, comforting him, till his screams died in sobs. Jenny stood by the window, her back to them, looking out, rubbing her arm where Dan's tight grip had bruised the flesh. She said without turning:

'You're home early, John.'

'I must go to Ellsworth tonight,' he explained in an empty voice. 'Colonel Black sent for me.' He picked Mat up and went toward the door, and Dan followed him. He carried Mat to the room the two youngest boys shared, down the hall; and then, gentle as any woman, he eased the baby and quieted him and bathed him and put him at last to bed, while Dan tried to tell him what had happened.

But John did not listen, his own thoughts in a dark confusion, until Dan cried at last in a boyish passion:

'And I hate her! I hate her! I wish she'd just die!'

John looked at him then in a grave concern. He said strongly: 'No, you don't, Dan. Never think such things, much less say them. Your mother was upset, that's all.'

He quieted Dan as he had quieted Mat, till the youngster, gulping down stale sobs, began to be at peace; and he said again: 'Don't ever think so of mother, Dan. Remember it's our job — yours and mine and your brothers' — to love her and take care of her always.' Mat was asleep, and he said in a low tone: 'Now you go find the others, Dan. Mother and I want to have a little talk. But everything's all right, son. Everything is fine.'

They left Mat, walked along the hall together. Through the open door they saw Jenny still standing by the window in the big room. John touched Dan's shoulder reassuringly. Then he went in and behind him closed the door.

II

When John found himself alone with Jenny, he was for a moment half-afraid, wishing Dan were here, wishing anyone were here. She must have heard him come in, but she had not turned, had not acknowledged his presence in any way. He hesitated, watching her; and she seemed so small and lonely there that he forgot everything in a fine tenderness. He crossed to stand beside her, not looking at her; and he put his arm lightly around her shoulders, still without speaking, both of them looking out of the window toward the gardens where there was a mass of bloom.

But after a moment she freed herself, turning away from him, turning back into the room, moving to and fro, chafing with her hand that spot on her arm where Dan's desperate grip had bruised the flesh. John watched her, wondering what to say. That cruel birch switch lay where she had dropped it, by the foot of the bed. She picked it up and took it to the closet and put it carefully away there.

In the action there was something hard and determined which roused a slow anger in John. He went to the closet, took the switch, broke it into many little bits and stuffed the bits down behind the birch logs in the fireplace. When he stood erect again after doing this, Jenny spoke at last.

'John,' she said evenly, 'I will not permit you to interfere between me and the children.'

He felt his color rise. 'I think you must be insane,' he protested. Mat's small garments lay here and there on the bed and the floor. She picked them up, bundled them together, went to the door and threw them out into the hall. She held the door open, asked: 'Are you going to Ellsworth now?'

He shook his head. 'What happened, Jenny? What had Mat done?'

'Does that matter? He deserved to be punished.'

'He didn't deserve to be — flogged like an animal!'

'Oh, don't be self-righteous, John.' She closed the door again. 'You can be so tiresome.'

'I'm sorry,' he said. 'I'm just trying to understand you. What did he do, Jenny?'

'That is entirely my business,' she assured him. 'Mat has always been unruly. I will not spare the rod and spoil the child.'

'Do you know you whipped him so hard that you broke the skin in several places?'

'He deserved it.'

John made an impatient gesture. 'Don't be ridiculous! He's just a baby!' He said reproachfully: 'I suppose you're still angry at me about Atticus and took it out on Mat. You mustn't do that, Jenny.'

'Will you prevent me, John?' Her tone was almost sweet.

He said miserably: 'I don't understand you. You can be so wonderful to all of us. You are, most of the time. But — you can be so cruel, too.'

'Cruel, darling?' She smiled a little. 'It's true you don't understand me, John.' Her voice hardened. 'So — if you're wise — don't try to tell me what I must — or must not — do.'

He was between anger and bewilderment. 'You can make me so damned miserable, Jenny.' He tried to smile, tried to appease her. 'I love you, you know. Nothing can ever change that. And that means you can hurt me more than I can be hurt by anyone else in the world. But — when you want to hurt me — please don't do it through the boys.'

She came close to him, facing him calmly, her countenance composed and still. 'I tell you not to interfere,' she said softly.

'I am interfering,' he insisted, angry in his turn, his voice stern now. 'I will interfere. Jenny, you simply must not do this sort of thing again.'

'Must not?' Her eyes were flaming.

'Must not,' he repeated inflexibly. There was in him in that moment a firm strength which as their eyes met beat her eyes down and mastered her. She turned away, looked back at him, half-smiling.

'I wonder what you'd do . . .' she murmured, more to herself than to him. 'Would you — beat me, John?' Then she turned to face him again, and now she was really smiling, in a malicious mirth which touched him with cold fear. 'You do love me, don't you, my dear,' she reflected thoughtfully.

'Yes.'

'You righteous, good man — trying to tell me what I must and must not do!' There was a bite like acid in her tones. She came nearer, walking in a strangely feline way, slowly and gracefully, watching him as she drew near. She came close, stood looking sweetly up at him.

'John, darling,' she said, almost whispering. 'You've never really known the strange woman you married. Do you remember all the things Ephraim told you? About me? Before you ever saw me?' He could not speak, and she insisted: 'He told you that I tried to seduce him and that I tried to persuade him to kill Isaiah and that I took Ruth's place in her bed and he did not know me till morning. Do you remember, John?'

He wetted his dry lips, unable to speak, paralyzed with fear of the irrevocable word that was to come.

'Do you remember?' she insisted.

He made a hoarse sound, no more than her name. 'Jenny!'

She said implacably: 'You said a moment ago that you don't understand me. Well, I must help you, John — help you to understand. You see, darling — everything Ephraim told you about me was true.'

VI

Elder Pittridge

I

LINCOLN PITTRIDGE was born in 1800, in Haverhill, Massachusetts, three or four months after the death of his father. He was an only child. His mother within a year or two married a man named Ball, who, when Lincoln was five or six years old, moved to Old Town and set up a double sawmill at the lower village. He died in 1809, without having fathered any children; and Linc's mother took her son — then nine years old — back to Haverhill. There she 'went out by the day' to help other women with their housework; and Linc earned small sums by doing what chores were within his power.

They lived in two rooms; but Linc, though he knew they were desperately poor, found only happiness in this close companionship. His mother lavished on him a bountiful tenderness, and his earliest memories were of lying in her arms, his every sense revelling in her nearness. As he now grew older, she jealously monopolized not only his life but his affections too; so that there was never while she lived any other girl or woman in his life. She absorbed him completely. He lived for her, and as a child and a young man her love was the deepest happiness he knew.

She was a devout church woman — increasingly so as she grew older — and she early decided that her son should become a minister. Linc found himself enrolled at the Theological Seminary in Andover; but after a period there, without explanation she announced that they were going back to Maine. In Bangor she rented a small house on Harlow Street. He entered the Theological Seminary while she set up a baking business, making cakes and pies and even bread which she sold to housewives willing either to help a worthy woman with their patronage, or to relieve the burden on their own kitchens.

When a few weeks later she died, the foundations of Linc's life were destroyed. He was left at once emptied and solitary, having no normally easy and friendly relationship with anyone in the world. But worse was to come. Immediately after her death he was called before the trustees of the Seminary and cross-examined about a certificate which his mother had presented on his behalf, and which declared that he was a suitable person to receive charitable assistance in preparation for the ministry. This certificate was signed by a deacon of the church in Haverhill, and also it was signed by Linc himself.

Linc saw his own signature with a shock of surprise. He had known nothing of this certificate, and he realized at once that his mother must have forged his name. But since she had done it to win for him the education he could not otherwise have achieved, he forgave her; and to protect her name, he said that he had prepared the document. He was then asked what his means were, and he answered that he and his mother had very little, that they had lived with the utmost frugality, and that his mother had been forced to work at her baking to piece out their small income.

The trustees thereupon denounced him as a forger and as a liar. Mrs. Pittridge's frugal way of life had excited in Bangor some surprise, for there were those who knew that when her husband died she had sold his mill for a substantial sum. A few inquiries even before her death had developed the fact that she had money in the bank, that her poverty was pretense; and this led to an investigation. Letters were dispatched to Haverhill. The deacon there whose name was signed to the certificate which procured Linc's admission to the Bangor Seminary denied his signature; and he added indignantly that a similar imposition had been practised by Mrs. Pittridge on the trustees at Andover and that when it was discovered, she had withdrawn her son and moved away.

Mrs. Pittridge died before she could be called to account, but the trustees confronted Linc with these facts, and loyalty to his mother led him, by acknowledging his signature, to convict himself of participation in her greedy fraud. He was denounced as destitute of moral principle and told that he had shown such a disregard for truth as was painful to witness; and his dismissal from the Seminary was immediate.

So at one blow the young man — he was then just twenty years old — not only lost his beloved mother, but learned beyond question that she had been a liar and a cheat. He found himself endowed by her death with a modest fortune; but except in worldly ways he was bankrupt, disgraced and without friends. For a few weeks he moved like a ghost through the empty house on Harlow Street, seldom appearing in the haunts of men; but thereafter, in unbearable loneliness, he turned to the taverns and the dives for companionship. Within the year, his debauched life was a matter of awed wonder even to his boon companions, and his debasement seemed complete.

When he left Bangor, no one missed him. He drifted eventually to Albany, where he married a young woman who was attracted by his unhappiness and sure that her love would reform him; but he went from bad to worse, and she presently left him and returned to her father's house. Linc proceeded to Hartford, where — his money by this time all wasted — he began to teach school; but a few months later he seduced one of his pupils and — since his previous marriage prevented his making the conventional amends — he was driven out of Hartford by the indignant townsfolk.

He was in Boston when his alcoholic excesses led to a protracted illness so that he lay for weeks at the point of death, tended by the wife of the tavern keeper where he had been taken ill. Her sympathies had been enlisted by the tragic unhappiness which she sensed in him; and she persuaded her husband to give Linc shelter while she nursed him back to life. When he recovered, he vowed never to touch liquor again in any form; and at the same time, as sometimes happens, he made other resolutions. He went back to Albany to seek a reconciliation with his wife, but since their separation she had died. He returned to Hartford to offer marriage to his victim there, only to find her happily wed to a decent farmer outside of town. Since in these directions no atonement could be made, he turned to Bangor, passionately vowing to redeem there not only his own past but his mother's memory.

For a while after this return, still weak from his long illness, he thought that his dead mother sometimes communicated with him; and he attracted some attention from morbid minds by pseudo-psychic manifestations, going into self-induced trances, muttering mumbo-jumbo, seeing and hearing sights and sounds not visible to normal eyes. When gradually his health improved, this half-madness passed, but there was no slackening in his moral force. He found work as a laborer, lived frugally, saved every penny; and as soon as he was able, he began to repay to the Seminary the sums of which his mother had defrauded that institution. This so pleased the trustees that he was invited to resume his studies there. He did so, perfecting himself in the various categories of Systematic Theology, Ecclesiastical History, Sacred Rhetoric and Literature, and Pastoral Duties, till he was found ready for ordination as a minister; but without cant he humbly avowed that he felt himself unworthy to lead other men in spiritual ways. The fact that he had justified his mother's faith and fulfilled the letter of her hopes contented him and brought him peace. He was quickly accepted as one of the most respected members of the congregation to which as a lay member he attached himself; and his ecclesiastical education earned for him the appellation of 'Elder' which he thereafter wore.

II

When his studies were done, to find some avenue of self-support, Elder Pittridge opened a school — not for children, but for ladies and gentlemen — designed to teach composition and grammar. His success was considerable; but it was not always convenient for his pupils — most of whom were men — to come to classes at regular hours, so the school gradually became a system of tutoring. There were many men in Bangor who, as the riotous speculation of the thirties got under way, suddenly found themselves possessed of means, and — arriving at a consciousness of their intellectual deficiencies — sought him out to learn how to speak and to write with a certain elegance.

Among his private pupils was, for a short time, Rufus Dwinel himself; and when in 1832 Mr. Dwinel, Ira Wadleigh and Asa Babcock organized the project to build the Bangor, Old Town and Milford Railway, Dwinel promised Elder Pittridge a part in the work of bringing that dream to life. Three years later, when stock began to be sold to build the road from Bangor to Old Town, Elder Pittridge, out of commissions which he received for selling stock, was able to buy one of the thousand shares; and when the construction work began, he followed it with a lively interest, not only in the road itself but in the moral welfare of the men employed.

His interest in railroad construction, which was aroused during these years, continued. After the original Bangor-Old Town road was completed, he explored the possibility of building another along the riverfront; but though he enlisted capital and the work was begun, the objections of property-owners along the projected route put an end to it. He surveyed a right of way from Bucksport to Milford, some twenty-eight miles, and estimated the probable cost of construction, including cars and storehouses, at eight thousand dollars a mile. He was one of the first to urge that a railroad should be built from Bangor to Portland, and to advocate state aid for the work.

In his enthusiasm for the Old Town road he had come into friendly contact with Sam Smith, and Sam first advised him to buy and then to sell timber lands, so that Elder Pittridge found himself after the panic of 1837 swept the city reasonably well-to-do. This fact won for him the respect of men of business, just as his diligent and honorable life, and his loyal advocacy of every good cause, had earned for him a universal esteem.

III

Elder Pittridge first met Jenny in the winter before Isaiah's death. In view of his own former dissipations, it was not surprising that he had become an ardent advocate of the temperance cause; and at public meetings where the subject was discussed he proved himself a persuasive speaker. He was a tall, gaunt man with dark hair and sallow skin, thin to the verge of emaciation, and he seemed to burn with an inner fire of conviction which he was able to pass on to his hearers. Jenny on her part was equally zealous; and their common interest in the fight against the rum traffic led to a certain bond between them. She found in him much to admire, and although his interest in her was scrupulously impersonal, she seemed to him remarkable for the clarity of her thinking and for the spiritual strength which was evidenced by the purity and beauty of her habitual expression.

When the news of Isaiah's death reached Bangor, he called upon her to offer sympathy and prayers; and when afterward Ephraim, crushed and shattered by his sense of guilt and shame, turned to the dives of the town, she asked Elder Pittridge to try to save the wretched young man. That she should turn to him was natural enough, since the Elder's own early dissipations were as well known as his present fine way of life. He was eager to serve her in any way. So long as Isaiah lived, his thoughts of her had been admiring and respectful; but now in her widowhood he allowed himself to remember that she was beautiful, and young, and that in a year or two she might marry again. There was already a spiritual sympathy between them. He dreamed of a more personal attraction.

At her request, he sought Ephraim out and labored with him; but Ephraim grinned in cheerful mockery.

'She sent you, I suppose!' he jeered, without naming Jenny. 'And you trotted to do her bidding. Look out for her, Mr. Pittridge! She's ruined a better man than you will ever be.'

'You're wrong to talk so,' Pittridge assured him, and since Ephraim's words hit so near the mark, his color rose resentfully. 'She's almost your only friend in Bangor today. She alone has defended you when others said your cowardly folly was the cause of your father's death. It's true that she sent me, yes; but it was her truly Christian kindliness which led her to do it!'

Ephraim watched him in a dry amusement. 'Got you hooked already, has she?' he challenged. The phrase made Elder Pittridge stiffen with anger. 'Well, look out for yourself, or you'll end up where I am!'

'You're a lost man,' the Elder said severely. 'You've chosen your own damnation, so damned you shall be!' And he left Ephraim to his cups.

But when he reported to Jenny the result of his interview, she was deeply distressed. 'I don't know what to do,' she said ruefully, in that soft, warm tone which seemed to him so deeply moving. 'I want to help him, but I don't know how.'

It was his suggestion that Ephraim's only chance was to leave Bangor and seek redemption where his crime was not known. He helped her draft that letter to Ephraim which John Evered presently would read, and he went with her to consult Deacon Adams about it and get his approval. It was he and Pat Tierney who put Ephraim on the Bangor, and it was he who gave the letter, and Ephraim's money, to Captain Howes.

When later Jenny, having discovered that Ruth was to bear Ephraim's child, and learning from Mr. Richardson that Ephraim was in New York, came to Elder Pittridge for advice, he offered to find Ephraim and bring him home; but Jenny insisted that it was her duty to do this. He wished to go with her, to protect her against the hazards of the journey; but she reminded him gently that if they went away together, even on such an errand, people might not understand; and he was touched by her wise and tolerant understanding.

The news of her marriage to John Evered, when it came back to Bangor, filled him at first with a stern reprobation. He had not realized the hold which even thus soon she had laid upon him, did not in fact realize it now. He thought it was not jealousy he felt, but disapproval of this unseemly marriage so soon after her husband's death. But when he found that almost without exception everyone else in Bangor was glad she had so soon found the happiness she deserved, after her loyal years with old Isaiah whom few liked, he held his tongue, spoke no critical word, blamed himself for his own thoughts, and prayed sincerely and honestly enough that he might become a better and more Christian man.

When Pat and Ruth were married, he proposed to write and tell Jenny the news; and he was disappointed when Pat said they wished to surprise her. The thought of writing to her had evoked in him such a deep pleasure that he awoke to the necessity of remembering that she was now another's wife; but when he heard from Pat of her imminent return, he could not resist going to the wharf, lurking unseen in the crowd there. He saw happiness writ plain in her eyes; and he told himself that John was a fine-looking young man, was surely the husband she deserved.

Yet in the weeks that followed, it was the fact that she was in the audience which lent his speeches at the temperance meetings in the Hammond Street vestry such eloquent passion. His eyes were apt to fix upon her countenance as though he drew from that spring his inspiration. At the first opportunity, she introduced him to her husband, and Elder Pittridge liked John and cultivated the friendship between them, finding in it an anchorage against the uneasy disturbances which in his solitary thoughts of Jenny might still shake his soul. He was often at the house when John was not there, helping Jenny draft that temperance petition from Bangor women to the Legislature, skilfully counterfeiting a feminine style in thought and phrasing; advising her in organizing her sewing circle to work for good, and in the project to found a children's home which she and her friends presently put under way. As the years passed and her children were born, he found an honest pleasure in his friendship with Jenny and John too, and the ghost that for a while had haunted his thoughts walked no more. These two were happy together, the firm union between them a beautiful thing to see; and Elder Pittridge, liking them both, was at peace with himself and with the world.

IV

When Captain Philbrook brought Atticus to Bangor, Elder Pittridge was inclined to agree with John that they should be prepared to yield up the slave if his master came to fetch him; but Jenny's insistence moved him too. When John went to Augusta, there had been no word from the Savannah man, but Elder Pittridge was in John's office when Mr. Sagurs came there.

The Southerner introduced himself, and asked for Mr. Evered, and Elder Pittridge explained that John was out of town. 'I've come for my slave, Atticus, Mr. Pittridge,' the Georgia man said in stern formality. 'He stowed away on Mr. Evered's schooner when she was in Savannah. I assume he's been held for me?'

Elder Pittridge hesitated, uncertain what course to pursue, wishing John were here; but he knew what Jenny would wish him to do. 'He's not in jail, if that's what you mean,' he answered. Then, to gain time to warn Jenny, he said: 'If you'll wait, I'll send a man to find him.'

Mr. Sagurs said he would wait, and Elder Pittridge wrote a hurried note:

> Dear Jenny: Mr. Sagurs is at the office, come from Savannah to recover his Atticus. I have told him I am sending a man to find the slave LINC

He dispatched this message. 'Your negro has been working as a gardener for Mr. Evered,' he explained to Mr. Sagurs. 'He has made no attempt to escape, so we did not lock him up. He should be here within the hour. May I offer you some hospitality in the meantime?' And he added: 'We're proud of our city here. I'd be glad to show you around.'

The Southerner doubtfully agreed; and they strolled down to the wharves. A hundred and twenty-one million feet of boards would be surveyed in the port that year, the largest figure thus far attained. The river was full of vessels ready to load, rafts of sawed timber coming down-river daily from the mills at Old Town; and Mr. Sagurs listened with real interest to Linc's enthusiastic description of the thriving industry.

The two men in that hour arrived at an almost friendly footing; but when they came back to Linc's office, a note was waiting. Jenny had written:

> Dear Linc — Thank you. Atticus is safe where Mr. Sagurs can never find him.
>
> JENNY

Elder Pittridge felt a surprising pleasure in this alliance between himself and Jenny; but he told Mr. Sagurs in regretful tones: 'I've bad news for you, sir. Apparently your man heard of your arrival. He has disappeared.'

Mr. Sagurs' chubby countenance burned red. He rose with a rigid dignity. 'Sir, I offer no comment — though I suppose I am free to make any conjectures that seem justified. Since we can no longer meet on a friendly basis, I shall consult your local authorities — if there is any authority in your lawless town.'

And without waiting for a reply, he strode away.

Elder Pittridge wished to go at once to Jenny, but Mr. Sagurs might be keeping a watch upon his movements; so he waited till evening before walking out to the house. She opened at his knock.

'I thought you would come, Linc,' she said. 'Atticus is safe hidden in the barn mow. They came looking for him today, but I told them he was gone.'

'I wish John were here to handle this,' he confessed. 'It can lead to trouble.'

'We can handle it, you and I,' she said. 'John is too apt to remember his responsibilities as a citizen, and to forget his duties as a man.'

He hesitated, said in slow surprise: 'I've never heard you criticize John before.'

She smiled. 'Have you not? John is not perfect, Linc.'

He said warningly: 'Mr. Sagurs seemed a determined man. He'll not be easily put aside.'

She smiled. 'If he can't find Atticus, what can he do?'

There was no answer to that, and Linc admitted it. He rose to return to town, but she persuaded him to stay awhile. 'With John away, I'm lonely,' she confessed. 'I'm never one to go early to bed, you know; and when he's not here, evenings are long.' The night was warm, and they moved out of doors and sat in the chairs on the lawn in quiet talk awhile; and the murmur of her soft voice in the darkness was warm and beautiful. When he said good night at last, she said: 'Come soon again, Linc. I always enjoy seeing you.' She added: 'You're my oldest good friend, you know. I knew you even before I knew John.'

Elder Pittridge strode back to town in a strange, blind haste, looking back over his shoulder now and then like a man who fears pursuit. He had thought any feeling he might once have had for Jenny was forgotten long ago; but the suggestion of a lack of understanding between her and John woke something new in him. There were turbulences in him which he had long controlled; but now in his middle forties he found himself sometimes reviving hot, youthful memories. The forces in any man which, too long held under bond, rebel at last at long disuse, were stirring in Elder Pittridge now.

He did not see Jenny again till after John's return from Augusta she came to the office to chide John for the indiscretion that had delivered Atticus up to his master. Elder Pittridge heard what passed between them, and while John stood silent in the face of her cold rage, he thought there was in her tones no least hint of love remaining. No woman, he thought, could speak so to her husband unless she hated him through and through.

The understanding filled him with an exultation which he dared not recognize. He spoke to John after she was gone, empty words of comforting; but his lips were hot and dry.

2

ELDER PITTRIDGE thought that moment in John's office must leave between John and Jenny a gulf plain to every eye; but this did not happen. During the days that followed, Atticus seemed to be forgotten, and between John and Jenny and Elder Pittridge and Margaret Saladine the old friendship went on as before. John and Jenny seemed on the surface to be as happy as they had ever been; but in his new awareness of her Elder Pittridge thought that Jenny was more beautiful every day, as now in her full maturity she came to bloom.

One day in August these four friends took the boys for a picnic at Pushaw Lake. The lake lies about six miles north of Bangor, and during the boom times it had begun to attract pleasure parties as well as fishermen. Now, to cater to such groups, there were two hostelries, the Pushaw House of which Captain Burgess was proprietor, and the Perch House kept by John Hasey. John had promised young Dan to take him fishing there; and the picnic was arranged to carry out that promise. Pat Tierney borrowed for the day a hay cart from the nearest farm and they started soon after breakfast behind plodding farm horses for the easy two-hour journey. John drove, and young Dan sat beside his father and sometimes was permitted to hold the reins. The others made themselves comfortable on the hay in the cart bed. The Elder, watching Jenny, thought there was a shadow in her eyes; but outwardly she was gay enough, happy with the children or talking quietly with Margaret while he kept the youngsters amused.

The jolting ride was dusty and wearying for all of them; but when it ended, discomforts were forgotten. John drove past the Perch House and down across an open meadow to a knoll above the water. He and Elder Pittridge, with Dan trying to help, unharnessed the horses and led them down to the lakeside to drink and then tethered them in a clump of young oaks where there was no underbrush, so that the breeze would keep away the worst of the flies. Jenny and Meg opened the hamper Mrs. McGaw had packed with good things and spread the feast. Dan in his eagerness to begin fishing could hardly wait to eat; but John told him cheerfully:

'Might as well, son. Fishing's no good in the middle of the day, anyway.'

'It might be,' Dan urged.

'Oh, we'll try it,' his father chuckled. 'Don't worry about that. And we'll stay till they start to bite, even if we have to wait till dark. But there's plenty of time. It's going to be hot out there in the sun. Eat while you can.'

Dan did his best, and Will, who had been promised that he might go in the boat with them and perhaps hold a line, nevertheless did full justice to Mrs. McGaw's provisions. When they were finished, John said: 'Well, Dan, here we go! Linc, you want to come along?'

Elder Pittridge shook his head. 'I'm no fisherman,' he said. 'I'll stay and mind the youngsters.'

So John and the two boys departed. He had arranged with Mr. Hasey for the use of a boat, and the others, watching from the shady knoll, presently saw them set out, John rowing, Dan in the stern, Will perched high in the bow. Then young Tommy declared that he wanted to go wading, and Mat loudly announced a like desire. Elder Pittridge rose to take them down to the lake shore; but Meg said:

'No, I'll go, Linc. You stay here.'

'I'll come help you,' he urged.

Jenny said smilingly: 'Better stay, Linc. I see a wicked gleam in Meg's eyes. I expect she'll go wading, herself, unless you tag along so she can't!'

'Of course I will!' Meg laughingly agreed. 'There's a sandy beach in the next cove, where I'll be out of your sight.' She challenged: 'Don't you want to come, Jenny? The water will be so cool!'

'I'll stay and keep Linc company,' Jenny told her, and her eyes met his.

So Meg and the two boys went down toward the lake, and Elder Pittridge and Jenny were left together. He stood above her, and though they had often been thus alone before, something he had seen in her eyes a moment ago now made his pulse pound hard. John and the older youngsters were in sight, half a mile along the shore, sitting patiently in the sun with dangling lines; but when Meg and the younger children had disappeared, there was no one near. The horses stamped in the oak clump a little way off. A great pine, many-branched and therefore neglected by the lumbermen who had stripped this locality, shaded them, and its spills lay in a soft mat everywhere, fragrant in the sun. Jenny, in a checked gingham dress that made her seem like a girl, sat with her feet tucked under her wide skirts, resting one hand upon the ground. Her head was bare, her dark hair escaping softly from its coils to shadow her brow. Her eyes were downcast, and she picked up a twig, snapping it between her fingers. Elder Pittridge, standing above her, saw a single white thread in her dark hair, and he felt for her a great tenderness and a wistful sorrow that she must grow older. Because when his eyes rested on her his throat was full, he looked again toward the distant boat.

'They don't seem to be catching anything,' he said.

For a moment she did not speak, and when she did it was with a quiet gravity. 'Sit down, Linc,' she told him. 'I must talk to someone — and you're my closest friend.'

He obeyed her, trying to find a word to say. 'What is it, Jenny? I've guessed you were — troubled today.'

She nodded. 'You always do understand,' she said gratefully and met his eyes; and her eyes were wide, as though she had unveiled them with that glance, admitting him to read her heart. She told him slowly: 'John and I have quarrelled.' And after a moment she repeated: 'We had a dreadful quarrel.'

He said in lame jocularity: 'Don't married people have lots of quarrels, Jenny?'

'Oh, those, yes,' she agreed, smiling a little. 'When they're both angry, and say things they don't mean. But this was different, Linc. We weren't angry. If we had been, I would know it didn't matter. Being angry is just one way of — loving. This was a perfectly calm, reasonable — final quarrel.'

'Final?' His heart beat in his throat.

'Yes,' she said. 'Final. Nothing can ever be the same between John and me again.' And she asked: 'Do you mind my talking to you? I must talk to someone. I warn you, if you are still my friend, John may accuse you of — hideous things.' She smiled affectionately: 'He may even say I am in love with you.'

'I'm your friend and his too,' Elder Pittridge said quickly. 'You two — and Meg — are the only real friends I have.'

'I value your friendship,' she assured him. 'Always know that, Linc. But if you'd rather I didn't talk to you —— Yet I'm so unhappy, I must talk to someone or weep.'

'You know I'd do anything for you — for either of you,' he added carefully, and he urged: 'Surely this will pass, Jenny. Aren't you making too much of it?'

'No, it's final,' she insisted. 'Oh, I don't mean that we will part —

at least not in the world's eyes — or be divorced. We've the children, so for their sakes we must go on. But — John has left my room, Linc.' Her low voice was like a wail. 'And oh, I'm so wretched and so miserable!'

He wetted his dry lips, cleared his throat. 'If you want to talk — I'll listen. I might even be able to help.'

She nodded. 'I do want to talk,' she said. 'But promise me you won't blame John? I couldn't bear to have this make any difference between you two. You and he have always been such friends.'

'I won't do anything you don't want.'

'You're so fine,' she told him gratefully. And after a moment she went on: 'I can see now that this has been coming on for a long time. John and I think differently about so many things. He thought I was wrong about poor Atticus. You remember that. That was just one of many things, but they go back to the first year we were married. As long as we loved each other, they didn't matter; but since little Mat was born I've known that John didn't love me, and my love for him has slowly died. This last quarrel was really the first moment in years when we've been honest with each other.'

He waited and she said: 'This was about the children, Linc. You see, John has always spoiled them. Oh, I know it's because he's so proud of them; but he indulges them in every way, and I have to do all the discipline. They can't be allowed just to run wild. So it is always I who must tell them what to do, and make them do it, and punish them if they don't. Mustn't I, Linc?'

He nodded. 'Of course. But the boys are fine, Jenny.'

'If they are, it's I who have made them so. John always protested whenever I punished them at all. I've had to wait till he was away from home, because if he heard them cry he interfered — and you must see how unfair that was, for him to seem to rescue them from me!'

'Of course.'

'Well,' she murmured, 'the last straw came three days ago. I had to punish little Mat . . .'

'Mat?' he echoed in astonishment. 'He's too young, surely, to do anything very wrong!'

She smiled. 'I assure you he deserved every stroke I gave him, Linc. He deliberately and defiantly disobeyed me — and of course I couldn't allow that, so I switched him.' She added rebelliously: 'I didn't really hurt him; but while I was doing it, and he was screaming — you know they always make as much noise as they possibly can, pretend I'm just killing them, so I'll stop the quicker — John came home.

'He was furious, Linc. He told me I must never do it again.' Her voice caught. 'And Linc, he threatened me! He said that if I ever whipped one of the boys again, he would whip me.' She pushed up her sleeve to show the dark bruise Dan's small hands had left there. 'See where he gripped my arm,' she whispered pitifully.

His fist clenched in a dark rage. That mark on her white flesh, seen thus in the clear light of a fine August afternoon, was somehow shameful and appalling; and he felt a passionate anger toward John who had done this to her.

She laughed a little, bravely. 'I was afraid of him, Linc,' she confessed. 'He's so big and so strong, he could break my neck between his fingers. I'm not very big, you see. He almost broke my arm, just taking hold of it that way. I was afraid, so I talked as bravely as I could. I told him if he ever struck me I'd kill him, Linc.' She smiled wistfully. 'That seems funny now, the idea of me being able to hurt anyone as strong as he. But he let go of me.'

She added ruefully: 'And then he took his things into the other room, the room next mine. I've had to lie about that to Mrs. McGaw and to Ruth. I told them I wasn't sleeping well, that I was nervous, that John and I would sleep apart awhile. I don't know whether they believed me or not, but it was the only thing I could think of to say.'

He tried to find some anchorage in the storm which shook him. 'It will come out all right,' he predicted. 'Time heals all these things.'

'Perhaps,' she agreed, and smiled, this time almost happily. 'I know it's done me good to tell you about it — as though by sharing it with you the burden were lighter. Thank you for letting me do it, Linc.'

He said, as steadily as possible: 'You know I'll do anything for you.'

Her eyes met his. 'I know you will, Linc.' Then her eyes fell and suddenly her cheeks were scarlet. She whispered: 'I've always known that, even before Isaiah died, it seems to me.'

II

Elder Pittridge would never forget the hour that followed when they sat together under the pine, talking quietly together, drawing nearer to each other. It seemed to him that each word they spoke had two meanings; that behind the simplest phrase lay connotations of understanding and sympathy and of affection firmly founded and coming now into a rich warmth and beauty. He had never found in her so much sweetness, such a yielding deference, such dependence upon his strength and wisdom. No sense of danger warned him. Surely no harm could come from this quiet talk between two friends there under the old pine upon the knoll and in the clear light of a fine summer afternoon.

Yet there were changes in him which he did not suspect before at last Meg and the two small boys came back from their wading. The youngsters promptly wandered off toward the horses, devising some game of their own among the oaks there; and Elder Pittridge rose to go after them, to keep them clear of any harm. As he moved away he heard Meg say in distressed tones:

'Jenny, when I took off little Mat's shoes and stockings so he could wade, I saw that his legs are all covered with red marks, crisscrossed every way. Whatever are they?'

'I think he must have scratched himself in his sleep,' Jenny said easily. 'He's had a touch of hives. You know how they itch.'

'These didn't look like scratches,' Meg protested.

Elder Pittridge was by that time too far away to hear Jenny's answer, but for that matter he had hardly heard what Meg said. All his senses were confused. He was like a man blinded by looking too long upon the sun.

They stayed by Pushaw Lake till dusk, and young Dan caught his fill of fish before John brought the boat back to the landing. There was enough left over of the provisions in Mrs. McGaw's hamper so that they could eat supper here, and they did so. Jenny, Elder Pittridge thought, was even more quiet than usual, and Meg too; but John seemed perfectly normal, laughing with his sons, speaking easily to Jenny, teasing Meg as he sometimes liked to do. The older man resented John's composure, finding in it something hard and heartless. Now and then Jenny's eyes met his in a glance that was a reminder of what had passed between them; and he was proud to think that in her distress she had called him to stand by her side. When he remembered that bruise which John's hard clasp had left upon her arm, he was shaken with anger which was the more violent because he knew his own physical inability to make that anger effective. He wished to smash John and to beat him — but he knew he could not do this, even if a pretext were afforded.

While they ate supper and afterward during the moonlit homeward drive, when Meg and Jenny, sitting in the cart bed with the younger children, sang softly, he said scarce any word. The moon was bright, so that he could see Jenny's face as she sang. Her voice was a firm, clear soprano; Meg's a warm contralto. Their tones blended in a rich perfection, and their two voices played on him, just as a glass may be set vibrating by a fiddle string. He had long since taught himself not to think of Jenny's beauty; but tonight those lessons were forgotten. There had been a time in his life when he was no anchorite. His thoughts ran like unbridled horses now.

III

When they came home, John said Pat would drive Elder Pittridge and Margaret back to town; but Meg protested: 'Oh, no, John! Linc and I will walk. It's such a fine night.' And when he would have insisted, she cried laughingly: 'Be tactful, John! After all, we may prefer to walk home!' She smiled. 'We might even be a little sentimental, in the moonlight.'

John laughed. 'All right, if you want it so. But I can't imagine old Linc getting sentimental, even with you, Meg!'

Elder Pittridge bit his lip in angry resentment. He was by almost ten years the oldest of them, a gaunt man, his black hair well streaked with gray, his face deep-lined, but the reminder tonight annoyed him. Even Meg cried: 'That's not a very nice thing to say!' She took his arm and they turned toward the door.

They were in no hurry. These two, through the friendship for John and Jenny which had drawn them together, had long since arrived on an understanding and comfortable basis; they could be silent together without embarrassment when they chose. It was so tonight. His thoughts, though they led nowhere but simply raced in a ceaseless circle, nevertheless made him forget everything except Jenny with her soft hair loosely shadowing her brow, Jenny with her eyes so wide and open and honest, Jenny whose mouth was like a child's soft eager mouth, Jenny whose quiet tones could start a deep vibration in a man, Jenny whose flesh bore a bruise John had set there, Jenny who loved John no more. The thought of her filled him tonight as he walked homeward in the soft south wind and the moon.

Margaret at first showed no desire for speech, quiet beside him, her eyes straight ahead as his were. Only when they came opposite the house Isaiah had built for Jenny, she turned and looked up at him and saw his deep abstraction; and after a moment then she said:

'Linc, I think I will tell you my great news.'

He roused almost with a start. 'News? Oh, yes, Meg. What news?'

She asked: 'Do you know — of course you do — Cap'n Pawl?'

'Yes. Not well, but I know him.' Captain Chester Pawl was

a Searsport man, and his Lucy brig plied in the lumber trade. He was one of those who had been satisfied, during the speculation in timber lands, to make a modest fortune and then turn to less profitable but more substantial activities. He was a few years younger than Elder Pittridge, who knew him only as a bluff individual no different from a dozen or a score of other seamen.

'I'm sorry you don't know him better,' Margaret said. 'Father handles his law business, and he usually has dinner with us when he comes to town. His mother's a wonderful old lady, and their home in Searsport is delightful. We've been down there several times. I know you'll like her.'

He looked at her curiously. 'What is it, Margaret? What's your news?'

'Cap'n Pawl has asked me to marry him,' Margaret explained. 'He's away, won't be back till next month. He didn't try to persuade me, didn't argue or anything. He just told me he wanted to marry me, and said I could take time to think it over and let him know when he comes back. But I've decided. I decided today — seeing how happy John and Jenny are together — that I would.' She made a little mirthful sound. 'So you're the first one to know.'

He was struck by the irony of this; that she should marry Captain Pawl because John and Jenny were so happy, when in fact their life together was shattered now for good and all. 'Have you told Jenny?' he asked.

'No, no one but you.' She added: 'In fact, I didn't really decide until a moment ago. I've been thinking about it all day.' They approached her door and paused.

'Tell Jenny,' he urged. If Meg told Jenny, then Jenny might confess her own unhappiness; might save Meg from this marriage which — since her consent to it was based on a mistake — must be wrong. 'Tell Jenny. See what she says.'

But Margaret shook her head. 'No. No, I must tell Cap'n Pawl before anyone else knows.' She added: 'Yet I had to tell you, Linc. I was so happy in my decision, in having made up my mind. Marriage can be a sort of rescue, don't you think — a safe harbor against so many storms.'

'Will you still live in Bangor?'

'No, in Searsport, with his mother — unless sometimes I go on voyages with him.'

'We'll miss you — we three, John and Jenny and I. We've done so much together.'

She said: 'I know. But such pleasant years don't last, Linc. Soon or late there always comes a change.' She added in a strange, still urgency: 'I hope you'll find some fine girl and marry, too, Linc. You ought to. You'd be so much happier, and safer, too.'

After he had said good night to her, walking on to his own home, he puzzled over those astonishing words. It was as though she had said, explicitly: 'I am marrying to find safety, Linc. You had better do the same.' But — what danger was it from which she sought to escape? What possible danger threatened her — or him?

3

Soon after that day at Pushaw Lake, and without having seen Jenny again, Elder Pittridge went to Augusta to attend the meeting of the State Temperance Society, and to seek among the legislators converts to the cause. He stayed there several weeks, coming for the first time into personal contact with Neal Dow. Dow, a man of means, born of Quaker parents and reared in a fine tradition of decency and truth, early enlisted in the fight to drive rum-sellers out of Maine. When he was thirty he assisted in organizing the State Temperance Society, but its willingness to compromise and to accept half measures did not satisfy him; and in 1838 he and those who felt as he did founded the Maine Temperance Union, devoted to the cause of total abstinence. The following year in his home city of Portland he secured a referendum on the question of licensing the liquor trade. He lost that fight, but three years later he won a similar referendum.

Then he plunged into the battle for a state-wide law, appealing not only to the legislators but to the voters, flooding the state — largely at his own expense — with tracts and pamphlets so that he was able to say years later: 'Maine was made a prohibition state by sowing it knee-deep with Temperance literature.' He circulated, too, petitions to the Legislature; and when Elder Pittridge now met him in Augusta he was seeking support for a bill designed to curb the traffic. The measure had passed the House in February, but it had been defeated in the Senate; and taking that defeat as a challenge to greater efforts he now threw all his energies and a considerable part of his fortune into the fight, determined to turn that first defeat into an eventual victory.

He told Elder Pittridge success was sure. 'But first we must purge the legislative councils of those who oppose us.' His utterances rang with such passion that the Elder thought he meant physical violence, but Dow added: 'We'll clean these halls as a farmer cleans his tie-up — but with ballots, not with shovels.' He was at the time about forty years old, of commanding physique and with an eloquent tongue. He wore side whiskers, his brow was high, his hair was parted on the right with a lock usually hanging over his left eye. His eyes had an extraordinary burning quality; and the ferocity of his habitual zealous concentration had carved perpendicular wrinkles between his heavy brows.

Elder Pittridge was himself set on fire by the flame in this man. He felt himself cleansed and purified by his new loyalty; and Jenny drifted into the background of his thoughts. Here in Neal Dow he found a leader to whom, forsaking all others, he could cleave. But when early in October he returned to Bangor it was to find that John had gone away up-river for an indefinite stay. The demand for lumber was in these years steadily increasing; and the Bingham lands were being logged on an expanding scale. John went ostensibly to oversee the setting up of camps for the winter's operations, and his going was thus natural enough; but to Elder Pittridge his departure for what might be a long absence seemed proof that the rupture between him and Jenny remained unhealed, and this realization revived those treacherous thoughts which Neal Dow's magnetic charm had for a while driven into the background. The Elder wished to see Jenny. He told himself this was because he wanted to tell her about Neal Dow and to report what was happening in Augusta; but he knew in his heart that this was not the only reason, that it was in fact no more than a pretext. Doubts restrained him, doubts of himself. He went instead to Margaret Saladine, and she welcomed him happily.

'I began to think you wouldn't be here for my wedding,' she declared. 'Cap'n Pawl and I will be married on the fourteenth, you know.'

He asked smilingly: 'So it's not a secret now?'

'He's coming, he and his mother, tomorrow, to stay with us two or three days,' she explained. 'Will you have dinner with us one day? I do want you to know him, Linc.'

'Of course.' He hesitated. 'Meg, they tell me John is gone up-river.'

'Yes.' Her tone was shadowed. 'He'll be away all winter, Jenny says.'

'All winter?' Their eyes met, and she nodded; and he said lamely: 'She'll miss him.'

'She'll keep busy. She does so much.'

He tried to laugh, changed the subject. 'Well, so you're really going to be married, and our good times together, the four of us, you and me and Jenny and John, are done.'

'I told you, such things have to end after a while.' And she said again, gravely watching him: 'Linc, you ought to marry too.'

He laughed the suggestion aside, but he faced the fact, during the days that followed, that with John away for weeks or months he could no longer easily see Jenny, could not without provoking the clatter of loose tongues go freely to the house. He tried to persuade himself that as John's closest friend he had certain privileges; but his guilty certainty that it was not friendliness for John which made him want to see Jenny prevented his accepting his own arguments.

He saw her first at Judge Saladine's house when they and others of Meg's friends gathered to dine and to greet Captain Pawl. Jenny was there before him, and she met him easily and without restraint; and when he said: 'How are the boys? I've been meaning to get out to see them as soon as I could find the time,' she smiled in full understanding.

'Don't apologize for not coming, Linc,' she said. 'There never need be any explanations between you and me.'

She wore during the few moments before they went in to dinner a gaiety he had never seen in her before, her lively tongue keeping not only him but others laughing; and this provoked in him a quicker wit to respond to hers. Her beauty moved him too. Her dark gown with snug bodice and full skirt was cut low in a deep curve from shoulder to shoulder, and he wondered as a man will what feminine magic kept it in position. Her hair was dressed smoothly, with soft curls on the left side. Her cheek was bright, and a warmer hue tinted the ivory of her throat and bosom, exquisitely fleshed. To look at her left him breathless. There was about her something ethereal and remote, as though she were a goddess to be worshipped from a distance; but when they went in to dinner, she said a word that brought her suddenly within a man's reach. Margaret had asked him to take her in; and they followed Judge Saladine, who bore Captain Pawl's mother on his arm. Jenny whispered in delicious amusement that the switch which old Mrs. Pawl wore was slipping.

'It will be down around her ear before long,' she predicted, and she added: 'And did you ever see such an impressive bustle?' She looked up at him, her eyes twinkling mischievously. 'You know,

Linc, if I'd been trying to find a name for a bustle I'd have called it a rump-us!'

He was by the indelicacy of this jest at once startled and excited. She who had seemed so far beyond his reach was suddenly a flesh-and-blood woman — and therefore attainable. Until woman herself — in generous love or in light wantonness — descends to earth, man by habit sets her on a pedestal. Jenny had always seemed to him so completely and perfectly decorous that not even his thoughts could touch her; but now she had put herself within his reach, and his thoughts ran a hot race. He talked for a while only to her, his eyes devouring her, till he saw Margaret's troubled glance upon him and turned to old Mrs. Pawl on his other side.

Afterward, when the ladies withdrew, he cultivated Captain Pawl. The man Margaret would marry was heavy without being fat, with powerful physical force in his every line; but in Margaret's presence or when he spoke of her to Elder Pittridge now, he became altogether gentle, even his voice subtly changing, so that he testified in a thousand ways his tender and devoted reverence for the lovely woman who was to be his bride.

When awhile after they joined the others the evening ended, Jenny was one of the first to leave. Pat Tierney called for her, and Elder Pittridge, though he wished to offer her his escort, stood silent and watched her depart. She made smiling good-byes to them all, but when her eyes met his he thought he read a personal message in them. He stayed till most of the others were gone, and Margaret, bidding him good night, asked smilingly:

'Do you like my Captain, Linc?'

'Yes,' he said, honestly and gladly. 'Yes, Meg, I do.'

She pressed his hand and let him go.

II

He and Jenny met again at Margaret's wedding. After the Captain and his bride had driven away, they drew together, and he spoke regretfully of the fact that John could not be here.

'I don't think he wanted to be,' Jenny admitted. 'He and Meg were fond of each other, you know.' She smiled. 'I think he even thought she was in love with him. Men are so ready to believe that of a woman.'

He wondered whether she meant to warn him against such a presumption. 'We used to joke about that, all of us,' he reminded her.

'I know, but I don't think it was quite a joke to John,' she insisted. 'The day she told us she was to be married, after she was gone he fairly raged, said she was throwing herself away, till I showed him how absurd he was. He was sure she would never be happy.'

'She certainly looked happy today, and — peaceful, as though she were finding something she had always wanted!'

'She found refuge,' Jenny said, and he remembered that Meg had said the same thing. Then she added frankly: 'She has always loved John, you know. He's quite right about that — though I wouldn't tell him so. And her feeling for John — since he was my husband — made her unhappy. Now when she has taken this definite and final step, she is at least at peace in her own mind.'

The many voices around them merged in one general note of which now and then a word or two were audible. 'Lovely bride.' 'Able man.' 'Should have married long ago.' 'At Searsport.' 'A dear old lady, but a tyrant!' With a remote part of his mind, he heard these words and phrases; but they seemed to come from a long way off. What Jenny had said made many things clear to him, just as when a lightning flash momentarily illuminates the scene at night, trees, buildings, hills and rivers are for an instant fixed upon the retina in their mutual relations, persisting for seconds after darkness comes again. In the light of Jenny's word he saw with an extraordinary clarity not only that Meg had long loved John, but also that Meg must somehow have known that John and Jenny were no longer one. While they were united, Meg could love John safely enough, knowing him altogether another's; but if he were not altogether Jenny's — then there were dangers for Meg in loving him. From those dangers she had fled to marriage with Captain Pawl.

For a moment he saw thus clearly; and then Jenny said: 'The boys have missed you. You haven't been out to the house for so long.'

'I spent some time in Augusta.'

'I know.'

He told her, almost absently: 'I met a great man, over there, Jenny. Neal Dow, of Portland. He's a living, walking inspiration. You know of him.'

'I've heard of him, of course.'

'He'll come here to speak, some day. You'll see then what I mean. Jenny, he's sure the law can be passed, next time, in another year or two.'

She said wisely: 'It will have to be such a law that the legislators can still get rum to drink! You know, everyone thinks liquor is bad for the other man, but not for himself.'

He nodded. 'He knows that, so this first law will be a mild one, chiefly planned to put the principle of the control of rum-selling on the statute books. He proposes a law to license dealers, and to provide that they can sell only by the barrel. Poor men can't afford to buy more than a few drinks at a time, so that will protect them against themselves — and still let those who can afford it buy liquor.' He added: 'And the penalties will be light, almost negligible. But once this law is passed and the principle established, the next law will be stronger.'

Because in this discussion they were on safely impersonal grounds — so that he could have the happiness of being with her and of talking to her without any sense of guilt — he talked for long, earnestly and eloquently, trying to blind himself to her beauty and to the softness in her eyes, till she said at last, interrupting him in mid-flight, forcing him back to more personal things:

'John was sorry not to see you before he went up-river.'

He accepted her guidance. 'Meg says he'll be away all winter?'

'Yes. But you mustn't be a stranger, Linc. You know he would want you to come, as you always have. And of course I want you, too — as much as the children do.'

'I will,' he promised. He tried to laugh. 'I'll come so often you'll soon be tired of having me around.'

She smiled. 'When I am, I'll surely tell you, Linc,' she promised. 'But till I do — you may be sure you're welcome. Come when you can.'

III

After they parted, he remembered her every word and intonation and every glance of her eye. She, clearly, recognized as he did the risk of gossip which his coming to the house involved; yet she had bidden him dare that risk and come. But his thoughts so far outreached the present moment that even for him to go to see her — since his thoughts were what they were — seemed to him like a betrayal of John. Whosoever lusted after a woman in his heart was already an adulterer; and he reminded himself of this with a guilty vehemence, and prayed for an honest mind. He could not control his thoughts, so he felt himself already damned; but he could control his physical actions, and he did not go to her till she sent for him, wrote him: 'Come when you can. I've something I'd like to discuss with you.'

The boys, when he appeared, welcomed him almost shyly. It was so long since he had seen them that he was, especially to the younger ones, half a stranger; and he had to invite them to that exploration of his pockets which they had used to initiate. Jenny smilingly watched them press around him, and for a while they had him to themselves; but then she sent them away.

'I wanted your advice about a problem that has come up at the Children's Home,' she reassuringly explained. She had refused a place on the board of managers there, but by her singleness of purpose she dominated the direction of the institution. When Miss Folsom resigned as matron to marry Deacon Skinner of Brewer, Jenny had been dissatisfied with Mrs. Quimby, her immediate successor, and she had led the managers to replace Mrs. Quimby with Mrs. Norton. She told Linc now about a difficulty which had arisen with Mrs. Norton; and although the matter seemed to him of no importance — it concerned the question whether Mrs. Norton should be required to teach the children their lessons, as Miss Folsom had done, or whether a teacher should be engaged — she discussed it at length, laying out every argument for or against, requiring his opinion.

He answered emptily. To be alone with her here in the big living room, the doors closed, the bright fire crackling, was at once blissful and affrighting. Dusk presently would darken the windows, and they would sit here in the firelight, with the flames giving just enough light so that he could see how lovely she was, and at last the house, except for them, would be all asleep, and — if he stayed so long — they might go quietly and secretly up the wide stairs together. His ravenous thoughts, watching her while she talked of Mrs. Norton and of these unimportant matters, clung to her alone. Was it possible, he asked himself, that she was as unconscious as she seemed of the potency and of the peril of this quiet hour? If he rose and crossed to where she sat and drew her into his arms — what would she say? What do?

Her words were of matters wholly impersonal. She spoke earnestly and strongly of her perplexities about the Home, and her eyes were intent, and her countenance wore an extraordinary purity. He found it impossible, looking at her untouched beauty now, to believe that she had borne John four children; that she and John had been these ten years devoted and passionate lovers.

And yet — was it impossible? Was there not something of invitation, even of surrender, in her eyes? Was there not in her glances a lambent fire he had never seen before?

They talked about the Children's Home till he was fretfully

weary of that subject; and he asked questions on his own account. Had she heard from John? Had the boys been well, escaping all the ills of childhood? 'I feel as though I were all out of touch,' he admitted. 'I haven't seen them since the day we went to Pushaw Lake.' He hoped she might refer to their conversation there, bring them thus to that more intimate footing he wished somehow to achieve.

But she only said that life went smoothly in its usual courses. She smiled and added: 'Only some stray pigs got into my garden one night and almost ruined it!' Swine in greater or less numbers had always run wild in the Bangor streets and still did so, dodging out of the way of passing teams with querulous squeals. 'They must have rooted in my flower beds all night long,' she said. 'It was sickening. I threatened to put out poison for them, but John wouldn't let me.'

'You can't poison dumb animals,' he agreed. 'They're not to blame.'

'Then I'd like to poison the people who let them run loose,' she declared, laughing at her own heat. 'Bangor's full of pigs — and the human ones are the worst!'

It had been mid-afternoon when he came to her. He stayed long, wondering whether she would invite him to supper, but she did not; and at last he began to see a smile in her eyes, as though she were amused at his lingering. He rose to say good-bye, hoping for protests, longing to hear her whisper: 'No, Linc. Stay.' But she let him go.

IV

John came home for Christmas, making the trip with a caravan of teams sent to fetch supplies. He would stay a few days, and he invited Elder Pittridge home with him to supper. They met at John's office, where Pat would pick them up; and John with a boyish enthusiasm displayed a writing machine which someone wished to sell him, and which printed small capital letters, clearly and neatly, on a piece of paper. 'But I'm not buying it,' he said. 'It's still new. I doubt it will work.' He produced with some pride another new device, elastic bands useful for holding letters and bills in packets for filing, made by a Mr. Goodyear, of Providence, Rhode Island.

John laid such emphasis on these small matters that Elder Pittridge thought the other was uneasily making conversation, and he was glad when the carriage came for them. On the way home John said in friendly reproach:

'Jenny says you've been neglecting her. You mustn't do that, Linc. She likes to go to concerts and entertainments and the Lyceum lectures and such things; but she can't well do it without an escort. And with me gone and Meg married and living down in Searsport, Jenny has no one now but her sewing circle and her church friends. It's a lonely winter for her.'

'I've been busy,' Elder Pittridge admitted. 'The cold winter has caused a lot of distress, you know. With the mills shut down, there are many idle men, and families with no income. I try to do what I can to help them along.'

'I know,' John assented. 'Jenny does a lot of that too, of course. There are dozens of women and children in Bangor who would go hungry if it weren't for her and her friends. She tells me she's given away eleven Franklin stoves and airtights this winter to people who couldn't even keep warm; and since I've been at home there are children at the house every day to beg for food. Mrs. McGaw and Jenny always feed them.' He added: 'It's the fact that we haven't enough jobs here from November to May that's making so many Maine men move to Massachusetts. That's the weakness in the lumber business, Linc. Most of the work — so far as Bangor is concerned — is concentrated in the summer. We'll cure that some day.' He added in friendly urgency: 'But you ought to find time to see your friends.'

'Well, you know, John, if I saw much of her, some clatter-tongues would start wagging.'

John laughed. 'What of it? Those whose opinion I value won't think harm of Jenny — or of you. Why pay attention to the others?' And as they drew up to the door: 'So here we are.'

Jenny made much of that reunion of the three of them. 'It's a pity Meg can't be here,' she said. 'But she couldn't come without her Captain, so it wouldn't be the same.' She told John: 'You should have come back for her wedding, my dear. There was never so happy a bride.'

'Wish I could have,' John agreed; and Elder Pittridge thought there was no reservation in his tone. 'I'd go down and see them if I had the time; but it can't be managed.'

He told them at the supper table how his winter was being spent. He was overseeing the work of half a dozen camps scattered along twenty miles of river. 'We'll have the biggest single drive that ever came down-river,' he declared. 'I want to see some men here tomorrow, see if the drive on the whole river can't be organized as one proposition.' And he explained the plan he had in mind. The extension of large-scale lumbering up the West

Branch had begun sixteen years before, when Steve Bussell and nine or ten others cut off some monster pines in the Millinocket Lake region; but not even a systematic exploration of the upper river was made till 1837, and then primarily with the idea of opening a route of travel to Canada.

'Now there are gangs lumbering all along the river,' John told them. 'But every man drives his own logs. There's a dam at Chesuncook that helps give a head of water, and pays General Veazie as much in tolls every year as it cost him to build it; and there's another at North Twin Lakes. But a company that went into it right, handled the drive for the whole river, could afford to put up dams and sluices wherever they're needed, and take out rocks in the main channel, boom the coves, and so on. They could drive cheaper than any one outfit, and make a good profit for themselves doing it.'

His plan was for a mutual company, membership open to any man owning timber land or engaged in lumbering along the river. 'We'd have to work it out in proportion to the size of the operation, maybe give every owner one vote, and give every operator a vote for each six-ox team he's got working. We'd assess costs, and divide profits. I'm going to see Ira Wadleigh about it tomorrow. I've talked with Aaron Babb, and he says he could save a lot of money for all of us if he could run the whole drive. He figures he could drive from Chesuncook Dam to Argyle for seventy-five cents a thousand, or maybe less. That beats the best we can do.'

Listening, Elder Pittridge felt renewed in him that strong affection for the other man which had been almost forgotten. There was something in John Evered at once youthful in eagerness and zest, and mature in wisdom. Certainly there was no weakness in him anywhere. If now between him and Jenny a gulf had opened which John would not cross, yet to the world she would always hold her place as his wife, receiving his respect and deference if not his love. Elder Pittridge for this hour tonight remembered his own thoughts of her as though he saw them through John's eyes, and he felt a sick contempt for those treacherous hungers in him which he had not been strong enough to stifle. When John urged again that he should see as much of Jenny as he could, he promised to do so — and swore to himself that from seeing her no harm should come.

v

So after John went back into the wilderness, Elder Pittridge went sometimes to the house; and three or four times he escorted Jenny to a concert, or to some other function which she wished to attend. If they were criticized for this he never knew it, nor was there ever anything, any word or sign, between them to make him uneasy; and his fears slept. He enjoyed being with her, and since no harm came of their hours together, he felt at last secure. Winter relaxed its grip upon the land and spring began to come. The drifts settled, the first birds appeared, the ice went out of the river, and at last after a night of soft rain the ground was left almost bare of snow. The first warm days tinted the dull brown of last year's grass with green.

Spring had in Bangor one manifestation which was not beautiful. When the ice went out and the lumber fleet worked up the river, the sailors trooped ashore; and when the gangs came out of the woods they made straight for Bangor; and when the drives were down, the rivermen rushed to taste the delights of town. To welcome them, scores of dives along Washington and Hancock and Exchange and Harlow Streets waited with open doors. Taverns and grogshops, lodging houses and restaurants and forthright bawdy houses from March to November did a thriving business.

The establishments — sometimes secretly or openly financed by Bangor men — knew no scruples. Lena Tempest's place, with its pretty little harlots, enjoyed a certain distinction. Her doors were open only to those elect whom she chose to admit, and she herself kept the peace in her house, by force if need be. But elsewhere the customers were a brawling, truculent lot to whom a fight was a welcome part of any holiday; so every saloon and gaming hall and catch-penny joint had its staff of ruffians alert not so much to keep the peace as to protect property against physical damage. If a fight started indoors, whether it involved two men or a dozen, the combatants quickly found themselves in the street, sometimes with bumped heads, cut faces, or broken teeth as evidence of the ruthless methods of the bouncers.

But there was other and more secret violence. When a man came out of the woods with money in his pockets, it was good business to rid him of it as quickly as possible; and if the individual was stubbornly slow to lose himself in a helpless intoxication, there were ways to hurry the process, relieve him of everything he possessed and be rid of him. If sometimes violence went too far — why, the river ran with a scouring tide to the sea.

The Devil's Half Acre was part of Bangor, but only one part. There was another Bangor made up of families who had travelled widely, of people of cultivation and taste who lived quietly and decently. There was a group characterized by steadily increasing wealth; there was the Bangor of the lumbermen, and there was the Bangor of the seafarers, the builders of ships and their owners and their captains. But the backbone of the city was made up of small merchants and sober and respectable artisans; joiners, coopers, painters, masons, stonecutters, turners, smiths, cord-wainers, block-makers, coppersmiths, curriers, fishmongers, hostlers, shipwrights, housewrights, wheelers, tanners, toolmakers and the like; yeomen and farmers, men who lived diligently and frugally, bred children and protected them and planned what their lives should be.

To these sober folk spring was a season to be dreaded, since, in the weeks before the ice went out, the dives began to be reopened; and every stage brought from Augusta and Portland and even from Boston rough men and women coming to repopulate that district along the Stream. It was the shameful scenes to be encountered there which turned public opinion among decent folk more and more against the rum traffic; and this year Elder Pittridge, feeling within himself new powers and anxious to carry through to victory the long fight for a temperance law, began to go down to Exchange Street at night to see at first hand what went forward there, gathering ammunition which he used at the regular meetings of Friends of Temperance in the Hammond Street vestry.

As they felt their position increasingly endangered by the rising tide of public sentiment, the people of the Devil's Half Acre were in a mood to fight back. One night when Elder Pittridge passed McPhail's Tavern in an alley off Exchange Street, he was recognized and seized by three or four men and dragged indoors. He found himself the centre there of a drunken, angry crowd, damning him for his crusading efforts against them; and he faced them boldly, haranguing them for their crimes until someone on a happy inspiration filled a bucket with rum and, coming quietly behind him, emptied it over his head, drenching his clothes. The spectacle he presented suggested to their hilarious minds a further procedure; and despite his desperate struggles, they pinned him fast and poured rum down his throat until he was thoroughly drunk and presently became insensible.

In this condition he was deposited on the doorstep of Deacon Adams, and at dawn the Deacon found him there, snoring heavily. On a sheet of paper pinned to his coat the word 'Rummy' had been painted in large letters.

Deacon Adams took him indoors and kept him till he was himself again; and when Elder Pittridge told him what had happened, the Deacon accepted his report as true. But the perpetrators of the jest liked it too well to let it be forgotten, and the tale was spread abroad. It was, of course, distorted. Elder Pittridge, they insisted, had come down to McPhail's and drunk himself into a stupor.

His enemies and the enemies of his cause professed to believe this; and he himself, having told the truth to Deacon Adams, made no further protestation of his innocence. But when in May the County Temperance Society planned a meeting in the City Hall to discuss and reprehend the seasonal renewal of activity in the Devil's Half Acre, he, as a sort of martyr who had suffered for the right, was scheduled to be the principal speaker.

VI

The hall on the appointed night was crowded with people who had come from friendship, from enmity, or from a simple curiosity to hear what he would say; and Elder Pittridge, waiting his turn to speak, saw Jenny in the audience. He listened grimly while those who came before him said what had been said many times before, speaking generalities, deploring the disgrace which the existence of Devil's Half Acre imposed upon the city. The Mayor and the Chief of Police in their turn gave the usual assurances that disorders would be dealt with, but they suggested that decent citizens might be well advised to avoid the quarter, and they pointed this advice by referring to the atrocious treatment which Elder Pittridge had encountered.

These references evoked some amused smiles and some glances in his direction, so when at last he rose to speak, there was a burning rage in him. He was always a ready and a forceful talker; but today he was by his own anger inspired. Yet he began easily enough, controlling his voice, speaking with a sardonic moderation.

'I have attended many such meetings as this, in the years that are gone,' he said. 'Most of you here have attended those same meetings. For me tonight, as for all of you, it has been as though we heard over again all the things that have been said here in other years. Of course what was said in other years is still true. We still daily see our fellow beings — some of them once respectable — falling into the mud in our streets, and when down not able to rise. We hear every winter of men insensible with liquor freezing to death in the snow. We still see grogshops everywhere, making drunkards by thousands.

'We still deplore the vices of others — and ignore our own. We condemn intemperance, yet I see some here who themselves indulge.' His voice began to rise from its easy level. 'How can you assist in this work whilst you are in the habit of the common and daily use of ardent spirits? The youth with his first drink in his hand replies to your remonstrance: "Why do you upbraid or advise me? You drink. Why should not I?" You may tell him that you do not drink to excess, but will he believe it — or admit that he is not your equal in self-restraint?

'Drunkenness itself is praised by no one. The very sight of the drunkard is enough to disgust all who see him. But who made him a drunkard? From what class do drunkards come? Let no one presume to say: "I am safe. Am I a dog that I should become a drunkard?" No one goes to ruin all at once. No one plunges headlong into the pit. It is the little foxes that gnaw the vines, the little surrenders that corrupt us in the end. We venture near the edge, we skirt it, perilously near; till suddenly we find ourselves falling — beyond redemption!'

His eye met Jenny's, and he thought suddenly that she was a peril which in reckless folly he regularly courted. At the thought his words acquired a savage and ironic force. His eye while he spoke found her in the crowded hall, and his glance returned to her again and again, almost accusingly, till it was as though he spoke to her alone.

'All these things you have heard over and over and over!' he cried. 'And you have listened with nodding heads, and strong Amens, wishing your neighbor to believe that you accented these reproaches instead of wincing beneath them.' He flung his hand high. 'But the time has come when nods and Amens are not enough. It is time for passion, for wrath and passion, for striking down this thing.' His eye found Jenny again, and for a moment his voice changed, so that he seemed to be speaking to himself as he repeated:

'Yes, it is the little surrenders that destroy us. We say: "I will drink a little wine for the stomach's sake, but I will not take ardent spirits." Yet let us sip enough wine and our steps become uncertain and we stumble and are lost. It is the little foxes that gnaw the vines. No one deliberately says: "I will now destroy myself!" He says: "I am strong and sure of foot and wise. I can skirt the pit in safety." Till he falls.

'So here today we have heard said the same old things. Down in Devil's Half Acre, the gaming hells are waiting, and the rum-sellers are waiting, and the bawds are waiting; and young men come to our city, from the clean meadows of the sea, from the frozen beauty of our forests, from the river sparkling in the sun, to be robbed of money and of manhood and of life in the traps and pitfalls we allow to be set for them. And our Mayor and our police officers tell us to close our eyes, to turn our backs and hold our noses, while this stinking thing crawls in slime around our heels!

'They speak to us of patience and of calmness and of composure; but I tell you tonight: The time for patience is past! The time for halfway measures is past! While we assure ourselves that we are safe — if we will only turn our backs and pretend not to smell and hear what goes on behind us — young men are being debauched with our permission and consent. We are all alike guilty of their destruction! We are as guilty as though we pressed the cup into their reluctant hands!

'The time for patience and long waiting and for whispering disapproval is past! A hundred brave men could lay all that sink of iniquity in ashes in a night, and make our city clean! I see your heads are not nodding now. Perhaps you deplore my heat and violence. Well, I deplore your shaking, disapproving heads. It is time for violence! It is time for passion!'

He flung up his hands in a wide gesture, towering above them, flaming with his own earnestness. 'Arise!' he cried. 'Arise and be men! If this leprous scab of iniquity is allowed to survive, it will devour the whole city in the end. If Devil's Half Acre be a good thing, let us say so and stop this womanish mewing! If it be a bad thing, why, then with God's help let us wipe it out, so that the place where it was shall know it never more!'

He finished, his strong voice ringing in the silent hall, and stood a moment shaken with his own emotion. He saw Jenny, saw no one but her, for the long instant that he stood there; and then, suddenly tired, he turned and sat down.

VII

Before with decorous words the meeting was adjourned, Elder Pittridge slipped out by a side door and away, unwilling now to face anyone. He came into the cool sweetness of the night and at a rapid stride, avoiding any who might have followed him, moved off. He did not know which way he took. The soft air was grateful on his brow. He walked at random, headlong.

He walked till a carriage overtook him and passed him and then pulled up, and when he came abreast of it, Jenny spoke to him. 'Linc!'

He stopped and saw her, Pat Tierney on the box. He rubbed his hand across his eyes; and she said:

'Linc, I tried to find you after the meeting. Will is sick. He

wants you to come and see him. Can you come?' And when he
hesitated, she said: 'Get in.'

He obeyed her silently, his pulses thrumming. He sat beside
her, and Pat lifted the horses to a trot. He felt her close to him,
yet it was as though she were far away, on the horizon of a world
seen redly through hot flames; but after a little she said quietly:
'You spoke splendidly tonight, Linc.' At her word, he filled his
lungs deeply, as though he had held his breath till now. 'You were
fine,' she told him.

He did not speak, and she said no more till the carriage stopped
at her door. Then she bade the Irishman: 'Wait, Pat, to take
Mr. Pittridge home. He'll only be a minute here.'

'I will that, ma'am,' Pat assured her. 'It's late, to be sure.'

But Elder Pittridge did not hear the disapproval in Pat's tones.
He went in with her. In the hall when the door was closed they
were alone. She turned to speak to him in her soft voice. 'You
moved me tonight, Linc,' she said, and came near him, 'You
stirred me deeply. I will always remember a word you said. You
said: "It is time for passion." Do you remember?'

She stood before him and her eyes were coals. He took a blind,
groping step; and so, suddenly, she was in his arms, clinging, pressing close and closer as though she could not come close enough
to him, her lips devouring his.

Then from the upper hall Mrs. McGaw, unseen, called down:
'Is that you, Mrs. Evered?'

Instantly, though their eyes still grappled, she was free, stepping
back from him.

'Yes,' she said, in her usual calm, unshaken tones; and he wondered at her composure after that embrace which had left him
shaken and helpless. 'And I've brought Uncle Linc to see Will.
We're coming right up.'

She took one step, expecting him to follow; and then, smiling because for this moment he could not move, she returned to catch
his hand and lead him toward the stairs.

VIII

Will was restless and miserable, and Mrs. McGaw said Doctor
Mason had been here and thought the youngster was developing
measles. 'He left some Indian Vegetable Pills for him,' she said,
'and some manna.' Jenny asked what this was, and she explained:
'Doctor says it's like spruce gum, comes off an ash tree in Europe
somewhere. He says it's a de —' She hesitated. 'Well, it was de-

something or other, but he says it will keep Will's throat from getting too sore. And the pills will keep his fever down.'

Elder Pittridge stayed only a few minutes, since Pat was waiting with the carriage to take him back to town. In the carriage, staring blindly at Pat's broad shoulders, he licked his lips that were still dry and bruised from the hot pressure of hers upon them; and convulsions shook him, deep shudders that seemed to loose his tendons from the bones, that left his joints weak and his flesh fibreless, as though at a touch his whole body might fall apart into its component and useless parts. Yet this body of his over which he had no longer any firm control, so that when he alighted at his own door he stumbled and almost fell, was nevertheless a vessel which contained boiling forces so violent it seemed impossible any man could endure them and survive. He slept not at all that night, moved haggardly the next day and the next; but Will had made him promise to come soon again and at last reluctantly he did so, walking out to the house with many hesitations, vowing he must not see Jenny, praying for strength to stay away from her, yet still trudging helplessly toward where she waited.

But the days that followed lulled him into a false security. Jenny met him easily and in a completely impersonal fashion which denied all recollection of that moment he could never forget. The two younger boys caught the measles almost at once, and Jenny nursed the three with a tireless tenderness, so Elder Pittridge saw her only with them. Dan fell ill last of all, when the others were nearly recovered, and he was sicker than the others had been; but by mid-June he too was convalescing.

When he began to be better every day, Jenny sent Mrs. McGaw — who had exhausted herself in caring for the children — to visit her daughter in Brewer and rest awhile, and Ruth assumed the household cares while Jenny spent every hour with Dan. Elder Pittridge — his misgivings reawakening as the household returned to something like a normal routine — went to see them not so often now; but one morning he met Jenny as she emerged from a consultation with Miss Robinson, the tailoress, and he asked how Dan was.

'He's missed you,' she said. 'Why not come out and cheer him up this afternoon?'

'Is he still in bed?'

'Yes.' She added: 'You know Meg insisted on having the other three down to Searsport for a visit, as soon as they could stand the trip; so I've only Dan to take care of now, but I'm keeping him quiet for a few days longer. Won't you come this afternoon, early?'

He hesitated, torn and distracted. 'I'm not sure I can,' he said in a low tone, evasively, fighting to control his voice.

She held his eyes. 'I've heard from John,' she told him quietly. 'He'll be home tomorrow; but Dan and I would like to see you today. Do come?'

There was a strong insistence in her tone, but he scarce heard her. John would come home tomorrow! That fact offered at once a promise of security against this thing which threatened to engulf him and an end to those dreams which at once attracted and repelled him. Yet since Dan was still at the house, he could safely go today. He submitted. 'I will, then,' he agreed.

She turned away, almost hurriedly, as though fearing he would change his mind; and he watched her, thinking he had never noticed how gracefully she walked, suddenly conscious as he looked after her now of all the co-ordinated parts of her, the perfect articulation of her joints, the controlled tensions and relaxings of her muscles. His palms were moist, his throat throbbing. When she disappeared, he roused like a man half asleep, moving on about his own concerns.

But after dinner he turned out Main Street to go to her. He had reached the corner of Adams Street when he saw her carriage approaching with Pat on the box; and in the seats behind were not only Ruth and her children but also Dan, wrapped snug in blankets, tucked and warm. Elder Pittridge hailed them, and when Pat pulled up he said:

'Well, Dan, you're well again!'

'Yes,' Dan told him gleefully. 'And now I'm going down to Searsport to visit Aunt Meg. We're all going, Pat and everybody except mother. She's going to stay at home and rest and bring father down tomorrow.'

Linc's fists clenched at his sides. 'Why, fine!' he assented. 'Give my love to Aunt Meg.'

He stepped back as the carriage moved on; and he stood a moment, watching it out of sight, thinking now with perfect clarity and certainty. Jenny was alone in the big house; alone, expecting him, awaiting him. And—knowing he was coming—she had sent Dan away; had sent everyone away.

Yet—perhaps this decision to send Dan to Searsport was a sudden one. Perhaps if he went to her she would say: 'I'm sorry. Dan was so much better that I sent him down to Meg's. Too bad you walked so far for nothing.' But if that were the case, she would have bidden Pat tell him not to come; and Pat had given him no such message.

So she was waiting for him!

He knew in his heart that this was the moment of decision, to go back or to go on. To go on to what irrevocable end? He refused to look so far as in sudden madness he continued more swiftly now upon his way. He thought remotely of the swine possessed of devils racing toward the precipice, plunging headlong to their own destruction. He was like them, as lost and mad as they, but the thought did not slow his pace. If there were devils in him, he could fight them now no more.

When he came to the door, she opened it. She was slender and small, like a child, in a white dress buttoned down the front, fitting snugly from throat to slim waist; and her hair was soft above her brow. She smiled and said: 'Come in, Linc,' and when the door was closed she said: 'Dan's waiting for you.' She turned at once away.

Without speaking, accepting her guidance, letting her determine the event, he followed her up the stairs. She did not hurry. There was again in her walk that catlike, smooth perfection of movement which he had seen for the first time a few hours before. At the head of the stair she said softly:

'He's here in my room.'

She led the way, opened the door and stood aside to let him pass and then closed the door and leaned her shoulders against it, her hands behind her back. His eyes swept the empty room, and then he turned to face her; and she smiled, and those faint inverted crescents on her cheekbones made her seem like a child about to cry. She whispered teasingly:

'You don't ask where Dan is?'

'I saw him on his way to Meg's.' His voice was hoarse so that he scarce recognized it. 'I knew he wouldn't be here!'

Her cheek burned bright as flame, and he thought it would be hot to touch. 'You knew!' she whispered. 'You knew, as I did!'

Then with a motion swift as a snake's striking head, her hand flew to the topmost button at her throat to loose it. An instant later she struck him in the face with both small fists as he caught her in his arms.

4

ELDER PITTRIDGE, walking back to town late that afternoon, stumbled and wavered like one suddenly struck blind; and he moved with hanging head, unwilling to meet any eye, feeling that the first person he met must see him as he was, a betrayer of his friend, a befouler of the home in which so long he had been a welcome visitor. Jenny in this hour he hated and abhorred, and he vowed never to see her again, swore weakly to himself that he would leave Bangor, go far away, put behind him forever this woman who embodied in her person all the evil iniquities which led men to their dark destruction. In these hours now irrevocably past, which never could be recalled, he had destroyed all that he had wished to make out of his life, all those intangible ideals of decency and self-respect and loyalty and service to which he had clung. He was debased and unclean, would never be clean again; and in a passion of hopeless regret he accepted this fact. He despised Jenny as much as he despised himself. They had been companions in the foulest act of which man and woman were capable, and he not only admitted this, he wished to shout it aloud in abject humiliation; he wished to mortify and to mutilate the flesh which had betrayed him. He thought of self-destruction, thought of it almost hungrily. Such men as he were not fit to live, and the world would be well rid of him, a better place without him. From his earlier debaucheries Elder Pittridge had gone to the other extreme, to a worship of what seemed to him good which was as passionate and frenzied as his previous conduct had been debased and mean. It was the man he had made out of himself, that almost holy man, who judged him now, and not with the stern remoteness of a serene mind but with the merciless cruelty of the Inquisition which damned without recourse.

He was lost, lost, lost! It was himself he had contaminated and befouled. To think of Jenny now was to provoke in himself waves of actual nausea. But before he came to his own door his thoughts took a new turn and he began to blame John. If John had lived in love and faith and trust with the wife to whom God had joined him, then he himself would never have been tempted to come between those two. It was John who by turning against his wife had thrust Jenny and himself together; and he damned John in his heart, cursing the man with mumbling lips, seizing on this hatred of John as on an anodyne which could help him forget his own crime.

As for Jenny, he vowed he would never see her again!

II

But he forgot that vow. John returned, and urged Elder Pittridge to be one with them as in the past, and the Elder in his thoughts damned John's eternal soul to hell for leading him thus into temptation. Yet he was already lost, so he had no more to lose; and in an ironic wrath he surrendered to John's cordial friendliness.

But John after a few weeks at home was often absent, so that at night after the city was asleep, Elder Pittridge could go to Jenny, meeting her in the garden below the house, or with her hand to guide him through the darkened halls slipping secretly up to her room. Again and again he swore to come to her no more, and told her so; and he might have broken free, but she said: 'If you won't come to me, Linc, I shall come to you.' And when he argued and pleaded and implored, she said firmly: 'I care for none of that, my dear; and I warn you, I am not to be treated lightly — nor in any other way except as I desire.' When he said he must go away to Augusta or to Portland, she told him simply: 'If you do, I shall follow you.' There was in her none of the regrets which tortured him. Instead of withdrawing in shame and horror from their contacts, she was forever demanding; and sometimes when he cried out in self-condemnation, she watched him with a quizzical smile, her head on one side; and when he was silent she might say: 'You're really good, aren't you, Linc? I like making you do things you think are wicked. It torments you so!'

At such moments she was frightening, but she was not always so composed, and he was sometimes dismayed by the storms which shook her, as though she were being riven by forces beyond control. Once, lying appeased at last in his arms, she began to weep uncontrollably, sobbing aloud, crying: 'Oh, Linc, I'm not like this really! What makes me so? What makes me so?' And she protested in a tragic despair: 'I'm a good woman, Linc! You know I am! Oh, why, dear God, why?'

He, as torn as she, could not comfort her. He was slowly broken on the rack, pulled one way by forces he could not combat, pulled the other by all the convictions on which for years his life had been based; till he lost all will of his own.

She worked upon him in other ways, as though she sensed the fact that if he could be led to hate John altogether, he would be completely hers. Twice during the summer, when Cap'n Pawl was away on the Lucy brig, Meg came home to visit her father; and on these occasions she and Elder Pittridge and John and Jenny were much together as of old. After the second time Jenny asked challengingly:

'Linc, did you watch John and Meg today? Did you see the way she looks at him, and he at her?'

'They're as they've always been.'

'Exactly,' she retorted. 'Under my eyes, for years!'

'But Jenny,' he protested, 'Meg's married now.'

'Am I not married, darling? And have I been the less generous to you on that acount?'

He said in weak loyalty: 'You're not fair to John!'

'To John?' She smiled. 'John's no anchorite, Linc. I could tell you some things . . . ' She hesitated faintly, added then: 'You wouldn't believe me, but you'll know better some day.' There was suddenly a quiet ferocity in her still tones. 'Everyone will realize what John really is, before I'm through. He's not so fine as he pretends, be sure of that. I know.'

There was more than a casual threat in her tone. Elder Pittridge questioned her, uneasily, wondering what she meant to do; but she would tell him nothing, so he had no more explicit warning of what was to come than was contained in her words and tone.

III

A new paper was started in Bangor that summer by a man named Andrew Lebbeus. Lebbeus had formerly lived in Old Town, and then in Bangor. He was the younger son of an English county family who had left his own country in some disgrace and who astonished and shocked the good people of Old Town while he lived there by his habit, when — as was usually the case — he was in his cups, of delivering lengthy orations on the high moral values of free love. He spent most of his time in the taverns, and lumbermen just out of the woods or off the river hilariously encouraged him to talk. He was a cultivated man, with a vocabulary which expanded with every drink he took. One of his gleeful audience remarked one night in an awed delight:

'By God, I've been doing it ever since I was old enough to wear britches, but I never heard it called so many fancy names!'

He subsisted on moneys sent him by his family; and at intervals, flushed with sudden wealth, he went to Boston for a month or two. From one of these excursions he returned to Bangor with a floridly decorative young woman whom he introduced as Miss Thorne. Their relationship was an open scandal, an affront to the town; but Lebbeus laughed at protests till he and she were haled into court on a charge of living together without benefit of clergy. Judge Saladine was at that time on the bench and he took a short way to settle the case. He asked:

'Mr. Lebbeus, do you propose to show the court that you are married to this woman?'

Lebbeus replied in a sardonic tone: 'We are married, Your Honor, in the eyes of God and in the light of our own consciousness!'

'Do you love this woman well enough to take her for your wife?'
'I do.'

The Judge asked: 'Madam, do you love this man enough to take him for your husband?'

The young woman said amiably: 'Why, I just certainly do, Judge.'

Judge Saladine nodded. 'Good! Then by the authority vested in me by the laws of Maine, I do pronounce you man and wife! Go and sin no more!'

The result of this judgment of Solomon was not happy for Mr. Lebbeus. His wife clung to him like a harpy for years, making his life a long torment; and he blamed Judge Saladine for his distresses. But during the boom period she left Bangor with a successful speculator and never returned; and Lebbeus, free from her demands, presently came into a small inheritance and found himself possessed of comfortable means. In this summer of 1845 he started a paper in Bangor called the *Star,* whose guiding editorial principle was a violent opposition to the Bingham interests. Since John was Colonel Black's right-hand man, he was one of the *Star's* occasional targets. Late in October there appeared in that scurrilous sheet the following:

YOUNG WOMAN INSULTED

We are requested to publish the affidavit herewith in the interest of morality and decency, and as an imperative act of justice, that the humblest female may be secure from insult on the street or elsewhere. The character of the person signing the affidavit is fully vouched for by the lady in whose house the aggrieved is employed:

AFFIDAVIT

BANGOR, *October* 17, 1845

I, Mattie Hanson, residing on Harlow Street in the city of

Bangor, and working as a servant by the day in the house of Ira Hodder, make the following statement on oath:

That until last July I was employed one day a week to do washing in the family of John Evered; and that I quit that employment because Mr. Evered used to come to where I was washing clothes and talk to me and pinch me.

That a week ago last Saturday evening on my way home from Mr. Hodder's to Harlow Street Mr. Evered walked close up to me, and talked to me, asking if I was married and if I had any children and said he would not want anyone only if they were willing; and Mr. Evered has spoken in the same way at least six times since I went to work in his house and has asked me to go riding with him and I have felt insulted every time he has spoken to me.

Mattie Hanson

State of Maine, Penobscot, SS. Oct. 17, 1845. Personally appeared the above-named Mattie Hanson and made oath to the truth of the foregoing statement, made and signed by her. Before me,

Levi S. Spree,
Justice of the Peace.

IV

Elder Pittridge was not a subscriber to the *Star*; but within half an hour of the paper's publication, Sam Smith came to find him and to show him the offending passage.

'Here, take a look at that!' he said in a strong indignation. 'John's in Boston, won't be back till next week; but somebody's got to do something about this quick — and you're John's best friend in town.'

So Elder Pittridge read the damning paragraphs. He remembered seeing Mattie Hanson at the house, busy over her tubs in the shed or hanging out the clothes; remembered her as a plump young negress with white teeth in the shining black expanse of her face. Though he hated John, this affidavit was obviously absurd; and reading it he remembered those half threats Jenny had made against her husband. He took time to think before he spoke.

'I'll go see the rascal who printed that,' he said then. 'Do you know him?'

'Lebbeus? Yes, certain. He has a one-room office with a printing press in the cellar, down on Water Street.' He added: 'Of course this is a hit at the Bingham crowd. Lebbeus has always hated them since Judge Saladine married him to that woman.'

Elder Pittridge looked at the affidavit again. 'Who's Ira Hodder?'

'He's a no-account loafer,' Sam told him. 'Used to be a good housewright till the speculation. Then he made some big profits, dressed Mrs. Hodder up in fine clothes, bought a carriage, built the house on Harlow Street — and lost all his money. Now he owes everyone in town.' He laughed. 'If this girl works for him, she must work for nothing.'

'She's colored,' Elder Pittridge said. 'I've seen her out at the house.'

'Colored!' Sam stared at him. 'Well, I'll be damned!' Then he said: 'Come along. I'll go with you to talk to Lebbeus.'

They found Lebbeus in his office. The publisher of the *Star* was a lean, gangling individual with a watery eye, sallow and unhealthy skin, and yellow buck teeth that were conspicuous when he grinned. Elder Pittridge, not yet sure of his course, stood looking down at the man, who did not rise; and he asked uncertainly:

'Why did you print this scurrilous affidavit?'

Lebbeus grinned. 'In the interests of public decency, Elder Pittridge. You and I are crusaders in the same cause, you see.'

'How did it come into your hands?'

'Levi Spree brought it to the office. He and Mr. Hodder.' The publisher largely explained: 'It appears that this girl came home in tears after fighting off your friend Evered's carnal advances; and Mrs. Hodder comforted her, got her story, and thought something should be done to put a stop to such goings on. That was a conclusion, if I may say so, with which I thoroughly agree.'

Elder Pittridge looked uneasily at Sam Smith; and he began to say: 'You know it's a ridiculous——' But before he could finish, the door behind him opened. He turned and saw Jenny there, and beside her Pat Tierney; and Pat had his slender whip in his hand.

Jenny looked at Elder Pittridge without speaking, passed him, faced Lebbeus. 'Are you the publisher of the *Star*?' she asked in low tones.

Lebbeus, still without rising, said mockingly: 'I have that honor, Mrs. Evered!'

Jenny without a word took the whip from Pat. Lebbeus at her movement dodged back, overturning his chair; but the whip cracked across his shoulders, once and then again. The whip was light, the hurt not great; but Lebbeus leaped toward the door that led to the cellar. Sam Smith sprang before him to block his way. Sam was enjoying this. 'Give it to him, ma'am!' he cried. Lebbeus, the whip still snapping across his back, dodged to the street door and out; and Jenny followed to give him a last stroke before he escaped beyond her reach. Lebbeus, since she could not pursue him, was satisfied to keep his distance; and he bowed and said profoundly:

'Thank you, Mrs. Evered, for the attention you have thus attracted to my humble paper. Your indignation does credit to your loyalty, if not to your wit. Yet I can see that the truth struck home.' He chuckled. 'Made the galled jade wince!'

A curious crowd had been quick to collect. Jenny spoke evenly. 'I have nothing to say to you.' She turned to the carriage, and Pat helped her in.

Elder Pittridge and Sam had followed them out of the little office, stood now as they drove away. Lebbeus came toward them, shrugging his shoulders to ease the smart of the whip.

'That wench cuts hard,' he said dryly. 'As for you, Elder, have you finished what you were saying?'

Elder Pittridge hesitated, but others were watching, and something was expected of him. 'Not quite,' he said, and struck an awkward yet a powerful blow, so that the other man staggered backward and went down. Sam cheered, and the crowd pressed closer, hooting an appreciation, eager to see more; but Lebbeus did not rise. Elder Pittridge said hoarsely: 'I advise you to put Bangor forever behind you before Mr. Evered returns.'

And, thinking he had done all anyone could expect of him, he brushed through the crowd and walked away.

v

By the time John Evered came home from Boston, everyone in Bangor had read that affidavit in the *Star*; and John and Jenny, Elder Pittridge and Judge Saladine met at the Judge's house to discuss what should be done.

'I'm sorry you and Jenny took it so seriously,' John told Elder Pittridge. 'It might have been the sooner forgotten.'

'I didn't stop to think, John,' Jenny confessed. Her tones were low-pitched as always. 'I was so angry at any attack on you.'

Elder Pittridge looked at her in a sort of wonder, astonished as he always was at her capacity for such dissimulation; and Judge Saladine said quietly: 'We can't silence this thing by blows. The wise procedure is to sue for libel, bring Lebbeus into court, and the Hodders, and this negress — if we can find her. She left for Boston before the libel was published, but I've set afoot some inquiries there. I hope to bring her back. I'd like to cross-examine that young woman, find out who prompted her to this.'

Jenny spoke quickly. 'We don't need her to prove this is a lie. John was at home with me that evening.'

John said in surprise: 'Wait a minute, Jenny. I came down town, remember? Right after supper?'

'But you were at home till after eight,' Jenny insisted.

John seemed about to speak, hesitated, looked at Judge Saladine. 'She doesn't say just what time this is supposed to have happened, does she?'

'She says it was on her way home from the Hodder house. That would be after she had done the supper dishes. We can fix the time through them.' John looked again at Jenny, and Judge Saladine said strongly: 'In any case, I advise bringing suit, bringing the whole thing into court. Only in that way can we end the whispering.'

In the end, that was their decision. John had expected to go up-river again this winter; but his plans were of necessity changed. He stayed at home to wait for the trial; and Elder Pittridge was relieved to find that Jenny was now as ready as he to move discreetly.

'I'm worried about what may happen, Linc,' she confessed, one afternoon when he had come to supper and they were waiting for John to arrive. 'You know — I've told you — John's not blameless. Since we began to live separate lives, I know many disgraceful things he has done, not only here but in Boston and elsewhere, and I'm afraid Mr. Lebbeus may find them out.' She added ruefully: 'Mr. Spree came to see me, last week.' Levi Spree, who had taken the colored girl's oath to that affidavit, would be counsel for Lebbeus in the approaching trial. 'He asked me so many questions. It's not easy for me to lie, Linc. You saw how willing John was to let me lie about the time he left the house that night. I hope I don't have to go on the witness stand; but if I'm called, I must, and I must lie; for John did go down town early that night, you know.' And she added, almost vengefully: 'Sometimes I think I'd like to tell the truth, let people know John as I know him.'

'You half-believe this, don't you?'

'She said ruefully: 'I don't know. But — when Mattie left me, she said John was the reason. That's what hurt me worst, Linc; that right here under our roof he should turn to a colored girl!'

He said helplessly: 'She must be lying!'

'I'm not sure,' she admitted. 'I saw John with her once, from the storeroom window. She was hanging out the wash and he was talking to her, standing near her. I couldn't hear what they said, but I could see that he was laughing and she was mad!' He colored in a red anger at John who had hurt her so; but then he saw a shrewdness in her eyes, and his own expression must have changed, for she said evenly: 'I see you don't believe me.'

Before he could answer, John appeared, so they said no more; yet Jenny's assertion left Elder Pittridge bewildered and confused. He told himself it was impossible she could have prompted the colored girl to this accusation; and yet his doubts of her persisted. She had certainly no love left for John; and it would have been so easy to bribe the girl to make this affidavit and then to disappear.

But he remembered the Jenny the world knew, active in every worthy cause, sacrificing money and time and energy to help the unfortunate, beloved by so many of the poorer folk of the city whom she had befriended, and respected and esteemed by every good man and woman who knew her. To such a woman, the thing he imagined must have been impossible. He fought his suspicions down, and as the alternative he began to accept the idea of John's guilt. He had cause enough to hate John as we hate those we have wronged; and Jenny, even while she pretended to defend her husband, fed this hatred, till Elder Pittridge was ready to believe the other man guilty of any shame.

He learned in these weeks to dissemble, too; for during the months before the trial — it was set for the second week of February — he saw John often. When on the first of January Ike Billings, to win a wager, working in Aaron Wingate's blacksmith shop, forged two hundred and ten horseshoes from the bar in ten and a half hours with one sledge man to help, John and Elder Pittridge were among those who watched and cheered the feat. Meg often came up from Searsport — Captain Pawl was at sea — to join them in loyal friendliness; and once they all drove out to Pushaw Lake in a jingling sleigh for supper at John Hasey's Tavern there, coming home through the still, cold, moonlit night while their runners squeaked on the snow. Mr. Lebbeus must have heard of that excursion, for he wrote in the *Star*:

> Sleighing parties are now the rage. The delightful weather, the brilliant moon, the charming company of a carefree social party in an ample hotel, and a good frolic — perfectly harmless of course — are all thought to be excellent for brushing from the mind and heart the cobwebs of morbid care which dread of an imminent appearance in court may have spun there.

They attended together the temperance meeting where Mr. Kellogg of Ohio lectured on the evils of drink, they heard Professor Goodwin's Lyceum lecture on Goethe's *Faust*, they were seen publicly at every opportunity. It was Jenny who insisted on this, pointing out that she and they could thus best demonstrate to the world their trust in John. Elder Pittridge lent himself to this play-acting, but his hatred of the other man was whetted by the necessity for such dissimulation.

Also, he saw that Jenny was suffering under the long strain, thinner, her color fading; and he blamed John — of whose guilt he had by this time no doubt at all — for imposing this torment on her. Long before the day set for the trial arrived he had persuaded himself, or Jenny had persuaded him, that John deserved the contempt of every honest man.

VI

When the trial opened, the courtroom was crowded to the doors, with people standing everywhere. Neither Jenny nor Meg was present, but Elder Pittridge sat among the spectators; and he watched John at the table beside Judge Saladine with a white hostility. Judge Saladine with his first witnesses made formal proof of publication. He called Charles Page, the printer, to testify that Mr. Lebbeus had handed him the copy for the offending paragraphs and that he had set it up and printed it. He called Mr. Lebbeus himself to admit that he had written the introductory lines and had given the copy to Mr. Page, and to describe the circumstances under which the affidavit came into his hands. It was brought to him, Mr. Lebbeus said, by Levi Spree and Ira Hodder.

Judge Saladine asked no further questions; but Mr. Spree inquired: 'Now, Mr. Lebbeus, why did you print this affidavit?'

'In the interests of public decency,' Lebbeus amiably assured the court. 'To try to protect respectable young women — even though colored — from insult on our streets.'

'And with no malice?'

'None whatever.'

'You have no feeling against Mr. Evered personally?'

'Not at all.'

Judge Saladine rose for another inquiry. 'On this question of malice, Mr. Lebbeus, have you any feeling against me?'

'None whatever.'

'I ask you to recall the circumstances of your marriage.'

That incident was so well remembered that a murmur of mirth went through the courtroom; and Lebbeus colored angrily. Mr. Spree rose to object that the Judge sought to impeach his own witness, but Judge Saladine protested: 'Not at all. I seek only to clarify the testimony he gave under cross-examination.' He asked:

'Now, Mr. Lebbeus, did you resent my marrying you in the way I did?'

'I thought you presumptuous.'

'Do you know that Mr. Evered and I are associated in serving the Bingham interests?'

'Yes.'

'Do you know, then, that to that degree anything which hurts him hurts me?'

'Why should it?'

Judge Saladine smiled and excused him. He called Ira Hodder to describe the circumstances under which the affidavit was made. Hodder testified that Mrs. Hodder brought Mattie to tell him her story; and he said he and she agreed that something should be done. 'So I took her to Mr. Spree,' he explained.

'On the Saturday night in question,' Judge Saladine asked kindly, 'what time did you finish supper?'

'Why, the usual time, I guess.'

'What is the usual time?'

'Maybe half-past six or some earlier.'

'Did Mattie wash the dishes afterward?'

'I guess so. She's supposed to.'

'What time did she leave your house for her home?'

'I don't know. I didn't say good-bye to her! I'm no nigger lover!'

At this reference to those taunts which had been directed at John after the affair of Atticus, a smiling stir ran around the crowded courtroom; but Judge Saladine said, unmoved: 'Let's go at this patiently, Mr. Hodder. We ought to be able to fix at least some broad limits.' He pursued the point with a gentle, tireless persistence till in the end Mr. Hodder was persuaded to say positively that Mattie must have left the house before eight o'clock.

When the Judge finished, Levi Spree asked only one question. 'And you acted, Mr. Hodder, purely as a public-spirited citizen and out of kindness toward this humble representative of an enslaved and downtrodden race?'

'That's right.'

Judge Saladine rose again. 'Did your interest in Mattie lead you to follow her fortunes after she left Bangor?'

'How's that?'

'Do you know why she left Bangor?'

'She was scared. Some of her colored friends said Mr. Evered would have her put in jail.'

'Do you know where she went?'

'She quit her job and told Mrs. Hodder ——'

'Excuse me. You're not allowed to say what she told Mrs. Hodder. Mrs. Hodder herself can tell us that when she takes the stand. Thank you, that is all.'

Mrs. Hodder was in the courtroom. As her husband resumed his seat, she bristled expectantly; but Judge Saladine ignored her. 'To complete our proof of publication,' he said, 'I would like to put my learned brother, Mr. Spree, on the stand — but of course not without his consent.'

Mr. Spree rose. 'Defendant admits publication, Your Honor,' he announced.

Judge Saladine bowed. 'In that case,' he said, 'if the publication of the libel is admitted, I await the defense my brother proposes to offer.'

'We propose to prove that the facts are as stated in the affidavit,' Mr. Spree assured him. 'If the truth is no defense, then a technical libel is admitted; but the question of damage depends on malice, and also on the reputation, before and since the libel, of plaintiff; and on this question of damage we wish to offer testimony.

'First, to prove the facts, I desire to put in evidence the original deposition of Mattie Hanson. Is there any objection?'

Judge Saladine said: 'If the Court please, we have tried without success to find Miss Hanson. I assume my learned brother in his very proper zeal for his client has done the same. Her deposition is of course valueless as evidence, since she was not subjected to cross-examination. We therefore object to its admission as evidence of what happened; but we are willing to accept this document as evidence that Mattie Hanson made and swore to the statements there recorded.'

'That will serve,' Mr. Spree assented. He spoke to Judge Saladine. 'As one of our witnesses,' he said, 'I shall wish to call Mrs. Evered. She is not in court today. Will it be necessary for us to summon her?'

'Not at all,' Judge Saladine assured him. 'She will be here at any hour you name.'

'This afternoon, then?' Mr. Spree requested, and he said: 'Now we will begin with Mrs. Hodder.'

Mrs. Hodder rose with a brisk energy. She was a large, aggressive woman with a jutting chin, and she marched forward like a General surveying the field of battle and took her place upon the witness stand. But Elder Pittridge did not wait to hear her testimony. The fact that Jenny must face the ordeal of testifying here filled him with an angry consternation. He slipped out to go to her, to warn her before the fact.

He found Jenny and Meg together at Judge Saladine's home. Meg was pale and troubled, but Jenny seemed perfectly composed. 'Tell us what's happening,' she bade him.

'You're going to have to be a witness, Jenny,' he said unhappily. 'Mr. Spree wants you in court after dinner, and Judge Saladine promised you'd be there.'

'Of course,' she assented. 'I'll go. I hate it, but I want to help John.'

Meg protested: 'Couldn't father prevent that, Linc?'

'He would have done so if he could,' Jenny reminded her. 'Don't worry, Meg. I'll be all right.'

'It's so hard for you, though,' Meg insisted. 'And you haven't been well lately, Jenny. You're short of breath, and thin and peaked-looking. I'm worried about you.'

'Nonsense!' Jenny told her, quietly and yet with a surprisingly aggressive defiance in her tone. 'Don't be absurd, Meg! There's nothing the matter with me. I'm fine.'

'You don't look fine!' Meg insisted. 'Oh, I know it isn't tactful to say so, but you look drawn and miserable. Of course you've reason enough, with this awful business hanging over you all winter.' She leaned to whisper, half-laughingly, in Jenny's ear; and Jenny said with some asperity:

'Don't be ridiculous!' She added in a teasing tone: 'And as for that, Meg — is Cap'n Pawl well? Has he used you properly? I think he has, for you're a little pale yourself!'

Meg's cheeks flamed; and Elder Pittridge, suddenly uncomfortable at this interchange which he must be presumed not to understand, said: 'I'll go back, I think. Mr. Spree warned me this morning that he means to call me, too.'

'You?' Meg exclaimed in surprise. 'What can you tell him?'

'He said it was on the question of damage to John's reputation.'

Meg laughed. 'Oh, that! Certainly nothing can really hurt John.'

When Elder Pittridge left them, he thought in a deep rage at John that what Meg had said about Jenny's pallor was at least to some degree true. The long waiting for the trial had been for her an exhausting ordeal — and for that, John was to blame. The virulence of Elder Pittridge's feeling toward the other man was by Jenny's suffering increased and intensified. His passion for her, as though the very frailty which she wore more and more inflamed him, in these last weeks when he dared not go to her had gnawed at him like rats; and a bitter virulence of anger burned in the man in this hour.

VII

Before court opened that afternoon Elder Pittridge met Judge Saladine in the corridors, and the Judge said: 'Mr. Spree means to call you, Linc.'

'I know,' Elder Pittridge assented. He added: 'I left court this morning, went to tell Jenny he wanted her, took a long walk afterward. What happened?'

'Very little.' Judge Saladine smiled. 'Mrs. Hodder helped us. I managed — with very little difficulty — to get her angry; and she became increasingly dogmatic. She says positively that the colored girl left her house that night at half-past seven. She remembers because she gave Mattie her pay. Jenny — and Pat Tierney and Mrs. McGaw — will all testify that John was at home till long after that.' He added: 'Mrs. Hodder also admitted that she dislikes John because he once prosecuted her brother for stealing Bingham lumber.' And he explained: 'After her testimony Mr. Spree put on a collection of rag-tag and bobtail, a dozen or fifteen men to swear that John's reputation was bad. I was able to show that most of them had grudges against him. I think we're doing very well.' He saw the other's nervous tremors and urged: 'Don't take it so hard, Linc. Just keep calm and answer Mr. Spree's questions. I'll take care of you.'

Nevertheless, when court resumed, Linc was wet with nervous perspiration, his fists clenched tight upon his knees. Jenny, coming in after he did, passed where he sat on her way to the witness stand, and for a moment he was blinded, his eyes swimming. When he could see again, she stood facing them all, calm and outwardly serene; and her voice, answering Mr. Spree's questions, was perfectly composed.

When preliminaries were done, Mr. Spree said raspingly: 'Now Mrs. Evered, I may tell you, since you were not in court this morning, that fourteen witnesses have testified that your husband's moral reputation, his reputation for chastity, is bad. What do you say to that?'

'I say it is ridiculous.'

'You mean,' he suggested in apparent uncertainty, 'that his reputation is ridiculous?'

Jenny said serenely: 'I mean that the statement that Mr. Evered is anything but a fine and upright man is ridiculous.' She was so small and so brave, standing steadily there, that Elder Pittridge's heart swelled with tenderness and pity and love; and he looked toward John and his teeth set in hard fury at that man because he subjected her to this.

'I see. What is your own estimate of your husband's moral character?'

'He is in every way the finest man I know.' Her voice rang clear and proudly through the packed courtroom.

'Very proper, to be sure. But on what do you base that opinion?' Jenny smiled faintly. 'On our life together for ten years.'

'Ah, yes. Let us inquire into that. What are your relations?'

'Those of a loving and devoted husband and wife.'

'Then of course you occupy the same room?'

Jenny hesitated only for an instant. 'Not at present, no,' she admitted, in a faint confusion.

Mr. Spree seemed surprised. 'You and your devoted husband occupy separate rooms?'

'Yes.'

'How long has that been the arrangement?'

'For a few months past.'

'What is the reason for that arrangement?'

Jenny said quietly: 'I was troubled with sleeplessness. I sleep better if there is nothing to disturb me, no one in the same room.'

'Did you and Mr. Evered have some discussion before arriving at this arrangement?'

'Yes, naturally. I reluctantly suggested it, and he, since he is always thoughtful of me, at once assented. I slept better afterward, so the arrangement continued.'

'There was no other cause — no feeling on your part prejudicial to your husband's character?'

'Certainly not.'

'Did you suggest this arrangement after or before you suspected undue familiarity between your husband and Mattie Hanson?'

Jenny said icily: 'I never had cause to suspect anything of the sort.'

'I did not inquire as to whether you had cause. Wives are often suspicious without cause. I spoke only of your suspicions.'

'I had none. I trust Mr. Evered completely.'

Mr. Spree looked toward where John sat and bowed profoundly. 'My congratulations, Mr. Evered.' He turned to Jenny again, his voice grating like a file. 'But though you trust your husband, and love him, you do sleep apart?'

'Yes.'

Mr. Spree dismissed her, and Judge Saladine rose. 'Just one or two questions, Mrs. Evered,' he said. 'You have read this affidavit?'

'Yes, the day it was printed. I horsewhipped Mr. Lebbeus that day!' Lebbeus made a comical grimace and winced elaborately, and the spectators smiled. Elder Pittridge, watching her so steady and serene under these bitter questions, felt a murderous anger toward John, and a great tenderness for her.

'On the evening referred to in the affidavit,' the Judge inquired, 'what were your husband's actions?'

'He had supper at home with me and our sons. We talked with our sons till their bedtime.'

'What is their bedtime?'

'We start Mat to bed at half-past seven. They're all tucked in, usually, by eight.'

'Were they, that night?'

'No. John — my husband — told them a story. It was a long story, and they enjoyed it and so did he. It was almost half-past eight before we bade them good night.'

'Did your husband then do something?'

'He came to town.'

'Ride or walk?'

'Pat Tierney drove him to his——'

'We will let Pat tell us about that. You saw him leave the house?'

'Yes.'

'Did anyone else know when he left the house?'

'Pat, and Mrs. McGaw.'

Elder Pittridge thought grimly that they would lie to save John, as she was lying; as she had told him she must lie to save her husband. She — or John — must have suborned them too.

'When did he return?'

'I had gone to bed just before ten o'clock. He came in to say good night to me a few minutes after.'

Elder Pittridge looked toward where John sat. John's lips were firm set, his cheek white; but that he should permit her thus to lie filled Elder Pittridge with such a black madness that he had to fight to hold back a furious cry. He saw Judge Saladine sit down, saw Mr. Spree rise once more; heard the ironic question:

'But in spite of everything — or perhaps because of everything, Mrs. Evered — you and your husband do occupy separate rooms?'

At that repeated inquiry Jenny suddenly was terribly pale. She swayed and, drooping like a flower, went down. Judge Saladine and John leaped to her side. A moment later Jenny passed where Elder Pittridge sat, leaning on John's arm, her cheek still white as snow, her head bowed. She and John went out of the room together. Then Elder Pittridge heard his own name called.

VIII

This man was during the moments he spent on the stand almost wholly insensible of his surroundings. He saw only the lean, fox-like countenance of Mr. Spree; and he saw like a shadow beside it the imagined face of Jenny, pale and fainting from the long torture which John had imposed on her. Yet he heard the questions, heard his own harsh grating voice as he answered them.

'You are acquainted with John Evered?'

'I am.'

'For how long?'

'I have known him intimately for almost ten years, our acquaintance beginning soon after he came to Bangor.'

'You have been friends?'

'Yes.'

'Has he discussed with you the alleged damage to his reputation by this publication?'

'He said no one would believe it.'

'But if that is true, then his reputation has not suffered?'

'Certainly his reputation has not suffered.'

'We have had some testimony here as to just what his reputation is. Did you hear that testimony?'

'No.'

'Do you know his reputation?'

'I suppose I do.'

'Has anyone ever discussed his moral character with you?'

Elder Pittridge did not answer, drawing back from that pit in a sharp affright; for Jenny's name had been on the tip of his tongue. Jenny had most certainly discussed with him her husband's reputation, but he must not say so. He was silent, and Mr. Spree urged: 'Come, what is your impression of Mr. Evered's general reputation as to chastity, as to morals?'

Elder Pittridge said with a venomous precision, grimly relishing his own words and the astonishment they would evoke, and the hurt they would do John: 'I'm afraid it is bad.'

There was at that word a sharp stir in the courtroom, and then an intense silence. Mr. Spree, if he were surprised, made no sign. He nodded almost casually. 'That is all.'

He sat down, looking in sharp triumph at Judge Saladine. For a moment the Judge did not speak. Then he said mildly:

'I have no question to put to Mr. Evered's good — friend.'

Elder Pittridge winced at those quiet words. He looked at Judge Saladine as though to plead for questions, but the Judge ignored him. Impaled by every eye, Elder Pittridge left the stand. When he came into the aisle, he was conscious of low murmurs, of withdrawings all around. The seat he had left was when he reached it filled. He stood a moment uncertainly beside it, but none made room for him; and he passed out of the door.

In the hall he met John, and Evered spoke to him. 'Are they through with you, Linc?' Elder Pittridge nodded, and John gripped his hand. 'Thanks, Linc,' he said. 'I sent Jenny home with Pat and Meg. Go to her, will you? This was hard for her. She needs you.'

Elder Pittridge nodded again and so moved on.

But he did not go to Jenny. He wondered in a dull abstraction whether he would ever see her again. He knew in sudden, full prescience now all that he had done, knew that none of those he had counted his friends would hereafter wish to touch his hand.

5

ELDER PITTRIDGE saw Jenny twice more. Once she was with John. This was ten days after the trial ended. The jury had given John a verdict of forty-eight hundred dollars damages; a tremendous sum, representing complete vindication. The heavy judgment and Judge Saladine's prompt action to enforce it left Lebbeus for the time bankrupt, deprived him of his press and plant, and sent him to Boston to await his next remittance from England.

The verdict silenced, too, the last whisper in Bangor against John; but it did not help Elder Pittridge. He met everywhere a quiet contempt which no one troubled to conceal; and his own recognition of the fact that this scorn was deserved made it the more bitter. He thought of John now, in a strong revulsion, as of an almost Christlike virtue and nobility; thought of himself as Peter who thrice denied his Master. His hatred was forgotten, and by the very wrong he had inflicted, John was in his thoughts magnified. Remorse tore at him with raking talons from which he could not escape. If he could have lost himself again in Jenny's arms, he might have mustered a swaggering bravado convincing to himself if to no other; but it was months since he had been alone with her except for an occasional casual word when John was near, and there had been since the day the libel first was published no invitation in her eyes nor in her tones. He knew instinctively that she had discarded him, that they would never again be to one another what they had been in those mad months of spring and summer when he alternated between a frenzied abandon in which the world seemed like to end and a shamed and wretched scorn of himself and of her. She had cast him aside; and now those he met, men and women he had known for years and whose respect he had earned and valued, likewise turned their backs on him.

The account of the trial was published at length in the *Whig and Courier;* and Sam Upton, the editor, printed Elder Pittridge's testimony verbatim, but without comment. Any comment would have been better than that silence. To contradict the eighty-odd witnesses — drawn from the lowest quarters of the town, and most of them with an admitted reason to hate John — who testified that his reputation was bad, Judge Saladine had called General Veazie, Rufus Dwinel, Deacon Adams, Colonel Black, and two or three others, men of the highest standing. For Elder Pittridge to read his own name in the shabby company of those who testified against John made his brooding regrets the more bitter.

He thought — as he had thought many times in these months — of killing himself. To that pitch he did not come; but like the flagellants he scourged himself not only with words but with actual violence, so that he wore welts and bruises and raw, unhealing wounds and from the very hurt of them derived a grotesque comforting.

Yet he did not immediately reach these depths; and for a while he haunted familiar scenes, hoping for some kindly glance or word. He went to church the first Sunday after the trial only to find himself isolated and alone in that company where he had always been a respected leader. He attended the concert given by the Washington Quartette Club of amateur singers, where as the *Whig and Courier* said: 'A highly intelligent and fashionable audience of the élite of the city in matters of taste' were pleasantly entertained. But there, too, he found himself ignored, and Jenny was not in the company. On the following Sunday, a hopeless longing led him to pass the Congregational Church as the service ended, in the hope of seeing her. Pat Tierney with the carriage — on runners, since this winter snow lay deep everywhere — was waiting for the worshippers to emerge, and Elder Pittridge spoke to him with a brave cheerfulness.

'Morning, Patrick! A fine day,' he said.

Pat pretended not to see him. He stared at the ears of his horses and flicked at them with the whip, and the tassel came so near the Elder's cheek that he moved back hastily. Yet when a moment later the congregation began to emerge after the service, he returned to meet John and Jenny as, with Judge Saladine and others near, they reached the carriage.

John spoke to him, extending his hand. 'Good morning, Linc,' he said clearly, so that those near-by could hear. 'You've made yourself a stranger. Come and see us.'

Elder Pittridge clung to that offered hand almost desperately. 'Why, I will, John,' he said, his voice shaking.

'I'm going up-river Friday,' John explained, 'to have an eye on things when the drive starts. So come soon.'

The Elder nodded and he hopefully sought Jenny's eye; but she passed him without a glance. John helped her into the carriage and they drove away.

He did not go out to the house where he had so long been welcome during the week that followed; but after John departed up-river, he went one evening secretly to knock on the door. There was some delay before it was opened, not by Jenny herself but by Mrs. McGaw. When she saw Elder Pittridge and before he could speak, she closed the door with a quiet emphasis and a firm finality; and he went hopelessly back to town.

February ended and March came in, and the lonely man turned to company he once had scorned. The lumbering crews would soon now be coming out of the woods; and down in Devil's Half Acre their welcome was preparing. The population of the district along the east side of the Stream near its mouth, which in winter shrank to a skeleton, began to grow again. When he first went that way Elder Pittridge was met with suspicious glances, and with an occasional jeering taunt; but he ignored the glances and the taunts and ordered rum and drank it, sitting alone, sinking into a sodden stupor which was nevertheless release from the ordeal of keeping his own company. As in the succeeding days his collapse became increasingly complete, the jeers were silenced, and he began to be met in his new haunts with tolerance, and at last with pity that was not far from friendliness.

But in his sober hours he still longed to see Jenny; and he went to the Lyceum lecture on 'The State of Poetry in England,' hoping vainly to encounter her there. That was his last venture into the circles where he had once been always welcomed. After that, so far as his old friends were concerned, he moved alone.

II

His last encounter with Jenny occurred in the hours between midnight and dawn on the morning of Sunday, the twenty-ninth of March. For almost the full month preceding, he had lived as a solitary, more often drunk than not, sleeping sometimes in his own bed, sometimes in the tavern or den where insensibility overtook him; and in his maudlin state he might be seen to pluck at his arms and body and legs with fingers like pincers, as though he tried to pull the flesh away from his bones, so that the crowds in the grogshops he frequented watched him in a wondering curiosity. He was apt, halfway from semi-sobriety to complete drunkenness, to become argumentative, truculent and quarrelsome. Once, far gone in rum, he attempted to take part in a loud discussion of the Oregon Question, and he made a speech in McNeill's Tavern to a cheering audience which was indifferent to the issues involved but highly amused by his oratorical flights. He was encouraged to new efforts, and having exhausted the one topic, turned to another.

'And I will say a few words to you now,' he cried, 'about a condition here in our fair city which is a shame and a disgrace to our good name! I refer, ladies and gentlemen —' Good-humored cheers from his mixed audience drowned him out for a moment till with uplifted hands he commanded silence and so went on. 'I refer, my friends, to the swine which everywhere run loose in our streets. It is nothing but hog, hog, hog, go where you will, into the streets, lanes, gardens, front yards, back yards, woodsheds —'

Someone shouted amiably: 'Don't leave out the privies, Brother Pittridge!'

Elder Pittridge bowed. 'I thank you. The privies, yes, and even the kitchens of our homes, if the doors are left open for a moment. Wherever you go, swarms of miserable, half-starved and shivering hogs meet you at every step. Every person who can raise the means to scare up the skeleton of a swine with just enough life left in it to feel the pangs of unsatisfied hunger does so; and the miserable creatures range from door to door through cold and snowdrifts, squealing and suffering!'

A woman laughed in shrill amusement. 'Now, ain't that terrible about the poor pigs?'

The tall, gaunt man levelled at her a bony finger. 'You may well say so. But waste no sympathy on the swine! You too may wander one day from door to door.' He flung up his arms, losing the track of his discourse, turning to a familiar topic. 'It is all a part of rum's horrid work. Not a month ago a party of honest lumbermen left their axes and their saws to go to Mattawamkeag for a debauch. A Troy man named Robert Lytell — I doubt not that some of you knew him — lagged behind his fellows on the way back to camp, and froze to death beside the road. He left a wife, gentlemen; a wife and six small babies, homeless, fatherless.' His voice broke in a sob. 'There's rum for you! That's what rum will do for you, my poor brothers and sisters!'

The man nearest him laughed and put a cup of raw liquor into his hand, and he drained it with a shudder and went on, his voice at a higher pitch. Usually his orations entertained his audience, but this was not always true. When his denunciations of rum became too violent, or when in rolling Biblical phrases he damned the strange woman and all her works, someone as truculent as he might take issue with him. At such times he seemed to welcome physical combat, courting the hardest blows as though pain were bliss to him. The fact that in these fights he was always worsted, and with an almost contemptuous ease, did not deter him on the next occasion; and there was seldom a day during this month of March that he did not wear on his countenance, in swollen mouth or nose or discolored eyes, the marks of losing battles.

For a while, to 'get old Pittridge started' was a favored form of entertainment in the resorts he frequented, till the rapid decline of his faculties muddled his speech. He began to repeat himself, not always lucidly; and his discourses lost the vigor and fire which had at first distinguished them. He came to be a bore, more likely than not to be shouted down; and he learned at last to sit in a bitter, brooding silence, plucking at himself with claw-like hands, listening to the talk around him, but without attempting to take part in it at all.

III

With the approach of the time when the ice might be expected to go out of the river, the spring break-up gradually pushed Mexico and Oregon and the tariff and all such remote affairs out of the minds of Bangor men. The lumbering crews were emerging from the woods, and they reported an unprecedented amount of anchor ice in the river, six to eight feet deep almost everywhere, while in some places here on tidewater the ice was thirty feet thick. A succession of unusually low tides in the lower river had left this mass for the most part undisturbed, and a well which had been dug near the piers of the Bangor-Brewer Bridge found fourteen feet of ice there, most of it solid. The snow blanket in the woods was heavy, and warm rains, melting that snow overnight, would almost certainly produce a dangerous freshet.

On the seventeenth of March the rain began, turned to snow and then to sleet and then to snow again, and finally to rain once more. Word came from Old Town that the rising water there was beginning to break the two or three feet of blue ice which covered the river, and bring it down to jam at every narrow sluice. By the twenty-fourth of the month the jam filled the river solidly from above Old Town to within two miles of Bangor. A small channel was open from the foot of the jam to the bridge, and ice-pokers were at work loosing big blocks and freeing them in this channel, so that they might pass harmlessly away.

But on the twenty-sixth a thundershower came down the valley, with wind and heavy rain. Elder Pittridge, sprawling in his chair in the corner of McNeill's Tavern, heard dimly through the alcoholic fog which obscured his senses the reports from each newcomer, and a man fresh from Old Town, shouting his news, had for a while the attention of them all.

'They're getting hell up there,' he cried, 'and worse to come! The new ice slides under the old till it hits bottom. River's full of it, so no water can get through; and it's rising all the time. Bridges are gone a'ready, and if the jam don't draw tonight, the mills will float right off their foundations.'

McNeill said positively: 'She won't draw tonight. There's a high run of tides, water in my cellar right now. That'll hold her back!'

'By God, she'd better!' the other insisted. 'Or half the mills in Old Town and Stillwater will come down-river by morning.'

But the jam did not draw, and the rain continued. Up-river above the jam, the water rose thirty feet higher than its normal level. The Basin Mills at Old Town lifted off their foundations, floated off and packed into the jam; the City Mills followed them.

'And that means we can't get the winter's cut sawed this year,' McNeill announced. 'Half of it will rot, or be lost. They'll have to hold it up-river, anywheres they can.'

There was still debate as to whether flood conditions would hit Bangor. Above the wharves the river was a mass of ice, rising higher than the usual level of the water, locked and motionless.

Elder Pittridge, half-sobered by the excitement in the air, Saturday morning walked out on the bridge to look upstream. The ice above the bridge was a tumbled chaos, in which the pressure of the water, exerting tremendous force, caused constant small upheavals. Blocks of ice as big as a cart might be squeezed upward between two others, rising slowly to their full height above the level of the jam before toppling on their sides. The air was full of a grinding, groaning noise; there was a rumbling and a squealing everywhere in the ice mass; and the men and boys watching from the vantage of the bridge stood in a silent wonder at the sight.

Elder Pittridge, scanning the ice through one of the windows of the bridge with dull, blinking eyes, found his attention fixed at last on a small object almost directly beneath where he stood. It lay on the ice that had packed against the bridge piers, and for a long time he did not realize what it was, his thoughts far away. But then something about it stirred recognition in him and he saw that this was the body of a baby, new-born and naked, lying face down in a pale huddle there.

When he was sure, he went back to find Jerry Skinner, the toll-taker; and Jerry came out with him to the spot to see for himself. Others gathered to discover what it was these two looked at so intently. The baby's body lay some distance from the pier, but Jerry thought they might reach it; and at his word men ran to bring ladders. Elder Pittridge, sobered by the sight, asked:

'How did it get there? How came it there?'

'Some woman that didn't want it threw it off the bridge,' Jerry guessed. 'Might have been a woman from one of the houses on Exchange Street.' And then he said in sudden memory: 'I mind now, three girls came across late last night. I didn't know who they was, shawls around their heads. Likely it was one of them.'

The lost man shuddered. 'Was it alive then, do you think?'

'Might have been at first, but it wouldn't last long down there. Just the fall would kill it. Or maybe it was dead before.' The men bringing ladders were near when he cried loudly: 'There it goes!'

While they watched, the ice cake upon which the small body lay rose under the pressure it sustained. It tipped almost on edge, and the dead infant slid a little, then rolled over, then fell into a crevice in the ice. Instantly the crevice closed like jaws, ice cakes splintering against one another, grindingly.

'Well, there wa'n't any use in getting it, anyway,' the toll-gatherer said philosophically; and he told the men as they arrived: 'Don't need the ladders now, boys. It's gone.'

He turned away; but Elder Pittridge stayed behind, watching

with dark brooding eyes the ice in which the baby now lay entombed. There was a life, of so many potentialities, which had ended before it began; yet perhaps those potentialities were evil ones. Were there not many men who might better have died as infants? How much misery and shame might have been saved them — and the world — if their mother had pinched them out, just as the owner of a bitch which whelps destroys the maimed and weak among the litter. He wondered what mother, what poor shameless one among the creatures in Devil's Half Acre, had thus ridded herself of an unwanted child; and his eyes filled with a wringing sympathy for her. No matter how hardened, she must have suffered in the doing, must always suffer in the memory of her action.

Yet it was as much for himself as for her he wept, in a weak and spineless self-commiseration.

IV

His thoughts clung to the dead baby, and to its unknown mother, till a movement on the river attracted his attention. A small section of the upper jam broke away and came with a ponderous slowness downstream, carrying with it the wreckage of the City Mills. It struck the ice immediately above the bridge with a terrific concussion, and fragments were thrown up in huge sheets and piles, some of the smaller flying clear to fall upon the mass and shatter with explosive sounds. The bridge on which Elder Pittridge stood shuddered under that shock; and instantly the water followed till — checked again by the jam above the bridge — it began to overflow the banks on either side.

The people on the bridge had scattered before the approaching impact, running either way; but Elder Pittridge stayed where he was, not caring how soon death reached for him. On the Brewer side where a line of houses fronted the water he saw the flood pouring into windows, saw women and children running for safety from those houses to the higher land; and almost indifferently he turned that way in an automatic move to help them. But before he reached the other end of the bridge, he saw that those in the houses must have escaped, so he turned back.

On the Bangor side, the sudden rising water had begun to sweep away lumber piled on the wharves awaiting shipment; and some of the wharf buildings were already shifting as the rising water lightened them to the floating point. By the time he reached the Bangor end of the bridge, scores of men were at work moving lumber back from the encroaching flood, carrying furniture and smaller objects out of the houses and buildings which the water had already reached. Elder Pittridge joined them, working with a desperate and driving energy, working as zealously as though these were his own possessions here in peril. He labored all that day, tirelessly, as long as there was light to see, rejoicing that in this common effort his help was welcomed. The waters of the Stream, backed up by that portion of the jam below its mouth, began to overflow the low ground on both sides of its banks. Before dark the buildings between the Stream and Exchange Street were flooded; but at dark the situation was no worse, and the jam was under increasing pressure with every hour that passed. When it should give way, unles it packed again in the narrows at High Head, the flood would pour down-river to the Bay.

So with darkness there was for a while some respite, and men had time to snatch a bite to eat; but Elder Pittridge did not seek food. He waited by the river above the Bangor end of the bridge, listening in the darkness for the first sounds that would indicate the jam was moving. The night was almost warm, the stars hidden, the air filled with misty haze rising from the ice. There were torches and lanterns everywhere in the watching crowd, and bonfires here and there around which men, wet and weary from their exertions during the day, huddled to await what was to come. But the light from these penetrated only a little distance; the river itself was hidden in hazy darkness.

It was almost midnight when there came in the constant grumbling and complaining of the ice a new note; a shrill and ominous sound. Elder Pittridge heard himself shouting: 'There it draws!' The cry ran along the margin of the flood and up through the city; and a clamor of church bells began, every bell clanging out the warning. From the banks it was impossible to see what was happening; but the roar from the river was deafening. He heard the splintering crash as one section of the bridge was carried away; and then the tail of the jam, loosened and lifted by the steadily rising water, spread out to brush along the banks as it moved downstream. The crowds fled, drawing back from its encroaching advance, shouting and screaming in the darkness; and Elder Pittridge heard the scrape and slither and thump of lumber piles dissolving into their component parts as the ice ground planks to splinters or the water swept them away.

When the tail of the jam passed below the bridge, the water which thrust it on began to fall to lower levels. He followed the receding flood, gauging by it the movement of the jam — unseen in the darkness — in the river below. He came down toward the lower ground along the Stream, the water withdrawing before him till it was no more than eight or ten feet above its normal level; but then suddenly he felt it around his feet, and almost at once, before he could take a backward step, it had risen to his knees.

He knew what that meant. The jam had stopped again, packing in the narrows at High Head; and the combined waters of the river and the Stream, piling up behind it, rose with incredible speed. All along the margin of the flood, others had been as quick as he to guess the truth; and a general shout of many men and the shrill cries of women filled the night, and people everywhere fled blindly to safety. The grinding roar of the ice, tumbling and cracking as it wedged solidly in the narrows below the town, was even at this distance deafening; and the mighty river, draining rain and melting snow off seven thousand square miles of wilderness, rammed that ice plug hard home till it was an impenetrable dam rising from the river bed high above the normal level of the water. Barred thus from escape to sea, the flood banked high and then recoiled; and like a herd of stampeding cattle which begins to mill and then to spill in every direction, it overflowed the banks on both sides, and it came in swirling torrents and eddies, with hissing, sucking sounds that were terrifying in the steamy blackness of the pitch-dark night, surging up across the low flats along the east bank of Kenduskeag Stream.

Elder Pittridge had no more than realized that the water was rising before it threatened to overwhelm him. He backed stubbornly away till he reached Exchange Street, knee-deep, thigh-deep, knee-deep again as he encountered inequalities in the ground; and he felt earth treacherously crumble under him, and a raft of loose floating planks banged against his legs in the darkness so that he found his way through them in half panic. He had been less quick than others to take flight, so the sound of human voices receded and he was alone in the midst of the flood. He worked clear of the floating lumber and sought to make greater haste; but even on Exchange Street he was thigh-deep. All around him in the night there were the sounds of panic flight, the crash of collapsing buildings, the crushing impact of collisions when ice masses pounded against frail, wooden walls still standing; and as he sought to wade up Exchange Street to higher ground, the church bells still sang in startling clangor in the town, their voices coming muffled through the thickening river fog.

The water was deeper all the time, so he swung aside into a narrow alley between two buildings — a store block on one side, a house on the other — thinking to escape that way more readily to dry land. All around him and between him and the Stream was dark, but he saw a lighted window on the second floor of the house beside him; and he looked up, and a woman opened the window and leaned out.

He could not see her face, but he knew who she must be. This was Lena Tempest's house, and its fame was wide. He shouted to her: 'Get out of there, quick as ever you can! The whole river's coming in on you! Get your girls out quick, or you'll all drown!'

Lena did not answer him. She drew back and closed the window and disappeared; and Elder Pittridge, in a sudden rage at her stupidity which might cost her life, felt along the wall and found the door and thrust it open. Water was better than knee-deep inside. There were no lights on the ground floor, but a lamp was burning in the upper hall; and he raced up the stairs.

Lena came striding to meet him there. She had not kept that flaxen comeliness which she had worn fifteen years before. She was heavier, with the solid weight which muscular women sometimes put on; and her face was like a man's, leathery and lined and strong; and her eyes were old and wholly wise and leaden, flat and without depth, like those of a fish. The only obviously feminine thing about her was an absurd and hideous set of frizzed curls, too brightly hued to match the color of her own faded yellow hair, which was pinned above her ears and dangled all askew across her brow.

She met Linc at the stairhead and without a word set her hard hand against his face and pushed him backward. His nose bones grated as though that push which was half blow had broken them. His grip on the rail saved him from falling; but he was flung to his knees. He scrambled to his feet, two or three steps below her, and he shouted in pain and rage:

'Come out of here, you fool!' Then in that blazing voice of his, suddenly moved to a dark hysteria, he cried: 'Come, you shameless trull! "Behold the works of the Lord, what desolation he hath made in the earth!" Jehovah has let lose the flood waters of the deep to purge away your iniquities!'

Lena said briskly: 'I'll purge you, you long, slick limb of hell! Get out of my house before I kick your ribs in!' She gathered up her skirts to free her booted feet.

But before he could speak or move, a low voice came from that lighted room behind her; a low, laughing, familiar voice.

'Why, that sounds like Elder Pittridge, Lena!' said that voice in amused contempt. 'Bring him in to me.'

He knew that voice. It was Jenny's. Jenny was here!

v

When Elder Pittridge, Lena's heavy hand upon his shoulder pushing him forward, came into that small, lighted room, he was already shaken and mumbling with astonishment and terror. He saw a bed in which a woman lay; but his eyes were blurred and blinded. Not till he came nearer did his vision clear.

This was indeed Jenny, lying here very small and frail, yet smiling mirthlessly up at him. He wetted his dry, cracked lips, trying to speak, staring down at her. After a moment and without a word she turned down the coverlet which covered her so that he could see the round poll of a baby, newly born, there in the crook of her arm.

He shuddered in a sickening horror, and something made him remember that other infant which the ice had today engulfed. That unwanted baby had been thrown there by some lost girl; perhaps by one of the very girls whom Lena housed here and who now were fled to escape the flood. How many other babies, born in this house, had gone that same cold road to the sea? Perhaps before dawn this red and wrinkled infant, so like the other, would by Lena's hard and ruthless hands be committed to the hungry, icy waters. He stared down at the small head in the crook of Jenny's arm as though at a frightful apparition, shaking with convulsions like sobs.

Jenny spoke in mocking amusement. 'Don't look so scared, Linc,' she protested. 'Aren't you glad to see our daughter? Look! She's not yet three hours old.'

He mumbled: 'Ours?' Then, in full, helpless comprehension: 'Oh, my God!'

'Yes, ours, of course,' she told him in those low, calm tones which suddenly to him were terrible. 'Why are you surprised, my dear? Can I not conceive and bear, like other women?'

'But — why didn't you tell —— How could you hide ——'

She laughed. 'What are stays for, Linc? But you remember Meg did say I was a little breathless sometimes! Yet it did our daughter no harm. She's fine! Lena says she never saw a finer baby.'

Elder Pittridge looked around at Lena Tempest, a grim and scowling figure. How many other babies had her hard hands twitched into the world — to live a little while and die? 'What are you going to do with her?' he asked in dull terror, turning to Jenny again.

Jenny smiled. 'Oh, just leave her here. Lena will take care of her. I can't well take her home, you know. John would know she wasn't his.'

'Here?' His heart recoiled. Here in this house? The river would be better than Lena Tempest's house, for any girl child; and this baby was his child, sprung from his loins. He began to sob aloud in babbling delirium, his reason at last unseated, lost in the bitter winds that blow between the worlds.

Jenny watched him in amused, malicious contempt. 'I think so, yes.' Then, in icy scorn suddenly unmasked: 'Do you think Lena's house not good enough for her, Linc, when she had such a father as you?' Her voice was pitiless. She turned her head as though weary of him. 'Lena, throw him out,' she said.

Lena's great hand clamped on Elder Pittridge's nerveless arm. She propelled him to the stairs, pushed him headlong down.

VI

Water was deeper in the alley now. Elder Pittridge half-waded and half-swam through the icy flood, groping in darkness, his knees giving way, not knowing where he went or why. After Lena Tempest thrust him out into the night, no one wittingly saw him again. There was a rumor next day that a man whom no one knew, but who was obviously insane, had been seen beating himself sickeningly with his fists and writhing on the ground in self-inflicted pain till someone tried to seize him and he scrambled to his feet, screaming as he fought them off and ran away. There was another rumor that someone, trying to cross Smith's Bridge through water waist-deep, had been overwhelmed by the raging stream; but this rumor was discredited. When after the flood subsided he was missed — great bales of temperance literature sent to him by Neal Dow for distribution accumulated on his doorstep and were never claimed — it was assumed that he had gone away; but no inquiry was made. He was gone, and none regretted him; gone forevermore.

VII

Dan Evered

I

DAN EVERED's first memory was of his mother. In this memory she sat in a big, comfortable chair by a sunny window in the front bedroom where she and his father slept; and the bed itself was disordered, so that he knew she had just left it. She was dressed in something soft and voluminous, with a cashmere shawl around her shoulders. The window was open and a warm breeze came in, and the air seemed to him in remembrance to have been faintly scented with a pleasant fragrance of roses. His mother in his early memories of her always smelled like roses.

On this day which he remembered, he and Will came into her room, and Will ran and climbed into her lap, and she cautioned him smilingly not to hurt their new little brother; and Dan drew nearer to see the very small, red baby with a wrinkled nose and eyes tight shut. The baby lay in the curve of his mother's arm while Will perched on her knee; and Dan, since there was no room on her lap for him, moved away a little, feeling lonely and sad. His mother must have seen this, for she called to him in melting tenderness:

'Danny boy — come here to me!'

So he pressed close to her, careful not to hurt the new baby, and she embraced them all three, hugging his head and Will's together against her breast, laughing and crying at the same time; and Dan felt the soft warmth he loved, and smelled a sweet, milky, maternal smell, and she cried:

'Oh, I'm so proud and happy with my three big, big boys!'

Dan did not think of himself as big, and certainly the new baby was absurdly small; but Aunt Meg came in while they were all there and she too exclaimed at the newcomer's size. 'I declare, Jenny,' she cried admiringly, 'you hardly show it beforehand, but they're always tremendous!'

Jenny laughed, ignoring the fact that Dan was listening, assuming as older people so often and so unwisely do a lack of comprehension in children. 'I know it,' she agreed. 'Dan weighed ten and a half pounds, and Will was almost eleven, and Tommy here was a little over ten.'

Aunt Meg cried admiringly: 'And you don't have a bit of trouble!

It's as easy for you as opening an umbrella, and you're always up in no time afterward!'

'Tommy's only eight days old,' Dan's mother proudly assented.

So Dan could always date his first memory as going back to eight days after Tommy was born. During the next two or three years, his life began to be well studded with incidents which he remembered. Most of them were fun, but one was frightening. Usually his mother was quick to forgive his youthful crimes, but one day when he was not conscious of any wrongdoing, she summoned him up to her room; and there was something in her bearing which made him afraid of her. She closed the door and slipped the bolt on it and said quietly:

'Dan, someone picked all my nasturtiums. Was it you?'

Dan, mysteriously alarmed by her tone, began to cry. 'No, mother,' he said, honestly enough. 'Ruth picked some to bring in the house, but I didn't pick any.'

'Not even one, Dan?' she insisted.

He had, it is true, picked one blossom. He knew this was against the rules of the garden in which his mother took such pride; but the one he picked had seemed to him particularly beautiful, and he had kept it secretly in his pocket till it was crushed and faded. He stood appalled at his own crime now, and she said in her even tones that could be so terrifying:

'I saw you, you know, from my window. I must teach you not to tell lies, Dan.'

Then she made him take down his breeches, and she whipped him with a limber birch switch on his bare thighs. She whipped him almost savagely, yet in a controlled and quiet way which made him awfully afraid, so that he screamed as much from fear as from pain; and he heard Will howling in sympathetic terror outside the bolted door. Then suddenly his mother dropped the switch and caught him in her arms and carried him to the chair by the window and sat down there, hugging him and kissing him; and she was crying now too, not with tears, but with dry, shuddering sobs that made her shake all over, and whispering to herself in a terrible aching tone: 'Oh, why do I? Dear God, why do I?' In the end it was he who sought to comfort her, patting her cheek and kissing her and begging her in a sort of panic not to cry any more.

II

Dan loved his father as much as he loved his mother, but in a different way. Toward his mother he began while he was still very young to feel a devotion not only possessive — he always spoke of her to Will and the others as 'our mother,' while of John he always said simply 'father'—but protective too. One morning he woke early and became conscious of a sound which he presently realized was his mother's voice; but she was uttering strange, muffled cries, and he jumped out of bed and ran along the hall to their door and burst in, his eyes wide with alarm.

His father and mother were tussling together by the window, still in their nightclothes, standing in the streaming morning sun; and his mother was pounding at his father with her fists and he was laughing and dodging the blows and trying to catch her hands, and she was making growling sounds exactly like a cat till she saw Dan and said in a quick, low tone:

'Don't, John! There's Dan!'

They faced Dan together, and she was as pink as a rose, and his father said amiably: 'Hello, son. Anything wrong?'

'I heard mama crying,' Dan confessed. 'I thought someone was hurting her.'

His father laughed. 'We were just playing,' he explained. He looked at Jenny and chuckled. 'In fact, she was hurting me, instead of its being the other way around! Did you see her pound me, Dan?'

Dan knew he did not completely understand, but also he knew that everything was all right. There was something warm and happy and comfortable in the very air of the room here; and he grinned and said: 'She hit you some good ones, didn't she!'

Jenny said tenderly: 'Poor Dan, so scared, and running to protect his mother! Come in bed with me, darling, while papa gets dressed.'

Dan at that invitation whooped with delight, and his cry woke the other boys and they all came running for the rare and perfect treat of a lazy morning hour with her, climbing over her, squabbling for the privilege of being next to her, revelling in her nearness; and their father laughed at them and said they were like so many bugs in a rug, and went into his wardrobe to dress. But he called Dan in there to speak to him confidentially.

'Don't tell the other boys what you saw, Dan,' he said. 'Nor anyone else, for that matter. People wouldn't understand. We'll keep that a secret among the three of us, mother and you and me.'

Dan promised, and he kept his word; but he always remembered that morning because of the particularly strong and heartening and beautiful happiness which he had felt between them when he came into the room and afterward. He often had this sense of a rapturous and sweet communion between his father and mother; and once, shyly, he asked his mother about it, and she said:

'That's just because we love each other so, Dan.'

He never spoke of this to his father, feeling in the big man's presence a reticence that was a part of his almost worshipful love and pride, so overpowering that he could not bear to think of it. When he was alone with his father he was shy, as a young girl may be in the presence of a man she admires. It was a rare thing for them to talk of any but impersonal matters; yet many things passed between them without the necessity of words. If John spoke of something that had happened in the city, telling Jenny how this man had behaved worthily, or that one had done ill, Dan early began to understand that his father was really speaking to him, teaching him to understand what things were a mistake and what other actions and principles were good and perfect altogether. John did not say to his sons: You must do thus; you must not do so and so. But he spoke of the deeds of others in terms of strong approbation or of sober disapproval, in words so simple and clear that even a boy could understand. While he was still a youngster, Dan began to acquire John's code; and he knew his father was transmitting this code to him, and accepted it because what his father said was *per se* true. Good men did not lie. They did not cheat nor play devious tricks. They did not do one thing, nor refrain from doing another, because they were afraid. They were afraid of nothing but fear. They did not deviously evade responsibility for their actions. They did what seemed the best and wisest thing to do — and accepted for good or ill the consequences. They did not abuse their own strength nor take advantage of the weaknesses of others. Those beliefs and many another came little by little to be a part of Dan; they combined to form a pattern, a rule from which any deviation brought regrets.

Yet Dan's father never laid down a moral precept. His teaching was all by indirection. He had a tremendous fund of anecdote, had many stories to tell; and some of them were stirring and some made the boys howl with glee; but through them all ran one consistent strain, which Dan came by degrees to recognize as the character of his father, as the distilled essence of all John Evered was and tried to be.

And everything that was his father, Dan learned to love with a fierce yet humble devotion, and with a pride so keen that just to think of the man might make the boy's eyes fill happily.

III

There were other people in Dan's youthful world. Mrs. McGaw in the kitchen, and Pat Tierney and Ruth and their children, were almost part of the family. Mrs. McGaw was outwardly querulous, sharp-tongued, forever scolding; but she did not mean half she said, and the boys knew it. The cooky jar was always filled; and if she were frying doughnuts and the delicious fragrance drew them to the kitchen door, she would give them samples, hot out of the boiling grease, so hot they could hardly be held at all and must be passed rapidly from one hand to the other while they cooled. The boys plagued her affectionately till she said they would be the death of her; but when Jenny one day offered to keep them out of the kitchen, Mrs. McGaw said briskly: 'Thank you for nothing! I'll never see the day I can't run my own kitchen. Any time I want to be rid of them, I can scatter them like so many chickens. No, ma'am, leave them be.' She had been widowed when her own son and daughter were babies, and she went sometimes now to her daughter's in Brewer to see her grandchildren. Her son was the boss of a lumber crew, in the woods all winter, with a small farm down Bucksport way and grown sons now of his own; but Mrs. McGaw did not like her son's wife and spoke darkly of her goings on and never went there unless her son was at home.

Pat Tierney welcomed the boys to the stables which were his particular province and taught them to ride almost before they could walk. They delighted to help him curry the horses and brush them till their coats shone; and they helped him clean the harness and wash the carriages, and as they grew older they learned to harness the horses. Dan always remembered as a triumph the day he first succeeded in bridling old Charley, standing on the mounting block to do so, under Pat's watchful eye. Pat kept them busy helping him with all the chores around the place. They cleaned stalls and raked the driveway and the paths, and cut the grass and clipped the borders and weeded garden beds and raked leaves in the fall and kept Mrs. McGaw's woodbox filled — Pat himself carried the big logs for the fireplaces — and in summer they helped with the haying on the meadow lands behind the house, pitching on as soon as they were tall enough to do so, treading down the hay as Pat spread it in the great mow.

Pat they liked and trusted, but they were always a little afraid of Ruth. She was a quiet woman who flew sometimes into shrill tempers which passed as quickly as they came. She was much younger than Pat, and she preserved a youthful appearance, while Pat's red hair was long since tinged with gray. Dan, for no reason he could define, was always a little sorry for her, and that made him like her. She was devoted to Pat, yet in her not infrequent fits of temper she berated him with outright violence, sometimes coming down into the stable to give him a piece of her mind. He at such times never defended himself, standing quietly under the storm; but when she was gone he would wink at Dan and say wisely:

'Sure and she'll feel better now that's out of her system!'

Dan unconsciously acquired from Pat a habit of thinking of all womankind — except of course his mother, who was unique and incomparable — as weaker vessels, capable of being all sweetness and content, but subject to storms and stresses from which man was immune and with ways no man could understand. He understood that for woman's frailties it was necessary to make allowances, and this conception fitted well with Dan's own mysterious sympathy for Ruth, his feeling that she was unhappy and in need of kindliness. He adopted toward her Pat's attitude, so that if she laid her tongue on him he attributed her wrath to what Pat called 'the vapors' and waited for it to pass.

She and Pat had three children, never any more. The oldest, named after Pat himself, was a year or so older than Dan; but young Pat was frail, with sandy hair and an appealing grin. Also, the truth was not in him. He was a chronic liar, and he was addicted even as a child to petty thieving, stealing not only Mrs. McGaw's goodies out of the kitchen — that was a venial sin which they all committed — but such things as straps out of the harness room, the bright medallions attached to the cheek strap of bridles, or even on one or two occasions small treasured possessions belonging to Dan or the other boys. Dan hated and despised young Pat as soon as he was old enough to form an opinion. It puzzled him sometimes to see that Ruth seemed to prefer her oldest son to her other children; but he thought she hid this preference from Pat himself, as though it were something of which she was ashamed.

Their younger children were red-headed like Pat himself. The oldest, named John out of compliment to Dan's father and called Jack, was Will's age, freckled, full of a lively instinct for harmless mischief, and with a faculty for clowning which delighted Dan and the others. Elizabeth — Lizzie for short — two years younger, was like her mother quiet and reserved, but with none of those storms of temper which Ruth sometimes displayed. Except for young Pat, the children were all congenial enough, doing many things together; but young Pat was more apt to be alone or with his mother than with them.

Of the older people who came to the house which was at first Dan's world — Judge Saladine, Elijah Hamlin, Colonel Black, Deacon Adams, General Veazie, Rufus Dwinel and all the leading citizens of the city — Aunt Meg and Uncle Linc were the only ones who made on Dan as a youngster any particular impression. He liked them both, but he found in Uncle Linc as in Ruth something wistful and unhappy and therefore curiously appealing. When Uncle Linc brought them small presents, Dan understood that the man did this to win their liking; and he always pretended to be delighted with these gifts in order to please Uncle Linc. It would always be true of Dan that sympathy and affection went hand in hand. For him to be even a little sorry for a person was to like him.

So he liked Uncle Linc, but for Aunt Meg, on the other hand, he had a warm and forthright affection in which there were no qualifications. She was just pretty and nice and jolly and he loved her. He had loved her ever since he could remember; not as he loved his mother, possessively and protectively, but with a warm and merry adoration which was undiluted happiness. He never saw her without delight; and when as sometimes happened they were alone together and she talked to him — not as so many grown-ups talk to children but as to one as mature as she — he enjoyed it completely.

One of the things he liked best about her was her frank affection for his father. He liked to tell her of the pleasures he and his father had together, and of the things they planned to do 'when I grow up,' and he might repeat to her some of the stories John had told him, and they would laugh together at these tales. In many ways the happiest times Dan had, until Aunt Meg married Captain Pawl, were when he talked about his father with her. She seemed to know so exactly how he felt, seemed so completely to agree that his father was all the splendid, unnamed things which Dan knew him to be.

IV

When he was very young, Dan used to feel in the very air of his home the strong happiness which lay between his father and his mother. Without knowing why, he nevertheless knew that when he was with them he felt virtuous and warm and calmly content; and to see the way they looked at each other and how when their eyes met even casually each might become for a moment still and smiling, to hear them laugh together, to see their quiet amusement as they watched him and Will and little Tom and Mat, to listen while they talked to each other in grave, low tones about things he did not in the least understand — all these experiences contributed in secret and subtle ways to his own happiness. The first time he heard any other than a note of fondness in their tones frightened him almost to tears. That was while Mat was still a very young baby, no more than two or three months old; and his mother was perched on his father's knee as though she too were a child, teasing his father, pulling his nose, tickling him, her finger boring into his neck under his ear, whispering to him, begging for something, saying: 'Please, please, pretty please! Pretty please, John?' Dan thought she was incredibly sweet and beautiful, her cheek flushed, her eyes curiously lustrous; and he thought no one could deny her anything. But his father, though when this teasing began he had laughed good-humoredly enough, began as Dan could see to be a little irritated and severe; and once he said sternly: 'Hush, Jenny! Dan's watching you!' But she laughed and buried her face against his neck, and pretended to bite his ear, worrying it with little growl-ing sounds, till his father pushed her away. Dan could feel his father's anger, oppressive and alarming, in the very air; and as though in response to it, his mother suddenly was angry too, for she got up off his father's knee and walked toward the door, and she said over her shoulder in a hard, scornful tone:

'I'm sure you're admirably continent!'

She left the room, and Dan was embarrassed and unhappy; but an hour later his father and mother were laughing together again.

But after that there were other occasions when he felt this hard antagonism between them. Sometimes, passing their door, he heard in their voices an inflexible and unforgiving tone that made him uneasy.

Usually when Dan's father and mother were thus at odds, it was over some issue which they veiled behind obscure phrases, or which even though they spoke plainly Dan could not understand; but he did understand their differences over Atticus, the black man who for a while helped Pat take care of the lawn and garden. Atticus appeared mysteriously one morning, having arrived after the boys were abed the night before; and at once he and the boys were on the best of terms. Their first shy curiosity led them to question him; his chuckling good humor made them like him; and they listened in fascination to the interminable tales he loved to tell, and they discovered that he could sing queer, haunting, form-less songs about God and his children, and about heaven and hell, and they followed him around the place like cats behind a fish-monger's cart, teasing him to sing while he worked.

They thought it hilariously funny because to him even pleasant summer days seemed uncomfortably cold; and when one night there was almost a frost and he appeared in the morning wearing two suits of their father's old clothes and with chattering teeth, they laughed to the point of tears. He said this was the coldest winter he ever did see, and they told him scornfully that this was summer, and they boasted about how cold real Bangor winters were, and showed him on the trees how deep the snows might drift, and told him how water might freeze in their bedrooms at night even with the windows closed. They showed him the air-tight stoves, stowed away for the summer in the shed, which in the fall would be set up indoors to keep the house warm; and they assured him, happily exaggerating, that even with fires in all the stoves they often wore heavy coats and shawls indoors. They reduced the colored man to a state of real and lively apprehension; till he said one day, wagging a rueful head:

'M-m-man! Time it gits tuh be cold lak dat, I'm gwine wish't I'd stayed in Savannah, Gawguh!' He worried about the fact that there was no heat and no provision for a stove in the small room in the shed where a bed had been placed for him. 'What I gwine do when it gits tuh be cold lak you say, Mistuh Dan?' he protested dolefully. 'Savannah, Gawguh — da's de place I'm gwine want tuh be.'

Atticus began in fact to suffer from something like homesick pangs, and he would talk for hours about the charms and beauties of his life as a slave, his snug warm cabin, his Nancy, his Mr. Sagurs who valued him so highly. Dan told his mother that Atticus wanted to go home to Savannah, but she said Dan was foolish, that no one could possibly prefer to be a slave! Dan tried to argue with her. 'I told him that, mother,' he declared, 'and he said being a slave was just having a good master and plenty to eat and a warm cabin and having it warm weather all the time.' But she silenced him almost indignantly, assuring him that Atticus did not mean what he said.

Dan was conscious of the fact that his father and mother disagreed about Atticus, and when two men came one day and took the negro away, he saw the frightening wrath in her, and knew that she was angry at his father. For most of the week after Atticus was taken away, she did not speak to Dan's father at all, except with such a dreadful politeness that Dan and the other boys moved in hushed misery.

Since Mat was born it had been increasingly often true that there hung about Dan's father and mother this red and angry cloud. On the occasions, more and more rare as time went on, when they were again completely happy together, Dan and the other children were apt to run and shout and laugh in sheer exuberance because all was once more well between their father and mother — and therefore in their world.

v

Dan never took sides between his father and mother even in his thoughts until a day soon after Atticus went away, and that day it was rather an instinct on his part to defend Mat than any other consideration which ranged him against his mother. She and his father had been at odds at breakfast; and after his father went away to the office, she paced up and down the living room, so engrossed in her own thoughts that once when Dan came to the door and spoke to her she did not even hear him. He watched her for a moment in a puzzled and increasing uneasiness and at last slipped quietly away, but he came back, drawn by a fascination he could not resist, to spy upon her; and he saw that as she walked and walked, her fists were clenched, and presently she began to beat her fists against her hips and to make low, wordless sounds. Dan was wholly frightened now, and he tiptoed away to the end of the hall, and out to the barn.

Later, he saw her go past the barn toward the woodlot behind the house. She walked purposefully, and yet with slow, hard steps as though someone were pushing her against her will, and he watched her through the window of a horse stall and saw her cut off a young birch sapling. It was not so long as the switch which she kept hanging behind the woodshed door and which these last two or three years, and especially on those days when she and Dan's father were at odds, she had been apt to use at the most trivial offense. She brought the switch toward the house, stripping off the leaves as she came, and Dan stayed hidden in the stable till she went indoors.

Dan's father came home to dinner; and at table she was quiet while his father joked with them as he always did. Afterward Pat drove John back to town and returned to take Mrs. McGaw to Brewer to see her daughter; and Dan and Will and the other children begged to go along, but their mother said no. She sent Ruth instead, and she even let Ruth take her children; and Dan thought it unfair that they should go while he and his brothers must stay at home. The ride to Brewer, across the covered bridge, stopping to pay the toll, was an adventure which they all enjoyed.

The carriage drove away, and the four boys wandered across the front lawn, idly seeking a way to amuse themselves. Mat was by that time a chubby youngster who already displayed a will of his own, and who promised to be some day the biggest of them all. He and Dan were both large for their age, and Dan had once heard his mother tell Aunt Meg that they were like her father. Mat was a rowdy, with a trick of shouting down all opposition till he got his way. The other brothers, Will and Tom, were of slender mold, and though Will was tall enough for his years, Tom, despite the advantage in age which he possessed, was only a little taller than Mat, and not much heavier; and he lacked completely Mat's bold truculence.

At the foot of the lawn, Jenny was planning to put in a lattice to support some climbing vines; and Pat had dug the holes in which two stout cedar posts would presently be set. The boys examined these holes and began to argue about how deep they were. Tom thought they were over his head, and Will said scornfully that he was crazy, and to prove his point Tom slid down into one hole. The top of his head did not reach the level of the ground, but Will accused him of scrooching down to make the hole seem deeper than it was, and demanded that Tommy let Mat get down into the hole to make an honest test.

It proved necessary to use some force to insert Mat into the hole. Tommy was slender enough to wiggle in and out of it with no great difficulty, but Mat showed a tendency to stick; and once he was down in the hole, a sense of suffocation seized him and he pleaded for rescue. This excited the other boys, who began to tease him, threatening to go away and leave him stuck in the hole; and the threats produced in him a sort of frenzy. He reached out and caught Tommy's bare leg and set his fingernails in it so deeply that Tommy yelled in turn, dragging his leg free of Mat's claws at the cost of astonishingly deep and bloody scratches.

Tommy fled toward the house, blood running down his torn leg, and Jenny called sternly from her bedroom window: 'Dan, pull Mat out of that hole and send him in to me.'

They were all sobered by the sight of Tommy's blood, and they escorted a subdued Mat into the house where Jenny silently cleaned and bandaged Tommy's wounds, bidding Mat stand and wait her pleasure, ignoring the uneasy and placating remarks of the older boys. When Tommy was bandaged, she took a silent and rather pale Mat by the hand and marched him up the stairs to her room.

The others waited, white and breathless, at the stair foot till they heard Mat's first piercing cry. At that sound, Tommy frankly fled, and Will too edged away; but Dan stood his ground. The steady screams of mingled terror and pain which sounded from that upper room were after a moment more than he could bear. He ran up the stairs, himself by that time sobbing nervously, and burst open the door.

Mat's outcries must have covered the sound of the opening door, for Dan's mother did not turn her head. She was holding Mat, stark naked, face down on the bed, lashing him with that many-branched birch sapling Dan had watched her cut. At every stroke, red lines drew themselves on Mat's soft white flesh, and his screams were shrill and terrible.

Dan ran forward and came on her from behind and caught her upraised arm, his muscular small hands gripping hard. She tried to fling him aside, but he still clung, crying: 'Stop, mama! Stop! Please stop, mama!' She released Mat to tear Dan's hands off her arm, and in doing so she swung around and Dan saw his father there in the open bedroom door.

So Dan ran to his father, sure that now everything would be all right again, sobbing with relief as he clung to the big man's hand.

VI

But in the weeks that followed, Dan slowly came to realize that the world was not all right again. His father and mother were pleasant together, and he never again heard between them an outright angry word; but neither did he ever again feel that comfortable, warm happiness which had seemed almost visibly to cloud around them when he was little; and the way his mother spoke to his father, in quiet, cruel tones, was often worse than quarrelling. Also there was a tangible change in their way of living. His father now slept in a small bedroom down the hall, and his clothes and all his things were there; and as far as Dan knew he never again went into the big room he and Dan's mother had always shared.

For another thing, Dan's father now seemed more anxious to do things with him and with his brothers. They had a picnic at Pushaw Lake with Aunt Meg and Uncle Linc, and there were other occasions that summer when Dan and sometimes Will went on such excursions with their father but without the others. Twice John took Dan to fish for trout in near-by brooks, showing him how to select a properly straight and not too heavy black alder pole, and how to attach to it a band from Mrs. McGaw's spinning wheel which Dan had at his father's instigation begged, with a bit of black linen thread at the end to attach the hook.

'For a trout has sharp eyes,' his father explained, 'and we have to try to fool him, make him think this worm has just dropped into his pool off the bank.' At the brookside his father made Dan crawl under low-growing hemlocks till he was near enough to lower his worm into the water. 'Now just let it lie on the bottom, Dan,' John advised. 'Wait till I tell you.'

Dan obediently waited, hardly breathing, till his father said: 'All right, lift your pole a little; and if you feel anything, give a jerk to set the hook and then haul out your trout.'

Dan obeyed, cautiously raising the heavy pole. He felt a heavy, twitching tug, and jerked with spasmodic energy; but the low boughs of the trees over his head stopped the pole's upward swing, and something almost frighteningly strong was yanking at the stiff pole. He crawled backward away from the brook, dragging the pole behind him, dragging thus ignominiously up over the low bank a tremendous trout, which thrashed and pounded on the ground till, abandoning his pole, he pounced upon it with both hands, gripping the cold, muscular body still full of vibrant strength, whooping with delight, and happiest of all when he saw the fine pride in his father's eyes.

But though they had many such fine days together, during that summer and fall after the picnic at Pushaw Lake, two unhappy things happened to Dan. For one, Aunt Meg came one day and told them she would be married. Dan did not know Captain Pawl, and the name meant nothing to him, but he was very much in love with Aunt Meg; and to think of losing her—he had no doubt that when she married she would go out of their lives forever—was terrible. She was so pretty and jolly and nice in every way, and he loved to be with her and to talk to her, particularly about his father. Sometimes when they were thus together her eyes would shine and he felt in watching her the same peace and content which he found in being with his father and mother in their happy hours. That she should now marry someone and go away to Searsport to live seemed to him terrible, and he grieved in a secret wretchedness. She guessed this, and she took him in her arms and told him he mustn't look so miserable; and he could not tell her what he really felt, so he tried to be very manly and told her he was all right, and she respected his reticence and said: 'There, of course you are!'

But even worse than Aunt Meg's approaching marriage was his father's decision to go into the woods to be away all winter. He took Dan to town with him one day, and they had dinner together like two men, at the Bangor House, and afterward he announced his plan, and he told Dan what he would be doing up-river, locating logging camps and seeing that they were well run. Dan said miserably: 'I wish I could go, too,' and his father said: 'I'll take you, some day. But this winter, son, you'll have to stay home and be the man of the family, take care of your mother and your brothers. Mother's going to be lonely with me gone, so she'll need all your love and thoughtfulness, and you must see to it that your brothers don't make her unhappy. It's a lot of responsibility for you, but I know you can handle it. I'm trusting you, son!'

So Dan swallowed hard, and promised to try, and soon afterward his father went away.

VII

That was a long and lonely winter. Dan and Will and Tommy went to school, and Dan's mother was very busy with other ladies in the sewing circle and the temperance societies of which she was a member and in church affairs. One rather terrible experience — in which nevertheless Dan came to feel a secret pride — was the church entertainment when the three boys were required by their mother to memorize and perform a 'dialogue' for the delectation of their elders. This dialogue had been written by Miss Merrill, their teacher; and their mother devised and she and Mrs. McGaw made their costumes. The dialogue was called, 'A Lump in the Side,' and the characters were three. Dan himself played the part of Bill Johnson, a mechanic. Tommy was 'Mr. Abbott, President of the Temperance Society,' and Will was the villain of the piece, 'The Landlord.'

Miss Merrill was tremendously pleased with her first dramatic effort, and she drilled the three boys tirelessly in their lines. When the great day came and their turn arrived, the improvised curtains were drawn back to reveal Dan, in rough clothes and a hat much too big for him, with a considerable bulge in the pocket of his shirt, alone upon the stage. He faced the pleased audience, his eyes shamedly avoiding every familiar countenance, and stiffly recited:

'*One year ago I was a miserable drunkard. One year ago today I signed the pledge, not only on paper but in my own heart; and I have kept it. What a change it has made! I am now a happy and prosperous man. Now that the year of my promise is up, shall I fall back into my old poverty and sin? No; I'll sign again. Ah! Here comes Mr. Abbott, the President of the Temperance Society; I'll ask him about it.*'

Dan realized as he finished that he had forgotten Miss Merrill's instructions to look, as he spoke these last lines, toward where Tommy, as Mr. Abbott, in a beaver hat and a long black coat cut down and made over from one of his father's, was waiting to make his entrance; but Tommy, even without that warning glance from Dan, picked up his cue. He marched stiffly up on the platform and in his character of Mr. Abbott said as rapidly as possible:

'*Good morning, William. I was on my way to your home, to speak to you about that pledge. You know we let you have your own way of signing. There is your written promise.*' He handed Dan a slip of paper. '*It will not bind you after today.*'

Dan reached for the paper and missed it, and it fluttered to the floor, slid off the edge of the platform and was irretrievably lost. Dan blushed to the ears and stared down at it hopelessly while he recited:

'*This little slip of paper has done great things for me. How well I remember when I wrote it.*' The bit of paper was beyond his reach, but he held up an imaginary slip with both hands, and pretended to read: '*"I William Johnson pledge myself to drink no more intoxicating drinks for one year."*'

Tommy demanded, all in one breath, so that it sounded like a single word: '*Are you not going to renew the pledge?*'

Dan was by this time determined to finish this ordeal as quickly as possible. He spoke almost as rapidly as Tommy. '*Well, I don't know but I will. I've done pretty well so far; will you let me sign it again my own way?*'

Tommy blurted: '*O yes, any way, so that you will not drink rum.*'

Dan, as Tommy spoke, remembering what he was supposed to do next, felt a sudden stark alarm. He looked appealingly at Miss Merrill in the front row, hoping for rescue, but she was pale with helpless dismay. The emergency which he faced was a real one. He was expected at this point to write out a new pledge, and a table and pen and paper should have been provided for the purpose; but Miss Merrill had forgotten these properties! She looked now so despairing that Dan was sorry for her, and in that moment of sympathy he rose to the occasion and proceeded magnificently to ad lib his lines.

'*I'll need a piece of paper. This will do,*' he said, and jumped down off the platform, recaptured the lost pledge, climbed back up to the platform again and spread the paper on the palm of his hand and pretended to write, while he went on with his lines:

'*"I, William Johnson, sign this pledge for nine hundred and ninety-nine years, and if living at the end of that time I intend to take out a lease for life." There, I think that'll do, Squire Abbott; but here comes my old Landlord.*' A murmur of approbation from the audience had applauded his composure under difficulties, and stimulated by that approval he was now master of himself. He remembered to look at Will, waiting in his part of the villainous Landlord to come on. 'He knows my time is up. See him eye me as a hawk does a chicken. Stand by, Mr. Abbott, you'll see game.'

When Will stumped up the steps to the platform, his appearance was so satisfactorily villainous that he was greeted with a gust of applause. His very garments were sinister, his hands were in his pockets, he swaggered ominously, and a tremendous black mustache of burnt cork almost covered his small countenance. While he waited his turn, he had perspired in nervous excitement, and the mustache had run a little at either side of his mouth. The effect was tremendous, and Tommy incontinently giggled; but Dan, approaching his big scene, did not even grin. He bent double as though with pain, pressing his hand against that bulging shirt pocket, and in a high falsetto expressive of the most intense agony he cried:

'O Landlord, I have such a lump on my side!'

Will grunted villainously. 'That's because you have stopped drinking; you won't live two years longer at this rate.'

'If I commence drinking,' Dan piteously begged, 'will the lump go away?'

'Yes; but if you don't, you'll have another just such a lump on the other side.'

'Do you think so, Landlord?'

'I know it,' Will assured him. 'You will have them on your arms, back, breast, and head; you will be covered all over with lumps.' He spoke with a careful precision, went on in hearty tones: 'Come, Bill, let's drink together; come over to the tavern; I've got some prime brandy there.'

'No, I can't, for I've signed the pledge again.'

'You haven't, though! Well, you are a fool!'

Dan said dolefully: 'Yes, the Squire coaxed me hard. I couldn't get off.'

'What a blockhead, to sign away your liberty.'

There was at this an embarrassing pause. Tommy had the next speech, but some stray fleck of dust, drifting through the air, had lodged in his nose, and it tickled and stung. He was rubbing his nose so hard that he forgot his lines till Dan nudged him. That brought him back to his immediate obligations, but at the same time it precipitated a volley of sneezes. His anxiety to say what he must say before the next sneeze could interrupt him increased the tempo of his utterances, so that he said — or exploded — something like this:

'Ha-chew! Let-me-tell-you-friend-what-liberty-he — Ha-chew! — has-signed-away-his-elbows-and-knees-are — Ha-ha-hachew!—not-at-liberty-as-they-were-his-head-and-feet-are-not-so-much-at-liberty-the— Ha-chew! — cold-wind-and-rain — Ha-chew! — have-no-liberty-to-enter-his-house-he-has-lost-the-liberty — Ha-chew! Ha-chew! Ha-ha-hachew! — to-lie-in-the-gutter-all-night-without-interruption-and-to-beathisfamilywhenhegoeshome. Ha-chew!'

He finished in an indistinguishable blur of words, but no one heard him, for even Miss Merrill joined in the peals of helpless laughter which swept the audience. Dan and Will ignored this disturbance, and their lips could be seen to move, even though no words at first were audible. Dan led off in this final interchange.

'Yes, thank Heaven; and I don't want such liberties restored.'

'Well, how long do you go this time?' Will raised his voice, trying to be heard.

'For nine hundred and ninety-nine years!' Dan bawled.

The audience began to quiet. 'You won't live a year!' Will said, above the diminishing sound of laughter, finding himself suddenly shouting in a reasonably complete silence, and hurriedly and guiltily lowering his voice again on the last word.

'Well, if I drink, you are sure the lump on my side will go away?' Dan demanded.

'Yes, in less than a week!'

Dan plunged with vast relief into his last lines. 'Well, I guess I won't drink; here's the lump.' He drew that bulge out of his pocket and revealed a handful of genuine bills which Jenny had provided for the occasion. 'There's a hundred dollars in it.' There was actually this amount in the roll, and Dan was so proud of this miraculous fact that his tone became increasingly impressive. 'And you say I'll have more such lumps if I don't drink, and that's what I want!'

The curtain, as he finished, was drawn hurriedly, and Miss Merrill came swiftly around from her seat to tell them — and particularly Dan — that they were wonderful. From beyond the curtain the storming applause confirmed her verdict. Now that the ordeal was over, Dan felt pleased. He guessed they had really been pretty good.

VIII

John Evered came home for Christmas, but this only made them miss him more when he went up-river again. Uncle Linc for some reason now seldom called at the house, and when he did he seemed changed, awkward and uncomfortable and almost shy. As spring began to come, Will caught the measles, and Tommy and Mat and finally Dan fell ill in turn. The other boys recovered and went to Searsport to visit Aunt Meg while Dan was still sick in bed; but he began to get better, and then one day his mother came home from town with shining eyes, somehow excited and tensely happy, and told Dan he was well enough to go to Searsport too; and in no time at all he was bundled into the carriage with Pat and Ruth and their children for the long drive down the river road, and Dan was still weak enough so that the happiness of going to see Aunt Meg made him cry, and young Pat jeered at him for crying like a baby, but Dan didn't care.

He had a wonderful time at Aunt Meg's. Captain Pawl was at home, and he and Aunt Meg took them for a two-day trip in a little sloop the Captain hired, down the western Bay and around Isle au Haut and home through Eggemoggin Reach; and they were allowed to steer and to help hoist the mainsail and jibs and to stow the sails neatly when they anchored for the night in a sheltered, solitary cove. Will decided that he would be a sailor when he grew up, but Dan, thinking of his father, was sure he himself would be a lumberman.

His father was much away that summer; but whenever he was at home, he was forever planning excursions to delight his sons. Then in October something happened, something involving Mattie Hanson, who had done their washing for a while. Dan did not at all understand what this was till young Pat Tierney enlightened him. Young Pat said his father was a nigger lover, and Dan fought him for that, and whipped him soundly, beating Pat into the ground and pounding him till Pat squalled for mercy; but there was for Dan no satisfaction in that victory because he knew quite well that something was terribly wrong in his father's world. So a day or two later he asked Pat for more information and got it, so explicitly that he was sick at his stomach.

'My father wouldn't do that!' he cried.

Pat jeered at him. 'Well, I guess he would. Everybody does.'

'My father doesn't!'

'Your father does and your mother does too!'

Dan, choking with rage and shame, cried: 'You're a dirty old liar!'

'Yah!' Pat cried. 'You're a baby! Don't know anything! They had to do it before you were born, and before Will was born, and Tommy, and Mat! Four times! They did too!'

Dan, helpless in his own ignorance, was nevertheless strong in his faith in his father and his mother; so he thrashed young Pat again, and when old Pat intervened and demanded to know what the matter was, Dan told him through sobs of hurt rage; and old Pat marched his son indoors by the ear, and young Pat's squeals of anguish for a while came muffled from one of the empty stalls.

Through the days when the case was being tried, Dan and the other boys stayed home from school, and Dan suffered torments of fear — fear of the unknown; but he was happy afteward in the happiness of his father and Aunt Meg and Judge Saladine. The only shadow on his happiness was his secret feeling that his mother did not share it, and his vague understanding that in connection with the trial Uncle Linc had done something for which he would not be forgiven. Uncle Linc came no longer to the house, and when the following summer Dan asked where he had gone, his father could only say:

'I don't know, Dan. He went away.'

IX

At the time of the big flood, Dan's father was up-river overseeing the drive. As the danger of high water became obvious to everyone, Dan begged his mother to take him to see the ice jam which began to fill the river from Old Town down; but she would not, and she forbade him to go near the river. During the week of suspense before the high water hit Bangor, she stayed much of the time in her room, appearing only for meals, moving stiffly about the house, declining Mrs. McGaw's offers of small attentions.

Saturday morning, Mrs. McGaw went to Brewer to see her daughter. This was her usual custom; but when Pat came home, he reported that the crisis of the flood was near. 'It won't be safe to go across the bridge to fetch Mrs. McGaw home, ma'am,' he said. 'The bridge might go out while I was on the other side.'

'Then don't risk it,' she agreed. 'Let her stay till the danger is past.'

Dan cried: 'Oh, mama, can't we please go watch and see what happens? Please, mama! Pat can take care of us!'

His mother hesitated. Her lips were white, and it was clear that she felt badly; but she said at last: 'Why, yes, Dan, I think you may. All of you.' They shouted with delight and she added: 'If Pat will take care of you.'

'To be sure I will, ma'am,' Pat promised. 'And it would be a pity for them not to see it, at that, for a rare sight it is.'

'Only, be home by dark,' she warned them, and Pat promised, and they all trooped down into town to watch the frantic efforts of those who along the riverfront worked to move lumber piles which a further rise of water might wash away. Pat held fast to Will and Tommy all the time, and Dan held Mat's hand, and they clung to safe vantages, and came home at dark, so tired that even Dan was ready enough to go to bed right after supper.

They missed the climax of the flood, which befell during that night; for not even the church bells woke them. Jenny did not come down to breakfast in the morning; and Ruth said she had left word that she might sleep late, might even stay abed all day and was on no account to be disturbed. Assuming her consent, Dan and the other boys, with Pat dutifully shepherding them, roamed the town to see the damage done by the now receding waters, to exclaim at the marks which showed that the flood had at one stage been seven feet deep in the stores on West Market Place, to hear how the Drew Block on Kenduskeag Bridge had been swung around cock-billed and then miraculously set squarely on its foundations again. Dan thrilled to the story of how when the flood invaded the post office, General Miller hurried the clerks up the stairs to safety, but one of them lingered below and the General shouted.

'Hey, Calvin, what the hell you doing?'

The lagging clerk answered cheerfully: 'Coming right up. I had to wait to stamp these paid letters!'

They saw in the lower streets huge ice blocks, masses twenty feet square, cast high and dry and left there to obstruct the highways till they melted away; and vessels building on the ways had been crushed or buried under mud and miscellaneous débris; and they came home at dusk with many a tale to tell. But Ruth said their mother was still asleep.

'Or anyways, she hasn't rung for me all day,' she said, 'and you're not to go pestering her. Keep quiet too, and let her rest if she can. I've had sick headaches myself and I know what they can do to you.'

So their reports of what they had seen had to wait till next morning when Dan went to listen at her door and she heard him and called him in. She was still in bed, and she looked so pale and weak and small that his eyes widened with concern.

'Are you sick, mother?' he asked huskily.

'A little, Dan,' she confessed. 'But I'll soon be all right now.' She added: 'The worst was Saturday night.' There was an almost mischievous twinkle in her eyes. 'I had something on my stomach that was bothering me, but I got rid of it, so I'll be better soon.' She told him to bid Ruth bring her breakfast. 'I'll need another day or two in bed,' she said. 'I get over these attacks quickly, just by resting, so don't you worry, Dan.'

She must have been pretty sick, Dan decided, for she stayed in bed all that week; and once, outside her door, Dan heard her crying in such a desperate and terrible way that he dared not even go in to comfort her. But most of the time she was cheerful, and he and the other boys spent long hours with her, telling her all about the flood.

They did not tell her that Pat and Ruth thought someone had broken into the house Sunday night, because there were muddy footprints in the hall and on the stairs Monday morning; and also Pat had found where a cart had left the road below the house, cutting deep ruts and leaving hoof marks in the lawn. But nothing, so far as they could see, had been stolen out of the house; so at Ruth's insistence they protected their mother from any alarm by telling her nothing at all till she was about again.

When they did tell her, she said calmly that they must have imagined these things. She suggested that it might have been Dan's shoes which tracked the hall and stairs and that the horse which wandered on the lawn was probably a stray. Dan saw that Pat Tierney did not accept these explanations, receiving them in silence, but Pat did not argue the point with her.

Before John came home she warned them all to say nothing to him of these matters.

'And don't tell your father I was sick,' she said. 'It would worry him so.'

2

For months after the great flood, the wounds it had inflicted on the city still left their scars. The most conspicuous was the broken bridge. The superstructure had floated down-river as far as Bucksport where it was secured; but it would be a year before the bridge was rebuilt, and Mrs. McGaw had to go back and forth to her daughter's home by the ferry. When Dan's father returned, a fortnight after the flood, Dan and Will persuaded him to take them down to Bucksport to see the wreckage of the bridge at anchor there; and they in turn showed him all the ravage nearer home, excitedly describing the great event, delighted when he exclaimed in wonder and amazement. They were as proud of that flood as though it had been their own production; and John was satisfyingly impressed by all they showed him.

That summer they made a sort of family pilgrimage — all six of them — to see Grandmother Evered in Freeport. Jenny had not wished to make the trip with them, and Dan heard her urge John to go and take the boys and leave her at home; but she was somehow persuaded, and once they were on the Portland steamer she seemed to have as good a time as anyone. Dan's grandmother had several times come to visit them in Bangor, until as she grew older travel became burdensome; and Dan remembered her from these visits as a quiet little old woman with merry twinkling eyes, but who never had much to say. He had sometimes suspected that she was a little shy and afraid in their big house with the servants to wait on her and the roaring city so near; but at her own home on this visit she was charming, mistress of herself and of all about her, making them welcome in every way, showing the boys old treasured things that had belonged to their grandfather or their father, telling them hilarious tales of their father's boyhood, telling them about her other sons. She and Jenny were happy together, too; and Dan's mother seemed during the visit now to love John as she used to. Dan himself felt that there was something mysteriously pleasing in the fact that although at home his father and mother had rooms of their own, here they shared the same bed; and his mother was rosy and bright all the time, and sometimes in ways Dan could not understand she teased his father, with twinkling eyes and words that did not seem to mean quite what they said. Yet Dan never felt that fine warming happiness in them which he had used to feel, and once he thought his mother was frightened and faintly desperate and unhappy, and he wished he knew how to comfort her.

Before they left for home, Grandmother Evered gave each of the boys a ring. 'I gave a ring to each of my own sons when they went away,' she explained, 'to remind them.' Dan asked what the ring was to remind them of, and she told him: 'To remind them that wherever they might go they were still a part of our family, and that we were all sharing our common strength and were stronger because of it. You see a ring is strong, until there is a break in it. After it is broken, the rest of it is weaker because of that break.'

Jenny told her: 'In our family it is John whose strength we all share.' And she said, as though she had only just remembered this: 'When we built our house, I persuaded John to use a huge oak timber for the ridgepole, the roof tree; and I've always thought of that and John together. He's the rooftree of our house, the keystone of our arch. We all lean on him and are strong for doing so.'

Dan had seen that huge timber running the length of their attic home; but he had never heard this, and he found it deeply moving and beautiful. He saw Grandmother Evered's eyes fill with pride.

'My John's a fine man,' she assented.

Jenny smiled, and said in that tone she always used when she was teasing John: 'Yes, and so awfully strong!' Dan was glad his father was not there to hear, for he knew her teasing during this visit had disturbed him.

When they set out for the return journey, the gaiety and tenderness which she had worn at Grandmother's fell away from her and she looked tired and sad; and on the steamer an hour after they sailed, Dan went down to her cabin to summon her to join them on deck and found her crying desperately, thrown across the bunk, sobbing aloud. He was frightened and tried to comfort her; but without lifting her head she pleaded in a choking passion:

'Go away! Oh, for God's sake, go away!'

He felt like crying himself. On deck he drew his father aside and told him about her tears; and he saw John's lips whiten. Then his father went below and later he and Jenny came on deck together and she was again serene.

That was Dan's only visit to his grandmother, although his father still went to see her every two or three months as he always had. When she died a few years later, Dan was surprised to find how sorry he felt, and how deeply he shared his father's quiet grief.

They took another trip that summer, down to Searsport to picnic on the shore and eat clams and lobsters with Aunt Meg and Captain Pawl, and Dan had an undefined impression that there was something queer in Aunt Meg's appearance; but he did not at the time connect this with the fact that toward the end of summer she had a baby, a girl named Elizabeth. The birth of Aunt Meg's baby seemed to Dan to write a finish to the brightest chapter in his life. He had loved her for years, and even after her marriage, the fact that Captain Pawl was years older than she, and bald besides, somehow made her seem younger and lovelier than ever, and still remotely attainable. But when now he heard about the baby, she receded forever beyond his reach. He thought of himself as nobly enduring an irreparable loss and wore for a few days an air of sad detachment which provoked impatient questions from his brothers, who accused him of putting on airs.

II

In October, Dan discovered that his career as an entertainer was not, as he had hoped, ended. His composure in a trying hour during the rendition of that famous dialogue had won him a reputation which he was now required to sustain. The first law regulating the sale of liquor in Maine had passed at last; and the Friends of Temperance, seeking to consolidate their gains and to prepare for new conquests, proposed to organize a 'concert' which should both win converts and earn money for the cause. For that occasion, Dan under his mother's calm insistence was required to memorize a lengthy speech, an address originally delivered — as the title-page of the printed copy read — in 'The Brick Meeting House in Danvers, before the Society in that town for Suppressing Intemperance and Other Vices and for Promoting Temperance and General Morality,' by a man named George Osgood. Those tremendous packages of temperance tracts sent by Neal Dow, which after Uncle Linc's disappearance continued to arrive addressed to him, had been turned over to Dan's father; and among them Dan's mother discovered scores of copies of Mr. Osgood's address, and thought it wonderful.

She drilled Dan painstakingly in its delivery, teaching him what seemed to her appropriate gestures. Mr. Osgood had begun in the most pessimistic vein, announcing that: *'Vice has been a prominent trait in the human character from the first history we have of man down to the present time.'* Dan's mother taught him to deliver these gloomy words in slow and measured tones; and some of the sentences and paragraphs which followed would remain all his life deep graven in his mind. The words, *'unused to declamation in public it is with no small degree of diffidence that I attempt it on a subject that requires so much delicacy in its management,'* he was trained to speak with a proper and becoming humility; but when he recited the effects of intemperance, it was in ringing tones. *'The use of ardent spirits weakens the strength of a nation. In some it impairs, in others totally obliterates, religion in the heart. It is an insidious but sure poison, destructive of the life of those who indulge in its use.'* There followed an engrossingly detailed discussion of the results on the stomach of such indulgence, and a suggestion for a well-balanced diet free from alcohol. A kind word was spoken for tea and coffee. *'It is being too rigid to deprive the community of these dainties.'* Then came a pathological explanation of the way in which ardent spirits produce disease; an analysis of the economic ills to which indulgence leads; and a long passage describing the *'secret sighs and silent tears'* of the family of the afflicted.

Dan found a delicious pleasure in reciting, in a voice full of the most piercing sweetness, the paragraph which began: *'It always affords pleasure to an ingenuous mind to dwell on those traits of the female character that adorn and add loveliness to their charms. We admire that modesty of deportment, that delicacy of sentiment and that purity of thought that characterize most of the fair sex.'* He always thought of Aunt Meg when he launched on this passage, and to remember her inspired in him a laudable eloquence.

He memorized this address, and the day came when he found himself declaiming the rolling periods to an appreciative audience which included a large number of boys of his own age or a little older. The occasion was a meeting called to organize the Cadets, a junior order designed to attract those still too young to be members of the Sons and Daughters of Temperance. Dan's mother was an instigator of this enterprise; and he, by virtue of his ability to stand on his feet and face an audience without losing the power of speech, became one of the leading spirits in the organization. As he approached his 'teens he took it with some seriousness.

This was partly because he thus found release from the increasing unhappiness of his life at home. There was no longer on Jenny's part — so far as her private life was concerned — any pretense of affection for Dan's father. Publicly she held toward him a loyal, proud and happy manner, moving graciously beside him; and to anyone who saw her thus — Dan, watching her, often wondered how she could be so different from her normal self — she and John would have seemed the pattern of an affectionate and self-respecting couple. But at home when she spoke to Dan's father, her low, quiet tones more often than not were edged and stinging.

She had a trick of showing young Pat Tierney an affection which Dan — who roundly hated him — could not understand; nor could he understand why this demonstrativeness on her part disturbed his father, but he knew this was true. One Sunday afternoon he and his father were inspecting the garden, appreciating the rich bloom everywhere; and she came out to join them, moving toward them down the lawn. Then Will raced around the corner of the house with young Pat on his heels in a game of tag, the other children trooping after them; and Dan's mother called affectionately:

'Oh, Pat! Come here. I haven't seen you all day!'

So Pat gave over the pursuit and came to her, and she put her arm around his shoulders and walked with him thus toward Dan and his father. But Pat wished to escape. 'I'm "It," Mrs. Evered,' he said. 'I've got to catch Will.'

She smiled and kissed him. 'All right, run along.' He raced away and she said, looking toward her husband: 'He's such a dear boy, John. I think he has all his father's sweetness, don't you?'

Dan had never thought of old Pat as sweet! In fact, for months now Pat had been dour and brooding, as though there were some unhappy secret in his mind; so Dan thought her remark rather silly. Also, he felt anger like actual heat in his father as John said quietly:

'He seems to me a malicious, rather unpleasant, definitely dishonest little boy.'

'Mercy!' She laughed in a tinkling way. 'Malicious! Dishonest! Well, perhaps he is; but don't women have to learn to overlook such qualities?' The words in themselves were nothing, yet her tone made them a reproach; and Dan was not surprised that his father turned away. When he was gone, Dan protested in sore distress:

'Mother, what makes you so mean to father?'

She smiled at him wistfully. 'Do you feel that I am, Dan?'

'Yes, I do,' he said bravely. 'He's unhappy just about all the time when he's at home. I guess that's why he goes away so much.'

'I've tried to make his home attractive to your father, Dan,' she said in still tones. 'But he finds happiness elsewhere — in what strange places I don't always know.'

For some reason beyond his own understanding, that made him angry to the point of tears. 'He does not!' he blurted. 'He doesn't either!'

She said gently: 'I hope you can always keep your faith in him, Dan. I trusted him, too, for years.' She walked slowly away across the lawn, her head bowed, sadness in the very line of her shoulders. and Dan looked after her in an angry helplessness.

III

Dan was ten years old at the time of the flood. The golden days of '49 ushered in his 'teens. California was far away, but gold was a magic word, and it ran on every tongue for weeks and then for months. From Bangor scores of men set out for California to make their fortunes. The Penobscot Mining and Trading Company, organized one night at the Bangor House, enlisted a hundred and twenty members, each contributing four hundred dollars to a general fund; and Pat Tierney caught the fever and added his name to the roll. They chartered Captain Pawl's Lucy brig to carry them around the Horn to California, and Captain Pawl himself would command her on that voyage.

When Pat came to John Evered to announce his decision to go with the others, John tried to dissuade him; and Dan, listening to their talk together, seeing Pat's stubborn determination which outran his father's best persuasions, remembered the old Irishman's sombre bearing in these three years since the flood, and thought Pat was glad to get away from some secret unhappiness which beset him here, was seizing this chance to escape.

John tried to laugh the Irishman out of his intent. 'You've said yourself you weren't meant to be a rich man, Pat!' he reminded the other. 'You're comfortable here, well fixed, and nothing to worry about. You don't want to go back to pick and shovel work again!'

But Pat would not be dissuaded. He had made his plans in detail before he spoke to John. Ruth and the children would go to live with her widower brother on his farm in Waldoboro. 'I've saved my money, Mr. Evered,' he said, 'and she'll have all she needs. Her brother wants her, him with no woman to his name and two young ones, and she'll get along — till I come back with my pockets full of gold, to be sure!'

There was at his own word a twinkle in his eyes, as though he laughed at himself; but Dan suddenly knew Pat never would come back at all.

His mother said the same thing when she heard Pat's decision. 'He's tired of Ruth, that's the fact of it.' She added: 'Men do grow tired of their wives, you know, John.'

Dan sensed the malice in her word, but he thought it more likely that Ruth was tired of Pat. It was years since he had seen her show Pat any tenderness or outward affection, and her shrewish tongue grew sharper all the time.

'I don't think it's that,' Dan's father dissented. 'I'm sure it's not. There's something on Pat's mind, something that distresses him. I've noticed it before.' And he said thoughtfully: 'Whatever it is, it developed suddenly. He's never been the same, never at ease with me, since the flood three years ago. It's as though he wanted to tell me something and couldn't bring himself to do so. In fact, I've asked him what the trouble was, but he always denied there was anything at all.'

Dan had a sharp impression that his mother was frightened. She said quickly: 'If he's dissatisfied, by all means let him go.'

'I hate to. I like the old man — and if he's troubled about something I'd like to help him.'

'Nonsense,' she insisted. 'He's caught the gold fever, that's all. Let him go!'

In the end Pat had his way. He took Ruth and the children to Waldoboro a few days before his departure; and on the day the Lucy brig would sail from Searsport they all went down to see her depart and to stay the night with Aunt Meg. Beth, Meg's daughter, who had been born the summer of the flood, was now three years old, and on this occasion she took an immediate fancy for Dan, and he for her. She followed him everywhere, and she was in his arms on the wharf when the brig's lines were loosed.

In that last moment, Meg clung to Captain Pawl, whispering loving farewells; and old Mrs. Pawl, crippled with rheumatism, sat in the big chair in which she had been carried down from the house and with stony composure watched her son sail away. They stayed on the wharf till the brig was under full sail, and then went back to the house, since from the front stoop they could still see her work down the Bay. Old Mrs. Pawl in her chair on the walk below the stoop watched the departing vessel with unwinking eyes; and Meg brought a shawl to draw around her shoulders and said comfortingly:

'There, mother! Cap'n Pawl has a fine breeze to clear the Bay, hasn't he!'

Dan was near Meg as he liked to be, little Beth clinging possessively to his hand. Old Mrs. Pawl said quietly, her eyes never leaving the distant vessel: 'I've always known there'd be one time he'd sail away and I'd never see him again. This is the time, Meg.'

'Now, mother, you're just fine!' Meg tenderly protested. 'And he'll be back before you know it. He's not going to stay in the gold fields, you know. The sea's his place. He'll stick to it; and he'll come safely home.'

'Aye,' the old woman agreed. 'He'll come home to you, my dear; but I'll not be here.' She smiled a little, and patted Meg's hand, and Dan marked how old and dry her hand was, the knuckles swollen, the dark veins showing, while Meg's hand was so slender and soft and smooth. 'But I know I'll never see him again, and so does he. Don't distress yourself, Meg. We've said our good-byes.'

Dan was a little frightened by her words, but he felt in her a deep peace curiously reassuring; and he saw that she was not afraid.

She died, in fact, in January of the winter following; died quietly in her sleep, and Dan heard his father tell his mother: 'Meg found her in the morning — as though she had known she was going —

lying straight and all composed, with her crossed hands on her breast.'

Dan felt a mystic sweetness in that, but his mother said quietly: 'I suppose you'll hurry down to Searsport to comfort Meg.'

His father looked at her in a still fashion, not speaking; but they all went down for old Mrs. Pawl's funeral, and Jenny was serene and strong, and Aunt Meg drew strength from her.

'I'm scared, Jenny,' Dan heard her say. 'She knew she was going to die before Cap'n Pawl came home, and now I'm worried about him.'

Jenny said reassuringly: 'Don't be worried, Meg dear.' Dan sometimes thought that his mother did not like Aunt Meg, but certainly no one could have guessed it from her manner now, just as no one could guess, seeing her and his father together, that she was anything but a devoted wife. 'He'll come home one day safe and sound, Meg. Never fear.'

So Aunt Meg was comforted; but Captain Pawl never did come home again, nor any word of him, nor of the Bangor men — Pat and the others — who sailed aboard the brig. The Lucy had been sighted off the east coast of South America, and she was in good order then; but no one ever saw her on the Pacific side. There were months of waiting, months of fading hope before at last it came to be accepted that she had somehow met disaster in her attempt to round the Horn, crashing on some hidden ledge, smashing into a floating berg, dismasted and swept under in some gale, or perhaps carried far southward to be lost forever in Antarctic ice. She was last sighted in late December, and there were some who thought, with a sense of dark, unseen forces in the world, that perhaps old Mrs. Pawl and her son had died at the same hour, their spirits ten thousand miles apart leaving their bodies for a swift and eternal reunion; but no one ever knew. Margaret, after a year or two of waiting had killed the last hope of her husband's return, sold the Searsport house and came back to Bangor, she and Beth, to live with her father again. This meant that Dan saw them often, and Beth was rapturously fond of him, watching him with a shy pleasure whenever he was near.

IV

There were in the world during these years so many great events that the far-off death of Captain Pawl did not greatly move Dan. He was proud of his place in the Cadets, and when Neal Dow himself came to Bangor to speak to a tremendous gathering in a grove out at the end of Broadway, he lodged at their house, and Dan felt the driving force in the man and was hypnotized by his energy and zeal. Neal Dow was at this time approaching his hour of triumph. The prohibitory legislation which he himself had drafted was presently to be submitted to the Legislature. 'It may fail this year,' he told Jenny. Dan was near, proud that he was himself in a small way one of the crusaders whom this man commanded and inspired. 'But if it fails now, another year will surely bring success. The time will come when no political party can survive in Maine unless it accepts prohibition as the settled policy of the state.'

'We want so to help,' Dan's mother told him.

'The heart and soul of the movement are the church members engaged in it,' the great man assured her. 'The liquor traffic exists only by the sufferance of the churches. Seek to win your whole congregation to the work. The problem is simple. There is the grogshop. When you say "go" and when your husbands vote "go," it will go.'

Dan was breathless with wonder at the man, and Neal Dow went on: 'Victory is near, but with victory our most dangerous hour will strike; for when the law is passed, it must be enforced.' He said he himself would be a candidate for Mayor of Portland on the platform of enforcement. 'It will be a hard fight at first,' he predicted. 'But a good one, a fight worth winning.' His nostrils dilated, so that Dan thought of a horse, excited and prancing. 'We will win,' he said.

Dan carried for a long time in his heart the memory of Neal Dow, feeling himself ennobled by that contact. He confided this to his father. John at the time of Neal Dow's visit was not at home, having gone to Ellsworth to consult Colonel Black, who as he grew older began to be infirm and his sight to fail so that he seldom came to Bangor. Dan's father agreed with him that Neal Dow was a great man.

'And it's a good thing to know great men, and to admire them, Dan,' he said. 'To recognize and to be moved by greatness in others is one way to become fine and strong ourselves.'

These two could talk more frankly now as Dan grew older, and between them an increasingly strong bond was developing. John, if he were to be away, always reminded Dan that he was during these absences the head of the family, bound to be helpful to his mother in every way; and Dan tried to carry out these instructions. He had sometimes to check incipient rebellion in Will and Tom. While Dan and Mat were as much like their own father in disposition as they were like Tim Hager in stature and outward appearance, the other two were of a swifter temper and of a quick and impatient mind. They had when they chose endearing qualities which made Dan think of his mother, who when she would could be so altogether lovable; but by the same token, they were more often at odds with her, quicker to argue, quicker to resent her directions and commands. Dan more than once had to interfere to end these discords, protecting her.

v

Jenny's work in the temperance cause did not use up all her energy. When the cholera epidemic hit Bangor — a hundred and sixty people died before the terror passed — she threw herself tirelessly into the effort to do everything possible for the sick and dying. Marshal Farnham, as directing head of the forces which kept order in the town, organized not only the doctors but as many ladies as would serve to bring what comfort was possible to the sick and dying, and Dan's mother and Aunt Meg worked together among these volunteers.

It was during this epidemic of the cholera that Will — he was just thirteen — told Dan one day that when he grew up he intended to become a doctor. This ambition was a secret between the two boys for years, although Will himself confided in Doctor Mason, who had attended them through their many youthful ailments; and he told Dan he had done so.

'He's going to let me come and see him and he's going to teach me things,' he said happily. 'He says doctors don't really know very much. He says he used to know a lot about curing people, but now he knows he didn't really know anything. He says most people when they're sick just get well anyway, and he says a doctor can help them mostly just by keeping them from being scared. He says people are always scared when they're sick; but if they send for a doctor and he comes and they see he's not worried about them, they get over being scared, and then they get well.'

Will in the years that followed was forever repeating to Dan the things Doctor Mason told him, and the Doctor's every word remained firmly imprinted on his youthful mind. Tom and young Mat were not so quick to decide on what they wished to do, but as he came into his 'teens Tom began to spend much time along the waterfront, watching the vessels loading there. The steady growth of the lumber business, since all the lumber was shipped by water — Bangor had no rail connection with Portland and the outer world till 1855 — meant that during the ice-free months the river was crowded, and the harbor master had a harrowing time finding berths for new arrivals. Schooners and brigs came loaded with coal and departed with lumber stowed in their holds and piled on every clear foot of deck space. Lime, cement, iron, salt, grain — everything the city had to import arrived by water; and there was always a cargo of lumber ready so that no vessel, large or small, had to leave Bangor empty. Hay too was shipped out by water, with deck loads, as high as the handling of the sails would permit, bulging out over the rails. There were times when craft waiting to load filled the river so completely that an agile boy could cross to the Brewer shore, just below the bridge, by leaping or swinging from one vessel to another or by using the rafts of sawed lumber lying alongside to be loaded as stepping stones upon the way.

In this fine rich confusion of shouting men, creaking yards and complaining cables, Tom spent long summer days, loving the smell of sawed pine and of the great piles of cedar shingles and of tar, loving the voices of the men and the aroma of far places and of forgotten cargoes which each vessel brought with it; and he told Dan one day that when he grew up he wanted to go to sea. The younger boys were always apt to confide in Dan. He had a strength beyond his years, developed by the fact that his father so often impressed upon him the necessity for accepting responsibility; and they found in him a readiness to listen without dissent or protest and a capacity for keeping their secrets which they early learned to value.

As for Dan himself, when he was sixteen he worked during the early summer at the sorting boom up-river above Old Town, where the great logs were held as the drive came down till they covered every inch of the water for miles. The whole drive was handled by a single organization, which John had been instrumental in organizing years before, and to which every operator along the river contributed; so the logs in the boom had many owners, and each bore a distinguishing mark, usually of a sort which could be easily made with an axe. There were diamonds, double darts, crow's feet, anchors, girdles — and these and other marks appeared not only singly but in many combinations. It was the business of the boom crew to sort logs by ownership, securing each operator's logs in rafts held together by warps and wedges, ready to be moved down-river to the mills.

Dan loved the work, the long days on the water with no footing except the huge logs, some of them so tremendous that his weight seemed to have no effect on them; and since he was already over six feet tall and with strength to match his size, he held his own with the men among whom he worked. He came home when the logs were all sorted toughened and hardened, with calloused hands and shoulders which seemed inches broader than they had been in the spring. His father was not at home on the day of his return, had gone to Ellsworth on some business matter, and when he arrived at the house Will and Tom and Mat were away upon their own concerns; so he and his mother had an hour alone. He had not known how much these weeks had changed him till he saw himself through her eyes — and through her words. When they met she looked at him for a moment as though he were a stranger.

'Why, Dan!' she cried, almost breathlessly. 'You're not my little boy any more. You're a grown man!' She laughed in a rich, husky fashion entirely unlike her usual laughter. 'You've grown so much that sleeves are too short, Dan.'

He colored with embarrassed pleasure, and she stood on tiptoe, pulling his head down to kiss him, making him sit in the great chair, perching on his knee, rumpling his dark shock of hair. 'My, my, darling!' she said teasingly. 'What a lot of feminine hearts will turn topsy-turvy when they see you!' And she added: 'Why, I feel as if I had a new sweetheart myself!'

'Well, you have! I guess you're the only sweetheart I want for a few years yet,' he told her. He had forgotten how beautiful this mother of his could be. Just now it was easy to forget that she was anything but a lovely girl smiling on his knee, waiting to be kissed.

She asked curiously: 'Haven't you really anyone at all?'

'Just you and Beth!'

She laughed. 'Beth's cunning, isn't she. But you ought to have a real grown-up someone. I know the men you worked with all had, even if it was only in the grogshops at Old Town. Or here in Bangor.'

He flushed uncomfortably. 'I guess so.'

'You must have seen some of them in Old Town,' she insisted, watching him curiously. He nodded, and she kissed him quickly. 'There, dear! You know, you're a sweet boy.' Her head tipped prettily on one side and she said: 'I'm not sure you're not just about the sweetest boy I ever saw! It makes me feel like a girl again, just to see you.'

'You look like one,' he assured her. 'I've never seen anybody that could match you — and Aunt Meg. You're both just about as pretty as anyone can be.'

Her eyes darkened as a sunny hillside is darkened by a passing cloud. 'You think Aunt Meg's lovely?'

'Yes.' He grinned at himself. 'I've always been sort of in love with her, you know, since I was little.'

For a moment she did not speak, and her eyes were sombre. 'You're like your father,' she said then, in a low tone, in that way which always made him mysteriously uncomfortable. 'He's always — liked her, too, since long before we were married.' Then she laughed. 'I'm glad you didn't like any of the tavern girls, Dan. But — weren't they pretty too?'

'Gosh, no!' he told her. 'I was always sort of sorry for them.'

Her face suddenly set in lines of angry pain. 'You men!' she exclaimed. 'You're always so high and mighty, sorry for every woman who tries too hard to please you!' She rose from his knee, moving her arms in a nervous way as though to forget some strange hurt. 'I don't want anyone to be sorry for me!' she said in low-voiced, resentful protest. 'I won't have anyone sorry for me!'

VI

Next morning, John — Dan was now by an inch the taller of the two — took him to his office, as he was apt to do when some decision was to be considered. 'I've been talking to Miss Merrill, Dan,' he began. The boys all attended Miss Merrill's school. 'She says you're a fine student — and she says you should go to college. You know I went to Harvard College. Would you like to go?'

Dan had never foreseen this possibility. He had a natural aptitude for study, his work had never seemed to him hard, and he knew Miss Merrill ranked him highly; but this prospect at first alarmed him. 'I don't know, father,' he admitted. 'I've always kind of thought I wanted to be in the lumber business when I grow up, and — I liked working at the boom.'

His father smiled with pleasure. 'Well, college needn't interfere with that,' he reminded Dan. 'I went to Harvard, you know.' He added: 'And I'm glad you feel that way. We'll make a team. I'm about ready to start in for myself.' He leaned back in his chair. 'But the lumber business is changing, son. The big pine is being cut off pretty fast. A lot of it has been culled out already.'

He talked quietly, and Dan listened almost without interruption while the older man went on, as though he were thinking aloud.

'Up to ten years ago, the logs rafted up at the boom where you worked this summer averaged about three hundred and fifty board feet to the log,' he said. 'This year the average size was under two hundred feet for the first time. For five years now, there has been more and more spruce cut. In another ten years you'll see more spruce than pine in the river.' He looked at his son. 'You know Mr. Hersey?'

'I just know who he is. I've seen him.'

'He tells me he's thinking of buying some western land, in Michigan and Minnesota. He believes lumbering here is near its peak, about ready to start down grade. He says anyone who bothers with spruce is crazy. But there'll be virgin spruce on the mountains up-river after the pine is gone. It's harder to move, but we'll find ways to get it to the water.

'And there are men enough who see a big future here. General Veazie's mills will be just as profitable sawing spruce as pine.' He chuckled. 'There's a great man, a great businessman, Dan. You know he's thinking of getting the upper part of Ward Seven set off as a town, to be named after him. He's asking the Legislature to do it next winter. He'll have his own town — own most of it, and own just about all the business in it — and he can run it the way he wants to, levy his own taxes and collect them too. He'll run it the way he used to run the boom. You know, he was the whole corporation, held meetings all alone at his house, voted himself in as President and Clerk and the Board of Directors. Of course he sold out to Mr. Pingree five years ago; but he could afford to. He's made his money out of mills and the boom and the dam at Chesuncook — that paid him close to eighty per cent a year from the first. And of course he's in the banking business, too.

'Rufe Dwinel's another who's not ready to quit.' John smiled again. 'The trouble is, Rufe would rather fight than 'tend to business. Like the Telos War. But he's one of the biggest operators on the river.

'And Colonel Black says Maine timber lands have never yet brought what they're really worth. He's in a position to know. Outside of the Bingham interests, he's a tremendous operator on his own account, not only cutting lumber and milling it, but shipping it too, and usually in his own vessels, vessels he's built. He worked up markets years ago in every port along the coast; not only Boston, but Taunton and New Bedford and Nantucket. Now most of his lumber goes to Boston. He'll ship over four million feet to Boston this year, and he's beginning to ship to Brett and Vose in New York.'

'His own lumber?' Dan asked.

'Yes. You see, he had the same arrangement with the Bingham interests that I have with him; a salary plus the right to buy stumpage cheap. He's been selling off the Penobscot Million right along. Most of the Bingham land up-river is in other hands now. His personal operations are to the eastward. And of course George is a keen business man, too.' He smiled. 'Colonel Black sent George one day to see about a mill he had heard was for sale, and at noon he asked George about it and George had bought it for himself!

'I don't think George and I would pull together. The Colonel's an old man now. Mrs. Black died last fall, you know. I don't think he'll live long. When he dies — or maybe before — I'll go in for myself. I've sold some of my stumpage rights from time to time, bought some land with the proceeds. It's a long way up-river, but it's easier to take supplies and teams that far now, going by road to Moosehead and up the lake by steamer and across the new Moosehead railroad to the river. And when the time comes I'll cut my pine myself.' He looked at Dan, and Dan guessed what was coming, watching this man whom he loved so proudly, seeing through his father's eyes the greatness of these enterprises. 'Maybe I'll take you four boys into the woods with me, for one winter anyway, if mother thinks she can spare you. Would you like that?'

'Yes, sir.' Dan's throat was for some reason full. He wetted his lips. 'Yes, I would,' he said.

John considered his son for a moment. He said: 'I haven't seen as much of any of you, these last few years, as I wish I had; don't know any of you as well as I'd like to. By the way, Doctor Mason tells me Will wants to be a doctor.'

Dan said with a shy discretion: 'I guess you'd better talk to Will about that, father, see what he says.'

'I need to get better acquainted with all of you,' John repeated. 'But things have been developing so fast these last few years that I've been kept busy with business, other people's business.' He smiled. 'It's about time I began to 'tend to my own.' He returned to the point. 'Do you want to go to college, son?'

'Well — do you want me to?'

'Only if you want to. But — yes, I think it would be a good thing.'

'Why, then — I'll go,' Dan agreed. 'I guess I'd like to.'

His father nodded. 'Good!' he said. He hesitated, smiled in a way which made Dan love him. 'It will be your first time away from home, Dan.' There was suddenly something diffident about this big man. 'You'll run into things you haven't encountered before.' Dan began to guess what was in the other's mind before his father suggested: 'Have you — any questions you want to ask me, son? Is there anything you want to know?'

Dan, eager to help this embarrassed man he loved, said: 'I guess you mean about women?'

'Yes.' John relaxed in relief, this hurdle crossed. 'Yes, that's it, son.'

'I know about — going with women,' Dan said reassuringly. He hesitated. 'I've heard boys talk about it. Young Pat was talking once about you and mother, and he made it sound bad. I was just a kid, and I called him a liar and licked him. Pat heard us fighting, and he whipped him, too; but he told me the straight of it, afterward. It didn't sound bad the way he told me. And of course, I've been working with men up at the boom, heard them talk, so I know about it.'

John watched his son in a slow regret. 'I'm sorry I didn't talk to you before, Dan; sorry you had to find out these things for yourself. Perhaps I can fill up some gaps in what you know.' He asked curiously: 'Do your brothers — do you all — I mean, did Pat talk to all of you?'

'No, just to me.'

'Well, see here, suppose we get the other boys and go for a walk this afternoon, and you can help me explain things to them?'

Dan approved of that. They spent an afternoon he would always remember; an afternoon that shone with a sort of glory in his thoughts as long as he lived. He saw cleanness and beauty and wonder in things which once had been not only mysterious but ugly and degrading; and he loved his father more and more.

3

When Dan returned from his first year at Cambridge, he was astonished and unhappy at the change in his mother. It was as though the fair flesh which had clothed her in loveliness so long were now attacked and corrupted from within, just as a pine rotten at the heart may seem sound and fine outside till the inner rot breaks through the bark and spreads to overrun the whole. Her hair, which once had been so full of warm loveliness, began to lose its lustre. Without turning gray, it nevertheless faded into a nondescript hue. Her eyes began to be framed in fine lines like crow's feet, assuming sometimes an expression astonishingly cold and cruel. Her mouth, which had been soft and warm, pursed narrowly. She and Aunt Meg were of about the same age, in their middle forties, yet Aunt Meg now seemed years the younger, with no suggestion of lines in her face, and jolly friendly eyes.

Dan decided that the difference between Aunt Meg and his mother might lie in the fact that Aunt Meg was happy and at peace with herself while his mother was not; but unhappiness in anyone had always enlisted his sympathy, so he tried tentatively to draw near his mother, paying her small attentions, seeking to make her smile. She always welcomed his company, but he was tormented by the fact that more and more often she spoke about his father in a way he hated, as though the inner corruption which was destroying the bloom of her loveliness attacked her thoughts too. There had been a time when he did not know what she meant by these reflections on his father; but after a year in college he was wiser. Once when in this way she named Aunt Meg, Dan protested:

'Mother, you know as well as I do that what you're trying to make me believe just isn't true!'

She smiled patiently: 'I certainly don't want to hurt your faith in your father — or in Aunt Meg, Dan!'

'You can't,' he said stubbornly. 'You're just making yourself miserable, thinking such things about them.' And he urged: 'And you ought not to say things like that to us, to Will and Tom and Mat and me.' He appealed to her: 'Remember what you told Grandmother Evered about father's being the rooftree, and our all sort of leaning on him? It's true, so you oughtn't to try to make us believe he's rotten.'

'Sometimes I wake in the night,' she said softly, 'and think of that huge timber at the top of the house and think some day it will fall and crush us all.'

'Father'll never fall, as long as we — stand by him!' He tried to put his arms around her. 'You know that, really, mother.'

But she put his embrace aside, smiled in that patient fashion he always found so infuriating and turned away.

Once he went frankly to his father to confess how she troubled him. He saw as he spoke a great weariness bow the older man's shoulders; and he talked on, afraid to stop, anxious, now that he had begun, to say all he had to say. When he was done, John Evered said slowly, and with nothing but simple truth in his tones:

'Dan, your mother is the only woman in my life, has always been, always will be as long as she lives.'

'I know that, father,' Dan assured him. 'But she keeps saying things and insinuating things.' He spoke awkwardly. 'Father — you and she don't sleep in the same room. Why don't you? Don't you — love each other?' His voice suddenly was husky. 'You used to. I can remember how happy we all were when you and she were happy together.'

'Well, Dan, marriage includes a lot of things,' John explained. 'Sleeping together is one of them. It's a beautiful, happy part of marriage. But sometimes that part of marriage has to end, and there's nothing that can be done about it. It just ends.

'But marriage goes on, Dan. People once married are always married. Your mother is my wife, just as surely as she is your mother; and she always will be. That can never be changed. I shall always be as good a husband as I can — just as you will always be a good son.' He smiled ruefully. 'That's all I can promise you, Dan.'

'She's so grand in so many ways,' Dan said miserably. 'Everyone likes her and just thinks she's wonderful.'

'Exactly,' John agreed. 'And they're right, Dan. Don't ever think hardly of her.'

'I'm so darned sorry for her — and for you.'

John said quietly: 'Never be sorry for me, Dan. No one need ever be sorry for me as long as I have a son like you.'

II

It was during Dan's college years that he first awoke to any personal interest in the great national political question which now approached its crisis. He knew that his mother was an abolitionist; but he knew also that his father felt less strongly on the subject. His own opinion, if he had any, was actually nothing but a memory of Atticus. Atticus was a slave, yet Dan knew Atticus had preferred to return to slavery rather than face a Bangor winter; so it was impossible for him to think of slavery as the outrage on humanity which his mother held it to be. Certainly she had been wrong about Atticus. It was reasonable to think she might have been wrong about the institution of which Atticus was a part.

But in the summer of 1856, this feeling on his part underwent a change. When he read in the papers how Hannibal Hamlin, Bangor's great man, had arisen in the United States Senate to announce his withdrawal from the Democratic Party, Dan felt a quickening sense of something imminent and vital in which — since he would soon be twenty-one, and old enough to vote — he would have a part. While he was at home that summer, Senator Hamlin spoke in Norombega Hall, and Dan went with his father to hear him.

The hall was crowded, and Dan and John, to be sure of finding places, were early on hand. Elijah Hamlin, the Senator's brother, a Whig all his life while Senator Hamlin had always until now been a Democrat, was elected chairman. Noah Barker of Exeter, recently returned from Kansas, described the terrorism there; Lot Morrill followed with a formal renunciation of his adherence to the Democratic Party; and then Senator Hamlin came forward.

He began by embracing his brother, glad that at last they were politically united in their opposition to the extension of slavery; and Dan's eyes filled and his throat ached as he joined in the shouting approval of that scene. But thereafter, intent on hearing every word, he resented the applause which occasionally interrupted the speaker; and when Senator Hamlin sat down, Dan was convinced that upon the new Republican Party all the hopes of every right-thinking man must centre.

Next day Senator Hamlin and a group of men came to dinner at the house, and Dan at John's suggestion joined them at the table. The group included Judge Saladine, still apparently hale but actually with only a few months to live; Colonel Black, upon whom age had laid a heavy hand, but who, despite the fact that his vision was almost completely gone, spoke with authority in any company; his son George, Elijah Hamlin, General Veazie, and half a dozen others. Dan listened to their talk with a glowing interest. There was a rocklike strength in Hannibal Hamlin's clean-shaven face, his heavy jaw a little protruding, his broad upper lip and deep-shadowed eyes. For a while they spoke of things that happened long ago, questioning the Senator; and he told them about the growth of anti-slavery sentiment which had led to the founding of the new party. He said the slave states had tried to surrender Oregon to England, and he declared that the Mexican War was part of the South's design to extend slave territory. He spoke of the Clayton Bill and the Wilmot Proviso and the compromises of 1850; and though Dan, whose years in college had left him almost completely ignorant of the things most important for any young man to know, the recent history of his own country, understood none of these references, he felt in the Senator's tone their profound importance.

'Doctor Bailey of the *National Era* did more than any other individual to bring anti-slavery men together,' the Senator told them. 'His home in Washington was a place where we could meet in cosy, congenial surroundings and where we could find intellectual and physical refreshment after our long labors.

'Now we can foresee eventual victory, but there is much still to be done, and it will not be easy. The troubles in Kansas are an earnest, I'm afraid, of what is to come. The South is ready for violence. The assault upon Senator Sumner is no more than a symptom of the disorder in the minds of the slavery men as they see their defeat approaching.

'If there is to be a trial of strength,' he continued, 'why, then, I say, let it come. But it was always from the firm certainty in my mind that the people of Maine were behind me in the great fight that I have drawn what powers I possess. I asked John Evered to bring you together today because I want to know you are still of the same mind.'

Judge Saladine said: 'We are, Senator. In fact, we hoped you would be named for President, at the Philadelphia Convention.'

'I have no desire for the office,' Senator Hamlin assured him. 'The ambition to be President has ruined the public usefulness of many an able man. I can be more valuable if I can keep my bonnet clear of that bee.' He smiled grimly, and then he added: 'Fremont is a good man; but of course we will lose this election. The country has yet to be made to see the issue clear and plain.'

His immediate appeal to them had to do with the coming campaign in the state. He was looked upon as the inevitable nominee for Governor at the Republican State Convention to be held in Portland on July 8; but he was reluctant to accept without assurances of strong support. They discussed the question gravely. There was still among sober men of business a lingering respect for the right of property in slaves; but Dan, listening, watching their faces, saw in each one a growing conviction of the justness of the Republican position which expressed itself at last in their unanimous insistence that the Senator should accept the nomination. Old Colonel Black said quietly:

'We Maine folks trust you, Senator. Eastern Maine will follow you to a man. The size of your majority will surprise you.'

Dan carried away from that gathering a profound and stirring sense that he had seen a great man. He heard the Senator speak three times during that summer's campaign; and when the returns were in and Hamlin's sweeping victory, greater than even the most optimistic had foreseen, was known, Dan felt an almost personal triumph, a feeling of having shared in the birth of a fine and splendid thing.

III

Dan finished college and came home with a sense of new beginnings, of changes in process and to come. He looked forward to a closer association with his father. Colonel Black and Judge Saladine had died within a few weeks of each other, and John's long connection with the Bingham interests was done. In his letters during Dan's last year in college he had proposed that he and his sons spend the coming winter in the woods together.

Dan exulted in the prospect, but his father wrote that there was some question about the others. Will was still bound to become a doctor; and for three or four years he had been almost constantly with Doctor Mason, learning to compound prescriptions, visiting patients, reading every volume the Doctor could put into his hands. 'So I don't know about Will,' John explained. 'He's anxious to make a beginning at his doctoring. He's grown a beard to give himself a properly mature look.' Dan himself had a mustache, satisfyingly dark and conspicuous, and he touched it lightly as he read. 'And he imitates Doctor Mason, talks a little ponderously. Be careful not to smile at this when you come home. I've assured him that what with accidents and wet and cold and stomachaches, he'll have patients enough in our woods gang to give him practice if he goes with us; but I'm afraid he'll go his own gait when the time comes.'

Of Tom, too, there was some doubt. 'I'd be as well pleased if Tom did go to sea for a year or two,' John said in another letter. 'He's inclined to run wild, a headstrong youngster. He seems to have a remarkable attraction for young ladies, too — even for those somewhat older than himself. Your mother and I see him very little.' He added, as he often did, a message from Jenny. 'Your mother sends all her love and counts the days till you come home. You're the oldest, and mothers always have a special place in their hearts for their oldest sons. She's dreading next winter, dreading your going away, so it may be just as well if Tom — and Will too — stay here with her; but we'll see.'

When Dan came home Jenny was forty-seven years old, and time had set its mark on her. Not only was her face increasingly lined, but the life had gone out of the skin on her cheeks and on her hands, so that it was dry and dull, as the skin of an orange or a lemon becomes dull and lifeless when the natural oils have evaporated; and there were blue shadows under her eyes. Under her jawbones on either side the skin sagged, while her throat was deeply lined. Something in her eyes suggested that she had suffered pain; and Dan, seeing this, felt toward her more tenderness than he had felt for years, and during his first days at home he tried in every way to please her and to make her smile.

One day through the dining room window he saw her on the lawn, while she looked off toward the river as though unseeingly. He came out to her and she turned to him with a faint start, and smiled a little and he asked on sudden impulse:

'Mother, are you all right?'

'Why, yes, of course, Dan. Why?'

'You were just sitting here, thinking.'

'Hardly even thinking,' she confessed in her patient tones. 'Just sitting here.'

'You looked unhappy.'

'None of us is completely happy, Dan.'

'Are you well? I mean, really well?'

'Oh, I suppose so. No woman my age is really well.' Dan knew only vaguely what she meant, and his ignorance kept him from pushing the question. 'I'm well enough,' she said.

'You're not sick, are you?'

'Not in a physical way, no.'

He said in half impatience: 'What other ways are there?'

'None, perhaps,' she assented. 'Although I sometimes think that one of these days wise doctors will be more concerned with ills of the heart and spirit than of the body.'

'There's nothing wrong with your heart and spirit,' he protested, almost angrily, trying to stifle the irritation, the faintly defensive antagonism which she so often aroused in him. 'Your heart and spirit are fine!'

She smiled. 'I wonder if people who are dying of a broken heart show it?' she murmured.

He laughed, conscious of the harsh note in his laughter, trying to mend it. He wished to protest, to say hotly: 'Why do you talk like that when father and all of us just spend our time trying to keep you happy?' But he knew that if he did, she would say something critical of his father. He felt baffled and helpless and half-angry.

'I've been worried about you,' he said, almost curtly, 'afraid you were sick. I'm glad you're all right.'

'Oh, I'm quite all right, I suppose,' she agreed.

IV

With her he tried to be kind, but one day he confessed explosively to Will: 'She makes me so damned mad. I can't do anything with her!'

'She's having change of life,' Will explained. 'Doctor Mason told me about it. It makes her nervous and short of breath and she has hot flashes, so she feels hot all over, the way your foot feels when you go to sleep.'

Dan said wonderingly: 'Hot? Her hands are cold when you touch them, and her lips are cold and dry when she kisses you. They always used to be warm and moist.' He shivered faintly, with a sense of repulsion he could not down. 'I used to like to kiss her, but I don't any more.' Will told him that women slept ill at these times; that their nerves were forever on edge; that sometimes they actually became insane; and Dan asked: 'Do they get over it?'

'Oh, yes,' Will said. 'They're fine again, after a while; but she's really sick now. She can't help herself.'

'I hate the way she talks about father. It's so damned hard on him.'

Will said wisely: 'He understands about it. I've told him.' Will, a year younger than Dan, nevertheless wore with that fine beard of his a sober manner and a maturity of bearing which prevented Dan's finding anything ludicrous in the thought of Will's telling their father anything. As a result of Will's explanation, Dan was thereafter even more gentle toward Jenny; but Tom, always inclined to be hot-headed, had no patience with her.

'What if she does feel bad, some of the time?' he protested. 'I guess everyone does, as far as that goes; but the rest of us don't go around making everyone miserable. I've had about all of it I'm going to stand!'

Nevertheless he kept his temper and held his tongue, until a day in late July. They were all together that evening at the supper table. Jenny's rose garden had been for many years her particular pride; and tonight she said resentfully: 'John, someone stole a lot of my buds last night, deliberately cut them, at least a dozen! I counted eleven stems that had been snipped off.'

'Why, that's too bad, Jenny,' he said sympathetically. Then — Dan recognized the attempt to please her — he added: 'You've the best roses in Bangor. Probably some young man wanted to offer a particularly lovely gift to his fair.'

'I think I'll put a set gun loaded with rock salt to surprise the next thief,' Jenny declared; and John chuckled and said:

'That's always dangerous. Maybe it was one of the boys!' They laughed at that presumably absurd suggestion — all except Jenny — and John added: 'Reminds me of the time Doc Webster up at Old Town set out to catch the men who were stealing his potatoes. He asked John Rollins to help him, and John agreed to do it. John had an old Queen's arm, and that night Doc came to his house and they loaded it up with four fingers of powder and four fingers of rock salt. The Doc's potato field was opposite the Temple place, and it backed down on a big patch of bog along the river. Doc and John sat down in the middle of the field to wait, and along about midnight they heard the rails rattle as someone climbed the fence.'

Dan saw that his father was trying to make her forget her grievance; but Jenny paid no attention. She sat looking at her plate, her head bowed, as though enduring an unwelcome interruption, and Dan watched her resentfully as John went on.

'They could tell there was a crowd of the thieves,' he said. 'They were making a lot of noise, talking — some of them like Germans, and Irish, and so on — and Doc whispered: "'Y Godfrey, John, there's more here than we can handle! We better lay low!"

'But Rollins told him not to worry. "They'll scatter when we give the word," he said; and when the crowd came near them he sung out: "Now I've got you. I'll salt your tail!" And he hauled up the old fusil and let her go.'

John laughed, and Dan and the others began to grin, and John explained: 'Well, sir, it missed fire. Rollins had tipped off some of his friends, so they could have some fun with Doc Webster; and he saw to it that the gun didn't go off. But when the lock snapped, the other crowd had guns too and they began to shoot, and Rollins yelled: "We're licked, Doc! Run for your life!"

'So Doc ran, and the only way for him to go was into the swamp. That was a bog hole of a place, all hoop-pole stuff and cat-tails. Rollins, telling the story, used to say: "He like to never did get out; and when he did, there wa'n't enough left of his britches to call 'em such. It was broad daylight by then and he had to hide till dark before he dast come home!"'

Dan and the others found this extravagantly funny, partly because of their father's zest in the telling, but Jenny did not even smile. The sun, low in the west, had begun to shine through the windows directly into her eyes, and while they still laughed she rose and went to draw the curtain there. Dan, too late to do it for her, protested:

'Mother, why didn't you ask me to do that?'

'It doesn't matter,' she said patiently. 'I'm used to looking out for myself.' She returned to the table and said in her low tones which had an icy, controlled frigidity about them: 'Tom — what your father said made me think it possible — did you cut my roses?' Dan looked at her in astonishment. Since they were children they had known that her flowers must never be touched, so the question surprised him; but he was the more surprised by the fact that Tom did not instantly deny it. Jenny explained: 'I remember you asked me the other day if you could have a bouquet to take to one of your little friends.'

'Yes, and you said I couldn't,' Tom told her resentfully.

'Exactly. Tom — did you go against my word?'

The moment suddenly was dreadful. Tom rose, standing very tall, his cheek red with guilty anger; and at the same time John came to his feet and moved as though protectingly to Tom's side. Then Tom spoke, almost as quietly as she.

'Yes,' he said. 'I cut the roses.'

'You stole them,' said his mother.

Tom nodded, a sort of resignation in his tones. 'I stole them if you like,' he agreed. 'I cut them yesterday afternoon, took them to Betsy Thatcher.' And he asked defiantly: 'Why shouldn't someone enjoy them, instead of just leaving them to fade and die?'

Jenny looked up at her son — and at her husband standing by Tom's shoulder. 'You're like your father, Tom,' she said evenly. 'A liar and a thief.' Her voice was icy cold. 'But I suppose there is no escape for me, from either one of you.'

Tom did not speak, his eyes as bleak as her tones; and she rose with no other word and left the room.

When she was gone, for a moment no one moved. Then John very gently touched Tom's shoulder, and then he followed her. They heard his steps go up the stairs, and Tom's rigid posture relaxed. He looked around at them all, and suddenly they were all on their feet; coming close to him, pressing together in this troubled moment with an instinct that went back to their earliest days, cleaving one to another.

Tom said thickly: 'She'll never say that to me again!'

Dan put his arm around the other's shoulder; and Mat urged: 'Don't feel bad, Tom! She gets upset all the time about something.'

Will nodded wisely. 'Remember how Ruth always use to be, with Pat, Tom?' he suggested. 'Always raising Cain about any little old thing?'

Tom seemed to hesitate, as though warily. 'I know. Yes,' he assented.

Dan at the other's tone felt a chill like terror. He said warmly:
'Come on, Tom, let's walk it off, talk it off.'

Tom accepted readily enough, and they turned out of doors,
the others following. They swung at random along the road to
Old Town, and at first they went in silence. Tom was the first
to speak.

'The thing that makes me so damned mad,' he confessed, 'is that
we just have to grin and take it, anything she wants to say or do.
We're like dogs with a man. The man can kick the dog around
all he wants to, but the dog keeps hoping the man will treat him
better after a while. She's sarcastic and cold and horrible most of
the time, and we roll over on our backs like puppies begging to be
forgiven, but the minute she's good-natured we bounce up and start
wagging our tails and loving her again.'

Will said gently: 'That's the whole trouble, Tom. We do love
her.'

'Don't I know it!' Tom exclaimed. 'She knows it too, takes
advantage of it all the time.'

Mat echoed Tom. 'She uses the fact that we love her to bully us
and to bully father! I can stand it myself, but I hate to see the way
she treats him — and I hate the way she talks about him to us.'

'I guess women all bully their menfolks,' Will pointed out.
'Maybe it gives them a sense of power, makes them forget how
weak they are, to know they can treat us like dirt and then smile,
and we'll thank them for the smile and forget the meanness.' He
grinned. 'They keep reminding men how helpless and abused they
are — so they can get their own way. They're really stronger than
men — or cleverer, anyway.'

Tom said harshly: 'I don't believe it's just because they want to
be boss. I think they like to make a man miserable! I think mother
likes seeing us unhappy, just the way she used to like to whip us.
I think she gets some sort of satisfaction out of being just as mean
to us as she can! And of course she knows how we all feel about
father, so she hurts us through him.'

'Maybe she sees we like him best and is jealous,' Mat suggested.

'Then why doesn't she try to make us like her?' Tom exclaimed.
'We're all ready to, if she'd give us a chance.'

The talk went on, arriving nowhere; but Dan took no part in
their discussion. He listened, and weighed what they said; but he
thought, with a deeper understanding than theirs, that his mother
herself suffered more than they in these moments when she lashed
them with her stinging, quiet tongue.

When they came home, Tom seemed no longer angry; but four

days later he failed to appear for supper. Dan was concerned, and his father and the others too; but Jenny took Tom's absence calmly.

'He's probably stayed at Betsy's,' she suggested. 'It wouldn't occur to him to send word, or to think of the concern — and the inconvenience — he might cause us.'

They ate without him, and Dan persuaded himself that his mother was right, that Tom would spend the evening with Betsy and come late home; but when he went up to the room he and Tom shared, there was a note under his comb on the lowboy.

> *Dear Dan* — I'm sailing on the Lucy B, Captain Morse, for Norfolk, Savannah, Galveston and the West Indies. You can tell the others. I guess you know I haven't been happy at home for quite a while; and the other day when mother called me a liar and a thief finished it for me. I've always wanted to go to sea; so I'm going to try it.
>
> Tell mother I love her, but I think we'll get along a lot better apart than together. You and Mat could always get along with her. You're both sort of slow and easygoing; but I get mad — and so does Will, only he doesn't show it so much. Maybe I ought to grow a beard, the way he did, so people couldn't tell what I was thinking. Maybe I will before I come home.
>
> I'll be home some day, all right, but I probably won't have a chance to write you, so you won't know I'm coming till I just walk in.
>
> Don't blame mother. It's not her fault. I just had to get away for a while. Tell father I wish I was going up-river with you all, this winter, but I couldn't wait. Will had better stay home and take care of mother while you and Mat and father are gone. She'll need someone to bully!
>
> Your Brother,
> Tom

Dan read this letter by candlelight — the house was outside the part of the city into which the new illuminating gas had thus far been piped — and after a moment he went along the hall to his father's door. The older man read the letter slowly, and Dan, watching him, saw small beads of moisture form upon his brow. He finished and Dan said:

'I thought you might want to tell mother, so she won't worry.'

His father looked at him thoughtfully. 'The Lucy B — your mother owns her, Dan,' he said in an absent tone. 'I used to manage mother's affairs; but for several years now she's been handling them herself. Cap'n Morse wouldn't have shipped Tom without letting mother know. So she knew he was gone.'

Dan protested in surprise: 'But she pretended to think he'd gone to see Betsy Thatcher or someone!'

His father did not reply. 'It's the first break in our family,' he said, half to himself. 'My mother used to say that a family was like a ring, strong as long as it clung together, weak when it was broken.'

'He'll be back,' Dan urged; and the older man smiled and said quietly:

'Yes, of course. He'll be back, to be sure.'

But Tom did not come back. He wrote, saying that he had left the schooner at Savannah. The sea, he admitted, had proved a disappointment. He was sick all the time, with a sickness from which there seemed to be no recovery; and he said:

> If I have to come home by sea, I may never come at all. I'm going to visit a lady and her daughter who took passage with us when we stopped at Norfolk; a Mrs. McPherson and Miss Bunty McPherson. They live at a place called Midway, and we're going down there this afternoon, to their plantation. I'm hurrying this off while I can.

Jenny, when she heard this, said in a quiet fury: 'So—my son is to be waited on by slaves; to be the guest of slave-owners.'

Dan tried to reassure her. 'You know how Tom is, mother. Probably Miss McPherson is a lovely young lady, and they say Southern girls are all coquettes, and Tom always had a lively eye. But you'll never have to worry about Tom in the end.'

'I never thought any son of mine would make friends with slave-owners,' she insisted. 'But then, of course, he's John's son too.'

▼

In mid-September, Dan and Mat and his father started up-river, to be gone all winter. Will had finally decided to stay at home.

Dan, despite himself, felt a deep relief when at last they were upon the road, as though a load he bore had been lifted; and his father was happier too. No sooner had they set out than in a sudden exuberance John was full of things to say. He spoke jubilantly of the prospect of a fine market for the pine they would cut this winter. Two years before, a hundred and twenty-three million feet of pine lumber had been surveyed in the port of Bangor; but a year ago the figure fell to a hundred and two million, and this year was less.

'There'll never be another year when a hundred million feet of pine will come down to Bangor,' John predicted. 'But that means better prices for us now.'

In Old Town he had business to do before they went on; and he rejoined them, laughing at something he had just heard. 'I was talking to George Sewall,' he said. 'He's a lawyer here, went to Congress in '51. They tell about him that when he was in Congress, some long-winded speaker kept taking a drink of water during his speech, till Sewall rose to a point of order, said he'd never before seen a windmill run by water!' They laughed, as much at his own enjoyment of the jest as at his words, and he went on: 'He was just telling me about a trick he played on old Colonel Rollins, a few years ago. They were neighbors, and they both needed some cedar posts. Colonel Rollins proposed to cut them on Bingham land. He was to do the cutting, and Sewall the hauling. They went out to locate some cedar and Sewall led the way to a big cedar swamp, and the Colonel cut a lot of posts and a big pine too — Sewall took the butt log of the pine and the Colonel took the rest — and the Colonel didn't find out for three months that they were on his land, stealing his own lumber instead of ours, all the time.'

That was the first of many tales he told them through the long, easy days of their journey. He told them about Jonathan Farrar, who tapped both ends of a rum barrel and sold the rum from one end for forty cents and from the other for fifty. 'And everyone agreed that the fifty-cent rum was better,' he declared. He told them about old Isaiah Powers who said of an extremely loud-voiced orator that he was like a bell, with a noisy tongue and an empty head; and he told them about the drunken Indian who went to sleep in his canoe and went over the falls at Old Town unharmed; and he told them about Jim Percival who was never bested in the game of pinch, till he tackled Eb Husted when Eb had a bullet mold in his hand and Jim failed to realize this till he was pinched black and blue; and he told them about Judge Howard who when a culprit was brought before him and asked whether he needed counsel said: 'Counsel be damned! I'll fine you two dollars and all the counsel in the world won't do you any good'; and about Asa Wadleigh who when his tail crew let a drive of logs get hung up told the men they ought to work for nothing a day and be cheated out of their pay every night. He told about old Jonathan Bridges, who came to Deacon Hannon's store one cold winter day, sent by his wife to buy some butter. The Deacon was busy at the time, and Jonathan went to the rear of the store where the butter and the rum barrel were side by side. He thought no one was watching him, so he clapped a ball of butter into his hat, drew a jug of rum, and tendered payment for the rum without troubling to mention the butter. But the Deacon had seen the butter disappear, and he made old Jonathan sit by the stove to warm himself and kept him there till the butter melted and ran down his cheeks in streams so conspicuous that some notice had to be taken, and the Deacon said:

'Well, I declare, you're hog fat, Jonathan! You're sweating pure grease.'

And he reached out and snatched off Jonathan's hat and the half-melted lump of butter fell into the old man's lap, and Jonathan stared at it and said in innocent surprise:

'Well, I'll be switched! Now where in time did that come from?'

John had an inexhaustible supply of these tales, drawn from the accumulating folklore of the town along the river; and Dan and Mat laughed with him at the telling. But his tales were not all of the river. Sometimes he talked of his own boyhood; and one night when they huddled under the overturned batteau to escape a cold driving rain, he told them about that night on Coetue when he and their mother fought bitter death and won; and often he spoke of incidents in their own boyhood, which they themselves could not remember. Jenny was always in these tales; and when he spoke of their mother they saw her through his eyes as young and tender and beautiful. Afterward, rolled in his blankets, Dan might lie awhile awake, summoning his own bright memories of her, wondering wretchedly and hopelessly what it was which had changed her so.

John spoke of her daily, and always loyally, on that long trip up-river. They travelled alone, three stalwarts, the two sons each taller than their father, in a light batteau with setting poles to negotiate the rapids and paddles for the quieter reaches of the river and for the lakes. They saw dams and piers and booms built by the Penobscot Log Driving Association, and John explained to them the uses of each one. He told them tales of tremendous pines so huge that even the men who laid them low wondered at their size; of a Mattawamkeag tree that was eighty-two feet to the first branch; of another which required fourteen yokes of oxen to haul it, and sawed six and a half thousand board feet of lumber; and he told them of one tree he himself had cut.

'It was an old punkin pine,' he said. 'I dropped some small trees to make a cradle for it first and then went at it. It was better than six feet through, where I tackled it, about four feet from the ground, and I was an hour and a quarter bringing it down. That pine was sixty-five feet to the first branch. It made five logs; and a six-ox team took three trips to handle it. At that, the butt log was so big that we couldn't float it in the spring, had to leave it behind. That one log would have been worth fifty dollars at the boom.'

Dan smiled and said: 'Father, you like to remember old times, don't you; to talk about them.'

'Why — yes,' John assented, and he tried to explain. 'You see, Dan, the things men remember together become a part of their common strength. The fact that a group of men know and love the same tales unites them. There's no stronger force than the bond of a common tradition. Any tradition is a good thing, a steadying thing.' He added, suddenly grave: 'We're going to need all these unifying forces in the Northern states one of these days, Dan. You see, the South has a common tradition, the slave tradition; and it makes them all think in the same way. We in the North are nowhere near being united, not even in opposing slavery. Some of us — even in Bangor — sympathize with the South. Senator Hamlin thinks it may come to the point of fighting; but while the South will fight in a minute to keep their slaves, the North won't fight — not yet, anyway — to free them. Some man will have to come along who will find a way to unite the North as the South is united; to give us up here a common loyalty. And it will be hard, because we're a big country.' He chuckled and said: 'If the whole North was in the lumber business, it would be easy, because we'd have these common traditions, this trick of laughing at the same things, of being proud of the same things.'

VI

They carried for provisions some ship's bread, salt pork, tea, sugar and molasses, and a gun and fishing lines to supplement their rough fare. Their blankets, a teakettle, a tin dipper, a frying pan and an axe completed their equipment. At night if the weather was stormy, the overturned batteau gave them shelter. Otherwise a few boughs laid across a frame of poles was cover enough. They made camp each day in time to be secure before dark, were up and about at first gray dawn. They followed the main river for eleven days, turned aside at last to ascend a considerable tributary stream that came in from the north, and when they stopped for the night John said:

'Well, we're here. From now on we'll foot it, scout the land, lay out what we want to do.'

The days that followed were for Dan pure delight. On the first morning they climbed a horseback which traversed the lower lands for miles; and about mid-morning John said:

'Now it's time to take a sight.'

He selected a tall spruce whose lowest limbs were some thirty feet from the ground and undercut a smaller tree to fall and lodge against it as a sort of ladder. 'You go up, Dan,' he said. 'Climb high enough so you can see all around. You'll be able to see any clumps and veins of pine for miles across the low lands, because they stand up fifty or sixty feet above the spruces. Shout down to us what you see.'

So Dan began the climb, ascending the smaller tree till he reached the larger, where the branches were a ladder to help him higher. When he had climbed as high in the spruce as he could safely go, he hooked his knee over a branch and began his survey of the leagues of forest which surrounded them. There were mountains, some not distant, some far away, all uniformly clad in spruce and hemlock and cedar and pine; but since the best pine was likely to be found in the lower lands, it was to the nearer scene that he gave the most searching scrutiny. He saw a dozen groups of pines, some including only half a dozen trees, some apparently covering acres; and he called to those below:

'There's pine everywhere, father.'

'Pick out the nearest big vein,' John directed. 'What direction is it?'

Dan said: 'There's a big one about four or five miles away, but I don't know the direction.' The day was cloudy and overcast so that he could not locate the sun. 'It's over that way.'

He pointed, but the ground was far below, the intervening branches thick, and they could not see him. At his father's instruction he broke off a small branch, stripped it of twigs so that it would not catch on the lower foliage, and threw it as far as he could toward the stand of pine he had chosen. John, far below, marked where it fell and shouted up to him:

'All right, we've got a compass bearing now! Come along down.'

So Dan descended, and following the compass they made their way to the tract Dan had spied. During the days that followed they located in this fashion all the nearer veins of pine, and John taught his sons how to calculate the number of trees in each one, how to recognize concussy pines which, rotten at the heart, were not worth the cutting, and how to appraise the task of getting logs from each tract to the nearest water. At the end of a week he had determined where the winter's work should centre, and had chosen the sites for three camps, so located that a plentiful supply of meadow hay could be cut from intervales along the river to feed the oxen, with water and firewood near, and never too far from the trees that were to be cut nor from the landings where the logs would be accumulated against the break-up in the spring.

By the time this was done the first of the men came up-river and John set them to work putting up hay, stacking it on staddles made by driving poles into the ground and laying other poles across them to keep the hay clear of possible flood waters. When the hay was cut, it was piled in cocks on two poles and men carried these cocks between them to the growing stacks. Since in the process their hands were both engaged, the flies and mosquitoes had free play on them; and each day's end saw their faces converted into swollen, bloody smears.

Day by day more men arrived, and the camps began to be built. John — and Dan under his instruction — directed this work. The ground had first to be cleared and levelled; then walls were raised, built of notched spruce logs, eight feet high in front and half that in the rear. The camps were roofed with poles and split shingles of spruce or cedar, held down in turn by other poles, and covered for greater warmth with fir and spruce and hemlock boughs. The walls were calked with moss. The beds along the rear walls were no more than a shelf of split planks on which boughs were thrown, and the men slept there side by side. The bunks, the kitchen — John had a cook stove as well as a box stove for each camp — and the dining room were all under the same roof; and the deacon seat, a hewed plank high enough to serve as a comfortable bench, ran along the foot of the long bed.

Before the camp was ready, the last batteaus arrived with the winter's supplies, flour and beans and pork, potatoes, coffee and tea and molasses. John had warned the men when he hired them that there would be no rum in camp. The hovels that would house the oxen were thrown up; and as cold weather came and the river closed, the teams began to arrive. They had come by way of Moosehead, made the last stages of the long journey on the frozen river. Road-building was already under way; and Dan and Mat worked with the men, cutting brush and trees to clear roads a dozen feet wide, filling holes, hauling great boulders out of the way, and as the first snows came watering the roads every night till they were paved solidly with ice as hard as iron.

By that time the work in the woods was organized; choppers, swampers, barkers, loaders and teamsters were each hard at his particular task. Dan saw the first tree come down. Bed pieces had been laid to break its fall; and after it was undercut, a smaller tree was toppled against it to knock it over. It tipped a little with a splintering groan as every fibre in the huge trunk complained at the new stresses suddenly imposed, then crashed down upon the bed pieces with a tremendous, ground-shaking impact that Dan could feel in the soles of his feet. At once the men swarmed upon it, some of them knocking off the smaller branches and severing the tip while the barkers stripped down to the white wood that smaller end which would drag upon the ground.

Dan watched while with skids and rolling chain the butt was rolled upon the sled; and then six yokes of oxen, straining at the load, began to drag it to the iced road and off to the landing. It seemed to him incredible than any number of oxen could move that tremendous mass, almost four feet through at the butt. He measured it, found it was twenty-one paces long; yet the oxen hauled it along the well-iced road to the landing where it was cut into four shorter logs, ready for driving in the spring that was still months away.

VII

There was about that winter in the woods a certain fine monotony, in which small incidents assumed tremendous proportions. Once they found a hibernating bear and killed it; and venison was a regular addition to their fare. With the venison — or rabbit meat if deer were scarce — the cook made a studjo, a meat and potato stew; and if there was no fresh meat in camp, dinner was dunderjunk, bread and pork and molasses all baked together. But usually game was plenty, and several times they heard wolves, and though Dan himself never saw one, others did. At the west camp a teamster named Jeff Hazard was killed. His loaded sled outran his oxen on a mild grade, and it was assumed that he had tried to swerve them off the road; but in doing so he himself fell, and the sled crossed his body and pinned him down. He was on a haul of a mile or more, and it was some time before — when he failed to return — men came to look for him. They found him still alive, but in the agony of his efforts to be free he had gnawed halfway through the stout spruce pole that made the railing of the sled. He died almost at once, but that was the only case during the winter where a man was killed.

Dan liked the work, and he liked too the long idle Sundays, when men slept, or mended their clothes, or went tramping off through the woods to hunt spruce gum or on some other pretext. This might be to find white ash or rock maple, or elm or hornbeam useful for axe helves. Some went hunting, and a few men ran a line of deadfalls, visiting the traps once a week. But if the weather was evil, everyone stayed in camp, the teamsters mending harnesses or yokes or tending their oxen — a good yoke of oxen was worth a hundred dollars or a little more, and their owners gave them every care — the men telling long tales or singing come-all-ye's in roaring, surprisingly tuneful voices.

For the last month before the break-up, John put Dan in full charge of the east camp. It was Dan's first experience in handling men; and since his gang knew their jobs and did them, he had wit enough not to interfere. For three weeks John did not come to the camp at all; and when he did, Dan was at the cutting so he did not see his father till night. John had by that time a full report of him, and he said approvingly:

'You've pulled your weight, Dan. The work's kept up, and the men like you. I'm pleased with you, son.'

Dan grinned with pleasure. 'But it's no credit to me,' he said. 'I haven't tried to drive them, or to interfere at all. I just gave a hand where I could. They'd have done as well without me.'

John smiled. 'Then you've learned the first lesson in how to be a good boss,' he said. 'To leave well enough alone.'

That winter there had been scant snow in the woods, so their operations were handicapped; but despite this they had a good cut of pine at the landings. John explained to Dan the necessary preparations for the break-up. From this east camp the logs would have to go down a stream that was not much more than a brook till they reached the main river; and Dan put men to work at once to cut a channel through the ice and roll the logs into it as fast as room could be made for them. The channel was made wide enough to take three or four logs abreast, and men extended it downstream day by day, not only cutting out the ice and hauling it clear, but removing trees and bushes which tended to hang the logs. To get the logs into the channel was hard, driving work; and the men, with pries and handspikes and swing dogs were sometimes waist-deep in the icy water for most of the day. Mat came to help with this work; and Dan, quick to give a hand at the worst spots, inspired the men, leading them more than he drove. Before the break-up of the main river, the brook was choked with logs from the landings down. Well ahead of time, on his own initiative, Dan had set the men to build a rude dam above the landing, holding back the water so that the logs were barely afloat. When the river opened he broke the dam a little at a time, and out of the winter's cut at this east camp not a log was hung and lost in the bushes along the brookside or upon the occasional bars.

Once in the river, the logs passed into the hands of the driving crews, and the great bulk of the men headed for Bangor to spend their winter's pay; but John and his sons followed more slowly, watching the drive, marking how each hindrance to its progress was met and solved. Dan enjoyed this easy trip down-river, savoring every hour of every day, trying not to admit to himself that he was reluctant to come home again. He reminded himself how fine and sweet his mother had used to be, and assured himself she would be glad to see them; but secretly — and more and more as they approached journey's end — he dreaded seeing her, dreaded living once more under the daily sting of her acid tongue.

Yet day by day they came nearer home. In Old Town they saw Bill Hale and heard from him how Joe Peavey, watching men breaking a jam on the Stillwater with swing dogs, had figured out a new tool for the work. Bill, himself a boss driver, had one to show them. The hook was fixed, so that it would swing up and down but not sidewise, and there was a spike in the end of the shaft. 'It's the handiest God damned rig I ever did see,' he told them in a rare enthusiasm. 'Take a rig like that and a couple men with the heft to him of these boys of yours and I'd like to see the log they couldn't move!'

They admired the new tool, and John agreed that it would make a riverman's work easier; and then they hired a team for the last reach of their homeward journey. Dan, as familiar scenes began to come into view, thought there was a change in his father. He was quieter, no longer so ebullient and gay; and Dan himself, thinking of his mother, wondered whether she were happier now, whether she would be glad to see them, whether she were well. She must be, of course. Will would have made her take care of herself. Yet it was almost eight months since he had seen her. So many things might have happened in that time.

They turned aside at last along the familiar road and saw the house ahead. Mat was the first to discover her. 'There's mother!' he cried. 'Working in her garden!' He shouted a greeting as they turned into the drive, and Dan leaped to the ground to run toward her.

She waited, not moving. He thought she seemed smaller, pitifully withered and shrunken; and the shadows under her eyes were deep blue. Nevertheless he swept her into his arms and swung her high, and kissed her before he set her down.

She said: 'Mercy, Dan, you need to bathe!' Mat kissed her boisterously; John put his arms around her, but Dan saw that she turned her face away. 'You all need to bathe,' she said, in her low, unmoved tones.

For a moment none of them spoke, and Dan was heartsick with disappointment at this unmoved welcome; but he said determinedly: 'My, it's fine to see you again, mother! You look so well. Doesn't she, father? Where's Will?'

'Will?' she echoed, as though the word were only faintly familiar. 'Will? Oh, Will's gone away.' They stared at her in a flat surprise and dismay; and she explained that Will had said he was going West to be a doctor. She said he had announced his intention without warning, had left within the hour. 'He did not consult me,' she told them in her level tones. 'He just packed his things and took the Boston steamer.' She added quietly: 'That was a month ago. I've had no word from him since.'

So the happiness of this homecoming, to which Dan had looked forward with an unadmitted hope that things might now be different, was ended. Not only was Will gone — with all his departure implied of long patience worn to shreds — but also in Jenny's demeanor there was more strongly marked than ever a hard and bitter anger, all cruelty and pain.

Of Will there was no more to say. The level finality of Jenny's tone put an end to questions. But after a moment Dan asked: 'What's the news from Tom?'

She said, her words like icy drops: 'He married that young woman.' Her lip twisted in a faint grimace. 'He has become a Southern planter, raising rice and cotton, with a whip in his hand to cut the backs of his slaves.'

This called for a thousand questions, but the implacable anger in her eyes warned them to silence. Only John ventured to say: 'Where are Tom's letters? We'd like to read them.'

'I burned them,' Jenny said simply. 'The last one I did not even open. They are gone.'

Her tone said that Tom, too, was gone, was no longer a part of their lives; and it said that her decision in this matter was final, and binding upon them all, and that if they opposed her they too would be thrown into the outer darkness of her anger. She repeated now, standing quietly beside the rose bed where they had found her:

'You had all best go and bathe. You smell of smoke, and animals, and dirty men.'

VIII

During that summer Dan found that Will's departure and Tom's marriage had the effect of erecting an invisible wall in their home. Jenny was alone on one side of that wall, Dan and Mat and his father were together on the other. Jenny herself erected this barrier. They had spoken of Will at supper, a day or two after their return, wondering how soon a letter from him would reach them; and Jenny said:

'Oblige me, please, by not mentioning either Will or Tom in my hearing. They have left my house and my life. I wish to hear no more of them.'

Dan urged in tender teasing: 'Pshaw, mother, you know you love them as much as we do! When they come back, think how glad you'll be to see them.'

She did not deny this, simply looked at him; but under her eyes he flushed and was silent, and afterward John told him and Mat: 'Best not speak of the boys before her. She loves them so much that she's broken-hearted at their going, that's all. Every word reopens the wound.'

So they were careful thereafter to keep silent as he suggested. When a letter came from Tom they read it together — it was gay and happy, full of amusing detail, contrasting plantation ways with what his life in Bangor had been — but they did not speak of that letter to Jenny; for in it Tom said:

And father, don't let Bangor people think that they can ever make Southerners give up slavery. The people around here are kind to their slaves. Mr. McPherson is a good friend of Thomas Spaulding of Sapeloe — that's a wonderful island outside the marshes, facing the ocean, ten or fifteen miles long — and he believes as Mr. Spaulding does that slaves should never be sold, and never bought except fresh from Africa. Our slaves are better off than if they were free. As far as slavery is concerned, I'm beginning to see some sense and justice in their point of view down here.

The people around here don't believe in all this talk of secession, either; but their loyalty is to the State of Georgia, not to the National Government. And they're hot-tempered, ready to fight for little or no excuse, with each other or with outsiders. They even fight duels, and they think they can whip the North if they have to.

Such words, they were sure, would anger Jenny beyond bearing; but Mat declared that the life Tom described sounded attractive to him. 'I'd like to go down and visit him,' he said. He was an indolent young giant, now in his later 'teens; and he added with a grin: 'I wouldn't mind having five or six slaves to wait on me! Remember old Atticus? He didn't mind being a slave, and I liked him.'

They had letters too from Will. The first, from Philadelphia, was addressed to Dan.

Dear Dan

I expect you are all at home again now and surprised to find me gone. I wanted to stay till you came, and I stood it as long as I could. I'll tell you about it, but don't tell father. It would just make him more unhappy than he is.

Mother started complaining as soon as you went away. She pretended to think that you weren't going up-river right away. She said father was in love with a woman in Old Town and that he had gone to see her; and I thought I could persuade her that wasn't true, so we drove up to Old Town next day and asked around and found out you'd gone straight on. But then she said he probably had women waiting for you somewhere up beyond.

She kept it up all winter, Dan. You know how she is, always hinting; but sometimes she'd come right out with it. I knew she was really sick and didn't mean anything she said, and I kept trying to talk her out of it, till she got mad and sometimes she wouldn't speak to me at all for two or three days at a time. I was almost crazy myself, trying to find some way to make her happier.

When she wasn't talking about father, it was about Tom; and after he married down South she was terrible for a while, pinching herself black and blue, grinding her teeth, saying she wished he was dead. She never told anyone where Tom was and wouldn't let me tell. She just said, if people asked her, that he was at sea, on a ship somewhere halfway around the world.

When I tried to stand up for him she got mad at me, so I kept quiet; but she said I was against her, and finally she ordered me out of the house. She said it was her house, built with her money, and she wouldn't have any enemies in it. I told her I wasn't her enemy, but I couldn't make her believe anything. She said I had to go.

The only ones she has any use for are you and Mat, and she thinks father is trying to turn you two against her. I told her how wonderful father was, and how lovingly he always spoke of her, but she said he was a hypocrite, in love with a lot of other women.

I'm sorry I had to come away. I did the best I could. I'm going to Cincinnati and then maybe settle somewhere in Ohio. I'll write you again as soon as I know where I'll be. I mean I'll write father. Probably you'd better not tell him any of these things. He has it hard enough without.

Your loving Bro,

WILL

IX

Dan sometimes thought that summer at home, and the others which followed it, would have been unbearable if he had not been able to turn often to Aunt Meg and Beth. Since Judge Saladine's death they lived alone in the big house on Essex Street, and they were always glad to see him. Beth was twelve years old, and her devotion to Dan, which had begun in her early babyhood, not only persisted but grew stronger. She liked to stand beside his chair, pressing against him while his arm lay around her small waist; and after she discovered that it delighted him when she rubbed his head, twining her slender fingers in his hair, she might do this, laughing when he pushed his head against her hand as a dog does when its ears are rubbed. There was a warm sweetness about her which made her dear to him. He and Meg sometimes laughed together — when she was not with them — at her love for him.

'It's natural for little girls her age to fall in love with tall young men,' Meg said.

He smiled, remembering. 'I was in love with you in the same way,' he reminded her. 'When I knew you were going to marry Cap'n Pawl, it seemed to me like the end of the world. And you didn't even invite me to your wedding! I hid outside the church and cried.'

They laughed together at that. 'I knew how you felt,' she admitted. 'You looked at me so accusingly, as though I had betrayed you. That's the reason I didn't ask you to the wedding. I was afraid to face you!'

'I'd probably have bawled or something!'

She asked smilingly: 'Who has taken my place, Dan?'

'No one.' He laughed. 'Oh, of course I don't mean I still feel the same way about you! Not quite.'

'You've outgrown that. But isn't there someone else about whom you're beginning to be just a little serious?' Her eyes were shining as she teased him. 'I know at least a dozen young ladies who are sighing over you!'

He chuckled, reddening. 'They haven't let me hear them.' He considered himself in a sudden surprised appraisal, no longer joking. 'I don't know why I'm not — thinking about someone,' he confessed. 'I've seen a lot of pretty girls, nice ones too, in Cambridge and here; and I always got along fine with them, but I've never even thought about being serious with any of them. I'd a lot rather be here with you and Beth than with any of them.'

She smiled affectionately. 'You're like your father,' she said, and he saw her eyes softly fill with old memories. 'Did you know he and I knew each other before he married your mother? Down at Colonel Black's in Ellsworth? Your father was so big and nice and shy. I'm afraid I set my cap for him, shamelessly. I taught him to dance — or tried to — but he was so miserable that I took pity on him. I don't think he ever looked at anyone but your mother.'

'No,' he agreed. 'No, I guess not.' He saw her cheeks bright at her own thoughts. 'I expect you were lovely,' he said, watching her. 'You must have been. You always have been, since I can remember. I used to think you were more beautiful than anyone except mother.' And he added honestly: 'She's changed a lot, lately, but you haven't. I suppose you have, really; but it's in good ways. You always look so happy and — at peace.'

'I am,' she assented. 'I've had some griefs, Dan, but they've been tender and beautiful too.' She asked: 'Is Jenny well? Sometimes I think she looks ill. I'm worried about her. She's not strong, but she gives herself so unsparingly whenever she can do good, wears out her strength.'

'I guess she's well,' he said. 'She has a lame back sometimes, but that's all.'

x

Dan spent much time that summer in his father's office. The lumber business was still in a period of steady growth; and Bangor grew with it. The population of the city had doubled in Dan's lifetime, and some enthusiasts predicted that the next census, two years hence, would tally twenty thousand people in the city. Andrew Lebbeus, who had published that libel against John years before, came back to Bangor and revived his old paper, calling it again the *Star*. He and Marcellus Emery, the editor of the *Democrat,* set themselves against the rising strength of the Republican Party and took the Southern side of the slave question which began to be the only issue in the public mind. Mr. Emery was a lawyer, a graduate of Bowdoin and a man of ability, and he kept his partisan editorials on a respectable plane; but Lebbeus wrote with a scornful and derisive pen, escaping reprisals by confining his attacks to national figures whose Bangor supporters were not sufficiently moved to seek to silence him.

Dan took no public part in the political discussions of the day. Under Senator Hamlin's influence he had long ago decided that he was against the extension of slavery, but the issue of union against disunion was not yet clearly formed; and he was in any case too busy with the beginnings of his business career to become engrossed in politics.

For another reason, too, he avoided expressing any fixed opinions. His mother had a single mind, hating slavery and all its works and all who countenanced it. He could not, remembering Tom, agree with her; but neither could he argue with her. Mat tried it sometimes, and Mat alone among them sometimes spoke to her of Tom; but when he did so, she was driven to such a stony anger that Dan — or his father — again and again had to intervene.

It was perhaps her unforgiving hatred for Tom which made her relent toward Will; and before the summer ended she was glad to hear his letters read aloud. He had pushed on from Ohio to Wisconsin and settled in a small town there, buying books and medicines and a horse and saddle and beginning a practice which grew rapidly; and he wrote much about the cases he handled. In one letter he said:

> Write me as soon as you get this. I wish mother were here
> to tell me what to do sometimes. I hope she will write to me.
> I love her and all of you.

Jenny did write to him; and Dan thought she was happier for having done so.

That winter and the next, though his father stayed in Bangor, Dan spent in the woods; and he was happy in the hard toil there. But he learned to dread his homecomings, to dread his mother's increasing malevolence. On his return in the spring of 1859, she seemed to him to have shrunk and contracted within herself; and although his father assured him that things went well, Mat told him the truth.

'She's been terrible,' he said rebelliously. 'Specially this spring.' In February, Congressman Sickles of New York had shot and killed Philip Key, the son of the author of 'The Star-Spangled Banner,' on the streets of Washington, because Key had seduced his wife. The Congressman's trial was broadcast in every newspaper in the country, and the proceedings were recorded at length in the Bangor *Jeffersonian*. Mat spoke of this, reciting the facts for Dan. 'And mother kept talking about it,' he said, 'and when Congressman Sickles was acquitted she said a woman ought to have the same right to shoot her husband if he went with other women. She said it in such a way that I knew it was father she meant. Then there was a man named Potter in Lee, and his wife was carrying on with two or three men, and he killed five people and set fire to the houses to burn up the bodies, and she talked about that too, and said he did the right thing.' Mat's voice fell almost to a whisper. 'I think she's crazy, Dan! I can't hardly stand being at home, the way she is all the time.'

Dan tried to reassure his brother; but that was an ugly summer, and he was glad to start up-river again. When he returned in mid-May of 1860, his father met him at Old Town; and his first news was that Mat had left home the previous fall, going to Georgia to join Tom there. Dan saw that even his father was shaken by this, and he himself had a helpless sense of irreparable loss, prompted not alone by Mat's going. That was only the capstone to the structure of his grief. Tom and Will and Mat were all gone now; and Dan, lonely for them, missing them always, recognized the fact that it was his mother who had driven them away.

4

DAN and his father drove home from Old Town together, and the older man warned Dan not to mention Mat's name to his mother. 'There's sure trouble coming between us and the Southern States,' he said, 'and mother feels that Tom and Mat have gone over to the enemy. Will's really her only comfort. She reads his letters over and over, so proudly.' He added: 'She's not well, Dan. She's losing weight all the time, and her back bothers her more and more.'

'Why did Mat leave finally?' Dan asked. 'Was there any special trouble at the end?'

John nodded. 'Yes, one day at dinner he was bound to read Tom's last letter aloud to her. She tried to leave the room, but he teased her, laughing at her, daring her to stay, and she did. But when he finished she said if he was so fond of his nigger-loving brother he'd better go to Georgia himself. That made Mat mad and he said: "By God I will!" And he did.'

'I wish she could be happy.'

'She'll be happy seeing you again,' John reminded him. 'You've always had a special place with her, you know.'

Dan when he saw his mother was shocked by the change in her. Her cheek was a dry yellow, her eyes sunken and deeply shadowed. Her chief happiness, Dan found, came from poring over Will's letters, and she read them aloud to him. Will wrote of his successes, proudly and openly; but Dan knew he was not so much boasting as telling Jenny the things he knew would make his mother happy. Once he said:

> The doctors with whom I had to compete here helped me: That is, they recommended me to a lot of people who couldn't afford to pay their bills.

Dan could imagine the quiet amusement in Will's eyes as he wrote the words.

> But that really did help, because I was pretty successful in curing putrid sore-throat. Before I came here it killed about all the people who had it, but I have not lost one case where I was the first called. I didn't have many women patients at first, but about five weeks since I had a bad case of obstetrics, a young woman in her first labor with a deformed pelvis. I thought she must have instrumental aid, but they called another doctor and he went on about eighteen hours, exhausting her strength with stimulants until prostration came on and she was about dead, so he called on me. She came through fine, and that has placed me all right with the women, and with the doctors too. I have about eight hundred dollars in money owing me and not much paid yet, but I'm doing a lot of work and better all the time.

And there was a postscript:

> No, mother, I am not married yet. That is an accident that has not happened to me.

There were five of Will's letters which Jenny read aloud to Dan; but for news of Tom and Mat he turned to his father. Tom's first baby had been a boy, and another was expected. Mat when he left Bangor had gone direct to join Tom in Georgia, and Tom said that in spite of the fact that they were from the North, Mat had made many friends. He wrote:

> Mat already thinks as I do that people down here have a fine, gracious, friendly way of life. The people here are so polite and friendly and at the same time so brave and self-respecting that you can't help liking and admiring them. None of the gentlemen I know want Georgia to secede; but they say Georgia will have to do it if the other states do, and South Carolina is sure to unless she gets her way.

They talk a lot more about politics down here than we do
at home. We were always so busy — or maybe it was just
because I was so young — that I never thought much about
such things; but the men I know don't do much except ride
around their plantations and hunt foxes and turkeys and
ducks and go visiting, so they have lots of time to talk and
they're more interested in politics than in anything else.

Dan read Tom's letters — and Mat's hasty, lusty scrawls — with
a lively interest, yet with misgivings too. Since his first meeting
with Senator Hamlin he had shared the Senator's expectation that
sooner or later the differences between the North and the South
would lead to fighting; and it seemed to him that if that happened, Tom and Mat might find their positions difficult.
He had been home only a few days when Lincoln and Hamlin
were nominated by the Republican Convention to head the ticket.
Jenny saw in these nominations the sure success of the Republican
Party and the end of slavery; but Dan and his father did not share
her certainty. Tom's letters had persuaded them that if Lincoln
were elected, the South would secede. What would happen then,
no one could foresee; but Dan voiced the thought in both their
minds when he said:
'If there's trouble, father, will Tom and Mat come home?'
John shook his head. 'I don't know, Dan,' he said. 'I don't know.'
Dan ventured a day or two later to write to his brothers. He
said that Jenny was not well, suggested that Tom and Mat come
North and bring Tom's family for a visit and to avoid the summer
hot weather; but it would be weeks before an answer to his letter
came.

II

Within a few days after the conventions, the campaign got
under way. There were four parties in the field, and the split
between the Breckinridge and the Douglas Democrats made Republican success probable. To Dan the Republican platform seemed
fair and just, leaving to every state the right to control its own
internal affairs, with the corollary that just as a Southern state
could maintain slavery within its boundaries, so could a Northern
state refuse to admit the institution. He was too young to realize
that this was a dangerous oversimplification of the dispute in which
passion now replaced reason. Southern editorials damning the
Northern Republicans as nigger-lovers and fanatics were reprinted
in the *Whig and Courier;* and when Barnwell Rhett in a speech in

Charleston asserted that Hannibal Hamlin was a mulatto, even Mr. Lebbeus in the *Star* and Mr. Emery in the *Democrat,* though they consistently opposed the Republican ticket, published editorials ridiculing the charge.

The effect of Mr. Rhett's speech was to increase the pride of Bangor men in Mr. Hamlin, and when he came to Maine in June for the party convention his welcome was tremendous. At the convention Israel Washburn of Freeport was nominated for Governor. He was one of seven brothers, all remarkable men. Three of them had served in the national House of Representatives at the same time and from as many different states, and the others were equally distinguished in their several fields. Mr. Washburn was generally credited with having been the first to suggest founding the Republican Party, calling anti-slavery members of Congress together after the passage of the Wilmot Proviso to lay the proposal before them. Dan's father knew and admired him, and his nomination went a long way to persuade John that the Republican Party was the country's best hope.

Dan had no doubts of the long wisdom of the Republican position; and as the campaign got under way he joined the Wide Awakes, and marched with them in torchlight parades, and worked with them in the vigorous fight to give Washburn the largest possible plurality. The pleasure barge, Fairy of the Waves, was launched toward the end of June from Isaac Dunning's shipyard in Brewer; and the Wide Awakes chartered her for a trip down the river. She was decorated with flags and bunting, almost fifteen hundred people crowded aboard her, the Bangor Cornet Band played all day long, and men shouted the campaign songs.

> 'There's a sound like the surges of ocean
> Or winds sweeping forest and lea;
> It comes from a nation in motion
> From the millions who've sworn to be free . . . ,

Beth Pawl was fourteen that summer, and she found Dan in his marching uniform a splendid figure. She had a pleasing voice — she was taking piano lessons too, from Madame Zimmerman — and at one of the mass meetings, very lovely in starched white on the flag-draped platform, she sang this song, and the crowd joined in the smashing chorus, picking up the last lines of the stanza:

> 'Here's to Lincoln and Hamlin! God bless them!
> And bless, too, our country and cause!

'And bless, too, our country and cause!
And bless, too, our country and cause!
Here's to Lincoln and Hamlin! God bless them!
And bless, too, our country and cause!'

Beth's clear small voice was drowned by that mighty surge of sound; and Dan, watching her, felt a sudden fulness in his throat, she stood so straight and proudly there above the packed ranks of men, her small head high. There were songs and then some speech-making and then more songs; and when the meeting ended, Dan went to find Beth and to escort her home, offering her his arm as gravely as though she were a young lady instead of a child, smiling to himself at her demure composure as she walked happily by his side.

Aunt Meg was at home before them, and when Beth went upstairs to change her dress, leaving them alone, Meg said smilingly:

'You made her mighty happy, Dan, bringing her home. You know she thinks that after you were made, the mold was broken.'

'She's mighty sweet!'

Meg looked at him thoughtfully, her eyes shadowed by some faint concern. 'She takes you so seriously, dreams about you, writes in her diary about you.' She added, smiling again: 'But of course she'll get over it.'

'I don't want her to get over it,' he declared, chuckling a little. 'I like her too.'

'You'll be falling in love pretty soon, though,' she reminded him. 'Finding someone and getting married. I hope she gets over it before that happens.'

He laughed. 'I haven't seen anyone I want to marry, yet,' he said. 'Maybe I'll wait for Beth.'

III

During that summer the campaign filled Dan's mind. He gave only what time he must to business. Lumber was in demand. On the fourteenth of July, sixty vessels made up Bangor River seeking cargoes. But the drouth had made logs scarce, and mill after mill was forced to shut down; and there was a cry for new industries to give employment to the idle. One result of the hardships of the period was an increase in the number of incendiary fires, and piles of lumber, wharf buildings, sheds and mills were from time to time set alight. A reward was offered by the city government for the capture of the incendiaries, but the fires went on, and as the water fell lower, even those mills which had logs on hand were forced to shut down.

The election of Governor Washburn by a fine plurality forecast the Republican victory which followed in November; and the election of Lincoln and Hamlin was welcomed with complacent satisfaction by the Republicans. The *Whig and Courier* said editorially that in the face of this demonstration of the firm will of the North, Southern threats of secession would evaporate, and predicted a long era of peace and prosperity; but Dan and his father, reading the letters that came from Tom, thought there was more hope than wisdom in this prediction. Tom wrote:

> There's trouble coming, sure. They're calling Lincoln an ape down here, and saying that he's not really President because a minority elected him. Up in South Carolina they're shouting for secession, and saying the South ought to unite with Mexico and make a new nation. The only chance I see — judging by the talk I hear — is that something may happen to prevent Lincoln's being inaugurated. If he's as bad as they say he is, then the South is in for it. You know I think the real trouble down here is they're scared. They're afraid what Lincoln will do. And they're sure they can secede without having any trouble.

Dan wrote hopefully to suggest again that Tom and Mat come home. 'I don't think Mr. Lincoln will let the South secede,' he said. 'And if the South starts a fight, the North won't back down. If there's fighting, you'll be in an unpleasant position down there.' But Tom — and Mat signed the letter too — replied:

> This is our home down here now, Dan. We like these people. They've been good to us, and if there's trouble, we'll stay and do our share with them. I hate it, but you have to stick with your neighbors and relatives. I've a Southern wife, you know, Dan, and a Southern baby. There's nothing else I can do.

Dan showed this letter to his father, explaining his invitation which had prompted it. John nodded in sober acceptance of Tom's decision. 'I'm not surprised, Dan,' he said. 'They're both grown men, old enough to know their own minds. They'll have to decide for themselves what they want.' Yet he added: 'It's going to be hardest on mother. I can see some justice on both sides, but she is sure the South is wrong.'

Dan nodded. 'And she hasn't mentioned Tom or Mat for months,' he said. 'She won't let me talk to her about them at all.'

IV

During that winter, when the long uncertainty kept every man uneasy in his mind, Dan and his father both wrote Tom and Mat, accepting their decision and without recriminations. Congress met and President Buchanan in his message said the Government had no power to prevent secession. In Bangor the *Star* and the *Democrat* each argued that the union was a federation of sovereign states from which any state could at will withdraw. Little by little, secession rather than slavery became the dominant issue. When South Carolina demanded the surrender of the harbor forts, the immediate crisis drew nearer. In mid-February, Senator Hamlin left Bangor for Washington for the inauguration, and a line of sleighs a mile long escorted him to the station. The Bangor papers recorded his progress to Washington and reported the throngs which cheered him at Worcester, Hartford, Meriden, New Haven, and all along his route. Dan read every dispatch, and through the weeks that followed he forgot personal and business considerations in the breathless suspense which held the nation.

But if Dan and his father still hoped that the tension would somehow pass, Jenny was by this time serenely sure what was to come. 'There will be war,' she said confidently. 'The Southerners are cowards, forever bragging and bullying, but cowards all the same. They've been needing a whipping for years. I'd like to see every slave-owner whipped till his back is as raw and bleeding as the lacerated backs of his miserable slaves. They've been talking fight for years. Well, they shall have it now!'

Dan, though he still hoped for peace, had some of his mother's feeling that the North had been patient too long, that this thing must be settled for good and all. Then Sumter was attacked and fell; and the *Whig and Courier* printed an editorial: 'Has the War Begun?' and another, two days later: 'The People Aroused, The War Begun'; and then grimly: 'A Call for Troops from Maine.'

When there was no longer any doubt, as though during the months of tightening tension men had waited poised for action, things happened fast. From Augusta came orders to the Major-Generals of Militia to enroll ten thousand volunteers, and when the Legislature in special session authorized the raising of ten regiments, the State Arsenal in Bangor became the focus of activity that went on twenty-four hours a day. As recruiting got under way, the Arsenal became a general rendezvous into which poured squads and companies from the whole Penobscot Valley. The place was like a hive, not only with recruits, but with hundreds of small boys gathered to watch the excitement, and with Bangor folk come to see and hear.

Every day in the *Whig and Courier* there were dispatches which increased the steadily rising anger against the South. Two Scots, woodsmen who had been getting out ship timbers in the hard-pine forest of South Carolina, arrived in Bangor with a lurid story of their narrow escape from being forced into the Confederate armies. Three Belfast vessels were reported seized on the same South Carolina river. Jenny began to organize Bangor ladies to take care of the sick and wounded who with the first fighting would begin to come home; and she helped collect subscriptions for the fund that was being raised to take care of the families of soldiers. She was instrumental in drawing up a schedule of advice for volunteers, warning them not to wear cotton stockings, and suggesting that even woollen stockings be soaked in tallow to prevent blisters. Mayor Stetson received from S. H. Ruggles, Esq., of New York a specimen of the Havelock Cap Cover, designed to protect troops in a hot climate against sunstroke. It included a loose cloth flap to hang down over the back of the neck, and had been devised by General Havelock at Lucknow. Jenny's sewing circle and a dozen other groups of ladies bought up all available linen cloth and began to make these cap covers by the dozens, finding in this way an outlet for their emotional enthusiasm, and blissfully sure that they would thus save many a soldier's life. The young men who received the first of these products vowed that a Havelock made by lovely Bangor hands was a better ward against harm than any armor.

Dan was, of course, one of the first to volunteer. He joined the Second Regiment, which within a fortnight after the fall of Sumter was already filled and organized. It numbered some two hundred officers of all grades and about seven hundred men, and there were in it so many tall woodsmen that someone suggested forming a regiment of six-foot grenadiers to terrify the enemy by their colossal size. One proud lumber operator boasted that the thirty men in his crew were all of the required height; and he wrote the *Whig and Courier* that of twenty-five passengers on the river steamer on a recent trip, twenty-two were over six feet. It was proposed to call the regiment the Infants; and a dozen people told Dan he should withdraw from the Second to join this new organization.

But he preferred the Bangor regiment. As soon as it was organized, preparations were put under way to transport the men to Long Island, there to be mustered into the United States Service. On May 13, the regiment was ordered to leave by rail on the following day; but not all the men were as yet outfitted and equipped, and Dan was among those who stayed behind to go forward later.

He was glad of that respite, of that longer time at home, finding on the eve of departure a nostalgic pleasure in reviewing and revisiting familiar sights and scenes. Even to read the *Whig and Courier* with its familiar advertisements — of Mr. Williams' Hair Cutting and Shaving Saloon, of the Fresh Teas and Pure Coffees to be had at the China Tea Company, of Mr. Kirkpatrick's new shipment of skirts, of Doctor Swett's Infallible Liniments and Doctor Langley's Root and Herb Bitters, of the new carpet hooks so much superior to tacks for laying carpets — was a quiet pleasure. He read, too, quotations from Southern papers which said that the North was bent upon a war of extermination, and he read Beauregard's proclamation that the Northern armies would seek to invade the South and lay predatory hands upon Beauty and Booty alike. When the Little Singers of Bangor gave an entertainment with tableaux directed by Mr. William Wilder, he went to hear Beth sing 'The Flag of Our Union' and assured her afterward that hers was the sweetest voice of all. When the *Democrat* published the statement that forty thousand Democrats in Maine were opposed to the war, he told his father that Marcellus Emery was a liar and should be tarred and feathered; but he was appeased when next day the *Democrat* attacked the New York *Tribune,* calling it one of the disguised organs of rebellion in the North, because it had said this was a politicians' war.

Before he left Bangor, a letter came from Will in Wisconsin.

Dear mother and father and Dan —

Well, this war has upset all my plans and I can think of nothing else but being in it. I have a good practice here, more debts than pay, but there will be good crops this fall and they will have money to pay, but I won't be here. There is a company going from this place, and I will go in that and then try to get a place in the surgical department. I don't mind a good fight when it is just a question of hitting the other fellow some licks and getting some yourself, but when it comes to bullet holes and killing I would rather cure than kill, if I can. Anyway, even if it is just to carry a musket, I would like a hand in settling our national difficulties. Maybe I ought to stay here, because I can do some good here, but there is so much excitement of war and so much necessity for all to turn out that I do not think I can stay home at peace with myself. The Northern people are on the right side of the question and must succeed in whipping the South and putting down this rebellion. I want to help do it.

Write to me as soon as you get this, before I leave here. I want to hear from all. Write me who are going ahead in war matters there. This war makes me miserable. I hate it and should like to help close it.

Your loving son and bro —   WILL

John read this aloud at supper that night, and when he was done, Jenny took it to read over and over to herself. Dan wrote to Will that night to say that he had volunteered — he was commissioned Captain — and that he would soon leave Bangor to join his regiment at the front; but Jenny did not write to her son that day or the next. Then at supper on the third evening she said:

'Dan, I've written a letter to Will. I want to read it to you after supper, because I want to say the same thing to you.'

Something hard and cruel in her level tones disturbed him; and he saw concern in his father's eyes. There was often this spring a hint of controlled pain in Jenny's countenance and in her voice; a tightening of her lips, an aching hollowness in the way she spoke. Once or twice Dan had asked her if she were all right, but she always said indifferently: 'Just my back. It gives me a twist sometimes.' The long excitement of the campaign which led to Lincoln's election, and the suspense all this past winter while they waited for the inauguration and what would follow it, had seemed to make her forgetful of her own distress; and while she was thus less mindful of herself she had been happier.

But tonight Dan thought there was a change in her; and he half-guessed what she might have written Will, guessed its tenor if not its actual content, before in her quiet and precise tones she read to him and to his father the letter.

Dear Will —

I am proud to know that you are taking arms to destroy the cruel, brutish beasts who have so long held under the lash millions of their fellow human beings. I hope to see the South conquered and I hope to see every man who has owned slaves himself reduced to slavery, forced to bitter labor in the fields under a baking sun, with a whip across his shoulders when he lags; and may the wives and the daughters of those men be debauched as they have debauched the wives and daughters of others, and may their sons be born in bondage and never know freedom. For this I pray.

Dan knew then that his guess was correct. He met his father's eyes and saw that John too foresaw what was to come. Jenny, her low voice dry and burning in the quiet room, read on.

I am proud that you and Dan, my true and only sons, will help to bring these things to pass. Dan will be fighting. I do not know whether you will be a fighter or a surgeon. If you are a fighter, kill and kill and kill. If you are a surgeon, save our men when you can.

But Will, for my sake, never give a wounded Rebel so much

as a drink of water to wet his parched lips while he dies in screaming pain! For my sake, Will, remember this.

She paused a moment then, to meet Dan's eyes, as though bidding him pay attention to what she was about to read.

There are two young men from Bangor, two young men you know, who chose to go to the slave South and mingle their blood with that of the slave-masters, and forget their birth and their upbringing here. No one knows what will happen in this war that is beginning; but it may be that, if your are in the fighting lines, some day in a Rebel soldier you will recognize one of these two traitors. If you do, aim straight, Will. Kill him. Or it may be that when our armies ravage the South you will come to a house where one of these men lived. Burn it. Lay waste the lands around it. Spare nothing that is theirs, except the helpless slaves they have abused. Or if you become a surgeon and they come wounded into your hands, leave them to die, or rub salt into their wounds. Do this for me!

Her eyes met Dan's again in a bleak insistence; they even turned to John, as though warning him not to interfere. Then she went on:

You may think me an unnatural mother. It is true that I am the mother of unnatural and alien sons, who have betrayed us all. I have cast them out of my life and out of my heart together; and I wish I had plucked them still-born from my womb. Kill them, Will. Kill them if you can. You and Dan are my only sons.

Your loving
MOTHER

She read this letter through with no variation of emphasis, letting the blazing words speak for themselves. Dan while she read watched his father; but John sat with his eyes lowered, his hands resting on his knees. Dan thought how firm those hands were and how strong, and he wished suddenly to hold to them, to feel his father's handclasp, to draw strength from the older man. His mother as she read seemed to him no longer human; not even like a beast, but like some sentient horror of a sort man had never seen and should not see. Perspiration beaded his forehead and ran coldly down his cheeks and he was sick at his stomach so that he wished to retch and vomit, and he shook with terror and thought to run, to escape from her low tones which beat upon his ears.

Then suddenly she was done and she spoke to him, forcing him to look at her, saying:

'So, Dan! You heard me?' He made some miserable sound, and she said: 'To you I give the same bidding. The chance may never come; or if you meet these two, they may kill you by some treachery before you can destroy them. I know they will if they can. That is the habit of traitors and murderers. But if you can, kill them, Dan. Kill them, if you love me.'

Dan could not speak, but John said gravely: 'Jenny, you say more than you mean.'

'I say not half of all I mean!' she insisted in her dreadful soft voice. 'Killing is too easy for them. I want them to suffer a long time before they die!'

John shook his head. 'You've lost yourself in anger. This isn't your heart, Jenny, speaking so of brother killing brother. It's anger, brooding anger like madness. Please believe me.'

Dan, staring at her, praying for some yielding in her, saw for a moment something in her eyes at once mocking and truculent, naked as a skull. Then she said gently, in a way that burned, half-smiling as she spoke:

'But John darling, you know I'm quite capable of — thoughts of death and pain.'

Her words hinted of dark things, hideous and unspeakable and frightening; and Dan saw that even his father was shaken. A gust of panic seized him. Unable to endure this moment longer, he came to his feet and fled. Behind him he heard his father rise and stride grimly toward his mother's chair, as though to lay a hard hand on her. He rushed out of doors, blundered through the darkness, hurrying away.

5

Dan, commanding a detachment of seventy-five men, left Bangor on the third of July to join his regiment; and for more than two years he saw neither Jenny nor his father again. The Second Maine had reached Washington on the thirty-first of May. Dan joined it at Falls Church, Virginia, in time to face the Confederates at Bull Run. The regiment lost almost fifty men in killed and wounded and a hundred missing in that disaster. They wintered at Hall's Hill, had a share in the siege of Yorktown, fought at Hanover Court House, and during the dreadful Seven Days and at Malvern Hill they learned their trade and learned it well — only to suffer with others at Second Manassas when the command was put into Pope's unskilful hands. Back in Washington again they welcomed McClellan's reappointment to command, and under his leadership had a part in that miracle of reorganization which culminated at Antietam. There the Second was held in reserve; but at Shepherdstown soon afterward they were badly shot up in an attempt to ford the Potomac, and at Fredericksburg in December their losses were again heavy. Their last great battle was Chancellorsville, in May of '63.

Through these long months Dan had at irregular intervals letters from home; from his father and his mother, from Aunt Meg and Beth and from others too. Jenny's letters were full of a dark rancor against the South which Dan, who by fighting Southerners had learned to respect them, could not share. Aunt Meg's were straightforward and cheerful and heartening, rarely mentioning the war at all; and Beth's, written in the stilted unnatural style taught her in school, packed with long words and polished phrases, completely unlike her straightforward self and by their very perfection suggesting that they had been laboriously written and rewritten before the final fair copy, made him chuckle. She began them: 'Dear Friend,' and signed herself: 'Your Sincere Friend, Beth.' She said his father was well and his mother seemed better and that her mother and she herself were well and that she hoped he was well. She spoke of her piano lessons and her singing; of how much sewing she and her mother did for the soldiers; of the weather; of his friends whom she had seen and who were, she assured him, well; and rarely she spoke of the war — never of battles that were past — saying that everyone hoped it would soon be over, and that she hoped he was well. What she wrote was nothing, but the faithfulness with which she continued to write pleased him; and once when she confessed: 'I very much fear that my poor merits as a correspondent cannot hope to interest one so absorbed in more important matters as yourself,' he replied: 'Your letters are grand, Beth. I eat them up, every word. I wish I could have a fresh one every day.'

He became conscious as the months passed that a change in her letters marked the change which must be taking place in her, and he realized that she was growing out of girlhood and wished he had kept her earlier letters for comparison. Toward the end of 1862 he began to keep every line he had from her.

His father's letters he had from the first preserved, reading them over and over, not so much for what they said as because they brought his father close to him. John wrote meticulously about whatever Bangor happening he thought would interest his son. In a letter which John received when after Bull Run the regiment was in garrison at Fort Corcoran, John enclosed a clipping from a Western paper criticizing the Bangor *Democrat* for its opposition to the war, and another which quoted a Southern paper as applauding the *Democrat* for speaking out 'against the damnable usurpations of Abe Lincoln and his cowardly abettors'; and he explained:

> These clippings will tell you that the *Democrat* did not change its tune after you went away. Mr. Emery continued to sing a song of treason until the natural result followed. Mayor Stetson saw trouble coming and tried to prevent it, but one day a crowd of men got together and when Mr. Emery and everyone in the office were gone to dinner they went in and threw his presses, his paper and types and cases and everything out of the window into the street. That was four stories and that wrecked the presses, but then they burned everything that would burn and threw everything else into the Stream. Mr. Emery came along and tried to stop them and it looked for a while as if he'd get hurt, but they got him away from the crowd. I hear he's left town. Mr. Lebbeus has sung low in the *Star* since then. I don't like violence; but in war you've got to be on one side or the other, and Mr. Emery was on the wrong side to suit most of us here. I didn't want to see this war start; but it wasn't our fault that started it, and now it's started I want to see it won.

John wrote, then and in his later letters, of many things. The races at the Trotting Park the day after Dan's departure had drawn a big crowd. The *Whig and Courier* had printed in full President Lincoln's message calling for 400,000 men and $400,000,000 to finance the war. 'Your mother and Aunt Meg and Beth and I went to hear Madame Charlotte Varian James sing "The Star-Spangled Banner" and other songs at Norombega Hall,' he reported. 'Beth said she didn't sing very well, but your mother enjoyed it, and the people clapped so hard she had a time of it to finish.' The *Whig and Courier* thought there ought to be defenses against Confederate privateers along the coast and down the Bay. Letters from soldiers were being printed in the papers, but they were mostly brag and blow. There were claims of Confederate cruelties to prisoners after Manassas, but John did not believe them. Most people blamed the

Union generals for letting forty thousand Northern troops attack anywhere from sixty to ninety thousand entrenched Confederates, but John guessed there weren't quite that many Southerners. 'It looks to me they outfought us,' he commented. 'Sounds to me like a boy I used to know in Freeport who got licked in a fight once and said: "Well, maybe I can't lick you but I can make faces at your sister!"' The list of the Second Regiment's killed and wounded had been printed, and Bangor people felt pretty bad about that, but steady too. The state was paying twenty-two dollars for recruits. Wambold and Company's Great Double Show was in town early in September, but not many went to see it. In 1861, for the first time, more spruce than pine had come down-river. They were asking for three-year enlistments now, and John guessed that judging by what happened at Manassas a soldier had to learn his trade like anyone else.

Dan found these letters had the very flavor of his father's talk, wise and tolerant and cheerful. In the spring of 1862 John wrote that business was slack. The arrivals of vessels had fallen the year before to a scant seventeen hundred, about half the figure for 1860. There was no demand for lumber. Two pine logs, one fourteen feet long and the other ten feet long, had sawed up into 2541 feet of boards. The ice went out on April 18, and there was quite a freshet, so that the bridges were weighted down to keep them from floating away. The young ladies of Rescue Division, Sons of Temperance, had held a levee with tableaux and music to raise money for a melodeon, and Beth sang and there was a collation of oysters, ice cream and coffee. Beth was getting to be a young lady and a mighty pretty one. One tableau called 'How Jemima Took Him Down a Peg' was funny. The latest joke in Bangor was that if you wanted your clocks never to stop running you could oil them with oil out of a Rebel's heel, but John hadn't noticed that the Rebels were any quicker to run than some others he could mention. There were a lot of fires being set and the city had offered a reward of five hundred dollars for anyone who would catch the guilty party.

In each letter, too, there was some word of Jenny. She was more cheerful than she had been — or less so. She was better — or worse. Her back bothered her more — or less. In the winter of 1862 John wrote that she was badly off. 'I don't think she'll ever be well again,' he confessed. 'She has dreadful pain, and keeps her bed, and it is terrible to see her. She speaks much of you.' He added further word of business conditions. In July of that year, the ship S. E. Smith sailed from Bangor to Liverpool with over a million feet of lumber, the largest cargo ever shipped from Bangor. Jenny had refused to let her ships be used in the ice trade because fresh water rotted them. The sudden closing of the river on the fifth of December caught twenty vessels and froze them in for the winter. There was talk of building a Soldiers' Monument. Not much first-class pine remained uncut anywhere on the river, certainly not south of Medway. The labor shortage was worse all the time as more men went to war.

Dan drew strength from these long, cheerful letters; but he began to look forward to the end of his enlistment. The Second had been mustered in for two years, and after Chancellorsville their time was almost up. The regiment, that originally numbered close to a thousand men, was by service losses and despite replacements reduced to about half that number. Some of the replacements had been three-year men, but the rest of the regiment would return to Bangor to be mustered out.

Dan expected to go with them, but a day or two before his time expired, something happened to change his mind. A letter came through from his father saying that Jenny was better; and it enclosed one from Will.

Dear Father —

I read between the lines of your letters your trouble, but I know the strength of your honest mind which has always been true to itself, to yourself and to us, and I know you can support everything.

As for me, I am at last to take my part in this war. You remember I meant to go first as a Lieutenant in a company I helped to raise; but Colonel Thomas said there was plenty of time, that the war would be a long one and surgeons would be needed, and recommended me to finish my medical course. I came out this spring with my diploma and honors. I then went before the military board of the State and passed successfully and was appointed Assistant Surgeon to the Sixth Regiment, Wisconsin Volunteers, which is now at or near Belle Plaine, Va. I am starting at once for Washington and then to join my regiment.

Dan read this with a sudden quickening of attention. Will's letter was dated in mid-April. He must be with the Sixth Wisconsin now, and Dan longed to see him again if only for an hour. He read on:

I do not know what to say as to mother. I know she is not right in her mind, so all we can do is not pay attention to what she says or does. It is a form of insanity which it is doubtful if she will ever recover from; but you have strength to stand it. I know you have had trouble enough to kill any ordinary man. I can understand now things that happened when we were boys that did not mean anything to me then. Mother can't help herself, and I think she is more unhappy than she ever makes anyone else. Tell her not to be discouraged. I don't think she is sick so much as her disposition, and now in the spring she will probably get better.

There was more about Will's hopes and plans. He expected to be married when the war was over, and he wrote:

The young lady wished to be married now, but I have told her it is better to wait till I come back, and I think I have persuaded her to wait. If not I will just have to bear it. Her name is Miss Margaret Wellcome, and she is very sweet. I have told her all about you, which made her like me.

Your loving son,

WILL

Then at the bottom of the last page:

Miss Wellcome decided she did not want to wait. She said if my brothers had married Southern girls I might do the same if I went to war before we were married, so we are going to marry this afternoon and I leave tomorrow. Your new daughter sends her love to you and mother and so do I.

Dan chuckled as he read this. It sounded so like Will, who was always apt to have a twinkle in his eye; and Dan decided that if he could be with Will it would be worth changing his decision to go home. The Army of the Potomac after its disastrous spring campaign was losing thousands of two-year troops whose time had run, and there were recurrent rumors of a movement by the Southern Army to take advantage of this weakness, so those soldiers who like Dan were willing to re-enlist could within reason make their own terms. Dan sought and received permission to re-enlist in Will's regiment, and early in June he reported to the Sixth Wisconsin at White Oak Church.

II

The two brothers met after these many years almost with diffidence. Dan knew Will at once, but Dan too now wore a beard and for a moment Will did not recognize him. They clasped hands in a strong happiness, and then they began a cautious series of questions and answers, building a bridge across the gap between the present and the past. Will wanted to know how Dan came into a Wisconsin regiment, and Dan told him, and Will said Dan's beard made him look a lot older.

'I feel older,' Dan assented. 'I've had two years of this, you know. It takes the tuck out of a man.'

Will nodded gravely. 'Have you been hit at all?'

'Nothing to matter. A nick in the arm, and a cut head. I've never been in hospital.'

Will asked questions about the service Dan had seen, about many impersonal things. At last, hesitantly, he inquired: 'Have you heard anything from Tom and Mat?'

'I saw a Lieutenant out of a Georgia regiment, a prisoner, who knew them.' And Dan added eagerly, glad to have this news to tell: 'He says Mat was married in the fall of '61.'

'That's good,' Will declared, and he colored a little. 'You know I'm married, too.'

'Yes, father sent me your last letter,' Dan assented. 'That's how I knew where you were.'

'Are you married yet?'

Dan shook his head. 'No.' He thought suddenly of Beth, and with a surprising pleasure. She must be sixteen now, nearly seventeen, almost a young lady. 'No,' he repeated, and laughed and said jokingly: 'I'm waiting for Beth to grow up! You've all beaten me. Tom has two children, you know. Two, anyway.'

Will chuckled. 'Beth? She always did like you.' He asked awkwardly: 'Are they all right, Mat and Tom?'

'As far as anything I've heard.' Dan wanted to ask whether Will had ever received that letter from Jenny, in which she wished Tom and Mat dead, but he could not bring himself to do so. Not even between him and his father had that moment been mentioned since.

Will turned again to impersonal matters. 'They tell me these Southerners are hard fighters.'

'They're fine infantry,' Dan agreed. 'So are ours, but the Rebels are better led. But our artillery is better than theirs, better guns and better handled.'

'I haven't been in a battle yet,' Will confessed.

'I thought you might have been at Chancellorsville.'

'No. When I wrote father, I expected to start for Washington next day, but after we decided to be married I asked for extra leave, so I didn't go to Washington till the second of May, and no one knew just where the Sixth was. I joined them here on the eighth.'

Dan asked: 'Been here ever since?'

'We marched down the Northern Neck.' He grinned. 'But the only thing that happened, a horse loaded with gear for the head-quarters mess fell off a bridge and got rid of his load.' And he asked: 'Dan, do you think the Rebels will attack us here?'

'No,' Dan said positively. 'No, not if Lee's smart — and he is. Of course, he might beat us, but even if he did, it would be just another battle won, and he's already won a lot of battles without settling anything. Fighting the North is like punching pillows, Will. The South is going to lose Vicksburg. That's just a question of time, and it will be bad news when it comes. Lee needs some big success to counteract that, to cheer up the South — and maybe change England's mind, make them recognize the Confederacy. I think he'll invade the North, go up the Valley into Pennsylvania.'

'What if he does?'

'Why — we'll go after him, keep between him and Washington.'

Will asked in a shy way: 'Are you afraid, in a battle, Dan?'

'Everybody is,' Dan assured him.

'I think I'll probably be,' Will confessed. 'But if I can keep busy, I won't run away.'

Dan chuckled. 'You'll be scared,' he assented. 'But you won't run.'

Not till days later did it occur to Dan as strange and saddening that though they talked for an hour longer, they did not at that first reunion speak of their mother at all.

III

This camp near White Oak Church, pleasantly situated in a fine grove, faced the Rappahannock, and the Southern pickets on the opposite bank were not two hundred yards away; but both armies were quiet, there was no firing to and fro, and unless there were officers about, the pickets occasionally met to exchange newspapers and trade Northern coffee for Southern whiskey in the friendliest way. Nevertheless, this close proximity of the armies made both commanders nervous, and several times during the days that followed the regiment was turned out ready to move; but each time the orders were countermanded.

Dan told Will: 'It's just that every time a few Rebels march across a field, the balloon spots them and we have to get ready.' General Hooker's reconnoitering balloon, hanging in the air behind the lines, was a fair target for every jest. 'Our men say Johnny Reb enjoys fooling the balloon!'

Through the first week of June these alarms were frequent, and once the troops had to lie in line of battle under a baking sun till

their tempers ran short; but on the morning of June twelve—
though none knew why—the regiment moved at last, marching
twenty miles through dust and sun to Deep Run, moving on to
Bealton Station, and on the third day to Bull Run. Dan told Will
that night:

'This is my third time here at Manassas. We were licked the
first time and the second; but maybe this time we'll be let off. I
think Lee backed away from the Rappahannock and crossed into
the Valley and headed north. If that's so, we're racing to catch him
now.'

He was right in this guess, for they pushed steadily northward;
and the first batch of newspapers brought word that Lee's foragers
were already in Pennsylvania. Dan and Will read the papers together.

'If his advance is that far north,' Dan pointed out, 'it means he's
got a big start on us. Hooker's balloon didn't do us any good. Lee
got away without our knowing it.' One paper predicted another
battle at Antietam, and he added: 'I hope that doesn't happen. I
never want to see the place again. We were in reserve—I was in
the Second Maine then—but we were one of the first into Sharpsburg after the Rebels pulled out, and I saw more dead men there
than I've ever seen anywhere.'

Will nodded, and he said soberly: 'Major Hauser tells me that
the Sixth was slaughtered in the cornfield there.' This Major
Hauser was a German, with a background of training in European
military schools. At Thun, in Switzerland, he had been a fellow
student with Louis Napoleon, and he liked to tell in a roaring
voice of the hilarious debauches they had together. He had served
on Garibaldi's staff, and his particular duty in the Sixth was to act
as drillmaster of the line officers. He had made it a point to be
friendly with Will, explaining cheerfully that a wise soldier always
cultivated the surgical staff, so that if he were wounded he could
count on some personal care.

They halted for two days at Broad Run, and since the newspapers
said Lee's men were foraging as they pleased in Pennsylvania, Will
could not understand this delay. 'Why don't we go climb his
frame?' he demanded. 'We're doing no good here!'

'We're protecting Washington!' Dan told him in sardonic scorn.
'That's Hooker's only idea. As long as Lee lets Washington alone
—to hell with Pennsylvania! Hooker'll edge along, keep between
Lee and Washington, let Lee go clear to New York if he wants to.
We'll never fight Lee again if Hooker's in command! He's had his
belly full.'

But they did move northward presently, marching all day and all night with occasional brief halts to Edwards Ferry, and then on through Poolsville to Barnesville. The next day they were early on the road through deep mud and a drizzle of rain which half-obscured the mountain wall to the west, beyond which Dan knew the main Confederate army was likewise pushing north up the Shenandoah Valley in a race to pour its main forces after its van-guard into the heart of Pennsylvania, to Harrisburg, or Philadel-phia, or to Baltimore. He wondered if Tom and Mat were with that army, wondered whether in the coming conflict they would meet at last, remembered his mother's injunction with a deep sor-row like a prayer.

On the long marches he felt within himself a constant impulse to hurry, hurry; and he was forever conscious of that other army over beyond the mountains which was racing northward along parallel lines. That army of Lee's they were bound to intercept and to beat and to sweep off the last foot of Northern soil. He watched his men, helped the stragglers, multiplied himself as though he alone could win this race and the battle that was to come. The men were wet to the skin, eating soggy hardtack and salt pork, sleeping at night in wet blankets; but rain and mud were better than dust and sun. It was at least blissful to be cool.

They had better than two weeks of forced marches, with only a short respite at Broad Run, while that breathless race went on. The twenty-seventh saw them at South Mountain. Next day they marched to Frederick through the continuing rain, and then went on to Emmittsburg. On the evening of the thirtieth of June they made their bivouac on Marsh Creek, four or five miles southwest of Gettysburg.

They had heard a report two days before that Meade had relieved Hooker. Dan knew nothing of Meade or of his merits. 'Anyone's better than Hooker,' he told Will. 'But of course this may not be true.' A constant flood of rumors, true and false, ran along the marching columns day by day. Men said that Confederate cavalry had cut the telegraph wires to Washington, and that Lee had cap-tured Harrisburg and was marching on to Philadelphia, and that Lee was massing troops to hit their flank at Emmittsburg, and that Lee was coming down the Susquehanna to Baltimore, and that Lee was laying waste all Pennsylvania. The men discussed every rumor, but they were veterans, not easily disturbed by any tale. When the report of Meade's appointment to the command was confirmed, the whole army felt a lift of spirit, glad to be free of Hooker, damning him and his balloons!

On this last day's march they had had for the first time a feeling that their immediate goal was near. The Sixth had been the first regiment to cross the Pennsylvania line; and at Emmittsburg, students of the college there turned out to greet the troops and marched a few miles with them, watching the advance guard and flankers feeling for the enemy. That day small Confederate foraging parties scattered before the advance, and in the bivouac tonight dozens of curious farm folk came to welcome them as deliverers. Dan and Will talked with one of them, a fat and amiable man who rode a small horse which seemed half-smothered under the weight he carried, and who said his name was Berrows. The man had a curious impediment in his speech which made him substitute the letter 'r' for 'l' in many words; and as though to conceal this he talked very loudly and with little prompting.

'Say, it's high time you boys were showing up!' he declared. 'Folks around here have been acting rike so many chickens with their heads off. Major Harrer came arong ten days ago making a big speech about defending our homes, and they tried to get up a cavarry company around here. Wanted my horse, but I said I had to have him to run away on when Ree comes. They been out chasing Reb pickets and getting chased theirserves. It was horses mostry the Rebs wanted, so I kep' out of their way.'

Dan asked: 'Any Rebs around here now, except the stealing parties?'

'Nope. There was a rot of them came to Hagerstown and went on to Chambersburg and nigh to Harrisburg. Major Harrer sent one regiment out the Chambersburg Pike, here three-four days ago, but they run into the Rebs and got their hair singed and got chased back to Harrisburg. Then the same day some Rebs rode into Gettysburg shooting off their guns and hooting rike a bunch of Indians. Come arong some sordiers after them, five-six thousand by my guess, and the raggedest, dirtiest, tiredest rot of boys they was I ever see. Yes sir, I was sorry for them. They stayed in Gettysburg Friday night, wanted us to give them I don't know what — or five thousand cash. Town Council tord 'em we didn't have the one or the other, so they went on to York. I heard York gave them twenty-eight thousand cash to get out of town.'

Will said: 'It's been hard on you folks who live around here.'

'Hard doings,' Mr. Berrows agreed. Dan found himself wondering whether the man's name was really Berrows or Bellows. 'They've took what they wanted, gave scrip for it, craimed the scrip would be worth more than our money in a few days. But they got worried and reft, and some of our cavarry came day before yester-

day. They're out west of town now. But I'm grad you boys have
got here, just the same. A man on a horse, if he don't want to fight
he can run away; but you boys that have to wark, you can't get
away if you want, so you have to stay and fight. Yes sir, you rook
good to me.' He added: 'And you better get ready, too. There's
a heap of Rebs camped out arong the pike. Ree's whore army's
handy, what I hear, coming through Cashtown Gap to head you off.
Some of them came in as far as the Seminary this morning and
put some pickets in Shead's house, but they backed off toward
Cashtown again. Buford's cavarry scared them off, maybe; but I
rook to see them back tomorrow, rooking for a fight.'

He said good night at last. 'See you in the morning,' he promised.
'Give 'em what for, boys!' And he ambled away. When he was
gone, Dan said:

'You know, Will, if Lee's whole army's near, that's maybe a
hundred thousand men.'

'Why doesn't General Meade wait till the rest of our men get
here?'

Dan laughed. 'You can't always have your druthers in war,
Will — not even if you're a General. Meade won't fight at long
odds unless he has to, but maybe he can't help himself. But we
don't have to worry about him.' He chuckled, slapped Will's
shoulder. 'You never have to worry in the army, Will. You just
do what you're told.'

IV

That night of the thirtieth of June was quiet, and the drizzle
which had beset them on so much of their march north from Virginia had given way to clearing skies; but Dan slept little. He had
no desire to sleep, anticipating the morrow. An easy two-hour
march would bring them to Gettysburg. Probably, Dan thought,
the nearest Confederates were no farther away to the westward;
and he wondered whether it would be possible from some low hill
— for instance, from the little rocky summit which before dark he
had seen a mile or so northeast of their bivouac — to see the fires
in the Confederate bivouacs. He found himself remembering some
of the Confederates he had come to know, prisoners whom he had
questioned, or enemy pickets ready enough to pass the time of day
and discuss the war with you. War, he thought, in a remote lucidity, was a strange institution. You met a man some sunny morning
by a brookside between the lines where each of you had gone to
bathe, and the uniform he took off was gray, and the clothing you

removed was blue; but when you were naked you looked much alike except that he was a little thinner than you. There were other slight differences. He talked in an easy, soft, friendly drawl; and he slurred his 'r's' and this Southerner washing himself in the same brook — which he called a creek — was a little more ready to talk about himself than you were. But otherwise you were much alike, and you met in friendly ways.

But if the next day some officer told you to fight, and some other officer told that other man to fight, you would both do it. He might come bounding at you with his mouth open, screaming like a murderous maniac, and letting off his musket at you; and you would shoot at him, and if you missed him he would be at you with his bayonet unless you pinned him first, or cracked his skull with your musket butt. You and he could have been friends, given the opportunity; but you were ready enough to kill each other if someone told you to do so.

Dan wondered why, but at once he knew the answer. You were ready to fight each other because fundamentally that man believed one thing and you believed another. Perhaps it would never have occurred to either of you to fight over your beliefs if you had been let alone; but men — presumably wiser, certainly more passionate than either of you — had decided that you should fight, and you accepted their decision, and they appointed men to tell you when to fight, and you did it — freely and eagerly. And once a man began to fight, he would go on until he won or was beaten, if he were a man; but unless someone told you that the hour for fighting had come, you and that Rebel could be friends just the same.

The enigma was curious and perplexing and sorrowful, yet Dan thought to be a soldier was on the whole surprisingly peaceful and contenting. Now and then you had a job of fighting to do, and when that happened men were nothing but counters in a game, and the more of them you knocked over, the quicker you won, and blood and brains and guts and amputated arms and legs heaped in a pile outside the hospital tents ceased to be sickening evidence of the destruction of other human beings like yourself, but became just the meaningless débris which the game left behind on the playing field. But whether in battle or between whiles, you had never to make decisions; you just did what you were told.

You felt nothing in a fight. Beforehand, of course, you were afraid. That is, your hands perspired and your stomach was a knot of crawling worms, and your mouth was so dry you couldn't spit. But once the thing began, you were like a spectator, seeing everything that happened with an extraordinary clarity, remembering scenes like tableaux in which every actor was motionless; and you were completely cool and calm even though you might hear yourself utter toneless screams of hate and rage as you fought. Then when the fighting was done you might be sick, and then if you were allowed to do so you slept for hours and hours and hours, as though you would never wake.

Dan wondered whether Will was sleeping tonight. Will would be busy tomorrow in the hospital tents somewhere, or in a house or a barn, cutting and hacking useless flesh off maimed bodies just as one stripped bark off a felled pine and lopped the branches. He wondered again whether Tom and Mat were in that invading army he and the Sixth were come to fight. That Lieutenant who knew them had told him they were in the Fourteenth Georgia, in General Thomas' brigade and Pender's division. That division was in Hill's Third Corps, and probably Hill and Ewell and Longstreet were all with Lee on this great enterprise, so presumably Tom and Mat would be in tomorrow's fight. Dan thought he would like to see them, and he wondered whether he would know them. Probably they were bearded as he was, and older. He remembered his mother's prayers to him to kill them if he could; and he thought ruefully that this might happen as easily as not, in the smoke and moil and sudden clash of battle. They might not even know each other — yet he thought he would know Mat by his great size.

And he thought pityingly of his mother, who had been unhappy for so many years, torturing herself with doubts of John, torturing herself with many hates. He thought of her with a remote, dispassionate tenderness, a feeling completely impersonal, feeling no bond between him and her except his sympathies. But he thought of John with a fine strengthening pride; and finding as he always did that he could borrow peace from thus thinking of his father, toward dawn he fell at last asleep.

v

The Sixth Wisconsin was in General Wadsworth's division of the First Corps; and when the men had snatched a hurried breakfast the Sixth was the last regiment in the marching order for the day. The brigade guard of a hundred men was the only unit behind them. The regiment mustered three hundred and forty officers and men. Colonel Dawes, while they waited to fall into their place, ordered the drum corps to the front, and the regimental colors were unfurled. At eight o'clock, the drum corps struck up 'The Campbells are Coming,' the men filed into the road, closed ranks and swung into step toward Gettysburg. On their right and a little ahead, a mile or more to the northeast, there was that rocky hill which Dan had noticed yesterday. It rose to a peak some three hundred feet above the valley through which they marched. The hill was wooded, and another like its smaller twin lay just north of it, and from them a low ridge led on toward Gettysburg. Between the road and these wooded hills lay a rocky slope strewn with great boulders and grown up to underbrush. Another low ridge topped with woods paralleled their road on the west. They passed a fine-looking peach orchard and a four-corners, and beyond there were wheatfields on either side of the road. Up the shallow valley they could see the first houses of the town, and on the right the small white stones that marked the cemetery, with other wooded hills rising beyond.

But before they were halfway to the town, they heard sudden cannon fire to the north; and almost at once the head of the column left the road, breaking down the fences, and struck across the wheatfields on the left directly toward the firing that was still four or five miles away. The ground was wet and soft from the continued rain, and the marching men broke down the young wheat, trampling it into the mud. They began to climb the easy slope of the western ridge which rose only a little above the level of the wheatfields they were crossing. The firing ahead was louder all the time, but the action there was hidden from their view by the ridge, except that Dan saw smoke clouds drifting upward above the trees. Not till they reached the high land, filing around an orchard and through a gap in the woods, did the full roar of the battle strike their ears. Then an officer galloped to meet them with orders, and Dan had his part to do in seeing those orders executed. The brigade advanced by regiments in echelon, the Sixth on the left flank and rear. They went forward at the double, loading their muskets as they ran. Dan saw ahead of them, on the western slope of the ridge and descending westerly into a dark ravine, a thick clump of woods several acres in extent; and from its depths came the steady rattle of musketry, the yells of fighting men, and all the dreadful clamor of a hot contention, while among the trees and above them the thinning smoke clouds rose.

The foremost regiments of the brigade plunged into this battle in the woods, taking cover, dodging forward through the trees; but another aide brought Colonel Dawes orders to halt the Sixth where they were, and at the Colonel's command the men lay down to rest and to avoid the spent bullets that came their way. At the same time, the brigade guard was put in order on either flank of the Sixth so that there were about four hundred and fifty men in the immediate command.

During this lull, with the steady clatter of the opening battle to the west and north, Dan, sitting by his men, had time to look around. Behind him toward Gettysburg, there was another patch of woods; and above the crests of the trees he could see the roof and bell-tower of a large building like a church or seminary. To his right a road ran east and west between rail fences, and in the field beyond that road a Union battery was firing toward the still unseen enemy to the west. In the woods below him, where the other regiments of the brigade had disappeared, there was the sound of steady battle.

The regiment lay here refused on the slope above the wood for what seemed to Dan no more than minutes. By the fact that the sounds of battle in the dark forest below somewhat receded, he judged that the Confederates were being pushed back out of the ravine there; but then he saw the battery in the field beyond the road to the north suddenly begin to withdraw. He sprang to his feet to watch that movement. It could only mean that there on the brigade's right flank the Federal troops were being beaten back; and he was not surprised when a moment later another aide came with orders to put the Sixth in line of battle facing toward the turnpike.

The move was made at the double. The regiment trotted north and then swung at right angles to the east and halted, turning to face the road. As the movement was completed, Dan saw Colonel Dawes' horse go down; but before anyone could reach him the Colonel scrambled free and rose, unhurt, and the men shouted in a hoarse cheer.

There was the steady clangor of battle to the west, but until this moment the Sixth had not fired a gun. Now through the smoke Dan saw beyond the fenced road which they faced a ragged line of gray-clad men come running up the rising ground from the west, driving scattered Union forces in headlong flight toward Gettysburg. At the colonel's order, the regiment moved briskly forward to the fence, steadying their muskets on the rails; and from this position they poured in a careful, well-aimed fire on the flank of the Confederate line. When the smoke from their own weapons rose and cleared away, the result of that fire could be seen. Except for scattered dead and wounded, the nearest enemies were gone. Those not hit were scurrying away from the road, tumbling into a raw new ditch which ran parallel with the turnpike about two hundred yards away. The Sixth's flanking fire, enfilading their line, had broken their charge, driven them to cover there.

Colonel Dawes shouted an order to climb the fences which lined the turnpike and advance on the ditch where the Confederates now lay. Dan, warning his men to reload, swung over the first fence at a bound. At the same time, men around him began to fall as the Confederates in the ditch opened a steady fire. Before he climbed the second fence, he saw along the road to the west another regiment moving with them, the men pouring across the fence to form lines of battle. An officer came running from that direction, and Colonel Dawes met him, and a moment later while the Sixth, having crossed the fence, ordered their lines, Colonel Dawes shouted:

'Forward! Charge! But hold your fire!'

Dan felt a sharp relief. To advance was better than to stand here, facing the ditch yonder which was hidden now behind the smoke from many muskets as the Confederates fired, with the sodden sound of bullets striking flesh all around you, and your comrades going down. He shouted to his men: 'Come on! Don't shoot! Come on!'

He — and the whole line — moved forward together. Colonel Dawes at their front repeated over and over a shouted order: 'Close up on the colors! Close up on the colors!' Men were dropping at every step as the line advanced; but when gaps opened they were as quickly closed, each man stronger for feeling a friendly shoulder against his own. Twice Dan saw the color-bearer shot down, but other hands were always quick to seize the fallen flag. He watched the men of his own company, marching with them, shoulder to shoulder, taller than any man of them; and unconsciously he stretched out his arms as though to shepherd them forward.

They moved at a fast walk, steadily and without faltering, their weapons poised. The enemy fire slackened and spurted again and slackened once more as the Confederates reloaded. In these brief intervals between volleys the smoke each time lifted a little, so that Dan could see for a moment the heads and shoulders of the men crouching in the ditch ahead; and each time the volleys came, looking along the line of his own regiment, he saw men fall forward on their faces with a clattering thump, or lag and drop to their hands and knees and then lie down as the line moved on; and each time he and the other officers repeated the command: 'Close up! Close up on the colors! Close up! Hold your fire!' Many men were falling. When the regiment crossed the turnpike they numbered with the brigade guard four hundred and fifty men; and marching shoulder to shoulder they made a fine line that stretched far to right and left. Dan's company was near the centre. To his right the line extended well over a hundred yards; to his left it joined up with that other regiment which was advancing with them. But at once, as they began this advance on the ditch, the line began to shrink as gaps were made and closed; and Dan, looking to the right, saw the line grow shorter and shorter, so that he thought of the elastic bands which his father used to fasten together bunches of papers and with which he had as a boy liked to play, pulling them out to the greatest possible length and then allowing them to contract again. Thus the line of the regiment contracted now, till as they approached the ditch it was no more than half as long as it had been when they crossed the road.

The moment of contact was near. The ditch, he saw with a remote interest, was actually a railroad cut; and he thought of the sunken road at Waterloo, and wished his men were cavalry so they could go faster. It was hard to move so slowly when men were shooting at you. He saw the enemy colors on the edge of the cut not ten yards ahead, and then another burst of fire and smoke hid everything, and Corporal Eggleston sprang toward that flag to seize it and fell forward into the cut, and Dan saw the man who had shot him, and a musket butt split that man's skull.

Then Dan was standing on the lip of the cut. To right and left the Union forces had reached it, and the cut was full of Confederates, milling in confusion. Most of their muskets were empty, so that they were helpless under the still-loaded weapons of the Sixth. Two or three scattering shots were fired, and something tripped Dan and he fell. He tried to rise, but his right foot gave way under him and he looked down at it in astonishment and caught it in his hands and a red flood spilled through his fingers. A bullet had struck him fairly in the ankle, and under his hands he felt the grating bones.

Yet he was conscious of no pain, and he knew a calm surprise at that; and then the men of the Sixth here all around him were shouting: 'Throw down your muskets! Down with them!' Along the railroad cut Dan saw hundreds of Confederates sullenly dropping their empty weapons. A group of the Sixth ran into position to enfilade the cut, and Colonel Dawes, here just beside Dan, shouted in a great voice:

'Where is the Colonel of this regiment?'

An officer stepped forward and reached up to hand Colonel Dawes his sword. His men, already disarmed, stood in huddled groups along the cut. Dan forgot his own hurt, looking all around. Back toward the fence from which they had come the ground was littered with men in blue, some lying motionless, some like himself sitting up, some propped weakly on one arm watching what went forward here; and some of them were shouting, and Dan heard himself utter a yell of triumph, a long, thin howl of exultant pride.

Then he watched the disarmed Confederates fall in, and he saw Major Hauser march them away, and he saw Colonel Dawes throwing out a line of skirmishers to face the enemy to the westward where the roar of battle still was strong. At the same time some men of the Sixth began to trundle a gun — abandoned by the battery which had been firing here — across the field toward the turnpike; and the line of skirmishers moved westward to meet the battle there, and Dan realized that he was dreadfully sleepy, and his head fell slowly on his arms and he lay down.

He wished drowsily that Will were here to take care of him. His foot hurt a little, now, but he was too sleepy to mind. Probably Will was in Gettysburg, where Chief Surgeon Preston would be likely to establish his hospital. Dan decided that pretty soon he would make his way to town. He was always sleepy after a fight, so it did not occur to him that it was loss of blood which made him wish now to close his eyes and rest awhile.

VI

Dan never knew how long he lay asleep or fainting there by the railroad cut, but when his senses began to clear, the sounds of new battle were about him, and the feet of hurrying men pounded past where he lay. He saw men of the Sixth filing eastward through the cut, and he knew that they were being driven back toward the town, and he tried to get to his feet to join them, but his leg would not support him. He must follow them to town; but it would be hard walking along the railroad ties, so he began to crawl painfully toward the road. It was a long way. He judged the distance to be almost two hundred yards; and he estimated, tallying the dead and wounded all around, that a fair half of the Sixth had fallen in that short advance from the road to the railroad cut. But he remembered proudly that they had captured a regiment of the enemy.

He went on, on hands and knees, dragging his leg; and when he reached the fence, soldiers in blue were retreating along the turnpike, looking over their shoulders toward the Confederates who pressed the pursuit. Dan crawled through the fence and propped himself up there beside the road. His foot by that time was a hot ball of pain, and thirst tormented him. He found a full canteen on the body of a dead man, but the warm water seemed only to make his thirst worse. Just beyond where he lay, the Federals stood for a moment to return the Confederate fire before withdrawing stubbornly again. Then a little gust of men in gray came pressing up along the pike and through the fields on either side, and Dan with a remote interest watched them approach and pass where he lay. They were lean, bony men; and old and young were bearded alike; and their faces were powder-stained and some of them had bloody smears across their cheeks from minor wounds; and they shouted with shrill, panting cries as hounds yelp upon a hot trail, running forward, pausing to fire, reloading as they came on again. None of them noticed him, their eyes all intent upon the retreating Federal troops whom they pressed hard toward the town.

Then abruptly Dan saw among them a great man he knew; and his heart leaped and he shouted: 'Mat! Mat!'

Mat, coming up the turnpike at a trot, checked and looked all around, uncertainly; and Dan called his name again. They were not a dozen feet apart, but Dan had to cry out with all his voice before over the tumult of the battle Mat surely heard him and saw him and knew him and came bounding to his side. The big man dropped to his knees by Dan and caught his shoulders and growled hoarsely:

'Dan! God damn you, is it you?'

Dan grinned, gripping the other's hands that clasped his shoulders. 'Me, yes!' he said.

Mat looked at him, looked the length of him, saw his grimed and bloody foot. 'Hit?' he exclaimed.

'Yes,' Dan assented. He asked: 'What's happened?'

Mat's eyes glowed redly with battle light. 'We're driving you like sheep!' he cried. Then more gently: 'We turned your right, Dan.' He demanded, touching his brother's leg: 'When did you get this?'

'There was a regiment of yours in the railroad cut over there.' Dan pointed. 'We climbed the fences here, charged across this field. We lost half our men, but we captured the lot of yours. They hit me just as I got to the cut.'

'Just now?'

'Awhile ago. I don't know. I went to sleep.'

A tall Confederate officer stopped beside them and said harshly: 'Here, you, what are you skulking for?' He struck Mat's shoulder lightly with his naked sword. 'Go on, man,' he said cheerfully. 'You're missing all the fun!'

Mat rose to face him. He said: 'This is my brother, sir.' He spoke through his teeth, and Dan thought he knew that tone

The officer had better be reasonable, or Mat would be on him like a breaking log jam, smashing him down.

But the officer was more than reasonable. 'Your brother?' he echoed. Then he grinned, his teeth white in his smoke-blackened face. 'He's as big as you are!' His tone was friendly. He looked along the road toward Gettysburg, considering. 'Well, we don't need you for the moment,' he said. 'We've got them on the run. Take care of him. We'll have the town in half an hour. Get him to town, to a bed somewhere, and then rejoin your command.' He looked at Dan. 'Your brother, is he?' he repeated curiously.

'Yes, sir,' Mat told him. 'Bangor, Maine. I'm Lieutenant Evered, Fourteenth Georgia. I moved South before the war, but he stayed in Bangor.'

The officer nodded almost sadly. 'Brothers? That's what makes this such a hell of a war. All right, see him comfortable.'

He moved on. Dan said: 'There's a good man.'

Mat stared after the departing officer. 'There are damned few that aren't good men, either side,' he commented. He asked: 'Can you walk with my shoulder, or shall I carry you?'

Dan grinned. 'I think you could. You're big enough! But maybe I can walk.'

From where Dan lay it was a long way into the town. They made it slowly, waiting while the battle marched before them. When they crossed the ridge and began to descend toward the first houses, they could see the Confederate force that had turned the Federal right swinging down from the north toward Gettysburg; and from the hill beyond the town Union cannon were playing on these troops. The brothers paused for many rests. Dan's foot began to bleed again, and Mat stopped that; and he asked where Will was, and Dan said:

'He's somewhere here. He's assistant surgeon of the Sixth Wisconsin. He always wanted to be a doctor. Remember? I was in the Second Maine, but when my time expired I joined them to be with him.' And he asked for Tom.

'Tom's my Captain,' Mat said. 'But he got a bullet through the body at Fredericksburg. They pulled a silk handkerchief through the hole, and he's still in hospital, but he'll get well.' He asked: 'How's father?'

'Fine! I haven't been home since the war began, but I get his letters. He's always the same.'

Mat nodded. They were resting for a moment by the roadside, sitting on the bank. 'That's what I remember about him. He was always the same. I'd like to see him again.' He said in a low tone:

'But I couldn't stand it at home.'

'We wanted you to come home, before the war began.'

'Tom and I talked it over,' Mat assented. 'But Tom's family was down there, and the people had been good to us. We liked them.' He asked awkwardly: 'Is mother the same as ever, Dan?'

'She's sick,' Dan told him. He added honestly: 'But I guess she'll never change.'

Mat said slowly: 'Father's a great man. We all know that. Feeling about him the way we do holds us four together — no matter where we live.'

Dan nodded. He said: 'I heard — some Georgia prisoners told me — that you're married, Mat.'

Mat grinned. 'Yep! I went home last winter to see my son.'

'Is he going to be as big as you?'

'Bigger!' Mat bragged. 'He'll begin where I left off.'

There began to be a lull here about them. The fighting ahead seemed to have passed beyond the town. As they moved on, wherever the Federal troops had made a stand they saw dead men and wounded men in blue and in gray, and all the dreadful wreckage of the battlefield; and once they met a file of more than a hundred Federal prisoners, marching under guard, and drew aside to let them pass. They came into the town and Mat said: 'I'll find a place to leave you somewhere here, send one of our surgeons to look out for you tonight if I can.'

He watched hopefully the houses along the way, and presently a woman came out on her front stoop to watch them pass. They stopped and Mat asked: 'Ma'am, can you take this man in?'

She said in strong tones: 'I've a spare bed he can have, yes — but no Rebel's going to cross my doorstep!'

Mat took off his hat. 'I'm your servant and your debtor, ma'am,' he told her gravely. 'This is my brother, Captain Evered of the Sixth Wisconsin.' He helped Dan toward the steps.

'Sixth Wisconsin?' she repeated. 'We've had Captain Harris and two Lieutenants of that regiment here already, but they got away before the Rebs came along. Sergeant Evans is still here.' She was speaking to Dan. 'So come you in.'

Dan stood on one foot and she gave him her shoulder. Mat said: 'I'll send a surgeon, Dan. Tell father that Tom and I love him Good-bye!'

Dan tried to speak steadily. 'Good-bye, Mat. Take care of yourself.' Then he hopped painfully into the house, leaning on the stout shoulder of the woman who had offered him asylum here.

VII

She was Mrs. Hollenger, and as soon as Dan was indoors her daughter Julia came to help her tend him. They put a bed for him in the room with Sergeant Evans.

'They got me in the legs, sir,' the Sergeant explained, recognizing Dan. 'That was right at the edge of the railroad cut. I saw you go down a minute after.' He lowered his voice cautiously. 'When that lot surrendered, I could walk, with a couple of muskets for crutches, and Colonel Dawes gave me their battle-flag to keep. I wrapped it around my body and got this far with it. Miss Julia cut a slit in the bedtick and hid it there and I'm lying right on top of it, so it's safe and sound till we drive the Rebs out of here again.'

Dan was too tired and weak to care about flags, or about anything but sleep. He was almost indifferent when hours later the surgeon Mat had sent came to dress his wound, and thought the foot might be saved. 'We won't know for a day or two,' he said. 'It will be stiff the rest of your life, anyway. I'll try to come back later.'

But Dan never saw him again. Next day through a fog of fever he heard the roll of guns and the steady musket fire during the bloody battle to the southward; and Mrs. Hollenger, coming to pack wet cloths upon his head and to bathe and bandage his torn foot, told him there had been dreadful fighting down between Mr. Sherfy's peach orchard and the hill called Round Top. Dan remembered the orchard past which they had marched the day before, and the rocky underbrush where that battle must have been fought; and his fever-spurred imagination peopled those rugged thickets with yelling Rebels, men who leaped out from behind great boulders, their mouths wide open showing yellowed teeth like fangs, their red eyes glaring madly. That night he fought over many fields in his disordered sleep, and screamed with rage and battle lust, and Mrs. Hollenger and Julia took turns in easing him. In the morning of the third day his senses were clear again, till somewhere near-by a tremendous cannonade began; and the thundering detonations shook the house where he lay, and thirst tormented him so that the women wetted his parched lips hour on hour. He had intervals when he knew everything that passed; and once Julia Hollenger came like an angel with shining eyes to tell her mother that the Rebels were beaten, and Dan yelled with triumph and pride. That night he heard marching feet in the street outside, and he saw Julia and Mrs. Hollenger watching at the windows of the room where he and Sergeant Evans lay, and he heard Sergeant Evans telling the women that the Rebs were retreating, going back the way they had come. 'And we'll be on their tail,' the Sergeant cried exultantly. 'Damned few of them will ever get home again.'

For hours, either in sleep or in delirium, Dan lost all sense of his surroundings; but when the sun rose his mind was clear. Sergeant Evans was moving, limping about the room, and Dan saw him draw out from the bedtick the captured colors. 'I'm going to take them to the Colonel,' he told Dan; and by him Dan sent a message to Will. He was clear-headed enough when toward noon Will came; but he thought Will had aged ten years in these three days. The other's eyes were red with sleeplessness.

'I'd have come sooner, Dan,' he said. 'But I've been at it steady, taking care of the poor devils. This was hell and repeat!' He was streaming with sweat, dusty, haggard, stained. 'Sergeant Evans said your foot was smashed.' His tone was empty of all feeling, bleak with dreadful fatigue.

'You've had it hard,' Dan said.

'How much of it were you in?'

So Dan told him, speaking slowly, all about that first day. When he spoke of Mat, Will asked no questions, but he leaned forward to listen more intently. Dan finished, and Will nodded. He pulled his chair nearer the bedside and began to remove the bandages on Dan's foot, talking in dull tones while he did so.

'We came on into town that day,' he explained. 'But that afternoon we saw the Rebels coming down from the north so we pulled back behind the cemetery.' He removed the last bandage and made a little woeful whistling sound at what he saw, but he spoke steadily enough. 'The brigade cleaned the Rebs out of the woods you saw them go into,' he said. 'And what the Sixth did at the railroad cut rolled up a whole Rebel brigade and they drove the Rebs back a mile or two; but then the Rebs brought up more men and flanked our line and pushed it back into town here. The Sixth damned near got cut off. They had to crawl through a high board fence, like a lot of boys stealing apples, but they made it, and went on to a hill east of town. Culp's Hill they call it.' He wiped his forehead. 'Dan, the brigade lost eleven hundred men out of eighteen hundred, that first day. They had some hard fighting the second day, too; but yesterday they had it pretty quiet.' His tone did not change. 'I guess I've cut off a hundred legs. I'll have to cut off your foot, Dan. I'll go get some men to hold you.'

'I thought you'd have to,' Dan assented. 'I didn't like the smell of it. But you won't need any men, Will. I'll lie still. Mrs. Hollenger and Miss Julia will get you what you need. Go ahead.'

'Like hell I will! I can't have you jerking around right in the middle of the job.'

'I'll lie still,' Dan repeated. 'Go ahead.'

Will hesitated. 'Oh, all right,' he said then in a dead weariness. 'I guess you can. You're like father. You can do anything. I'll call the women!'

What followed was not, on the whole, as bad as Dan had thought it would be. When the saw touched the bone, he set his teeth to fight back waves of dreadful faintness, and the plucking and the tugging at his torn flesh made his stomach sick; but presently the thing was done.

The wound healed readily, and in late July, Dan started on the long journey home.

6

BANGOR's contribution to the war had been from the first a heavy one. The city served as the focal point for all martial activities east of Augusta, and Bangor industries had turned in large measure to war work. The foundry of Hinckley and Egery remodelled and rifled eighteen old smooth-bore cannon, making them potentially usable for coast defense; and the guns were mounted in Portland, Wiscasset, Rockland and elsewhere. Wheelwright, Clark and Company manufactured cloth for uniforms for eight of the Maine regiments recruited in 1862. The city itself undertook to provide support for the families of men absent on service; and except for the relatively small group of secessionists — the Peace Party had thirty-one votes out of nineteen hundred and ninety-two cast at the election in September, 1861 — public sentiment was strong and unified in support of the war.

In the first year there were nine hundred and fifty-eight volunteers from the city, out of a population of some sixteen thousand, and before the war ended, twenty-seven hundred Bangor men would go into the national service and three hundred of them would never return. Throughout the war there were so many volunteers and substitutes provided by Penobscot Valley towns that most of them had to furnish no drafted men; but in this summer of 1863 when Dan came home there was talk in a few localities of resisting the draft. Dexter was occupied by a detachment of the State Guard, with some light field guns, to handle expected trouble there, while even in Bangor preparations were made to deal with any riots that might occur. The arms and ammunition in the State Arsenal, to prevent their capture by rioters, were removed and put in what seemed to Mayor Dale safer places, and Joseph Downe was placed in command of the city and made responsible for keeping order. His preparations were so thorough that those who might have contemplated violence thought better of their plans.

The city, in addition to its direct sacrifices, suffered indirectly from the collapse of the lumber business. Men were too sorely needed on Southern battlefields to be spared for the big north woods. Along with the decline of trade, silver currency disappeared from circulation. General Veazie's bank put out scrip in denominations of ten, twenty-five and fifty cents to supply the need for fractional currency, and almost a hundred thousand dollars' worth of his paper circulated in eastern Maine until the Government scrip came to supersede it.

II

Dan was not the first Bangor man to come home maimed, nor was he alone in his homecoming. A score or so of returning soldiers, some wasted by disease, some like himself minus a foot or a hand or a leg or an arm, some weakened by wounds which had been slow to heal, were in that company on the train. Despite their weakness, when they saw from the windows the rising hills and familiar contours of this land that was their home, their spirits lifted; and when, some on crutches and each helping each, they descended from the train into welcoming arms, there was in them a gladness so great that they were half-amazed at the tender tears which greeted them.

Dan, as the train slowed to a stop, saw his father standing, scanning the windows of the cars; and beside John was Jenny, and Meg was there too, and a tall young woman whom at first Dan did not recognize as Beth. The watching crowd raced along the platform to keep up with the car in which the homecoming soldiers rode; and Dan was suddenly a little ashamed of that leg of his which ended in a neatly sewed-up fold of his trousers. He dreaded to face so many eyes. Nevertheless he rose, steadying himself on one foot and adjusting the crutches to which he was not yet well accustomed, and followed the others to the car door. When he appeared upon the platform, below him there was a compact mass of men and women and children, each grouped around some one of the soldiers; but he saw his father making a way gently through the press, and John called some smiling word and lifted his hand, and Dan eased himself down the steep steps of the car and so into his father's arms.

They kissed each other, as though Dan were a boy again; and then John said: 'Here's mother, Dan.' So Dan, balancing himself on one foot, his father's steadying hand under his arm, swept her close.

Jenny was outwardly as composed as ever; but he felt her twitching and trembling against his breast. Her lips on his were dry and hot and fevered, and she was thin and wasted, her arms like slender cords around him, her bony frame seeming to wear no garment of flesh at all, so that it was as though he held a skeleton. He felt a strong revulsion and compassion too, his heart full of tenderness and sorrow for her while his healthy flesh shrank from touching her, feeling the abhorrence a man feels for a serpent on the ground or for any miserable hurt and wretched thing, wishing to destroy it forever.

Meg was near, watching them; and even while Dan held Jenny in his arms, he saw Beth. She was smiling through streaming tears, and her lips were moving, saying his name in a queer, choking rush over and over. She was as tall as Meg, and as lovely as Meg had always seemed to Dan to be, with her mother's clear eyes and open countenance in which no shadows lay, and no unrest, but strength and peace and long content; and Dan, looking now at Beth, had a contrasting memory of stricken battlefields and dead men and hurt men screaming and he remembered the struggles of a horse he had seen at Sharpsburg. The horse had been hit by a cannon ball that ripped open its belly and tore its leg half away so that the dangling leg was all entangled in its own spilled intestines. The memory of that horse had haunted him more persistently than any memory of human suffering, spoiling his dreams, waking him sometimes to shuddering, sweating terror; and it was strange that to see Beth now should bring it back to him — until in that same moment, while he still held his mother in his arms, meeting Beth's eyes, the blunt horror of that memory faded and was gone, and he knew it would never torment him more. Beth was the cure for it. Merely to see her made all the ugliness and pity of these years seem distant and unreal — and yet at the same time these things which he had seen and done were now no longer meaningless, but became part of an ordered and somehow splendid whole.

And he thought even in this moment that women can always look on birth and on death with calm and steady glance, understanding and unafraid, finding neither in birth nor death that mystery which lends them terror; and he thought that a man without a woman is not complete and whole.

Thus his thoughts in the long seconds while he held Jenny straining in his arms. Then he turned to Aunt Meg, and her arms were strong and firm, and she kissed him, and she was as beautiful as he remembered, but in more generous and finer ways. Then Beth was strongly gripping his hand, smiling through tears; and all of them were saying empty words — words that were empty because there were no words for the things they wished to say. And then John helped him with his crutches, and they moved toward the carriage, and Jenny bade Meg and Beth come to supper, and Aunt Meg said smilingly:

'Not tonight, Jenny. You'll want him to yourself tonight.'

Beth added: 'And Dan's tired. He'll need to go to bed, to rest.' Her eyes did not leave his.

Then John helped Dan into the carriage and so they were driving home; and the streets were the same and the people were the same; and when they turned into the drive their own house, staunch and strong with that great beam for a rooftree, was as it had been and would be for a hundred years and more.

III

Jenny, when they came indoors, went directly to bed; but she insisted that they must eat supper with her in her room on a table set there, and John promised they would do so. When she had gone upstairs he told Dan:

'She got up to go to meet you, son, but it was hard for her. She's been in bed most of the time since last winter, and she's very weak; but for a fortnight now, since we heard from Will that you would soon be coming home, she's been getting up awhile every day, walking, gaining strength to meet you.'

'She's awfully thin and weak. Is she sick?'

'Yes,' John assented. 'Her back is worse all the time, hurts her more and more.' He hesitated, said soberly: 'I don't think she'll ever get well, Dan. I think she's dying.'

Dan thought so too, thought the mark of death was on her, yet he asked: 'What's the matter with her?'

John did not answer directly. 'I've had every doctor in town,' he said, 'till she won't let them come any more.' He asked awkwardly: 'Want me to help you upstairs, son?'

'I'm getting pretty good with these things,' Dan said in cheerful reassurance, handling his crutches. He looked down at his leg. 'It's just my foot that's gone, you know; and Will says that I can have a sort of high boot made with stiff bracing in it, and have it come up to just under the knee and strap it on and I'll be able to manage fine. But I'll have to wait till the — stump's completely healed before I can put any weight on it.'

John cleared his throat. 'We'll work that out,' he agreed. He came behind Dan to the stairs; but at the stair foot he checked Dan to say quietly:

'Son — Will wrote me that you saw Mat at Gettysburg.'

'Yes, he helped me to town after I was hurt — maybe saved my life.'

'I didn't tell your mother about that,' John confessed. 'You'd better not. She never mentions him or Tom, but I'm sure her bitterness toward them is as strong as ever. Don't say you saw him.'

Dan nodded in reluctant agreement, and they climbed the stairs. They talked not long that night. Dan now and then saw Jenny's face set hard when some stark pinch of pain gripped her, and he saw perspiration on her brow, but her voice was steady enough. It was pitched even lower than he remembered, in a sort of husky whisper. She had many questions, first about himself and Will, and then about the war; and Dan told her that the North would surely win, that after the invasion which ended at Gettysburg the South would never be able to make an equal effort. He had to repeat this in a dozen different forms, to reassure her again and again; but also he had to tell her about the battles he had seen, had to describe scenes of dreadful conflict, and the clash of fighting men, and the havoc of the cannon. She seemed to him to have a morbid appetite for the ugliest detail, urging him with many questions. Once or twice John tried to interfere, but she ignored him, pressed Dan more and more.

She wished not so much to hear the results of each battle as to be told how the Confederates had suffered, asking again and again when Dan described some bloody field: 'Were there many Rebels dead? And many wounded? Did your surgeons take care of the Rebels the same as our men?' Half a dozen times he thought she was about to ask whether he had seen Tom or Mat; and at last, when they had talked long and she was weary and he and John prepared to leave her, she did so in straightforward terms, demanding: 'Did you ever see your brothers, Dan?'

He had decided what to say, and he answered her, steadying himself on his crutches while he felt his father's eyes upon him. 'Mat's a Lieutenant and Tom a Captain in a Georgia regiment,' he said.

'Are they still alive?' she insisted.

'They were, the last I heard.' He added: 'One man told me Tom was shot through the body at Fredericksburg, but that he was recovering.'

She said in low tones: 'I hope he dies.' She lay still for a long moment, her face becoming set and stony white, and Dan thought he could feel as though they tore his own flesh the talons of pain which ripped at her. Then she whispered almost soundlessly: 'Good night, Dan. Come to me when you wake. I'm glad you're home.'

IV

After Dan's homecoming, Jenny never left her bed, and John told him her suffering seemed stricter all the time; but she was hungry for Dan's company, kept him much by her side. To be with her was an ordeal which he dreaded, yet because she welcomed him he gave her long hours. John was grateful to him.

'I know it's hard on you, son,' he said, 'but she hates to be alone.' He added ruefully: 'Why, this winter past, she's even been glad to have me for company. Often I've sat with her all day, and sometimes half the night. It doesn't seem to make her any happier when I'm with her — I wish it did — but she will never let me go unless I must. Now it's you she wants most.'

'I'll take your place,' Dan agreed. 'Give you some rest. You're pretty tired yourself, father.'

So he was much with her, leaving her only when he could no longer endure the horror of this long watch beside a shrivelling hulk of mortifying flesh which retained no animating qualities except an unbreakable will to live and a capacity for ascending mountainous peaks of pain. To look at her was like looking at a sun-dried cadaver which had escaped the burial parties on some Southern battlefield; yet at the same time she was so much alive that Dan could not easily accept the fact that there was nothing to be done for her.

His father told him that not only Doctor Mason but Doctor Brown and Doctor Laughton had seen her regularly, till she refused

to let them come again; and Dan went to question them. Doctor
Mason he had known always, as the wise and kindly man who
brought healing to him and to his brothers when childhood ills
beset them; but with the others he was not so well acquainted.
Doctor Brown was a Bowdoin man, and like Will he had read
medicine with Doctor Mason; but he had supplemented this by
three courses of lectures in the Medical Department at Harvard
University and had worked at the Tremont Street Medical School
in Boston before going abroad for further study. He had prac-
ticed for a while in St. Louis, returning to Bangor at the outbreak
of the war. Doctor Laughton was an older man who had come to
Bangor from Foxcroft in 1849, and who had a wide reputation
as a surgeon.

Doctor Mason, to whom Dan naturally turned first, said honestly
that Jenny could not hope to be better. 'I could give her drugs to
ease her pain,' he said. 'But she won't have them. You know how
brave she is, Dan.'

'Can't anyone do anything to cure her?' Dan pleaded.

The old man shook his head. 'Your father-asked me the same
question,' he explained. 'So I called in Doctor Brown and Doctor
Laughton. Doctor Brown knows as much about women's ailments
as anyone, and Doctor Laughton has performed some of the great
operations in surgery. You can talk to them, but you'll find that
they agree with me that beyond easing her pain — which she will
not permit — there is nothing we can do.'

Dan was not satisfied till he had seen the others for himself.
He came back to Doctor Mason afterward, beaten; and he asked
the older man in straightforward words: 'Then you mean she's
just going to die?'

The Doctor nodded honestly. 'Yes, Dan.'

'How long will it be?' Dan whispered.

Doctor Mason shook his head. 'That's as God wills, Dan. She's
very brave, you know, and her resolution will keep her body alive
where another would go quickly.'

'I can't bear to see her suffer so,' Dan confessed. 'Isn't there some
thing we could give her without her knowing it?'

The old man said gravely: 'She has the right to decide that, Dan.
Her mind is clear. But she wants to go on as she has, till the end.'

'Will you come and talk to her about it?'

'If she wants me.'

So Dan tried to persuade Jenny to send for Doctor Mason, but
she would not. Yet she was ready enough to see others, and she
had many visitors, the Elders of her church, and the women with

whom for so many years she had worked for the public good. Aunt Meg came often, and at first Beth came too, till Jenny forbade this. She sent that word through Dan. 'Tell Aunt Meg Beth's too young and pretty to see me the way I am now,' she said; and thereafter Beth stayed away.

Once or twice Jenny insisted that the Sewing Circle of which she had so long been a leading member meet with her, and they did so; and she took a continuing interest in the Children's Home, and members of the Board of Managers called several times to discuss with her the sudden increase in the number of children — orphaned by the war — who must be cared for, and to get her advice on the selection of an assistant to the Matron. Also, after Dan came home she conceived a new design, and during that fall and winter she urged it on all those who called upon her; a project to establish a 'Rest' to receive sick and disabled soldiers. To this plan she gave much time and thought, and during the winter the project assumed a definite shape. She herself made a substantial contribution to the funds that were raised for the purpose; and it was in connection with this project for a Soldiers' Rest that she did at last see a physician, Doctor Morison, who had been a surgeon attached to the Second Maine Regiment. She proposed to him to take charge of the new hospital, and offered to compensate him in advance for any loss of practice or of income he might suffer from doing so. She kept Dan with her for that interview. Doctor Morison thanked her, but he said:

'I've put myself at the disposal of wounded soldiers since I came home, Mrs. Evered; and so has every other doctor in town. We'll continue to do so.'

She said, smiling thinly: 'You make it hard for a woman to help as much as she wishes to. Then this, Doctor. There will be times when you could ease pain, or bring comfort, by some expenditure beyond your pocketbook. I will put a sum of money in your hands to be spent at your discretion, whenever you think wise. Will you let me do that?'

'Of course,' he assented eagerly. 'And a fine thing, too!'

When afterward Dan took him to the door, the Doctor said: 'You've a grand woman for a mother, Dan. I've been practicing in Bangor for a good many years; and every doctor in town knows how often she has quietly done just such things as this, to make life a little easier for afflicted folk.'

'I know,' Dan agreed. 'She's done a lot of good.' He said in a husky voice: 'It seems awful to me that she can't be kept from suffering so. Can't you give her opium or something?'

But Doctor Morison said quickly: 'I'm not her physician, Dan. Doctor Mason can do as much for her as anyone.'

v

These various interludes when Jenny was engaged with her friends or with matters of business — she had long since taken full charge of her own affairs, and attended to them even now — gave Dan an occasional respite from his close attendance upon her; and when he was free, he was always apt to turn to Aunt Meg and to Beth. Judge Saladine's old house on Essex Street was like a haven. It was a frame structure, built narrow and high so that it might more easily be heated, with a small, seldom-used parlor on one side of the front hall, a sitting room and dining room connected by folding doors and with a wide fireplace in each room on the other. The outside was shingled and painted brown, so that Meg sometimes laughed at the dark and gloomy appearance it presented; and the windows were small, and even in summer the rooms were never bright. But there was something warmly comfortable about them. The very chairs had learned to shape themselves hospitably to their users. The woodwork was painted white and the wallpaper was bright and cheerful; and except on the warmest days Aunt Meg liked to have at least a small fire burning.

Dan sometimes thought that Meg and Beth would have given any house a fine and friendly atmosphere. They were both so jolly and gentle that to be with them was like a healing. Beth was seventeen, and she thought of herself as a young woman; but Dan was ten years older than she, and to him she seemed more a child than ever, while in her young and vivid presence he felt like an old man. His two years of service had been like ten, or twenty, packed with more hardship and suffering and tragedy and death than is compassed in the span of a hundred normal lives; while she was in the first ripeness of life, unscarred and unwearied. He felt old enough to be her father.

When he was with Beth, too, since she was so complete and perfect in every way, he could never forget his mutilation; and there were dark hours when he thought it set him apart from the company of normal men and women. Aunt Meg and Beth may have guessed this; for it was they who put on foot a series of experiments, calling in old Ezra Hooker, the bootmaker, to help, which by a process of trial and error produced at last a boot that Dan could wear.

They kept this a secret between them till the boot was done and while Dan learned to walk without his crutches. When he came to their house he would put on the boot, and Beth, kneeling at his feet, secured the straps which held it in place; and it was with Meg to steady him on one side and Beth on the other, that he took his first steps. They laughed together at his awkwardness, finding in this laughter relief from unbearable pity and sorrow. At first the boot had a tendency to turn sidewise on his leg, with ludicrous results; and when this happened, they were all hilarious together.

Once, when Beth was helping him put on the boot, shaping the padding in the empty foot of it, adjusting it on his leg, he said, looking down at her wonderingly: 'It's too bad for you to do that.'

'Why?' she protested. 'I like it.'

'Doesn't it — make you sort of sick?'

Her eyes met his for a silent moment, as though there were much she wished to say; but she only shook her head and told him quietly: 'No, it doesn't bother me.'

He could not fail to see that she loved him. He knew she had always loved him; but this was a warmer, more mature affection in her now. She showed it in so many ways: in the gladness with which she met him always; in her merry laughter — a laughter full of tenderness — at his first efforts to walk; in her intent solicitude to be sure the boot was properly adjusted on his foot; in the way her hand tightened on his arm when while she was supporting him he stumbled; in her quick-caught breath when he winced with pain; in the way she watched his face while she tightened the straps around his leg; in the way her eyes widened and filled with tears the first time he walked unassisted toward her across the wide room; in her very tones when she spoke to him. Meg saw it, too. Once he said to her:

'I hate having Beth handle this — stump of mine. No matter what she says, it must be hard for her.'

Meg smiled and shook her head. 'No, Dan. Women are not easily distressed by the things that upset a man. Specially ——' She hesitated, did not go on except to say: 'No, Dan, be sure Beth's happy helping you.'

He knew what was in her mind, knew what it was she did not say; and as summer passed he came at last frankly to acknowledge to himself that Beth meant the world to him. But there was, must always be, a gulf between them; for she was young and he was old, an old, crippled fragment of a man.

VI

In their long hours alone together Jenny talked to Dan. Even sitting close beside her bed he had sometimes to lean closer to hear her, she spoke in such low, dry, faintly husky tones; and sometimes in mid-sentence pain gripped her so that her breath caught and she lay rigid, staring upward at the ceiling, no movement in her anywhere. She never cried out nor uttered any least complaint, never spoke of the agonies she endured; but he came to recognize these moments, to share them with her so that he was racked as she was. When surges of pain shook and battered her she made no sound, but after a while, minutes, half an hour, she would speak again, perhaps taking up what she had been saying and continuing, perhaps abandoning it to turn to other thoughts.

Once, soon after he came home, she asked, lying with closed eyes: 'Dan, did Will really have to amputate your foot?' Her tone was eloquent of the fierce anger at Will of which she might be capable if he had erred.

'Yes, of course,' Dan said. 'The bones were all shot to pieces, you know, and the whole foot was — dying. He did well to save this much of my leg.'

She questioned him in low, curiously avid tones. 'Did it hurt, Dan? How did he do it?'

'Why, Mrs. Hollenger and Miss Julia helped him — only mostly Miss Julia just held my hand. I had to lie still, of course.'

'Did it hurt awfully?'

He remembered that moment when the saw bit into the bone, and his flesh crawled at the thought, but he said: 'Not as much as you'd think.'

'How did he do it?' she insisted, and when he did not speak she opened her eyes, turned her head, looked at him. 'Tell me, Dan. I want to know.'

So he described the mechanics of the operation as Will had described it to him, and she made him repeat over and over all he knew. He thought she derived a dark satisfaction from contemplating the pictures his words evoked, as though to think of his suffering somehow eased her own. More than once on other days she came back to the matter, asking him new, searching questions. It seemed to him strange and moving that though she relished this ugly topic she would never admit her own agonies, never speak of them.

Sometimes to be with her was terrible, but there were other hours when he yearned over her, wishing in every way to ease her long ordeal. There was so often in her a humble sadness, when she spoke in retrospect, spoke of her life and his. Thus once, her head a little turned so that her inflamed and weary eyes rested on his countenance, she murmured: 'You always loved John more than me, Dan, all four of you, even when you were babies.' He uttered some quick denial, but she said softly: 'Sh-h-h-h, Dan! I've always known. And you were right, too!' She nodded, almost archly, to emphasize her words. 'Yes, you were right to love him, Dan! He's much better worth loving than I.' And she said with a sort of prescience: 'If you had loved me best, I would have ruined all of you. I've ruined everyone who ever loved me, Dan, everyone but John. It was loving him that saved you.'

Dan thought honestly enough that this might be true. Certainly their shared love for their father was a bond between him and his brothers. She may have read his thoughts, for she said accusingly: 'But if you had loved me, I might have been different, Dan. When you were all little, I tried so hard to be. But you always loved him best. Maybe that's why I began to hate him!' And she confessed: 'I do hate him, you know; but I used to love him, too. I loved him as hard as I could, Dan, because I thought loving him hard would make me a good woman.' And she murmured: 'Loving him has made you good, Dan. You're good even to me. You don't hate me, the way the others do. They hate me, you know, all but you and John. If he had ever hated me, I'd be happier, I think. He had reason to hate me, long ago; but he wouldn't. He never would.'

At first, when she spoke thus Dan tried to protest, defending her against herself; but he found that this might anger her and he understood in the end that in thus accusing herself she found a sort of solace, a strange comforting. So he learned to sit silent, neither assenting nor denying, sometimes for hours on end while she spoke like one in the confessional, drawing aside the curtain which hid the past, letting him see, even though dimly, things he would rather not have seen at all. Thus once she said:

'Do you remember Mattie Hanson, Dan? The negro girl? She used to do our washing when you were a little boy. I hired her to swear that your father had made love to her, and then I hired her to go away, because I knew she couldn't stick to that lie if she were questioned. I thought people would believe it, but John was a good man and no one did believe it, and when I saw that, I went to court and testified for him, and everyone thought I was noble and brave.' There was an ironic amusement in her tones. 'People are so willing to think well of a pretty woman, Dan! Everybody thinks I'm nice and generous and wise, and so full of religion; but really I'm just plain bad! I wonder if lots of people are as bad as I am in their thoughts, but just don't do the bad things they want to do? Is it worse to do awful things than to think them and wish you dared do them? As a man thinketh in his heart, so is he.' She was silent, and she lay long rigid in a catalepsy of pain endured; and as he watched her, sweat dripped from his brow, and after an interminable time she asked: 'Do you remember the day I bit your arm till it bled, when you were a little baby? But of course you were too young. But you do remember the time I whipped Mat? I loved doing that, Dan. I used to love to whip all of you, and when I did, I had to be careful not to just beat you to ribbons, till you died!' Then she whispered: 'I killed a man once, Dan, in a way.' Her head moved suddenly from side to side in a lost woe. 'But I mustn't tell you that. I mustn't tell you that . . .'

And once she said: 'I was a sly, awful little girl, Dan. Ever since I can remember, I've known that if I did some things to men they would do anything I wanted. My father was big, Dan, a big man; bigger than you; and he would have been fine if I hadn't been so sly and clever and cruel, driving him to do crazy, awful things till he hated himself and wanted to die. Oh, Dan, Dan, Dan . . .'

But she was not always thus contrite. Sometimes she spoke with a dry, rancorous bitterness, mocking him, mocking John, scorning them all; and sometimes, when her friends had been here to see her, she talked to Dan about them, deriding them, hating them. 'The silly fools, thinking me so fine and generous and brave. The silly fools! The silly fools!' There was a sudden violent passion in her tones against these simple decent folk who liked her well. 'I'd like to spit in their smug faces! I'd like to tell them . . .' Her eyes narrowed with a sudden thought and she spoke under her breath. 'I'd like to tell them that other, too! Oh, I'd like to tell them that and see their faces. Most of all I'd like to tell them that!'

But then caution checked her and she looked at him shrewdly and said: 'Dan, you don't believe I'm wicked, do you?' And then in scorn again: 'No, indeed, you're too like John to think evil of anyone! But don't ever believe me when I say terrible things about myself, will you, Dan!'

There were many such hours. There was no day from his homecoming till she died when he was not for at least part of the time with her; and the months were for him a long crucifixion. To endure the ordeal he drew strength from his father, and more and more from Beth; but always, too, he tried to help his mother, to bring her some faint cheer. When in October he first came to her without his crutches she was for a moment almost gay, till he told her that it was Aunt Meg and Beth who had helped him learn to walk again, and then she sulked like a sullen child.

Before Dan had been a month at home he knew he wished to marry Beth, but he told himself he could not. She was so young and so perfect, and he was maimed. To turn to her could make him forget his dreadful hours with Jenny, yet, since he recognized more and more certainly Beth's feeling for him, he thought he should avoid seeing her so often. But because he hoped to be assured this was not true, one day in late fall — he had found her alone — he said to Aunt Meg:

'You know, I've been thinking. I'm afraid I — ought not to be so much with Beth.'

Meg hesitated for a moment, carefully not smiling; then asked quietly: 'Aren't you happier here than anywhere?'

'Yes. But — Beth ought to be seeing more of — younger people. I take all her time.'

She said, half to herself and half to him: 'Of course you know Beth's loved you since she was a baby, Dan.'

'I know the way you mean, but she'll be a young woman, soon, ready to fall really in love with someone.'

'She's a young woman now, Dan,' Meg told him simply. 'And she's in love with you.'

He knew this was true, and he said in sudden, half-angry challenge: 'But see here, would you be willing for her to marry a — wreck like me?'

Meg smiled. 'I'd be proud and happy, Dan; but I don't think what I felt would matter. Beth has a mind of her own. You'd have to ask her. Whatever she wanted, I would want too.'

He considered this, asked uneasily: 'What do you think she'd say?'

'What do you think, yourself?'

'But she's not old enough to know her own mind, Meg,' he protested. 'Of course I'm a soldier, crippled and home from the war, and that sort of thing means a lot to a girl her age; but I have to be fair to her.'

'I don't think Beth's a silly little fool,' Meg assured him, almost sternly. 'I think she knows her own mind — and her heart, too.' And suddenly her eyes warmed and she said slowly: 'I wouldn't tell you to ask her, Dan, unless I were sure what the answer would be. I wouldn't want you hurt, my dear.'

Yet Dan still lacked the courage and the will to speak, till one day Meg came to see Jenny, and when he went downstairs to meet her she told him to go to Beth. 'I said I'd send you,' she explained.

'I'll stay with Jenny. Go along, Dan. You need a rest from things here.' And after an instant, smiling, she rose on tiptoe to kiss him. 'Run along, my dear,' she said, and went away up the stairs.

Dan when she was gone began to tremble uncontrollably, and he stared in wonder at his shaking hands. He was at once passionately eager and doubtfully uncertain, half-desiring and half-dreading this hour that was to come. He decided after a moment to walk to town. He might have driven, but the crisp November day was fine, so he took his cane and set out. He walked by this time with some certainty.

On the way he met old friends and stopped and spoke with them; yet when he left them he hurried on. Only at the very end did his steps lag and he came halting to Beth's door.

She must have been watching for him, for before he could lift the knocker she opened the door and bade him in. 'Did you walk?' she asked, in a smiling excitement.

'All the way!' It was the first time he had walked so far.

'Oh, fine!' she said happily. They turned into the sitting room and she made him sit down, but she herself stood by the hearth, by the blazing fire. For a moment neither of them spoke, yet watching her he felt a deep excitement warm him. Then she asked how Jenny was, and he told her soberly:

'Why — she suffers more all the time. And she's weaker every day.'

'It's hard on you, being so much alone with her.'

'It's what she wants.'

They were silent then again. She asked incuriously: 'Do you — just sit and talk together all day long?'

'She does most of the talking. She likes to talk to me.' His fists for a moment clenched as he remembered some of the things his mother had said. 'She's really not talking to me,' he explained. 'It's more as if she were thinking aloud, about all her life, and about when we were children.' He said: 'She's terribly unhappy sometimes.'

'I know,' she assented. 'She's never been happy since Tom and Mat went South. I wish they hadn't gone, Dan. It hurt her so. Because of course she was always against the South.' He nodded, and she said pityingly: 'It isn't fair that she should be unhappy, and should suffer so. She's always been so good, doing so much for so many people. Everyone loves her.'

It seemed to him incredible that Beth could believe this; but he remembered that everyone who knew his mother would have said the same. 'She's fine,' he assented. 'And she's so brave, Beth. It breaks my heart to watch her.'

'I wish it didn't have to come so hard on you.'

'I'm glad I can help her.' He said thoughtfully: 'She has something on her mind, something she wants people to know.'

'What is it?'

'I don't know. She's said, several times, speaking of people here in town: "I wish I could tell them that." '

'Why doesn't she tell you?'

He repeated: 'I don't know. I think it's some sort of joke. She always sort of laughs when she speaks of it.' He hesitated, remembering his impression of malicious amusement in his mother when she spoke of this secret matter, warily said no more.

Beth did not question him. She turned, looking down into the fire, her head bowed; and he watched her, content to be silent here with her, remembering that Meg had sent him here today, sure there had been a purpose in that sending, thinking of the things he wished to say and dared not. Beth spoke again of casual matters, not looking at him; and he answered her, and this meaningless talk ran awhile and died and between them silence lay again.

She had been standing with her eyes upon the fire, but she turned at last to face him, and met his eyes and smiled. For what may have been a long time they spoke no word. She stood with her back to the fire, and their eyes held, at last unsmilingly, and he knew she was waiting for him to speak, waiting in a fine serenity. He remembered moments long ago when, seeing his father and mother happy together, he himself had felt warm and comfortable and full of a fine delight, sharing their happiness; and meeting Beth's eyes a like sense of calm content began to fill him now.

But he did not speak, and after a moment she stood more erectly, with a lifting of her shoulders as though in decision. Then she came toward him across the room in a steady way that made him remember how he and the men of the regiment had walked calmly across that bloody field between the turnpike and the railroad cut, never faltering. Nor did she falter now. She stopped just in front of him, looking down into his eyes; and he saw that she was as if transfigured, her eyes melting, her cheeks warm.

For a moment more that was all. She stood before him, waiting, grave and serene and sure; and her eyes held his, and this glance between them was enough without words. There was in him no need for speech. It seemed to Dan all was determined in that marriage of their eyes.

But for her this was not enough. She moved one hand in a

little gesture almost of appeal, smiling again. 'Hello, Dan,' she said, in a low tone, half-mirthful.

He chuckled, felt his heart lift its beat. 'Hello, Beth.'

She folded her arms tightly, as though her hands were trembling and she must quiet them. She said: 'Remember when I was little?'

'Yes, Beth.'

She nodded vigorously. 'So do I. I remember all about everything. All about us.' Something like fear swept him; a strange fear that this could not be true, that if he moved she would vanish, that this moment was too fragile to endure. She said: 'I've always thought you were wonderful.'

'You've been mighty sweet to me.'

She nodded. 'I asked Mother to send you today.'

There was no more fear, yet he did not speak. Almost he forgot her, while out of his mind and heart the ghosts of dark memories withdrew; memories of dreadful battlefields; older memories of his boyhood when he had been unhappy; memories of hours with his mother in the months since he came home. Beth, standing here before him, by her nearness banished them all; swept the innermost parts of him clean of everything that cast a shadow there. She was like a healing flood sweeping through his soul. He had no wish to speak, no need of words.

She still stood with arms folded. 'Dan,' she said bravely, 'I asked mother to send you to me because she says you want me to marry you.' He thought that to look at her was like looking at the brightness of full dawn. She asked, still steadily: 'Do you, Dan?'

He spoke gladly. 'I want it more than anything, Beth.'

She nodded in a slow way. 'I know it,' she said. Then she laughed, with a soft, chuckling sound, and pressed her hands to her burning cheeks. 'Am I terrible?' she whispered. 'Mother said I might have to make you ask me. Well, I did, I guess.' Then, in sudden rueful pleading: 'Only you haven't really asked me yet, Dan!'

He tried to rise, but there was no need; for at his first move she was on her knees, pressing close between his knees, her arms around him, drawing his head down upon her bosom, laughing with happy tears, crying: 'Oh Dan, Dan, Dan!' Just to speak his name at first contented her, and she whispered over and over: 'Dan, Dan, Dan!' holding him close and cherishingly; till he found her cool lips and silenced her and felt her happy tears upon his cheek where it pressed hers.

They stayed there for a long time, she at his feet, he bent above her. murmuring many things. Once he said: 'But you're so young, so wonderfully young, Beth; and I feel old, old.'

She moved quickly, freeing herself, facing him, still on her knees, yet thus, since he was seated, as tall as he. Her eyes were flashing. 'You're not! Oh, you're not!' she cried. She caught his shoulders with her hands, protesting in tender wrath: 'Why, sometimes you seem just like my baby, Dan, and I have to take care of you!' Then, as he smiled, wishing to be reassured in turn, she cried: 'But I'm awfully young, Dan. I don't know anything. You'll have to teach me, darling, how to be all the things you want me to be.'

He drew her close again. 'I want you what you are, forever and ever.'

'Oh, no!' she protested. 'No one can stay the same, dear.' She laughed up at him. 'You wouldn't want that. Think, when you're old and gray and ever so dignified, how silly we'd look if I were the way I am now!' They laughed together at the picture she drew; and she said with mischievous amusement: 'I know women like that, who keep on acting like young girls when they're old enough to know better. I always think how their husbands must just shrivel up, being so embarrassed by the way they act. So many women don't ever grow up. Men keep maturing and developing as they grow older. I want to grow up with you, Dan.'

He held her tenderly, laughing in a rich content; and then more thoughtfully he said: 'You're so wise. Father used to tell us, when we were youngsters, that a sensible young man would always be sure to marry someone wiser than he — and then try to live up to her. Well, that's what I'm doing! You're worth a dozen of me!'

She smiled, her head on one side, her eyes dancing. 'Do you really think so?'

'I know it!'

'Then that makes thirteen of us,' she pointed out. 'One of you and twelve of me! Because there aren't — there isn't any "you and me" any more. There's just us!' And she cried in a swift, unsmiling ardor, breathless in his arms: 'But Dan, if I were a hundred times what you think, all of me would still be always yours. I'm glad there are twelve of me, because twelve of me can be so much sweeter to you than just one of me could be.' And she whispered, pressing close to him: 'If we live a thousand years, I'll never be able — the whole twelve of me will never be able — to show you how completely I'm all yours, Dan. Forever and ever, Amen!'

He whispered: 'Forever and ever, Beth. Forever and forevermore!'

VIII

Dan was sure that his mother must not know what had happened, sure that she would resent losing to another any part of him; and Beth agreed that he was right, that they must wait. They did not say they must wait till she should die, though this was in both their minds. So they waited, but the waiting was not hard. They had time to grow together, to come happily nearer one another, to weld between them an even firmer bond. They told Aunt Meg and John, but no one else; and from his hours with Beth, Dan drew strength to support him through long days by his mother's side.

When winter had laid its bonds upon the city and while the months took their slow way, Jenny grew weaker day by day. She could no longer lie motionless through the worst spasms of her torment. Sometimes Dan heard her teeth chatter behind her closed lips, and saw the vibration of her jawbone; and little by little she began to surrender under stress of pain to small writhing movements when her knees rose under the coverlets, and her fists clenched and lifted, to fall back again in a sort of submission as the worst passed. Also, as her sufferings increased, she became more rancorous toward John. Whenever he came to her, as he did daily, his presence seemed to awake in her a mocking strength. If she spoke to him at all, it was heartlessly and with a dry scorn in her tones, and she never urged him to stay.

But she clung to Dan, and when sometimes he rose, unable to endure watching her, wishing to go, she might whisper through clattering teeth: 'Stay, Dan, stay! Don't go away!'

There was no longer any flesh upon her bones. Her countenance was a skull-like mask on which her skin, too large, hung in sagging folds and wrinkles. As she lay on her back — her position seldom changed — there was a deep wrinkle beneath a skin flap in front of her ears; and below her chin, dry yellowed skin lay in slack folds. Once she saw in Dan's eyes as he watched her something of the horror he could not help feeling, and she said, almost teasingly, answering his thoughts:

'Yet I was pretty once, Dan; lovely and desirable. But I was more than that. There was something inside me that many men felt, and it set them burning. No one looked at me then as you are looking at me now.' And she whispered half to herself: 'You know, Dan, I was always two people, two women; and one of them was good and true and generous and fine, and one was ugly and terrible. The good one is gone now, Dan. The bad one used to hide inside her, but now the good one's gone, and only the bad one is left. It's the worst of me you see.' But then she pleaded in those straining, husky tones: 'Yet there's some good left in me, Dan. That part that always loved you.'

She had, alone with him, rare moments of breathless sweetness when her intonations and her words made him weep with an almost forgotten love for her, made him forget the wreck of skin and bone and straggling lifeless hair which she had become; and sometimes, when he and the servingmaid tended her, to see the emaciation of her tormented body, her legs no more than knobby bones, her arms so thin and small, was unbearably pitiful.

One day in March, as the long winter neared its end, a letter came from Will with news which gladdened and excited Dan and his father to a new hope; and that day Dan spoke to her for a while of the years when he and the others were boys together here, and when he named Tom and Mat she heard him without protest, so he risked reading Will's letter to her. Will had written:

Dear Mother and Father and Dan —
 Your letters reach me pretty well now and I am sorry to hear Mother is still afflicted. I am in hopes she will be better come spring. The war will be over some day and I can come home. I wish this cussed rebellion could be ended and the South whipped into the true way of thinking. My own plans afterward are not sure. If I remain in the army I can be surgeon, and have an income maybe better than building up a new practice, or I may bring my wife home to Bangor to see you all and maybe to try there. Tell Mother not to be discouraged. We are all sick with this war, but it will end sometime.
 Father, I have seen Mat and Tom. They were wounded in the fighting in East Tennessee and captured, and Tom sent word to me through one of our surgeons who took care of them. A piece of shell tore Mat's leg, but the leg was saved. Tom got another ball through him, but it didn't hit anything vital. They are both tough ones, you know, and they will get well. I got leave to take care of them for a week, and they gave their parole till they are exchanged. I think I could get permission for them to come home when they can travel, as we are not exchanging prisoners because the Rebs just go back to fight us some more. If Mother would like to see them, they could come home, probably in June, if I vouch for them. You can tell me what you think about this.

Dan looked at his mother, but she lay with closed eyes, making no sign, so he read on. The rest of Will's letter, he thought, had been written in such a way that it might be read aloud to her without disturbing her. It was full of Will's slow wit, and Dan smiled now and then as he read, and hoped she was amused.

Then at the last Will had written:

> Let me know how Mother would take it if they came home. If they have to go to prison it will be hard. The prisons are crowded and bad. But if I stand back of them they can go home and maybe stay till the war is over.

Dan read this, too, and he finished and waited for her to speak, hoping to find relenting in her; but almost at once, as though his silence were a question, she said in her low tones:

'I told you and Will to kill them if you had the chance. Why doesn't Will do it?' He shook his head wearily, and she said: 'Let them wait to come home till I am dead.' Her husky voice had that inflexible note which had always given her least word the force of a command.

Yet he ventured one word more. 'It might be their wives and children could come, too — and Will's wife. We could all have a real reunion.'

She turned her head, her eyes opening, meeting his, searching his; and after a moment she said remotely: 'I'm glad you've never married, Dan.' Before he could speak, she went on: 'When a son marries, his father and mother lose him, as we lost Tom and Mat, forever. The boy who was a child in their house becomes a master in his own, meeting problems about which he can't even talk to them. A daughter can come to her mother, if marriage troubles her — though my mother ran away with a British Lieutenant when I was a baby and died in a bawdy house somewhere, I suppose — but a son, once married, is gone into a world of his own.' And she asked: 'Why haven't you married, like your brothers, Dan? Was it because you love me?'

There was a pleading hope in her words, but resentment at her unchanging anger toward Tom and Mat prevented his hearing this; and also, the question in her eyes demanded truth from him. He heard himself saying:

'I'm going to be married soon, mother.'

When he saw her lips twist with pain, he wished to recall the words, but it was too late. She said wearily, her eyes closing:

'I thought you loved me?'

'I do, mother.'

'Who is it?' Her voice was low and cold. 'Who are you going to marry?'

'Beth Pawl.'

She looked at him again, with a sharp movement; and a flame came into her eyes. 'Beth? Meg's daughter?' He did not speak, wincing under her tone; and she began to laugh in a dreadful way. 'John always loved Meg, too,' she murmured. 'He left me for her — as you now leave me for her daughter. Like father, like son!' Then she said evenly: 'Aren't you afraid Beth is your father's daughter, Dan?'

He rose as though he had been struck. He stood above her, a giant above her frail enfeebled helplessness; and he wished to crush her, stamp upon her, expel from her small withered body what spark of malicious life remained. He turned sharply toward the door.

But she called to him then, her voice for once rising. 'Dan! Dan, don't go!' He hesitated, and she began to cry, shaking weakly with terrible racking sobs, so that he came reluctantly back to her; and she wailed: 'Oh Dan, Dan, my dear! Why do I? What makes me? Oh please, Dan, Dan, Dan!'

She wept like a child, twisting weakly on her side, burying her face, crying thinly: 'Oh, why don't I die? Why can't I die? I always loved you, Dan!' In despair he knelt beside her, his arm across her shaking shoulders, forgetting everything except that she was racked and broken and dying, squeezed to death in a red-hot vise of pain.

IX

For an hour they clung together, mother and son, and she put on a sweetness he had almost forgotten, begging his forgiveness, swearing to him that she loved them all. She told him to write Will that if Tom and Mat could come home in June they would be welcomed here, and she bade Dan bring Beth to see her.

'I'll give you my blessing, Dan,' she promised. 'You shall see! I'll be sweet to her, and love her because she loves you.'

But also, she gave Dan that day another errand to do. 'This is to be a special secret between you and me, son,' she said, her tone full of promises. 'And especially from your father. It's a matter of business, and I should have attended to it long ago.' And she explained: 'There's a man — you know him — a lawyer, Mr. Levi Spree. Bring him to see me, Dan, tomorrow morning, after your father has gone.'

Dan knew Levi Spree by evil reputation, and her injunction disturbed him; but he would not risk changing her from this sweetly affectionate mood, so he promised to do what she asked. Levi Spree seemed surprised at the summons, but he obeyed it, coming with Dan to the house. While she talked with the lawyer she sent Dan away, smilingly dismissing him. Mr. Spree was with her for an hour. Dan was glad to see him leave, but Mr. Spree came again that afternoon with Mr. Lebbeus, the publisher of the *Star*, and two other men; and Jenny sent Dan away again and was alone with them.

Dan wished to confide this matter to his father, but his mother had his promise and he kept it; and after that day Mr. Spree did not come to the house again.

In mid-April, when the world was waking to the touch of spring, Jenny drifted at last into a merciful unconsciousness. Dan and his father were alone with her for long hours before the end, sitting gravely, watching her faint breathing fail and cease at last, and she was gone.

7

JOHN thought to have Jenny's funeral services quietly at home, but her friends dissuaded him. There were so many who wished to do her honor that the house could not accommodate them; and when the hour came, not only was the church, where till she became ill she had always been a regular attendant, crowded to the doors, but scores of people, unable to find seats, waited outside to follow her casket to the grave.

The pulpit of the church was vacant at the time, the place of the Reverend Edward Gilman not having been filled; and the Reverend Johnson of the Hammond Street Church conducted the services. He was a graduate of Yale Theological Seminary, and had served in a small Illinois town and in the Bowdoin Street Church in Boston till 1861 when he was called to the Bangor pulpit. At that time Jenny was already ill, seldom appearing in public, so he knew her good works only by report; but he spoke eloquently today of her long life of service to her neighbors and to the community, in church affairs, in the fight for temperance, in the organization of the

Children's Home, as a leader in the abolitionist cause, and as a generous contributor to the Soldiers' Rest now soon to be established. He referred, too, to her many private benefactions.

'The sum of them will never be known,' he said, 'since she moved always quietly and without ostentation in her generous ways; but certainly multitudes have had cause to call her blessed.'

The cortège which proceeded from the church to the cemetery was a long one. Dan, riding with his father, wished Tom and Mat and Will could have been here to see, and to feel a fine pride in this tribute which Jenny's neighbors and friends thus mutely offered her. The carriages moved slowly, and behind them came many humble folk on foot, mechanics and workmen with their wives and their children, all decked in their sober best, each gratefully cherishing the memory of some much-needed benefaction. This long procession, and the people in it, were visual evidence of the place which Jenny had earned in the hearts of Bangor folk.

At the grave, the brief service of committal kept them not long; but Dan, looking around him, seeing everywhere the evidences of spontaneous and genuine grief, forgot all the things in his mother's life which he had hated and resented, and remembered only that she had once been beautiful and tender, and that she had loved him always as he now loved her. One moment at the graveside moved him profoundly. Eight little girls from the Children's Home sang together the hymn called Bangor, from which seventy years before old Parson Noble had borrowed a name for the newly incorporated town. There was something poignant and profoundly moving in the moment when their thin, clear voices rose.

'Hark, from the tombs a doleful sound!
Mine ears, attend the cry —
Ye living men, come view the ground
Where you must shortly lie!'

After the service, as the clods began to fall, Dan and his father moved together toward their carriage; but there were many who spoke a comforting word to them upon the way. Mrs. Smith, the Matron of the Home, thanked them for letting the little girls sing.

'They so wanted to,' she explained. 'Of course, only a few of them knew Mrs. Evered, she'd been ill so long; but we always spoke of her in our daily prayers.'

George Thatcher and Mrs. Thatcher were among their oldest friends. Mr. Thatcher said to them that the Reverend Johnson's eulogy had been eloquent and moving, and Mrs. Thatcher added: 'But of course he did her less than justice. He did not know her as we did, Mr. Evered. Yet I suppose he did as well as, without knowing her whole life, anyone could have done.'

Mrs. McGaw's daughter had come from Brewer for the funeral and she pressed John's hand and told him: 'What she did for us, time and again, no one will ever know, Mr. Evered, and there's many can say the same.'

Dan, standing beside his father, seeing all around them these humble folk watching and wishing to come near to add their word, knew this was true. But if these dozens and scores were silent, there were others who did speak to them before they left the cemetery. Elijah Hamlin brought a message of condolence from the Vice-President himself, and Doctor Morison told John: 'You know, Mr. Evered, her benefactions will live after her, through the fund she put into my hands to help our wounded soldiers.' Doctor Mason stayed with them a moment, his hand on Dan's shoulder; and Dan heard him muttering under his breath: 'A fine woman. A damned noble woman!' General Veazie blew his nose and told John: 'She was always on the right side, John. Bangor will miss her, now she's gone.' Chief Justice Appleton spoke in quiet tribute; and Doctor Laughton, and Joe Littlefield; and Rufus Dwinel, who had always a gift for the right word at the right time, said to Dan: 'Sir, if I had ever met another woman to match your mother I would not have remained a bachelor.' Mr. Hardy, the painter, who had made that portrait of Jenny when she was young, stopped them for a moment. 'I knew Mrs. Evered before you did, John,' he said. 'And I admired her and esteemed her as we all did. I've always been sorry I did her less than justice in that likeness long ago.' Dan wondered what he meant by that. The portrait had always seemed to him beautiful.

There were others; and when at last Dan and his father stepped into the carriage they were warmed and comforted by many strong and friendly assurances. They stayed for supper with Aunt Meg and Beth, and these four sat in quiet talk awhile; and afterward Dan and his father walked out Main Street to the big, strangely empty house together. They spoke little, and then of unrelated things, each with his own thoughts. Only, when they said good night, John told his son:

'She left a fine memory behind her, Dan.'

Dan nodded. It was true. He thought there was not another woman in Bangor whose death would have caused more widespread and genuine sorrow; and he remembered the ways in which he himself had sometimes thought of her with a rueful shame. Surely these others were right and he was wrong.

II

Jenny was buried on a Monday. John decided to spend the next day at home with Dan, and they were quiet together there till while they were at dinner the knocker sounded. Dan went to the door and found a small boy who pressed a wrapped newspaper into his hand.

'For Mr. Evered,' he said. 'Compliments of Mr. Lebbeus.' And he turned and ran as though afraid he would be pursued.

Dan looked at the paper curiously, returning with it to the dining room. 'From Mr. Lebbeus, father,' he said. While his father removed the wrapper, Dan remembered that Mr. Lebbeus had come with Mr. Spree to see his mother, on that day not long ago; and a shapeless terror turned him cold.

John tore the wrapper and unfolded that day's issue of the *Star*. On the front page, two columns wide, conspicuously displayed but without any comment, there was this:

MRS. EVERED'S WILL

I, Jenny Hager Poster Evered, of Bangor in the County of Penobscot and State of Maine, being of sound and disposing mind, declare this to be my last will and testament.

I give and bequeath as follows:

1. To my husband, John Evered, the silver-headed cane in the locked pine box in the attic of my house, which was the property of Ephraim Poster, once my lover, son of my first husband and friend of said John Evered, whose place John Evered took in my affections, and whose word he foolishly scorned when he married me.

2. To my oldest son, Daniel Evered, the painting of me made by Mr. Hardy, so that he may forget my aspect in my later years.

3. To my second son, William Evered, the sum of one dollar, to remind him that he refused to grant the last request I ever made of him, my injunction to destroy his traitorous and rebellious younger brothers if they ever came into his hands.

4. To my sons Thomas and Matthew, who betrayed me and their country, nothing, with the assurance that I hated them till I died.

5. To Levi Spree five thousand dollars in full payment of all claims he may ever make against my estate.

6. To Andrew Lebbeus five thousand dollars in full payment for the publication of this my last will and testament in the *Star*.

7. All the rest and residue of my estate, including the house

in which during my lifetime I permitted my husband and my
sons to live, and including all other real estate, and all my
ownership of vessels in whole or in part, and all moneys in
hand and debts collectible, and all other property, real and
personal, of whatever description, I give and bequeath to my
daughter Molly, who was born on the night of the flood of
1846, in the bawdy house then and now kept by Lena Tempest, and who was acknowledged during the first hours of her
life by her father, Elder Lincoln Pittridge, who had become
my lover a year before; said Molly being still an inmate of said
bawdy house; and out of this bequest I ask but do not require
that said Molly set aside a sufficient sum of money for the
erection of a monument to my memory whenever the good
people of Bangor, whose esteem I have always valued, may
so direct.

8. I appoint Levi Spree as executor of this my last will and
testament, and I require of him no bond. I direct that he cause
the publication of this my will in a prominent position in the
Bangor *Star* as soon as possible after my funeral.

In Witness Whereof, and in the presence of the under-
signed witnesses, I have set my hand and seal.

JENNY HAGER POSTER EVERED

III

John, and Dan, standing at his father's shoulder, read this together; and Dan's hand rested on the older man's arm, his fingers
tightening there. For a long time, long enough to read Jenny's
will three or four times over, neither of them moved. Then Dan
returned to his chair and sat down, and automatically they addressed themselves to their unfinished dinner. They ate slowly,
as if to go on in accustomed ways were a duty that must be done.

When at last they were finished, for a moment more they sat
quietly, their eyes meeting. Then John said:

'Dan, we must go to town, after all.'

'I'll go with you,' Dan agreed. 'We'll walk. The fresh air will
do us good.'

So they set out together, the tall man and his taller son. From
the front door they turned down the drive, and Dan thought more
of his father than of the house they had left. He thought more of
his father than of himself, full of a great tenderness for the man
beside him, wishing to find the just word that would ease the
other's pain.

They came to the road and John paused and turned to look back
at the big house, and Dan stopped too, looking from the house to
his father. John said in a low tone:

'It's been our home since you were born, Dan. The only home you've ever known.'

Dan read the thought in his father's mind and he gripped the other's arm. 'Father,' he said. 'For me — and for the others — home wasn't just that house. Home for us was wherever you were. It will always be.'

So John's head lifted and his eyes met Dan's and he smiled in a quick, boyish way, deeply happy and proud.

They looked back no more, moving down toward Main Street, taking the way toward town. The day was fine and they spoke of this, and they spoke of the far-off progress of the war, and of what General Grant was likely to accomplish this summer, and of the last letter from Will. He had written from camp near Culpeper on the twenty-second of March, saying that the General was to arrive there next day and establish his headquarters. It was cold, he said, with six inches of snow on the ground. He had not when he wrote received Dan's letter saying that Jenny was willing for Tom and Mat to come home, and they spoke of this now, and John said:

'If Will comes to know General Grant, I'm sure he can arrange it. I hope so. I'd like to see the boys.'

Halfway to town they met General Veazie in his carriage driving toward Old Town, and the General bade his man pull up and alighted and came to speak to them, gripping John's hand and then Dan's. He cleared his throat tremendously. 'A fine day,' he said.

'Fine, yes,' John agreed.

'This would have been a great winter for lumbering, plenty of snow — if we'd had the men.'

'Why, yes, it would,' John assented.

The General blew his nose. 'See here,' he said. 'Let me carry you to town. Dan, you ought not to overdo on that leg of yours.' He shouted to his driver: 'Turn around.'

John hesitated, then accepted; so they came into town in the General's carriage, and that ride was like a triumphal progress. Again and again they had to stop while men came to speak to them: George Thatcher; and Amos Roberts, who was the most extensive operator on the river; and the Reverend Enoch Pond, President of the faculty at the Theological Seminary; and Doctor Brown; and George Pickering, banker, merchant, shipowner, lumberman, and one of the founders of the Hammond Street Church. There was a certain similarity in the greeting of each one: the same strong handclasp; the same word about the weather, or about business, or about the war; the same lingering, as though, without

having anything to say, each of these men was unwilling to depart.
Dan, his throat full, thought: They act as if they were proud to be
seen with us. God bless them!

At John's office General Veazie insisted on coming in, and he
stayed for the hour or two they remained there. Joe Littlefield,
the school teacher, stopped for a moment; and old Doctor Mason
joined them and sat for an hour, muttering to himself; and Elijah
Hamlin came to discuss politics, and General Hersey to talk business, and Judge Godfrey of the Probate Court, and Freeman Duren,
whom John had always liked, and Moses Giddings, and Mayor
Dale each came in, if only for a handshake and a casual, friendly
word. Dan thought it was as though there were a conspiracy among
them to show his father and him their regard and their unspoken
sympathy. They talked of impersonal matters, not referring in the
remotest way to the *Star* or to what it had printed that morning.
They told tales and laughed at them. They seemed unhurried,
content to be here with John, testifying in a thousand ways the
strong, salty, masculine affection in which they held him, and
careful to include Dan in all they said till he found himself trembling with gratefulness. Oh, men were fine, sensitive and delicate
and tender as no woman would know how to be.

Only at the end, when it was time to leave, was there any reference, even indirectly, to what was in all their minds. Then General
Veazie, as John rose, said:

'Well, John, I'll carry you home.'

John answered quietly: 'Why, thank you, Sam; but Dan and I
are going to live at the Bangor House for a while.'

General Veazie seemed at that to remember that the house was
no longer theirs, and he cleared his throat like a trumpet blast. 'To
be sure! To be sure!' he agreed. He clapped his hand on John's
shoulder. 'But I'll want to see you every day!'

John smiled. 'I'll always be here,' he promised. 'Thank you, Sam.'

When Dan and his father walked up to the Bangor House
together, the day was almost gone. Dan thought that this black
noontime when they had read his mother's will could already begin
to be forgotten, for the sun set fine and the next day would be fair.

IV

Dan and Beth were married at once. They had planned still to
wait awhile, but now Beth would not. 'I want to be with you, Dan,'
she said. 'I want to be with you every minute, always.'

Aunt Meg agreed, and when Dan consulted his father John said:

'Yes, Dan. Don't wait.' His voice was firm and strong. 'There's no need of waiting, not now.'

'You'll be alone,' Dan said. 'I can't bear to think of you alone.'

'I'm as well off alone, son.' He smiled faintly. 'It will give me time to lick my wounds.' And he said in a strong certainty: 'Mother would have torn up that will, Dan, if she'd lived a little longer. You know that. She changed from day to day. Some days she was fine.'

'I can remember so many fine things about her.'

'Always remember them,' John adjured him. 'This other will be forgotten in a while.' He added huskily: 'Forgotten at least by everyone but us.' And he said: 'Yes, marry Beth, son. You've long happiness ahead.'

Dan touched his father's arm in a shy gratefulness. 'I want you to know,' he told the older man. 'It's you who have given all of us — Will and Tom and Mat and me — what strength there is in us.' And he said: 'I always remember a true thing she said once, that you were like the big beam that makes the ridgepole of the house, the rooftree. Remember?'

'She said that long ago, when we built the house,' John assented, his eyes clouding.

'We four have always known we could turn to you, and that you'd be strong, and understanding.' Dan confessed almost diffidently: 'Whenever I think of you, I think about that line in the Bible: "Be ye therefore steadfast." You're always the same.'

John clapped him on the shoulder, smiling. 'We're a good lot, all of us,' he said. 'Marry Beth, Dan. She's fine.'

v

Dan and Beth lived at first with Aunt Meg, and Dan found a richness in Beth of which he had not dreamed. They never spoke of what Jenny at the last had done, but Beth — and Meg too — were apt to remember and to remind Dan of old times, of bright days he had forgotten. At first Dan dreaded that he might encounter Mr. Spree or Mr. Lebbeus upon the streets, but he never did; and he learned long afterward that — under what compulsion he never knew — they had left Bangor almost at once. General Veazie undoubtedly had a hand in their departure, for Dan later heard that the General had bought the house on Exchange Street where Lena Tempest had lived so long, on condition that Lena and the girl Molly should leave Bangor and never return. The house was torn down, and a business block took its place; yet all this was managed by their friends so quietly that neither John nor Dan knew of it at the time.

The world conspired to protect them, and at home Dan had always Beth, wise in silences, rich in understanding, ready to meet his every wish just as a dog is happiest in doing what its master desires; yet she began to lead him too, so that without knowing it he learned to forget all those things that need not be remembered and to laugh and love with her.

Dan lived with Beth and Meg, and John lived at the Bangor House; but he came often for supper with them. Once late in June he brought a letter from Will, written from a field hospital near Cold Harbor.

> Dear Father and Dan —
>
> I was happy to hear that Dan is married. I remember Beth always was crazy about him even when she was a baby; and if she's as nice and pretty now as she was then, and I'll bet she's nicer, it's fine for Dan. And it's fine for her too, Dan. She's lucky to get you.
>
> I wish I could have been there, but now there's no knowing when I can come home. I don't think I can come till the summer's campaign is over. I'm in charge of the Medical Dept. of the Reg. The surgeon has resigned and I expect to be promoted to fill his place. If they do not give it to me I will resign. I shall know in a few weeks and let you know.
>
> We have had very hard fighting during this campaign. We crossed the Rapid Ann River on the fifth of May into a place known as the Wilderness where we fought from then till the 17th. One Regt lost in killed 60, wounded 200, missing 40, in all 300 men and 15 of them officers, 5 known to be killed, 7 wounded, 3 missing supposed to be killed. We lost no more till we came here on the 1st of June. Here we have lost one officer and 10 men.
>
> Gen. Grant is an obstinate fighter. Our line is a semicircle about 7 miles long, the centre at Cold Harbor 9 miles from Richmond, our left at Meadow Bridge. Our base for supplies is White-house landing on the York River. We throw up entrenchments as we go and so do the Rebs, and in some parts our lines are less than a hundred yards apart where if a man shows his head above the breastworks a dozen bullets come to get him.
>
> No one can conjecture what is to be the result of this campaign. I would like to see you very much, but I can't come home now.
>
> I have to say that Tom and Mat are not coming home. They sent their love to you both, after I told them about Mother

and her will, and they would like to help you face it down, but they took back their parole and are now in prison to stay till the war is over. Then they say they will go home to Georgia, because they know the South will be beaten and they will be needed after the war when the South will be hard put to it to get along. Father, they say they think you would want them to take the hard part down there, instead of bringing their families to Bangor to have it easy with you. They say going back to where they have made their own homes in Georgia is what you would do. I think they will escape from prison and get back to the fighting if they can. I guess you would say that the time to fight hardest is when you know you're going to be whipped, and the South knows that now, and is fighting harder than ever and Tom and Mat will too. Father, I think you and Dan are proud of them. I am.

As for me, I will come and bring my wife when I can to see you all.

Your loving son and bro.
Will

They had other letters from Will that summer, and from him and from the dispatches in the papers they had the story of that bloody campaign, and of the weary winter; and in spring they followed day by day with a deep, exultant thankfulness the news of the last battles of all. With the word of victory came spring, faintly at first and then in a pulsing tide that rose higher every day. Beth's son was born in May, and they named him John; and Dan's father looked at him and said with a chuckle:

'Well, that's the first of my grandchildren I've seen. He's not much to look at, Dan; but I wouldn't wonder if he turned out all right in the end.'

Dan laughed. 'With you for a grandfather, he'll have a sure chance!'

That night after Beth was asleep, Dan and Aunt Meg sat together for a while; and Dan, watching Aunt Meg, thought she looked younger than she had a year ago. There had been for these long months since Jenny died a steady thought in his mind unspoken; but tonight the time had come to put it into words.

'Aunt Meg,' he said, 'I've been thinking. You know grandmothers always spoil babies. It's time Beth and I had a home of our own, to get our baby away from you!'

She looked at him in a slow surprise. 'Do you mean it, Dan? I thought we were all happy here.'

'Well, I partly mean it,' he admitted. 'But mostly it's something else.' He hesitated. 'Aunt Meg, do you remember I talked to you once about marrying Beth, and you said it was all right; but I was so slow that you finally had to manage it.'

Meg smiled. 'Do you blame me for meddling? Hasn't it worked out all right?'

'Yes,' he said, simply. 'Yes, it has. But now it's my turn to meddle.' He hesitated. 'Beth had a lot of trouble with me, bringing me to admit the way I felt,' he reminded her, smiling. Then his eyes sobered and his voice fell. 'Aunt Meg — father and I are a lot alike. I wouldn't ask Beth, for fear it wasn't fair to her. But I knew she loved me.' She sat silent, waiting. 'Father loves you,' he said then gently. 'But he's like me. He'll never ask you to marry him. But I think you want him to.'

For a long time she did not speak, and she stared at her own hand where it lay on the arm of her chair, turning it palm upward, inspecting it as though she had never seen it before. Dan waited, and there was an excitement in him that made his breath catch in his throat, till finally her eyes met his and she spoke.

'I met John in Ellsworth thirty years ago, Dan,' she said. 'I know now that I loved him then. But I didn't know it for many years — not till the time came when I realized that he and your mother were no longer happy together.' She hesitated. 'Then I knew, Dan,' she said. 'Then I knew I loved him, had always loved him. But I was afraid I might let him see it. That was why I married Cap'n Pawl, so I'd be sure never to let John know.'

His eyes were hot and stinging. 'I've always known you were the best and finest person anywhere, except my father.'

'I think John loves me, too,' she said. 'I think he always has. But he'd never let himself know it, not after he and your mother were married.' Her eyes filled and she smiled. 'But I've learned to be happy, Dan,' she said. 'And he's been happy too, happy as a man is in doing what he should.'

He rose. He said strongly, smiling down at her: 'All right, you're two wonderful people. But now you need someone to meddle, just the way you did with Beth and me! I'm going down town, Aunt Meg. I'm going to find father. I'll bring him here to you. Then I'll go to bed.' He chuckled. 'Even when you sent me to Beth, she had to do the talking,' he confessed. 'You'll have to do the talking, too. Will you?'

He waited for her assent, and after a moment she nodded, laughing in a breathless way; and she said softly: 'Yes. But it's been so long. Oh hurry, hurry, Dan.'

THE END